Where Are You Going, Where Have You Been?

Where Are You Going, Where Have You Been?

Selected Early Stories

Joyce Carol Oates

Ontario Review Press / Princeton

"The Fine White Mist of Winter" was first published in *The Literary Review;* "First Views of the Enemy" in *Prairie Schooner;* "At the Seminary" in *The Kenyon Review;* "What Death with Love Should Have to Do" in *The Literary Review;* "Upon the Sweeping Flood" in *Southwest Review;* "In the Region of Ice" in *The Atlantic Monthly;* "Where Are You Going, Where Have You Been?" in *Epoch;* "Unmailed, Unwritten Letters" in *The Hudson Review;* "Accomplished Desires" in *Esquire;* "How I Contemplated the World from the Detroit House of Correction and Began My Life Over Again" in *TriQuarterly;* "Four Summers" in *The Yale Review;* "Love and Death" in *The Atlantic Monthly;* "By the River" in *December;* "Did You Ever Slip on Red Blood?" in *Harper's Magazine;* "The Lady with the Pet Dog" in *The Partisan Review;* "The Turn of the Screw" in *The Iowa Review;* "The Dead" in *McCall's;* "Concerning the Case of Bobby T." in *The Atlantic Monthly;* "In the Warehouse" in *The Transatlantic Review;* "Small Avalanches" in *Cosmopolitan;* "The Widows" in *The Hudson Review;* "The Translation" in *TriQuarterly;* "Bloodstains" in *Harper's Magazine;* "The Molesters" in *The Quarterly Review of Literature;* and "Silkie" in *The Malahat Review.* "Daisy" first appeared in a special limited edition published by Black Sparrow Press. "The Fine White Mist of Winter," "First Views of the Enemy," "In the Region of Ice," "Where Are You Going, Where Have You Been?," "Unmailed, Unwritten Letters," "Accomplished Desires," "How I Contemplated the World from the Detroit House of Correction...," "The Dead," and "The Translation" were reprinted in *Prize Stories: The O. Henry Awards.* "The Fine White Mist of Winter," "First Views of the Enemy," "Upon the Sweeping Flood," "Where Are You Going, Where Have You Been?," "By the River," and "Silkie" were reprinted in *The Best American Short Stories.* "Four Summers" was reprinted in *The American Literary Anthology.*

Library of Congress Cataloging-in-Publication Data

Oates, Joyce Carol, 1938–
    Where are you going, where have you been? : selected early stories /
    Joyce Carol Oates
      I. Title
    PS3565.A8W43   1993   813'.54—dc20   92-44899
ISBN 0-86538-077-5
ISBN 0-86538-078-3 (pbk.)

ONTARIO REVIEW PRESS
Distributed by W. W. Norton & Company, Inc.
500 Fifth Avenue, New York, NY 10110

CONTENTS

Edge of the World

S HELL WAS EIGHTEEN just the day before his unlucky race with Jan. He stood a proud five feet ten inches, weighed a hundred sixty pounds—all dressed, that is, wearing his boots—on the scales in front of the drugstore, and drove a motorcycle with a white fur seat. He was known up and down the highway but thought nothing of that—they had heard of him, Shell, when he was fifteen; the older guys had known him back as far as that. "He's got blood there," guys would say, two years ago, even, when he was only a kid. "He's got blood in him"—so they had yelled, cheering, his own friends now, when he had beaten out every other cyclist the Sunday before at the Eden Crick turkey run.

Driving up to Jan's, Shell had sung in the wind. He had sucked in the air, swelling with it, singing against the noise of the motorcycle and not once looking back at his two friends, who must have stayed behind him on purpose, watching him, maybe imitating the way he drove with his head tilted a little back, so, his hair shooting out straight in the wind. Shell could picture himself: his shoulders looking big, muscular, under the khaki jacket, his hands clumsy and strong in the thick cotton gloves, grasping the handles, Shell with the sailor's cap, streaked with dirt and oil, pulled down tight over his forehead, so he had to tilt his head back slightly to look at the road. His eyes were hidden by the merciless gleam of sunglasses, so that he looked impersonal, secret, and vaguely threatening—he pictured himself so, and indeed had just been looking at himself in the candy-machine mirror back at the garage. The Sunday before, everyone had watched him: getting off the motorcycle slowly, his jeans tight about his legs and hips, his feet big in the grease-stained old boots, his eyes just streaks of light, while his friends crowded around him, and girls too, and others just coming through the tall grass to congratulate him. "You drew blood there," one of the guys shouted, and Shell felt the words make him hot, dizzy, blind. "That old guy with the bald head. He never got past them rocks."

On their way to Jan's, on the narrow road, Shell had been struck as always by a queer sensation of falling, of being drawn toward something; and the proud vision of himself had vanished. He and the boys had followed the winding road for a mile or two out of town, through farmland and woods; they had smelled burned grass in the air, and the clear hot smell of sunlight itself. But after a while the woods had given way, the fields had given way, and their eyes were assaulted by the great sweep of Jan's land, as far as the eye could dart, an incredible expanse of what looked like reflections at first, a painful glaring—the sunlight here sheered off hundreds of old automobiles and trucks with something like the swift, clean stroke of a surgical instrument.

These cars and trucks were not in rows but were simply set down at random in the wild grass. Some of them had human looks, Shell thought, with doors swung open like arms, or torn off completely; cars lying still on their sides with the dust-covered grease of the undersides showing, like something indecent. In the hot sunlight the windows were winking at Shell, and the twisted metal had a look of tenseness, of rigidity, like muscles braced against something. And the cars were nearly all the same color: a dirty rain-washed gray. "Old Jan!" Shell had suddenly said aloud. He felt an unaccountable surge of anger, of frustration. "Goddam junk yard—" Here and there bright pools of oil stretched between the cars, and rubbish burned in piles, smoke rising slowly as if through water. This smoke Shell could almost taste. It had been in the air for some time and he spat viciously, trying to get the taste out of his mouth. The smell made him angry and he felt his legs and arms begin to twitch as he slowed to turn into the drive.

"A goddam junk yard here!" he had yelled back to Nick and Tony.

Jan always emerged in Shell's mind out of the smell of dust and oil and perpetually burning rubber. He was a big old man, over six feet tall, with thick filthy arms like hacked wood, angular and bursting with strength. His head he carried high and tilted as any game cock's, and his hair, grown gray and wispy, moved softly about his head like a cloud. His working clothes, matted and dirty and shapeless about him, looked like parts of his body, grown to him, stiff with grease. That spring he had dragged the sick-looking strip of land on the far side of the junk yard to plant corn, using a borrowed horse and plow. Going by on the road, people had watched him silently—the horse and the man about the same size, moving with the same ponderous, indifferent strength, eyes closed dreamily against the white, hot haze. Saturdays in town they would see him, dressed up in a black suit coat with leather patches sewed on the elbows, tight across his shoulders, opening pompously upon his big stomach. His young wife would be at his side, walking as if she were in a parade—a back-country girl said to be his cousin, or maybe his niece, with streaked hair and a broad, flat, satisfied look, a look that made men watch her. She would always stop and pull Jan to a stop before the mirror on the scales in front of the drugstore, and lick her lips, and stare seriously at herself in the mirror, the only time she looked serious at all. Later on in the afternoon, down at the saloon, or out by the fair grounds where the motorcyclists gathered, everyone would hear Jan's voice—slow and easy in its strength, its expansiveness. "It was on Cherry River that bastard got kilt, and nowhere else," Jan would say, evoking in his listeners looks of calculation, of admiration, ending arguments with his blank pitiless stare, with the edge of humor that threatened them more surely than his anger.

Shell and the other guys had come over to poke around the junk and to drive on Jan's track. Each time Shell had seen Jan this summer the older man's importance had dwindled a little, to Shell, and now Shell made no pretense of hiding his contempt. Stopping to comb his hair, peering in the motorcycle's mirror at his blemished face—he stiffened a little when he saw it, for the sunlight was too clear—Shell was conscious of the old man's contempt for him as well, as if it were this and nothing else that drew them together. Shell drew out the ritual of combing his hair; he sucked at his lip with deliberation. He lifted his left hand slowly, his arm in the thick khaki sleeve bending clumsily, deliberately, to shape his hair on top, while with his right hand he combed the thick front lock, heavy and dull with grease. Then he wiped the comb on his thigh and took up the dirty sailor's cap again; and again, slowly, ceremoniously, peering all the while into the mirror, he replaced it on his head and pulled it down over his brow. Shell shivered with excitement; he did not know why.

"Yah, it don't matter what you say," Jan muttered. His expression must have been funny because they all laughed—the four or five older men who stood around the edge of the track. For a moment Shell felt isolated by their laughter. Then he turned slowly and glanced at his friends—Nick and Tony, like him sitting on their motorcycles. They grinned back encouragingly, and he felt all right.

"A old man like you shouldn't talk so much," Shell said. He peered at himself thoughtfully in his mirror. "He ain't got just that much time left to breathe in." He heard them laugh again, this time Nick and Tony too. He felt good. The shiver of excitement returned, and he had a vision, in just that instant, of striking old Jan with his bare fists, his fingers, nails, digging at the man's face—he had a vision of setting fire to all of Jan's land, his junked cars, trucks, motorcycles, the squat little shanty in the middle, even. . . .

Shell put the comb into his pocket. He turned slowly, luxuriously. He felt good. He felt he could see himself in the other men's eyes: younger than they were, stronger, healthier. He leaned back in the fur seat and pulled his sailor's cap a little farther down on his forehead. He was conscious of entering into the ritual once more—of giving in to, indeed bringing about, the dialogue between himself and old Jan that had started at the beginning of the summer, when he had won his first real race. Before that, in the years before that, he had sometimes felt the old man's eyes on him, he had felt something in the old man's behavior that was peculiar—peculiarly harsh, even for Jan—as if the man was singling Shell out for something. When he was just a kid he and the other guys would stand in the high burnt grass at the edge of tracks, listening to Jan or other men arguing about racing, recalling races, victories, deaths.... It seemed to Shell that they had stood there, so, on the edge of tracks for years, listening and watching; and now they were on the tracks themselves, they were looked at, applauded; they tore through the blurring visions of these old men and discovered finally that they had no concern for these men, no care at all, except maybe an irritable impatience to be rid of them, an impatience for them to die.

"Yah," Jan said almost pleasantly, "I'll be breathin' when your blood runs along the track, you wait an' see. I'll walk acrost your blood in the dirt. You wait for that, kid."

Shell did not move. He felt Nick and Tony watching him, and the other men—the old men of forty or so, in farm clothes, dirty, shapeless, without identity—holding their faces tight, ready to smile or laugh out loud. "I'll wait for it," Shell said.

"You don't have anybody good to go against anymore," Jan said. He had a short piece of copper wire wound around his fingers; he pointed at Shell with it. "Not a one of you. If you'd been around here when I—when I was—"

Shell and the boys hooted with laughter. One of them, Nick or Tony, began pounding on the seat of his motorcycle. "That's what I come to hear!" Shell cried. "Old Jan! Goddam old Jan! I speck your wife'd like to hear that too, she ain't heard it much these last years!" He saw the men finally give in and begin smiling. He saw Jan's eyes narrow. "I speck she'd like to hear it again. How come she ain't out here? What's she doin'?"

When Jan did not answer, Shell went on excitedly, "How come she ain't here? She ain't even seen this-here thingmajig I bought for the handle here," he said, caressing the white fur ornament, a thing the shape of a giant rabbit's foot. Caressing the fur, glancing around toward the little shanty, he felt another surge of excitement. Then he gave in to his excitement, chanting breathlessly and mindlessly: "May! You, May! May! May! You come on out! You come on out an' listen to goddam old Jan an' his junk yard! How he ust to race! May—"

The other boys joined in, pounding at the seats of their motorcycles. "You leave off that noise," Jan said.

Shell stopped. He was wet with perspiration. The khaki jacket was too hot, now that he was no longer on the road, but he did not want to take it off. He grinned and wiped his forehead. "It might be I got to show you somethin' myself one of these days," Jan said. "It might be there ain't nobody your own age to do it to you."

Shell laughed. "Old Jan an' his junk yard," he said.

"It might be you just don't know enough about the world and what it does to you," Jan said.

Shell hesitated; he felt confused, then angry. "Ah, hell," he said. "How would you know yourself? A goddam big lot of talk. How would you know? You never go anywheres yourself. You always stay here. What do you think, this is the middle of the world? This place here—" He looked around with what was meant to be an expression of careless, enveloping contempt, taking in the whole of the lot, the whole of the country, perhaps. "You ought to get somewheres! You ought to do something!" He was leaning forward now, tense and excited; and when he thought of how he must look he relaxed. He sat back and laughed. "Stick to one place all your life like a goddam grazin' cow," he said. He thought that was good.

"I know all I need to know," Jan said quietly. "I meet all the people there is to meet. Why, I been drivin' since I—" But here Jan too caught himself. He went on sarcastically, "There's always a young kid like you, thinks he knows everything, gets himself something like this-here—" He kicked the front wheel of Shell's motorcycle. "You get yourself one of these an' think that buys you everything. Well—you come to the right place if you want to learn about . . ."

"Don't you kick this!" Shell said.

"What?"

"You heard me!"

Jan looked at him. "You heard me," Shell said. "You ain't got nothin' in this whole place as good as this. This place! I ought to come here some night, you an' your wife asleep snorin', an' get me a big thing of gasoline an' spill it half acrost an acre! I ought to! An' then take a match an' let it go! Fire it up! Fire up Jan's goddam old junk field! That's what I ought to do, you old— goddam old—"

Shell's words ran out. But the excitement of the moment stayed static, loud in the air about them. Shell understood something of his own threat when he saw the beginning of fear in Jan's eyes. Jan looked at him, twisting the piece of copper wire slowly around his dirty fingers; no one spoke. Then there was movement somewhere—coming across the field—and they saw Jan's wife crossing, a bright splash of color against the burnt field and the fog of smoke beyond. Shell forgot his tenseness. "You, May!" he shouted. "Hey! You look here, look what I got for myself!"

May's big grin seemed to come on ahead of her. She wore a bright blue scarf loosely about her hair, and her blond streaked hair glinted in and out of the sunlight. "I heard you all talkin' out here," she said. "I heard your voices all the way back home." She was looking at Shell. "What's that?" she said. "Is that a new thing? Well, look at that—ain't it pretty—"

She laughed; Shell grinned foolishly. She stepped delicately through the high grass, self-consciously, still laughing, and came to Shell's side and poked at the fur piece with her finger. "I seen one of these things before, on a car antenna. I always thought it was the prettiest thing."

"We got to listen to old Jan again," Shell said boldly, with more courage than he had believed he possessed. "We got to listen to how he beat off everybody, sixty years ago when he was a kid! We got to listen to how he—"

May laughed again. She ran her finger around the rust-flecked edge of the motorcycle mirror. "He ain't at that again, is he?" she said.

"Acts like he's got somethin' good as this out in all that junk," Shell said.

May looked around at Jan. "Now, don't you say that. You know it ain't true. Don't you go an' say anything. You know how much Shell paid for this."

"For that? What do I care?"

"It beats anything you got here," Shell said. "This old junk yard! You expect you can talk to me, *me*, when all you own for yourself is junk!"

"I got one good cycle here," Jan said slowly. "It ain't new but it's faster than that—"

"Where? Where is it?"

"It ust to belong to a guy drove a regular racer, too; he had to quit an' let me have it!"

"Where is it? Let's see it!"

"You mean that old thing?" May said. "That old thing you had out here the other day? Is that what you're talkin' about now?"

"You be quiet."

"Is that it? That thing you give him fifty dollars for, like a regular fool?"

"You be quiet!"

"Like a regular fool—"

"You be *quiet!*"

May stepped back, her arm still outstretched, her forefinger still touching the top of the mirror. They saw, after a moment, that she was smiling again, tightly, that she was glancing now and then at her reflection in the mirror. "You don't need to get so loud," Shell said. He pulled the sailor's cap off, wiped his forehead with the back of his hand, and put it on again so low on his forehead that he had to tilt his head back to look at Jan. Then he twisted his identification bracelet around, back and forth on his wrist. "Don't need to go all crazy over some motorcycle you prob'ly ain't even got. I wonder you wouldn't—" He looked at May. "You, too, I wonder you wouldn't go all crazy, stuck here in a place like this. Why, you don't even know what they're makin' any more—an' all you got here is old junk, old tires an' parts— You don't own a thing close to what I got!"

Jan began smiling. His grin took on a harsh and indecent look. Shell, under the impact of that look, suddenly got off his motorcycle and walked around it. He kicked at the dust on the track. Some dirt came up onto his pant leg, and he kicked angrily, aimlessly, into the air. "You an' this goddam cemetery you come to die in! Well, I got more than this! I got more than you! It don't even matter what you think—here— Because this is only here. Where do you ever go? What do you ever see? All you do is stay here, this little place, this little—"

"What are you sayin'?"

"This little world here!" He was still kicking at the track. When he looked around at Jan the old man's face seemed all angles and sharp, clear planes, as though his features had been struck out of rock. "This little world."

Still Jan looked at him, smiling coarsely, and the other men, and Nick and Tony, and May too, all watched him. Shell felt blinded and dizzy by their attention. "I mean to go a far way from here!" he said. He began talking faster and faster. "I ain't stayin' out here in the country to die!"

"No place is ever diffrent," Jan said.

"No." Shell began circling Jan slowly, self-consciously, aware that he might look a little ridiculous. He shook his head. "No. You got to go somewhere. You got to do something."

"What?"

"You got to do something with yourself!"

They waited; May was staring at him. "But you do a lot of things right now, Shell," she said. "What are you talkin' about? Do you know what he's talkin' about?"

"This ain't enough," Shell said. "This place here, this ain't enough for me!"

"Do you know what he's talkin' about?"

Shell stopped to look at her. "There's all kinds of places you ain't seen yet, or I ain't—there's all kinds of things we ain't done. We ain't even thought of! If I just knew which way to go...."

Jan began to laugh. Shell was gripped with anger again, with an anger verging on madness. "You shut up! You keep out of this! I only come over here today to show you this, to show you I got somethin' better than you! I did! What the hell do I care about you? I never wanted your opinion on it—I never asked it—I never asked it once, all the time I been here today! Did I? Did I? Or any time since I got this-here motorcycle! Did I? Never once! Now you know it, now I tole you, now I'm goin'. This cheap little dump, a place to crawl an' die in, I ain't ever comin' back here again—" He jerked his head suddenly, slapping at his cheek, at a fly about to alight on his face. "An' you know what I'm goin' to do? You know what? I'm goin' to get on that, I'm goin' to keep right on an' on as fast as I can, right out of here and this whole land—this whole time—I ain't ever comin' back!"

"Where are you goin'?"

"I ain't ever comin' back!" Shell shouted. "I ain't ever goin' to see you again! A goddam place like this to die in, an' the world goin' on an' on out away from it, on all sides, in all ways! Out to the edge of the world! A windy place! A wild place!" Shell fell into the somehow comforting familiarity of chanting, as he twisted the tarnished bracelet around his wrist. This was the way they urged drivers on at the tracks, or joked with each other, their voices falling into short low breathless phrases, the words themselves meaningless, only the gesture itself important. "Out far away from here! This goddam cemetery to die in—ought to burn it up—burn you up with it—burn it all up, up to the sky! An' you in it—you in it cryin'—cryin' for me to stop!"

He fell quiet. No one spoke. Then Jan said slowly, slyly, "But anywhere you go ain't no diffrent than here. Don't you know that?"

Shell looked at him. He was panting with excitement; his face was covered with sweat. Jan went on expansively, his big hands caught in his straining belt, "That's how this-here world was put together. It ain't no diffrent, one side or another; an' there ain't no edge to it, neither, but only one side that keeps on goin' around. An' the people— Why, the people might look a little diffrent, maybe, but they're the same ones—the same people.... They just act like they don't know you, but they're all the same. You act like you don't know them; you do it yourself, without thinkin'. Yet it's all the same, it never changes, it keeps the same in spite of you."

Shell felt he could not understand. The sunlight buzzed and throbbed at him. In the middle of it Jan watched him with brown eyes, eyes the color of earth, dirt; and his face, the color of hardened earth too, seemed posed flatly and blindly and permanently at Shell. "You lyin' old bastard," Shell said.

One of the men slapped at his arm. "These flies here," he said. "They're bitin' like skeeters today."

"Must be goin' to rain."

"What? Goin' to rain? There ain't any clouds at all."

One of the men coughed. "I don't care, it feels like rain anyhow. Just the wind, how it is—it feels so hot, it feels so heavy—"

"You shut up!" Shell cried. "You're drivin' me crazy!" He stopped; he met their eyes in alarm; then his face changed again, he felt it change. "Or I don't care. Talk all you want. I'm gettin' out of here anyway."

Jan stepped over to him. One minute he stood a few feet away, so heavy, so solid that he might never be able to move, even; the next minute his big dirty boot was right next to Shell's. "Just a minute," he said. "You ain't leavin' yet."

Shell faced him. "The hell I ain't," he said. He waited for the moment to assess itself, for his friends to shout approval or to say, "You drew blood there, Shell!" But no one spoke. The way Jan looked at him, a person could tell he had control of the silence as well as of whatever was said.

Finally he said, "You don't mean to leave without me teachin' you a lesson."

"A lesson!"

"A lesson in drivin'."

"You can't teach me anything," Shell said.

"Are you afraid?" The old man, with the copper wire still twisted jaggedly about his fingers, pointed at Shell, smiling a little.

"I ain't afraid of anybody," Shell said.

"You get on that motorcycle then, an' wait till I bring mine around."

"You think so!" Shell cried pointlessly. He looked around at the others and laughed suddenly. He began pounding the palm of one hand with the fist of the other. "Did you hear that?" he said. "Did you hear how crazy he's got now?"

May put her hand to her mouth. "It must be the heat drove him crazy," he said.

"You ain't leavin' without this," Jan said. His glance flicked from Shell's face to May's. "What are you laughin' at?" he said. "You! You get on back to the house!"

"I guess I can stay here."

"You go on."

"I guess I can stay here, watch you make a fool of yourself. I ain't seen that for a while lately."

"And I'll bet anything you want! You just name it to me!" Jan said suddenly. He pointed at Shell again; Shell could see the jagged wire trembling. "I'll put it up against nothin' from you— you don't need a thing to back it up."

"I got some money," Shell said. His words came in a rush, as if he had at last discovered a point about which he could argue. "You say how much. You say it."

They faced each other, a few feet apart. "I don't want anything of yours," Jan said. "All I want is to show you somethin'. But you, you name it— You go on and say anything."

Shell was still striking his palm, laughing a brief, humorless laugh. He looked around—at his friends who stood waiting and eager, oddly silent, their expressions exactly alike, at the older men with their looks of savage contentment, at May, at Jan himself. Then he looked away; his gaze dropped. "No. I don't want anything either. I'm as much a man as you."

"I'm waitin'."

"I said no. I said nothin'."

"Come on." Jan's chest swelled; his voice came deeper, calmer. "Come on, I'm waitin'. You name it."

"No."

"I said you name it."

"No."

"Come on."

"No—nothin'—"

"Say *her*. Come on."

Shell's gaze jerked back up. "Wouldn't you like that!" he said.

"Come on. Say it."

"So you could—"

"Come on!"

"So you could kill me!"

"Come on. Come on."

Shell shook his head. "No. I ain't sayin' a word. You go get that old thing an' I'll race you for nothin'. I will. You needn't get all crazy over it."

Jan seemed pleased with something. "I spose you do think I'm crazy," he said. "All right. All right, you stay here. Three times around this track, then, three times—"

"Three times!" Shell cried. "An' then see who's faster!"

Jan had turned; he now hesitated. He looked around. "Faster?" he said. "See who's faster? Why, did you spose the race was for that?"

Shell blinked at him. One of the men ducked his head suddenly, as if he did not want to show his laughter. "Ain't you smarter'n that?" Jan said. He grinned broadly, showing his gray teeth, a big man with a thick, muscular neck, with a proud set to his head, a proud hard smile—not an old man, really, Shell saw, but a man who had always looked as he did, stood as he did, a man who had never been any younger, had never cared to be younger—a man who had waited for Shell, standing just so, for years. Shell felt the heat vibrate and throb about him. "A big man like you," Jan said, "ain't you smarter'n that?"

Jan turned and crossed through the field. Shell felt dizzy, uncertain, he could not understand Jan's words or the looks of the men who watched him. "Three times around!" he said loudly, his mind jerking back to that phrase. "You come on! I'm waitin' here! Crazy old— Must be crazy, gone crazy with the sun an' that-there smell around here!" Shell went back to his motorcycle suddenly, as if he had just remembered it. He pushed May aside. "You stand off an' watch," he said. He spoke furiously. "Wanted me to bet with him! Well, I ain't goin' to! I ain't goin' to bet a thing, or say a word, he could use to get mad on— I heard some of the things he done already, over that."

"You're not afraid of him?" May said.

"I ain't afraid of anybody," he said. "I don't care how it would hurt to die; I just don't want to get kilt now. I want to keep on drivin' for a while, I want to go somewheres and do things, you know, I want to go around tracks like this with guys— That's what I want, that's all I want, I don't want to get kilt here, to have it all end here, nothin' done, no place seen, a goddam cemetery to come to— Only he could never do it," Shell said abruptly. "He could never kill me." He looked at May. Then he looked at Nick and Tony. But they did not share any expression with him, any common thought. Shell looked past them to the shanty, to Jan beside it, bent over something, working with something that gleamed; and in that same instant he believed he could see himself as he must look to these people, his queer narrowed look, his frightened silence, channeled toward their indifferent curiosity out of the whole day—the whole vista of wind, and heat, and dust, and the smell of burning rubber—a communication to them of other days they had seen, surely, in other summers, days such as this with the burning odor in the air and the sunlight pressing down against one's chest like a weight, or an opened hand; with the backs of men stained with perspiration above the tall grass; and beyond them the track itself with the choked roar of the motorcycles, now loud, now sucked away, a drifting, weightless speed which never really touched the ground—until something would happen and the design would shift, the men would be running out onto the track and a cloud of dust would ease away to the fields. And afterward small boys would go out onto the deserted track and point out in the dust where the skidding had begun, and they would be able to see in the dirt the dark stains straining inward, toward the center where weeds grew beneath a veil of dust; browned, wind-blown weeds with bright blue flowers.

Shell faced with contempt the weak encouragement of the boys. He put out his hands toward them, ceremoniously, very seriously. "Give me some dirt for it," he said.

The Fine White Mist of Winter

S OME TIME AGO in Eden County the sheriff's best deputy, Rafe Murray, entered what he declared to the sheriff, and to his own wife and man-grown sons, and to every person he encountered for a month, white or black, to be his second period—his new period, be would say queerly, sucking at his upper lip with a series of short, damp, deliberate noises. He was thirty-eight when he had the trouble with Bethl'em Aire, he would say, thirty-eight and with three man-grown sons behind him; but he had had his eyes opened only on that day; he was born on that day; he meant to keep it fresh in his mind. When the long winter finally ended and the roads were thick and shapeless with mud, shot with sunlight, the Negro Bethl'em and his memory had both disappeared from Eden County, and—to everyone's relief, especially his wife's—from Murray's mind too. But up until then, in those thick, gray, mist-choked days, he did keep what had happened fresh in his mind; memories of the fine driving snow that fell on that particular day, and of his great experience, seemed to recur again and again in his thoughts.

He and the Negro Bethl'em, whom he had arrested out in a field, had been caught in a snowstorm driving in to the sheriff's office. At the wheel, Murray had muttered that he had never seen such snow; and every time he exploded into a brief, harsh, almost painful series of curses, the snowstorm outside the car grew thicker. Murray was a big proud man, with eyes that jutted a little out of his head, as if with rage, and these he turned to the swirling world beyond his windshield while the Negro sat silent and shivering beside him, his own eyes narrowed, discreet, while Murray swore at the storm. Never had a man been so tricked by the weather, so confused by his own country, as Murray thought himself to be; and it seemed to him too, though he pushed the idea right away, that he was lost and would never find his way back again.

Back in the sheriff's office they would be waiting for him, the windows warm and steamy, the men sitting around the stove with their legs outstretched, smoking, surely talking of him—of this queer bad luck that had come to Murray, the best deputy, the only man beside Walpole himself good enough to bring in Bethl'em Aire. Murray grimaced to himself at the picture. He saw the men, and he saw in turn their picture of him: Murray with his big, proud shoulders, his big hands, but no common farmer either, no common country farmer; Murray with his felt hat stuck tight on his head, the filthy band fitting right on his forehead as if it had grown there, his black felt hat, like a symbol of something, or like a pot overturned above his face. So his face would emerge beneath the hat broad and tanned, but raw-looking too, stung by the December wind, and his eyes blinking and squinting as if there were a glare. He would have on his overcoat, as great as any horse blanket, stiff and looking from a distance like wood or iron; always braced as if in a wind or just emerging out of one; he would have on his leather gloves as fine and gleaming as new leather could be, his big boots dully gleaming with grease or melted snow; and these he would kick against the stove, ceremoniously, grunting, first the left foot and then the right, with his chin lowered so upon his chest, or down to where the big coat seemed to swell out from his body. No sheriff's deputy carried himself like Murray, no country son of them had his look, or his voice, or could be trusted to bring in such a one as Bethl'em Aire....

But sitting in the cold car, Murray felt the vision slip away. He was looking at the snow, the crazy whirling of flakes. Not that these seemed infinite, or even numerous—they looked instead simply like a constant shuffling and reshuffling of the same flakes, the same specks, gleaming back at him like little white eyes in the glare of the headlights. On either side they fell away into a mass of gray, like a cloud. Murray grinned and swore, spitting at the storm. Now and then he saw stiff, shocked trees along the roadside, bare things as naked in the cold as if someone had peeled all their bark off with a jackknife, peeled it off and tossed it up to be sucked away by the wind. It was then that Murray noticed the Negro Bethl'em staring at the trees too. "This won't last long," Murray said. "It's just a freak storm, and a freak cold too, and you know it as well as me."

It was good to hear his own voice again. He went on: "When I lived farther up north there were storms *there!* That's where they really were—snow up past the first-floor windows of houses, there—and my father would have to dig his way out to see about the stock. People used to die, there, in storms like that! People who were alone . . . ." He wondered why his conversation had taken that turn. His voice had simply gone on that way by itself. He waited for the prisoner to say something; but they only sat for a minute or two in silence, listening to the wind. Then Murray laughed, harshly and humorlessly, and found himself continuing: "They wouldn't find them till maybe a month afterwards," he said, "—old people who lived all alone, old men, frozen to death in their homes. There was one caught in a schoolhouse, one old man; he'd sleep there to save wood at home. He got caught in the schoolhouse when a storm come on and he couldn't get home, and burned all he could—books and desks and all. . . . That old man, I remember him, I remember him coming around, asking to shoe horses in the summer. . . ." Murray wondered at himself, at the odd sound of his voice. He went on immediately. "That was it, then. A man caught so all alone in the winter, that would happen to him—then or now, up there or right here, anywhere. A man is got to stick with others, doing how they do, their laws, obeying their laws, living with them—not off by himself, with his own laws. . . . The ones that think diffrent are the ones get kilt—or we bring them in to get..."

He stopped talking and drove on a while, silent, impressed with his own words and also with the peculiar feeling he had of the closeness of that old man's death; it was just as if it had happened out there in the snowstorm he now faced. Then he shook his mind clear of the thought and decided they ought to stop. "We'll wait this goddam wind out," he said. The wind kept on. Before him the road reared out in broken, bare stretches, as if it had been torn out of the drifts of snow on either side. "Wait it out," Murray muttered. He had not glanced at his prisoner for some time; he did not do so now. He knew, and the prisoner knew, that he had been talking to himself. But now he went on to ask, "You know where we are now?"

The question hung in the air between them. Murray looked around in surprise, as if the Negro had spoken to him. The Negro Bethl'em, however, just sat there, as big a man as Murray, his puffed black face turned right to him; and his eyes, too, small and close together the way Murray supposed a pig's eyes would be, these were staring right at Murray's face or maybe at those queer words Murray had just heard himself say. Bethl'em, a well-known country Negro, well known up and down the road, who worked for hire in the summertime, hay mowing and such, now looked to Murray no longer like himself, but like someone else, or a statue of someone else—all hard and cold and ageless, as if he had been staring at Murray or someone like him, just that way, with those pig's eyes, for centuries. Then he began to cough—not bothering to turn his head aside, coughing in a wracking, terrifying, almost spiteful way.

"Yah, you wouldn't know, would you," Murray said. He felt his cold cheeks tighten. "Cough your goddam heart out, your black tonsils out, then. Go on." He drove on, sitting near the edge of the seat, his knees apart and rubbing against the steering wheel. Murray stared at the storm, his face distorted with the effort of peering ahead. "There—something over there," he said. The prisoner had stopped coughing. Murray pressed the car forward slowly. A ridge of land to his left seemed to fly right up out of the ground, a giant swelling of white like the side of a mountain. "There's a garage somewhere here; I'm damned if there ain't... I know it, I seen it enough times." He spit out his words, almost as if he expected the garage to appear as soon as he spoke, as if his words would make it appear. "It must be here somewhere," he said a little more quietly. "Out here somewhere...." Next to Murray the Negro began coughing again. Murray stared at him for a moment; then he looked away. "Are you all right?" he said.

Bethl'em did not answer. "Most likely getting sick," Murray went on harshly, even angrily, as if he were talking to the snow. "Running all that ways without a coat, like a goddam fool nigger.... Well, you cough all you like. I'm getting out here." He had stopped the car, or allowed it to stop, or allowed the wind to stop it. "I'm going out to see what's here. I think there's a building here." He switched off the ignition but left the lights on. He could barely open the door of the car, and when the first gust of wind hit his face he grunted with surprise and looked back at Bethl'em. He saw the Negro sitting there, watching him.

Murray carried the picture of the man with him as he made his way—bent awkwardly against the wind, against the terrific onslaught of snow—around the front of the car and off the frozen road. Now the snow seemed to mock Murray: Murray with all his pride, all his strength, stumbling first in one direction and then stopping, slyly perhaps, and turning in another, now walking as if he had really caught sight of something. When he finally found himself actually looking at two shapes, oblong and upright with long narrow drifts extending out behind them like angels' wings, he could only gape at them in confusion. Then he saw the dim flicker of a light behind them, a light that grew stronger as he stared at it, shielding his big face with his hands. The wind flung pulsing clouds of snow, like handfuls of fine hard sand, against his face.

While helping Bethl'em out of the car and to the building he had just discovered, Murray had to grab hold of him once to keep him from falling—the ground underfoot was ice—and stood for a moment with his feet far apart, bracing both of them: the prisoner, with his wrists tied behind him, could not help himself. Murray put his arms tightly around the man's shoulders and in this way, panting, with both their heads bowed, the line of snow slashing at their foreheads as if they were no more than the gasoline pumps they could now make out, they made their way through to the little wasteland of shelter in front of the garage. Murray slammed at the door with his foot. He bent to look through the glass of the door, and despite his blurred vision was able to see two men at the back of the garage, a stove, and a lamp of some sort. Muttering with impatience, he saw one of the men advancing slowly and hesitantly toward the door.

When the door opened, Murray pushed Bethl'em inside and then stepped in himself to a warm surge of air and to a startling scene—how startling only Murray himself could have said, and yet it could not really have been a surprise to Murray, who knew this country so well. The man in overalls who had opened the door—a man whose black-and-red plaid shirt was unexpectedly clean—was a Negro. And at the back of the room another Negro sat up straight, staring at them with the look of a rabbit or chipmunk or any small animal who believes himself camouflaged by the foliage around him and not really visible, and thus has an air of absurdity about him. Murray, who was still a little shaken by his efforts outdoors, turned to close the door; and for an instant he stared at the frosted glass, and the sense of his isolation among these men welled up and subsided within him, leaving him a little weak. Then he turned back. "We only come to sit out this storm," he said.

The first Negro was staring at him and, past him, at Bethl'em, with a look of muffled recognition. "You c'n come in here," the Negro said slowly. "By the stove an' get warm . . . I was . . . I was scairt for a minute who was out there."

It was warmer at the back of the garage. The other Negro, a younger man, watched them. He was sitting in a swivel chair before a large office desk, an old-fashioned, ridiculous piece of furniture with scratches and initials on its surface. The older Negro went to the side of the desk and picked up a screwdriver, idly. He looked back at Murray over his shoulder.

"We thank you for this," Murray said, nodding brusquely. He had begun to feel oddly warm. Now, as if performing before these men—whom he believed he recognized vaguely—but at the same time not really performing for them at all, but for his own satisfaction, his own delight, Murray began ceremoniously to unbutton his coat. He had taken off one of his fine leather gloves, and this he now stuck in his pocket, as if it were an ornament, and then with one glove on and one glove off he began to unbutton the big plastic buttons of the coat, frowning, his face distorted with concentration. The Negroes watched him. When he had pushed the last button out of its buttonhole he sighed and straightened his shoulders and made a gesture— even Murray could not have said how he did it—so that the older Negro gave a slight start and came over to take Murray's coat. Murray watched him carry it off gingerly in his arms and then hang it on a peg, brushing snow off it, yet doing that gingerly too, as if he knew he was being closely watched. With his right hand Murray took hold of the red wool scarf his mother had knitted for him the first winter he was a deputy and began to unwind it, again ceremoniously, while the others watched. This too he handed to the Negro, who hung it by the coat. Murray was about to take off his hat, but he only touched it; for some reason it suddenly struck him that it might look better on, though it was wet. Then he turned with ceremony to Bethl'em and, while the others stared, began to brush some of the snow off the man. "Stand by the stove," he said. Bethl'em turned to it almost blindly. The stove was an old one, made of iron, a large, squat, ancient stove that gave forth a low roaring murmur and glowed, in spots, a hard-looking yellow. Murray patted Bethl'em's shoulders and untied his wrists, and he saw now that the cord had cut into the man's flesh, that it had made raw red lines in his skin. "Look at that," Murray said in disgust. He held the cord at arm's length. "Never even told me it was too tight."

He faced the two Negroes boldly, as if they were somehow involved in this. They were watching him, looking at his uniform. They had evidently both been sitting at the desk, on either side of an open drawer with a piece of stiff cardboard over it, playing cards; some of the cards now lay inside the drawer, blown there when the door was opened. The finger-worn, soiled surfaces, the drunken-looking, glazed faces of the kings and queens and jacks, seemed to be gazing idly at Murray. "Expect we could offer them some coffee," the young Negro said. "It's a purely cold night out."

Murray's mouth watered. But no one moved; and he caught his confusion quickly enough to keep it from showing. The older Negro, who stood picking at the desk halfheartedly with the screwdriver, as if he thought he should look busy, said, "If there's trouble with the car we ain't any help. We ain't up to these new cars. We just give out gas, now."

"No trouble with the car," Murray said.

"That's luck for you," the other Negro said. He and the older man—Murray supposed they were brothers—laughed shortly. The young man leaned back in the swivel chair. He took a pack of cigarettes out of his pocket. "Ain't much luck for your friend you got there, though." Again he and his brother laughed. "Say. Ain't goin' to tie us up with that, are you?"

Murray saw that he was still holding the cord. He shrugged his shoulders and tossed it to the floor. The brothers were grinning identically. At the stove Bethl'em stood with his arms out as if to embrace the heat; his eyes were averted. "That had us purely scairt for a minute," the young Negro said. He was lighting a cigarette. His movements were slow and self-conscious. Still moving slowly, he got to his feet. "You, boy. I expect you'd like a cigarette too." He was grinning at Murray, showing his teeth; but when he extended the pack it was to Bethl'em. Murray, watching cautiously out of the corner of his eye, saw the prisoner's fingers take a cigarette. "What's he done to get himself arrested so?" the young Negro said. "He hurt some white folks somewheres?"

The young man's chest seemed swollen when he sat down again, leaning back precariously in the swivel chair; and now his brother had begun to smile too, looking up from the scratches he was making on the desk. Alarmed, Murray realized that not only did they look alike but they seemed now to be sharing the same expression: a sly, knowing, inviting look. The young man smoked his cigarette. "Maybe you can't talk none," he said. Murray blinked at his words. "We got to let you in here, or anything you want, but you never need to talk to us. But I

expect we already know what he done, anyhow. That Bethl'em
Aire, there, there was talking all up an' down here about him.....
He never left off fightin' too early. Ain't that right?"

Murray glanced at the prisoner, who stood with his eyes
lowered, as if he were listening to something forbidden. His
face, though, looked as if it had thawed. "What they goin' to do
to him?" the older Negro asked suddenly.

Murray stiffened. "A matter of the law," he said.

"What they goin' to do?"

Murray stared at them. The brothers met his stare equally,
easily, like burlesques of himself, or like negatives of himself
mocking him.

"Seems that takin' a man in to somethin' like he's goin' to get,
there, an' not even know for sure what it is—that ain't the way
to do," the young man said seriously. "You, Bethl'em. You think
that's the way to do? Takin' a man in, an' him sure to be kilt for
it...."

"Wait," Murray said. His voice sounded quite young. But
what most surprised him was that whatever concern he felt,
whatever alarm, was not for himself but for Bethl'em.

The word evidently came as a pleasant surprise, however, to
the young Negro, who now lounged in the chair with the
cigarette in his teeth. "That sheriff Walpole knows me fine, an'
he might of come through here an' tole me somethin'," he said.
"Yes. He might of tole me somethin' about Bethl'em. An' I surely
wouldn't want to trade no place with that boy there."

Murray glanced from the prisoner's strong back to the brothers. The brothers had drawn closer together; the older man,
standing, was leaning against the desk; the younger sat up
slowly in the creaking chair. He shook some ashes deliberately
onto the concrete floor. "It ain't easy to consider a man that's
alive right now," he said grandly, as if beginning a speech, "an'
is goin' to be dead in a time. Why, that-there blood goin'
through him right now, only think—only think how it'll get all
cold an' hard like grease in the cold.... How a man can go from
alive to dead in such a time! Not just black but white too or any
color. Ain't that so? A thing no more'n that-there screwdriver,
for puttin' in screws an' pickin' around here an' scratchin' the

ice off the window, why, set up against any man's forehead an' pushed in only a bit—any man at all, why . . . "

Murray felt his face burn, and he felt something—at first quite small, like a pinprick—touch coldly at his heart. When he looked around to the prisoner he saw the man was staring at something invisible on the top of the stove. Murray could no longer stand still but began to shift his weight from one foot to the other, grimacing as if in impatience at the storm. But when he spoke it was not of the storm. His words seemed to explode from him. "But I helped him," he said suddenly. "I did. I found him half a mile out in a field trying to run up a hill that was all drifted, and it was sundown, dark in a hour. . . . And this storm coming. . . . He would have died there."

Now the young man laughed. "One place, here or there, another place; there ain't much diffrence." He and his brother laughed quietly. "You, Bethl'em. You see much diffrence?"

Bethl'em did not look around. "He would have got lost in the storm anyway," Murray said. "Lost and frozen, all alone. What good is it for a man all alone? By himself, thinking by himself. . . . He did that just to get away from me. That's what I can't get used to," he said strangely, "them always running away. Goddam fools, don't know what's for their own good, what's all thought up to help them! They don't understand anything but how hungry they are, they live by their stomach, you can't talk to them for five minutes explaining any law—about deer or bass or anything—without their eyes going all around to something else, something over your shoulder: a bird in a tree, or the tree itself, or the sky . . . "

"Hey, what's that?" the young man said. "What's that you're sayin'?"

Murray was breathing hard. He felt more words crowding and jumbling inside him.

"Somethin' about a bird in a tree," the older brother said.

"An' the sky too. Bethl'em, you hear that? You s'pose you're goin' to see much of a sky? Huh? Where you're goin'?"

When Bethl'em turned they all must have thought he was crying. Two almost even trickles of water had run down his face. But it was only from the snow in his hair, and he licked his lips and spat and glared at them. He held the cigarette without smoking it. "I got nothin' to say," he muttered.

"Got nothin'? Why, you better have!" the young man said gaily. "What you think they're bringin' you in for? Why, to talk, Bethl'em, to talk—you got to answer questions polite. You know that sheriff? Don't you s'pose he's got things to ask you? He'll hit right on that trouble with that-there man at the saloon, you know, an' how you done somethin' with your knife you oughtn't of; an' you ain't goin' to like it, no, but you got to answer polite for him." The young man began gathering up the playing cards, which had been blown back into the desk drawer. He picked them up one by one, nodding, clicking his tongue as if in agreement with something. "Yes," he said. "You got to answer polite. An' you know what, Bethl'em? You know what?"

The young man's expression was inscrutable, serious, and knowing, all at once, and he sat nodding at the dirty cards, picking them up and inspecting them, putting them into a pile. "You know what?" He looked right past Murray to the prisoner. "There ain't goin' to be a person at that trial, later, only maybe the wife of the guy you cut, an' his kids or somethin', no, not a person, sheriff or judge or nobody, that ain't goin' to be glad for what you done. They'll all be pleased fine with it." He nodded again, looking at Murray. Murray could see the glazed faces on some of the cards, kings and queens, whose eyes, like those of the Negroes, were turned toward him. "Ain't that right, mister deppity? You tell him. Ain't that right?"

Murray turned away; he walked blindly toward the front of the garage. "Ain't that right!" the young man cried; there was joy in his voice. "Ain't it! An' nobody here ain't explained the diffrence between lettin' a man die a good way, a clean way, by himself out in the snow, in his own land, an' bringin' him in so they can make a fuss out of it—a show out of it." His words tumbled about themselves. "Yes," he said loudly, "that ain't been tole to me yet. Or to Bethl'em either. He ain't got much time to be tole it in. If you're goin' to take a man in to be kilt you better explain to him why. You—"

Murray tried to calm himself. He stared out the window, but his hand was on his pistol. Most of all he was conscious of

Bethl'em's eyes on him, on his back; and he could feel his heart cringing inside him, in shame, a shame that was all mixed up, that had no direction in which to go. The best deputy, Murray thought, the best one of them, as good almost as Walpole himself.... And he saw a picture of himself suddenly: tall and proud, with his hat stuck so tightly on his head, his broad face sick and pale, like uncooked dough, just a mockery of the old Murray, the one everyone along the road knew, Murray with his hard chin and his sunburned, wind-blown good looks.... Outside the snowstorm had thinned a little, the wind had nearly stopped; there was a bright moon somewhere that lit up everything with a delicate whiteness, a crystalline whiteness. It was so clean, so white, it would be painful to the touch, burning to the breath. "A man let loose in all this cold wouldn't last," the young man said loudly. "He'd walk off by himself further an' further, all alone, an' never need for any white folks to do it to him. Any man is got a right...."

Murray stared out at the great banks of white, toppled and slanted in the dark. Beyond his surface paralysis, he felt something else, something peculiar—a sense, maybe, of the familiarity of the landscape. He had watched such scenes as this almost every night in the winters of his childhood farther north, when he used to crouch at his bedroom window in the dark and peer out at the night, at the snow falling or the fine whirling mist, which held no strangeness, he felt, except what people thought strange in it—the chaos of something not yet formed.... Outside the garage the earth seemed to roll out of sight, like something too gigantic to conceive of. And Murray felt again the isolation not only of himself but of the prisoner and the other Negroes as well; and he knew too that the time was approaching when he would have to do something by himself—not with the sheriff behind him, or with any laws to back him up, but by himself alone.

When Murray turned back, his heart was pounding. Bethl'em had straightened; he now stood taller than any of them. He was sucking in his breath slowly, moving his eyes slowly about Murray's face and behind his head as if it were all the same thing, doing something with his hands—rubbing his wrists—

and grinding out the cigarette on the floor. The brothers had not moved; they grinned toward Murray, their smiles fixed and expectant, and the younger one went on quietly, proddingly, "Now you, Bethl'em, you maybe got your only chance now. We're behind you. We ain't goin' to stand by to see such things happen—we ain't now, that's true—an' that-there deppity what's-his-name, that I seen ridin' around in the back seat of Walpole's old car enough times, he knows what's good for him, he ain't goin' to interfere—he ain't!" The young man's arms came loose. "You go on now, Bethl'em," he said. "You go on! You're a man, an' you got your right to."

Murray waited. Both he and the prisoner were breathing strongly, almost at the same time, their big chests taut, filling with air and then falling; they were standing stiffly, rigidly, waiting, their eyes tied up together as if they were counting the steps between one another. But Bethl'em's look was so unflinching, so intense, so knowing of what was right, what was just, that Murray thought he could not bear it any longer—that look pierced him like a sliver of glass, and he looked away. Now the young Negro's chanting voice, even his words, which ought to have sounded so provoking to Murray, seemed only familiar, only right, exactly what he would have expected, almost what he should have said himself. "You are a man," the young Negro said, "an' there's no law here—not here, not tonight. Where is there any law? Where is it? Or any one of us better'n another? All of us caught here in a storm, a blizzard, who's to say if there's anything left but us? Any laws? Any ol' sheriff? You surely got a right to your own life. You got a right. You got a right to...."

Neither Murray nor the prisoner had moved. They seemed locked by their eyes, as if in an embrace, with the air swelling about them, around their ears, so that Murray was sure that in a moment it would explode into him, deafening him and crushing his brain. Then he saw something he did not at first believe: the young Negro now standing behind Bethl'em's shoulder, *winking*, and at Murray, too. But there the young man stood, nodding brightly, grinning incredibly, with one eye shut tight and wrinkled. Murray gaped; he sucked at the air, at its tremendous pressure. "You...you..." he stammered. His fingers were so tight on the revolver handle that he could not move them. "You! What are you...? What..."

Just as Bethl'em was about to move, the young Negro and his brother began laughing. To Murray, even their teeth seemed to laugh, and he felt their laughter tear through him, just as he knew it must be tearing through Bethl'em. "Look at that Bethl'em, now!" the young man cried. His delight so shook him that he jerked like a puppet, his arms loose, his shoulders rocking. "Just look! Here he thinks he's goin' somewhere! He ain't never goin' to get along with no white men—ain't one time goin' to learn!"

Bethl'em's shoulders relaxed just a little. His face stayed tight like a mask, staring straight at Murray's shamed face. "Now, you, Bethl'em, now," the young man said, dancing around, "don't you get mad at *me*. I ain't done a thing. It ain't a fault of mine you come to believe so much!"

Murray went to the prisoner and took his arm. He could not look at the man's face, so he looked at his collar instead and at the wet hair that grew so far down his neck. Murray stood there for a minute or so. Then be said, "We're leaving now. The storm's let up." Murray could hear nothing but the prisoner's slow, even breath and the almost noiseless laughter of the brothers. "You, Bethl'em," he said. "You go on out to the car. You get in and wait." He stopped for a moment. "Go on," he said.

Bethl'em went to the door and left. Murray did not watch him, nor did he look at the brothers. At first he did not know where to look; he did not know what to do; he could not, right now, even think beyond the terrible shame he had seen. He felt weak and sickened at the thought of it. Then he turned briskly; he stiffened his shoulders; he took his red scarf very carefully off the peg and began winding it around his neck. It took him some time to dress. The young Negro kept on, a little louder now: "That Bethl'em's a big man, a good big man, I known him too long a time already. A big man up an' down this road! Hey!"

Murray finished buttoning his coat. He did not hurry. He kept his attention on himself; he kept his attention on putting on his gloves. When he was ready to go he knew there was something left wrong, unfinished; but he could not think what it was, his mind still buzzed and was crowded so. "An' you tell that sheriff, too," the young man was saying. "Will you? You tell him." The laughter had suddenly drained out of his face. "Mister deppity—wait.... Wait a minute!"

Murray was staring at him. Then he saw the cord on the floor; he bent over slowly, picked it up, and put it in his pocket. He went to the door. The young man hurried along behind him. He took hold of Murray's arm. "You, mister," he said. "You tell the sheriff how I did here. You tell him that. An' how you caught on to the game right away an' played it too. You tell him. He'll like that. He will. I know that sheriff, he comes out here sometimes.... He buys gas here sometimes...."

Murray stared at the man. "That black boy out there don't demand no more consideration than any other one. He is got to have it done to him too. Is he any diffrent?" The young man spoke quickly and a little shrilly. "Why, there ain't a one of us ain't had it done to him," he said proudly, "an' ain't a white man here don't know it.... That's how it is. An' him too, him too, he is got to have it done to him too...."

He smiled shakily as Murray opened the door and the cold air fell upon them. Murray stepped out. "Wait, wait!" the young Negro said, pulling at his arm. "Mister, you wait. You tell the sheriff, huh? Huh? Will you? You tell him how I did—he'll laugh—you say it was me, here, this garage.... He knows me good.... Why, look here, mister," he said, and he pulled up one of his trouser legs, so quickly that Murray hadn't time to look away, all the way up to the knee so that Murray couldn't fail to see the queer mottled scars. "They sic'd the dogs on me once, had them chase me for fun down by the crick; I wasn't fifteen then; they chased me a long ways, I kept runnin' with them right on my legs an' somebody tole the sheriff an' he come to see me himself an' ast about it, an' looked sorry, but there couldn't be nothin' done.... Why, I never needed to knife no man first, did I? But I had it done, it's how it is; I never even thought much on it. So that black boy you got ain't no diffrent.... You tell the sheriff. He'll remember which one I am, he'll remember me...."

Murray let the door close behind him. Crossing to the car—
he saw with a shock he had never turned the lights off—he
thought he could sense the young man leaning against the glass,
his arms up and embracing the window. Murray did not look
back. The wind pulled at his hat, and he pressed it down tighter.
He went around and got in the car, grunting, his body as heavy
as if he were dragging himself out of water. The air inside the
car was frozen and painful. It turned his breath to steam before
him. Murray sat quietly, resting, his hands on the steering
wheel, looking out at the white world—as Bethl'em himself was
looking, without speaking—and Murray felt the heat of that
shame only now begin to cool. A strange, sinister, diffuse shame
it was; it reached out to all of them, touched them all. He saw
that the fine white mist of the storm, all its queer, brutal power,
its primeval power, had settled, and that all that remained were
forms of sculptured whiteness, familiar forms that reminded
him of the familiar world to which he would return. But still he
sat behind the window tapping his stiffened fingers on it,
thinking, knowing that his behavior not only did not puzzle
Bethl'em but did not even touch upon him.

Murray thought that some time before very long, surely in a
minute or two, he would again continue on his way.

First Views of the Enemy

JUST AROUND THE TURN, the road was alive. First to assault the
eye was a profusion of heads, black-haired, bobbing, and a
number of straw hats that looked oddly professional—like straw
hats in a documentary film; and shirts and overalls and dresses,
red, yellow, beflowered, dotted, striped, some bleached by the
sun, some stiff and brilliant, just bought and worn proudly out
of the store. The bus in which they were traveling—a dead dark
blue, colored, yet without any color—was parked half on the
clay road and half in the prickly high grass by the ditch. Its old-
fashioned hood was open, yanked cruelly up and doubled on
itself, and staring into its greasy, dust-flecked tangle of parts
was the driver, the only fair, brown-haired one of the bunch.
Annette remembered later that as her station wagon moved in
astonishment toward them, the driver looked up and straight at
her: a big indifferent face, curious without interest, smeared
with grease, as if deliberately to disguise himself. No kin of
yours, lady, no kin! he warned contemptuously.

Breaking from a group of children, running with arms out for
a mock embrace, a boy of about seven darted right toward
Annette's car. The boy's thick black hair, curled with sweat,
plastered onto his forehead, framed a delicate, cruelly tanned
face, a face obviously dead white beneath its tan: great dark

eyes, expanded out of proportion, neat little brows like angels'
brows—that unbelievable and indecent beauty of children ex-
ploited for art—a pouting mouth, still purple at the corners
from the raspberries picked and hidden for the long bus ride,
these lips now turning as Annette stared into a hilarious grin
and crying out at her and the stricken child who cringed beside
her, legs already drawn up flatly at the knees—

In agony the brakes cried, held: the scene, dizzy with color,
rocked with the car, down a little, back up, giddily, helplessly,
while dust exploded up on all sides. "Mommy!" Timmy
screamed, fascinated by the violence, yet his wail was oddly still
and drawn out, and his eyes never once turned to his mother.
The little Mexican boy had disappeared in front of the car. Still
the red dust arose, the faces in the bus jerked around together,
white eyes, white teeth, faces were propelled toward the windows of the bus, empty a second before. "God, God," Annette
murmured; she had not yet released the steering wheel, and on
it her fingers began to tighten as if they might tear the wheel off,
hold it up to defend her and her child, perhaps even to attack.

A woman in a colorless dress pushed out of the crowd,
barefooted in the red clay, pointed her finger at Annette and
shouted something—gleefully. She shook her fist, grinning, others grinned behind her; the bus driver turned back to his bus.
Annette saw now the little boy on the other side of the road,
popping up safe in the ditch and jumping frantically—though
the sharp weeds must have hurt his feet—and laughing, yelling,
shouting as if he were insane. The air rang with shouts, with
laughter. A good joke. What was the joke? Annette's brain
reeled with shock, sucked for air as if drowning. Beside her
Timmy wailed softly, but his eyes were fastened on the boy in
the ditch. "He's safe, he's safe," Annette whispered. But others
ran toward her now—big boys, tall but skinny, without shirts.
How their ribs seemed to run with them, sliding up and down
inside the dark tanned flesh with the effort of their legs! Even a
few girls approached, hard dark faces, already aged, black hair
matted and torn about their thin shoulders. They waved and
cried, "Missus! Missus!" Someone even shouted, "Cadillac!"
though her station wagon, already a year old, was far from

being a Cadillac. As if to regain attention, the little boy in the ditch picked up something, a handful of pebbles, and threw it at the car, right beneath Timmy's pale gaping face. A babble of Spanish followed, more laughter, the barefoot woman who must have been the boy's mother strode mightily across the road, grabbed the boy, shook him in an extravagant mockery of punishment: sucked her lips at him, made spitting motions, rubbed his head hard with the palm of her hand—this hurt, Annette saw with satisfaction, for the child winced in spite of his bravado. At the bus the American man's back swelled damply and without concern beneath his shirt; he did not even glance around.

Annette leaned to the window, managed a smile. "Please let me through," she called. Her voice surprised her, it sounded like a voice without body or identity, channeled in over a radio.

The boys made odd gestures with their hands, not clenching them into fists, but instead striking with the edges of their hands, knifelike, into the air. Their teeth grinned and now, with them so close (the bravest were at her fender), Annette could see how discolored their teeth were, though they had seemed white before. They must have been eating dirt! she thought vaguely. "Please let me through," she said. Beside her, Timmy sat in terror. She wanted to reach over and put her hand over his eyes, hide this sight from him—this mob of dirty people, so hungry their tongues seemed to writhe in their mouths, their exhaustion turned to frenzy. "Missus! Missus! *Si, si,* Cadillac!" the boys yelled, pounding on the front of the car. The women, men, even very old people—with frail white hair—watched, surprised and pleased at being entertained.

"Please. Please." Suddenly Annette pressed on the horn: what confidence that sound inspired! The boys hesitated, moved back. She toyed with the accelerator, wanting to slam down on it, to escape. But suppose one of them were in the way.... The horror of that falling thud, the vision of blood sucked into red clay, stilled her nervousness, made her inch the big car forward slowly, slowly. And in the back, those unmistakable bags of groceries, what would be showing at the tops? Maybe tomatoes, pears, strawberries—perhaps picked by these people a few days ago—maybe bread, maybe meat— Annette's face burned with something more than shame. But when she spoke, her voice showed nothing. "Let me through, please. Let me through." She sounded cool and still.

Then she was past. The station wagon picked up speed. Behind her were yells, cries no longer gleeful, now insulted, vicious: in the mirror fists, shouting faces, the little boy running madly into the cloud of dust behind the car. He jerked something back behind his head, his skinny elbow swung, and with his entire body he sent a mud rock after the car that hit the back window square, hard, and exploded. With her fingers still frozen to the steering wheel, Annette sped home.

Beside her the child, fascinated, watched the familiar road as if seeing it for the first time. That tender smile was something strange; Annette did not like it. Annette herself, twitching with fear, always a nervous woman, electric as the harassed or the insanely ill are, saw with shock that her face in the mirror was warm and possessed. That was she, then, and not this wild, heart-thumping woman afraid of those poor children in the road.... Her eyes leaped home, her mind anticipated its haven. Already, straightening out of a turn, she could see it: the long, low orange brick home, trees behind the house not yet big enough for shade, young trees, a young house, a young family. Cleared out of the acres of wheat and wood and grass fields on either side, a surprise to someone driving by, looking for all the world as if it and its fine light green grass, so thin as to look unreal, and its Hercules fence had been picked up somewhere far away and dropped down here. Two miles away, on the highway that paralleled this road, there were homes something like this, but on this road there were only, a half mile ahead, a few farmhouses, typical, some shacks deserted and not deserted, and even a gas station and store; otherwise nothing. Annette felt for the first time the insane danger of this location, and heard with magical accuracy her first question when her husband had suggested it: "But so far out.... Why do you want it so far out?" City children, both of them, the hot rich smell of sunlight and these soundless distances had never been forbidding, isolating. Instead, each random glance at the land strengthened in them a sense of their own cleverness. Children of fortune, to withdraw from their comfortable pasts, to raise a child in such safety! —It was fifteen miles to the nearest town where Annette did her shopping and Timmy went to school, and fifty miles to the city where her husband worked.

Annette turned in the driveway, drove slowly into the garage. Still in a trance, angry at herself, she got out of the car but stood with her hand still lingering on the steering wheel. A thin, fashionably thin young woman, for years more woman than girl, in a white dress she stood with a remote, vague smile, hand lightly on the wheel, mind enticed by something she could not name. Perplexed, incredulous: in spite of the enormity of what threatened (the migrant workers were hardly a mile away), she felt slowed and meaningless, her inertia touched even Timmy, who usually jumped out of the car and slammed the door. If only he would do this and she could cry, "Timmy! *Please!*" calm might be restored. But no, he climbed down on his side like a little old man, he pushed the door back indifferently so that it gave a feeble click and did not even close all the way. For a while mother and son stood on opposite sides of the car; Annette could tell that Timmy did not move and was not even looking at her. Then his footsteps began. He ran out of the garage.

Annette was angry. Only six, he understood her, he knew what was to come next: he was to help her with the packages, with the doors, open the cupboards in the kitchen, he would be in charge of putting things into the refrigerator. As if stricken by a sudden bad memory, Annette stood in the garage, waiting for her mind to clear. What was there in Timmy's running out? For an instant she felt betrayed—as if he cherished the memory of that strange little boy and ran out to keep it from her. She remembered the early days of her motherhood, how contemptuous she had been of herself, of what she had accomplished—a baby she refused to look at, a husband neurotic with worry, a waiting life of motherhood so oppressive that she felt nausea contemplating it: is this what I have become? What is this baby to me? Where am I? Where am *I?* Impassioned, a month out of college and fearful, in spite of her attractiveness, that she would never be married, Annette had taken the dangerous gamble of tearing aside her former life, rejecting the familiar possessions and patterns that had defined her, and had plunged, with that intense confident sharp-voiced young man, into a new life she was never quite sure had not betrayed the old, stricken the old: her parents, her lovely mother, now people to write to, send greeting cards to, hint vaguely at visiting to....

Sighing, she began to move. She took the packages out of the car, went outside (the heat was not brilliant), put them down, and with deft angry motions in case Timmy was secretly watching, pulled down the garage door and locked it. "There!" But when she turned, her confidence was distracted. She stared at the house. Shrubbery hiding the concrete slab—basements were not necessary this far south—rosebushes bobbing roses, vulnerable, insanely gaudy, the great picture window that made her think, always, someone was slyly watching her, even the faint professional sweep of grass out to the road—all these in their elaborate planned splendor shouted mockery at her, mockery at themselves, as if they were safe from destruction! Annette fought off the inertia again, it passed close by her, a whiff of something like death; the same darkness that had bothered her in the hospital, delivered of her child. She left the packages against the garage (though the ice cream in its special package might be melting) and, awkward in her high heels, hurried out the drive. She shielded her eyes: nothing in sight down the road. It was a red clay road, a country road that would never be paved, and she and her husband had at first taken perverse pride in it. But it turned so, she had never noticed that before, and great bankings of foliage hid it, disguised its twistings, so that she could see not more than a quarter mile away. Never before had the land seemed so flat.

She hurried. At the gate the sun caught up with her, without ceremony. She struggled to swing the gate around (a few rusty, loosened prongs had caught in the grass), she felt perspiration breaking out on her body, itching and prickling her, under her arms, on her back. The white dress must have hung damp and wrinkled about her legs. Panting with the exertion, she managed to get the gate loose and drag it around; it tilted down at a jocose angle, scraping the gravel; then she saw that there was no lock, she would need a padlock, there was one in the garage somewhere, and in the same instant, marveling at her stamina, she turned back.

Hurrying up the drive, she thought again of the little Mexican boy. She saw his luxurious face, that strange unhealthy grin inside his embracing arms—it sped toward her. Cheeks drawn in as if by age, eyes protruding with—it must have been hunger, dirty hands like claws reaching out, grabbing, demanding what? What would they demand of her? If they were to come and shout for her out in the road, if she were to offer them—something—milk, maybe, the chocolate cookies Timmy loved so, maybe even money? Would they go away then, would they thank her and run back to their people? Would they continue their trip north, headed for Oregon and Washington? What would happen? Violence worried the look of the house, dizzied Annette! There were the yellow roses she tended so fondly, rich and sprawling against the orange brick. In the sunlight their petals, locked intricately inside one another, were vivid, glaringly detailed, as if their secret life were swelling up in rage at her for having so endangered their beauty.

There the packages lay against the garage, and seeing them, Annette forgot about the padlock. She stooped and picked them up. When she turned again she saw Timmy standing just inside the screen door. "Timmy, open the—" she said, vexed, but he had already disappeared. Inside the kitchen she slammed the bags down, fought back the impulse to cry, stamped one heel on the linoleum so hard that her foot buzzed with pain. "Timmy," she said, her eyes shut tight, "come out in this kitchen."

He appeared, carrying a comic book. That was for the look of it, of course; he had not been reading. His face was wary. Fair, like his mother, blond-toned, smart for his age, he had still about his quiet plump face something that belonged to field animals, wood animals, shrewd, secret creatures that had little to say for themselves. He read the newspaper as his father did, cultivated the same thoughtful expression; encouraged, he talked critically about his schoolteacher with a precocity that delighted his father, frightened Annette (to her, even now, teachers were

somehow *different* from other people), he had known the days of
the week, months of the year, continents of the world, planets of
the solar system, major star groupings of the universe, at an
astonishing age—as a child he approached professional perfection; but Annette, staring at him, was not sure now that she
could trust him. What if, when the shouting began outside,
when "Missus! Missus!" demanded her, Timmy ran out to
them, joined them, stared back at her in the midst of their white
eyes and dirty arms? They stared at each other as if this
question had been voiced.

"You almost killed him," Timmy said.

His voice was soft. Its innocence showed that he knew how
daring he was; his eyes as well, neatly fringed by pale lashes,
trembled slightly in their gaze. "What?" said Annette. "What?"

The electric clock, built into the big white range, whirred in
the silence. Timmy swallowed, rustled his comic book, pretended to wipe his nose—a throwback to a habit long outgrown—hoping to mislead her, and looked importantly at the
clock. "*He* hit the car. Two times," he said.

This was spoken differently. The ugly spell was over. "Yes,
he certainly did," Annette said. She was suddenly busy. "He
certainly did." After a moment Timmy put down the comic
book to help her. They worked easily, in silence. Eyes avoided
each other. But Annette felt feverishly excited; something had
been decided, strengthened. Timmy, stooping to put vegetables
in the bottom of the refrigerator, felt her staring at him and
peered up, his little eyebrows raised in a classic look of wonder.
"You going to call Daddy?" he said.

Annette had been thinking of this, but when Timmy suggested it, it was exposed for what it was—a child's idea. "That
won't be necessary," she said. She folded bags noisily and
righteously.

When they finished, mother and son wandered without enthusiasm into the dining room, into the living room, as if they
did not really want to leave the kitchen. Annette's eyes flinched
at what she saw: crystal, polished wood, white walls, aqua
lampshades, white curtains, sand-toned rug, detailed, newly
cleaned, spreading regally across the room—surely no one ever

walked on that rug! That was what *they* would say if they saw it. And the glassware off in the corner, spearlike, transparent green, a great window behind it linking it with the green grass outside, denying a barrier, inviting in sunlight, wind, anyone's eyes approaching— Annette went to the window and pulled the draw drapes shut; that was better; she breathed gently, coaxed by the beauty of those drapes into a smile: they were white, perfectly hung, sculpted superbly in generous swirling curves. And fireproof, if it came to that.... Annette turned. Timmy stood before the big red swivel chair as if he were going to sit in it—he did not—and looked at her with such a queer, pinched expression, in spite of his round face, that Annette felt a sudden rush of shame. She was too easily satisfied, too easily deluded. In all directions her possessions stretched out about her, defining her, identifying her, and they were vulnerable and waiting, the dirt road led right to them; and she could be lured into smiling! That must be why Timmy looked at her so strangely. "I have something to do," she murmured, and went back to the dining room. The window there was open; she pulled it down and locked it. She went to the wall control and turned on the air conditioning.

"Run, honey, and close the windows," she said. "In your room."

She went into the bedroom, closed the windows there and locked them. Outside there was nothing—smooth lawn, lawn furniture (fire-engine red) grouped casually together, as if the chairs made of tubing and spirals were having a conversation. Annette went into the bathroom, locked that window, avoided her gaze in the mirror, went, at last, into the "sewing room" that faced the road, and stood for a while staring out the window. She had never liked the color of that clay, really—it stretched up from Louisiana to Kentucky, sometimes an astonishing blood red, pulsating with heat. Now it ran watery in the sunlight at the bend. Nothing there. Annette waited craftily. But still nothing. She felt that, as soon as she turned away, the first black spots would appear—coarse black hair—and the first splashes of color; but she could not wait. There was too much yet to do.

She found Timmy in the living room again, still not sitting in the chair. "I'll be right back, darling," she said. "Stay here. It's too hot outside for you. Put on the television—Mommy will be right back."

She got the clipping shears out of the closet and went outside, still teetering in her high heels. There was no time to waste, no time. The yellow rosebush was farthest away, but most important. She clipped roses off, a generous amount of stem. Though hurried—every few seconds she had to stare down the road—she took time to clip off some leaves as well. Then she went to the red bushes, which now exclaimed at her ignorance: she could see they were more beautiful, really, than the yellow roses. Red more beautiful than yellow; yellow looked common, not stunning enough against the house. It took her perhaps ten minutes, and even then she had to tear her eyes away from the lesser flowers, over there in the circular bed, she did not have time for them—unaccountably she was angry at them, as if they had betrayed her already, grateful to the migrant workers who were coming to tear them to pieces! Their small stupid faces nodded in the hot wind.

Timmy awaited her in the kitchen. He looked surprised at all the roses. "The big vase," she commanded. In a flurry of activity, so pleased by what she was doing that she did not notice the dozens of bleeding scratches on her hands, she lay the roses on the cupboard, clipped at leaves, arranged them, took down a slender copper vase and filled it with water, forced some roses in, abandoned it when Timmy came in with the milk-glass vase (wedding present from a remote aunt of hers). The smell of roses filled the kitchen, sweetly drugged Annette's anxiety. Beauty, beauty—it was necessary to have beauty, to possess it, to keep it around oneself!—how well she understood that now.

Finished abruptly, she left the refuse on the cupboard and brought the vases into the living room. She stood back from them, peered critically . . . saw a stain on the wood of the table already, she must have spilled some water. And the roses were not arranged well, too heavy, too many flowers, an insane jumble of flowered faces, some facing one another nose to nose, some staring down toward the water in the vase in an indecent way, some at the ceiling, some at Annette herself. But there was no time to worry over them, already new chores called to her, demanded her services. What should she do next? —The answer hit her like a blow; how could she be so stupid? The doors were not even locked! Staggered by this, she ran to the front door, with trembling fingers locked it. How could she have overlooked this? Was something in her, some secret corner, conspiring with the Mexicans down the road? She ran stumbling to the back door—even that had been left open, it could have been seen from the road! A few flies buzzed idly, she had no time for them. When she appeared, panting, in the doorway, she saw Timmy by the big white vase trying to straighten the flowers.... "Timmy," she said sharply, "you'll cut yourself. Go away, go into the other room, watch television."

He turned at once but did not look at her. She watched him and felt, then, that it was a mistake to speak that way to him—in fact, a deliberate error, like forgetting about the doors; might not her child be separated from her if they came, trapped in the other room? "No, no, Timmy," she said, reaching out for him— he looked around, frightened—"no, come here. Come here." He came slowly. His eyes showed trust; his mouth, pursed and tightened, showed wariness, fear of that trust. Annette saw all this—had she not felt the same way about him, wishing him dead as soon as he was born?—and flicked it aside, bent to embrace him. "Darling, I'll take care of you. Here. Sit here. I'll bring you something to eat."

He allowed her to help him sit at the dining room table. He was strangely quiet, his head bowed. There was a surface mystery about that quietness! Annette thought, in the kitchen, I'll get through that, I'll prove myself to him. At first cunningly, then anxiously, she looked through the refrigerator, touching things, rearranging things, even upsetting things—a jar of pickles—and then came back carrying some strawberry tarts, made just the day before, and the basket of new strawberries, and some apples. "Here, darling," she said. But Timmy hesitated; while Annette's own mouth watered painfully, he could only blink in surprise. Impatiently she said, "Here, eat it, eat them. You love them. *Here.*" "No napkins," Timmy said fearfully.

"Never mind napkins, or a tablecloth, or plates," Annette said angrily—how slow her child seemed to her, like one of those empty-faced children she often saw along the road, country children, staring at her red car. "Here. Eat it. Eat it." When she turned to go back to the kitchen, she saw him lifting one of the tarts slowly to his mouth.

She came back almost immediately—bringing the package of ice cream, two spoons, a basket of raspberries, a plate of sliced chicken wrapped loosely in wax paper— She was overcome by hunger. She pulled a chair beside Timmy, who had not yet eaten—he stared gravely at her—and began to eat one of the tarts. It convulsed her mouth, so delicious was it, so sweet yet at the same time sour, tantalizing; she felt something like love for it, jealousy for it, and was already reaching for another when she caught sight of Timmy's stare. "Won't Daddy be home? Won't we have dinner?" he pleaded.

But he paused. His lips parted moistly and he stared at his mother, who smiled back at him, reassuring him, comforting him, pushing one of the tarts toward him with her polished nails. Then something clicked in his eyes. His lips damp with new saliva, he smiled at her, relieved, pleased. As if a secret ripened to bursting between them, swollen with passion, they smiled at each other. Timmy said, before biting into the tart, "*He* can't hit the car again, it's all locked up." Annette said, gesturing at him with sticky fingers, "Here, darling. Eat this. Eat. *Eat.*"

At the Seminary

M R. DOWNEY LEFT THE EXPRESSWAY at the right exit, but ten minutes later he was lost. His wife was sitting in the back seat of the car, her round serious face made unfamiliar by the sunglasses she wore, and when he glanced at her in the rearview mirror she did not seem to acknowledge him. His daughter, a big girl in a yellow sleeveless dress, was bent over the map and tracing something with her finger. "Just what I thought, that turn back there," she said. "That one to the left, by the hot dog stand. I thought that was the turn."

His stomach was too upset; he could not argue. He did not argue with his daughter or his wife or his son Peter, though he could remember a time when he had argued with someone—his father, perhaps. His daughter, Sally, sat confidently beside him with her fingernail still poised against a tiny line on the map, as if she feared moving it would precipitate them into the wilderness. "Turn around, Daddy, for heaven's sake," she said. "You keep on driving way out of the way."

"Well, I didn't notice any sign," his wife said suddenly.

His daughter turned slowly. She too wore sunglasses, white plastic glasses with ornate frames and dark curved lenses. He could see her eyes close. "You weren't watching, then. I'm the one with the map anyway. I was pretty sure that was the turn, back there, but he went by too fast. I had to look it up on the map."

"Why didn't you say anything before?"

"I don't know." Sally shrugged her shoulders.

"Well, I didn't see any sign back there."

They had argued for the last hundred miles, off and on. Mr. Downey tried to shut out their voices, not looking at them, concentrating now on finding a place to turn the car around before his daughter complained again. They were on a narrow blacktop road in the country, with untended fields on either side. Mr. Downey slowed. "There's a big ditch out there," Sally said. She tapped at the window with her nails. "Be careful, Daddy."

"How much room does he have?"

"He's got—oh—some room yet— Keep on going, Daddy. Keep on— Wait. No, Daddy, wait."

He braked the car. He could tell by his daughter's stiff, alert back that they had nearly gone into the ditch. "Okay, Daddy, great. Now pull ahead." Sally began waving her hand toward him, her pink fingernails glistening roguishly. "Pull ahead, Daddy, that's it. That's it."

He had managed to turn around. Now the sun was slanted before them again; they had been driving into it all day. "How far back was that road," he said.

"Oh, a few miles, Daddy. No trouble."

They arrived at the crossroads. "See, there's the sign. There it is," Sally said. She was quite excited. Though she had been overweight by twenty or twenty-five pounds for years, she often bounced about to demonstrate her childish pleasure; she did so now. "See, what did I tell you? Mom? There it is, there's the sign. U.S. 274, going east, and there's the hot dog stand."

"It's closed."

"Yes, it's closed, I can see that, it's boarded up but it's there," Sally said. She had turned slightly to face her mother, the pink flesh creasing along her neck, her eyes again shut in patient exasperation.

They drove east on 274. "It's only thirty more miles," Sally said. "Can I turn on the radio now?" Immediately she snapped it on. In a moment they heard a voice accompanied by guitars and drums. The music made Mr. Downey's stomach cringe. He drove on, his eyes searching the top of the next ridge, as if he expected to see the handsome buildings of the seminary beckoning to him, assuring him. His wife threw down a magazine in the back seat. "Sally, please turn that off. That's too loud. You know you're only pretending to like it and it's giving your father a headache."

"Is it?" Sally said in his ear.

"It's too loud. Turn it off," his wife said.

"Daddy, is it?"

He began to shake his head, began to nod it, said he didn't know. "This business about Pete," he said apologetically.

Sally paused. Then she snapped off the radio briskly. She seemed to throw herself back against the seat, her arms folded so tightly that the thick flesh of her upper arm began to drain white. They drove for a while in silence. "Well, all right, turn it on," Mr. Downey said. He glanced at Sally, who refused to move. She was twenty-three, not what anyone would call fat, yet noticeably plump, her cheeks rounded and generous. Behind the dark glasses her eyes were glittering, threatened by stubborn tears. She wore a bright yellow cotton dress that strained about her, the color made fierce by the sun, as if it would be hot to the touch. "You can turn it on, Sally," Mr. Downey said. "I don't care."

"It gives you a headache," his wife said. She had thrown down the magazine again. "Why do you always give in to her?"

Sally snorted.

"She doesn't care about Peter!" his wife cried. Her anguish was sudden and unfeigned; both Mr. Downey and Sally stiffened. They looked ahead at the signs—advertisements for hotels, motels, service stations, restaurants. "Got to find a motel for tonight," Sally muttered.

"She doesn't care, neither of you cares," Mr. Downey's wife went on. "The burden always falls on me. He wrote the letter to me, I was the one who had to open it—"

"Daddy got a letter too. He got one right after," Sally said sullenly.

"But Peter wrote to me first. He understood."

"He always was a mommy's boy!"

"I don't want to hear that. I never want to hear that."

"Nevertheless," said Sally.

"I said I don't want to hear that again. Ever."

"Okay, you won't. Don't get excited."

Mr. Downey pulled off the road suddenly. He stopped the car and sat with his head bowed; other automobiles rushed past. "I won't be able to go on," he said. "Not if you keep this up."

Embarrassed, wife and daughter said nothing. They stared at nothing. Sally, after a moment, rubbed her nose with her fist. She felt her jaw clench as it did sometimes at night, while she slept, as if she were biting down hard upon something ugly but could not let go. Outside, in a wild field, was a gigantic billboard advertising a motel. From a great height a woman in a red bathing suit was diving into a bright aqua swimming pool. Mrs. Downey, taking her rosary out of her purse, stared out at this sign also, felt her daughter staring at it, thought what her daughter thought. In the awkward silence they felt closer to each other than either did to Mr. Downey. They said nothing, proudly. After a while, getting no answer, Mr. Downey started the car again and drove on.

The drive up to the seminary was made of blacktop, very smart and precise, turning gently about the hill, back and forth amid cascades of evergreens and nameless trees with rich foliage. It was early September, warm and muggy. The seminary buildings looked sleek and cool. Mr. Downey had the feeling that he could not possibly be going to see anyone he knew or had known, that this trip was a mystery, that the young man who awaited him, related obscurely to him by ties of blood and name, was a mystery that exhausted rather than interested him. Mr. Downey had been no more worried by his wife's hopes that Peter would become a priest than he had by her hopes that Sally would enter a convent; he had supposed both possibilities equally absurd. Yet, now that Peter had made his decision, now that Mr. Downey had grown accustomed to thinking of him in the way one thinks of a child who is somehow maimed and disqualified for life and therefore deserving of love, he felt as disturbed as his wife by Peter's letters. His son's "problem" could not be named, evidently; Peter himself did not understand it, could not explain it: he spoke of "wearing out," of "losing control," of seeing no one in the mirror when he went to look at himself. He complained of grit in his room, of hairs in food, of ballpoint ink he could not wash off his hands. Nothing that made sense. He spoke of not being able to remember his *name,* and this had disturbed Mr. Downey most of all; the hairs reported in his food had disturbed Mrs. Downey most of all. Nowhere had the boy said anything of quitting, however, and they thought that puzzling. If he had spoken in his incoherent letters of wanting to quit, of going to college, of traveling about the country to observe "life," of doing nothing at all, Mr. Downey would not have felt so frightened. He could not parrot, as his wife did, the words of the novice master who had telephoned them that week: Peter was suffering a "spiritual crisis." It was the fact that Peter had suggested no alternatives to his condition that alarmed his father. It might almost have been—and Mr. Downey had not mentioned this to his wife— that the alternative to the religious life had come to Peter to be no less than death.

God knew, Mr. Downey thought, he had wanted something else for Peter. He had wanted something else for them all, but he could not recall what it was. He blamed Peter's condition on his wife; at least Sally had escaped her mother's influence, there was nothing wrong with her. She was a healthy girl, loud and sure of herself, always her father's favorite. But perhaps behind her quick robust laugh there was the same sniveling sensitivity that had ruined Peter's young life for him. Sally had played boisterously with other girls and boys in the neighborhood, a leader in their games, running heavily about the house and through the bushes, while Peter had withdrawn to his solitary occupations, arranging and rearranging dead birds and butterflies in the backyard; but in the end, going up to bed, their slippers scuffing on the floor and their shoulders set as if resigned to the familiar terrors of the night, they had always seemed to Mr. Downey to be truly sister and brother, and related in no way to himself and his wife.

The seminary buildings were only three years old. Magnificently modern, aqua and beige, with great flights of glass and beds of complex plants on both the outside and the inside, huddling together against glass partitions so that the eye, dazed, could not tell where the outside stopped and the inside began: Mr. Downey felt uncertain and overwhelmed. He had not thought convincing the rector's speech, given on the day they had brought Peter up here, about the middle-class temperament that would relegate all religious matters to older forms, forms safely out of date. The rector had spoken passionately of the beauty of contemporary art and its stark contrast with the forms of nature, something Mr. Downey had not understood; nor had he understood what religion had to do with beauty or with art; nor had he understood how the buildings could have cost five million dollars. "Boy, is this place something," Sally said resentfully. "He's nuts if he wants to leave it and come back *home.*" "He never said anything about leaving it," her mother said sharply.

They were met by Father Greer, with whom they had talked on the telephone earlier that week and who, standing alone on the evergreen-edged flagstone walk, seemed by his excessive calmness to be obscuring from them the fact of Peter's not being there. He was dark and smiling, taller than Mr. Downey and many years younger. "So very glad to see you," he said. "I hope you had an enjoyable ride? Peter is expected down at any moment." Very enjoyable, they assured him. Sally stood behind her father, as if suddenly shy. Mrs. Downey was touching her hair and nodding anxiously at Father Greer's words. In an awkward group they headed toward the entrance. Mr. Downey was smiling but as the young priest spoke, pointing out buildings and interesting sights, his eyes jumped about as if seeking out his son, expecting him to emerge around the corner of a building, out of an evergreen shrub. "The dormitory," Father Greer said, pointing. A building constructed into a hill, its first story disappearing into a riot of shrubs, much gleaming glass and metal. Beside it was the chapel, with a great brilliant cross that caught the sunlight and reflected it viciously. The light from the buildings, reflected and refracted by their thick glass, blinded Mr. Downey to whatever lay behind them—hills and forests and remote horizons. "No, we don't regret for an instant our having built out here," Father Greer was saying. They were in the lobby now. Mr. Downey looked around for Peter but saw no one. "They told us in the city that we'd go mad out here, but that was just jealousy. This is the ideal location for a college like ours. Absolutely ideal." They agreed. Mr. Downey could not recall just when he had noticed that some priests were younger than he, but he remembered a time when all priests were older, were truly "fathers" to him. "Please sit down here," Father Greer said. "This is a very comfortable spot." He too was looking about. Mr. Downey believed he could see, beyond the priest's cautious diplomatic charm, an expression of irritation. They were in an area blocked off from the rest of the lobby by thick plates of aqua-tinted glass. Great potted plants stood about in stone vases, the floor was tiled in a design of deep maroon and gray, the long low sofa on which they sat curved about a round marble coffee table of a most coldly beautiful, veined, fleshly color. Father Greer did not sit, but stood with his hands slightly extended and raised, as if he were blessing them against his will. "Will you all take martinis?" he said. They smiled self-consciously; Mrs. Downey said that Sally did not drink. "I'll take a martini," Sally said without looking up. Father Greer smiled.

Someone approached them, but it was not Peter. A boy Peter's age, dressed in a novice's outfit but wearing a white apron over it, came shyly to take their orders from Father Greer. "Peter will be down in a minute," Father Greer said. "Then we can all relax and talk and see what has developed. And we'll be having dinner precisely at six-thirty, I hope, in a very pleasant room at the back of this building—a kind of fireside room we use for special banquets and meetings. You didn't see it the last time you were here because it's just been completed this summer. If anyone would like to wash up—" He indicated graciously rest rooms at the far end of the area, GENTLEMEN, LADIES. Mrs. Downey stood, fingering her purse; Sally said crudely, "I'm all right." She had not taken off her sunglasses. Mrs. Downey left; they could smell the faint pleasant odor of her cologne. "He said he would be down promptly," Father Greer said in a slightly different voice, a confidential voice directed toward Mr. Downey, "but he may have forgotten. That's one of the—you know—one of the problems he has been having—he tends to forget things unless he writes them down. We discussed it Tuesday evening." "Yes, yes," Mr. Downey said, reddening. "He was never like that—at home—" "His mind seems somewhere else. He seems lost in contemplation—in another world," Father Greer said, not unkindly. "Sometimes this is a magnificent thing, you know, sometimes it develops into a higher, keener consciousness of one's vocation.... Sometimes it's greatly to be desired." He made Peter sound mysterious and talented, in a way, so that Sally found herself looking forward to meeting him. "If you'll excuse me for just a minute," Father Greer said, "I think I'll run over to his room and see how he is. Please excuse me—"

Sally and her father, left alone, had nothing to say to each other. Sally peered over the rims of her glasses at the lobby, but did not take the glasses off. She felt hot, heavy, vaguely sick, a little frightened; but at the thought of being frightened of something so trivial as seeing Peter again her mouth twisted into a smirk. She knew him too well. She knew him better than anyone knew him, and therefore resented the gravity with which he was always discussed, while her "problems" (whatever they were; she knew she was supposed to have some) were discussed by her mother and aunts as if they were immortal, immutable, impersonal problems like death and poverty, unfortunate conditions no one could change, and not very interesting.

Her mother returned, her shoulders bent forward anxiously as if she were straining ahead. "Where did he go?" she said, gazing from Mr. Downey to Sally. "Nothing happened, did it?" "He'll be right back," Sally said. "Sit down. Stop worrying." Her mother sat slowly; Sally could see the little white knobs of vertebrae at the top of her neck, curiously fragile. When the novice returned he was carrying a tray of cocktails. Another boy in an identical outfit appeared with a tray of shrimp and sauce and tiny golden crackers, which he set down on the marble table. Both young men were modest and shy, like magicians appearing and disappearing. "Suppose we better wait," Mr. Downey said regretfully, looking at the drinks.

But when Peter did arrive, with Father Greer just behind him, they were disappointed. He looked the same: a little pale, perhaps thinner, but his complexion seemed blemished in approximately the same way it had been for years, his shoulders were inclined forward, just like his mother's, so that he looked anxious and hungry, like a chicken searching in the dirt. There were agreeable murmurs of surprise and welcome. Peter shook hands with his father, allowed his mother to hug him, and nodded to Sally with the self-conscious look he always directed toward her. He was a tall, eager boy with a rather narrow, bony face, given to blinking excessively but also to smiling very easily and agreeably, so that most people liked him at once though they did not feel quite at ease with him. In his novice's dress he took the light angularly and harshly, as if he were in strident mourning. And what could be the matter with him, Sally thought enviously, what secrets did he have, what problems that would endear him all the more to their parents? "Here, do have some of this. This looks delicious," Father Greer said, passing the tray of shrimp and crackers around. Sally's mouth watered violently, in spite of herself; she indicated with an abrupt wave of her hand that she did not want any. "Here, Peter, you always loved shrimp, every Friday we had to have shrimp," Mrs. Downey said in a trembling voice. She held the tray out to Peter, who had sat beside her. He hesitated, staring at the shrimp. "The sauce smells so good—" Mrs. Downey said coaxingly. At last Peter's arm moved. He picked up a toothpick and impaled a shrimp upon it; as they all watched, he dipped it into the sauce. Everyone sighed slightly. They settled back and crossed their legs.

They began to talk. Of the weather, first, and of the drive. The good and bad points of the expressway. Of all expressways, of encroaching civilization and the destruction of nature, yet at the same time the brilliant steps forward in the conquering of malignant nature. Peter chewed at the shrimp, Sally saw, but did not seem to have swallowed it. Talk fluttered about his head; now and then he glanced up, smiled, and replied. Sally, finding no one watching her, began to eat shrimp and could not stop. The more she ate, the more angry she felt at the people before her and at the boys who had served the drinks and food and at the seminary itself. She could feel her face freezing into that expression of disdain she hated in her mother but could not help in herself: so she faced everything she disapproved of, flighty vain girls no older than she in fur coats and glittering jewelry, young men in expensive sports cars, gossiping old ladies, old men who drank, young mothers who were obviously so proud and pleased with their lives they would just as soon spit in your eye when you passed them on the sidewalk, pushing baby buggies along as if that were a noble task! Sally did not approve of people talking in church or looking around, craning their bony old necks, nor did she approve of children— any children—who were noisy and restless and were apt to ask you why you were so fat, in front of everyone; she did not approve of people photographed on society pages or on maga- zine covers, or houses that were not made of brick or stone but were in poor neighborhoods with scrawny front lawns, but also she did not approve of lower-class white people who hated Negroes, as if they were any better themselves. She did not approve of high school boys and girls who swung along the sidewalks with their arms around each other, laughing vulgarly, and she did not approve of college students who did the same thing. While at college she had been so isolated by the sternness of her disapproval that no roommate had suited her and she had finally moved to a single room, where she had stayed for four years, studying angrily so that she could get good grades (which she did) and eating cookies and cakes and pies her mother sent her every week. She had loved her mother then and knew her mother loved her, since they never saw each other, but now that she was home and waiting for the placement bureau to send her notice of a decent job, something they evidently were not capable of doing, she and her mother hardly spoke and could feel each other's presence in the house as one feels or suspects the presence of an insect nearby. Her mother had wanted her to be pretty, she thought, and deliberately she was not pretty. (And Peter, there, still chewing, was homely too, she had never really noticed that before.) Sometimes she went to bed without washing her face. Certainly she did not wash her hair more than once a week, no matter what was coming up; and she had pretended severely not to care when her mother appropriated for herself the expensive lavender dress she had worn to the important functions at college when she had been twenty or thirty pounds lighter. She wore no make-up except lipstick, a girlish pink, and her shoes were always scuffed and marked by water lines, and she often deliberately bought dresses too large so the shoulders hung down sloppily. Everything angered her: the vanities of the world, the pettiness of most people, the banal luxuries she saw through at once—like this seminary, and the cocktails, when their own priest back home had new missions every week or new approaches to the Bishop's Relief Fund. She picked up the martini and sipped at it; its bitterness angered her. She put it down. She would not drink it and collaborate in this vanity. Even the graceful gleaming glass, finely shaped like a work of art, annoyed her, for beside it her own stumpy fingers and uneven nails looked ugly. What place was there in the real world for such things? She felt the real world to be elsewhere—she did not know where—in the little town they had passed through on the way up to the seminary, perhaps, where the ugly store fronts faced each other across a cobbled main street fifty years old, and where country people dawdled about in new shoes and new clothes, dressed for Saturday, looking on everything with admiration and pleasure. But what were these people talking about? She hunched forward in an exaggerated attitude of listening. Baseball. She was ashamed of her father, who spoke of baseball players familiarly, slowly, choosing his words as if each were important, so making a fool of himself. Father Greer, debonair and charming, was bored of course but would not show it. Mrs. Downey looked puzzled, as if she could not quite keep up with the conversation; the martini had made her dizzy. Peter, beside her, his awkward hands crossed on his knees, stared at something in the air. He was waiting, as they were all waiting, Sally supposed, for this

conversation to veer suddenly around to him, confront him in
his odd transfixed fear and demand from him some explanation
of himself. Sally sipped at the cocktail and felt its bitterness
expand to take in all of the scene before her. If Peter glanced at
her she would look away; she would not help him. She needed
no one herself, and wanted no one to need her. Yet she wondered why he did not look at her—why he sat so stiff, as if
frozen, while about him chatter shot this way and that to
ricochet harmlessly off surfaces.

The subject had been changed. "Peter made some particularly
perceptive remarks on the *Antigone* of Sophocles this summer,"
Father Greer was saying. He had finished his martini and rolled
the glass slowly between his palms, the delicate stem turning
and glinting against his tanned skin. "We study a number of
Greek tragedies in the original Greek. The boys find them
strangely intriguing. Puzzles." Mr. and Mrs. Downey were both
sitting forward a little, listening. "The world view of the Greeks,"
Father Greer said severely, "is so astonishingly different from
our own." Sally drew in her breath suddenly. "I wouldn't say
that, precisely," she remarked. Father Greer smiled at her. "Of
course there are many aspects of our civilizations that are
similar," he said. "What strikes us as most barbaric, however, is
their utter denial of the freedom of man's will." He thought her
no antagonist, obviously; he spoke with a faintly condescending
smile Sally detested because she believed she had been seeing it
all her life. "But that might not be so strange, after all," she
drawled. Her mother was frowning, picking at something imaginary on the rim of her cocktail glass. Her father was watching
her as if she were performing a foolish and dangerous trick, like
standing on her head. But Peter, sitting across from her with his
long fingers clasped together on his knees, his back not touching
the sofa, was staring at her and through her with a queer
theatrical look of recognition, as if he had not really noticed her
before. "And their violence," Sally said. "The violence of their
lives—that might not be so strange to us either." "There is no
violence in Greek drama," Father Greer said. Sally felt her face
close up, suddenly. Her eyes began to narrow; her lips pursed
themselves in a prim little look of defiance; the very contours of

her generous face began to hunch themselves inward.

An awkward minute passed. "You still on that diet?" Peter said.

Sally's eyes opened. Peter was looking at her with a little smile. Her face burned. "What? Me? I—"

"Why, Peter," their mother said. "What do you mean?"

Peter's gaze plummeted. He examined his fingers. Sally, more stunned than angry, watched him as if he had become suddenly an antagonist, an open enemy; she saw that his hands were streaked with something—it looked like red ink or blood, something scrubbed into his skin.

"Sorry," Peter muttered.

In this crisis Father Greer seemed to fall back; his spine might have failed him unaccountably. The very light turned harsh and queer; churned about gently in the air-conditioned lounge, it seemed not to be illuminating them but to be pushing them away from each other, emphasizing certain details that were not to be cherished: Peter's acne, Mrs. Downey's tiny double chin and the network of fine wrinkles that seemed to hold together her expression, Mr. Downey's sluggish mouth, drooping as if under the impact of a sudden invisible blow, even the surface gloss of Father Greer's professional charm dented by a dull embarrassed gleam at the tip of his nose. And Sally was glad of being fat and unattractive, with a greasy nose, coarse skin, a dress stained with perspiration, glad she could delight no one's eyes, fulfill no one's expectations of her—

"I don't believe you've seen our chapel," Father Greer said. He made a tentative movement that was not really tentative but commanding; Sally saw how Peter's shoulders and arms jerked up, mimicking the priest, before he himself had decided to stand. They all stood, smoothing their clothing, smiling down at the martini glasses and what was left of the shrimp and crackers, as if bidding good-by to acquaintances newly made. "It's very beautiful, we commissioned the Polish architect Radomski to design it for us—the same Radomski who did the campus at St. Aquinas University—you might remember the pictures in *Life?*"

They agreed vaguely, moving along. Father Greer seemed to

be herding them. Sally, at the rear, caught a glimpse of the young priest's face, as he turned, and was startled by the blunt, naked intensity of his concern—an instant's expression of annoyance, alarm, helplessness that immediately faded—and what an attractive man he was, in spite of his deep-set eyes, she thought, what a pity—a pity— But she did not know what the pity was for. Out of spite she kept her martini glass in hand; it was still half full. She wandered at the back of the small group, looking around, squinting through her dark glasses. Several young priests passed them, nodding hello. They walked on. The building smelled like nothing, absolutely nothing. It did not even have the bitter antiseptic smell of soap. Nothing had an odor, nothing was out of place, nothing disturbed the range of the eye: the building and its people might not yet have been born, might be awaiting birth and baptism, immersion in smells and disorder. On the broad flagstone walk to the chapel Sally walked with the martini glass extended as if it were a symbol of some kind, an offering she carried to the chapel under the secret gazes of all those secret boys, cloistered there in that faceless building.

In the chapel they fell silent. Sally frowned. She was going to take off her sunglasses, but stopped. The chapel was gigantic: a ceiling dull and remote as the sky itself, finely lined, veined as if with the chill of distance or time, luring the eye up and forward, relentlessly forward, to the great statue of the crucified Christ behind the altar. There it was. The walls of the buildings might have fallen away, the veneer of words themselves might have been peeled back, to reveal this agonized body nailed to the cross: the contours of the statue so glib, so perfect, that they seemed to Sally to be but the mocking surfaces of another statue, a fossilized creature caught forever within that crust— the human model for it, suffocated and buried. Father Greer chatted excitedly about something: about that sleek white Christ, a perfect immaculate white, the veins of his feet and throat throbbing a frozen immaculate white. About his head drops of white blood had coagulated over the centuries; a hard white crown of thorns pierced his skin lovingly, rendered by art into something fragile and fine. The chapel was empty. No, not empty; at the very front a figure knelt, praying. The air was cold and stagnant. Nothing swirled here; time itself had run out, run down. Sally felt perspiration on her forehead and under her arms. She had begun to ache strangely, her head and her body; she could not locate the dull throbbing pain. Her head craning stupidly, she stared up at the gigantic statue. Yes, yes, she would agree to Father Greer's questioning glance: was it not magnificent? Yes, but what was it that was magnificent? What did they know? What were they looking at? How did they know—and she thought of this for no reason, absolutely no reason—what their names were, their stupid names? How did they know anything? Her glance fell in confusion to her parents' nervous smiles and she felt she did not recognize them. And to Peter's awkward profile, so self-pitying; was it to tell them he could no longer believe in Christ that he had brought them to the seminary? But she understood, staring at her brother's rigid face, that he could no more not believe in Christ than she could: that the great milky statue itself could more easily twitch into life than they could disbelieve the ghostly contours that lay behind that form, lost in history—and that they were doomed, brother and sister, doomed in some obscure inexplicable vexing way neither could understand, and their parents and this priest, whispering rather loudly about "seating capacity," could never understand. The three adults walked toward the front of the chapel, down the side aisle. Peter stumbled as if a rock had rolled suddenly before his feet; Sally could not move. She stared up at the statue with the martini glass in her hand. She and Peter might have been awaiting a vision, patiently as always. Yet it will only end, she thought savagely, in steak for dinner—a delicate tossed salad—wine— And as her body flinched in outrage at this vision (so powerful as to have evoked in her a rush of hunger, in spite of herself) she felt a sudden release of pressure, a gentle aching relaxation she did not at first recognize. A minute flow of blood. She did not move, paralyzed, her mouth slowly opening in an expression of awe that might have been religious, so total and commanding was it. Her entire life, her being, her very soul might have been conjured up and superimposed upon that rigid white statue, so intensely did she stare at it, her horror transformed into a prayer of utter silence, utter wordlessness, as she felt the unmistakable relentless flow of blood begin in her loins. Then her face went slack. She looked at the martini glass, brought it to her mouth, finished the drink. She smirked. She had known this would happen, had thought of it the day before, then had forgotten. She had forgotten. She could not have forgotten but she did, and it was for this reason she grinned at the smudged glass in her hand. Now Peter turned and followed the others; she followed him. Bleeding warmly and secretly. Her gaze was hot upon the backs of her parents, her mother especially, cleanly odored well-dressed woman: what a surprise! What a surprise she had for her! "I'm afraid this is cloistered," Father Greer whispered. He looked sorry. They headed in another direction, through a broad passageway, then out, out and into a spacious foyer; now they could breathe.

"What beauty! Immeasurable beauty!" Father Greer said aloud. His eyes were brittle with awe, an awe perhaps forced from him; he looked quite moved. Yet what was he moved at, Sally thought angrily, what had they been looking at, what did they *know*? Peter wiped at his nose, surreptitiously, but of course everyone saw him. What did they know? What had they seen? What might they ever trust again in a world of closed surfaces, of panels just sliding shut? She was shaken, and only after a moment did she notice her mother glaring at her, at the cocktail glass and the sunglasses. Her mother's face was white and handsome with the splendor of her hatred. Sally smirked. She felt the faithful blood inside her seeping, easing downward. Father Greer pointed out something further—someone agreed— she felt the hot blood on her legs. She was paralyzed, charmed. The others walked on but she did not move. Her mother glanced around. "Sally?" she said. Sally took a step, precariously. Nothing. Perhaps she would be safe. She caught her mother's gaze and held it, as if seeking help, hoping for her mother to draw her safely to her by the sheer force of her impatience. Then, for no reason, she took a hard, brutal step forward, bringing her flat heel down hard on the floor. Then again. She strode forward, brusquely, as if trying to dent the marble floor. The others were waiting for her, not especially watching her. She slammed down her heel so that it stung, and the blood jerked free. It ran instantly down the inside of her leg to her foot. She was breathing hard, excited and terrified and somehow pleased, waiting for her mother to notice. Why didn't she notice? Sally glanced down, was startled to see how big her stomach was, billowing out in the babyish yellow dress she had worn here out of spite, and saw the delicate trickle of blood there—on her calf, her ankle (which was not too clean), inside her scuffed shoe and so out of sight! At the door the others waited: the slim priest in black, who could see everything and nothing, politely, omnipotently; her father and mother, strangers also, who would see and suffer their vision as it swelled deafeningly upon them, their absolute disbelief at what they saw; her brother Peter, who was staring down at the floor just before her robust feet as if he had seen something that had turned him to stone.

Sally smiled angrily. She faced her mother, her father. Nothing. They looked away, they did not look at each other. Father Greer was holding the door open. No one spoke. Sally wanted to say, "That sure must have cost a lot!" but she could not speak. She saw Father Greer's legs hold themselves in stride, she could nearly see his muscles resist the desperate ache they felt to carry him somewhere—the end of this corridor, through one of the mysterious doors, or back to the cloistered sanctuary behind them. "And these, these," he said, "these are tiny chapels—all along here— Down there the main sacristy—" His words fell upon them from a distance, entirely without emotion. He showed nothing. Sally stomped on the floor as if killing insects, yet he did not look around. She felt blood trickling down her legs, a sensation she thought somehow quite pleasant, and in her shoes her toes wriggled in anticipation of the shame soon to befall them. On they walked. At each of Father Greer's words they leaned forward, anxious not to be denied, anxious to catch his eye, force upon him the knowledge that they saw nothing, knew nothing, heard only what he told them. Sally began to giggle. She wanted to ask Father Greer something, but the rigidity of her hysteria was too inflexible; she found she could not open her mouth. Her jaws seemed locked together. But this isn't my fault, she cried mockingly to their incredulous accusing backs, I never asked for it, I never asked God to make me a woman! She could not stop grinning. What beauty! What immeasurable beauty! It was that she grinned at, nothing else. That immeasurable beauty. Each heavy step, each ponderous straining of her thick thighs, centuries old, each sigh that swelled up into her chest and throat, each shy glance from her brother, all these faded into a sensation of overwhelming light or sound, something dazzling and roaring at once, that seemed to her to make her existence suddenly beautiful: complete: ended.

Then Peter was upon her. He grabbed for her throat. His face was anguished, she was able to see that much, and as she screamed and lunged back against the wall her parents and the priest turned, whirled back, seemed for an instant to be attacking her as well. "Damn you! Damn you!" Peter cried. His voice rose to a scream, a girl's scream. He managed to break away from Father Greer's arms and struck her, his fists pounding, a child's battle Sally seemed to be watching from across the corridor, through a door, across a span of years— "Damn you! Now I can't leave! I can't leave!" he cried. They pulled him back. He had gone limp. He hid his face and sobbed; she remembered him sobbing that way, often. Of course. His habitual sob, sheer helplessness before her strength, her superior age, weight, complacency. She gasped, her body still shuddering in alarm, ready to fight, to kill, her strong competent legs spread apart to give her balance. Her heart pounded like a magnificent angel demanding to be released, to be set upon her enemies. Peter turned away, into the priest's embrace, still sobbing. He showed nothing of his face but a patch by his jaw, a splotched patch of adolescent skin.

Mr. Downey entered the expressway without slackening speed. It was late, nearly midnight. He had far to go. Fortified by alcohol, dizzily confident, he seemed to be driving into a wild darkness made familiar by concrete, signs, maps, and his own skillful driving. Beside him his daughter sat with the map in hand again, but they would not need it. He knew where he was driving them. The expressway was deserted, held no challenge to him, the sheer depthless dark beyond the range of his headlights could not touch him, fortified as he was by the knowledge of precisely where he was going. Signs, illuminated by his headlights, flashed up clearly and were gone, they were unmistakable, they would not betray him, just as visions of that evening flashed up to him, without terror, and were gone. They knew what to do. None of this surprised them. Nothing surprised them. (He thought of the confessional; that explained it.) A few weeks of rest, nothing more, the boy would be safe, there was nothing to worry about. And he felt, numbly, that there really was nothing to worry about any longer, that everything had been somehow decided, that it had happened in his presence but he had not quite seen it. The priests were right: Father Greer and the older priest, a very kindly Irishman Mr. Downey had trusted at once. Something had been decided, delivered over. It was all right. In the back seat his wife sat impassive and mindless, watching the road that led inexorably back home. Beside him his daughter sat heavily, her arms folded. She yawned. Then she reached out casually to turn on the radio. "Please, Sally," her mother said at once, as if stirred to life. The radio clicked on. Static, a man's voice. Music. "Sally," her mother said. Sally's plump arm waited, her fingers still on the knob. "It bothers your father," Mrs. Downey said, "you know it gives him a headache." "I'll turn it down real low," Sally said. Out of the corner of Mr. Downey's eye her face loomed blank and milky, like a threatening moon he dared not look upon.

What Death with Love Should Have to Do

A T LAST SHE SAID, "I'm bleeding," and in fear tightened her hold around him, her arms high against his ribs and her legs locked around his body as if she believed he would try to escape her. The motorcycle crashed through a thicket; stiff branches snapped back at them, across the dark green plastic of their goggles, stinging their cheeks. He would hear nothing.

They were in the open again. The motorcycle leveled suddenly, the sun slashed at them as if lurching precariously in the sky. Mae clung to Vale, her face against his wet back. They were in a lane, a cow path. Dust billowed up behind them, and flecks of straw, and churnings of grass. The sun tilted again and remained level. They were alone. The other cyclists were nowhere in sight; Vale had left them behind. The air smelled of empty heat, of hot, dry grass. There was a fine golden glow to the air that reminded Mae dreamily of love, and the roar of the motorcycle swelled out to obliterate all other sound: the usual country noises, birds and insects and dogs barking forlornly in the distance. Again the motorcycle dipped and recoiled up out of a rut. Mae cried out with pain. Vale absently caressed her hand and released it, as if he had just recalled her.

A fine day: they had noted it earlier, avoiding each other's eyes. Clumsy acting, in the diner (an old trolley up on blocks) down the street from the big dirty house in which they now lived: it made Mae suddenly conscious that she was young, after all, after so many years. Vale had said, frowning at his cigarette, "Are you sure you want to do it?" And Mae, thin and exhausted from the hot sleepless nights, had said, "For Christ's sake, *yes.*" Why did he have to be prodded always to do what he wanted to do? Staring at him, she imagined she could see the little flecks of his failings, his weaknesses, appear like pimples on his tanned face. "It wouldn't be your fault if anything went wrong," she said bitterly. "Went wrong?" said Vale. "You know things like that happen all the time." Later, out in the country, he had made her drink beer with him and the others. They joked; they danced around in their excitement. Mae drank the beer with her eyes closed, as if it were medicine. Now she could feel it in a tight hot circle in her stomach, waiting to force its way up.

She looked around, awakened by pain. Behind them the countryside jiggled crazily. They had cut down through someone's wheat field, down a hill, and their path was idly vicious—she stared back at it, as if she expected it to reveal some truth about herself and Vale. No one else was in sight; Vale would be proud. He was in the lead and straining to go faster. In moments of loneliness or terror (she did not know which this was) Mae murmured to herself *love, love,* that magic incantation, and there would come to her mind not just Vale's face (Vale sleeping: his boy's face, innocent and brutal, lips open slightly, a thread of saliva on his chin) but the faces of the other men, sometimes hopelessly mixed together, the eyes of one and the mouth of another, and even the faces of her brothers and sisters and the reserved, shadowed, secret face of her mother: an audience that stared in silence. As if resisting them, Mae pressed her mouth against Vale's back. Her lips were parched with dust, and yet she saw a faint spider-web pattern of blood on his shirt: she must have been cut somehow, by those branches probably. Vale strained forward, upward, the muscles in his shoulders and back asserted themselves, he shouted something back at her—

she embraced him desperately, just in time, for there was another crash, a jolt that hit her in the stomach. They had abandoned the lane and were crossing a field, bumping from rut to rut. She could feel Vale's chest expand with joy.

As always, the confusion of the race obscured all memories leading up to it. Once begun, all races were alike: they were perhaps the same race: their noises dispelled all mornings, all previous nights, fused them into a sameness that seemed a broad, thick, muddy stream to which everyone had to return. Vale had taught her to love these races, but he had also taught her to hate the return to rigid ground. Though she had been in love with Vale for only a few months, it seemed to her that her life had been a practice for such times: this dissatisfaction with the calm earth, this hatred of familiar things, of her own face in mirrors or reflected back to her from store windows, or (and this baffled her) even the delirious struggles of their love. At this thought her insides churned; she could feel the warm blood again, as if awakened. She closed her eyes and pressed the goggles against Vale's back, though she knew this irritated him, and for some reason thought immediately of her mother, who might be standing with the screen door pushed open as she often did, frowning out into the sunlight, waiting for Mae, able to hear—fifty miles away?—the insane roaring of Vale's motorcycle.

Another hill. They reared up out of the earth to land with great agility on a hillside well worn, pasture land with stumps of old trees here and there, not enough to be dangerous. No cows in sight; the farmers might have known about the race. Mae expected vaguely to see one appear out from behind a tree with a shotgun. Vale had been shot at more than once, so she had been proudly told; he had made his escapes down anonymous roads on this same motorcycle, not stopping, as he put it, to pass the time of day. Now the sun swerved again. Were they falling? No, for Vale was in control, they had turned and were plunging downhill. Mae saw a creek ahead. Her eyes refused this; she turned aside. She would tell him, would shout it at him. She would tell him she was bleeding. He had not heard. . . . And yet she said nothing, dreamily she closed her eyes and thought, for some reason, of an accident she had witnessed once: blood on the blue motorcycle, on the grass around it, flicked up onto the dusty indifferent weeds and even onto insects on these weeds, so that their hard black little shells were flecked with blood as they crawled lazily about.

Her muscles jumped by themselves. She gripped him in terror so that he grunted and slashed at her arm, without thinking. Her body had learned to resist, to draw itself back as if refusing to see what awaited; that was wrong. That was stupid. Vale's body, by contrast, urged itself forward, lunged forward into everything. He was not jolted because he became the jolting itself, became the careening, the speed. On the open road his body joined itself to the motorcycle as in love it joined itself to hers; he could not be hurt. She knew, jealously, that his mind dissolved out into the windy sunshine, into the roar of the motorcycle. There was no alien, unknown space to threaten him. He resisted nothing. She pretended to give herself, yet always resisted, and now as they rushed to the creek bank she held herself rigid as if hurtling through a dream that had betrayed her. The wheels churned viciously, striking bottom. Water surged against them, warm startled waves against their legs. Early September: the creek was shallow, and parched white rocks, flat rocks with moss baked onto them, dipped on either side and seemed to stare up, flat faces, in white, frenzied terror at what Vale was doing. Vale shouted something—she could not hear. Then something happened and she clawed at him and was knocked off the seat.

She did not know what had happened. She was sitting in the creek, leaning over clumsily to vomit in the dirty water. Vale splashed over to her. He shouted something but his words seemed to come to her through water, dazed and blurred. He loomed over her, began pulling her up. "Goddamn it, Mae, we got no time for it! No time!" he said. She could not get her breath. He yanked her to her feet and over to the motorcycle, not looking back at her. Please help me, aren't you going to help me? she thought, staring at his back, his strong shoulders. He had forgotten. He did not know her.

They went on. Heading for a road now, up a long incline

choked with weeds. The air was not so warm as it should have been. The motorcycle strained coyly, this was dangerous, they might tip back except that Vale knew what to do, knew how to snake about, to dance with it, tease it, to balance and unbalance it. Tall grass crackled about their feet as if it were on fire, torn by the wheels and sucked into the spokes. They ascended slowly to the road. At the top they barely moved. Mae groaned and urged them forward. "Come on!" she cried angrily. Then she felt Vale's sigh of relief: they had made it. They turned and moved on. How level this was! Mae had forgotten what roads were like. Now Vale fled as if death itself were pursuing him, or perhaps some cheap embarrassment (being beaten by one of his friends), leaning forward into the wind as if he were urging himself out of his body, weary of it, and away from Mae too, at last weary of her and her fragility. Behind them explosions of dust, great clouds of dust. The other cyclists could see the dust now from across the creek; they would know where Vale was. At the thought of them Mae's mind snapped back to the memory of that accident, last week, and to the knowledge of herself now, bleeding so secretly. She closed her eyes. She could not curse it because it was what they had wanted. Two months along, and to get rid of it so easily! Vale already had a child, a son, fifty miles away. That was why, perhaps, he had forgotten about her, could not guess her pain, would not cut the engine and drift along quietly and curve off the road so he might turn to her. She would tell him nothing.

Their speed was intoxicating; she would think of this. The wind and the sunlight were transformed into a golden buzzing, like liquid. Mae let her head fall back gently and opened her mouth to it. But it was just air, nothing more. She groped for something to hang onto: a memory, something. What came to her was the morning last April when she had gone over to the garage where Vale worked to get a Coke. He had been inside, squatting by his motorcycle, his eyes blinking at her through beads of sweat. She had wanted him and had gone to get him. She had been watching him for years, a boy much older than she; and back from the city where she had been living for a while, rested and home, sworn at and slapped and forgiven by her mother, allowed back in her old room, she had decided that Vale would be next. She had always liked his lean hard face, his muscular arms and shoulders, his nervous long legs and big feet. She remembered him from school, years ago. He had scowled then, imitating someone, and he scowled often now, even in his sleep, because of his work at the garage and his hatred for the people he had to give gas to, put air in tires for, check oil for. He hated them and so he had two vertical lines on his forehead. He spoke in bursts of words, often shouted, was vain and unsure of himself, was infatuated with Mae as (so she was told) he had once been infatuated with his wife, before she became his wife.

The countryside was blurred with their speed. Mae watched it through her lashes, distrusting it. Speed taught her that no sight was real: no appearance demanded faith in itself, since it changed so easily, flowed in and out of itself. Nothing stayed. Noise shattered Mae's thoughts, rattled and vibrated in her throat. She glanced down at her legs and was surprised to see no blood there. Her slacks were wet. She could not see her feet. The dirt road, clotted with pebbles, sped along. The air was suddenly thick with dust: someone was ahead of them. They rounded a turn too fast. Vale pulled out of the skid and they saw a pickup truck ahead of them, with children sitting in the back. A boy scrambled to his feet as Vale overtook them. In envy be stared; the seriousness of his look reminded Mae of one of her brothers, her favorite brother, now fourteen, a boy who hated her, she supposed, as they all did, who could not under-stand—as she herself could not understand—what she was doing. The boy on the truck platform hardly glanced at her. He was interested only in Vale.

Vale roared past. Mae slyly and contemptuously peered over at the driver of the truck, who stared at her (a middle-aged farmer with a large, brutal bald head) with hatred. She met his gaze solidly as they passed. Those looks were familiar: everyone looked at her that way. She was reminded of her father, that remote, dying old man, dead for years now, coughing into his handkerchief, and of her mother, still waiting at that screen door, waiting and listening and smelling the air. Mae had been gone for five months now, but her mother awaited her. Every morning, every night. At the dinner table no one would speak of her but, shivering with dread, everyone would think of her; she knew this; she did not have to be told. "Will you forgive me this time?" Mae thought. She would ask her mother this. "Will you let me in again?" The last time she had come home one of her younger brothers had been using her room, that closet behind the stairs she had once been so proud of, and the bed had been soiled from his dirty feet. The magazine pictures she had taped up on the wall were gone. "If you don't want me here I'll go back," Mae had said. "I'll catch the bus at the corner and go back!" Her mother would not speak to her for days: cold and pale, silent and suffering, a rosary entwined in her fingers. The other children hated her. They were afraid of her. But on the third day, so early in the morning it had not yet become light, her mother had come to her as always. Her eyes rimmed with shadow, her skin aging, coarse: never had she been so pretty as Mae! She had knelt at the bed and buried her face in the blanket. Mae, terrified, wanted to push her away, wanted to cry out that she hated her mother, hated her! That she did not know why she had come home! At the memory she dug her nails into Vale's chest. She had always hated her mother, and once Vale had said that he was sick to hell of her muling and puking, that she thought of her mother more than she did of him, did not hate her mother but loved her, more than she did him, and that he would not stand for it. She had slapped his mocking face. What did he mean, what did he know? He was brutal and ignorant, at the end of these races he would stagger about, drinking beer, laughing, showing everyone the nicks and scratches on his face and hands, as if there were something about blood that was funny.... But what has this to do with love, Mae thought dizzily, what has blood to do with love and why did they go together? Why were they related? She opened her eyes and saw trees with hazy leafed branches floating overhead, so blasted with Vale's deafening roar that they reared up as if in terror, straining to get away.

She embraced Vale but he did not notice. Her muscles, small and hard, would always relax, release, after a moment. She could not sustain an embrace. She was capable of strength, but only for seconds: passion reared her body, animated it as dying animates creatures wounded, blasted by shot, but left her then exhausted, panting, minutes closer to death. Mae rubbed her sunburned face against Vale's back and felt her strength flow into him, surging up into his arms, down into his thighs. They worked together. She leaned against him, her body groaning with the strain of the race; she sighed and let her head fall back again so that the sharp air slashed across her nose and parched lips. Vale swerved; pebbles were thrown up against the spokes; Mae leaned with him, felt the motorcycle respond gratefully to their skill. Ahead, the road dipped out of sight, bushes and nameless trees leaned to them, in patches the sky appeared, and mottled and indistinct, the gray-green mountains wavered behind miles of sunny mist. They slammed into a shallow, were stunned by something there—a rock, probably—careened up, swerved, skidded. But Vale had control. Mae gripped him, indifferent as always when there was real danger, staring sightlessly at nothing. At such times she understood she was alone. Everything drifted from her, memories of her past and of herself (for she saw herself, without regret, as the anonymous hard-faced girl surrounded by men, on tavern porches at night, at filling stations, in disreputable automobiles going past, jostling about street corners, taut and coquettish and frightened, stared at by safe, secure women with destinations who could feel only pity and hatred for her), memories even of Vale's body, his muscles, leaning away, away. She remembered the blood and her mind leapt at it. That was real. She knew what it meant. No baby this time, they had been too clever, no one had fooled them: Vale would want to celebrate. The first time they had been worried, he had taken her to a doctor in town and she had lain on the kitchen table, awake all the time, ten minutes (so Vale had told her later, proud of her), chewing on her agony, keeping it in. The doctor had been pale, shaken, not so much at Vale's threats as at Mae's stern sullen rigidity, her refusal to admit pain. Then the last time, which evidently had not been serious, on a turkey run like this, it had happened and without much pain: she had time then to be ashamed. The old shame of her young girlhood overtook her and she had thought, in the midst of Vale's delight, that this could not really be happening to her: she could not really have become this person. But this time it was different, somehow. Her body was exhausted. She knew that it had surrendered and that only the momentum of the race kept her going. She would say nothing to Vale, she would never tell him. As if in mockery of her pride, her teeth rattled suddenly. She clamped her jaws together. Her mouth was dry and filled with dust. She had seen Vale rinse his mouth out after a race, spitting out the mud with breathless boyish laughs....

Suddenly she could not remember where they were. She did not know how far they had to go or how long they had been driving. Had they been this way before? Nothing was familiar. Why had she seen so little with Vale after all, when it was Vale she loved, or almost loved? She felt her eyes burn suddenly behind the goggles. A bitter lament began itself, like a song (she was always haunted by songs, snatches of melodies heard on juke boxes and radios), a formless wail she wanted to deny, in panic and shame. This was not like her: this was someone else. Mae was not like this. She regretted nothing. She was afraid of nothing, nothing, not the operation that time, not that man, years ago, with the black hair frizzed and queer on his body, not her mother who waited for her so patiently. None of these frightened her, for she had chosen them. She had wanted them just as she wanted now this race and this stubborn pain. But everything was confused. She could not recall which race this was.... Did they really wait for her, sisters and brothers, the lost, dead father, the mother weeping in that helpless perpetual grief?

She fell. Her arms betrayed her, she was not strong enough to keep hold of Vale. She fell back slowly as the motorcycle sped on, and before she hit the ground she had time to wonder if he would notice, if he would glance around. Then she struck, hard on her side, and something snapped in her shoulder, some tiny brittle bone teased beyond patience. She did not lose consciousness but lay quietly and stared up at Vale's young panicked face. He leaned over her. His eyes were pale inside the goggles, white hollows against his dirty skin. Something in his face, some twitching muscle, could not acknowledge the end of the race. "Hey, honey, are you for Christ's sake okay?" he said. He took off his goggles. "Why'd you let go? Look, are you bleeding or something? Did it happen?" He pulled her up, propped and prodded her into sitting, as if that would make her all right. He squatted on the road and stared into her face as if staring into an abyss. "Honey," he said, shaking his head sadly, "I forgot about it, you ought to of told me.... Honey, look, don't die, I mean you're not going to die, are you? You're not hurt that bad, are you?"

Vale was a young man of twenty-six, newly married when he met Mae. He and his wife lived with their month-old son in a trailer not far from the girl's father's garage, an Esso service station on the outside of a village named Frothing. A small river bounded the village on one side; there was a sawmill, an old cider mill shut down, and a tavern with a water wheel lit up at night to attract tourists. Because a new highway had been opened north of the village, not so many tourists on their way to the mountains drove slowly through town as they once did. The Esso station had never done well anyway with tourists—they would brake and coast curiously by, staring at the dirt drive and the greasy, leaning garage with its array of tin signs advertising soft drinks and cigarettes and gasoline. Vale, who worked for his father-in-law, would sit smoking on a stump in front of the garage and stare coldly at the tourists—often middle-aged men and women—who showed such caution. He could see at the back of their minds a clumsy inert fear and would have liked to seize this fear and drag it out into the daylight.

Frothing was about half a mile long. There were a few stores and some boarded-up buildings and several frame houses that faced the old state highway; then the Esso station; then the bridge over the river, which was lively in the spring, showing flashes of white as the water streamed over the flat black rocks, but shallow the rest of the year. Vale had always hated Frothing.

He worked on his motorcycle when there was nothing else to do, though his father-in-law grunted in disapproval at this. He loosened parts and tightened parts, back and forth. Sometimes his wife ambled over with the baby. His wife was a tall girl with long brown hair. She wore colorful jeans or slacks, blouses without sleeves that showed her long, muscular, hair-flecked arms. She was eighteen but looked older; Vale thought of her as older than he was. Now that she was a mother she did not seem any different to Vale, who realized that she had always been one really, had always been so competent and controlled, so that the baby's crying did not weary her as it did Vale and did not even provoke her into answering Vale's aimless insults. Like her mother, she was robust and healthy, partial to bracelets and wide belts, imitation leather belts with rhinestones on them, that gave her a brusque cowboyish look. She had always been ready to laugh at remarks people, especially men, would make: that was what Vale had liked about her at first, the way she grinned and laughed, sometimes giggled helplessly, at his jokes. Now she often said, "Yeah, that's very funny, ha ha," and smirked at him, keeping her boyish laughter for Vale's friends. She did not laugh much around the garage, not down with Vale as he worked endlessly at his motorcycle without taking much notice of her (there was nothing to say anymore, and she stood around shifting her weight from foot to foot, cracking gum, sighing) or upstairs with her mother, who always had the radio on. Vale could hear his wife's heavy tread upstairs, and often the baby's crying, but he never could make out what his wife and her mother said, nor did he hear them laugh.

One morning Mae walked into the garage. The front door was always kept open and Vale glanced up to see her there with the dazzling glare from the dirt drive behind her. "You still got Cokes for sale here?" she said. Though her face was shadowed by the glare behind her, Vale recognized the taut suspicious expression she had always, even as a child, displayed. Vale, wiping the sweat out of his eyes, waved her over to the machine in the corner. "Yeah, well I need change," the girl said, holding out her hand, palm up. Vale felt his face go hot as he stood. He took the quarter from her and went over to the cigar box his father-in-law kept money in (the cheap old run-down bastard, Vale thought) to get change. The girl waited with one foot out slightly in front of the other, her ankles crossed. Vale gave her the change without smiling.

She drank the Coke in front of him. She had pale brown hair that had been cut jaggedly and was combed by her to stick out around her face stiffly, like doll's hair. She was small, thin, nervously agile; Vale sensed a peculiar tension in her movements as she lifted the bottle to her lips and brought it down again, watching him, a tension he understood. Even her features were stiff and arch, as if held rigid purposely. She had fine, intricate eyes, thickly lashed and outlined skillfully with black pencil; her eyelids had crescents of silvery blue. Her lips, deeply pink, sucked at the soft drink and pursed themselves with modesty and cunning. "Come home, huh?" Vale said finally. He did not know how to talk to her because he had always thought of her as a child. "Had enough of the city, huh?" he said, grinning without humor. She shrugged her small shoulders. "Here, you want some?" she said. She thrust the bottle out at Vale, who accepted it before he had time to think. He gulped it down; while drinking, some germ of childish revenge suggested itself to him and he finished the Coke, so that he handed the bottle back to her empty. "Yeah, thanks," he said, wiping his mouth. Their eyes met and they smiled. Then they looked away, laughing in embarrassment. "You're some sort of a pig, I guess," Mae had said, staring past him at the motorcycle. Vale looked down at her bare legs. "Are you glad you came home?" Vale said. She laughed again and turned away. Vale followed her out into the sunshine, still holding the empty bottle. "Hey, you," Vale said, swallowing, "you, Mae," as if he were reciting an incantation or something, not listening to what he was saying. Mae glanced back at him over her shoulder, showing her little white teeth in a smile, but did not stop; she was going home. Vale was seized by a sensation of alarm and despair—he could not understand. "You pig, little pig," he muttered, watching her.

Mae had run away from home four or five times, always with men, various men who worked in Frothing or were just on their way through. She ran off on Greyhound buses, in trucks, in automobiles. She came home the same way after a few months, and would appear with her family in church for Sunday Mass, sitting alone in new clothes and a new hat and lipsticked meditation while the rest of the family filed docilely out into the aisle and up for communion. When the girl had come home this time, jumping out of a car right in the middle of the street on Saturday afternoon, everyone had noticed but had not had much to say—there was nothing to say about her, and even those who hated her, like Vale's wife, shrugged their shoulders and said they "felt sorry" for her. There was something wrong with her. Vale always agreed, but now he knew it must be true: there was something wrong with her, her very stiffness, her self-conscious, deliberate cheapness, even the poised sweetness of that stupid, stupid innocence. His face stiffened at the thought of her into an expression of distaste. He wanted nothing to do with her.

That night he went out for a walk, something he never did, and walked the two miles down to Mae's mother's house. It was a warm spring night. Sounds of crickets, night birds, owls, dogs barking forlornly. Vale knew little about Mae's mother, who was a small, tidy woman of about fifty. She had married an old man with children half grown and her first child had been Mae; after her had come a succession of boys and girls, poking relentlessly out, sticking up their heads to be counted. The stepchildren were gone away, married. The old man had died when Vale was still in school. Vale had never paid any attention to them, having been busy with his own life. He remembered his own mother talking about Mae, telling of how her mother and the old man had beaten her, trying to make her behave, and, later, after the old man's death, how her mother had beaten her alone, furiously and hysterically, so that people on either side of them could hear. Apparently none of it worked. Mae was expelled from school when she was thirteen. She hung around the sawmill and around the bar. She took no notice of other children but had been interested only in men, at first men much older than she; but then as she grew older she would accept younger men, until Vale was the youngest of all: Mae then was sixteen. There were other bad girls, but Mae was somehow different. The others were stupid, some of them mentally retarded, or spiteful, or malicious, or desperate to leave home. Mae was happy with her home, showed no spite or malice, took care of her younger sister lovingly, went to church every week with her family, and to the world that was not made up of the certain men she wanted showed a hazy, smiling expression, more absent-minded than innocent.

The next night Vale returned. He had left his wife crying in the trailer, the baby in the plywood box crying harmoniously with her; but as soon as he had run out to the road he had forgotten about them. He could think only of Mae. He waited around on the road, went down to the tavern where he drank beer with some farmers, came back and prowled around in the field behind the house. Nothing. This went on for several nights. She did not peek out the window or come to the door. Though he waited patiently, she did not come to the garage. He waited. Her childish smile had magnified itself in his brain so that he could click it on at once and become intoxicated by it, blotting out the tedium of the garage and his father-in-law and his wife's doomed, bright chatter, her gestures of passion as he made love to her, pretending she was Mae.

Yet when she did come again he was not surprised. He had the motorcycle ready: it might have been for this that he had been preparing it. *"He's* been after me to sell it, the old bastard," Vale had whispered to Mae, nodding upstairs to indicate his father-in-law. "Wants me staying around. Don't want me driving off somewhere!" Mae carried a straw purse with a felt kitten on it, in white. Vale was so excited beneath her smiling, still gaze that he could not keep his hands still. "You ever take anybody for a ride on that?" Mae said. Vale sighed and was afraid to touch her; his blood pounded. They looked at each other. Mae giggled at his discomfort. They kissed and Vale had to step back, putting his hand down flat on the white fur seat of the cycle. "Christ, I don't know if I can drive," he said. "I'm not kidding." He was able to think clearly, though, as if he had planned this in advance: he took his transistor radio off the shelf and put it in the saddlebag, and went over to the cigar box and took the money inside (twelve dollars and some change). Because he felt it would be more of an insult, hours later when his father-in-law came in for the afternoon, he left the cigar box in its place on the shelf with the smudged cover closed.

That evening they were in the city (a town of about fifteen thousand people), where Vale felt they disappeared, sucked into it and each other. Vale had some friends there; Mae might have had, but said nothing. She was a secretive, quiet girl, embarrassed sometimes by Vale's passion for her but sometimes gloating over it, asking him about his wife and what she had been like. She would not say the word *love;* she taught Vale to be ashamed of it too. After they had been there a month he and another man drove her to a doctor they had heard of, in the same city. The doctor was sardonic, sallow, had a drooping, indifferent face. Confronted with Vale and the other man, he had sat at the old-fashioned table in his kitchen, rested his elbows on the oilcloth cover, and had covered his sunken eyes with his hands. "I don't do it for nothing. I don't do it anymore," he said. "Who sent you here?" Mae had stood behind them, shivering. Vale was forced to take hold of the man by what remained of his hair, at the very crown of his head, before he agreed. "She better not get hurt," Vale said. "You know what risk there is," the doctor whined, staring sideways at Mae. "You do a nice clean job and we won't bother you no more. See you get left alone," Vale said. "She may die," the doctor said. "No she don't," Vale said, as if he had been waiting for this. "No she don't, doctor. You'll see to that."

The next time she had not really believed she was pregnant, but Vale was nervous about it; he did not like the thought of her having a baby, of her body being changed. He was not sure he would be attracted to her so strongly afterward and something close to bitter tears threatened him at the thought of this loss, as if it were a part of himself, of his youth. They had practiced a turkey run until Mae, ashamed, had said, "It's enough. It's enough," and baby or no, pregnant or not, they had got by safely. It was Vale's theory that she had been pregnant just a little and that their acting so quick had brought it off; Mae herself said nothing. She would lie sleepy and sleepless for hours, her eyelids heavy, her lips slightly parted, oblivious to him. At these times she looked patient: as if she had been waiting for centuries. When they ran out of money she did not seem to care. Vale's wife had always fought with him about money, but Mae hardly noticed. He always got money when he needed it, working part time at garages or driving trucks, and a few times he and another young man had helped themselves to money lying unattended here and there, though they drew the line (he swore to Mae, who probably did not care) at real robbery; they did not like the risk of meeting people face to face, of having the temptation to hurt these people, maybe even kill them. "I wouldn't trust myself," Vale always said honestly. "I got a bad temper and I just wouldn't trust myself. I draw the line at that."

He never thought of his old life. He felt cleansed and young again. After a few weeks he could not always remember his wife's face. He thought of the baby as a younger brother, perhaps. Mae stunned him into remembering himself only once in a while, asking as she did (as if it were not a joke), "What year is it? Sometimes I can't remember what year it is." She spent time looking at the calendar, which had a picture of Niagara Falls on top. What she found there puzzled him; she lingered on dates, ran her fingers along the numbers, not really counting but caressing. Sometimes Vale thought of her while out driving alone and it was odd that his mind skipped past her as she was now (as if there were nothing there, really, but someone he had imagined) and settled upon her as a child, though at that time he had never noticed her in particular. He kept rummaging through these memories, sifting the garbage of his own late childhood, but could discover nothing more than a thin child with hair long and snarled underneath, as if someone in author-ity—her mother, no doubt—had insisted upon such long hair for the child's beauty, at the expense of her suffering. But he could not remember her before she had become "bad"; it seemed to him that even then, as a child of four or five, she had been as she was now, collaborating somehow in being "bad." This thought discomforted him, for he felt he could not understand her. But most of the time he thought of her with warmth. This had been her last flight from home, he thought, this flight would be permanent. He supposed that after a while his wife would get a divorce and he and Mae would get married. He never thought much about it. When an image of their future life suggested itself to him it was just another picture of their present, that furnished room with the open stairway outside and this particular stretch of road, reaching out dazedly into the future, obscured by dust.

While Mae was dying inside her mother's old farmhouse, Vale waited patiently down the road, smoking and drinking beer. The feed mill was closed down for the day. In front of it a rusted truck was parked, had been parked for years, surrounded by weeds and small prickly bushes. Out of a mound of clay atop its streaked hood small fine weeds grew, delicate as lace. Vale sat on the running board of the truck and waited. He was heavy with beer. Friends of his, one of them a cousin of his wife's, hung out down the road at the tavern (the Mill-Side Inn) and came out from time to time to look down at him. Now it was dark: they jostled each other in the gravel parking lot of the tavern, inside the halo of insect-dotted pink light. "Hey, you, Vale," one of them called. "Hey, you still there? Going to get yourself kilt?"

Vale had thrown up right on the road, but he could not stop drinking. He had bought six cans of beer and still had more to drink. He thought bitterly that inside the house the family was eating; he thought he could smell food, meat and potatoes. But he was not sure. The idea of food made him vomit again. When his vision cleared he saw the windows of the old house wink at him. The curtains inside hung filmy and rigid. The old house was lit by a sweet, stale, damp light, as it had always been lit, even before they had had electricity. All farmhouses looked alike. The doctor's car was in the driveway, parked near the front, and whenever Vale's eye happened upon it his brain flinched. There was a pickup truck there too, belonging to some relative, one of the stepbrothers probably; he knew he had serviced it but could not remember. It was not from nearby. Vale sat on the running board again, lighting a cigarette with his trembling fingers. He knew nothing. No one came to the door, no one looked out the window. He could see nothing through the curtains. Someone had warned him of trouble (Mae's step-brother was furious) but nothing would come of that: they had forgotten him. He leaned over to spit. His mouth was sour. A quarter of a mile away, out by the sparkling water wheel, two men stood and waved their arms and yelled drunkenly at him. Their harsh young voices came to Vale through a mist.

When someone opened the door of the house at last, Vale got to his feet. It was late now and the countryside was quiet. His head pounded. "Hey, hey you there," he called, stumbling onto the road. A boy ran out to the driveway. Vale crossed to him. "Hey, you. Is that you, Eddie?" The boy stared. He wore jeans and a shrunken undershirt; Vale could see his chest bones shadowed in the moonlight. "You tell me what's going on," he said. His voice was loud and frightened.

The boy considered running past Vale; Vale put out his arms in a vague, threatening embrace. "You got no right here," he whispered. "Ma said—"

"What happened to her?" said Vale.

The boy started to run by and Vale grabbed his arm. Vale could feel him shivering. "She's dead," he whispered. "I got to go down there to call the sheriff."

"What?" said Vale.

"I got to go use their phone," the boy said, and his voice broke into a whine. "She told me to go call! We got to report it right! The doctor said—"

"You little bastard!" Vale said. He began shaking the boy. "What are you lying for—you and that old bitch of a mother in there— Trying to tell me—" The boy jerked away in terror; Vale saw that he looked guilty. "Yes, you! You and them other ones and that bitch of a mother of yours! I never saw it till now, that *you* did it to her and not me—she didn't remember me, did she? Forgot me! She never paid any attention to me, she was always thinking of someone else that she loved better—all of you in there, bastards, son-of-a-bitches— Who sucked the blood out, got in there and sucked it out—" He threw something against the house: the can of beer. It rolled up onto the shadowed roof, approached the peak, paused, and turned to roll silently back down; it fell into the grass. Vale and the boy watched it. "You know but you won't let on," Vale said bitterly to the boy. He was exhausted; his mind buzzed; he could not get things straight. Already the little lights inside the trailer, peeking out from behind safety-pinned curtains, beckoned to him—he must rest so that he could understand what happened, so that he would know who had killed Mae. He must sleep. "There's so much of it I don't know," he said. "But those bastards. Those killers," he said, swaying, waving his empty hand vaguely as if he were conjuring shadows out of the unfamiliar night.

Upon the Sweeping Flood

ONE DAY IN EDEN COUNTY, in the remote marsh and swamp-
lands to the south, a man named Walter Stuart was
stopped in the rain by a sheriff's deputy along a country road.
Stuart was in a hurry to get home to his family—his wife and
two daughters—after having endured a week at his father's old
farm, arranging for his father's funeral, surrounded by aging
relatives who had sucked at him for the strength of his youth.
He was a stern, quiet man of thirty-nine, beginning now to lose
some of the muscular hardness that had always baffled others,
masking as it did Stuart's remoteness, his refinement, his faith
in discipline and order that seem to have belonged, even in his
youth, to a person already grown safely old. He was a district
vice-president for one of the gypsum mining plants, a man to
whom financial success and success in love had come naturally,
without fuss. When only a child he had shifted his faith with
little difficulty from the unreliable God of his family's tradition
to the things and emotions of this world, which he admired in
his thoughtful, rather conservative way, and this faith had given
him access, as if by magic, to a communion with persons vastly
different from himself—with someone like the sheriff's deputy,
for example, who approached him that day in the hard, cold
rain. "Is something wrong?" Stuart said. He rolled down the

window and had nearly opened the door when the deputy, an old man with gray eyebrows and a slack, sunburned face, began shouting against the wind. "Just the weather, mister. You plan on going far? How far are you going?"

"Two hundred miles," Stuart said. "What about the weather? Is it a hurricane?"

"A hurricane—yes—a hurricane," the man said, bending to shout at Stuart's face. "You better go back to town and stay put. They're evacuating up there. We're not letting anyone through."

A long line of cars and pickup trucks, tarnished and gloomy in the rain, passed them on the other side of the road. "How bad is it?" said Stuart. "Do you need help?"

"Back at town, maybe, they need help," the man said. "They're putting up folks at the schoolhouse and the churches, and different families— The eye was spost to come by here, but last word we got it's veered further south. Just the same, though—"

"Yes, it's good to evacuate them," Stuart said. At the back window of an automobile passing them two children's faces peered out at the rain, white and blurred. "The last hurricane here—"

"Ah, God, leave off of that!" the old man said, so harshly that Stuart felt, inexplicably, hurt. "You better turn around now and get on back to town. You got money they can put you up some-wheres good—not with these folks coming along here."

This was said without contempt, but Stuart flinched at its assumptions and, years afterward, he was to remember the old man's remark as the beginning of his adventure. The man's twisted face and unsteady, jumping eyes, his wind-snatched voice, would reappear to Stuart when he puzzled for reasons— but along with the deputy's face there would be the sad line of cars, the children's faces turned toward him, and beyond them in his memory, the face of his dead father with skin wrinkled and precise as a withered apple.

"I'm going in to see if anybody needs help," Stuart said. He had the car going again before the deputy could even protest. "I know what I'm doing! I know what I'm doing!" Stuart said.

The car lunged forward into the rain, drowning out the deputy's outraged shouts. The slashing of rain against Stuart's face excited him. Faces staring out of oncoming cars were pale and startled, and Stuart felt rising in him a strange compulsion to grin, to laugh madly at their alarm.... He passed cars for some time. Houses looked deserted, yards bare. Things had the look of haste about them, even trees—in haste to rid themselves of their leaves, to be stripped bare. Grass was twisted and wild. A ditch by the road was overflowing and at spots the churning, muddy water stretched across the red clay road. Stuart drove, splashing, through it. After a while his enthusiasm slowed, his foot eased up on the gas pedal. He had not passed any cars or trucks for some time.

The sky had darkened and the storm had increased. Stuart thought of turning back when he saw, a short distance ahead, someone standing in the road. A car approached from the opposite direction. Stuart slowed, bearing to the right. He came upon a farm—a small, run-down one with just a few barns and a small pasture in which a horse stood drooping in the rain. Behind the roofs of the buildings a shifting edge of foliage from the trees beyond curled in the wind, now dark, now silver. In a neat harsh line against the bottom of the buildings the wind had driven up dust and red clay. Rain streamed off roofs, plunged into fat, tilted rain barrels, and exploded back out of them. As Stuart watched, another figure appeared, running out of the house. Both persons—they looked like children—jumped about in the road, waving their arms. A spray of leaves was driven against them and against the muddy windshield of the car that approached and passed them. They turned: a girl and a boy, waving their fists in rage, their faces white and distorted. As the car sped past Stuart, water and mud splashed up in a vicious wave.

When Stuart stopped and opened the door the girl was already there, shouting, "Going the wrong way! Wrong way!" Her face was coarse, pimply about her forehead and chin. The boy pounded up behind her, straining for air. "Where the hell are you going, mister?" the girl cried. "The storm's coming from this way. Did you see that bastard, going right by us? Did you see him? If I see him when I get to town—" A wall of rain struck. The girl lunged forward and tried to push her way into the car; Stuart had to hold her back. "Where are your folks?" he shouted. "Let me in," cried the girl savagely. "We're getting out of here!" "Your folks," said Stuart. He had to cup his mouth to make her hear. "Your folks in there!" "There ain't anybody there— *Goddamn* you," she said, twisting about to slap her brother, who had been pushing at her from behind. She whirled upon Stuart again. "You letting us in, mister? You letting us in?" she screamed, raising her hands as if to claw him. But Stuart's size must have calmed her, for she shouted hoarsely and mechanically: "There ain't nobody in there. Our pa's been gone the last two days. *Last two days.* Gone into town *by himself.* Gone drunk somewhere. He ain't here. He left us here. LEFT US HERE!" Again she rushed at Stuart, and he leaned forward against the steering wheel to let her get in back. The boy was about to follow when something caught his eye back at the farm. "Get in," said Stuart. "Get in. Please. Get in." "My horse there," the boy muttered. "You little bastard! You get in here!" his sister screamed.

But once the boy got in, once the door was closed, Stuart knew that it was too late. Rain struck the car in solid walls and the road, when he could see it, had turned to mud. "Let's go! Let's go!" cried the girl, pounding on the back of the seat. "Turn it around! Go up on our drive and turn it around!" The engine and the wind roared together. "Turn it! Get it going!" cried the girl. There was a scuffle and someone fell against Stuart. "It ain't no good," the boy said. "Let me out." He lunged for the door and Stuart grabbed him. "I'm going back to the house," the boy cried, appealing to Stuart with his frightened eyes, and his sister, giving up suddenly, pushed him violently forward. "It's no use," Stuart said. "Goddamn fool," the girl screamed, "goddamn fool!"

The water was ankle deep as they ran to the house. The girl splashed ahead of Stuart, running with her head up and her eyes wide open in spite of the flying scud. When Stuart shouted to the boy, his voice was slammed back to him as if he were being mocked. "Where are you going? Go to the house! Go to the house!" The boy had turned and was running toward the pasture. His sister took no notice but ran to the house. "Come back, kid!" Stuart cried. Wind tore at him, pushing him back. "What are you—"

The horse was undersized, skinny and brown. It ran to the boy as if it wanted to run him down but the boy, stooping through the fence, avoided the frightened hoofs and grabbed the rope that dangled from the horse's halter. "That's it! That's it!" Stuart shouted as if the boy could hear. At the gate the boy stopped and looked around wildly, up to the sky—he might have been looking for someone who had just called him; then he shook the gate madly. Stuart reached the gate and opened it, pushing it back against the boy, who now turned to gape at him. "What? What are you doing here?" he said.

The thought crossed Stuart's mind that the child was insane. "Bring the horse through!" he said. "We don't have much time."

"What are you doing here?" the boy shouted. The horse's eyes rolled, its mane lifted and haloed about its head. Suddenly it lunged through the gate and jerked the boy off the ground. The boy ran in the air, his legs kicking. "Hang on and bring him around!" Stuart shouted. "Let me take hold!" He grabbed the boy instead of the rope. They stumbled together against the horse. It had stopped now and was looking intently at something just to the right of Stuart's head. The boy pulled himself along the rope, hand over hand, and Stuart held onto him by the strap of his overalls. "He's scairt of you!" the boy said. "He's scairt of you!" Stuart reached over and took hold of the rope above the boy's fingers and tugged gently at it. His face was about a foot away from the horse's. "Watch out for him," said the boy. The horse reared and broke free, throwing Stuart back against the boy. "Hey, hey," screamed the boy, as if mad. The horse turned in midair as if whirled about by the wind, and Stuart looked up through his fingers to see its hoofs and a vicious flicking of its tail, and the face of the boy being yanked past him and away with incredible speed. The boy fell heavily on his side in the mud, arms outstretched above him, hands still gripping the rope with wooden fists. But he scrambled to his feet at once and ran alongside the horse. He flung one arm up around its neck as Stuart shouted, "Let him go! Forget about him!" Horse and boy pivoted together back toward the fence, slashing wildly at the earth, feet and hoofs together. The ground erupted beneath them. But the boy landed upright, still holding the rope, still with his arm about the horse's neck. "Let me help," Stuart said. "No," said the boy, "he's my horse, he knows me—" "Have you got him good?" Stuart shouted. "We got—we got each other here," the boy cried, his eyes shut tight.

Stuart went to the barn to open the door. While he struggled with it, the boy led the horse forward. When the door was open far enough, Stuart threw himself against it and slammed it around to the side of the barn. A cloud of hay and scud filled the air. Stuart stretched out his arms, as if pleading with the boy to hurry, and he murmured, "Come on. Please. Come on." The boy did not hear him or even glance at him: his own lips were moving as he caressed the horse's neck and head. The horse's muddy hoof had just begun to grope about the step before the door when something like an explosion came against the back of Stuart's head, slammed his back, and sent him sprawling out at the horse.

"Damn you! Damn you!" the boy screamed. Stuart saw nothing except rain. Then something struck him, his shoulder and hand, and his fingers were driven down into the mud. Something slammed beside him in the mud and he seized it— the horse's foreleg—and tried to pull himself up, insanely, lurching to his knees. The horse threw him backwards. It seemed to emerge out of the air before and above him, coming into sight as though out of a cloud. The boy he did not see at all—only the hoofs—and then the boy appeared, inexplicably, under the horse, peering intently at Stuart, his face struck completely blank. "Damn you!" Stuart heard, "he's my horse! My horse! I hope he kills you!" Stuart crawled back in the water, crab fashion, watching the horse form and dissolve, hearing its vicious tattoo against the barn. The door, swinging madly back and forth, parodied the horse's rage, seemed to challenge its frenzy; then the door was all Stuart heard, and he got to his feet, gasping, to see that the horse was out of sight.

The boy ran bent against the wind, out toward nowhere, and Stuart ran after him. "Come in the house, kid! Come on! Forget about it, kid!" He grabbed the boy's arm. The boy struck at him with his elbow. "He was my horse!" he cried.

In the kitchen of the house they pushed furniture against the door. Stuart had to stand between the boy and the girl to keep them from fighting. "Goddamn sniffling fool," said the girl. "So your goddamn horse run off for the night!" The boy crouched down on the floor, crying steadily. He was about thirteen: small for his age, with bony wrists and face. "We're all going to be blownt to hell, let alone your horse," the girl said. She sat with one big thigh and leg outstretched on the table, watching Stuart. He thought her perhaps eighteen. "Glad you come down to get us?" she said. "Where are you from, mister?" Stuart's revulsion surprised him; he had not supposed there was room in his stunned mind for emotion of this sort. If the girl noticed it she gave no sign, but only grinned at him. "I was—I was on my way home," he said. "My wife and daughters—" It occurred to him that he had forgotten about them entirely. He had not thought of them until now and, even now, no image came to his mind: no woman's face, no little girls' faces. Could he have imagined their lives, their love for him? For an instant he doubted everything. "Wife and daughters," said the girl, as if wondering whether to believe him. "Are they in this storm too?" "No—no," Stuart said. To get away from her he went to the window. He could no longer see the road. Something struck the house and he flinched away. "Them trees!" chortled the girl. "I knew it! Pa always said how he ought to cut them down, so close to the house like they are! I knew it! I knew it! And the old bastard off safe now where they can't get him!"

"Trees?" said Stuart slowly.

"Them trees! Old oak trees!" said the girl.

The boy, struck with fear, stopped crying suddenly. He crawled on the floor to a woodbox beside the big old iron stove and got in, patting the disorderly pile of wood as if he were blind. The girl ran to him and pushed him. "What are you doing?" Stuart cried in anguish. The girl took no notice of him. "What am I doing?" he said aloud. "What the hell am I doing here?" It seemed to him that the end would come in a minute or two, that the howling outside could get no louder, that the howling inside his mind could get no more intense, no more accusing. A goddamn fool! A goddamn fool! he thought. The deputy's face came to mind, and Stuart pictured himself groveling before the man, clutching at his knees, asking forgiveness and for time to be turned back. ... Then he saw himself back at the old farm, the farm of his childhood, listening to tales of his father's agonizing sickness, the old people's heads craning around, seeing how he took it, their eyes charged with horror and delight.... "My wife and daughters," Stuart muttered.

The wind made a hollow, drumlike sound. It seemed to be tolling. The boy, crouching back in the woodbox, shouted: "I ain't scairt! I ain't scairt!" The girl gave a shriek. "Our chicken coop, I'll be goddamned!" she cried. Try as he could, Stuart could see nothing out the window. "Come away from the window," Stuart said, pulling the girl's arm. She whirled upon him. "Watch yourself, mister," she said, "you want to go out to your goddamn bastardly worthless car?" Her body was strong and big in her men's clothing; her shoulders looked muscular beneath the filthy shirt. Cords in her young neck stood out. Her hair had been cut short and was now wet, plastered about her blemished face. She grinned at Stuart as if she were about to poke him in the stomach, for fun. "I ain't scairt of what God can do!" the boy cried behind them.

When the water began to bubble up through the floor boards they decided to climb to the attic. "There's an ax!" Stuart exclaimed, but the boy got on his hands and knees and crawled to the corner where the ax was propped before Stuart could reach it. The boy cradled it in his arms. "What do you want with that?" Stuart said, and for an instant his heart was pierced with fear. "Let me take it. I'll take it." He grabbed it out of the boy's dazed fingers.

The attic was about half as large as the kitchen and the roof jutted down sharply on either side. Tree limbs rubbed and slammed against the roof on all sides. The three of them crouched on the middle beam, Stuart with the ax tight in his embrace, the boy pushing against him as if for warmth, and the girl kneeling, with her thighs straining her overalls. She watched the little paneless window at one end of the attic without much emotion or interest, like a large, wet turkey. The house trembled beneath them. "I'm going to the window," Stuart said, and was oddly relieved when the girl did not sneer at him. He crawled forward along the dirty beam, dragging the ax with him, and lay full length on the floor about a yard from the window. There was not much to see. At times the rain relaxed, and objects beneath in the water took shape: tree stumps, parts of buildings, junk whirling about in the water. The thumping on the roof was so loud at that end that he had to crawl backwards to the middle again. "I ain't scairt, nothing God can do!" the boy cried. "Listen to the sniveling baby," said the girl. "He thinks God pays him any mind! Hah!" Stuart crouched beside them, waiting for the boy to press against him again. "As if God gives a good damn about him," the girl said. Stuart looked at her. In the near dark her face did not seem so coarse; the set of her eyes was almost attractive. "You don't think God cares about you?" Stuart said slowly. "No, not specially," the girl said, shrugging her shoulders. "The hell with it. You seen the last one of these?" She tugged at Stuart's arm. "Mister? It was something to see. Me an' Jackie was little then—him just a baby. We drove a far ways north to get out of it. When we come back the roads was so thick with sightseers from the cities! They took all the dead ones floating in the water and put them in one place, part of a swamp they cleared out. The families and things—they were mostly fruit pickers—had to come by on rafts and rowboats to look and see could they find the ones they knew. That was there for a day. The bodies would turn round and round in the wash from the boats. Then the faces all got alike and they wouldn't let anyone come anymore and put oil on them and set them afire. We stood on top of the car and watched all that day. I wasn't but nine then."

When the house began to shake, some time later, Stuart cried aloud: "This is it!" He stumbled to his feet, waving the ax. He turned around and around as if he were in a daze. "You goin' to chop somethin' with that?" the boy said, pulling at him. "Hey, no, that ain't yours to—it ain't yours to chop—" They struggled

for the ax. The boy sobbed, "It ain't yours! It ain't yours!" and
Stuart's rage at his own helplessness, at the folly of his being
here, for an instant almost made him strike the boy with the ax.
But the girl slapped him furiously. "Get away from him! I swear
I'll kill you!" she screamed.

Something exploded beneath them. "That's the windows,"
the girl muttered, clinging to Stuart, "and how am I to clean it
again! The old bastard will want it clean, and mud over everything!" Stuart pushed her away so that he could swing the ax.
Pieces of soft, rotted wood exploded back onto his face. The boy
screamed insanely as the boards gave way to a deluge of wind
and water, and even Stuart wondered if he had made a mistake.
The three of them fell beneath the onslaught and Stuart lost the
ax, felt the handle slam against his leg. "You! You!" Stuart cried,
pulling at the girl—for an instant, blinded by pain, he could not
think who he was, what he was doing, whether he had any life
beyond this moment. The big-faced, husky girl made no effort to
hide her fear and cried, "Wait, wait!" But he dragged her to the
hole and tried to force her out. "My brother—" she gasped. She
seized his wrists and tried to get away. "Get out there! There
isn't any time!" Stuart muttered. The house seemed about to
collapse at any moment. He was pushing her through the hole,
against the shattered wood, when she suddenly flinched back
against him and he saw that her cheek was cut and she was
choking. He snatched her hands away from her mouth as if he
wanted to see something secret: blood welled out between her
lips. She coughed and spat blood onto him. "You're all right,"
he said, oddly pleased. "Now get out there and I'll get the kid.
I'll take care of him." This time she managed to crawl through
the hole, with Stuart pushing her from behind; when he turned
to seize the boy, the boy clung to his neck, sobbing something
about God. "God loves you!" Stuart yelled. "Loves the least of
you! The least of you!" The girl pulled her brother up in her
great arms and Stuart was free to climb through himself.

It was actually quite a while—perhaps an hour—before the
battering of the trees and the wind pushed the house in. The
roof fell slowly, and the section to which they clung was washed

free. "We're going somewheres!" shouted the girl. "Look at the house! That goddamn old shanty seen the last storm!"

The boy lay with his legs pushed in under Stuart's and had not spoken for some time. When the girl cried, "Look at that!" he tried to burrow in farther. Stuart wiped his eyes to see the wall of darkness dissolve. The rain took on another look—a smooth, piercing, metallic glint, like nails driving against their faces and bodies. There was no horizon. They could see nothing except the rushing water and a thickening mist that must have been rain, miles and miles of rain, slammed by the wind into one great wall that moved remorselessly upon them. "Hang on," Stuart said, gripping the girl. "Hang on to me."

Waves washed over the roof, pushing objects at them with soft, muted thuds—pieces of fence, boards, branches heavy with foliage. Stuart tried to ward them off with his feet. Water swirled around them, sucking at them, sucking the roof, until they were pushed against one of the farm buildings. Something crashed against the roof—another section of the house—and splintered, flying up against the girl. She was thrown backwards, away from Stuart, who lunged after her. They fell into the water while the boy screamed. The girl's arms threshed wildly against Stuart. The water was cold, and its aliveness, its sinister energy, surprised him more than the thought that he would drown—that he would never endure the night. Struggling with the girl, he forced her back to the roof, pushed her up. Bare, twisted nails raked his hands. "Goddamn you, Jackie, you give a hand!" the girl said as Stuart crawled back up. He lay, exhausted, flat on his stomach and let the water and debris slosh over him.

His mind was calm beneath the surface buzzing. He liked to think that his mind was a clear, sane circle of quiet carefully preserved inside the chaos of the storm—that the three of them were safe within the sanctity of this circle; this was how man always conquered nature, how he subdued things greater than himself. But whenever he did speak to her it was in short grunts, in her own idiom: "This ain't so bad!" or "It'll let up pretty soon!" Now the girl held him in her arms as if he were a child, and he did not have the strength to pull away. Of his own free will he had given himself to this storm, or to the strange desire to save someone in it—but now he felt grateful for the girl, even for her brother, for they had saved him as much as he had saved them. Stuart thought of his wife at home, walking through the rooms, waiting for him; he thought of his daughters in their twin beds, two glasses of water on their bureau.... But these people knew nothing of him: in his experience now he did not belong to them. Perhaps he had misunderstood his role, his life? Perhaps he had blundered out of his way, drawn into the wrong life, surrendered to the wrong role. What had blinded him to the possibility of many lives, many masks, many arms that might so embrace him? A word not heard one day, a gesture misinterpreted, a leveling of someone's eyes in a certain unmistakable manner, which he had mistaken just the same! The consequences of such errors might trail insanely into the future, across miles of land, across worlds. He only now sensed the incompleteness of his former life.... "Look! Look!" the girl cried, jostling him out of his stupor. "Take a look at that, mister!"

He raised himself on one elbow. A streak of light broke out of the dark. Lanterns, he thought, a rescue party already.... But the rain dissolved the light; then it reappeared with a beauty that startled him. "What is it?" the boy screamed. "How come it's here?" They watched it filter through the rain, rays knifing through and showing, now, how buildings and trees crouched close about them. "It's the sun, the sun going down," the girl said. "The sun!" said Stuart, who had thought it was night. "The sun!" They stared at it until it disappeared.

The waves calmed sometime before dawn. By then the roof had lost its peak and water ran unchecked over it, in generous waves and then in thin waves, alternately, as the roof bobbed up and down. The three huddled together with their backs to the wind. Water came now in slow drifts. "It's just got to spread itself out far enough so's it will be even," said the girl, "then it'll go down." She spoke without sounding tired, only a little disgusted—as if things weren't working fast enough to suit her. "Soon as it goes down we'll start toward town and see if there ain't somebody coming out to get us in a boat," she said, chattily and comfortably, into Stuart's ear. Her manner astonished Stuart, who had been thinking all night of the humiliation and pain he had suffered. "Bet the old bastard will be glad to see us," she said, "even if he did go off like that. Well, he never knew a storm was coming. Me and him get along pretty well—he ain't so bad." She wiped her face; it was filthy with dirt and blood. "He'll buy you a drink, mister, for saving us how you did. That was something to have happen—a man just driving up to get us!" And she poked Stuart in the ribs.

The wind warmed as the sun rose. Rain turned to mist and back to rain again, still falling heavily, and now objects were clear about them. The roof had been shoved against the corner of the barn and a mound of dirt, and eddied there without much trouble. Right about them, in a kind of halo, a thick blanket of vegetation and filth bobbed. The fence had disappeared and the house had collapsed and been driven against a ridge of land. The barn itself had fallen in, but the stone support looked untouched, and it was against this they had been shoved. Stuart thought he could see his car—or something over there where the road used to be.

"I bet it ain't deep. Hell," said the girl, sticking her foot into the water. The boy leaned over the edge and scooped up some of the filth in his hands. "Lookit all the spiders," he said. He wiped his face slowly. "Leave them goddamn spiders alone," said the girl. "You want me to shove them down your throat?" She slid to the edge and lowered her legs. "Yah, I touched bottom. It ain't bad." But then she began coughing and drew herself back. Her coughing made Stuart cough: his chest and throat were ravaged, shaken. He lay exhausted when the fit left him and realized, suddenly, that they were all sick—that something had happened to them. They had to get off the roof. Now, with the sun up, things did not look so bad: there was a ridge of trees a short distance away on a long, red clay hill. "We'll go over there," Stuart said. "Do you think you can make it?"

The boy played in the filth, without looking up, but the girl gnawed at her lip to show she was thinking. "I spose so," she said. "But him—I don't know about him."

"Your brother? What's wrong?"

"Turn around. Hey, stupid. Turn around." She prodded the boy, who jerked around, terrified, to stare at Stuart. His thin bony face gave way to a drooping mouth. "Gone loony, it looks like," the girl said with a touch of regret. "Oh, he had times like this before. It might go away."

Stuart was transfixed by the boy's stare. The realization of what had happened struck him like a blow, sickening his stomach. "We'll get him over there," he said, making his words sound good. "We can wait there for someone to come. Someone in a boat. He'll be better there."

"I spose so," said the girl vaguely.

Stuart carried the boy while the girl splashed eagerly ahead. The water was sometimes up to his thighs. "Hold on another minute," he pleaded. The boy stared out at the water as if he thought he was being taken somewhere to be drowned. "Put your arms around my neck. Hold on," Stuart said. He shut his eyes and every time he looked up the girl was still a few yards ahead and the hill looked no closer. The boy breathed hollowly, coughing into Stuart's face. His own face and neck were covered with small red bites. Ahead, the girl walked with her shoulders lunged forward as if to hurry her there, her great thighs straining against the water, more than a match for it. As Stuart watched her, something was on the side of his face—in his ear— and with a scream he slapped at it, nearly dropping the boy. The girl whirled around. Stuart slapped at his face and must have knocked it off—probably a spider. The boy, upset by Stuart's outcry, began sucking in air faster and faster as if he were dying. "I'm all right, I'm all right," Stuart whispered, "just hold on another minute...."

When he finally got to the hill the girl helped pull him up. He set the boy down with a grunt, trying to put the boy's legs under him so he could stand. But the boy sank to the ground and turned over and vomited into the water; his body shook as if he were having convulsions. Again the thought that the night had poisoned them, their own breaths had sucked germs into their bodies, struck Stuart with an irresistible force. "Let him lay down and rest," the girl said, pulling tentatively at the back of her brother's belt, as if she were thinking of dragging him farther up the slope. "We sure do thank you, mister," she said.

Stuart climbed to the crest of the hill. His heart pounded madly, blood pounded in his ears. What was going to happen? Was anything going to happen? How disappointing it looked— ridges of land showing through the water and the healthy sunlight pushing back the mist. Who would believe him when he told of the night, of the times when death seemed certain...? Anger welled up in him already as he imagined the tolerant faces of his friends, his children's faces ready to turn to other amusements, other oddities. His wife would believe him; she would shudder, holding him, burying her small face in his neck. But what could she understand of his experience, having had no part in it?.... Stuart cried out; he had nearly stepped on a tangle of snakes. Were they alive? He backed away in terror. The snakes gleamed wetly in the morning light, heads together as if conspiring. Four...five of them—they too had swum for this land, they too had survived the night, they had as much reason to be proud of themselves as Stuart.

He gagged and turned away. Down by the waterline the boy lay flat on his stomach and the girl squatted nearby, wringing out her denim jacket. The water behind them caught the sunlight and gleamed mightily, putting them into silhouette. The girl's arms moved slowly, hard with muscle. The boy lay coughing gently. Watching them, Stuart was beset by a strange desire: he wanted to run at them, demand their gratitude, their love. Why should they not love him, when he had saved their lives? When he had lost what he was just the day before, turned now into a different person, a stranger even to himself? Stuart stooped and picked up a rock. A broad hot hand seemed to press against his chest. He threw the rock out into the water and said, "Hey!"

The girl glanced around but the boy did not move. Stuart sat down on the soggy ground and waited. After a while the girl looked away; spread the jacket out to dry. Great banked clouds rose into the sky, reflected in the water—jagged and bent in the waves. Stuart waited as the sun took over the sky. Mist at the horizon glowed, thinned, gave way to solid shapes. Light did not strike cleanly across the land, but was marred by ridges of trees and parts of buildings, and around a corner at any time Stuart expected to see a rescuing party—in a rowboat or something.

"Hey, mister." He woke; he must have been dozing. The girl had called him. "Hey. Whyn't you come down here? There's all them snakes up there."

Stuart scrambled to his feet. When he stumbled downhill, embarrassed and frightened, the girl said chattily, "The sons of bitches are crawling all over here. He chast some away." The boy was on his feet and looking around with an important air. His coming alive startled Stuart—indeed, the coming alive of the day, of the world, evoked alarm in him. All things came back to what they were. The girl's alert eyes, the firm set of her mouth, had not changed—the sunlight had not changed, or the land, really; only Stuart had been changed. He wondered at it . . . and the girl must have seen something in his face that he himself did not yet know about, for her eyes narrowed, her throat gulped a big swallow, her arms moved slowly up to show her raw elbows. "We'll get rid of them," Stuart said, breaking the silence. "Him and me. We'll do it."

The boy was delighted. "I got a stick," he said, waving a thin whiplike branch. "There's some over here."

"We'll get them," Stuart said. But when he started to walk, a rock slipped loose and he fell back into the mud. He laughed aloud. The girl, squatting a few feet away, watched him silently. Stuart got to his feet, still laughing. "You know much about it, kid?" he said, cupping his hand on the boy's head.

"About what?" said the boy.

"Killing snakes," said Stuart.

"I spose—I spose you just kill them."

The boy hurried alongside Stuart. "I need a stick," Stuart said; they got him one from the water, about the size of an ax. "Go by that bush," Stuart said, "there might be some there."

The boy attacked the bush in a frenzy. He nearly fell into it. His enthusiasm somehow pleased Stuart, but there were no snakes in the bush. "Go down that way," Stuart ordered. He glanced back at the girl: she watched them. Stuart and the boy went on with their sticks held in midair. "God put them here to keep us awake," the boy said brightly. "See we don't forget about Him." Mud sucked at their feet. "Last year we couldn't fire the woods on account of it so dry. This year can't either on account of the water. We got to get the snakes like this."

Stuart hurried as if he had somewhere to go. The boy, matching his steps, went faster and faster, panting, waving his stick angrily in the air. The boy complained about snakes and, listening to him, fascinated by him, in that instant Stuart saw everything. He saw the conventional dawn that had mocked the night, had mocked his desire to help people in trouble; he saw, beyond that, his father's home emptied now even of ghosts. He realized that the God of these people had indeed arranged things, had breathed the order of chaos into forms, had animated them, had animated even Stuart himself forty years ago. The knowledge of this fact struck him about the same way as the nest of snakes had struck him—an image leaping right to the eye, pouncing upon the mind, joining itself with the perceiver. "Hey, hey!" cried the boy, who had found a snake: the snake crawled noisily and not very quickly up the slope, a brown-speckled snake. The boy ran clumsily after it. Stuart was astonished at the boy's stupidity, at his inability to see, now, that the snake had vanished. Still he ran along the slope, waving his stick, shouting, "I'll get you! I'll get you!" This must have been the sign Stuart was waiting for. When the boy turned, Stuart was right behind him. "It got away up there," the boy said. "We got to get it." When Stuart lifted his stick the boy fell back a step but went on in mechanical excitement, "It's up there, gotten hid in the weeds. It ain't me," he said, "it ain't me that—" Stuart's blow struck the boy on the side of the head, and the rotted limb shattered into soft wet pieces. The boy stumbled down toward the water. He was coughing when Stuart took hold of him and began shaking him madly, and he did nothing but cough, violently and with all his concentration, even when Stuart bent to grab a rock and brought it down on his head. Stuart let him fall into the water. He could hear him breathing and he could see, about the boy's lips, tiny flecks or bubbles of blood appearing and disappearing with his breath.

When the boy's eyes opened, Stuart fell upon him. They struggled savagely in the water. Again the boy went limp; Stuart stood, panting, and waited. Nothing happened for a minute or so. But then he saw something—the boy's fingers moving up through the water, soaring to the surface! "Will you quit it!" Stuart screamed. He was about to throw himself upon the boy again when the thought of the boy's life, bubbling out between his lips, moving his fingers, filled him with such outraged disgust that he backed away. He threw the rock out into the water and ran back, stumbling, to where the girl stood.

She had nothing to say: her jaw was hard, her mouth a narrow line, her thick nose oddly white against her dirty face. Only her eyes moved, and these were black, lustrous, at once demanding and terrified. She held a board in one hand. Stuart did not have time to think, but as he lunged toward her, he could already see himself grappling with her in the mud, forcing her down, tearing her ugly clothing from her body— "Lookit!" she cried, the way a person might speak to a horse, cautious and coaxing, and pointed behind him. Stuart turned to see a white boat moving toward them, a half mile or so away. Immediately his hands dropped, his mouth opened in awe. The girl still pointed, breathing carefully, and Stuart, his mind shattered by the broken sunshine upon the water, turned to the boat, raised his hands, cried out, "Save me! Save me!" He had waded out a short distance by the time the men arrived.

In the Region of Ice

S ISTER IRENE WAS A TALL, DEFT WOMAN in her early thirties. What one could see of her face made a striking impression—serious, hard gray eyes, a long slender nose, a face waxen with thought. Seen at the right time, from the right angle, she was almost handsome. In her past teaching positions she had drawn a little upon the fact of her being young and brilliant and also a nun, but she was beginning to grow out of that.

This was a new university and an entirely new world. She had heard—of course it was true—that the Jesuit administration of this school had hired her at the last moment to save money and to head off the appointment of a man of dubious religious commitment. She had prayed for the necessary energy to get her through this first semester. She had no trouble with teaching itself; once she stood before a classroom she felt herself capable of anything. It was the world immediately outside the classroom that confused and alarmed her, though she let none of this show—the cynicism of her colleagues, the indifference of many of the students, and above all, the looks she got that told her nothing much would be expected of her because she was a nun. This took energy, strength. At times she had the idea that she was on trial and that the excuses she made to herself about her discomfort were only the common excuses made by guilty people. But in front of a class she had no time to worry about herself or the conflicts in her mind. She became, once and for all, a figure existing only for the benefit of others, an instrument by which facts were communicated.

About two weeks after the semester began, Sister Irene noticed a new student in her class. He was slight and fair-haired, and his face was blank, but not blank by accident, blank on purpose, suppressed and restricted into a dumbness that looked hysterical. She was prepared for him before he raised his hand, and when she saw his arm jerk, as if he had at last lost control of it, she nodded to him without hesitation.

"Sister, how can this be reconciled with Shakespeare's vision in *Hamlet*? How can these opposing views be in the same mind?"

Students glanced at him, mildly surprised. He did not belong in the class, and this was mysterious, but his manner was urgent and blind.

"There is no need to reconcile opposing views," Sister Irene said, leaning forward against the podium. "In one play Shakespeare suggests one vision, in another play another; the plays are not simultaneous creations, and even if they were, we never demand a logical—"

"We must demand a logical consistency," the young man said. "The idea of education is itself predicated upon consistency, order, sanity—"

He had interrupted her, and she hardened her face against him—for his sake, not her own, since she did not really care. But he noticed nothing. "Please see me after class," she said.

After class the young man hurried up to her.

"Sister Irene, I hope you didn't mind my visiting today. I'd heard some things, interesting things," he said. He stared at her, and something in her face allowed him to smile. "I . . . could we talk in your office? Do you have time?"

They walked down to her office. Sister Irene sat at her desk, and the young man sat facing her; for a moment they were self-conscious and silent.

"Well, I suppose you know—I'm a Jew," he said.

Sister Irene stared at him. "Yes?" she said.

"What am I doing at a Catholic university, huh?" He grinned. "That's what you want to know."

She made a vague movement of her hand to show that she had no thoughts on this, nothing at all, but he seemed not to catch it. He was sitting on the edge of the straight-backed chair. She saw that he was young but did not really look young. There were harsh lines on either side of his mouth, as if he had misused that youthful mouth somehow. His skin was almost as pale as hers, his eyes were dark and not quite in focus. He looked at her and through her and around her, as his voice surrounded them both. His voice was a little shrill at times.

"Listen, I did the right thing today—visiting your class! God, what a lucky accident it was; some jerk mentioned you, said you were a good teacher—I thought, what a laugh! These people know about good teachers here? But yes, listen, yes, I'm not kidding—you are good. I mean that."

Sister Irene frowned. "I don't quite understand what all this means."

He smiled and waved aside her formality, as if he knew better. "Listen, I got my B.A. at Columbia, then I came back here to this crappy city. I mean, I did it on purpose, I wanted to come back. I wanted to. I have my reasons for doing things. I'm on a three-thousand-dollar fellowship," he said, and waited for that to impress her. "You know, I could have gone almost anywhere with that fellowship, and I came back home here—my home's in the city—and enrolled here. This was last year. This is my second year. I'm working on a thesis, I mean I was, my master's thesis—but the hell with that. What I want to ask you is this: Can I enroll in your class, is it too late? We have to get special permission if we're late."

Sister Irene felt something nudging her, some uneasiness in him that was pleading with her not to be offended by his abrupt, familiar manner. He seemed to be promising another self, a better self, as if his fair, childish, almost cherubic face were doing tricks to distract her from what his words said.

"Are you in English studies?" she asked.

"I was in history. Listen," he said, and his mouth did something odd, drawing itself down into a smile that made the lines about it deepen like knives, "listen, they kicked me out."

He sat back, watching her. He crossed his legs. He took out a package of cigarettes and offered her one. Sister Irene shook her head, staring at his hands. They were small and stubby and might have belonged to a ten-year-old, and the nails were a strange near-violet color. It took him a while to extract a cigarette.

"Yeah, kicked me out. What do you think of that?"

"I don't understand."

"My master's thesis was coming along beautifully, and then this bastard—I mean, excuse me, this professor, I won't pollute your office with his name—he started making criticisms, he said some things were unacceptable, he—" The boy leaned forward and hunched his narrow shoulders in a parody of secrecy. "We had an argument. I told him some frank things, things only a broad-minded person could hear about himself. That takes courage, right? He didn't have it. He kicked me out of the master's program, so now I'm coming into English. Literature is greater than history; European history is one big pile of garbage. Sky-high. Filth and rotting corpses, right? Aristotle says that poetry is higher than history; he's right; in your class today I suddenly realized that this is my field, Shakespeare, only Shakespeare is—"

Sister Irene guessed that he was going to say that only Shakespeare was equal to him, and she caught the moment of recognition and hesitation, the half-raised arm, the keen, frowning forehead, the narrowed eyes; then he thought better of it and did not end the sentence. "The students in your class are mainly negligible, I can tell you that. You're new here, and I've been here a year—I would have finished my studies last year but my father got sick, he was hospitalized, I couldn't take exams and it was a mess—but I'll make it through English in one year or drop dead. I can do it, I can do anything. I'll take six courses at once—" He broke off, breathless. Sister Irene tried to smile. "All right then, it's settled? You'll let me in? Have I missed anything so far?"

He had no idea of the rudeness of his question. Sister Irene, feeling suddenly exhausted, said, "I'll give you a syllabus of the course."

"Fine! Wonderful!"

He got to his feet eagerly. He looked through the schedule, muttering to himself, making favorable noises. It struck Sister Irene that she was making a mistake to let him in. There were these moments when one had to make an intelligent decision. . . . But she was sympathetic with him, yes. She was sympathetic with something about him.

She found out his name the next day: Allen Weinstein.

After this she came to her Shakespeare class with a sense of excitement. It became clear to her at once that Weinstein was the most intelligent student in the class. Until he had enrolled, she had not understood what was lacking, a mind that could appreciate her own. Within a week his jagged, protean mind had alienated the other students, and though he sat in the center of the class, he seemed totally alone, encased by a miniature world of his own. When he spoke of the "frenetic humanism of the High Renaissance," Sister Irene dreaded the raised eyebrows and mocking smiles of the other students, who no longer bothered to look at Weinstein. She wanted to defend him, but she never did, because there was something rude and dismal about his knowledge; he used it like a weapon, talking passionately of Nietzsche and Goethe and Freud until Sister Irene would be forced to close discussion.

In meditation, alone, she often thought of him. When she tried to talk about him to a young nun, Sister Carlotta, everything sounded gross. "But no, he's an excellent student," she insisted. "I'm very grateful to have him in class. It's just that . . . he thinks ideas are real." Sister Carlotta, who loved literature also, had been forced to teach grade-school arithmetic for the last four years. That might have been why she said, a little sharply, "You don't think ideas are real?"

Sister Irene acquiesced with a smile, but of course she did not think so: only reality is real.

When Weinstein did not show up for class on the day the first paper was due, Sister Irene's heart sank, and the sensation was somehow a familiar one. She began her lecture and kept waiting for the door to open and for him to hurry noisily back to his seat, grinning an apology toward her—but nothing happened.

If she had been deceived by him, she made herself think angrily, it was as a teacher and not as a woman. He had promised her nothing.

Weinstein appeared the next day near the steps of the liberal arts building. She heard someone running behind her, a breathless exclamation: "Sister Irene!" She turned and saw him, panting and grinning in embarrassment. He wore a dark-blue suit with a necktie, and he looked, despite his childish face, like a little old man; there was something oddly precarious and fragile about him. "Sister Irene I owe you an apology, right?" He raised his eyebrows and smiled a sad, forlorn, yet irritatingly conspiratorial smile. "The first paper—not in on time, and I know what your rules are.... You won't accept late papers, I know—that's good discipline, I'll do that when I teach too. But, unavoidably, I was unable to come to school yesterday. There are many—many—" He gulped for breath, and Sister Irene had the startling sense of seeing the real Weinstein stare out at her, a terrified prisoner behind the confident voice. "There are many complications in family life. Perhaps you are unaware—I mean—"

She did not like him, but she felt this sympathy, something tugging and nagging at her the way her parents had competed for her love so many years before. They had been whining, weak people, and out of their wet need for affection, the girl she had been (her name was Yvonne) had emerged stronger than either of them, contemptuous of tears because she had seen so many. But Weinstein was different; he was not simply weak—perhaps he was not weak at all—but his strength was confused and hysterical. She felt her customary rigidity as a teacher begin to falter. "You may turn your paper in today if you have it," she said, frowning.

Weinstein's mouth jerked into an incredulous grin. "Wonderful! Marvelous!" he said. "You are very understanding, Sister Irene, I must say. I must say...I didn't expect, really..." He was fumbling in a shabby old briefcase for the paper. Sister Irene waited. She was prepared for another of his excuses, certain that he did not have the paper, when he suddenly straightened up and handed her something. "Here! I took the liberty of writing thirty pages instead of just fifteen," he said. He was obviously quite excited; his cheeks were mottled pink and white. "You may disagree violently with my interpretation—I expect you to, in fact I'm counting on it—but let me warn you, I have the exact proof, right here in the play itself!" He was thumping at a book, his voice growing louder and shriller. Sister Irene, startled, wanted to put her hand over his mouth and soothe him.

"Look," he said breathlessly, "may I talk with you? I have a class now I hate, I loathe, I can't bear to sit through! Can I talk with you instead?"

Because she was nervous, she stared at the title page of the paper: "'Erotic Melodies in *Romeo and Juliet*' by Allen Weinstein."

"All right?" he said. "Can we walk around here? Is it all right? I've been anxious to talk with you about some things you said in class."

She was reluctant, but he seemed not to notice. They walked slowly along the shaded campus paths. Weinstein did all the talking, of course, and Sister Irene recognized nothing in his cascade of words that she had mentioned in class. "The humanist must be committed to the totality of life," he said passionately. "This is the failing one finds everywhere in the academic world! I found it in New York and I found it nere and I'm no ingénu, I don't go around with my mouth hanging open—I'm experienced, look, I've been to Europe, I've lived in Rome! I went everywhere in Europe except Germany, I don't talk about Germany.... Sister Irene, think of the significant men in the last century, the men who've changed the world! Jews, right? Marx, Freud, Einstein! Not that I believe Marx, Marx is a madman ...and Freud, no, my sympathies are with spiritual humanism. I believe that the Jewish race is the exclusive... the exclusive, what's the word, the exclusive means by which humanism will be extended.... Humanism begins by excluding the Jew, and now," he said with a high, surprised laugh, "the Jew will perfect it. After the Nazis, only the Jew is authorized to understand humanism, its limitations and its possibilities. So, I say that the humanist is committed to life in its totality and not just to his profession! The religious person is totally religious, he is his religion! What else? I recognize in you a humanist and a religious person—"

But he did not seem to be talking to her or even looking at her.

"Here, read this," he said. "I wrote it last night." It was a long free-verse poem, typed on a typewriter whose ribbon was worn out.

"There's this trouble with my father, a wonderful man, a lovely man, but his health—his strength is fading, do you see? What must it be to him to see his son growing up? I mean, I'm a man now, he's getting old, weak, his health is bad—it's hell, right? I sympathize with him. I'd do anything for him, I'd cut open my veins, anything for a father—right? That's why I wasn't in school yesterday," he said, and his voice dropped for the last sentence, as if he had been dragged back to earth by a fact.

Sister Irene tried to read the poem, then pretended to read it. A jumble of words dealing with "life" and "death" and "darkness" and "love." "What do you think?" Weinstein said nervously, trying to read it over her shoulder and crowding against her.

"It's very...passionate," Sister Irene said.

This was the right comment; he took the poem back from her in silence, his face flushed with excitement. "Here, at this school, I have few people to talk with. I haven't shown anyone else that poem." He looked at her with his dark, intense eyes, and Sister Irene felt them focus upon her. She was terrified at what he was trying to do—he was trying to force her into a human relationship.

"Thank you for your paper," she said, turning away.

When he came the next day, ten minutes late, he was haughty and disdainful. He had nothing to say and sat with his arms folded. Sister Irene took back with her to the convent a feeling of betrayal and confusion. She had been hurt. It was absurd, and yet— She spent too much time thinking about him, as if he were somehow a kind of crystallization of her own loneliness; but she had no right to think so much of him. She did not want to think of him or of her loneliness. But Weinstein did so much more than think of his predicament: he embodied it, he acted it out, and that was perhaps why he fascinated her. It was as if he were doing a dance for her, a dance of shame and agony and delight, and so long as he did it, she was safe. She felt embarrassment for him, but also anxiety; she wanted to protect him. When the dean of the graduate school questioned her about Weinstein's work, she insisted that he was an "excellent" student, though she knew the dean had not wanted to hear that.

She prayed for guidance, she spent hours on her devotions, she was closer to her vocation than she had been for some years. Life at the convent became tinged with unreality, a misty distortion that took its tone from the glowering skies of the city at night, identical smokestacks ranged against the clouds and giving to the sky the excrement of the populated and successful earth. This city was not her city, this world was not her world. She felt no pride in knowing this, it was a fact. The little convent was not like an island in the center of this noisy world, but rather a kind of hole or crevice the world did not bother with, something of no interest. The convent's rhythm of life had nothing to do with the world's rhythm, it did not violate or alarm it in any way. Sister Irene tried to draw together the fragments of her life and synthesize them somehow in her vocation as a nun: she was a nun, she was recognized as a nun and had given herself happily to that life, she had a name, a place, she had dedicated her superior intelligence to the Church, she worked without pay and without expecting gratitude, she had given up pride, she did not think of herself but only of her work and her vocation, she did not think of anything external to these, she saturated herself daily in the knowledge that she was involved in the mystery of Christianity.

A daily terror attended this knowledge, however, for she sensed herself being drawn by that student, that Jewish boy, into a relationship she was not ready for. She wanted to cry out in fear that she was being forced into the role of a Christian, and what did that mean? What could her studies tell her? What could the other nuns tell her? She was alone, no one could help;

he was making her into a Christian, and to her that was a mystery, a thing of terror, something others slipped on the way they slipped on their clothes, casually and thoughtlessly, but to her a magnificent and terrifying wonder.

For days she carried Weinstein's paper, marked A, around with her; he did not come to class. One day she checked with the graduate office and was told that Weinstein had called in to say his father was ill and that he would not be able to attend classes for a while. "He's strange, I remember him," the secretary said. "He missed all his exams last spring and made a lot of trouble. He was in and out of here every day."

So there was no more of Weinstein for a while, and Sister Irene stopped expecting him to hurry into class. Then, one morning, she found a letter from him in her mailbox.

He had printed it in black ink, very carefully, as if he had not trusted handwriting. The return address was in bold letters that, like his voice, tried to grab onto her: Birchcrest Manor. Somewhere north of the city. "Dear Sister Irene," the block letters said, "I am doing well here and have time for reading and relaxing. The Manor is delightful. My doctor here is an excellent, intelligent man who has time for me, unlike my former doctor. If you have time, you might drop in on my father, who worries about me too much, I think, and explain to him what my condition is. He doesn't seem to understand. I feel about this new life the way that boy, what's his name, in *Measure for Measure,* feels about the prospects of a different life; you remember what he says to his sister when she visits him in prison, how he is looking forward to an escape into another world. Perhaps you could *explain* this to my father and he would stop worrying." The letter ended with the father's name and address, in letters that were just a little too big. Sister Irene, walking slowly down the corridor as she read the letter, felt her eyes cloud over with tears. She was cold with fear, it was something she had never experienced before. She knew what Weinstein was trying to tell her, and the desperation of his attempt made it all the more pathetic; he did not deserve this, why did God allow him to suffer so?

She read through Claudio's speech to his sister, in *Measure for Measure:*

Ay, but to die, and go we know not where;
To lie in cold obstruction and to rot;
This sensible warm motion to become
A kneaded clod; and the delighted spirit
To bathe in fiery floods, or to reside
In thrilling region of thick-ribbed ice,
To be imprison'd in the viewless winds
And blown with restless violence round about
The pendent world; or to be worse than worst
Of those that lawless and incertain thought
Imagines howling! 'Tis too horrible!
The weariest and most loathed worldly life
That age, ache, penury, and imprisonment
Can lay on nature is a paradise
To what we fear of death.

Sister Irene called the father's number that day. "Robert Weinstein residence, who may I say is calling?" a woman said, bored. "May I speak to Mr. Weinstein? It's urgent—about his son," Sister Irene said. There was a pause at the other end. "You want to talk to his mother, maybe," the woman said. "His mother? Yes, his mother, then. Please. It's very important."

She talked with this strange, unsuspected woman, a disembodied voice that suggested absolutely no face, and insisted upon going over that afternoon. The woman was nervous, but Sister Irene, who was a university professor, after all, knew enough to hide her own nervousness. She kept waiting for the woman to say, "Yes, Allen has mentioned you. . . . " but nothing happened.

She persuaded Sister Carlotta to ride over with her. This urgency of hers was something they were all amazed by. They hadn't suspected that the set of her gray eyes could change to this blurred, distracted alarm, this sense of mission that seemed to have come to her from nowhere. Sister Irene drove across the city in the late afternoon traffic, with the high whining noises from residential streets where trees were being sawed down in pieces. She understood now the secret, sweet wildness that Christ must have felt, giving himself for man, dying for the billions of men who would never know of him and never understand the sacrifice. For the first time she approached the realization of that great act. In her troubled mind the city traffic was jumbled and yet oddly coherent, an image of the world that was always out of joint with what was happening in it, its inner history struggling with its external spectacle. This sacrifice of Christ's, so mysterious and legendary now, almost lost in time—it was that by which Christ transcended both God and man at one moment, more than man because of his fate to do what no other man could do, and more than God because no god could suffer as he did. She felt a flicker of something close to madness.

She drove nervously, uncertainly, afraid of missing the street and afraid of finding it too, for while one part of her rushed forward to confront these people who had betrayed their son, another part of her would have liked nothing so much as to be waiting as usual for the summons to dinner, safe in her room. . . . When she found the street and turned onto it, she was in a state of breathless excitement. Here lawns were bright green and marred with only a few leaves, magically clean, and the houses were enormous and pompous, a mixture of styles: ranch houses, colonial houses, French country houses, white-bricked wonders with curving glass and clumps of birch trees somehow encircled by white concrete. Sister Irene stared as if she had blundered into another world. This was a kind of heaven, and she was too shabby for it.

The Weinstein's house was the strangest one of all: it looked like a small Alpine lodge, with an inverted-V-shaped front entrance. Sister Irene drove up the black-topped driveway and let the car slow to a stop; she told Sister Carlotta she would not be long.

At the door she was met by Weinstein's mother, a small, nervous woman with hands like her son's. "Come in, come in," the woman said. She had once been beautiful, that was clear, but now in missing beauty she was not handsome or even attractive but looked ruined and perplexed, the misshapen swelling of her white-blond professionally set hair like a cap lifting up from her surprised face. "He'll be right in. Robert?" she called, "our visitor is here." They went into the living room. There was a grand piano at one end and an organ at the other. In between were scatterings of brilliant modern furniture in conversational groups and several puffed-up white rugs on the polished floor. Sister Irene could not stop shivering.

"Professor, it's so strange, but let me say when the phone rang I had a feeling—I had a feeling," the woman said, with damp eyes. Sister Irene sat, and the woman hovered about her. "Should I call you Professor? We don't ... you know ... we don't understand the technicalities that go with— Allen wanted to go here to the Catholic school; I told my husband why not? Why fight? It's the thing these days, they do anything they want for knowledge. And he had to come home, you know. He couldn't take care of himself in New York, that was the beginning of the trouble.... Should I call you Professor?"

"You can call me Sister Irene."

"Sister Irene?" the woman said, touching her throat in awe, as if something intimate and unexpected had happened.

Then Weinstein's father appeared, hurrying. He took long, impatient strides. Sister Irene stared at him and in that instant doubted everything—he was in his fifties, a tall, sharply handsome man, heavy but not fat, holding his shoulders back with what looked like an effort, but holding them back just the same. He wore a dark suit and his face was flushed, as if he had run a long distance.

"Now," he said, coming to Sister Irene and with a precise wave of his hand motioning his wife off, "now, let's straighten this out. A lot of confusion over that kid, eh?" He pulled a chair over, scraping it across a rug and pulling one corner over, so that its brown underside was exposed. "I came home early just for this, Libby phoned me. Sister, you got a letter from him, right?"

The wife looked at Sister Irene over her husband's head as if trying somehow to coach her, knowing that this man was so

loud and impatient that no one could remember anything in his
presence.

"A letter—yes—today—"

"He says what in it? You got the letter, eh? Can I see it?"

She gave it to him and wanted to explain, but he silenced her
with a flick of his hand. He read through the letter so quickly
that Sister Irene thought perhaps he was trying to impress her
with his skill at reading. "So?" he said, raising his eyes, smiling,
"so what is this? He's happy out there, he says. He doesn't communicate with us anymore, but he writes to you and says he's
happy—what's that? I mean, what the hell is that?"

"But he isn't happy. He wants to come home," Sister Irene
said. It was so important that she make him understand that she
could not trust her voice; goaded by this man, it might suddenly
turn shrill, as his son's did. "Someone must read their letters
before they're mailed, so he tried to tell me something by
making an allusion to—"

"What?"

"—an allusion to a play, so that I would know. He may be
thinking of suicide, he must be very unhappy—"

She ran out of breath. Weinstein's mother had begun to cry,
but the father was shaking his head jerkily back and forth.
"Forgive me, Sister, but it's a lot of crap, he needs the hospital,
he needs help—right? It costs me fifty a day out there, and
they've got the best place in the state, I figure it's worth it. He
needs help, that kid, what do I care if he's unhappy? He's
unbalanced!" he said angrily. "You want us to get him out
again? We argued with the judge for two hours to get him in, an
acquaintance of mine. Look, he can't control himself—he was
smashing things here, he was hysterical. They need help, lady,
and you do something about it fast! You do something! We
made up our minds to do something and we did it! This letter—
what the hell is this letter? He never talked like that to us!"

"But he means the opposite of what he says—"

"Then he's crazy! I'm the first to admit it." He was perspiring, and his face had darkened. "I've got no pride left this late.
He's a little bastard, you want to know? He calls me names, he's
filthy, got a filthy mouth—that's being smart, huh? They give

him a big scholarship for his filthy mouth? I went to college too, and I got out and knew something, and I for Christ's sake did something with it; my wife is an intelligent woman, a learned woman, would you guess she does book reviews for the little newspaper out here? Intelligent isn't crazy—crazy isn't intelligent. Maybe for you at the school he writes nice papers and gets an A, but out here, around the house, he can't control himself, and we got him committed!"

"But—"

"We're fixing him up, don't worry about it!" He turned to his wife. "Libby, get out of here, I mean it. I'm sorry, but get out of here, you're making a fool of yourself, go stand in the kitchen or something, you and the goddamn maid can cry on each other's shoulders. That one in the kitchen is nuts too, they're all nuts. Sister," he said, his voice lowering, "I thank you immensely for coming out here. This is wonderful, your interest in my son. And I see he admires you—that letter there. But what about that letter? If he did want to get out, which I don't admit—he was willing to be committed, in the end he said okay himself—if he wanted out I wouldn't do it. Why? So what if he wants to come back? The next day he wants something else, what then? He's a sick kid, and I'm the first to admit it."

Sister Irene felt that sickness spread to her. She stood. The room was so big it seemed it must be a public place; there had been nothing personal or private about their conversation. Weinstein's mother was standing by the fireplace, sobbing. The father jumped to his feet and wiped his forehead in a gesture that was meant to help Sister Irene on her way out. "God, what a day," he said, his eyes snatching at hers for understanding, "you know—one of those days all day long? Sister, I thank you a lot. There should be more people in the world who care about others, like you. I mean that."

On the way back to the convent, the man's words returned to her, and she could not get control of them; she could not even feel anger. She had been pressed down, forced back, what could she do? Weinstein might have been watching her somehow from a barred window, and he surely would have understood. The strange idea she had had on the way over, something about understanding Christ, came back to her now and sickened her. But the sickness was small. It could be contained.

About a month after her visit to his father, Weinstein himself showed up. He was dressed in a suit as before, even the necktie was the same. He came right into her office as if he had been pushed and could not stop.

"Sister," he said, and shook her hand. He must have seen fear in her because he smiled ironically. "Look, I'm released. I'm let out of the nut house. Can I sit down?"

He sat. Sister Irene was breathing quickly, as if in the presence of an enemy who does not know he is an enemy.

"So, they finally let me out. I heard what you did. You talked with him, that was all I wanted. You're the only one who gave a damn. Because you're a humanist and a religious person, you respect...the individual. Listen," he said, whispering, "it was hell out there! Hell Birchcrest Manor! All fixed up with fancy chairs and *Life* magazines lying around—and what do they do to you? They locked me up, they gave me shock treatments! Shock treatments, how do you like that, it's discredited by everybody now—they're crazy out there themselves, sadists. They locked me up, they gave me hypodermic shots, they didn't treat me like a human being! Do you know what that is," Weinstein demanded savagely, "not to be treated like a human being? They made me an animal—for fifty dollars a day! Dirty filthy swine! Now I'm an outpatient because I stopped swearing at them. I found somebody's bobby pin, and when I wanted to scream I pressed it under my fingernail and it stopped me—the screaming went inside and not out—so they gave me good reports, those sick bastards. Now I'm an outpatient and I can walk along the street and breathe in the same filthy exhaust from the buses like all you normal people! Christ," he said, and threw himself back against the chair.

Sister Irene stared at him. She wanted to take his hand, to make some gesture that would close the aching distance between them. "Mr. Weinstein—"

"Call me Allen!" he said sharply.

"I'm very sorry—I'm terribly sorry—"

"My own parents committed me, but of course they didn't know what it was like. It was hell," he said thickly, "and there isn't any hell except what other people do to you. The psychiatrist out there, the main shrink, he hates Jews too, some of us were positive of that, and he's got a bigger nose than I do, a real beak." He made a noise of disgust. "A dirty bastard, a sick, dirty, pathetic bastard—all of them. Anyway, I'm getting out of here, and I came to ask you a favor."

"What do you mean?"

"I'm getting out. I'm leaving. I'm going up to Canada and lose myself. I'll get a job, I'll forget everything, I'll kill myself maybe—what's the difference? Look, can you lend me some money?"

"Money?"

"Just a little! I have to get to the border, I'm going to take a bus."

"But I don't have any money—"

"No money?" He stared at her. "You mean—you don't have any? Sure you have some!"

She stared at him as if he had asked her to do something obscene. Everything was splotched and uncertain before her eyes.

"You must . . . you must go back," she said, "you're making a—"

"I'll pay it back. Look, I'll pay it back, can you go to where you live or something and get it? I'm in a hurry. My friends are sons of bitches: one of them pretended he didn't see me yesterday—I stood right in the middle of the sidewalk and yelled at him, I called him some appropriate names! So he didn't see me, huh? You're the only one who understands me, you understand me like a poet, you—"

"I can't help you, I'm sorry—I . . ."

He looked to one side of her and flashed his gaze back, as if he could control it. He seemed to be trying to clear his vision.

"You have the soul of a poet," he whispered, "you're the only one. Everybody else is rotten! Can't you lend me some money, ten dollars maybe? I have three thousand in the bank, and I can't touch it! They take everything away from me, they make me into an animal.... You know I'm not an animal, don't you? Don't you?"

"Of course," Sister Irene whispered.

"You could get money. Help me. Give me your hand or something, touch me, help me—please...." He reached for her hand and she drew back. He stared at her and his face seemed about to crumble, like a child's. "I want something from you, but I don't know what—I want something!" he cried. "Something real! I want you to look at me like I was a human being, is that too much to ask? I have a brain, I'm alive, I'm suffering— what does that mean? Does that mean nothing? I want something real and not this phony Christian love garbage—it's all in the books, it isn't personal—I want something real—look...."

He tried to take her hand again, and this time she jerked away. She got to her feet. "Mr. Weinstein," she said, "please—"

"You! You nun!" he said scornfully, his mouth twisted into a mock grin. "You nun! There's nothing under that ugly outfit, right? And you're not particularly smart even though you think you are; my father has more brains in his foot than you—"

He got to his feet and kicked the chair.

"You bitch!" he cried.

She shrank back against her desk as if she thought he might hit her, but he only ran out of the office.

Weinstein: the name was to become disembodied from the figure, as time went on. The semester passed, the autumn drizzle turned into snow, Sister Irene rode to school in the morning and left in the afternoon, four days a week, anonymous in her black winter cloak, quiet and stunned. University teaching was an anonymous task, each day dissociated from the rest, with no necessary sense of unity among the teachers: they came and went separately and might for a year just miss a colleague who left his office five minutes before they arrived, and it did not matter.

She heard of Weinstein's death, his suicide by drowning, from the English Department secretary, a handsome white-haired woman who kept a transistor radio on her desk. Sister

Irene was not surprised; she had been thinking of him as dead for months. "They identified him by some special television way they have now," the secretary said. "They're shipping the body back. It was up in Quebec. . . ."

Sister Irene could feel a part of herself drifting off, lured by the plains of white snow to the north, the quiet, the emptiness, the sweep of the Great Lakes up to the silence of Canada. But she called that part of herself back. She could only be one person in her lifetime. That was the ugly truth, she thought, that she could not really regret Weinstein's suffering and death; she had only one life and had already given it to someone else. He had come too late to her. Fifteen years ago, perhaps, but not now.

She was only one person, she thought, walking down the corridor in a dream. Was she safe in this single person, or was she trapped? She had only one identity. She could make only one choice. What she had done or hadn't done was the result of that choice, and how was she guilty? If she could have felt guilt, she thought, she might at least have been able to feel something.

Where Are You Going, Where Have You Been?

H ER NAME WAS CONNIE. She was fifteen and she had a quick, nervous, giggling habit of craning her neck to glance into mirrors or checking other people's faces to make sure her own was all right. Her mother, who noticed everything and knew everything and who hadn't much reason any longer to look at her own face, always scolded Connie about it. "Stop gawking at yourself. Who are you? You think you're so pretty?" she would say. Connie would raise her eyebrows at these familiar old complaints and look right through her mother, into a shadowy vision of herself as she was right at that moment: she knew she was pretty and that was everything. Her mother had been pretty once too, if you could believe those old snapshots in the album, but now her looks were gone and that was why she was always after Connie.

"Why don't you keep your room clean like your sister? How've you got your hair fixed—what the hell stinks? Hair spray? You don't see your sister using that junk."

Her sister June was twenty-four and still lived at home. She was a secretary in the high school Connie attended, and if that wasn't bad enough—with her in the same building—she was so plain and chunky and steady that Connie had to hear her praised all the time by her mother and her mother's sisters. June did this, June did that, she saved money and helped clean the house and cooked and Connie couldn't do a thing, her mind was all filled with trashy daydreams. Their father was away at work most of the time and when he came home he wanted supper and he read the newspaper at supper and after supper he went to bed. He didn't bother talking much to them, but around his bent head Connie's mother kept picking at her until Connie wished her mother was dead and she herself was dead and it was all over. "She makes me want to throw up sometimes," she complained to her friends. She had a high, breathless, amused voice that made everything she said sound a little forced, whether it was sincere or not.

There was one good thing: June went places with girlfriends of hers, girls who were just as plain and steady as she, and so when Connie wanted to do that her mother had no objections. The father of Connie's best girlfriend drove the girls the three miles to town and left them at a shopping plaza so they could walk through the stores or go to a movie, and when he came to pick them up again at eleven he never bothered to ask what they had done.

They must have been familiar sights, walking around the shopping plaza in their shorts and flat ballerina slippers that always scuffed the sidewalk, with charm bracelets jingling on their thin wrists; they would lean together to whisper and laugh secretly if someone passed who amused or interested them. Connie had long dark blond hair that drew anyone's eye to it, and she wore part of it pulled up on her head and puffed out and the rest of it she let fall down her back. She wore a pull-over jersey blouse that looked one way when she was at home and another way when she was away from home. Everything about her had two sides to it, one for home and one for anywhere that was not home: her walk, which could be childlike and bobbing, or languid enough to make anyone think she was hearing music in her head; her mouth, which was pale and smirking most of the time, but bright and pink on these evenings out; her laugh, which was cynical and drawling at home—"Ha, ha, very funny"—but highpitched and nervous anywhere else, like the jingling of the charms on her bracelet.

Sometimes they did go shopping or to a movie, but sometimes they went across the highway, ducking fast across the busy road, to a drive-in restaurant where older kids hung out. The restaurant was shaped like a big bottle, though squatter than a real bottle, and on its cap was a revolving figure of a grinning boy holding a hamburger aloft. One night in midsummer they ran across, breathless with daring, and right away someone leaned out a car window and invited them over, but it was just a boy from high school they didn't like. It made them feel good to be able to ignore him. They went up through the maze of parked and cruising cars to the bright-lit, fly-infested restaurant, their faces pleased and expectant as if they were entering a sacred building that loomed up out of the night to give them what haven and blessing they yearned for. They sat at the counter and crossed their legs at the ankles, their thin shoulders rigid with excitement, and listened to the music that made everything so good: the music was always in the background, like music at a church service; it was something to depend upon.

A boy named Eddie came in to talk with them. He sat backwards on his stool, turning himself jerkily around in semicircles and then stopping and turning back again, and after a while he asked Connie if she would like something to eat. She said she would and so she tapped her friend's arm on her way out—her friend pulled her face up into a brave, droll look—and Connie said she would meet her at eleven, across the way. "I just hate to leave her like that," Connie said earnestly, but the boy said that she wouldn't be alone for long. So they went out to his car, and on the way Connie couldn't help but let her eyes wander over the windshields and faces all around her, her face gleaming with a joy that had nothing to do with Eddie or even this place; it might have been the music. She drew her shoulders up and sucked in her breath with the pure pleasure of being alive, and just at that moment she happened to glance at a face just a few feet from hers. It was a boy with shaggy black hair, in a convertible jalopy painted gold. He stared at her and then his lips widened into a grin. Connie slit her eyes at him and turned away, but she couldn't help glancing back and there he was, still watching her. He wagged a finger and laughed and said, "Gonna get you, baby," and Connie turned away again without Eddie noticing anything.

She spent three hours with him, at the restaurant where they ate hamburgers and drank Cokes in wax cups that were always sweating, and then down an alley a mile or so away, and when he left her off at five to eleven only the movie house was still open at the plaza. Her girlfriend was there, talking with a boy. When Connie came up, the two girls smiled at each other and Connie said, "How was the movie?" and the girl said, "*You* should know." They rode off with the girl's father, sleepy and pleased, and Connie couldn't help but look back at the darkened shopping plaza with its big empty parking lot and its signs that were faded and ghostly now, and over at the drive-in restaurant where cars were still circling tirelessly. She couldn't hear the music at this distance.

Next morning June asked her how the movie was and Connie said, "So-so."

She and that girl and occasionally another girl went out several times a week, and the rest of the time Connie spent around the house—it was summer vacation—getting in her mother's way and thinking, dreaming about the boys she met. But all the boys fell back and dissolved into a single face that was not even a face but an idea, a feeling, mixed up with the urgent insistent pounding of the music and the humid night air of July. Connie's mother kept dragging her back to the daylight by finding things for her to do or saying suddenly, "What's this about the Pettinger girl?"

And Connie would say nervously, "Oh, her. That dope." She always drew thick clear lines between herself and such girls, and her mother was simple and kind enough to believe it. Her mother was so simple, Connie thought, that it was maybe cruel to fool her so much. Her mother went scuffling around the house in old bedroom slippers and complained over the telephone to one sister about the other, then the other called up and the two of them complained about the third one. If June's name was mentioned her mother's tone was approving, and if Connie's name was mentioned it was disapproving. This did not really mean she disliked Connie, and actually Connie thought that her mother preferred her to June just because she was prettier, but the two of them kept up a pretense of exasperation, a sense that they were tugging and struggling over something of little value to either of them. Sometimes, over coffee, they were almost friends, but something would come up—some vexation that was like a fly buzzing suddenly around their heads—and their faces went hard with contempt.

One Sunday Connie got up at eleven—none of them bothered with church—and washed her hair so that it could dry all day long in the sun. Her parents and sister were going to a barbecue at an aunt's house and Connie said no, she wasn't interested, rolling her eyes to let her mother know just what she thought of it. "Stay home alone then," her mother said sharply. Connie sat out back in a lawn chair and watched them drive away, her father quiet and bald, hunched around so that he could back the car out, her mother with a look that was still angry and not at all softened through the windshield, and in the back seat poor old June, all dressed up as if she didn't know what a barbecue was, with all the running yelling kids and the flies. Connie sat with her eyes closed in the sun, dreaming and dazed with the warmth about her as if this were a kind of love, the caresses of love, and her mind slipped over onto thoughts of the boy she had been with the night before and how nice he had been, how sweet it always was, not the way someone like June would suppose but sweet, gentle, the way it was in movies and promised in songs; and when she opened her eyes she hardly knew where she was, the backyard ran off into weeds and a fence-like line of trees and behind it the sky was perfectly blue and still. The asbestos "ranch house" that was now three years old startled her—it looked small. She shook her head as if to get awake.

It was too hot. She went inside the house and turned on the radio to drown out the quiet. She sat on the edge of her bed, barefoot, and listened for an hour and a half to a program called XYZ Sunday Jamboree, record after record of hard, fast, shrieking songs she sang along with, interspersed by exclamations from "Bobby King": "An' look here, you girls at Napoleon's— Son and Charley want you to pay real close attention to this song coming up!"

And Connie paid close attention herself, bathed in a glow of slow-pulsed joy that seemed to rise mysteriously out of the music itself and lay languidly about the airless little room, breathed in and breathed out with each gentle rise and fall of her chest.

After a while she heard a car coming up the drive. She sat up at once, startled, because it couldn't be her father so soon. The gravel kept crunching all the way in from the road—the driveway was long—and Connie ran to the window. It was a car she didn't know. It was an open jalopy, painted a bright gold that caught the sunlight opaquely. Her heart began to pound and her fingers snatched at her hair, checking it, and she whispered, "Christ, Christ," wondering how bad she looked. The car came to a stop at the side door and the horn sounded four short taps, as if this were a signal Connie knew.

She went into the kitchen and approached the door slowly, then hung out the screen door, her bare toes curling down off the step. There were two boys in the car and now she recognized the driver: he had shaggy, shabby black hair that looked crazy as a wig and he was grinning at her.

"I ain't late, am I?" he said.

"Who the hell do you think you are?" Connie said.

"Toldja I'd be out, didn't I?"

"I don't even know who you are."

She spoke sullenly, careful to show no interest or pleasure, and he spoke in a fast, bright monotone. Connie looked past him to the other boy, taking her time. He had fair brown hair, with a lock that fell onto his forehead. His sideburns gave him a fierce, embarrassed look, but so far he hadn't even bothered to glance at her. Both boys wore sunglasses. The driver's glasses were metallic and mirrored everything in miniature.

"You wanta come for a ride?" he said.

Connie smirked and let her hair fall loose over one shoulder.
"Don'tcha like my car? New paint job," he said. "Hey."
"What?"
"You're cute."
She pretended to fidget, chasing flies away from the door.
"Don'tcha believe me, or what?" he said.
"Look, I don't even know who you are," Connie said in
disgust.
"Hey, Ellie's got a radio, see. Mine broke down." He lifted his
friend's arm and showed her the little transistor radio the boy
was holding, and now Connie began to hear the music. It was
the same program that was playing inside the house.
"Bobby King?" she said.
"I listen to him all the time. I think he's great."
"He's kind of great," Connie said reluctantly.
"Listen, that guy's *great*. He knows where the action is."
Connie blushed a little, because the glasses made it impossible for her to see just what this boy was looking at. She
couldn't decide if she liked him or if he was just a jerk, and so
she dawdled in the doorway and wouldn't come down or go
back inside. She said, "What's all that stuff painted on your
car?"
"Can'tcha read it?" He opened the door very carefully, as if
he were afraid it might fall off. He slid out just as carefully,
planting his feet firmly on the ground, the tiny metallic world in
his glasses slowing down like gelatin hardening, and in the
midst of it Connie's bright green blouse. "This here is my name,
to begin with," he said. ARNOLD FRIEND was written in tarlike
black letters on the side, with a drawing of a round, grinning
face that reminded Connie of a pumpkin, except it wore sunglasses. "I wanta introduce myself, I'm Arnold Friend and that's
my real name and I'm gonna be your friend, honey, and inside
the car's Ellie Oscar, he's kinda shy." Ellie brought his transistor
radio up to his shoulder and balanced it there. "Now, these
numbers are a secret code, honey," Arnold Friend explained. He
read off the numbers 33, 19, 17 and raised his eyebrows at her to
see what she thought of that, but she didn't think much of it.
The left rear fender had been smashed and around it was

written, on the gleaming gold background: DONE BY CRAZY WOMAN
DRIVER. Connie had to laugh at that. Arnold Friend was pleased
at her laughter and looked up at her. "Around the other side's a
lot more—you wanta come and see them?"

"No."

"Why not?"

"Why should I?"

"Don'tcha wanta see what's on the car? Don'tcha wanta go
for a ride?"

"I don't know."

"Why not?"

"I got things to do."

"Like what?"

"Things."

He laughed as if she had said something funny. He slapped
his thighs. He was standing in a strange way, leaning back
against the car as if he were balancing himself. He wasn't tall,
only an inch or so taller than she would be if she came down to
him. Connie liked the way he was dressed, which was the way
all of them dressed: tight faded jeans stuffed into black, scuffed
boots, a belt that pulled his waist in and showed how lean he
was, and a white pull-over shirt that was a little soiled and
showed the hard small muscles of his arms and shoulders. He
looked as if he probably did hard work, lifting and carrying
things. Even his neck looked muscular. And his face was a
familiar face, somehow: the jaw and chin and cheeks slightly
darkened because he hadn't shaved for a day or two, and the
nose long and hawklike, sniffing as if she were a treat he was
going to gobble up and it was all a joke.

"Connie, you ain't telling the truth. This is your day set aside
for a ride with me and you know it," he said, still laughing. The
way he straightened and recovered from his fit of laughing
showed that it had been all fake.

"How do you know what my name is?" she said suspiciously.

"It's Connie."

"Maybe and maybe not."

"I know my Connie," he said, wagging his finger. Now she
remembered him even better, back at the restaurant, and her

cheeks warmed at the thought of how she had sucked in her breath just at the moment she passed him—how she must have looked to him. And he had remembered her. "Ellie and I come out here especially for you," he said. "Ellie can sit in back. How about it?"

"Where?"

"Where what?"

"Where're we going?"

He looked at her. He took off the sunglasses and she saw how pale the skin around his eyes was, like holes that were not in shadow but instead in light. His eyes were like chips of broken glass that catch the light in an amiable way. He smiled. It was as if the idea of going for a ride somewhere, to someplace, was a new idea to him.

"Just for a ride, Connie sweetheart."

"I never said my name was Connie," she said.

"But I know what it is. I know your name and all about you, lots of things," Arnold Friend said. He had not moved yet but stood still leaning back against the side of his jalopy. "I took a special interest in you, such a pretty girl, and found out all about you—like I know your parents and sister are gone somewheres and I know where and how long they're going to be gone, and I know who you were with last night, and your best girl friend's name is Betty. Right?"

He spoke in a simple lilting voice, exactly as if he were reciting the words to a song. His smile assured her that everything was fine. In the car Ellie turned up the volume on his radio and did not bother to look around at them.

"Ellie can sit in the back seat," Arnold Friend said. He indicated his friend with a casual jerk of his chin, as if Ellie did not count and she should not bother with him.

"How'd you find out all that stuff?" Connie said.

"Listen: Betty Schultz and Tony Fitch and Jimmy Pettinger and Nancy Pettinger," he said in a chant. "Raymond Stanley and Bob Hutter—"

"Do you know all those kids?"

"I know everybody."

"Look, you're kidding. You're not from around here."

"Sure."

"But—how come we never saw you before?"

"Sure you saw me before," he said. He looked down at his boots, as if he were a little offended. "You just don't remember."

"I guess I'd remember you," Connie said.

"Yeah?" He looked up at this, beaming. He was pleased. He began to mark time with the music from Ellie's radio, tapping his fists lightly together. Connie looked away from his smile to the car, which was painted so bright it almost hurt her eyes to look at it. She looked at that name, ARNOLD FRIEND. And up at the front fender was an expression that was familiar—MAN THE FLYING SAUCERS. It was an expression kids had used the year before but didn't use this year. She looked at it for a while as if the words meant something to her that she did not yet know.

"What're you thinking about? Huh?" Arnold Friend demanded. "Not worried about your hair blowing around in the car, are you?"

"No."

"Think I maybe can't drive good?"

"How do I know?"

"You're a hard girl to handle. How come?" he said. "Don't you know I'm your friend? Didn't you see me put my sign in the air when you walked by?"

"What sign?"

"My sign." And he drew an X in the air, leaning out toward her. They were maybe ten feet apart. After his hand fell back to his side the X was still in the air, almost visible. Connie let the screen door close and stood perfectly still inside it, listening to the music from her radio and the boy's blend together. She stared at Arnold Friend. He stood there so stiffly relaxed, pretending to be relaxed, with one hand idly on the door handle as if he were keeping himself up that way and had no intention of ever moving again. She recognized most things about him, the tight jeans that showed his thighs and buttocks and the greasy leather boots and the tight shirt, and even that slippery friendly smile of his, that sleepy dreamy smile that all the boys used to get across ideas they didn't want to put into words. She recognized all this and also the singsong way he talked, slightly mocking, kidding, but serious and a little melancholy, and she recognized the way he tapped one fist against the other in homage to the perpetual music behind him. But all these things did not come together.

She said suddenly, "Hey, how old are you?"

His smile faded. She could see then that he wasn't a kid, he was much older—thirty, maybe more. At this knowledge her heart began to pound faster.

"That's a crazy thing to ask. Can'tcha see I'm your own age?"

"Like hell you are."

"Or maybe a coupla years older. I'm eighteen."

"Eighteen?" she said doubtfully.

He grinned to reassure her and lines appeared at the corners of his mouth. His teeth were big and white. He grinned so broadly his eyes became slits and she saw how thick the lashes were, thick and black as if painted with a black tarlike material. Then, abruptly, he seemed to become embarrassed and looked over his shoulder at Ellie. "*Him*, he's crazy," he said. "Ain't he a riot? He's a nut, a real character." Ellie was still listening to the music. His sunglasses told nothing about what he was thinking. He wore a bright orange shirt unbuttoned halfway to show his chest, which was a pale, bluish chest and not muscular like Arnold Friend's. His shirt collar was turned up all around and the very tips of the collar pointed out past his chin as if they were protecting him. He was pressing the transistor radio up against his ear and sat there in a kind of daze, right in the sun.

"He's kinda strange," Connie said.

"Hey, she says you're kinda strange! Kinda strange!" Arnold Friend cried. He pounded on the car to get Ellie's attention. Ellie turned for the first time and Connie saw with shock that he wasn't a kid either—he had a fair, hairless face, cheeks reddened slightly as if the veins grew too close to the surface of his skin, the face of a forty-year-old baby. Connie felt a wave of dizziness rise in her at this sight and she stared at him as if waiting for something to change the shock of the moment, make it all right again. Ellie's lips kept shaping words, mumbling along with the words blasting in his ear.

"Maybe you two better go away," Connie said faintly.

"What? How come?" Arnold Friend cried. "We come out here to take you for a ride. It's Sunday." He had the voice of the man on the radio now. It was the same voice, Connie thought. "Don'tcha know it's Sunday all day? And honey, no matter who you were with last night, today you're with Arnold Friend and don't you forget it! Maybe you better step out here," he said, and this last was in a different voice. It was a little flatter, as if the heat was finally getting to him.

"No. I got things to do."

"Hey."

"You two better leave."

"We ain't leaving until you come with us."

"Like hell I am—"

"Connie, don't fool around with me. I mean—I mean, don't fool *around*," he said, shaking his head. He laughed incredulously. He placed his sunglasses on top of his head, carefully, as if he were indeed wearing a wig, and brought the stems down behind his ears. Connie stared at him, another wave of dizziness and fear rising in her so that for a moment he wasn't even in focus but was just a blur standing there against his gold car, and she had the idea that he had driven up the driveway all right but had come from nowhere before that and belonged nowhere and that everything about him and even about the music that was so familiar to her was only half real.

"If my father comes and sees you—"

"He ain't coming. He's at a barbecue."

"How do you know that?"

"Aunt Tillie's. Right now they're—uh—they're drinking. Sitting around," he said vaguely, squinting as if he were staring all the way to town and over to Aunt Tillie's backyard. Then the vision seemed to get clear and he nodded energetically. "Yeah. Sitting around. There's your sister in a blue dress, huh? And high heels, the poor sad bitch—nothing like you, sweetheart! And your mother's helping some fat woman with the corn, they're cleaning the corn—husking the corn—"

"What fat woman?" Connie cried.

"How do I know what fat woman, I don't know every goddamn fat woman in the world!" Arnold Friend laughed.

"Oh, that's Mrs. Hornsby.... Who invited her?" Connie said.
She felt a little lightheaded. Her breath was coming quickly.

"She's too fat. I don't like them fat. I like them the way you
are, honey," he said, smiling sleepily at her. They stared at each
other for a while through the screen door. He said softly, "Now,
what you're going to do is this: you're going to come out that
door. You're going to sit up front with me and Ellie's going to
sit in the back, the hell with Ellie, right? This isn't Ellie's date.
You're my date. I'm your lover, honey."

"What? You're crazy—"

"Yes, I'm your lover. You don't know what that is but you
will," he said. "I know that too. I know all about you. But look:
it's real nice and you couldn't ask for nobody better than me, or
more polite. I always keep my word. I'll tell you how it is, I'm
always nice at first, the first time. I'll hold you so tight you
won't think you have to try to get away or pretend anything
because you'll know you can't. And I'll come inside you where
it's all secret and you'll give in to me and you'll love me—"

"Shut up! You're crazy!" Connie said. She backed away from
the door. She put her hands up against her ears as if she'd heard
something terrible, something not meant for her. "People don't
talk like that, you're crazy," she muttered. Her heart was almost
too big now for her chest and its pumping made sweat break
out all over her. She looked out to see Arnold Friend pause and
then take a step toward the porch, lurching. He almost fell. But,
like a clever drunken man, he managed to catch his balance. He
wobbled in his high boots and grabbed hold of one of the porch
posts.

"Honey?" he said. "You still listening?"

"Get the hell out of here!"

"Be nice, honey. Listen."

"I'm going to call the police—"

He wobbled again and out of the side of his mouth came a
fast spat curse, an aside not meant for her to hear. But even this
"Christ!" sounded forced. Then he began to smile again. She
watched this smile come, awkward as if he were smiling from
inside a mask. His whole face was a mask, she thought wildly,
tanned down to his throat but then running out as if he had

plastered make-up on his face but had forgotten about his throat.

"Honey—? Listen, here's how it is. I always tell the truth and I promise you this: I ain't coming in that house after you."

"You better not! I'm going to call the police if you—if you don't—"

"Honey," he said, talking right through her voice, "honey, I'm not coming in there but you are coming out here. You know why?"

She was panting. The kitchen looked like a place she had never seen before, some room she had run inside but that wasn't good enough, wasn't going to help her. The kitchen window had never had a curtain, after three years, and there were dishes in the sink for her to do—probably—and if you ran your hand across the table you'd probably feel something sticky there.

"You listening, honey? Hey?"

"—going to call the police—"

"Soon as you touch the phone I don't need to keep my promise and can come inside. You won't want that."

She rushed forward and tried to lock the door. Her fingers were shaking. "But why lock it," Arnold Friend said gently, talking right into her face. "It's just a screen door. It's just nothing." One of his boots was at a strange angle, as if his foot wasn't in it. It pointed out to the left, bent at the ankle. "I mean, anybody can break through a screen door and glass and wood and iron or anything else if he needs to, anybody at all, and specially Arnold Friend. If the place got lit up with a fire, honey, you'd come runnin' out into my arms, right into my arms an' safe at home—like you knew I was your lover and'd stopped fooling around. I don't mind a nice shy girl but I don't like no fooling around." Part of those words were spoken with a slight rhythmic lilt, and Connie somehow recognized them—the echo of a song from last year, about a girl rushing into her boyfriend's arms and coming home again—

Connie stood barefoot on the linoleum floor, staring at him. "What do you want?" she whispered.

"I want you," he said.

"What?"

"Seen you that night and thought, that's the one, yes sir. I never needed to look anymore."

"But my father's coming back. He's coming to get me. I had to wash my hair first—" She spoke in a dry, rapid voice, hardly raising it for him to hear.

"No, your daddy is not coming and yes, you had to wash your hair and you washed it for me. It's nice and shining and all for me. I thank you sweetheart," he said with a mock bow, but again he almost lost his balance. He had to bend and adjust his boots. Evidently his feet did not go all the way down; the boots must have been stuffed with something so that he would seem taller. Connie stared out at him and behind him at Ellie in the car, who seemed to be looking off toward Connie's right, into nothing. This Ellie said, pulling the words out of the air one after another as if he were just discovering them, "You want me to pull out the phone?"

"Shut your mouth and keep it shut," Arnold Friend said, his face red from bending over or maybe from embarrassment because Connie had seen his boots. "This ain't none of your business."

"What—what are you doing? What do you want?" Connie said. "If I call the police they'll get you, they'll arrest you—"

"Promise was not to come in unless you touch that phone, and I'll keep that promise," he said. He resumed his erect position and tried to force his shoulders back. He sounded like a hero in a movie, declaring something important. But he spoke too loudly and it was as if he were speaking to someone behind Connie. "I ain't made plans for coming in that house where I don't belong but just for you to come out to me, the way you should. Don't you know who I am?"

"You're crazy," she whispered. She backed away from the door but did not want to go into another part of the house, as if this would give him permission to come through the door. "What do you . . . you're crazy, you . . ."

"Huh? What're you saying, honey?"

Her eyes darted everywhere in the kitchen. She could not remember what it was, this room.

"This is how it is, honey: you come out and we'll drive away, have a nice ride. But if you don't come out we're gonna wait till your people come home and then they're all going to get it."

"You want that telephone pulled out?" Ellie said. He held the radio away from his ear and grimaced, as if without the radio the air was too much for him.

"I toldja shut up, Ellie," Arnold Friend said, "you're deaf, get a hearing aid, right? Fix yourself up. This little girl's no trouble and's gonna be nice to me, so Ellie keep to yourself, this ain't your date—right? Don't hem in on me, don't hog, don't crush, don't bird dog, don't trail me," he said in a rapid, meaningless voice, as if he were running through all the expressions he'd learned but was no longer sure which of them was in style, then rushing on to new ones, making them up with his eyes closed. "Don't crawl under my fence, don't squeeze in my chipmunk hole, don't sniff my glue, suck my popsicle, keep your own greasy fingers on yourself!" He shaded his eyes and peered in at Connie, who was backed against the kitchen table. "Don't mind him, honey, he's just a creep. He's a dope. Right? I'm the boy for you and like I said, you come out here nice like a lady and give me your hand, and nobody else gets hurt, I mean, your nice old bald-headed daddy and your mummy and your sister in her high heels. Because listen: why bring them in this?"

"Leave me alone," Connie whispered.

"Hey, you know that old woman down the road, the one with the chickens and stuff—you know her?"

"She's dead!"

"Dead? What? You know her?" Arnold Friend said.

"She's dead—"

"Don't you like her?"

"She's dead—she's—she isn't here anymore—"

"But don't you like her, I mean, you got something against her? Some grudge or something?" Then his voice dipped as if he were conscious of a rudeness. He touched the sunglasses perched up on top of his head as if to make sure they were still there. "Now, you be a good girl."

"What are you going to do?"

"Just two things, or maybe three," Arnold Friend said. "But I promise it won't last long and you'll like me the way you get to

like people you're close to. You will. It's all over for you here, so
come on out. You don't want your people in any trouble, do
you?"

She turned and bumped against a chair or something, hurting
her leg, but she ran into the back room and picked up the
telephone. Something roared in her ear, a tiny roaring, and she
was so sick with fear that she could do nothing but listen to it—
the telephone was clammy and very heavy and her fingers
groped down to the dial but were too weak to touch it. She
began to scream into the phone, into the roaring. She cried out,
she cried for her mother, she felt her breath start jerking back
and forth in her lungs as if it were something Arnold Friend was
stabbing her with again and again with no tenderness. A noisy
sorrowful wailing rose all about her and she was locked inside it
the way she was locked inside this house.

After a while she could hear again. She was sitting on the
floor with her wet back against the wall.

Arnold Friend was saying from the door, "That's a good girl.
Put the phone back."

She kicked the phone away from her.

"No, honey. Pick it up. Put it back right."

She picked it up and put it back. The dial tone stopped.

"That's a good girl. Now, you come outside."

She was hollow with what had been fear but what was now
just an emptiness. All that screaming had blasted it out of her.
She sat, one leg cramped under her, and deep inside her brain
was something like a pinpoint of light that kept going and
would not let her relax. She thought, I'm not going to see my
mother again. She thought, I'm not going to sleep in my bed
again. Her bright green blouse was all wet.

Arnold Friend said, in a gentle-loud voice that was like a
stage voice, "The place where you came from ain't there anymore, and where you had in mind to go is cancelled out. This
place you are now—inside your daddy's house—is nothing but
a cardboard box I can knock down any time. You know that and
always did know it. You hear me?"

She thought, I have got to think. I have got to know what to
do.

"We'll go out to a nice field, out in the country here where it smells so nice and it's sunny," Arnold Friend said. "I'll have my arms tight around you so you won't need to try to get away and I'll show you what love is like, what it does. The hell with this house! It looks solid all right," he said. He ran a fingernail down the screen and the noise did not make Connie shiver, as it would have the day before. "Now, put your hand on your heart, honey. Feel that? That feels solid too but we know better. Be nice to me, be sweet like you can because what else is there for a girl like you but to be sweet and pretty and give in?—and get away before her people come back?"

She felt her pounding heart. Her hand seemed to enclose it. She thought for the first time in her life that it was nothing that was hers, that belonged to her, but just a pounding, living thing inside this body that wasn't really hers either.

"You don't want them to get hurt," Arnold Friend went on. "Now, get up, honey. Get up all by yourself."

She stood.

"Now, turn this way. That's right. Come over here to me.— Ellie, put that away, didn't I tell you? You dope. You miserable creepy dope," Arnold Friend said. His words were not angry but only part of an incantation. The incantation was kindly. "Now, come out through the kitchen to me, honey, and let's see a smile, try it, you're a brave, sweet little girl and now they're eating corn and hot dogs cooked to bursting over an outdoor fire, and they don't know one thing about you and never did and honey, you're better than them because not a one of them would have done this for you."

Connie felt the linoleum under her feet; it was cool. She brushed her hair back out of her eyes. Arnold Friend let go of the post tentatively and opened his arms for her, his elbows pointing in toward each other and his wrists limp, to show that this was an embarrassed embrace and a little mocking, he didn't want to make her self-conscious.

She put out her hand against the screen. She watched herself push the door slowly open as if she were back safe somewhere in the other doorway, watching this body and this head of long hair moving out into the sunlight where Arnold Friend waited.

"My sweet little blue-eyed girl," he said in a half-sung sigh that had nothing to do with her brown eyes but was taken up just the same by the vast sunlit reaches of the land behind him and on all sides of him—so much land that Connie had never seen before and did not recognize except to know that she was going to it.

Unmailed, Unwritten Letters

D EAR MOTHER AND FATHER,
     The weather is lovely here. It rained yesterday. Today the sky is blue. The trees are changing colors, it is October 20, I have got to buy some new clothes sometime soon, we've changed dentists, doctors, everything is lovely here and I hope the same with you. Greg is working hard as usual. The doctor we took Father to see, that time he hurt his back visiting here, has died and so we must change doctors. Dentists also. I want to change dentists because I can't stand to go back to the same dentist anymore. He is too much of a fixed point, a reference point. It is such a chore, changing doctors and dentists.

Why are you so far away in the Southwest? Is there something about the Southwest that lures old people? Do they see images there, shapes in the desert? Holy shapes? Why are you not closer to me, or farther away? In an emergency it would take hours or days for you to get to me. I think of the two of you in the Southwest, I see the highways going off into space and wonder at your courage, so late in life, to take on space. Father had all he could do to manage that big house of yours, and the lawn. Even with workers to help him it was terrifying, all that space, because he owned it. Maybe that was why it terrified him, because he owned it. Out in the Southwest I assume that no

one owns anything. Do people even live there? Some people live
there, I know. But I think of the Southwest as an optical illusion,
sunshine and sand and a mountainous (mountainous?) horizon,
with highways perfectly divided by their white center lines,
leading off to Mars or the moon, unhurried. And there are
animals, the designs of animals, mashed into the highways! The
shape of a dog, a dog's pelty shadow, mashed into the hot, hot
road—in mid-flight, so to speak, mid-leap, run over again and
again by big trucks and retired people seeing America. That
vastness would terrify me. I think of you and I think of protoplasm being drawn off into space, out there, out in the West,
with no human limits to keep it safe.

Dear Marsha Katz,
    Thank you for the flowers, white flowers, but why that
delicate hint of death, all that fragrance wasted on someone like
myself who is certain to go on living? Why are you pursuing
me? Why in secrecy? (I see all the letters you write to your
father, don't forget; and you never mention me in them.) Even if
your father were my lover, which is not true and cannot be
verified, why should you pursue me? Why did you sign the
card with the flowers *Trixie?* I don't know anyone named Trixie!
How could I know anyone named Trixie? It is a dog's name, a
high school cheerleader's name, an aunt's name . . . why do you
play these games, why do you pursue me?
    Only ten years old, and too young for evil thoughts—do you
look in your precocious heart and see only grit, the remains of
things, a crippled shadow of a child? Do you see in all this the
defeat of your Daughterliness? Do you understand that a Daughter, like a Mistress, must be feminine or all is lost, must keep up
the struggle with the demonic touch of matter-of-fact irony that
loses us all our men . . . ? I think you have lost, yes. A ten-year-
old cannot compete with a thirty-year-old. Send me all the
flowers you want. I pick them apart one by one, getting bits of
petals under my fingernails, I throw them out before my husband gets home.
    Nor did I eat that box of candies you sent. Signed "Uncle
Bumble"!

Are you beginning to feel terror at having lost? Your father and I are not lovers, we hardly see each other anymore, since last Wednesday and today is Monday, still you've lost because I gather he plans on continuing the divorce proceedings, long distance, and what exactly can a child do about that . . . ? I see all the letters you write him. No secrets. Your Cape Cod sequence was especially charming. I like what you did with that kitten, the kitten that is found dead on the beach! Ah, you clever little girl, even with your I.Q. of uncharted heights, you couldn't quite conceal from your father and me your attempt to make him think 1) the kitten suggests a little girl, namely you 2) its death suggests your pending, possible death, if Father does not return. Ah, how we laughed over that! . . . Well, no, we didn't laugh, he did not laugh, perhaps he did not even understand the trick you were playing . . . your father can be a careless, abrupt man, but things stick in his mind, you know that and so you write of a little white kitten, alive one day and dead the next, so you send me flowers for a funeral parlor, you keep me in your thoughts constantly so that I can feel a tug all the way here in Detroit, all the way from Boston, and I hate it, I hate that invisible pulling, tugging, that witch's touch of yours. . . .

Dear Greg,
We met about this time years ago. It makes me dizzy, it frightens me to think of that meeting. Did so much happen, and yet nothing? Miscarriages, three or four, one loses count, and eight or nine sweet bumbling years—why do I use the word *bumbling,* it isn't a word I would ever use—and yet there is nothing there, if I go to your closet and open the door your clothes tell me as much as you do. You are a good man. A faithful husband. A subdued and excellent husband. The way you handled my parents alone would show how good you are, how excellent. . . . My friend X, the one with the daughter said to be a genius and the wife no one has ever seen, X couldn't handle my parents, couldn't put up with my father's talk about principles, the Principles of an Orderly Universe, which he sincerely believes in though he is an intelligent man. . . . X couldn't handle anything, anyone. He loses patience. He is vulgar. He watches

himself swerve out of control but can't stop. Once, returning to
his car, we found a ticket on the windshield. He snatched it and
tore it up, very angry, and then when he saw my surprise he
thought to make a joke of it—pretending to be tearing it with his
teeth, a joke. And he is weak, angry men are weak. He lets me
close doors on him. His face seems to crack with sorrow, but he
lets me walk away, why is he so careless and weak...?

But I am thinking of us, our first meeting. An overheated
apartment, graduate school...a girl in dark stockings, myself,
frightened and eager, trying to be charming in a voice that
didn't carry, a man in a baggy sweater, gentle, intelligent, a little
perplexed, the two of us gravitating together, fearful of love and
fearful of not loving, of not being loved.... So we met. The
evening falls away, years fall away. I count only three miscarriages, really. The fourth a sentimental miscalculation.

My darling,

I am out somewhere, I see a telephone booth on a corner, the
air is windy and too balmy for October. I won't go in the phone
booth. Crushed papers, a beer bottle, a close violent stench.... I
walk past it, not thinking of you. I am out of the house so that
you can't call me and so that I need not think of you. Do you
talk to your wife every night, still? Does she weep into your ear?
How many nights have you lain together, you and that woman
now halfway across the country, in Boston, weeping into a
telephone? Have you forgotten all those nights?

Last night I dreamed about you mashed into a highway.
More than dead. I had to wake Greg up, I couldn't stop
trembling, I wanted to tell him of the waste, the waste of joy and
love, your being mashed soundlessly into a road and pounded
into a shape no one would recognize as yours.... Your face was
gone. What will happen to me when your face is gone from this
world?

I parked the car down here so that I could go shopping at
Saks but I've been walking, I'm almost lost: The streets are dirty.
A tin can lies on the sidewalk, near a vacant lot. Campbell's
Tomato Soup. I am dressed in the suit you like, though it is a
little baggy on me, it would be a surprise for someone driving

past to see a lady in such a suit bend to pick up a tin can.... I pick the can up. The edge is jagged and rusty. No insects inside. Why would insects be inside, why bother with an empty can? Idly I press the edge of the lid against my wrist; it isn't sharp, it makes only a fine white line on my skin, not sharp enough to penetrate the skin.

Dear Greg,

I hear you walking downstairs. You are going outside, out into the backyard. I am tempted, heart pounding, to run to the window and spy on you. But everything is tepid, the universe is dense with molecules, I can't get up. My legs won't move. You said last night, "The Mayor told me to shut up in front of Arthur Grant. He told me to shut up." You were amused and hurt at the same time, while I was furious, wishing you were...were someone else, someone who wouldn't be amused and hurt, a good man, a subdued man, but someone else who would tell that bastard to go to hell. I am a wife, jealous for her husband.

Three years you've spent working for the Mayor, His Honor, dodging reporters downtown. Luncheons, sudden trips, press conferences, conferences with committees from angry parts of Detroit, all of Detroit angry, white and black, bustling, ominous. Three years. Now he tells you to shut up. All the lies you told for him, not knowing how to lie with dignity, he tells you to shut up, my body suffers as if on the brink of some terrible final expulsion of our love, some blood-smear of a baby. When a marriage ends, who is left to understand it? No witnesses. No young girl in black stockings, no young man, all those witnesses gone, grown up, moved on, lost.

Too many people know you now, your private life is dwindling. You are dragged back again and again to hearings, commission meetings, secret meetings, desperate meetings, television interviews, interviews with kids from college newspapers. Everyone has a right to know everything! *What Detroit Has Done to Combat Slums. What Detroit Has Done to Prevent Riots,* updated to *What Detroit Has Done to Prevent a Recurrence of the 1967 Riot.* You people are rewriting history as fast as history happens. I love you, I suffer for you, I lie here in a paralysis of love, sorrow, density, idleness, lost in my love for you, my shame for having betrayed you.... Why should slums be combatted? Once I wept to see photographs of kids playing in garbage heaps, now I weep at crazy sudden visions of my lover's body become only a body, I have no tears left for anyone else, for anything else. Driving in the city I have a sudden vision of my lover dragged along by a stranger's car, his body somehow caught up under the bumper or the fender and dragged along, bleeding wildly in the street....

My dear husband, betraying you was the most serious act of my life. Far more serious than marrying you. I knew my lover better when he finally became my lover than I knew you when you became my husband. I know him better now than I know you. You and I have lived together for eight years. Smooth coins, coins worn smooth by constant handling.... I am a woman trapped in love, in the terror of love. Paralysis of love. Like a great tortoise, trapped in a heavy deathlike shell, a mask of the body pressing the body down to earth.... I went for a week without seeing him, an experiment. The experiment failed. No husband can keep his wife's love. So you walk out in the backyard, admiring the leaves, the sky, the flagstone terrace, you are a man whom betrayal would destroy and yet your wife betrayed you, deliberately.

To The Editor:

Anonymously and shyly I want to ask—why are white men so weak, so feeble? The other day I left a friend at his hotel and walked quickly, alone, to my car, and the eyes of black men around me moved onto me with a strange hot perception, seeing everything. They knew, seeing me, what I was. Tension rose through the cracks in the sidewalk. Where are white men who are strong, who see women in this way? The molecules in the air of Detroit are humming. I wish I could take a knife and cut out an important piece of my body, my insides, and hold it up ... on a street corner, an offering. Then will they let me alone? The black men jostle one another on street corners, out of work and not wanting work, content to stare at me, knowing everything in me, not surprised. My lover, a white man, remains back in the hotel, his head in his hands because I have walked out, but be won't run after me, he won't follow me. *They* follow me. One of them bumped into me, pretending it was an accident. I want to cut up my body, I can't live in this body.

Next door to us a boy is out in his driveway, sitting down, playing a drum. Beating on a drum. Is he crazy? A white boy of about sixteen pounding on a drum. He wants to bring the city down with that drum and I don't blame him. I understand that vicious throbbing.

Dear Marsha Katz,

Thank you for the baby clothes. Keep sending me things, test your imagination. I feel that you are drowning. I sense a tightness in your chest, your throat. Are your eyes leaden with defeat, you ten-year-old wonder? How many lives do children relive at the moment of death?

Dear Mother and Father,

The temperature today is _____. Yesterday at this time, _____. Greg has been very busy as usual with _____, _____, _____. This weekend we must see the _____s, whom you have met. How is the weather there? How is your vacation? Thank you for the postcard from _____. I had not thought lawns would be green there.

... The Mayor will ask all his aides for resignations, signed. Some he will accept and others reject. A kingly man, plump and alcoholic. Divorced. Why can't I tell you about my husband's job, about my life, about anything real? Scandals fall on the head of my husband's boss, reading the paper is torture, yet my husband comes home and talks seriously about the future, about improvements, as if no chaos is waiting. No picketing ADC mothers, no stampede to buy guns, no strangled black babies found in public parks. In the midst of this my husband is clean and untouched, innocent, good. He has dedicated his life to helping others. I love him but cannot stop betraying him, again and again, having reclaimed my life as my own to throw away, to destroy, to lose. My life is my own. I keep on living.

My darling,

It is one-thirty and if you don't call by two, maybe you won't call; I know that you have a seminar from two to four, maybe you won't call today and everything will end. My heart pounds bitterly, in fear, in anticipation? Your daughter sent me some baby clothes, postmarked Boston. I understand her hatred, but one thing: how much did you tell your wife about me? About my wanting children? You told her you no longer loved her and couldn't live with her, that you loved another woman who could not marry you, but ... did you tell her this other woman had no children? And what else?

I will get my revenge on you.

I walk through the house in a dream, in a daze. I am sinking slowly through the floor of this expensive house, a married woman in a body grown light as a shell, empty as a shell. My body has no other life in it, only its own. What you discharge in me is not life but despair. I can remember my body having life, holding it. It seemed a trick, a feat that couldn't possibly work: like trying to retain liquid up a reed, turning the reed upside down. The doctor said, "Babies are no trouble. Nothing." But the liquid ran out. All liquid runs out of me. That first week, meeting with you at the Statler, everything ran out of me like blood. I alarmed you, you with your nervous sense of fate, your fear of getting cancer, of having a nervous breakdown. I caused you to say stammering, *But what if you get pregnant?* I am not pregnant but I feel a strange tingling of life, a tickling, life at a distance, as if the spirit of your daughter is somehow in me, lodged in me. She sucks at my insides with her pinched jealous lips, wanting blood. My body seeks to discharge her magically.

My dear husband,

I wanted to test being alone. I went downtown to the library, the old library. I walked past the hotel where he and I have met, my lover and I, but we were not meeting today and I was alone, testing myself as a woman alone, a human being alone. The library was filled with old men. Over seventy, dressed in black, with white shirts. Black and white: a reading room of old men, dressed in black and white.

I sat alone at a table. Some of the old men glanced at me. In a dream I began to leaf through a magazine, thinking, *Now I am leafing through a magazine: this is expected.* Why can't I be transformed to something else—to a mask, a shell, a statue? I glance around shyly, trying to gauge the nature of the story I am in. Is it tragic or only sad? The actors in this play all seem to be wearing masks, even I am wearing a mask, I am never naked. My nakedness, with my lover, is a kind of mask—something he sees, something I can't quite believe in. Women who are loved are in perpetual motion, dancing. We dance and men follow to the brink of madness and death, but what of us, the dancers?— when the dancing ends we stand back upon our heels, dazed and hurt. Beneath the golden cloth on our thighs is flesh, and flesh hurts. Men are not interested in the body, which feels pain, but in the rhythm of the body as it goes about its dance, the body of a woman who cannot stop dancing.

A confession. In Ann Arbor last April, at the symposium, I fell in love with a man. The visiting professor from Boston University—a man with black-rimmed glasses, Jewish, dark-eyed, dark-haired, nervous and arrogant and restless. Drumming his fingers. Smoking too much. (And you, my husband, were sane enough to give up smoking five years ago.) A student stood up in the first row and shouted out something and it was he, my lover, the man who would become my lover, who stood up in turn and shouted something back...it all happened so fast, astounding everyone, even the kid who reported for the campus newspaper didn't catch the exchange. How many men could handle a situation like that, being wilder and more profane than a heckler?... He was in the group at the party afterward, your friend Bryan's house. All of you talked at once, excited and angry over the outcome of the symposium, nervous at the sense of agitation in the air, the danger, and he and I wandered to the hostess's table, where food was set out. We made pigs of ourselves, eating. He picked out the shrimp and I demurely picked out tiny flakes of dough with miniature asparagus in them. Didn't you notice us? Didn't you notice this dark-browed man with the glasses that kept slipping down his nose, with the untidy black hair? We talked. We ate. I could see in his bony knuckles a hunger that would never be satisfied. And I, though I think I am starving slowly to death now, I leaped upon the food as if it were a way of getting at him, of drawing him into me. We talked. We wandered around the house. He looked out a window, drawing a curtain aside, at the early spring snowfall, falling gently outside, and he said that he didn't know why he had come to this part of the country, he was frightened of traveling, of strangers. He said that he was very tired. He seduced me with the slump of his shoulders. And when he turned back to me we entered another stage of the evening, having grown nervous and brittle with each other, the two of us suddenly conscious of being together. My eyes grew hot and searing. I said carelessly that he must come over to Detroit sometime, we could have lunch, and he said at once, "I'd like that very much...." and then paused. Silence.

Later, in the hotel, in the cheap room he rented, he confessed to me that seeing my face had been an experience for him—did he believe in love at first sight, after all? Something so childish? It had been some kind of love, anyway. We talked about our lives, about his wife, about my husband, and then he swung onto another subject, talking about his daughter for forty-five minutes...a genius, a ten-year-old prodigy. I am brought low, astounded. I want to cry out to him, *But what about me! Don't stop thinking about me!* At the age of six his daughter was writing poems, tidy little poems, like Blake's. *Like Blake's? Yes.* At the age of eight she was publishing those poems.

No, I don't want to marry him. I'm not going to marry him. What we do to each other is too violent, I don't want it brought into marriage and domesticated, nor do I want him to see me at unflattering times of the day...getting up at three in the morning to be sick, a habit of mine. He drinks too much. He reads about the connection between smoking and death, and turns the page of the newspaper quickly. Superstitious, stubborn. In April he had a sore throat, that was why he spoke so hoarsely on the program...but a month later he was no better: "I'm afraid of doctors," he said. This is a brilliant man, the father of a brilliant child? We meet nowhere, at an unimaginative point X, in a hotel room, in the anonymous drafts of air from blowers that never stop blowing, the two of us yearning to be one, in this foreign dimension where anything is possible. Only later, hurrying to

my car, do I feel resentment and fury at him…why doesn't he
buy me anything, why doesn't he get a room for us, something
permanent? And hatred for him rises in me in long shuddering
surges, overwhelming me. I don't want to marry him. Let me
admit the worst—anxious not to fall in love with him, I think of
not loving him at the very moment he enters me, I think of him
already boarding a plane and disappearing from my life, with
relief, I think with pity of human beings and this sickness of
theirs, this desire for unity. Why this desire for unity, why? We
walk out afterward, into the sunshine or into the smog. Obviously we are lovers. Once I saw O'Leary, from the Highway
Commission, he nodded and said a brisk hello to me, ignored
my friend; obviously we are lovers, anyone could tell. We
walked out in the daylight, looking for you. That day, feverish
and aching, we were going to tell you everything. He was going
to tell his wife everything. But nothing happened…we ended
up in a cocktail lounge, we calmed down. The air-conditioning
calmed us. On the street we passed a Negro holding out
pamphlets to other Negroes but drawing them back when
whites passed. I saw the headline—*Muslim Killed in Miami Beach
by Fascist Police.* A well-dressed Negro woman turned down a
pamphlet with a toothy, amused smile—none of that junk for
her! My lover didn't even notice.

Because he is not my husband I don't worry about him. I
worry about my own husband, whom I own. I don't own this
man. I am thirty and he is forty-one; to him I am young—what a
laugh. I don't worry about his coughing, his drinking (sometimes over the telephone I can hear ice cubes tinkling in a
glass—he drinks to get the courage to call me), his loss of
weight, his professional standing. He didn't return to his job in
Boston, but stayed on here. A strange move. The department at
Michigan considered it a coup to get him, this disintegrating,
arrogant man, they were willing to pay him well, a man who has
already made enemies there. No, I don't worry about him.

On a television program he was moody and verbose, moody
and silent by turns. Smokes too much. Someone asked him
about the effect of something on something—Vietnam on the
presidential election, I think—and he missed subtleties, he

sounded distant, vague. Has lost passion for the truth. He has lost his passion for politics, discovering in himself a passion for me. It isn't my fault. On the street he doesn't notice things, he smiles slowly at me, complimenting me, someone brushes against him and he doesn't notice, what am I doing to this man? Lying in his arms I am inspired to hurt him. I say that we will have to give this up, these meetings; too much risk, shame. What about my husband, what about his wife? (A deliberate insult—I know he doesn't love his wife.) I can see at once that I've hurt him, his face shows everything, and as soon as this registers in both of us I am stunned with the injustice of what I've done to him, I must erase it, cancel it out, undo it; I caress his body in desperation. . . . Again and again. A pattern. What do I know about caressing the bodies of men? I've known only two men in my life. My husband and his successor. I have never wanted to love anyone, the strain and risk are too great, yet I have fallen in love for the second time in my life and this time the sensation is terrifying, bitter, violent. It ends the first cycle, supplants all that love, erases all that affection—destroys everything. I stand back dazed, flat on my heels, the dance being over. I will not move on into another marriage. I will die slowly in this marriage rather than come to life in another.

Dear Mrs. Katz,
    I received your letter of October 25 and I can only say
    I don't know how to begin this letter except to tell you
    Your letter is here on my desk. I've read it over again and again all morning. It is true, yes, that I have made the acquaintance of a man who is evidently your husband, though he has not spoken of you. We met through mutual friends in Ann Arbor and Detroit. Your informant at the University is obviously trying to upset you, for her own reasons. I assume it is a woman—who else would write you such a letter? I know nothing of your personal affairs. Your husband and I have only met a few times, socially. What do you want from me?
    And your daughter, tell your daughter to let me alone!
    Thank you both for thinking of me. I wish I could be equal to your hatred. But the other day an old associate of my husband's,

a bitch of a man, ran into me in the Fisher lobby and said, "What's happened to you—you look terrible! You've lost weight!" He pinched the waist of my dress, drawing it out to show how it hung loose on me, he kept marveling over how thin I am, not releasing me. A balding, pink-faced son of a bitch who has made himself rich by being on the board of supervisors for a county north of here, stuffing himself at the trough. I know all about him. A subpolitician, never elected. But I trust the eyes of these submen, their hot keen perception. Nothing escapes them. "One month ago," he said, "you were a beautiful woman." Nothing in my life has hurt me as much as that remark, *One month ago you were a beautiful woman....*

Were you ever beautiful? He says not. So he used you, he used you up. That isn't my fault. You say in your letter—thank you for typing it, by the way—that I could never understand your husband, his background of mental instability, his weaknesses, his penchant (your word) for blaming other people for his own faults. Why tell me this? He isn't going to be my husband. I have a husband. Why should I betray my husband for yours, your nervous, guilty, hypochondriac husband? The first evening we met, believe it or not, he told me about his *hurts*—people who've hurt him deeply! "The higher you go in a career, the more people take after you, wanting to bring you down," he told me. And listen: "The worst hurt of my life was when my first book came out, and an old professor of mine, a man I had idolized at Columbia, reviewed it. He began by saying, *Bombarded as we are by prophecies in the guise of serious historical research...* and my heart was broken." We were at a party but apart from the other people, we ate, he drank, we played a game with each other that made my pulse leap, and certainly my pulse leaped to hear a man, a stranger, speak of his heart being broken—where I come from men don't talk like that! I told him a *hurt* of my own, which I've never told anyone before: "The first time my mother saw my husband, she took me aside and said, *Can't you tell him to stand up straighter?* and my heart was broken...."

And so, with those words, I had already committed adultery, betraying my husband to a stranger.

Does he call you every night? I am jealous of those telephone calls. What if he changes his mind and returns to you, what then? When he went to the Chicago convention I'm sure he telephoned you constantly (he telephoned me only three times, the bastard) and joked to you about his fear of going out into the street. "Jesus, what if somebody smashes in my head, there goes my next book!" he said over the phone, but he wasn't kidding me. I began to cry, imagining him beaten up, bloody, far away from me. Why does he joke like that? Does he joke like that with you?

Dear Mother and Father,

My husband Greg is busy with _____. Doing well. Not fired. Pressure on, pressure off. Played golf with _____. I went to a new doctor yesterday, a woman. I had made an appointment to go to a man but lost my courage, didn't show up. Better a woman. She examined me, she looked at me critically and said, "Why are you trying to starve yourself?" *To keep myself from feeling love, from feeling lust, from feeling anything at all.* I told her I didn't know I was starving myself. I had no appetite. Food sickened me . . . how could I eat? She gave me a vitamin shot that burned me, like fire. Things good for you burn like fire, shot up into you, no escape. You would not like my lover, you would take me aside and say, *Jews are very brilliant and talented, yes, but . . .*

I am surviving at half-tempo. A crippled waltz tempo. It is only my faith in the flimsiness of love that keeps me going—I know this will end. I've been waiting for it to end since April, having faith. Love can't last. Even lust can't last. I loved my husband and now I do not love him, we never sleep together, that's through. Since he isn't likely to tell you that, I will.

Lloyd Burt came to see my husband the other day, downtown. Eleven in the morning and already drunk. His kid had been stopped in Grosse Pointe, speeding. The girl with him knocked out on pills. *He* had no pills on him, luckily. Do you remember Lloyd? Do you remember any of us? I am your daughter. Do you regret having had a daughter? I do not regret having no children, not now. Children, more children, children upon children, protoplasm upon protoplasm.... Once I thought I couldn't bear to live without having children, now I can't bear to live at all. I must be the wife of a man I can't have, I don't even want children from him. I sit here in my room with my head and body aching with a lust that has become metaphysical and skeptical and bitter, living on month after month, cells dividing and heating endlessly. I don't regret having no children. I don't thank you for having me. No gratitude in me, nothing. No, I feel no gratitude. I can't feel gratitude.

My dear husband,
    I want to tell you everything. I am in a motel room, I've just taken a bath. How can I keep a straight face telling you this? Sat in the bathtub for an hour, not awake, not asleep, the water was very hot....
    I seem to want to tell you something else, about Sally Rodgers. I am lightheaded, don't be impatient. I met Sally at the airport this afternoon, she was going to New York, and she saw me with a man, a stranger to her, the man who is the topic of this letter, the crucial reason for this letter.... Sally came right up to me and started talking, exclaiming about her bad fortune, her car had been stolen last week! Then, when she and a friend took her boat out of the yacht club and docked it at a restaurant on the Detroit River, she forgot to take the keys out and someone stole her boat! Twenty thousand dollars' worth of boat, a parting gift from her ex-husband, pirated away downriver. She wore silver eyelids, silver stockings, attracting attention not from men but from small children, who stared. My friend, my lover, did not approve of her—her clanking jewelry made his eye twitch.
    I am thirty miles from Detroit. In Detroit the multiplication of things is too brutal, I think it broke me down. Weak, thin, selfish, a wreck, I have become oblivious to the deaths of other people. (Robert Kennedy was murdered since I became this man's mistress, but I had no time to think of him—I put the thought of his death aside, to think of later. No time now.) Leaving him and walking in Detroit, downtown, on those days we met to make love, I began to understand what love is.

Holding a man between my thighs, my knees, in my arms, one single man out of all this multiplication of men, this confusion, this din of human beings. So it is we choose someone. Someone chooses us. I admit that if he did not love me so much I couldn't love him. It would pass. But a woman has no choice, let a man love her and she must love him, if the man is strong enough. I stopped loving you, I am a criminal.... I see myself sinking again and again beneath his body, those heavy shoulders with tufts of dark hair on them, again and again pressing my mouth against his, wanting something from him, betraying you, giving myself up to that throbbing that arises out of my heartbeat and builds to madness and then subsides again, slowly, to become my ordinary heartbeat again, the heartbeat of an ordinary body from which divinity has fled.

Flesh with an insatiable soul....

You would hear in a few weeks, through your innumerable far-flung cronies, that my lover's daughter almost died of aspirin poison, a ten-year-old girl with an I.Q. of about 200. But she didn't die. She took aspirin because her father was leaving her, divorcing her mother. The only gratitude I can feel is for her not having died.... My lover, whom you hardly know (he's the man of whom you said that evening, "He certainly can talk!"), telephoned me to give me this news, weeping over the phone. A man weeping. A man weeping turns a woman's heart to stone. I told him I would drive out at once, I'd take him to the airport. He had to catch the first plane home and would be on standby at the airport. So I drove to Ann Arbor to get him. I felt that we were already married and that passion had raced through us and left us years ago, as soon as I saw him lumbering to the car, a man who has lost weight in the last few months but who carries himself a little clumsily, out of absentmindedness. He wore a dark suit, rumpled. His necktie pulled away from his throat. A father distraught over his daughter belongs to mythology....

Like married people, like conspirators, like characters in a difficult scene hurrying their lines, uncertain of the meaning of lines... "It's very thoughtful of you to do this," he said, and I said, "What else can I do for you? Make telephone calls? Anything?" *Should I go along with you?* So I drive him to the airport.

I let him out at the curb, he hesitates, not wanting to go without me. He says, "But aren't you coming in . . . ?" and I see fear in his face. I tell him yes, yes, but I must park the car. This man, so abrupt and insulting in his profession, a master of whining rhetoric, stares at me in bewilderment as if he cannot remember why I have brought him here to let him out at the United Air Lines terminal, why I am eager to drive away. "I can't park here," I tell him sanely, "I'll get a ticket." He respects all minor law; he nods and backs away. It takes me ten minutes to find a parking place. All this time I am sweating in the late October heat, thinking that his daughter is going to win after all, has already won. Shouldn't I just drive home and leave him, put an end to it? A bottle of aspirin was all it took. The tears I might almost shed are not tears of shame or regret but tears of anger— that child has taken my lover from me. That child! I don't cry, I don't allow myself to cry, I drive all the way through a parking lot without finding a place and say to the girl at the booth, who puts her hand out expecting a dime, "But I couldn't find a place! I've driven right through! This isn't fair!" Seeing my hysteria, she relents, opens the gate, lets me through. *Once a beautiful woman*, she is thinking. I try another parking lot.

Inside the terminal, a moment of panic—what if he has already left? Then he hurries to me. I take his arm. He squeezes my hand. Both of us very nervous, agitated. "They told me I can probably make the two-fifteen, can you wait with me?" he says. His face, now so pale, is a handsome man's face gone out of control; a pity to look upon it. In a rush I feel my old love for him, hopeless. I begin to cry. Silently, almost without tears. A girl in a very short skirt passes us with a smile—lovers, at their age! "You're not to blame," he says, very nervous, "she's just a child and didn't know what she was doing—please don't blame yourself! It's my fault—" But a child tried to commit suicide, shouldn't someone cry? I am to blame. She is hurting me across the country. I have tried to expel her from life and she, the baby, the embryo, stirs with a will of her own and chooses death calmly. . . . "But she's going to recover," I say to him for the twentieth time, "isn't she? You're sure of that?" He reassures me. We walk.

The airport is a small city. Outside the plate glass, airplanes rise and sink without effort. Great sucking vacuums of power, enormous wings, windows brilliant with sunlight. We look on unamazed. To us these airplanes are unspectacular. We walk around the little city, walking fast and then slowing down, wandering, holding hands. It is during one of those strange lucky moments that lovers have—he lighting a cigarette—that Sally comes up to us. We are not holding hands at that moment. She talks, bright with attention for my friend, she herself being divorced and not equipped to live without a man. He smiles nervously, ignoring her, watching people hurry by with their luggage. She leaves. We glance at each other, understanding each other. Nothing to say. *My darling!* ...

Time does not move quickly. I am sweating again, I hope he won't notice, he is staring at me in that way ... the way that frightens me. I am not equal to your love, I want to tell him. Not equal, not strong enough. I am ashamed. Better for us to say good-by. A child's corpse between us? A few hundred miles away, in Boston, are a woman and a child I have wronged, quite intentionally; aren't these people real? But he stares at me, the magazine covers on a newsstand blur and wink, I feel that everything is becoming a dream and I must get out of here, must escape from him, before it is too late.... "I should leave," I tell him. He seems not to hear. He is sick. Not sick; frightened. He shows too much. He takes my hand, caresses it, pleading in silence. A terrible sensation of desire rises in me, surprising me. I don't want to feel desire for him! I don't want to feel it for anyone, I don't want to feel anything at all! I don't want to be drawn to an act of love, or even to think about it; I want freedom, I want the smooth sterility of coins worn out from friendly handling, rubbing together, I want to say good-by to love at the age of thirty, not being strong enough for it. A woman in the act of love feels no joy but only terror, a parody of labor, giving birth. Torture. Heartbeat racing at 160, 180 beats a minute, where is joy in this, what is this deception, this joke? Isn't the body itself a joke?

He leads me somewhere, along a corridor. Doesn't know where he is going. People head toward us with suitcases. A soldier on leave from Vietnam, we don't notice, a Negro woman weeping over another soldier, obviously her son, my lover does not see. A man brushes against me and with exaggerated fear I jump to my lover's side...but the man keeps on walking, it is nothing. My lover strokes my damp hand. "You won't...You're not thinking of...What are you thinking of?" he whispers. Everything is open in him, everything. He is not ashamed of the words he says, of his fear, his pleading. No irony in him, this ironic man. And I can hear myself saying that we must put an end to this, it's driving us both crazy and there is no future, nothing ahead of us, but I don't say these words or anything like them. We walk along. I am stunned. I feel a heavy, ugly desire for him, for his body. I want him as I've wanted him many times before, when our lives seemed simpler, when we were both deluded about what we were doing...both of us thought, in the beginning, that no one would care if we fell in love...not my husband, not his family. I don't know why. Now I want to say good-by to him but nothing comes out, nothing. I am still crying a little. It is not a weapon of mine—it is an admission of defeat. I am not a woman who cries well. Crying is a confession of failure, a giving in. I tell him no, I am not thinking of anything, only of him. I love him. I am not thinking of anything else.

We find ourselves by Gate 10. What meaning has Gate 10 to us? People are lingering by it, obviously a plane has just taken off, a stewardess is shuffling papers together, everything is normal. I sense normality and am drawn to it. We wander on. We come to a doorway, a door held open by a large block of wood. Where does that lead to? A stairway. The stairway is evidently not open. We can see that it leads up to another level, a kind of runway, and though it is not open he takes my hand and leads me to the stairs. In a delirium I follow him, why not? The airport is so crowded that we are alone and anonymous. He kicks the block of wood away, wisely. We are alone. On this stairway—which smells of disinfectant and yet is not very clean—my lover embraces me eagerly, wildly, he kisses me, kisses my damp cheeks, rubs his face against mine. I half-fall, half-sit on the stairs. He begins to groan, or to weep. He presses his face against me, against my breasts, my body. It is like wartime—a battle is going on outside, in the corridor. Hundreds of people! A world of people jostling one another! Here, in a dim stairway, clutching each other, we are oblivious to their deaths. But I want to be good! What have I wanted in my life except to be good? To lead a simple, good, intelligent life? He kisses my knees, my thighs, my stomach. I embrace him against me. Everything has gone wild, I am seared with the desire to be unfaithful to a husband who no longer exists, nothing else matters except this act of unfaithfulness. I feel that I am a character in a story, a plot, who has not understood until now exactly what is going to happen to her. Selfish, eager, we come together and do not breathe, we are good friends and anxious to help each other, I am particularly anxious to help him, my soul is sweated out of me in those two or three minutes that we cling together in love. Then, moving from me, so quickly exhausted, he puts his hands to his face and seems to weep without tears, while I feel my eyelids closing slowly upon the mangled length of my body....

This is a confession but part of it is blacked out. Minutes pass in silence, mysteriously. It is those few minutes that pass after we make love that are most mysterious to me, uncanny. And then we cling to each other again, like people too weak to stand by ourselves; we are sick in our limbs but warm with affection, very good friends, the kind of friends who tell each other only good news. He helps me to my feet. We laugh. Laughter weakens me, he has to hold me, I put my arms firmly around his neck and we kiss, I am ready to give up all my life for him, just to hold him like this. My body is all flesh. There is nothing empty about us, only a close space, what appears to be a stairway in some public place.... He draws my hair back from my face, he stares at me. It is obvious that he loves me.

When we return to the public corridor no one has missed us. It is strangely late, after three. This is a surprise, I am really surprised, but my lover is more businesslike and simply asks at the desk—the next plane? to Boston? what chance of his getting on? His skin is almost ruddy with pleasure. I can see what pleasure does to a man. But now I must say good-by, I must leave. He holds my hand. I linger. We talk seriously and quietly

in the middle of the great crowded floor about his plans—he will stay in Boston as long as he must, until things are settled; he will see his lawyer; he will talk it over, *talk it over,* with his wife and his daughter, he will not leave until they understand why he has to leave.... I want to cry out at him, *Should you come back?* but I can't say anything. Everything in me is a curving to submission, in spite of what you, my husband, have always thought.

Finally...he boards a plane at four. I watch him leave. He looks back at me, I wave, the plane taxis out onto the runway and rises...no accident, no violent ending. There is nothing violent about us, everything is natural and gentle. Walking along the long corridor I bump into someone, a woman my own age. I am suddenly dizzy. She says, "Are you all right?" I turn away, ashamed. I am on fire! My body is on fire! I feel his semen stirring in my loins, that rush of heat that always makes me pause, staring into the sky or at a wall, at something blank to mirror the blankness in my mind...stunned, I feel myself so heavily a body, so lethargic with the aftermath of passion. How did I hope to turn myself into a statue, into the constancy of a soul? No hope. The throbbing in my loins has not yet resolved itself into the throbbing of my heart. A woman does not forget so quickly, nothing lets her forget. I am transparent with heat. I walk on, feeling my heart pound weakly, feeling the moisture between my legs, wondering if I will ever get home. My vision seems blotched. The air—air-conditioning—is humming, unreal. It is not alien to me but a part of my own confusion, a long expulsion of my own breath. What do I look like making love? Is my face distorted, am I ugly? Does he see me? Does he judge? Or does he see nothing but beauty, transported in love as I am, helpless?

I can't find the car. Which parking lot? The sun is burning. A man watches me, studies me. I walk fast to show that I know what I'm doing. And if the car is missing, stolen...? I search through my purse, noting how the lining is soiled, ripped. Fifty thousand dollars in the bank and no children and I can't get around to buying a new purse; everything is soiled, ripped, worn out . . . the keys are missing . . . only wadded tissue, a sweet-ish smell, liquid stiffening on the tissue . . . everything hypno-tizes me. . . . I find the keys, my vision swims, I will never get home.

My knees are trembling. There is an ocean of cars here at Metropolitan Airport. Families stride happily to cars, get in, drive away. I wander around, staring. I must find my husband's car in order to get home. . . . I check in my purse again, panicked. No, I haven't lost the keys. I take the keys out of my purse to look at them. The key to the ignition, to the trunk, to the front door of the house. All there. I look around slyly and see, or think I see, a man watching me. He moves behind a car. He is walking away. My body still throbs from the love of another man, I can't concentrate on a stranger, I lose interest and forget what I am afraid of. . . .

The heat gets worse. Thirty, forty, forty-five minutes pass . . . I have given up looking for the car . . . I am not lost, I am still heading home in my imagination, but I have given up looking for the car. I turn terror into logic. I ascend the stairway to the wire-guarded overpass that leads back to the terminal, walking sensibly, and keep on walking until I come to one of the airport motels. I ask them for a room. A single. Why not? Before I can go home I must bathe, I must get the odor of this man out of me, I must clean myself. I take a room, I close the door to the room behind me; alone, I go to the bathroom and run a tubful of water. . . .

And if he doesn't call me from Boston then all is finished, at an end. What good luck, to be free again and alone, the way I am alone in this marvelous empty motel room! the way I am alone in this bathtub, cleansing myself of him, of every cell of him!

My darling,
    You have made me so happy. . . .

Accomplished Desires

THERE WAS A MAN SHE LOVED with a violent love, and she spent much of her time thinking about his wife.

No shame to it, she actually followed the wife. She followed her to Peabody's Market, which was a small, dark, crowded store, and she stood in silence on the pavement as the woman appeared again and got into her station wagon and drove off. The girl, Dorie, would stand as if paralyzed, and even her long fine blond hair seemed paralyzed with thought—her heart pounded as if it too was thinking, planning—and then she would turn abruptly as if executing one of the steps in her modern dance class and cross through Peabody's alley and out to the Elks' Club parking lot and so up toward the campus, where the station wagon was bound.

Hardly had the station wagon pulled into the driveway when Dorie, out of breath, appeared a few houses down and watched. How that woman got out of a car!—you could see the flabby expanse of her upper leg, white flesh that should never be exposed, and then she turned and leaned in, probably with a grunt, to get shopping bags out of the back seat. Two of her children ran out to meet her, without coats or jackets. They had nervous, darting bodies—Dorie felt sorry for them—and their mother rose, straightening, a stout woman in a colorless coat, either scolding them or teasing them, one bag in either muscular

arm—and so—so the mother and children went into the house
and Dorie stood with nothing to stare at except the battered
station wagon, and the small snowy wilderness that was the
Arbers' front yard, and the house itself. It was a large, ugly,
peeling Victorian home in a block of similar homes, most of
which had been fixed up by the faculty members who rented
them. Dorie, who had something of her own mother's shrewd
eye for hopeless, castoff things, believed that the house could be
remodeled and made presentable—but as long as he remained
married to *that woman* it would be slovenly and peeling and
ugly.

She loved that woman's husband with a fierce love that was
itself ugly. Always a rather stealthy girl, thought to be simply
quiet, she had entered his life by no accident—had not appeared
in his class by accident—but every step of her career, like every
outfit she wore and every expression on her face, was planned
and shrewd and desperate. Before her twenties she had not
thought much about herself; now she thought about herself
continuously. She was leggy, long-armed, slender, and had a
startled look—but the look was stylized now, and attractive.
Her face was denuded of make-up and across her soft skin a
galaxy of freckles glowed with health. She looked like a girl
about to bound onto the tennis courts—and she did play tennis,
though awkwardly. She played tennis with *him*. But so confused
with love was she that the game of tennis, the relentless slamming of the ball back and forth, had seemed to her a disguise for
something else, the way everything in poetry or literature was a
disguise for something else—for love?—and surely he must
know, or didn't he know? Didn't he guess? There were many
other girls he played tennis with, so that was nothing special,
and her mind worked and worked while she should have slept,
planning with the desperation of youth that has never actually
been young—planning how to get him, how to get him, for it
seemed to her that she would never be able to overcome her
desire for this man.

The wife was as formidable as the husband. She wrote
narrow volumes of poetry Dorie could not understand and he,
the famous husband, wrote novels and critical pieces. The wife

was a big, energetic, high-colored woman; the husband, Mark Arber, was about her size though not so high-colored—his complexion was rather putty-colored, rather melancholy. Dorie thought about the two of them all the time, awake or asleep, and she could feel the terrible sensation of blood flowing through her body, a flowing of desire that was not just for the man but somehow for the woman as well, a desire for her accomplishments, her fame, her children, her ugly house, her ugly body, her very life. She had light, frank blue eyes and people whispered that she drank; Dorie never spoke of her.

The college was a girls' college, exclusive and expensive, and every girl who remained there for more than a year understood a peculiar, even freakish kinship with the place—as if she had always been there and the other girls, so like herself with their sleepy unmade-up faces, the skis in winter and the bicycles in good weather, the excellent expensive professors, and the excellent air—everything, everything had always been there, had existed for centuries. They were stylish and liberal in their cashmere sweaters with soiled necks; their fingers were stained with ballpoint ink; and like them, Dorie understood that most of the world was wretched and would never come to this college, never, would be kept back from it by armies of helmeted men. She, Dorie Weinheimer, was not wretched but supremely fortunate, and she must be grateful always for her good luck, for there was no justification for her existence any more than there was any justification for the wretched lots of the world's poor. And there would flash to her mind's eye a confused picture of dark-faced starving mobs, or emaciated faces out of an old-fashioned Auschwitz photograph, or something—some dreary horror from *The New York Times'* one hundred neediest cases in the Christmas issue— She had, in the girls' soft, persistent manner, an idealism-turned-pragmatism under the influence of the college faculty, who had all been idealists at Harvard and Yale as undergraduates but who were now in their forties, and as impatient with normative values as they were with their students' occasional lockets-shaped-into-crosses; Mark Arber was the most disillusioned and the most eloquent of the Harvard men.

In class he sat at the head of the seminar table, leaning back in his leather-covered chair. He was a rather stout man. He had played football once in a past Dorie could not quite imagine, though she wanted to imagine it, and he had been in the war— one of the wars—she believed it had been World War II. He had an ugly, arrogant face and discolored teeth. He read poetry in a raspy, hissing, angry voice. "Like Marx, I believe that poetry has had enough of love; the hell with it. Poetry should now cultivate the whip," he would say grimly, and Dorie would stare at him to see if he was serious. There were four senior girls in this class and they sometimes asked him questions or made observations of their own, but there was no consistency in his reaction. Sometimes he seemed not to hear, sometimes he nodded enthusiastically and indifferently, sometimes he opened his eyes and looked at them, not distinguishing among them, and said: "A remark like that is quite characteristic." So she sat and stared at him and her heart seemed to turn to stone, wanting him, hating his wife and envying her violently, and the being that had been Dorie Weinheimer for twenty-one years changed gradually through the winter into another being, obsessed with jealousy. She did not know what she wanted most, this man or the victory over his wife.

She was always bringing poems to him in his office. She borrowed books from him and puzzled over every annotation of his. As he talked to her he picked at his fingernails, settled back in his chair, and he talked on in his rushed, veering, sloppy manner, as if Dorie did not exist or were a crowd, or a few intimate friends, it hardly mattered, as he raved about frauds in contemporary poetry, naming names, "that bastard with his sonnets," "that cow with her daughter-poems," and getting so angry that Dorie wanted to protest, no, no, why are you angry? Be gentle. Love me and be gentle.

When he failed to come to class six or seven times that winter the girls were all understanding. "Do you think he really is a genius?" they asked. His look of disintegrating, decomposing recklessness, his shiny suit and bizarre loafer shoes, his flights of language made him so different from their own fathers that it was probable he was a genius; these were girls who believed seriously in the existence of geniuses. They had been trained by their highly paid, verbose professors to be vaguely ashamed of themselves, to be silent about any I.Q. rated under 160, to be uncertain about their talents within the school and quite confident of them outside it—and Dorie, who had no talent and only adequate intelligence, was always silent about herself. Her talent perhaps lay in her faithfulness to an obsession, her cunning patience, her smile, her bared teeth that were a child's teeth and yet quite sharp....

One day Dorie had been waiting in Dr. Arber's office for an hour, with some new poems for him. He was late but he strode into the office as if he had been hurrying all along, sitting heavily in the creaking swivel chair, panting; he looked a little mad. He was the author of many reviews in New York magazines and papers and in particular the author of three short, frightening novels, and now he had a burned-out, bleached-out look. Like any of the girls at this college, Dorie would have sat politely if one of her professors set fire to himself, and so she ignored his peculiar stare and began her rehearsed speech about—but what did it matter what it was about? The poems of Emily Dickinson or the terrible yearning of Shelley or her own terrible lust, what did it matter?

He let his hand fall onto hers by accident. She stared at the hand, which was like a piece of meat—and she stared at him and was quite still. She was pert and long-haired, in the chair facing him, an anonymous student and a minor famous man, and every wrinkle of his sagging, impatient face was bared to her in the winter sunlight from the window—and every thread of blood in his eyes—and quite calmly and politely she said, "I guess I should tell you, Dr. Arber, that I'm in love with you. I've felt that way for some time."

"You what, you're what?" he said. He gripped her feeble hand as if clasping it in a handshake. "What did you say?" He spoke with an amazed, slightly irritated urgency, and so it began.

II

His wife wrote her poetry under an earlier name, Barbara Scott. Many years before she had had a third name, a maiden

name—Barbara Cameron—but it belonged to another era about
which she never thought except under examination from her
analyst. She had a place cleared in the dirty attic of her house
and she liked to sit up there, away from the children, and look
out the small octagon of a window, and think. People she saw
from her attic window looked bizarre and helpless to her. She
herself was a hefty, perspiring woman, and all her dresses—
especially her expensive ones—were stained under the arms
with great lemon-colored half-moons no dry cleaner could remove. Because she was so large a woman, she was quick to see
imperfections in others, as if she used a magnifying glass.
Walking by her window on an ordinary morning were an aged
tottering woman, an enormous Negro woman—probably
someone's cleaning lady—and a girl from the college on alumi-
num crutches, poor brave thing, and the white-blond child from
up the street who was precocious and demonic. Her own
children were precocious and only slightly troublesome. Now
two of them were safe in school and the youngest, the three-
year-old, was asleep somewhere.

Barbara Scott had won the Pulitzer Prize not long before with
an intricate sonnet series that dealt with the "voices" of many
people; her energetic, coy line was much imitated. This morning
she began a poem that her agent was to sell, after Barbara's
death, to the *New Yorker*:

> *What awful wrath*
> *what terrible betrayal*
> *and these aluminum crutches, rubber-tipped....*

She had such a natural talent that she let words take her anywhere. Her decade of psychoanalysis had trained her to hold
nothing back; even when she had nothing to say, the very
authority of her technique carried her on. So she sat that
morning at her big, nicked desk—over the years the children
had marred it with sharp toys—and stared out the window and
waited for more inspiration. She felt the most intense kind of
sympathy when she saw someone deformed—she was anxious,
in a way, to see deformed people because it released such

charity in her. But apart from the girl on the crutches she saw nothing much. Hours passed and she realized that her husband had not come home; already school was out and her two boys were running across the lawn.

When she descended the two flights of stairs to the kitchen, she saw that the three-year-old, Geoffrey, had opened a white plastic bottle of ammonia and had spilled it on the floor and on himself; the stench was sickening. The two older boys bounded in the back door as if spurred on by the argument that raged between them, and Barbara whirled upon them and began screaming. The ammonia had spilled onto her slacks. The boys ran into the front room and she remained in the kitchen, screaming. She sat down heavily on one of the kitchen chairs. After half an hour she came to herself and tried to analyze the situation. Did she hate these children, or did she hate herself? Did she hate Mark? Or was her hysteria a form of love, or was it both love and hate together . . . ? She put the ammonia away and made herself a drink.

When she went into the front room she saw that the boys were playing with their mechanical inventors' toys and had forgotten about her. Good. They were self-reliant. Slight, cunning children, all of them dark like Mark and prematurely aged, as if by the burden of their prodigious intelligences, they were not always predictable: they forgot things, lost things, lied about things, broke things, tripped over themselves and each other, mimicked classmates, teachers, and their parents, and often broke down into pointless tears. And yet sometimes they did not break down into tears when Barbara punished them, as if to challenge her. She did not always know what she had given birth to: they were so remote, even in their struggles and assaults, they were so fictional, as if she had imagined them herself. It had been she who'd imagined them, not Mark. Their father had no time. He was always in a hurry, he had three aged typewriters in his study and paper in each one, an article or a review or even a novel in progress in each of the machines, and he had no time for the children except to nod grimly at them or tell them to be quiet. He had been so precocious himself, Mark Arber, that after his first, successful novel at the age of twenty-four he had had to whip from place to place, from typewriter to typewriter, in a frantic attempt to keep up with—he called it keeping up with his "other self," his "real self," evidently a kind of alter ego who was always typing and creating, unlike the real Mark Arber. The real Mark Arber was now forty-five and he had made the transition from "promising" to "established" without anything in between, like most middle-aged critics of prominence.

Strachey, the five-year-old, had built a small machine that was both a man and an automobile, operated by the motor that came with the set of toys. "This is a modern centaur," he said wisely, and Barbara filed that away, thinking perhaps it would do well in a poem for a popular, slick magazine.... She sat, unbidden, and watched her boys' intense work with the girders and screws and bolts, and sluggishly she thought of making supper, or calling Mark at school to see what had happened ... that morning he had left the house in a rage and when she went into his study, prim and frowning, she had discovered four or five crumpled papers in his wastebasket. It was all he had accomplished that week.

Mark had never won the Pulitzer Prize for anything. People who knew him spoke of his slump, familiarly and sadly; if they disliked Mark they praised Barbara, and if they disliked Barbara they praised Mark. They were "established" but it did not mean much, younger writers were being discovered all the time who had been born in the mid- or late forties, strangely young, terrifyingly young, and people the Arbers' age were being crowded out, hustled toward the exits.... Being "established" should have pleased them, but instead it led them to long spiteful bouts of eating and drinking in the perpetual New England winter.

She made another drink and fell asleep in the chair. Sometime later her children's fighting woke her and she said, "Shut up," and they obeyed at once. They were playing in the darkened living room, down at the other end by the big brick fireplace that was never used. Her head ached. She got to her feet and went out to make another drink.

Around one o'clock Mark came in the back door. He stumbled

and put the light on. Barbara, in her plaid bathrobe, was sitting at the kitchen table. She had a smooth, shiny, bovine face, heavy with fatigue. Mark said, "What the hell are you doing here?"

She attempted a shrug of her shoulders. Mark stared at her. "I'm getting you a housekeeper," he said. "You need more time for yourself, for your work. For your work," he said, twisting his mouth at the word to show what he thought of it. "You shouldn't neglect your poetry so we're getting in a housekeeper, not to do any heavy work, just to sort of watch things—in other words—a kind of external consciousness. You should be freed from ordinary considerations."

He was not drunk but he had the appearance of having been drunk, hours before, and now his words were muddled and dignified with the air of words spoken too early in the morning. He wore a dirty tweed overcoat, the same coat he'd had when they were married, and his necktie had been pulled off and stuffed somewhere, and his puffy, red face looked mean. Barbara thought of how reality was too violent for poetry and how poetry, and the language itself, shimmered helplessly before the confrontation with living people and their demands. "The housekeeper is here. She's outside," Mark said. "I'll go get her."

He returned with a college girl who looked like a hundred other college girls. "This is Dorie, this is my wife Barbara, you've met no doubt at some school event, here you are," Mark said. He was carrying a suitcase that must have belonged to the girl. "Dorie has requested room and board with a faculty family. The Dean of Women arranged it. Dorie will babysit or something—we can put her in the spare room. Let's take her up."

Barbara had not yet moved. The girl was pale and distraught; she looked about sixteen. Her hair was disheveled. She stared at Barbara and seemed about to speak.

"Let's take her up, you want to sit there all night?" Mark snarled.

Barbara indicated with a motion of her hand that they should go up without her. Mark, breathing heavily, stomped up the back steps and the girl followed at once. There was no indication of her presence because her footsteps were far too light on the stairs. She said nothing, and only a slight change in the odor of the kitchen indicated something new—a scent of cologne, hair scrubbed clean, a scent of panic. Barbara sat listening to her heart thud heavily inside her and she recalled how, several years before, Mark had left her and had turned up at a friend's apartment in Chicago—he'd been beaten up by someone on the street, an accidental event—and how he had blackened her eye once in an argument over the worth of Samuel Richardson, and how—there were many other bitter memories—and of course there had been other women, some secret and some known—and now this—

So she sat thinking with a small smile of how she would have to dismiss this when she reported it to their friends: *Mark has had this terrible block for a year now, with his novel, and so . . .*

She sat for a while running through phrases and explanations, and when she climbed up the stairs to bed she was grimly surprised to see him in their bedroom, asleep, his mouth open and his breath raspy and exhausted. At the back of the house, in a small oddly shaped maid's room, slept the girl; in their big dormer room slept the three boys, or perhaps they only pretended to sleep; and only she, Barbara, stood in the dark and contemplated the bulk of her own body, wondering what to do and knowing that there was nothing she would do, no way for her to change the process of events any more than she could change the heavy fact of her body itself. There was no way to escape what the years had made her.

III

From that time on they lived together like a family. Or it was as Mark put it: "Think of a babysitter here permanently. Like the Lunt girl, staying on here permanently to help, only we won't need that one any more." Barbara made breakfast for them all, and then Mark and Dorie drove off to school and returned late, between six and six-thirty, and in the evenings Mark worked hard at his typewriters, going to sit at one and then the next and then the next, and the girl, Dorie, helped Barbara with the dishes and odd chores and went up to her room, where she studied . . . or did something, she must have done something.

Of the long afternoons he and the girl were away Mark said nothing. He was evasive and jaunty; he looked younger. He explained carefully to Dorie that when he and Mrs. Arber were invited somewhere she must stay home and watch the children, that she was not included in these invitations; and the girl agreed eagerly. She did so want to help around the house! She had inherited from her background a dislike for confusion—so the mess of the Arber house upset her and she worked for hours picking things up, polishing tarnished objects Barbara herself had forgotten were silver, cleaning, arranging, fixing. As soon as the snow melted she was to be seen outside, raking shyly through the flower beds. How to explain her to the neighbors? Barbara said nothing.

"But I didn't think we lived in such a mess. I didn't think it was so bad," Barbara would say to Mark in a quiet, hurt voice, and he would pat her hand and say, "It isn't a mess, she just likes to fool around. *I* don't think it's a mess."

It was fascinating to live so close to a young person. Barbara had never been young in quite the way Dorie was young. At breakfast—they ate crowded around the table—everyone could peer into everyone else's face, there were no secrets, stale mouths and bad moods were inexcusable, all the wrinkles of age or distress that showed on Barbara could never be hidden, and not to be hidden was Mark's guilty enthusiasm, his habit of saying, "*We* should go to...," "*We* are invited..." and the "we" meant either him and Barbara, or him and Dorie, but never all three; he had developed a new personality. But Dorie was fascinating. She awoke to the slow gray days of spring with a panting, wondrous expectation, her blond hair shining, her freckles clear as dabs of clever paint on her heartbreaking skin, her teeth very, very white and straight, her pert little lips innocent of lipstick and strangely sensual...yes, it was heartbreaking. She changed her clothes at least twice a day while Barbara wore the same outfit—baggy black slacks and a black sweater—for weeks straight. Dorie appeared downstairs in cashmere sweater sets that were the color of birds' eggs, or of birds' fragile legs, and white trim blouses that belonged on a genteel hockey field, and bulky pink sweaters big as jackets, and when she was dressed casually she wore stretch slacks that were neatly secured by stirrups around her long, narrow white feet. Her eyes were frankly and emptily brown, as if giving themselves up to every observer. She was so anxious to help that it was oppressive; "No, I can manage, I've been making breakfast for eight years by myself," Barbara would say angrily, and Dorie, a chastised child, would glance around the table not only at Mark but at the children for sympathy. Mark had a blackboard set up in the kitchen so that he could test the children's progress in languages, and he barked out commands for them— French or Latin or Greek words—and they responded with nervous glee, clacking out letters on the board, showing off for the rapt, admiring girl who seemed not to know if they were right or wrong.

"Oh, how smart they are—how wonderful everything is," Dorie breathed.

Mark had to drive to Boston often because he needed his prescription for tranquillizers refilled constantly, and his doctor would not give him an automatic refill. But though Barbara had always looked forward to these quick trips, he rarely took her now. He went off with Dorie, now his "secretary," who took along a notebook decorated with the college's insignia to record his impressions in, and since he never gave his wife warning she could not get ready in time, and it was such an obvious trick, so crudely cruel, that Barbara stood in the kitchen and wept as they drove out.... She called up friends in New York but never exactly told them what was going on. It was so ludicrous, it made her seem such a fool. Instead she chatted and barked with laughter; her conversations with these people were always so witty that nothing, nothing seemed very real until she hung up the receiver again; and then she became herself, in a drafty college-owned house in New England, locked in this particular body.

She stared out the attic window for hours, not thinking. She became a state of being, a creature. Downstairs the children fought, or played peacefully, or rifled through their father's study, which was forbidden, and after a certain amount of time something would nudge Barbara to her feet and she would descend slowly, laboriously, as if returning to the real world where any ugliness was possible. When she slapped the boys for being bad, they stood in meek defiance and did not cry. "Mother, you're out of your mind," they said. "Mother, you're losing control of yourself."

"It's your father who's out of his mind!" she shouted.

She had the idea that everyone was talking about them, everyone. Anonymous, worthless people who had never published a line gloated over her predicament; high-school baton twirlers were better off than Barbara Scott, who had no dignity. Dorie, riding with Mark Arber on the expressway to Boston, was at least young and stupid, anonymous though she was, and probably she too had a slim collection of poems that Mark would manage to get published . . . and who knew what would follow, who could tell? Dorie Weinheimer was like any one of five hundred or five thousand college girls and was no one, had no personality, and yet Mark Arber had somehow fallen in love with her, so perhaps everyone would eventually fall in love with her . . . ? Barbara imagined with panic the parties she knew nothing about to which Mark and his new girl went: Mark in his slovenly tweed suits, looking like his own father in the thirties, and Dorie chic as a *Vogue* model in her weightless bones and vacuous face.

"Is Dorie going to stay here long?" the boys kept asking.

"Why, don't you like her?"

"She's nice. She smells nice. Is she going to stay long?"

"Go ask your father that," Barbara said angrily.

The girl was officially boarding with them; it was no lie. Every year certain faculty families took in a student or two, out of generosity or charity, or because they themselves needed the money, and the Arbers themselves had always looked down upon such hearty liberalism. But now they had Dorie, and in Peabody's Market Barbara had to rush up and down the aisles with her shopping cart, trying to avoid the wives of other professors who were sure to ask her about the new boarder; and she had to buy special things for the girl, spinach and beets and artichokes, while Barbara and Mark liked starches and sweets and fat, foods that clogged up the blood vessels and strained the

heart and puffed out the stomach. While Barbara ate and drank
hungrily, Dorie sat chaste with her tiny forkfuls of food, and
Barbara could eat three platefuls to Dorie's one; her appetite
increased savagely just in the presence of the girl. (The girl was
always asking, politely, "Is it the boys who get the bathroom all
dirty?" or "Could I take the vacuum cleaner down and have it
fixed?" and these questions, polite as they were, made Barbara's
appetite increase savagely.)

In April, after Dorie had been boarding with them three and a
half months, Barbara was up at her desk when there was a rap
on the plywood door. Unused to visitors, Barbara turned clumsily and looked at Mark over the top of her glasses. "Can I come
in?" he said. "What are you working on?"

There was no paper in her typewriter. "Nothing," she said.

"You haven't shown me any poems lately. What's wrong?"

He sat on the window ledge and lit a cigarette. Barbara felt a
spiteful satisfaction to see how old he looked—he hadn't her
fine, fleshed-out skin, the smooth complexion of an overweight
woman; he had instead the bunched, baggy complexion of an
overweight man whose weight keeps shifting up and down.
Good. Even his fingers shook as he lit the cigarette.

"This is the best place in the house," he said.

"Do you want me to give it up to Dorie?"

He stared at her. "Give it up—why? Of course not."

"I thought you might be testing my generosity."

He shook his head, puzzled. Barbara wondered if she hated
this man or if she felt a writer's interest in him. Perhaps he was
insane. Or perhaps he had been drinking again; he had not gone
out to his classes this morning and she'd heard him arguing
with Dorie. "Barbara, how old are you?" he said.

"Forty-three. You know that."

He looked around at the boxes and other clutter as if coming
to an important decision. "Well, we have a little problem here."

Barbara stared at her blunt fingernails and waited.

"She got herself pregnant. It seems on purpose."

"She what?"

"Well," Mark said uncomfortably, "she did it on purpose."

They remained silent. After a while, in a different voice he
said, "She claims she loves children. She loves our children and

wants some of her own. It's a valid point, I can't deny her her rights...but...I thought you should know about it in case you agree to help."

"What do you mean?"

"Well, I have something arranged in Boston," he said, not looking at her, "and Dorie has agreed to it...though reluctantly...and unfortunately I don't think I can drive her myself ...you know I have to go to Chicago...."

Barbara did not look at him.

"I'm on this panel at the University of Chicago, with John Ciardi. You know, it's been set up for a year, it's on the state of contemporary poetry—you know—I can't possibly withdraw from it now—"

"And so?"

"If you could drive Dorie in—"

"If I could drive her in?"

"I don't see what alternative we have," he said slowly.

"Would you like a divorce so you can marry her?"

"I have never mentioned that," he said.

"Well, would you?"

"I don't know."

"Look at me. Do you want to marry her?"

A nerve began to twitch in his eye. It was a familiar twitch—it had been with him for two decades. "No, I don't think so. I don't know—you know how I feel about disruption."

"Don't you have any courage?"

"Courage?"

"If you want to marry her, go ahead. I won't stop you."

"Do you want a divorce yourself?"

"I'm asking you. It's up to you. Then Dorie can have her baby and fulfill herself," Barbara said with a deathly smile. "She can assert her rights as a woman twenty years younger than I. She can become the third Mrs. Arber and become automatically envied. Don't you have the courage for it?"

"I had thought," Mark said with dignity, "that you and I had an admirable marriage. It was different from the marriages of other people we know—part of it is that we don't work in the same area, yes, but the most important part lay in our understanding of each other. It has taken a tremendous generosity on

your part, Barbara, over the last three months and I appreciate
it," he said, nodding slowly, "I appreciate it and I can't help
asking myself whether . . . whether I would have had the strength
to do what you did, in your place. I mean, if you had brought
in—"

"I know what you mean."

"It's been an extraordinary marriage. I don't want it to end
on an impulse, anything reckless or emotional," he said vaguely.
She thought that he did look a little mad, but quietly mad; his
ears were very red. For the first time she began to feel pity for
the girl who was, after all, nobody, and who had no personality,
and who was waiting in the ugly maid's room for her fate to be
decided.

"All right, I'll drive her to Boston," Barbara said.

IV

Mark had to leave the next morning for Chicago. He would
be gone, he explained, about a week—there was not only the
speaking appearance but other things as well. The three of them
had a kind of farewell party the night before. Dorie sat with her
frail hand on her flat, child's stomach and drank listlessly, while
Barbara and Mark argued about the comparative merits of two
English novelists—their literary arguments were always witty,
superficial, rapid, and very enjoyable. At two o'clock Mark
woke Dorie to say good-by and Barbara, thinking herself admir-
ably discreet, went upstairs alone.

She drove Dorie to Boston the next day. Dorie was a mother's
child, the kind of girl mothers admire—clean, bright, passive—
and it was a shame for her to be so frightened. Barbara said
roughly, "I've known lots of women who've had abortions.
They lived."

"Did you ever have one?"

"No."

Dorie turned away as if in reproach.

"I've had children and that's harder, maybe. It's thought to
be harder, Barbara said, as if offering the girl something.

"I would like children, maybe three of them," Dorie said.

"Three is a good number, yes."

"But I'd be afraid...I wouldn't know what to do.... I don't know what to do now...."

She was just a child herself, Barbara thought with a rush of sympathy; of all of them it was Dorie who was most trapped. The girl sat with a scarf around her careless hair, staring out the window. She wore a camel's-hair coat like all the girls and her fingernails were colorless and uneven, as if she had been chewing them.

"Stop thinking about it. Sit still."

"Yes," the girl said listlessly.

They drove on. Something began to weigh at Barbara's heart, as if her flesh were aging moment by moment. She had never liked her body. Dorie's body was so much more prim and chaste and stylish, and her own body belonged to another age, a hearty nineteenth century where fat had been a kind of virtue. Barbara thought of her poetry, which was light and sometimes quite clever, the poetry of a girl, glimmering with half-seen visions and echoing with peculiar off-rhymes—and truly it ought to have been Dorie's poetry and not hers. She was not equal to her own writing. And, on the highway like this, speeding toward some tawdry destination, she had the sudden terrible conviction that language itself did not matter and that nothing mattered ultimately except the body, the human body and the bodies of other creatures and objects: what else existed?

Her own body was the only real fact about her. Dorie, huddled over in her corner, was another real fact and they were going to do something about it, defeat it. She thought of Mark already in Chicago, at a cocktail party, the words growing like weeds in his brain and his wit moving so rapidly through the brains of others that it was, itself, a kind of lie. It seemed strange to her that the two of them should move against Dorie, who suffered because she was totally real and helpless and gave up nothing of herself to words.

They arrived in Boston and began looking for the street. Barbara felt clumsy and guilty and did not dare to glance over at the girl. She muttered aloud as they drove for half an hour, without luck. Then she found the address. It was a small private hospital with a blank gray front. Barbara drove past it and circled the block and approached it again. "Come on, get hold of yourself," she said to Dorie's stiff profile, "this is no picnic for me either."

She stopped the car and she and Dorie stared out at the hospital, which looked deserted. The neighborhood itself seemed deserted. Finally Barbara said, with a heaviness she did not yet understand, "Let's find a place to stay tonight first. Let's get that settled." She took the silent girl to a motel on a boulevard and told her to wait in the room, she'd be back shortly. Dorie stared in a drugged silence at Barbara, who could have been her mother—there flashed between them the kind of camaraderie possible only between mother and daughter—and then Barbara left the room. Dorie remained sitting in a very light chair of imitation wood and leather. She sat so that she was staring at the edge of the bureau; occasionally her eye was attracted by the framed picture over the bed, of a woman in a red evening gown and a man in a tuxedo observing a waterfall by moonlight. She sat like this for quite a while, in her coat. A nerve kept twitching in her thigh but it did not bother her; it was a most energetic, thumping twitch, as if her very flesh were doing a dance. But it did not bother her. She remained there for a while, waking to the morning light, and it took her several panicked moments to remember where she was and who had brought her here. She had the immediate thought that she must be safe—if it was morning she must be safe—and someone had taken care of her, had seen what was best for her and had carried it out.

V

And so she became the third Mrs. Arber, a month after the second one's death. Barbara had been found dead in an elegant motel across the city, the Paradise Inn, which Mark thought was a brave, cynical joke; he took Barbara's death with an alarming, rhetorical melodrama, an alcoholic melancholy Dorie did not like. Barbara's "infinite courage" made Dorie resentful. The second Mrs. Arber had taken a large dose of sleeping pills and had died easily, because of the strain her body had made upon her heart; so that was that. But somehow it wasn't—because

Mark kept talking about it, speculating on it, wondering: "She did it for the baby, to preserve life. It's astonishing, it's exactly like something in a novel," he said. He spoke with a perpetual guilty astonishment.

She married him and became Mrs. Arber, which surprised everyone. It surprised even Mark. Dorie herself was not very surprised, because a daydreamer is prepared for most things and in a way she had planned even this, though she had not guessed how it would come about. Surely she had rehearsed the second Mrs. Arber's suicide and funeral already a year before, when she'd known nothing, could have guessed nothing, and it did not really surprise her. Events lost their jagged edges and became hard and opaque and routine, drawing her into them. She was still a daydreamer, though she was Mrs. Arber. She sat at the old desk up in the attic and leaned forward on her bony elbows to stare out the window, contemplating the hopeless front yard and the people who strolled by, some of them who— she thought—glanced toward the house with a kind of amused contempt, as if aware of her inside. She was almost always home.

The new baby was a girl, Carolyn. Dorie took care of her endlessly and she took care of the boys; she hadn't been able to finish school. In the evening when all the children were at last asleep Mark would come out of his study and read to her in his rapid, impatient voice snatches of his new novel, or occasionally poems of his late wife's, and Dorie would stare at him and try to understand. She was transfixed with love for him and yet—and yet she was unable to locate this love in this particular man, unable to comprehend it. Mark was invited everywhere that spring; he flew all the way out to California to take part in a highly publicized symposium with George Steiner and James Baldwin, and Dorie stayed home. Geoffrey was seeing a psychiatrist in Boston and she had to drive him in every other day, and there was her own baby, and Mark's frequent visitors who arrived often without notice and stayed a week—sleeping late, staying up late, drinking, eating, arguing—it was exactly the kind of life she had known would be hers, and yet she could not adjust to it. Her baby was somehow mixed up in her mind with the other wife, as if it had been that woman's and only left to her, Dorie, for safekeeping. She was grateful that her baby was a girl because wasn't there always a kind of pact or understanding between women?

In June two men arrived at the house to spend a week, and Dorie had to cook for them. They were long, lean, gray-haired young men who were undefinable, sometimes very fussy, sometimes reckless and hysterical with wit, always rather insulting in a light, veiled manner Dorie could not catch. They were both vegetarians and could not tolerate anyone eating meat in their presence. One evening at a late dinner Dorie began to cry and had to leave the room, and the two guests and Mark and even the children were displeased with her. She went up to the attic and sat mechanically at the desk. It did no good to read Barbara Scott's poetry because she did not understand it. Her understanding had dropped to tending the baby and the boys, fixing meals, cleaning up and shopping, and taking the station wagon to the garage perpetually... and she had no time to go with the others to the tennis courts, or to accompany Mark to New York... and around her were human beings whose lives consisted of language, the grace of language, and she could no longer understand them. She felt strangely cheated, a part of her murdered, as if the abortion had taken place that day after all and something had been cut permanently out of her.

In a while Mark climbed the stairs to her. She heard him coming, she heard his labored breathing. "Here you are," he said, and slid his big beefy arms around her and breathed his liquory love into her face, calling her his darling, his beauty. After all, he did love her, it was real and his arms were real, and she still loved him although she had lost the meaning of that word. "Now will you come downstairs and apologize, please?" he said gently. "You've disturbed them and it can't be left like this. You know how I hate disruption."

She began weeping again, helplessly, to think that she had disturbed anyone, that she was this girl sitting at a battered desk in someone's attic, and no one else, no other person who might confidently take upon herself the meaning of this man's words— she was herself and that was a fact, a final fact she would never overcome.

How I Contemplated the World from the Detroit House of Correction and Began My Life Over Again

Notes for an Essay for an English Class at Baldwin Country Day School; Poking Around in Debris; Disgust and Curiosity; a Revelation of the Meaning of Life; a Happy Ending...

I. EVENTS

1. The girl (myself) is walking through Branden's, that excellent store. Suburb of a large famous city that is a symbol for large famous American cities. The event sneaks up on the girl, who believes she is herding it along with a small fixed smile, a girl of fifteen, innocently experienced. She dawdles in a certain style by a counter of costume jewelry. Rings, earrings, necklaces. Prices from $5 to $50, all within reach. All ugly. She eases over to the glove counter, where everything is ugly too. In her close-fitted coat with its black fur collar she contemplates the luxury of Branden's, which she has known for many years: its many mild pale lights, easy on the eye and the soul, its elaborate tinkly decorations, its women shoppers with their

excellent shoes and coats and hairdos, all dawdling gracefully, in no hurry.
Who was ever in a hurry here?

2. The girl seated at home. A small library, paneled walls of oak. Someone is talking to me. An earnest, husky, female voice drives itself against my ears, nervous, frightened, groping around my heart, saying, "If you wanted gloves, why didn't you say so? Why didn't you ask for them?" That store, Branden's, is owned by Raymond Forrest who lives on Du Maurier Drive. We live on Sioux Drive. Raymond Forrest. A handsome man? An ugly man? A man of fifty or sixty, with gray hair, or a man of forty with earnest, courteous eyes, a good golf game; who is Raymond Forrest, this man who is my salvation? Father has been talking to him. Father is not his physician; Dr. Berg is his physician. Father and Dr. Berg refer patients to each other. There is a connection. Mother plays bridge with... On Mondays and Wednesdays our maid Billie works at... The strings draw together in a cat's cradle, making a net to save you when you fall....

3. *Harriet Arnold's.* A small shop, better than Branden's. Mother in her black coat, I in my close-fitted blue coat. Shopping. Now look at this, isn't this cute, do you want this, why don't you want this, try this on, take this with you to the fitting room, take this also, what's wrong with you, what can I do for you, why are you so strange...? "I wanted to steal but not to buy," I don't tell her. The girl droops along in her coat and gloves and leather boots, her eyes scan the horizon, which is pastel pink and decorated like Branden's, tasteful walls and modern ceilings with graceful glimmering lights.

4. Weeks later, the girl at a bus stop. Two o'clock in the afternoon, a Tuesday; obviously she has walked out of school.

5. The girl stepping down from a bus. Afternoon, weather changing to colder. Detroit. Pavement and closed-up stores;

grillwork over the windows of a pawnshop. What is a pawnshop, exactly?

II. CHARACTERS

1. The girl stands five feet five inches tall. An ordinary height. Baldwin Country Day School draws them up to that height. She dreams along the corridors and presses her face against the Thermoplex glass. No frost or steam can ever form on that glass. A smudge of grease from her forehead ... could she be boiled down to grease? She wears her hair loose and long and straight in suburban teen-age style, 1968. Eyes smudged with pencil, dark brown. Brown hair. Vague green eyes. A pretty girl? An ugly girl? She sings to herself under her breath, idling in the corridor, thinking of her many secrets (the thirty dollars she once took from the purse of a friend's mother, just for fun, the basement window she smashed in her own house just for fun) and thinking of her brother who is at Susquehanna Boys' Academy, an excellent preparatory school in Maine, remembering him unclearly ... he has long manic hair and a squeaking voice and he looks like one of the popular teen-age singers of 1968, one of those in a group, *The Certain Forces, The Way Out, The Maniacs Responsible.* The girl in her turn looks like one of those fieldsful of girls who listen to the boys' singing, dreaming and mooning restlessly, breaking into high sullen laughter, innocently experienced.

2. The mother. A Midwestern woman of Detroit and suburbs. Belongs to the Detroit Athletic Club. Also the Detroit Golf Club. Also the Bloomfield Hills Country Club. The Village Women's Club at which lectures are given each winter on Genet and Sartre and James Baldwin, by the Director of the Adult Education Program at Wayne State University.... The Bloomfield Art Association. Also the Founders Society of the Detroit Institute of Arts. Also ... Oh, she is in perpetual motion, this lady, hair like blown-up gold and finer than gold, hair and fingers and body of inestimable grace. Heavy weighs the gold on the

back of her hairbrush and hand mirror. Heavy heavy the candle-sticks in the dining room. Very heavy is the big car, a Lincoln, long and black, that on one cool autumn day split a squirrel's body in two unequal parts.

3. The father. Dr.   . He belongs to the same clubs as #2. A player of squash and golf; he has a golfer's umbrella of stripes. Candy stripes. In his mouth nothing turns to sugar, however; saliva works no miracles here. His doctoring is of the slightly sick. The sick are sent elsewhere (to Dr. Berg?), the deathly sick are sent back for more tests and their bills are sent to their homes, the unsick are sent to Dr. Coronet (Isabel, a lady), an excellent psychiatrist for unsick people who angrily believe they are sick and want to do something about it. If they demand a male psychiatrist, the unsick are sent by Dr.   (my father) to Dr. Lowenstein, a male psychiatrist, excellent and expensive, with a limited practice.

4. Clarita. She is twenty, twenty-five, she is thirty or more? Pretty, ugly, what? She is a woman lounging by the side of a road, in jeans and a sweater, hitchhiking, or she is slouched on a stool at a counter in some roadside diner. A hard line of jaw. Curious eyes. Amused eyes. Behind her eyes processions move, funeral pageants, cartoons. She says, "I never can figure out why girls like you bum around down here. What are you looking for anyway?" An odor of tobacco about her. Unwashed underclothes, or no underclothes, unwashed skin, gritty toes, hair long and falling into strands, not recently washed.

5. Simon. In this city the weather changes abruptly, so Simon's weather changes abruptly. He sleeps through the after-noon. He sleeps through the morning. Rising, he gropes around for something to get him going, for a cigarette or a pill to drive him out to the street, where the temperature is hovering around 35°. Why doesn't it drop? Why, why doesn't the cold clean air come down from Canada; will he have to go up into Canada to get it? Will he have to leave the Country of his Birth and sink into Canada's frosty fields...? Will the F.B.I. (which he

dreams about constantly) chase him over the Canadian border on foot, hounded out in a blizzard of broken glass and horns...?

"Once I was Huckleberry Finn," Simon says, "but now I am Roderick Usher." Beset by frenzies and fears, this man who makes my spine go cold, he takes green pills, yellow pills, pills of white and capsules of dark blue and green...he takes other things I may not mention, for what if Simon seeks me out and climbs into my girl's bedroom here in Bloomfield Hills and strangles me, what then...? (As I write this I begin to shiver. Why do I shiver? I am now sixteen and sixteen is not an age for shivering.) It comes from Simon, who is always cold.

III. WORLD EVENTS

Nothing.

IV. PEOPLE & CIRCUMSTANCES
CONTRIBUTING TO THIS DELINQUENCY

Nothing.

V. SIOUX DRIVE

George, Clyde G. 240 Sioux. A manufacturer's representative; children, a dog, a wife. Georgian with the usual columns. You think of the White House, then of Thomas Jefferson, then your mind goes blank on the white pillars and you think of nothing. Norris, Ralph W. 246 Sioux. Public relations. Colonial. Bay window, brick, stone, concrete, wood, green shutters, sidewalk, lantern, grass, trees, blacktop drive, two children, one of them my classmate Esther (Esther Norris) at Baldwin. Wife, cars. Ramsey, Michael D. 250 Sioux. Colonial. Big living room, thirty by twenty-five, fireplaces in living room, library, recreation room, paneled walls wet bar five bathrooms five bedrooms two

lavatories central air-conditioning automatic sprinkler automatic garage door three children one wife two cars a breakfast room a patio a large fenced lot fourteen trees a front door with a brass knocker never knocked. Next is our house. Classic contemporary. Traditional modern. Attached garage, attached Florida room, attached patio, attached pool and cabana, attached roof. A front door mail slot through which pour *Time Magazine, Fortune, Life, Business Week,* the *Wall Street Journal,* the *New York Times,* the *New Yorker,* the *Saturday Review, M.D., Modern Medicine, Disease of the Month* . . . and also . . . And in addition to all this, a quiet sealed letter from Baldwin saying: *Your daughter is not doing work compatible with her performance on the Stanford-Binet.* . . . And your son is not doing well, not well at all, very sad. Where is your son anyway? Once he stole trick-and-treat candy from some six-year-old kids, he himself being a robust ten. The beginning. Now your daughter steals. In the Village Pharmacy she made off with, yes she did, don't deny it, she made off with a copy of *Pageant Magazine* for no reason, she swiped a roll of Life Savers in a green wrapper and was in no need of saving her life or even in need of sucking candy; when she was no more than eight years old she stole, don't blush, she stole a package of Tums only because it was out on the counter and available, and the nice lady behind the counter (now dead) said nothing. . . . Sioux Drive. Maples, oaks, elms. Diseased elms cut down. Sioux Drive runs into Roosevelt Drive. Slow, turning lanes, not streets, all drives and lanes and ways and passes. A private police force. Quiet private police, in unmarked cars. Cruising on Saturday evenings with paternal smiles for the residents who are streaming in and out of houses, going to and from parties, a thousand parties, slightly staggering, the women in their furs alighting from automobiles bought of Ford and General Motors and Chrysler, very heavy automobiles. No foreign cars. Detroit. In 275 Sioux, down the block in that magnificent French-Normandy mansion, lives
himself, who has the C   account itself, imagine that! Look at where he lives and look at the enormous trees and chimneys, imagine his many fireplaces, imagine his wife and children, imagine his wife's hair, imagine her fingernails, imagine her

bathtub of smooth clean glowing pink, imagine their embraces, his trouser pockets filled with odd coins and keys and dust and peanuts, imagine their ecstasy on Sioux Drive, imagine their income tax returns, imagine their little boy's pride in his experimental car, a scaled-down C   , as he roars around the neighborhood on the sidewalks frightening dogs and Negro maids, oh imagine all these things, imagine everything, let your mind roar out all over Sioux Drive and Du Maurier Drive and Roosevelt Drive and Ticonderoga Pass and Burning Bush Way and Lincolnshire Pass and Lois Lane.

When spring comes, its winds blow nothing to Sioux Drive, no odors of hollyhocks or forsythia, nothing Sioux Drive doesn't already possess, everything is planted and performing. The weather vanes, had they weather vanes, don't have to turn with the wind, don't have to contend with the weather. There is no weather.

VI. DETROIT

There is always weather in Detroit. Detroit's temperature is always 32°. Fast-falling temperatures. Slow-rising temperatures. Wind from the north-northeast four to forty miles an hour, small-craft warnings, partly cloudy today and Wednesday changing to partly sunny through Thursday...small warnings of frost, soot warnings, traffic warnings, hazardous lake conditions for small craft and swimmers, restless Negro gangs, restless cloud formations, restless temperatures aching to fall out the very bottom of the thermometer or shoot up over the top and boil everything over in red mercury.

Detroit's temperature is 32°. Fast-falling temperatures. Slow-rising temperatures. Wind from the north-northeast four to forty miles an hour....

VII. EVENTS

1. The girl's heart is pounding. In her pocket is a pair of gloves! In a plastic bag! Airproof breathproof plastic bag, gloves

selling for twenty-five dollars on Branden's counter! In her pocket! Shoplifted!... In her purse is a blue comb, not very clean. In her purse is a leather billfold (a birthday present from her grandmother in Philadelphia) with snapshots of the family in clean plastic windows, in the billfold are bills, she doesn't know how many bills.... In her purse is an ominous note from her friend Tykie *What's this about Joe H. and the kids hanging around at Louise's Sat. night? You heard anything?...* passed in French class. In her purse is a lot of dirty yellow Kleenex, her mother's heart would break to see such very dirty Kleenex, and at the bottom of her purse are brown hairpins and safety pins and a broken pencil and a ballpoint pen (blue) stolen from somewhere forgotten and a purse-size compact of Cover Girl Make-Up, Ivory Rose.... Her lipstick is Broken Heart, a corrupt pink; her fingers are trembling like crazy; her teeth are beginning to chatter; her insides are alive; her eyes glow in her head; she is saying to her mother's astonished face *I want to steal but not to buy.*

2. At Clarita's. Day or night? What room is this? A bed, a regular bed, and a mattress on the floor nearby. Wallpaper hanging in strips. Clarita says she tore it like that with her teeth. She was fighting a barbaric tribe that night, high from some pills; she was battling for her life with men wearing helmets of heavy iron and their faces no more than Christian crosses to breathe through, every one of those bastards looking like her lover Simon, who seems to breathe with great difficulty through the slits of mouth and nostrils in his face. Clarita has never heard of Sioux Drive. Raymond Forrest cuts no ice with her, nor does the C   account and its millions; Harvard Business School could be at the corner of Vernor and 12th Street for all she cares, and Vietnam might have sunk by now into the Dead Sea under its tons of debris, for all the amazement she could show... her face is overworked, overwrought, at the age of twenty (thirty?) it is already exhausted but fanciful and ready for a laugh. Clarita says mournfully to me *Honey somebody is going to turn you out let me give you warning.* In a movie shown on late television Clarita is not a mess like this but a nurse, with

short neat hair and a dedicated look, in love with her doctor and her doctor's patients and their diseases, enamored of needles and sponges and rubbing alcohol.... Or no: she is a private secretary. Robert Cummings is her boss. She helps him with fantastic plots, the canned audience laughs, no, the audience doesn't laugh because nothing is funny, instead her boss is Robert Taylor and they are not boss and secretary but husband and wife, she is threatened by a young starlet, she is grim, handsome, wifely, a good companion for a good man.... She is Claudette Colbert. Her sister too is Claudette Colbert. They are twins, identical. Her husband Charles Boyer is a very rich handsome man and her sister, Claudette Colbert, is plotting her death in order to take her place as the rich man's wife, no one will know because they are *twins*.... All these marvelous lives Clarita might have lived, but she fell out the bottom at the age of thirteen. At the age when I was packing my overnight case for a slumber party at Toni Deshield's she was tearing filthy sheets off a bed and scratching up a rash on her arms.... Thirteen is uncommonly young for a white girl in Detroit, Miss Brock of the Detroit House of Correction said in a sad newspaper interview for the *Detroit News*; fifteen and sixteen are more likely. Eleven, twelve, thirteen are not surprising in colored ... they are more precocious. What can we do? Taxes are rising and the tax base is falling. The temperature rises slowly but falls rapidly. Everything is falling out the bottom, Woodward Avenue is filthy, Livernois Avenue is filthy! Scraps of paper flutter in the air like pigeons, dirt flies up and hits you right in the eye, oh Detroit is breaking up into dangerous bits of newspaper and dirt, watch out....

Clarita's apartment is over a restaurant. Simon her lover emerges from the cracks at dark. Mrs. Olesko, a neighbor of Clarita's, an aged white wisp of a woman, doesn't complain but sniffs with contentment at Clarita's noisy life and doesn't tell the cops, hating cops, when the cops arrive. I should give more fake names, more blanks, instead of telling all these secrets. I myself am a secret; I am a minor.

3. My father reads a paper at a medical convention in Los Angeles. There he is, on the edge of the North American con-

tinent, when the unmarked detective put his hand so gently on my arm in the aisle of Branden's and said, "Miss, would you like to step over here for a minute?"

And where was he when Clarita put her hand on my arm, that wintry dark sulphurous aching day in Detroit, in the company of closed-down barber shops, closed-down diners, closed-down movie houses, homes, windows, basements, faces... she put her hand on my arm and said, "Honey, are you looking for somebody down here?"

And was he home worrying about me, gone for two weeks solid, when they carried me off...? It took three of them to get me in the police cruiser, so they said, and they put more than their hands on my arm.

4. I work on this lesson. My English teacher is Mr. Forest, who is from Michigan State. Not handsome, Mr. Forest, and his name is plain, unlike Raymond Forrest's, but he is sweet and rodentlike, he has conferred with the principal and my parents, and everything is fixed... treat her as if nothing has happened, a new start, begin again, only sixteen years old, what a shame, how did it happen?—nothing happened, nothing could have happened, a slight physiological modification known only to a gynecologist or to Dr. Coronet. I work on my lesson. I sit in my pink room. I look around the room with my sad pink eyes. I sigh, I dawdle, I pause, I eat up time, I am limp and happy to be home, I am sixteen years old suddenly, my head hangs heavy as a pumpkin on my shoulders, and my hair has just been cut by Mr. Faye at the Crystal Salon and is said to be very becoming.

(Simon too put his hand on my arm and said, "Honey, you have got to come with me," and in his six-by-six room we got to know each other. Would I go back to Simon again? Would I lie down with him in all that filth and craziness? Over and over again

a Clarita is being betrayed as in front of a Cunningham Drug Store she is nervously eying a colored man who may or may not have money, or a nervous white boy of twenty with sideburns and an Appalachian look, who may or may not have a knife hidden in his jacket pocket, or a husky red-faced man of friendly countenance who may or may not be a member of the Vice Squad out for an early twilight walk.)

I work on my lesson for Mr. Forest. I have filled up eleven pages. Words pour out of me and won't stop. I want to tell everything...what was the song Simon was always humming, and who was Simon's friend in a very new trench coat with an old high school graduation ring on his finger...? Simon's bearded friend? When I was down too low for him, Simon kicked me out and gave me to him for three days, I think, on Fourteenth Street in Detroit, an airy room of cold cruel drafts with newspapers on the floor.... Do I really remember that or am I piecing it together from what they told me? Did they tell the truth? Did they know much of the truth?

VIII. CHARACTERS

1. Wednesdays after school, at four; Saturday mornings at ten. Mother drives me to Dr. Coronet. Ferns in the office, plastic or real, they look the same. Dr. Coronet is queenly, an elegant nicotine-stained lady who would have studied with Freud had circumstances not prevented it, a bit of a Catholic, ready to offer you some mystery if your teeth will ache too much without it. Highly recommended by Father! Forty dollars an hour, Father's forty dollars! Progress! Looking up! Looking better! That new haircut is so becoming, says Dr. Coronet herself, showing how normal she is for a woman with an I.Q. of 180 and many advanced degrees.

2. Mother. A lady in a brown suede coat. Boots of shiny black material, black gloves, a black fur hat. She would be humiliated could she know that of all the people in the world it is my ex-lover Simon who walks most like her...self-conscious and unreal, listening to distant music, a little bowlegged with craftiness....

3. Father. Tying a necktie. In a hurry. On my first evening home he put his hand on my arm and said, "Honey, we're going to forget all about this."

4. Simon. Outside, a plane is crossing the sky, in here we're in a hurry. Morning. It must be morning. The girl is half out of her mind, whimpering and vague; Simon her dear friend is wretched this morning...he is wretched with morning itself... he forces her to give him an injection with that needle she knows is filthy, she has a dread of needles and surgical instruments and the odor of things that are to be sent into the blood, thinking somehow of her father.... This is a bad morning, Simon says that his mind is being twisted out of shape, and so he submits to the needle that he usually scorns and bites his lip with his yellowish teeth, his face going very pale. *Ah baby!* he says in his soft mocking voice, which with all women is a mockery of love, *do it like this— Slowly—* And the girl, terrified, almost drops the precious needle but manages to turn it up to the light from the window...is it an extension of herself then? She can give him this gift then? *I wish you wouldn't do this to me* she says, wise in her terror, because it seems to her that Simon's danger—in a few minutes he may be dead—is a way of pressing her against him that is more powerful than any other embrace. She has to work over his arm, the knotted corded veins of his arm, her forehead wet with perspiration as she pushes and releases the syringe, staring at that mixture of liquid now stained with Simon's bright blood.... When the drug hits him she can feel it herself, she feels that magic that is more than any woman can give him, striking the back of his head and making his face stretch as if with the impact of a terrible sun.... She tries to embrace him but he pushes her aside and stumbles to his feet. *Jesus Christ* he says....

5. Princess, a Negro girl of eighteen. What is her charge? She is closed-mouthed about it, shrewd and silent, you know that no one had to wrestle her to the sidewalk to get her in here; she came with dignity. In the recreation room she sits reading *Nancy Drew and the Jewel Box Mystery*, which inspires in her face tiny

wrinkles of alarm and interest: what a face! Light brown skin, heavy shaded eyes, heavy eyelashes, a serious sinister dark brow, graceful fingers, graceful wristbones, graceful legs, lips, tongue, a sugar-sweet voice, a leggy stride more masculine than Simon's and my mother's, decked out in a dirty white blouse and dirty white slacks; vaguely nautical is Princess' style.... At breakfast she is in charge of clearing the table and leans over me, saying *Honey you sure you ate enough?*

6. The girl lies sleepless, wondering. Why here, why not there? Why Bloomfield Hills and not jail? Why jail and not her pink room? Why downtown Detroit and not Sioux Drive? What is the difference? Is Simon all the difference? The girl's head is a parade of wonders. She is nearly sixteen, her breath is marvelous with wonders, not long ago she was coloring with crayons and now she is smearing the landscape with paints that won't come off and won't come off her fingers either. She says to the matron *I am not talking about anything*, not because everyone has warned her not to talk but because, because she will not talk; because she won't say anything about Simon, who is her secret. And she says to the matron *I won't go home*, up until that night in the lavatory when everything was changed.... "No, I won't go home I want to stay here," she says, listening to her own words with amazement, thinking that weeds might climb everywhere over that marvelous $180,000 house and dinosaurs might return to muddy the beige carpeting, but never never will she reconcile four o'clock in the morning in Detroit with eight o'clock breakfasts in Bloomfield Hills.... Oh, she aches still for Simon's hands and his caressing breath, though he gave her little pleasure, he took everything from her (five-dollar bills, ten-dollar bills, passed into her numb hands by men and taken out of her hands by Simon) until she herself was passed into the hands of other men, police, when Simon evidently got tired of her and her hysteria.... *No, I won't go home, I don't want to be bailed out.* The girl thinks as a *Stubborn and Wayward Child* (one of several charges lodged against her), and the matron understands her crazy white-rimmed eyes that are seeking out some new violence that will keep her in jail, should someone threaten to let

her out. Such children try to strangle the matrons, the attendants, or one another...they want the locks locked forever, the
doors nailed shut...and this girl is no different up until that
night her mind is changed for her....

IX. THAT NIGHT

Princess and Dolly, a little white girl of maybe fifteen, hardy
however as a sergeant and in the House of Correction for armed
robbery, corner her in the lavatory at the farthest sink and the
other girls look away and file out to bed, leaving her. God, how
she is beaten up! Why is she beaten up? Why do they pound her,
why such hatred? Princess vents all the hatred of a thousand
silent Detroit winters on her body, this girl whose body belongs
to me, fiercely she rides across the Midwestern plains on this
girl's tender bruised body...revenge for the oppressed minori-
ties of America! revenge for the slaughtered Indians! revenge
for the female sex, for the male sex, revenge for Bloomfield
Hills, revenge revenge....

X. DETROIT

In Detroit, weather weighs heavily upon everyone. The sky
looms large. The horizon shimmers in smoke. Downtown the
buildings are imprecise in the haze. Perpetual haze. Perpetual
motion inside the haze. Across the choppy river is the city of
Windsor, in Canada. Part of the continent has bunched up here
and is bulging outward, at the tip of Detroit; a cold hard rain is
forever falling on the expressways.... Shoppers shop grimly,
their cars are not parked in safe places, their windshields may
be smashed and graceful ebony hands may drag them out
through their shatterproof smashed windshields, crying *Revenge
for the Indians!* Ah, they all fear leaving Hudson's and being
dragged to the very tip of the city and thrown off the parking
roof of Cobo Hall, that expensive tomb, into the river....

XI. CHARACTERS WE ARE
FOREVER ENTWINED WITH

1. Simon drew me into his tender rotting arms and breathed gravity into me. Then I came to earth, weighed down. He said *You are such a little girl*, and he weighed me down with his delight. In the palms of his hands were teeth marks from his previous life experiences. He was thirty-five, they said. Imagine Simon in this room, in my pink room: he is about six feet tall and stoops slightly, in a feline cautious way, always thinking, always on guard, with his scuffed light suede shoes and his clothes that are anyone's clothes, slightly rumpled ordinary clothes that ordinary men might wear to not-bad jobs. Simon has fair long hair, curly hair, spent languid curls that are like ... exactly like the curls of wood shavings to the touch, I am trying to be exact ... and he smells of unheated mornings and coffee and too many pills coating his tongue with a faint green-white scum.... Dear Simon, who would be panicked in this room and in this house (right now Billie is vacuuming next door in my parents' room; a vacuum cleaner's roar is a sign of all good things), Simon who is said to have come from a home not much different from this, years ago, fleeing all the carpeting and the polished banisters ... Simon has a deathly face, only desperate people fall in love with it. His face is bony and cautious, the bones of his cheeks prominent as if with the rigidity of his ceaseless thinking, plotting, for he has to make money out of girls to whom money means nothing, they're so far gone they can hardly count it, and in a sense money means nothing to him either except as a way of keeping on with his life. *Each Day's Proud Struggle*, the title of a novel we could read at jail.... Each day he needs a certain amount of money. He devours it. It wasn't love he uncoiled in me with his hollowed-out eyes and his courteous smile, that remnant of a prosperous past, but a dark terror that needed to press itself flat against him, or against another man ... but he was the first, he came over to me and took my arm, a claim. We struggled on the stairs and I said *Let me loose, you're hurting my neck, my face*, it was such a surprise that my skin hurt where he rubbed it, and afterward we lay face

to face and he breathed everything into me. In the end I think he turned me in.

2. Raymond Forrest. I just read this morning that Raymond Forrest's father, the chairman of the board at   , died of a heart attack on a plane bound for London. I would like to write Raymond Forrest a note of sympathy. I would like to thank him for not pressing charges against me one hundred years ago, saving me, being so generous... well, men like Raymond Forrest are generous men, not like Simon. I would like to write him a letter telling of my love, or of some other emotion that is positive and healthy. Not like Simon and his poetry, which he scrawled down when he was high and never changed a word... but when I try to think of something to say, it is Simon's language that comes back to me, caught in my head like a bad song, it is always Simon's language:

There is no reality only dreams
Your neck may get snapped when you wake
My love is drawn to some violent end
She keeps wanting to get away
My love is heading downward
And I am heading upward
She is going to crash on the sidewalk
And I am going to dissolve into the clouds

XII. EVENTS

1. Out of the hospital, bruised and saddened and converted, with Princess' grunts still tangled in my hair... and Father in his overcoat looking like a prince himself, come to carry me off. Up the expressway and out north to home. Jesus Christ, but the air is thinner and cleaner here. Monumental houses. Heartbreaking sidewalks, so clean.

2. Weeping in the living room. The ceiling is two stories high and two chandeliers hang from it. Weeping, weeping, though Billie the maid is *probably listening*. I will never leave home

again. Never. Never leave home. Never leave this home again, never.

3. Sugar doughnuts for breakfast. The toaster is very shiny and my face is distorted in it. Is that my face?

4. The car is turning in the driveway. Father brings me home. Mother embraces me. Sunlight breaks in movieland patches on the roof of our traditional-contemporary home, which was designed for the famous automotive stylist whose identity, if I told you the name of the famous car he designed, you would all know, so I can't tell you because my teeth chatter at the thought of being sued...or having someone climb into my bedroom window with a rope to strangle me.... The car turns up the blacktop drive. The house opens to me like a doll's house, so lovely in the sunlight, the big living room beckons to me with its walls falling away in a delirium of joy at my return, Billie the maid is *no doubt* listening from the kitchen as I burst into tears and the hysteria Simon got so sick of. Convulsed in Father's arms, I say I will never leave again, never, why did I leave, where did I go, what happened, my mind is gone wrong, my body is one big bruise, my backbone was sucked dry, it wasn't the men who hurt me and Simon never hurt me but only those girls...my God, how they hurt me...I will never leave home again.... The car is perpetually turning up the drive and I am perpetually breaking down in the living room and we are perpetually taking the right exit from the expressway (Lahser Road) and the wall of the rest room is perpetually banging against my head and perpetually are Simon's hands moving across my body and adding everything up and so too are Father's hands on my shaking bruised back, far from the surface of my skin on the surface of my good blue cashmere coat (dry-cleaned for my release).... I weep for all the money here, for God in gold and beige carpeting, for the beauty of chandeliers and the miracle of a clean polished gleaming toaster and faucets that run both hot and cold water, and I tell them *I will never leave home, this is my home, I love everything here, I am in love with everything here....*
I am home.

Four Summers

I T IS SOME KIND OF SPECIAL DAY. "Where's Sissie?" Ma says. Her face gets sharp, she is frightened. When I run around her chair she laughs and hugs me. She is pretty when she laughs. Her hair is long and pretty.

We are sitting at the best table of all, out near the water. The sun is warm and the air smells nice. Daddy is coming back from the building with some bottles of beer, held in his arms. He makes a grunting noise when he sits down.

"Is the lake deep?" I ask them.

They don't hear me, they're talking. A woman and a man are sitting with us. The man marched in the parade we saw just a while ago; he is a volunteer fireman and is wearing a uniform. Now his shirt is pulled open because it is hot. I can see the dark curly hair way up by his throat; it looks hot and prickly.

A man in a soldier's uniform comes over to us. They are all friends, but I can't remember him. We used to live around here, Ma told me, and then we moved away. The men are laughing. The man in the uniform leans back against the railing, laughing, and I am afraid it will break and he will fall into the water.

"Can we go out in a boat, Dad?" says Jerry.

He and Frank keep running back and forth. I don't want to go with them, I want to stay by Ma. She smells nice. Frank's face is dirty with sweat. "Dad," he says, whining, "can't we go out in a boat? Them kids are going out."

A big lake is behind the building and the open part where we are sitting. Some people are rowing on it. This tavern is noisy and everyone is laughing; it is too noisy for Dad to think about what Frank said.

"Harry," says Ma, "the kids want a boat ride. Why don't you leave off drinking and take them?"

"What?" says Dad.

He looks up from laughing with the men. His face is damp with sweat and he is happy. "Yeah, sure, in a few minutes. Go over there and play and I'll take you out in a few minutes."

The boys run out back by the rowboats, and I run after them. I have a bag of potato chips.

An old man with a white hat pulled down over his forehead is sitting by the boats, smoking. "You kids be careful," he says.

Frank is leaning over and looking at one of the boats. "This here is the best one," he says.

"Why's this one got water in it?" says Jerry.

"You kids watch out. Where's your father?" the man says.

"He's gonna take us for a ride," says Frank.

"Where is he?"

The boys run along, looking at the boats that are tied up. They don't bother with me. The boats are all painted dark green, but the paint is peeling off some of them in little pieces. There is water inside some of them. We watch two people come in, a man and a woman. The woman is giggling. She has on a pink dress and she leans over to trail one finger in the water. "What's all this filthy stuff by the shore?" she says. There is some scum in the water. It is colored a light brown, and there are little seeds and twigs and leaves in it.

The man helps the woman out of the boat. They laugh together. Around their rowboat little waves are still moving; they make a churning noise that I like.

"Where's Dad?" Frank says.

"He ain't coming," says Jerry.

They are tossing pebbles out into the water. Frank throws his sideways, twisting his body. He is ten and very big. "I bet he ain't coming," Jerry says, wiping his nose with the back of his hand.

After a while we go back to the table. Behind the table is the white railing, and then the water, and then the bank curves out so that the weeping willow trees droop over the water. More men in uniforms, from the parade, are walking by.

"Dad," says Frank, "can't we go out? Can't we? There's a real nice boat there—"

"For Christ's sake, get them off me," Dad says. He is angry with Ma. "Why don't you take them out?"

"Honey, I can't row."

"Should we take out a boat, us two?" the other woman says. She has very short, wet-looking hair. It is curled in tiny little curls close to her head and is very bright. "We'll show them, Lenore. Come on, let's give your kids a ride. Show these guys how strong we are."

"That's all you need, to sink a boat," her husband says.

They all laugh.

The table is filled with brown beer bottles and wrappers of things. I can feel how happy they all are together, drawn together by the round table. I lean against Ma's warm leg and she pats me without looking down. She lunges forward and I can tell even before she says something that she is going to be loud.

"You guys're just jealous! Afraid we'll meet some soldiers!" she says.

"Can't we go out, Dad? Please?" Frank says. "We won't fight...."

"Go and play over there. What're those kids doing—over there?" Dad says, frowning. His face is damp and loose, the way it is sometimes when he drinks. "In a little while, okay? Ask your mother."

"She can't do it," Frank says.

"They're just jealous," Ma says to the other woman, giggling. "They're afraid we might meet somebody somewhere."

"Just who's gonna meet this one here?" the other man says, nodding with his head at his wife.

Frank and Jerry walk away. I stay by Ma. My eyes burn and I

want to sleep, but they won't be leaving for a long time. It is still daylight. When we go home from places like this it is always dark and getting chilly and the grass by our house is wet.

"Duane Dorsey's in jail," Dad says. "You guys heard about that?"

"Duane? Yeah, really?"

"It was in the newspaper. His mother-in-law or somebody called the police, he was breaking windows in her house."

"That Duane was always a nut!"

"Is he out now, or what?"

"I don't know, I don't see him these days. We had a fight," Dad says.

The woman with the short hair looks at me. "She's a real cute little thing," she says, stretching her mouth. "She drink beer, Lenore?"

"I don't know."

"Want some of mine?"

She leans toward me and holds the glass by my mouth. I can smell the beer and the warm stale smell of perfume. There are pink lipstick smudges on the glass.

"Hey, what the hell are you doing?" her husband says.

When he talks rough like that I remember him: we were with him once before.

"Are you swearing at me?" the woman says.

"Leave off the kid, you want to make her a drunk like yourself?"

"It don't hurt, one little sip...."

"It's okay," Ma says. She puts her arm around my shoulders and pulls me closer to the table.

"Let's play cards. Who wants to?" Dad says.

"Sissie wants a little sip, don't you?" the woman says. She is smiling at me and I can see that her teeth are darkish, not nice like Ma's.

"Sure, go ahead," says Ma.

"I said leave off that, Sue, for Christ's sake," the man says. He jerks the table. He is a big man with a thick neck; he is bigger than Dad. His eyebrows are blond, lighter than his hair, and are thick and tufted. Dad is staring at something out on the lake without seeing it. "Harry, look, my goddamn wife is trying to make your kid drink beer."

"Who's getting hurt?" Ma says angrily.

Pa looks at me all at once and smiles. "Do you want it, baby?"

I have to say yes. The woman grins and holds the glass down to me, and it clicks against my teeth. They laugh. I stop swallowing right away because it is ugly, and some of the beer drips down on me. "Honey, you're so clumsy," Ma says, wiping me with a napkin.

"She's a real cute girl," the woman says, sitting back in her chair. "I wish I had a nice little girl like that."

"Lay off of that," says her husband.

"Hey, did you bring any cards?" Dad says to the soldier.

"They got some inside."

"Look, I'm sick of cards," Ma says.

"Yeah, why don't we all go for a boat ride?" says the woman. "Be real nice, something new. Every time we get together we play cards. How's about a boat ride?"

"It better be a big boat, with you in it," her husband says. He is pleased when everyone laughs, even the woman. The soldier lights a cigarette and laughs. "How come your cousin here's so skinny and you're so fat?"

"She isn't fat," says Ma. "What the hell do you want? Look at yourself."

"Yes, the best days of my life are behind me," the man says. He wipes his face and then presses a beer bottle against it. "Harry, you're lucky you moved out. It's all going downhill, back in the neighborhood."

"You should talk, you let our house look like hell," the woman says. Her face is blotched now, some parts pale and some red. "Harry don't sit out in his backyard all weekend drinking. He gets something done."

"Harry's younger than me."

Ma reaches over and touches Dad's arm. "Harry, why don't you take the kids out? Before it gets dark."

Dad lifts his glass and finishes his beer. "Who else wants more?" he says.

"I'll get them, you went last time," the soldier says.

"Get a chair for yourself," says Dad. "We can play poker."

"I don't want to play poker, I want to play rummy," the woman says.

"At church this morning Father Reilly was real mad," says Ma. "He said some kids or somebody was out in the cemetery and left some beer bottles. Isn't that awful?"

"Duane Dorsey used to do worse than that," the man says, winking.

"Hey, who's that over there?"

"You mean that fat guy?"

"Isn't that the guy at the lumberyard that owes all that money?"

Dad turns around. His chair wobbles and he almost falls; he is angry.

"This goddamn place is too crowded," he says.

"This is a real nice place," the woman says. She is taking something out of her purse. "I always liked it, didn't you, Lenore?"

"Sue and me used to come here a lot," says Ma. "And not just with you two, either."

"Yeah, we're real jealous," the man says.

"You should be," says the woman.

The soldier comes back. Now I can see that he is really a boy. He runs to the table with the beer before he drops anything. He laughs.

"Jimmy, your ma wouldn't like to see you drinking!" the woman says happily.

"Well, she ain't here."

"Are they still living out in the country?" Ma says to the woman.

"Sure. No electricity, no running water, no bathroom—same old thing. What can you do with people like that?"

"She always talks about going back to the Old Country," the soldier says. "Thinks she can save up money and go back."

"Poor old bastards don't know there was a war," Dad says. He looks as if something tasted bad in his mouth. "My old man died thinking he could go back in a year or two. Stupid old bastards!"

"Your father was real nice...." Ma says.

"Yeah, real nice," says Dad. "Better off dead."

Everybody is quiet.

"June Dieter's mother's got the same thing," the woman says in a low voice to Ma. "She's had it a year now and don't weigh a hundred pounds—you remember how big she used to be."

"She was big, all right," Ma says.

"Remember how she ran after June and slapped her? We were there—some guys were driving us home."

"Yeah. So she's got it too."

"Hey," says Dad, "why don't you get a chair, Jimmy? Sit down here."

The soldier looks around. His face is raw in spots, broken out. But his eyes are nice. He never looks at me.

"Get a chair from that table," Dad says.

"Those people might want it."

"Hell, just take it. Nobody's sitting on it."

"They might—"

Dad reaches around and yanks the chair over. The people look at him but don't say anything. Dad is breathing hard. "Here, sit here," he says. The soldier sits down.

Frank and Jerry come back. They stand by Dad, watching him. "Can we go out now?" Frank says.

"What?"

"Out for a boat ride."

"What? No, next week. Do it next week. We're going to play cards."

"You said—"

"Shut up, we'll do it next week." Dad looks up and shades his eyes. "The lake don't look right anyway."

"Lots of people are out there—"

"I said shut up."

"Honey," Ma whispers, "go and play by yourselves."

"Can we sit in the car?"

"Okay, but don't honk the horn."

"Ma, can't we go for a ride?"

"Go and play by yourselves, stop bothering us," she says. "Hey, will you take Sissie?"

They look at me. They don't like me, I can see it, but they take me with them. We run through the crowd and somebody spills a drink—he yells at us. "Oops, got to watch it!" Frank giggles.

We run along the walk by the boats. A woman in a yellow dress is carrying a baby. She looks at us like she doesn't like us.

Down at the far end some kids are standing together.

"Hey, lookit that," Frank says.

A blackbird is caught in the scum, by one of the boats. It can't fly up. One of the kids, a long-legged girl in a dirty dress, is poking at it with a stick.

The bird's wings keep fluttering but it can't get out. If it could get free it would fly and be safe, but the scum holds it down.

One of the kids throws a stone at it. "Stupid old goddamn bird," somebody says. Frank throws a stone. They are all throwing stones. The bird doesn't know enough to turn away. Its feathers are all wet and dirty. One of the stones hits the bird's head.

"Take that!" Frank says, throwing a rock. The water splashes up and some of the girls scream.

I watch them throwing stones. I am standing at the side. If the bird dies, then everything can die, I think. Inside the tavern there is music from the jukebox.

II

We are at the boathouse tavern again. It is a mild day, a Sunday afternoon. Dad is talking with some men; Jerry and I are waiting by the boats. Mommy is at home with the new baby. Frank has gone off with some friends of his, to a stock-car race. There are some people here, sitting out at the tables, but they don't notice us.

"Why doesn't he hurry up?" Jerry says.

Jerry is twelve now. He has pimples on his forehead and chin. He pushes one of the rowboats with his foot. He is wearing sneakers that are dirty. I wish I could get in that boat and sit down, but I am afraid. A boy not much older than Jerry is squatting on the boardwalk, smoking. You can tell he is in charge of the boats.

"Daddy, come on. Come on," Jerry says, whining. Daddy can't hear him.

I have mosquito bites on my arms and legs. There are mosquitoes and flies around here; the flies crawl around the sticky mess left on tables. A car over in the parking lot has its radio on loud. You can hear the music all this way. "He's coming," I tell Jerry so he won't be mad. Jerry is like Dad, the way his eyes look.

"Oh, that fat guy keeps talking to him," Jerry says.

The fat man is one of the bartenders; he has on a dirty white apron. All these men are familiar. We have been seeing them for years. He punches Dad's arm, up by the shoulder, and Dad pushes him. They are laughing, though. Nobody is mad.

"I'd sooner let a nigger—" the bartender says. We can't hear anything more, but the men laugh again.

"All he does is drink," Jerry says. "I hate him."

At school, up on the sixth-grade floor, Jerry got in trouble last month. The principal slapped him. I am afraid to look at Jerry when he's mad.

"I hate him, I wish he'd die," Jerry says.

Dad is trying to come to us, but every time he takes a step backward and gets ready to turn, one of the men says something. There are three men beside him. Their stomachs are big, but Dad's isn't. He is wearing dark pants and a white shirt; his tie is in the car. He wears a tie to church, then takes it off. He has his shirt sleeves rolled up and you can see how strong his arms must be.

Two women cross over from the parking lot. They are wearing high-heeled shoes and hats and bright dresses—orange and yellow—and when they walk past the men look at them. They go into the tavern. The men laugh about something. The way they laugh makes my eyes focus on something away from them—a bird flying in the sky—and it is hard for me to look anywhere else. I feel as if I'm falling asleep.

"Here he comes!" Jerry says.

Dad walks over to us, with his big steps. He is smiling and carrying a bottle of beer. "Hey, kid," he says to the boy squatting on the walk, "how's about a boat?"

"This one is the best," Jerry says.

"The best, huh? Great." Dad grins at us. "Okay, Sissie, let's get you in. Be careful now." He picks me up even though I am too heavy for it, and sets me in the boat. It hurts a little where he held me, under the arms, but I don't care.

Jerry climbs in. Dad steps in and something happens—he almost slips, but he catches himself. With the wet oar he pushes us off from the boardwalk.

Dad can row fast. The sunlight is gleaming on the water. I sit very still, facing him, afraid to move. The boat goes fast, and Dad is leaning back and forth and pulling on the oars, breathing hard, doing everything fast like he always does. He is always in a hurry to get things done. He has set the bottle of beer down by his leg, pressed against the side of the boat so it won't fall.

"There's the guys we saw go out before," Jerry says. Coming around the island is a boat with three boys in it, older than Jerry. "They went on the island. Can we go there too?"

"Sure," says Dad. His eyes squint in the sun. He is suntanned, and there are freckles on his forehead. I am sitting close to him, facing him, and it surprises me what he looks like—he is like a stranger, with his eyes narrowed. The water beneath the boat makes me feel funny. It keeps us up now, but if I fell over the side I would sink and drown.

"Nice out here, huh?" Dad says. He is breathing hard.

"We should go over that way to get on the island," Jerry says.

"These goddamn oars have splinters in them," Dad says. He hooks the oars up and lets us glide. He reaches down to get the bottle of beer. Though the lake and some trees and the buildings back on shore are in front of me, what makes me look at it is my father's throat, the way it bobs when he swallows. He wipes his forehead. "Want to row, Sissie?" he says.

"Can I?"

"Let me do it," says Jerry.

"Naw, I was just kidding," Dad says.

"I can do it. It ain't hard."

"Stay where you are," Dad says.

He starts rowing again, faster. Why does he go so fast? His face is getting red, the way it does at home when he has trouble with Frank. He clears his throat and spits over the side; I don't like to see that but I can't help but watch. The other boat glides past us, heading for shore. The boys don't look over at us.

Jerry and I look to see if anyone else is on the island, but no one is. The island is very small. You can see around it.

"Are you going to land on it, Dad?" Jerry says.

"Sure, okay." Dad's face is flushed and looks angry.

The boat scrapes bottom and bumps. "Jump out and pull it in," Dad says. Jerry jumps out. His shoes and socks are wet now, but Dad doesn't notice. The boat bumps; it hurts me. I am afraid. But then we're up on the land and Dad is out and lifting me. "Nice ride, sugar?" he says.

Jerry and I run around the island. It is different from what we thought, but we don't know why. There are some trees on it, some wild grass, and then bare caked mud that goes down to the water. The water looks dark and deep on the other side, but when we get there it's shallow. Lily pads grow there; everything is thick and tangled. Jerry wades in the water and gets his pants legs wet. "There might be money in the water," he says.

Some napkins and beer cans are nearby. There is part of a hot-dog bun, with flies buzzing around it.

When we go back by Dad, we see him squatting over the water doing something. His back jerks. Then I see that he is being sick. He is throwing up in the water and making a noise like coughing.

Jerry turns around right away and runs back. I follow him, afraid. On the other side we can look back at the boathouse and wish we were there.

III

Marian and Betty went to the show, but I couldn't. She made me come along here with them. "And cut out that snippy face," Ma said, to let me know she's watching. I have to help her take care of Linda—poor fat Linda, with her runny nose! So here we are inside the tavern. There's too much smoke, I hate smoke. Dad is smoking a cigar. I won't drink any more root beer, it's flat, and I'm sick of potato chips. Inside me there is something that wants to run away, that hates them. How loud they are, my parents! My mother spilled something on the front of her dress, but does she notice? And my Aunt Lucy and Uncle Joe, they're here. Try to avoid them. Lucy has false teeth that make everyone stare at her. I know that everyone is staring at us. I could hide my head in my arms and turn away, I'm so tired and my legs hurt from sunburn and I can't stand them anymore.

"So did you ever hear from them? That letter you wrote?" Ma says to Lucy.

"I'm still waiting. Somebody said you got to have connections to get on the show. But I don't believe it. That Howie Masterson that's the emcee, he's a real nice guy. I can tell."

"It's all crap," Dad says. "You women believe anything."

"I don't believe it," I say.

"Phony as hell," says my uncle.

"You do too believe it, Sissie," says my mother. "Sissie thinks he's cute. I know she does."

"I hate that guy!" I tell her, but she and my aunt are laughing. "I said I hate him! He's greasy."

"All that stuff is phony as hell," says my Uncle Joe. He is tired all the time, and right now he sits with his head bowed. I hate his bald head with the little fringe of gray hair on it. At least my father is still handsome. His jaws sag and there are lines in his neck—edged with dirt, I can see, embarrassed—and his stomach is bulging a little against the table, but still he is a handsome man. In a place like this women look at him. What's he see in *her?* they think. My mother had her hair cut too short last time; she looks queer. There is a photograph taken of her when she was young, standing by someone's motorcycle, with her hair long. In the photograph she was pretty, almost beautiful, but I don't believe it. Not really. I can't believe it, and I hate her. Her forehead gathers itself up in little wrinkles whenever she glances down at Linda, as if she can't remember who Linda is.

"Well, nobody wanted you, kid," she once said to Linda. Linda was a baby then, one year old. Ma was furious, standing in the kitchen where she was washing the floor, screaming: "Nobody wanted you, it was a goddamn accident! An accident!" That surprised me so I didn't know what to think, and I didn't know if I hated Ma or not; but I kept it all a secret...only my girlfriends know, and I won't tell the priest either. Nobody can make me tell. I narrow my eyes and watch my mother leaning forward to say something—it's like she's going to toss something out on the table—and think that maybe she isn't my mother after all, and she isn't that pretty girl in the photograph, but someone else.

"A woman was on the show last night that lost two kids in a fire. Her house burned down," my aunt says loudly. "And she answered the questions right off and got a lot of money and the audience went wild. You could see she was a real lady. I love that guy, Howie Masterson. He's real sweet."

"He's a bastard," Dad says.

"Harry, what the hell? You never even seen him," Ma says.

"I sure as hell never did. Got better things to do at night." Dad turns to my uncle and his voice changes. "I'm on the night shift, now."

"Yeah, I hate that, I—"

"I can sleep during the day. What's the difference?"

"I hate those night shifts."

"What's there to do during the day?" Dad says flatly. His eyes scan us at the table as if he doesn't see anything, then they seem to fall off me and go behind me, looking at nothing.

"Not much," says my uncle, and I can see his white scalp beneath his hair. Both men are silent.

Dad pours beer into his glass and spills some of it. I wish I could look away. I love him, I think, but I hate to be here. Where would I rather be? With Marian and Betty at the movies, or in my room, lying on the bed and staring at the photographs of movie stars on my walls—those beautiful people that never say anything—while out in the kitchen my mother is waiting for my father to come home so they can continue their quarrel. It never stops, that quarrel. Sometimes they laugh together, kid around, they kiss. Then the quarrel starts up again in a few minutes.

"Ma, can I go outside and wait in the car?" I say. "Linda's asleep."

"What's so hot about the car?" she says, looking at me.

"I'm tired. My sunburn hurts."

Linda is sleeping in Ma's lap, with her mouth open and drooling on the front of her dress. "Okay, go on," Ma says. "But we're not going to hurry just for you." When she has drunk too much there is a struggle in her between being angry and being affectionate; she fights both of them, as if standing with her legs apart and her hands on her hips, bracing herself against a strong wind.

When I cross through the crowded tavern I'm conscious of people looking at me. My hair lost its curl because it was so humid today, my legs are too thin, my figure is flat and not nice like Marian's—I want to hide somewhere, hide my face from them. I hate this noisy place and these people. Even the music is ugly because it belongs to them. Then, when I'm outside, the music gets faint right away and it doesn't sound so bad. It's cooler out here. No one is around. Out back, the old rowboats are tied up. Nobody's on the lake. There's no moon, the sky is overcast, it was raining earlier.

When I turn around, a man is standing by the door watching me.

"What're you doing?" he says.

"Nothing."

He has dark hair and a tanned face, I think, but everything is confused because the light from the door is pinkish—there's a neon sign there. My heart starts to pound. The man leans forward to stare at me. "Oh, I thought you were somebody else," he says.

I want to show him I'm not afraid. "Yeah, really? Who did you think I was?" When we ride on the school bus we smile out the windows at strange men, just for fun. We do that all the time. I'm not afraid of any of them.

"You're not her," he says.

Some people come out the door and he has to step out of their way. I say to him, "Maybe you seen me around here before. We come here pretty often."

"Who do you come with?" He is smiling as if he thinks I'm funny. "Anybody I know?"

"That's my business."

It's a game. I'm not afraid. When I think of my mother and

father inside, something makes me want to step closer to this man—why should I be afraid? I could be wild like some of the other girls. Nothing surprises me.

We keep on talking. At first I can tell he wants me to come inside the tavern with him, but then he forgets about it; he keeps talking. I don't know what we say, but we talk in drawling voices, smiling at each other but in a secret, knowing way, as if each one of us knew more than the other. My cheeks start to burn. I could be wild like Betty is sometimes—like some of the other girls. Why not? Once before I talked with a man like this, on the bus. We were both sitting in the back. I wasn't afraid. This man and I keep talking and we talk about nothing, he wants to know how old I am, but it makes my heart pound so hard that I want to touch my chest to calm it. We are walking along the old boardwalk and I say: "Somebody took me out rowing once here."

"Is that so?" he says. "You want me to take you out?"

He has a hard, handsome face. I like that face. Why is he alone? When he smiles I know he's laughing at me, and this makes me stand taller, walk with my shoulders raised.

"Hey, are you with somebody inside there?" he says.

"I left them."

"Have a fight?"

"A fight, yes."

He looks at me quickly. "How old are you anyway?"

"That's none of your business."

"Girls your age are all alike."

"We're not all alike!" I arch my back and look at him in a way I must have learned somewhere—where?—with my lips not smiling but ready to smile, and my eyes narrowed. One leg is turned as if I'm ready to jump away from him. He sees all this. He smiles.

"Say, you're real cute."

We're walking over by the parking lot now. He touches my arm. Right away my heart trips, but I say nothing, I keep walking. High above us the tree branches are moving in the wind. It's cold for June. It's late—after eleven. The man is wearing a jacket, but I have on a sleeveless dress and there are goose pimples on my arms.

"Cold, huh?" he says.

He takes hold of my shoulders and leans toward me. This is to show me he's no kid, he's grown-up, this is how they do things; when he kisses me his grip on my shoulders gets tighter. "I better go back," I say to him. My voice is queer.

"What?" he says.

I am wearing a face like one of those faces pinned up in my room, and what if I lose it? This is not my face. I try to turn away from him.

He kisses me again. His breath smells like beer, maybe, it's like my father's breath, and my mind is empty; I can't think what to do. Why am I here? My legs feel numb, my fingers are cold. The man rubs my arms and says, "You should have a sweater or something. . . ."

He is waiting for me to say something, to keep on the way I was before. But I have forgotten how to do it. Before, I was Marian or one of the older girls; now I am just myself. I am fourteen. I think of Linda sleeping in my mother's lap, and something frightens me.

"Hey, what's wrong?" the man says.

He sees I'm afraid but pretends he doesn't. He comes to me again and embraces me, his mouth presses against my neck and shoulder, I feel as if I'm suffocating. "My car's over here," he says, trying to catch his breath. I can't move. Something dazzling and icy rises up in me, an awful fear, but I can't move and can't say anything. He is touching me with his hands. His mouth is soft but wants too much from me. I think, What is he doing? Do they all do this? Do I have to have it done to me too?

"You cut that out," I tell him.

He steps away. His chest is heaving and his eyes look like a dog's eyes, surprised and betrayed. The last thing I see of him is those eyes, before I turn and run back to the tavern.

IV

Jesse says, "Let's stop at this place. I been here a few times before."

It's the Lakeside Bar. That big old building with the grubby siding, and a big pink neon sign in front, and the cinder

driveway that's so bumpy. Yes, everything is the same. But
different too—smaller, dirtier. There is a custard stand nearby
with a glaring orange roof, and people are crowded around it.
That's new. I haven't been here for years.

"I feel like a beer," he says.

He smiles at me and caresses my arm. He treats me as if I
were something that might break; in my cheap linen maternity
dress I feel ugly and heavy. My flesh is so soft and thick that
nothing could hurt it.

"Sure, honey. Pa used to stop in here too."

We cross through the parking lot to the tavern. Wild grass
grows along the sidewalk and in the cracks of the sidewalk.
Why is this place so ugly to me? I feel as if a hand were pressing
against my chest, shutting off my breath. Is there some secret
here? Why am I afraid?

I catch sight of myself in a dusty window as we pass. My hair
is long, down to my shoulders. I am pretty, but my secret is that
I am pretty like everyone is. My husband loves me for this but
doesn't know it. I have a pink mouth and plucked darkened
eyebrows and soft bangs over my forehead; I know everything,
I have no need to learn from anyone else now. I am one of those
girls younger girls study closely, to learn from. On buses, in
five-and-tens, thirteen-year-old girls must look at me solemnly,
learning, memorizing.

"Pretty Sissie!" my mother likes to say when we visit, though
I told her how I hate that name. She is proud of me for being
pretty, but thinks I'm too thin. "You'll fill out nice, after the
baby," she says. Herself, she is fat and veins have begun to
darken on her legs; she scuffs around the house in bedroom
slippers. Who is my mother? When I think of her I can't think of
anything—do I love her or hate her, or is there nothing there?

Jesse forgets and walks ahead of me, I have to walk fast to
catch up. I'm wearing pastel-blue high heels—that must be
because I am proud of my legs. I have little else. Then he
remembers and turns to put out his hand for me, smiling to
show he is sorry. Jesse is the kind of young man thirteen-year-
old girls stare at secretly; he is not a man, not old enough, but
not a boy either. He is a year older than I am, twenty. When I

met him he was wearing a navy uniform and he was with a girlfriend of mine.

Just a few people sitting outside at the tables. They're afraid of rain—the sky doesn't look good. And how bumpy the ground is here, bare spots and little holes and patches of crab grass, and everywhere napkins and junk. Too many flies outside. Has this place changed hands? The screens at the windows don't fit right; you can see why flies get inside. Jesse opens the door for me and I go in. All bars smell alike. There is a damp, dark odor of beer and something indefinable—spilled soft drinks, pretzels getting stale? This bar is just like any other. Before we were married we went to places like this, Jesse and me and other couples. We had to spend a certain amount of time doing things like that—and going to movies, playing miniature golf, bowling, dancing, swimming—then we got married, now we're going to have a baby. I think of the baby all the time, because my life will be changed then; everything will be different. Four months from now. I should be frightened, but a calm laziness has come over me. It was so easy for my mother. . . . But it will be different with me because my life will be changed by it, and nothing ever changed my mother. You couldn't change her! Why should I think? Why should I be afraid? My body is filled with love for this baby, and I will never be the same again.

We sit down at a table near the bar. Jesse is in a good mood. My father would have liked him, I think; when he laughs Jesse reminds me of him. Why is a certain kind of simple, healthy, honest man always destined to lose everything? Their souls are as clean and smooth as the muscular line of their arms. At night I hold Jesse, thinking of my father and what happened to him— all that drinking, then the accident at the factory—and I pray that Jesse will be different. I hope that his quick, open, loud way of talking is just a disguise, that really he is someone else— slower and calculating. That kind of man grows old without jerks and spasms. Why did I marry Jesse?

Someone at the bar turns around, and it's a man I think I know—I have known. Yes. That man outside, the man I met outside. I stare at him, my heart pounding, and he doesn't see me. He is dark, his hair is neatly combed but is thinner than before; he is wearing a cheap gray suit. But is it the same man? He is standing with a friend and looking around, as if he doesn't like what he sees. He is tired too. He has grown years older.

Our eyes meet. He glances away. He doesn't remember—that frightened girl he held in his arms.

I am tempted to put my hand on Jesse's arm and tell him about that man, but how can I? Jesse is talking about trading in our car for a new one.... I can't move, my mind seems to be coming to a stop. Is that the man I kissed, or someone else? A feeling of angry loss comes over me. Why should I lose everything? Everything? Is it the same man, and would he remember? My heart bothers me, it's stupid to be like this: here I sit, powdered and sweet, a girl safely married, pregnant and secured to the earth, with my husband beside me. He still loves me. Our love keeps on. Like my parents' love, it will subside someday, but nothing surprises me because I have learned everything.

The man turns away, talking to his friend. They are weary, tired of something. He isn't married yet, I think, and that pleases me. Good. But why are these men always tired? Is it the jobs they hold, the kind of men who stop in at this tavern? Why do they flash their teeth when they smile, but stop smiling so quickly? Why do their children cringe from them sometimes— an innocent upraised arm a frightening thing? Why do they grow old so quickly, sitting at kitchen tables with bottles of beer? They are everywhere, in every house. All the houses in this neighborhood and all neighborhoods around here. Jesse is young, but the outline of what he will be is already in his face; do you think I can't see it? Their lives are like hands dealt out to them in their innumerable card games. You pick up the sticky cards, and there it is: there it is. Can't change anything, all you can do is switch some cards around, stick one in here, one over here ... pretend there is some sense, a secret scheme.

The man at the bar tosses some coins down and turns to go. I want to cry out to him, "Wait, wait!" But I cannot. I sit helplessly and watch him leave. Is it the same man? If he leaves I will be caught here, what can I do? I can almost hear my mother's shrill laughter coming in from outside, and some drawling remark of my father's—lifting for a moment above the music. Those little explosions of laughter, the slap of someone's hand on the damp table in anger, the clink of bottles accidentally touching—and there, there, my drunken aunt's voice, what is she saying? I am terrified at being left with them. I watch the man at the door and think that I could have loved him. I know it.

He has left, he and his friend. He is nothing to me, but suddenly I feel tears in my eyes. What's wrong with me? I hate everything that springs upon me and seems to draw itself down and oppress me in a way I could never explain to anyone.... I am crying because I am pregnant, but not with that man's child. It could have been his child, I could have gone with him to his car; but I did nothing, I ran away, I was afraid, and now I'm sitting here with Jesse, who is picking the label off his beer bottle with his thick squarish fingernails. I did nothing. I was afraid. Now he has left me here and what can I do?

I let my hand fall onto my stomach to remind myself that I am in love: with this baby, with Jesse, with everything. I am in love with our house and our life and the future and even this moment—right now—that I am struggling to live through.

Love and Death

ONE FEBRUARY a man named Marshall Hughes returned to his hometown to visit his father, a widower. This is not really the beginning of the story, that is, not the true beginning; but it would be his idea of the beginning.

His father lived alone with an older sister, who was his housekeeper and nurse. His name was also Marshall; he had been "big Marshall" at one time; now it was Marshall, Jr. who was big and his father who was small, though perhaps that was just a trick of the light. "No, keep that shut," his father kept saying, wagging his fingers toward the window. "It hurts my eyes." He sat up in bed, or in a big armchair near the bed, reading newspapers. He was a sharp, petulant old man who still had money, coming in from sources he was secretive about. Good for him, Marshall thought, as if his father's financial stability protected them both from something; good, let him stay that way, let him die happy.

The family house was large and drafty, Victorian in style. It struck Marshall as the prototype for houses in the cartoons of certain sophisticated magazines—cartoons meaningful only to a generation that has abandoned such houses, with nostalgia. His wife could look back at such a family home too. Marshall and his wife were well matched, both intelligent and pleasant and accustomed to certain delicacies that are the result of money—money kept invisible, of course. They had both belonged to the same kind of social group; they had gone to the same kind of schools, had the same kind of teachers. They were bound together before they had even met by the queer pleasing network of names that made up their world. If Fran hadn't known Peter Applegate, the cousin of a friend of Marshall's, it was no surprise that she had known Gloria van Buren, who was the fiancée of another friend.

Marshall and Fran had been married for nine years in 1967, and they had three children. Marshall worked for a company that made electrical parts for other companies—an excellent business. And he needed to work, too, because the money that came to him and Fran from various sources was not enough to live on, no more than seven or eight thousand a year, and he felt a strange satisfaction at the thought of "having to work," because there was a kind of settledness in that thought, a sense of safety. They went to a Presbyterian church mainly for their children's sakes. And they lived in an excellent suburb in the Midwest, several hundred miles from their families and, it would seem, centuries beyond the influence of the past.

So Marshall went back to visit. His conscience nudged him, his wife said, "Why don't you? . . . " and he made up his mind to return, since his father wasn't well and it would be only a matter of time until the old man died. Marshall was worried that his father knew this. That was perhaps why his father kept saying sourly, "I'm going back to the office when the weather clears. This winter lasts too long."

"How is Dr. Fitzgerald?" Marshall said.

"Competent."

"Is his son doing well?"

"I wouldn't know about his son."

In such ways was Marshall's generation shouldered aside, squeezed out, ignored. Marshall, sensitive to his father's pride in himself and his power, never pursued any subjects that led to the forbidden subterranean world of time and mortality and death.

On the first evening of his visit he called Fran and was relieved to hear her voice—that cool, sane, immensely charming voice—that summoned up for him the elegant world of his home, his friends, his children, his wife. Whatever his father's people had achieved, there was none of the comfort of the new generation in it: its victories were grim, like its furniture. There was little joy in that generation. "How are the children?" Marshall asked over the telephone. Tears often stung his eyes when he called home from his business trips, asking about the children. He thought of them mainly when he was away; when he was home they somehow eluded his concern.

"Oh, they all miss you. They love you," Fran said.

"Tell them to be good."

There were odd embarrassed moments when he and Fran could not think of the next thing to say. This was not in spite of their politeness with each other but because of it.

"Please take care of yourself," Marshall said.

"Take care of your*self*," his wife answered.

The next morning he went out for a walk. He was prepared to see a decline in the neighborhood, but things weren't too bad. One or two of the old places were obviously vacant, another looked as if it must be a nursing home of some kind. He walked for quite a while. It was a mild, sunny day, suggesting spring. Marshall went all the way down to the post office, which looked smaller than he remembered; there were four windows inside but only one was open, so he had to stand in line, and he noticed a woman near the front of the line who looked familiar. He stared at the back of her head. She wore a cloth coat of a cheap cut. A flimsy pink scarf was tied about her hair, which was in no particular style, though bleached blond. Marshall himself wore a topcoat of a good, dark material, gloves, and his expensive shoes were protected by rubbers. He was a tall, fairly handsome man of about forty. When the woman turned away from the window he caught his breath—yes, he did remember her.

She went over to one of the closed windows and set her purse down on the counter, so that she could put stamps on some envelopes. He watched her. She had a thin, frail, careless profile, not quite as he had remembered. He had remembered her as more solid. She licked the stamps and put them on the envelopes, as oblivious of anyone around her as if she were in her own home. Marshall wondered whom she was writing to. He saw that her coat was too short for her skirt, which hung down an inch or so in an untidy way.

He kept watching her and thought surely she would notice him. He was almost at the window when she picked up her purse and turned to go, without seeing him. So there was nothing for him to do but follow her—he didn't want to call after her, and he didn't want her to get away. At the door he caught up with her and said, "Hello, it's Cynthia, isn't it? Cynthia?"

She turned and stared at him. He saw that she recognized him, and he saw also the sudden recoiling gesture, the half-demure protestation, as if he had caught her at a bad moment. "Oh, Marshall," she said flatly. Her eyes were a cold, critical gray. "Marshall Hughes."

He laughed in embarrassment, breathlessly. "I was sure it was you...."

"Are you back home again?"

"I'm visiting."

The corners of her mouth turned up, but not in a smile. Her lips were quite red. He was struck by the flat, blatant, tired look she was giving him, a look that must have been defensive. Her bleached hair, inside the scarf, had a festive and rather ludicrous appearance, framing so cold a face. Several strands of hair had been combed down onto her forehead in a style that was a little too girlish for her. Her nose was long, as he had remembered it, giving her a slightly hungry, impatient look, her nostrils were thin, nervous, her mouth sharply and ironically defined, with the shadows of lines at its corners. It was an intelligent look somehow imposed upon an ordinarily pretty woman's frail, conventional face; her plucked, arched eyebrows could have belonged to any unstylish woman, but that mouth looked as if it might have something to say.

"Well, it was a surprise, seeing you.... I was sure it was you," Marshall said vaguely. He kept staring at her. The woman laughed in a short, humorless way, as if he had said something funny. "Do you still live around here? I mean—with your mother?"

"With my mother?" she laughed.

"Yes, I thought—I mean, weren't you living with her?" He was conscious of having said something stupid, having confused facts. She stared at him mockingly. "Well, where do you live? Nearby?"

"Yes, nearby," she said. Her irony was crude; he felt a pang of revulsion toward her.

"Well, how are you?" he asked.

"All right."

"I live in Kansas City now myself. My wife and I have three children."

"That's nice."

"And you, are you married?"

"I *was* married."

He tried to smile, wanting her to smile. There was something cruel about her mouth. He resented her coldness and the proud, indifferent way in which she kept him there, asking her questions. The very look of his clothes embarrassed him; she looked so shabby, so sad, and there was no failure of his own that he could offer her.

"Where are you going now?" he said suddenly.

"Back."

"Back?..."

"A few blocks away."

She moved toward the door. He followed, awkwardly. His eyes traveled down to the hem of her coat. There was something sloppy and intimate about that, something vulnerable. "Did you walk all the way down here from your father's house?" she said.

"Yes. It's a fine day for a walk."

They descended the steps. He had the idea she wanted to get away, and he was anxious to keep her with him. He had to think of something to say. Years ago they had been involved with each other casually, and he had forgotten her, and yet now he did not want her to get away; her indifference made him uneasy.

"Could I buy you some coffee? Or lunch?"

"It's too early for lunch."

"It's after eleven."

"I didn't get up till ten."

Again he experienced a slight tug of revulsion. He himself always got up at seven, never slept later. "Some coffee then, down the street?"

"All right."

They went to a small restaurant that Marshall believed he could remember. He felt a little awkward in it, in his topcoat and suit, but the woman sat down and unbuttoned her coat and let it fall over the back of her chair as if she were quite accustomed to the place. She wore a deep pink sweater that was too tight for her, and with the coat off she looked younger, more gentle. The sweater was cheap, its neck stretched and a little soiled, but it cast up onto her face a soft pink tone that was flattering.

"How have you been all these years?" Marshall said.

"I've gotten along."

"It was quite an accident, running into you...."

"Yes," she said sarcastically. She was not yet smiling. Marshall was relieved when the waitress came to take their order. They were sitting across from each other at a small, wobbly table. The woman had not pulled her chair in, conscious of the smallness of the table, and so she sat back awkwardly. Marshall smiled at her. He folded his own coat neatly over a nearby chair, and with a deft neat movement that looked unplanned he pushed the table in toward her and drew his own chair up to it.

"Yes, it's quite a surprise," he said, rubbing his hands.

"Christ, do you have to keep saying that?"

"But I mean it." He flushed, as if embarrassed by her profanity. She had so much strength, mysterious strength, and he had none. Her eyes regarded him with an unsurprised, calculating look, a look he had never seen in any other woman, and he noticed with satisfaction that there were slight hollows beneath those eyes. She was about thirty-five now. In a few years she would age suddenly and there would be no strength then, none of this sullen independence. He could not understand why he had followed her out of the post office.

"Did you say you were married now?" he said.

"Who wants to know?"

"I do. I want to know," he said weakly.

"Maybe I am, what difference does it make? Maybe I kicked him out. It's the same old story—anyway, what difference does it make?"

"You certainly don't mean it makes no difference to you."

"No. I mean to you."

"But I care. I'm anxious to hear about you."

"Oh, Christ," she said. Her eyes moved about behind him with a remote, amused look, as if she were searching out someone to laugh with her over him. Marshall remembered that—he remembered this woman breaking off their conversation to gaze around in that stupid indifferent placid way, pretending she had better things to think about.

"How is your brother?" he said.

"Which one, Davey?" she said, more gently.

"Yes, what happened to him?"

"He's the same, he's married now. Working a night shift."

"And what about your mother?"

"Look, you know my mother died a long time ago. You know that."

Marshall frowned. He did not remember, and yet in a way he did remember. There was something sluggish about him. The woman leaned forward, crossing her arms at the wrists; her wrists were girlish and delicate. She said, "You certainly do remember. You're lying."

"What, lying?"

"You're lying." She smiled sourly. "Now tell me about your wife."

"But I want to talk about you."

She laughed. The waitress brought their coffee and Marshall resented the distraction. The woman said, "You want to talk about me? Why the hell about me? Do you have a cigarette?"

He took out his package of cigarettes at once, anxious to please her. She was so indifferent, so careless, that she might suddenly push her chair back and walk out, and he would not be able to run after her. Unwrapping the package, jerking the red cellophane strip around, he felt her eyes on his fingers and was nervous, thinking that there was something vaguely obscene about what he was doing. He finally got a cigarette to

stick out and she took it. Lighting her cigarette was another awkward thing but at last it was accomplished. He felt strangely weak before her sullen, indifferent silence.

"So your brother is still in town?"

"Yes. You liked him, didn't you?" she said curiously.

"Why do you ask?"

"You liked him because he kept his nose out of our business. That was what you liked about him, and what you didn't like about my mother."

This stirred some memory in him; he nodded slowly. It would be better to agree.

"Your own mother, of course, was a bitch of another type. We won't mention her."

"You never saw my mother."

"I certainly did."

"When did you see her?"

"My God, you know very well—we saw her one day downtown, the two of us. We saw her with some other fat bitches, all dressed up, and you pointed her out to me. I remember that."

Marshall was a little shocked, but he made himself smile. "But if you only saw her . . ."

"I knew all about her. You told me. And is your father still alive?"

"Yes."

"You're here visiting him?"

"Yes."

"How long are you going to stay?" But then she tapped ashes from the cigarette onto the floor, nervously, as if conscious of having said something wrong but not wanting to correct it.

"A few more days."

"Then you're going back—to Kansas City?"

"To St. Louis," he said slowly.

She smiled. "Oh, St. Louis, you live in St. Louis?"

He pushed the coffee cup aside, he had no desire for coffee. He watched her impatiently. "Well, never mind about that," he said. "What about you, are you married?"

"In a way."

"What does that mean?"

Love and Death

She shrugged her shoulders. With her thumb and two fingers she picked up the coffee cup, a precise little gesture of affectation that struck him. She was a pretty woman in spite of everything. There was something hungry and cynical about her, she had a way of looking steadily at him that no other woman had, yet still she was pretty in a way. Her hair was disheveled but clean, gleaming in the light from the window. He liked her hair. It was vulgar, that color, and showed that she wasn't so clever after all—what a phony color!—but still he liked it on her.

He said, "Your hair looks good."

She lifted one shoulder in a lazy gesture of indifference.

"You used to wear it long? . . . "

They sat for a while in silence. Then she said, "I have to leave now." She spoke stubbornly, as if arguing. Marshall said, hardly knowing what he would hear, "But where are you going?" Home, she told him. He asked what that meant; whom did she live with? She told him it was none of his business, was it? He could feel his heartbeat quicken and he asked her the question again. By herself, she said, she lived by herself; but she worked in the evening and she had some things to do, she had to wash things, go shopping. He asked her if he could come along. She swore in a gentle, weary, unsurprised way, staring at him; she shook her head. Marshall fumbled for the pack of cigarettes and put them away nervously. The woman kept looking at him. He felt guilty suddenly and had to fight down an impulse to look over his shoulder, to see if anyone had heard.

They had met many years ago in a bar. She had been with one crowd, he with another. He had been introduced to her, asked her her name and telephone number, and a few days later had called her up. She had lived then in a big ugly house, a very old house. He remembered that house, and his shyness, and the girl's carefully made-up, mocking face, and the very high heels of the shoes she wore.

"No, I have to leave," she said.

He helped her with her coat and put on his own, not bothering to button it. He caught up with her at the door.

"Where are you going now?"

"I told you, home."

"Where is that?"

"Close by." She looked sideways at him and smiled. "Do you want to walk me there?"

Her apartment was in a six-story building, an old building. Marshall had a vague impression of it but for some reason did not want to see more. He was in a hurry, his heartbeat was choked and rapid. On the stairs his feet ached to carry him up fast, faster than he was going. The woman kept glancing sideways at him, ironically. On the bannister her bare hand moved in jerks, a few inches at a time, and he watched this movement out of the corner of his eye.

At her door he watched as she put the key into the lock. This startled him, the way it went into the lock, forcing itself in and then quite at ease there, turning easily. He felt weak. She said, "You should go back down now, back down," indicating with a jerk of her head the stairs behind them.

"Couldn't I stay awhile? Talk to you?"

"Oh, talk, what do you want to talk about? Talk!" she said in disgust.

"Could I see you later, then? Tonight?"

She had opened the door. She seemed impatient to get away, yet something made her linger; like him, she felt a peculiar tugging between them, an undefined force that would not release her. Marshall waited. He remembered her making him wait, in the old days, this sluttish girl who had nothing, really nothing, except what men like himself wanted to give her. Her profile, nearly overwhelmed by the bunch of blond hair that looked resilient and unreal as a dummy's wig, put him in mind of his wife's profile for an instant. But the two women were quite different. His wife had a healthy, wholesome, friendly face; she played golf with women like herself, she dressed with simple, excellent taste. What reminded him of her, in this woman, was no more than the fact that he was standing close to the woman. He had been close to few people in his life.

"Could I come in now? For a few minutes?"

He was perspiring, he was not himself. Her fingers, tapping impatiently on the doorknob, seemed to be tapping against his body, teasing him. He said, begging, "I won't stay long."

He had no impression of the room except that it was small. Windows at one end with their shades drawn; mingled odors of food. He felt as if he had broken through to something, liberated and floating in a way he could not control. It was a strange feeling. All his life he had said silently to others, Let me alone, don't touch me, talk to me but don't touch me, because I'm afraid of—afraid of what? He was afraid, that was enough. He and his wife said this to each other, silently, Let me alone, don't touch me— Cynthia took off her coat angrily and looked around at him. "I don't know why the hell you're here. Do you think it's still fifteen years ago?"

This shocked him. "Fifteen years? Nothing ever happened—that long ago—" he said dizzily. He moved toward her. He put his arms around her, clumsy in his coat, and she stood there with a kind of contemptuous patience, a mockery of patience. "I don't think so much time went by—"

"All right."

"I've thought about you a great deal—"

"All right, sure."

"Could we go in there? Is that another room, could we go in there?"

"You'll have to give me some money."

"Yes."

"You used to give me money, right?"

"I don't know, yes, maybe—I don't remember. Did I give you money?" he asked, surprised. He thought about that. "No, I never gave you money. It wasn't like that."

"Certainly."

"I gave you money?"

"I was in love with you, sure, but I was never stupid," she said in her flat, amused voice. "What makes you think I'm stupid? Because I'm poor? Because I don't dress like your wife?"

"No, you're not stupid."

"Then give me some money, now."

He took out his wallet. He had the idea that she was degrading him in this manner, degrading herself, in order to block out the memory of their love together—that was all right, he under-

stood her. She was protecting herself. He took out a number of
bills and, smiling foolishly, handed them to her. She took them
and began to smile too. "Yes, you gave me money," she said.
"Otherwise why should I have bothered with you?"

They went into the other room. Marshall stopped thinking.
When he began to think again, a while later, his mind was
precise and he looked around the room as if memorizing it. And
when they went back out into the larger room, the woman
yawning and indifferent at his side, he looked around that room
too. He saw the cheap modern furniture, blond wood and green
cushions, a table with a formica top, flowered drapes, a worn-
out rug. He felt dislocated and quite empty. The room was so
ugly that it saddened him.

"Let me see you again. I want to see you again," he said.

"You can take me to dinner tonight."

"Dinner? Really?"

"Yes, dinner. Good-by."

He had to make excuses at home, saying he had met an old
friend on his walk. When his aunt asked who this friend was, in
her dry, suspicious spinster's voice, he really could not think of
a name for several seconds. It was embarrassing. His father
luckily paid no attention; he was reading newspapers. Marshall
watched the old man, jealous of the attention he paid to all those
papers while his son had traveled so far to see him.... He
noticed the way the old man pursed his lips, reading, working
his lips as if mumbling secret words to himself, flexing his jaws.
There was something outlandish and too intimate, almost indecent, in the way he worked his lips. Marshall looked away. Then
he looked back, fascinated. His father moved his narrow lips as
he read, not shaping silent words, but simply out of habit, as a
way of caressing himself.

Marshall called his wife again that afternoon. He asked how
the children were, how Fran was. Fine, fine. But there was
something—one of the boys had cut his leg. Out playing. No, he
hadn't been pushed, it was just an accident. Marshall tried to
keep talking and listening. It was easier to talk than to listen. His
wife's voice was very far away; the book-lined study in which
he sat seemed somehow very far away too, its indistinct walls

confining the air of another, older time into which he had
stepped accidentally. And he would step out of it again in a
moment.

When he came to the woman's apartment that evening he
was very nervous. She said, amused, "What's wrong with you?
In the post office you were another person, now you're back to
what you were fifteen years ago."

"But what was I fifteen years ago?"

"What you are now."

"But what is that?"

"I can't tell you. How can I describe you to yourself?"

They had dinner in a dark, ordinary restaurant. A big air-
conditioning unit was perched up above them on the wall, silent
and ominous; Marshall had the feeling that it was about to
topple off and fall on them. He was very uneasy, very nervous.
As they ate their dinner, uninteresting food he barely tasted, he
kept asking her about what she had meant, earlier—"Did I
really give you money?"

"Yes, of course."

"And you took it?"

"Why wouldn't I take it?"

"Do you remember how we met? The first time?"

"You came in a certain bar to make a telephone call. Your
friends were outside, waiting. You saw me and asked me
something—asked me for change for the telephone. You talked
to me. Then you went out and told your friends to drive on
without you, and you came back in, and the two of us went
somewhere...." She paused, thinking. "Yes. We went to this
place I sometimes stayed in, a flat a friend of mine rented."

"But it wasn't that way at all," Marshall said quickly.

"No? How was it, then?"

"Didn't I call you up later? Didn't I get your telephone
number?"

"Yes. You asked me for my number, after we went back to
that flat."

"Only after that?"

"Yes, what do you think? Don't you remember?"

He stared at her. Slowly, reluctantly, he began to remember.

She had been a thin girl in a black dress, trying to look older than she was. She had been sitting at a table near the telephone booth, in a corner. "So we went back to a flat? A friend of yours had a flat?"

"Yes. We only went there once."

"It wasn't someone else?"

"You mean, instead of you? There were other men, yes, but it was you as well, you were one of them."

"But you say we only went there once?"

"I lived at home then. I was with my family."

"Yes. I remember that, of course."

"You remember my mother?"

"Yes."

Her mother had screamed at him one day, a fat drunken woman who accused him of taking advantage of her daughter. Marshall had had to push her away, she had tried to strike him and scratch his face.... Yes, he remembered that fat bitch of a woman; he was glad she was dead.

"You were glad when she died," Cynthia said.

"I wouldn't say that...."

"Yes, I would say it," Cynthia said flatly.

After dinner he said, "Why haven't you done more with yourself? Why are you still living in the same neighborhood after so long?"

"I don't have any ambitions."

"You never got married?"

"I didn't say that."

"Or have children? None of that?"

"But that isn't of any interest to you. You know that."

"What do you mean?"

"My real life isn't of any interest to you, it's nothing. What do you care if I did get married? All right, I did. Then it was ended, like that. No children. I'm not like people you know, I don't have any ambition. I don't care."

"It seems impossible...."

"But I wouldn't want to be your wife. I wouldn't want that."

"You wouldn't want to marry me?"

She laughed. "No, I wouldn't. But I didn't mean that. I mean that I wouldn't want to be the woman who is your wife now—I wouldn't want to be that woman."

Marshall had to think for a moment, recalling his wife. His heart fluttered as if he were in danger.

"You are two very different people," he said slowly.

They went back to her apartment. Near as he could come to her, she always held him off, in a sense, observing him coldly. He could never get past the icy circle of her mind; she was always thinking about him, holding him apart from her. "What was your husband like?" he said. "Like anyone. An ordinary man," she said. "He didn't have money, did he?" he said. "Of course not," she said, "nobody has money except you." He wished he could see her face, to see what she meant by that.

He was reluctant to leave her; he wanted to stay all night, but his father would wonder about him; a vision of that ugly old mansion rose in his mind and made him stir guiltily. In the dark, it was difficult for him to know who he was. And yet it was a darkness that was not really unfamiliar.

She snapped on the light. "I hope that from now on we can be friends, and forget each other."

"Why should we forget each other?"

"But you forgot me before. You never sent me any money."

"I didn't know you wanted money."

"You must have known. Everyone wants money," she said, without bothering to emphasize any of her words, just pronouncing them. He felt that she did not believe this, that it was nothing more than a means of holding him off. She had a strange face, this woman, an unhappy, brooding, and yet careless look that her make-up seemed to parody. He was uncomfortable, beneath her gaze. She might have been assessing any man, himself or a stranger, making no distinction between them.

"I can send you some money, when I get home."

She said nothing. Marshall went on, anxiously, "I want to ask you something before I leave. Why do you think I came over to you?"

"When, today? Or the first time?"

"Either time."

"Because you liked me, I suppose."

"But why...why do you think I like you?"

She shut her eyes wearily. "You mean, it seems crazy to you that you should be here? All right, yes, it is crazy. But I do know why you're here, as a matter of fact."

"Why?"

"Don't you know? Can't you guess?"

He felt a slight pang of terror, at the very softness of her voice. "What? What is it?"

"Do you remember what you said to me, the first time we met? I mean after we went back to that flat."

"No. What did I say?"

"You asked me my age, how long I had been doing that sort of thing. You asked me about the men I knew. You were very curious, very excited. Of course, you were a young man then—"

"And you were young too," he said nervously.

"Not in the same way. You were always pestering me then, back then—don't you remember?"

"I think you're mixing me up with someone else."

"Oh, hell," she laughed. "Go on home, then."

"No, please. Couldn't you be mixing me up with someone else?"

"I don't forget things. There was a time when I loved you, and this time is closed off from what came before and what came after, and I can look back at it and remember it perfectly. What's strange is that you don't remember it."

"But I want to remember it...."

"You asked me about the other men. You came to see me all the time, it was crazy. You wrote me letters though we lived in the same city, you gave me presents—jewelry and clothes—you were always bothering me. You liked to tease me about those other men, you'd sit on the edge of the bed and ask me questions, lots of questions. Don't you remember that?"

"No," Marshall said dully. But even as she spoke he knew it was true, and a sense of revulsion and anger stirred inside him.

"What do you remember, then?"

"I asked you your telephone number and I called you up a

few days later," he said, as if reciting something. "I went to your house—your brother was working on his car, in the driveway. You introduced me to your mother. I think it was a Sunday, Sunday afternoon."

"But we met on Saturday night."

"This was the next day. You introduced me to your mother."

"Did you like that?"

"I thought it was nice."

"But you must have known I did it to make fun. My mother was always drunk and I wanted to see how you'd act. Didn't you know that?"

Marshall was silent for a moment. Then he said, "But I don't remember any flat."

"Of course you remember."

"I think you're mixing me up with someone else."

"So, you called me up, you met my mother, what else?"

"And then...we started seeing each other."

"What did we do?"

"We went to movies, out to dinner. We went dancing." He thought about this, watching her uneasily. Then his mind cleared and he remembered that it was Fran he had done those things with.

"We went to rooms, to hotels," she said. "We drove around in your car."

"But you didn't seem to mind—"

"Why should I mind? You paid me."

"I remember that vaguely—"

"Vaguely, hell!"

She wanted him to leave but he was reluctant. He clutched at something: "But you lied to me too. You said you had to work tonight."

"Did I?"

"I think you said that."

"Yes, I work some evenings. I have a real job, I'm a hostess in a restaurant. But I took tonight off."

"For me?"

She shrugged her shoulders. Of course, he had given her money—but he did not think that was significant.

She saw him to the door. He turned to leave, his face burning.

It seemed to him... that something was wrong, something was threatening. When he was out in the hall she said, in her low teasing voice, "Here's something else you won't remember either—how when we went out you talked to me about my life, how I was trapped, I had nowhere to go, no future—I'd get diseased or some maniac would kill me— You said you loved me, because I was just a tramp and my mother was a drunk and so on—and you really did love me, but you don't remember any of it."

He made up his mind not to see her again, and the rest of his visit was spent in the old house. He sat with his father while the old man read his papers, Marshall himself reading a newspaper, the two of them silent and bewitched by what they read, and quite oblivious of each other. Except from time to time Marshall glanced at his father and saw that queer silent smacking of his father's lips—again and again—and his very bowels seemed stirred by it, stirred to anger. He called Fran, as if in desperation. But her voice was distant and what she spoke of seemed trivial. He wondered whether, if he put the receiver down gently, he might cut her out of his life altogether.

But of course this was nonsense. He was frightened at himself, at such thoughts. He had never in his life had such thoughts before.... And he found himself recalling certain moments of his love-making with that other woman, when he had thought of the possibility of her being diseased and of the great risk he was taking. It excited him, to think of this risk. Yet that was all nonsense, all disgusting. He was anxious to return home again.

A strange thing: he began seeing things that weren't there. Or, rather, a foreign vision imposed itself upon them, distorting them violently. One day his aunt—a woman of over sixty, hefty, vague, sour, very religious—was cutting meat when he walked into the kitchen. He was eager to talk with someone. She was slicing pieces of raw meat off a large, fatty hunk, and something about her wet, bloodstained fingers, and the tender pink meat, and the flashing of the knife terrified him. He was almost sick. His aunt did not care to talk and so he passed on through to the breakfast room and so safely away.... And another time at dinner he watched his father finish a glass of water, lifting it to his mouth and drinking in rather audible gasps until nothing was left, and Marshall thought: in just that way do people make love. It was not a thought that made sense. But it flashed clearly through his mind as he watched his father empty the crystal goblet.

He was not going to call Cynthia, but on the last day he did. They talked vaguely as if they had nothing in common. "Now I'm leaving. I probably won't see you again," he said cautiously. She said, "Yes, good luck. I hope your father is well." The mention of his father startled him, for certainly she was thinking that he had to be back—didn't he?—when his father got worse, when his father died, he had to be back then and he'd call her up, wouldn't he? He was trapped. So he said irritably, "Of course he's well. And now I'm going back. You'll see—a person can do one thing and then do the opposite thing, it doesn't matter. I won't be seeing you again."

He arrived back home in time for a dinner party. Everything was confused, gaily muddled. He had to tell his wife about the visit while they dressed, the two of them already late, a little giddy with the prospect of a familiar excellent evening before them. Marshall felt good; he felt quite safe. He kept chatting to his wife about all sorts of things, and she in her turn chatted about the latest news, which friends she had had lunch with, who was in town. He was amazed at how rich and complex and yet safe this life was, out here.

It was several hours before he even remembered that woman. At about ten o'clock they went in to dinner, into an elegant dining room, and their host opened a bottle of wine. He worked at the cork, making jokes, and seemed to be looking at Marshall as if Marshall were somehow the main point of the joke. Marshall felt sweat break out on his body. He couldn't quite make out the joke, but he did watch with a kind of terror the man's fingers working at the cork. Something was straining for release, something threatened to spurt out— Then the moment passed, it was over. Wine was poured into glasses in an ordinary way and there was nothing behind it.

For more than a week he continued as his usual self, and then he had an overwhelming impulse to write to Cynthia. He was at his office and he used business stationery, with the firm's Kansas City address on it. Let her see it. He wanted to give her proof of how successful he was. He wrote her a long, aimless, unplanned letter. It was chatty and superficial. Rereading it, however, he saw that the letter was quite obviously a disguise for something left unsaid—but he did not know what that was.

She did not reply to it.

Angered, he wrote again. This time he typed out the letter, on the same stationery. He asked her specific questions, about her ex-husband, about her "present mode of living," about her plans for the future. This letter was five pages long, an inspired letter. Marshall had never been able to write letters to anyone and had always telephoned if he had anything to say, so he was both pleased and a little disturbed that he could write so much to that woman. She was so unimportant, after all.

He included in the letter a check for several hundred dollars, and this time she replied. She thanked him for the money and wrote a few more lines, just to be polite. He was enraged at this but did not know what he had expected. So he wrote again at once, ending his letter: "Write back. I want to hear anything you have to say. Tell me about your job, about your mother or anything."

As an afterthought he took some bills out of his wallet and slid them into the envelope. His fingers were shaking.

Her letter came a few weeks later. In ball-point ink she had written a few lines, mentioning the money. This was followed by a paragraph in pencil, evidently written at a later time, in which she did talk about her mother: "You both hated each other and yet you were curious about each other. She knew you had money and, who knows, she might end up with it herself—I'm sure that crossed her mind. And then, on the day she died, you had to hear everything about her and go right into her bedroom, though the poor woman had been in that bed a few hours before. And yet you two never really met except that one time and never talked to each other."

He read this and a fine dizzying film passed before his eyes. In such flat, blatant language, just as she spoke . . . what had she told him? Her mother's bedroom, what about that? He tried to remember but could not. Something seemed to be blocking his memory. So he wrote her again, careful to include a check this time (she had reproved him for sending money through the mail), and asked for more information. He waited eagerly for her to reply. But no reply came. He wondered if she had received the letter. He kept waiting, waiting for her to answer. When his wife mentioned that she had heard from a friend in Boston, Marshall turned to stare at her in amazement. Because it seemed to him that she was about to confront him with her knowledge of Cynthia, and he was excited not by the danger of his position but by the possibility of her having discovered a letter, having somehow intercepted it, and he would have allowed that if it meant he would at last hear from Cynthia.... But no, the letter was truly from a friend, no irony was intended.

He wrote Cynthia again, begging and demanding that she answer. He sent her another check, this time for a thousand dollars. Angry, frustrated, he believed that she was blackmailing him and that she was a criminal; she ought to be arrested and punished. Certainly she ought to be punished: she was a prostitute, taking money from men. He hated her for her power over him and thought of revenge he might take upon her. He would do something, yes. He did hate her. And yet when her letter arrived his heart pounded as if he were indeed in love.

She wrote: "You asked me about her room, about that apartment. You remember the living room—the ugly furniture, the religious junk on the walls. All right. My mother died of some kind of seizure while she was in bed. I went in and found her. Her face was awful, it was not her face at all or any human face. Her eyes were bulging. I went up to her and saw how it was, and so I went out to call the police. That night you came over. You wanted to take care of me, you said I must be very upset. You looked around the living room and asked me if you could see the bedroom. So I took you in. You were very quiet, you seemed sad. In that room you asked me about her, whether she'd known about me, how she had died, and you were very interested in hearing about it—because you hated her, I think that was the reason. Then you comforted me and put your arms around me, and you insisted that we make love in that bed. You insisted upon that. You begged me. I didn't care because a person can do one thing and then do the opposite, as you know. I didn't have a guilty conscience, because I had been good to my mother, so I didn't care. And while we were making love you asked me about her, about her eyes in particular, which had especially frightened me. Like what? What did she look like? you kept asking. Doesn't this all make you laugh now?"

He was sickened by that letter. "She's lying," he muttered, but at once he thought, "Yes, it was like that."

He reread the letter many times, as if hypnotized by it. He tried to get past the words and into that room again, into the man he had been, who had asked such things and had gotten such pleasure out of them, but what blocked him from entering into that man was not the gap of years between them but some terrified knowledge that he did not dare do that. He did not dare. Better for him to rip up the letter, forget it. Wasn't she blackmailing him already?

And he thought of the letters he had written her so recklessly. Certainly she could use them to blackmail him.

Feeling her power over him across the country, he began to send her things, to buy her off. He sent her some clothes, having them mailed from expensive shops. That ought to please her. And notes with checks enclosed now and then, anything to buy her off, shut her up. What was terrifying was that he had no way of knowing whether this would work, or whether his desperation would make her more bold. Suppose she wrote directly to his wife? Or went to see his father? He had given so much of himself to her, surrendered so much of his power, that she could destroy him if she wanted. And she never replied. What did her silence mean? He reread her letters again and again, lingering over the last one, sometimes lured into an erotic daze and unable to rouse himself—it was so vivid now, so real. Yes, he had certainly done that. He wanted very much to do it again. With Fran he was always too busy to talk, too tired to make love to her, and certainly this was a relief to her—she was not that kind of woman at all—yet his thoughts were preoccupied with his own body and its needs.

He thought, "When my father dies I'll have to go back."
But his father did not die. His father never wrote either. He
had to depend for news upon his own telephone calls, put
through every Sunday evening. But he kept calling, faithfully.
He had become quite a dutiful son now, at the age of forty.
And finally Fran said again, "Would you like to visit your
father?"

He had overheard her talking with a woman friend one
evening, about how hard it was for men to take their fathers'
deaths. Fran had been assured that, according to Freud, it was
the single most traumatic event in a man's life; therefore, with
Marshall, she had to be as sympathetic as possible. His father
was not dying yet, Marshall thought, but that seemed almost
irrelevant. The old man would die someday...perhaps. He
pretended to think it over, knowing all along that he would give
in and take the trip. It had been nearly a year since the last visit.

Planning for it, he was overcome with a strange lassitude. He
would sit in his office and daydreams forced themselves into his
mind, as if he were being invaded by an alien, sordid force. He
thought of that old flat—which he now remembered clearly—
and its clutter: the dishes and underwear lying around, the
stockings drying in the bathroom; he thought of Cynthia and
what they had done together, which was not at all what he and
Fran had ever done together; he thought of the money he had
given that woman—it gave him pleasure to think of this—and,
lingeringly, he thought of her mother's death, which seemed
somehow to have taken place in the room with Cynthia and
himself. He was tremendously excited by this. He did not
understand it except to know that his body ached and seemed
now to be the body of another man. It was hard to maneuver it,
even to walk normally. He felt that any moment he might take a
false step, lunge off a sidewalk, bump someone. It was especially difficult to get through an evening with friends because,
where once he had been able to imagine himself as a certain
person, a successful business executive named Marshall Hughes,
now he felt that his internal self had become impatient, as if
waking from a long sleep, and might demand recognition.

The more his wife chatted about her friends and her bridge

circle, the more he felt that he loved her and could forget about her. When she talked about the children she was his wife, she belonged to him. She could never disturb him. Their affection was the affection of friends or companions, there was nothing passionate or brutal about it. He loved her. He hated that woman who was blackmailing him, and his body stirred at the thought of her, excited and furious at the same time. Yes, he had to have his revenge on her! He could not spend the rest of his life being blackmailed by a prostitute.... And yet, at this thought he would fall off into another of his disturbing dreams, recalling her, shaking his head at the memory of her hair and her plucked eyebrows—she was so common, really—and he had to urge himself awake to get where he was going, to do his work or to reply to his wife, who had begun to look at him a little strangely. So he decided to go back to visit his father.

He wanted to talk with her just once more, to say good-by. He would ask her for his letters. Why should she have anything against him? He was prepared to write out one more check, a sizable check, and all she would have to do would be to return his indiscreet letters and promise to forget him... it disturbed him to think that she might not forget him. And yet it excited him. On the plane he sat rigid, thinking. It was not quite thinking, perhaps, but planning, groping, inching along as if with his fingers. Of his father he hardly thought; the old man could take care of himself. What did that old man, or any other old man, know of the terrible dangers of life? Marshall nearly wept to think that he had so many years to go before he drifted into the sanctity of old age and death, the final safety, far safer than his suburban life and marriage. "Those old bastards don't let us through. They block things up. They don't move along," he thought in anguish.

His body writhed at the thought of Cynthia, her silent stubborn face, all the secrets she possessed—and at the thought of her body too, which he did certainly hate for its power over him, and had always hated—but there was nothing he could do. His heart pounded strangely. The stewardess leaned over him and assured him that everything was fine, they would be landing soon. Her pretty, proper face reminded him of his wife's face and he was impatient to get rid of her. He did not want to be distracted.

At the airport he took a taxi out at once to her neighborhood. But, for some reason, he asked to be let out a few blocks away. His hands were shaking, he was quite terrified. The cab driver was silent, as if in the presence of a sick man. Marshall's palms were damp with sweat, his entire body was damp, he seemed in a kind of vague, outraged daze. He was both lunging forward and holding himself back. He did not think at all, except to say to himself: "I'll talk her out of it." He walked the several blocks quickly. Down on the sidewalk, he stood for a while staring up at her lighted windows. Again he thought of nothing, not really. His body seemed to be thinking for him. It was protecting all the people who stood behind him, his father, his family, the people who worked for him, the people who were his friends. After a while he went inside and up the stairs to her door. He knocked on it. The knocking echoed jarringly in his brain and he thought of all the letters he had written—so recklessly, and yet perhaps on purpose?—and he thought of the hours he had spent with that woman, losing himself in her, groveling in the darkness of her body and the mystery of her soiled, ugly life, and yet coming from her with no knowledge and no affection, nothing.

The door opened. A child of about twelve, a girl, leaned out and looked at him. "Whatdaya want?" she said.

"Who lives here?" Marshall said. "What—what happened to— Where is—?"

"You want my father?" the girl said.

"But—when did you move in here?"

"Last summer." The girl looked at him, chewing gum. She seemed to see something interesting in his face. "You looking for somebody else?"

He turned away. He began to weep. His breath came in gi at gulps, as if he had just saved himself from a terrible danger. Descending the stairs, he grasped the bannister and remembered the way she had held onto it, indifferently, lightly, and how, even then, he had wanted to reach over and snap her wrist. But it was better not to think of that. He would never think of it again, nor would he think of his having come to this apartment straight from the airport, drenched in sweat, his body stiffened and monstrous with desire; he would not think of that. When he felt better he called another taxi and went to his father's house.

The old man was about the same, perhaps getting senile. Not much change. He did not die for six years, and then his death was sudden. Marshall was nearly forty-seven at this time and his own health was unsteady, so he had an excuse not to go to his own father's funeral. But no one in the family believed him, even Fran did not really believe him, and they held it against him all his life: he was a man who had not even honored his own father's death.

By the River

H ELEN THOUGHT: "Am I in love again, some new kind of
love? Is that why I'm here?"

She was sitting in the waiting room of the Yellow Bus Lines
station; she knew the big old room with its dirty tile floor and its
solitary telephone booth in the corner and its candy machine
and cigarette machine and popcorn machine by heart. Everything was familiar, though she had been gone for five months,
even the old woman with the dyed red hair who sold tickets
and had been selling them there, behind that counter, for as long
as Helen could remember. Years ago, before Helen's marriage,
she and her girl friends would be driven into town by someone's
father and after they tired of walking around town they would
stroll over to the bus station to watch the buses unload. They
were anxious to see who was getting off, but few of the passengers who got off stayed in Oriskany—they were just passing
through, stopping for a rest and a drink, and their faces seemed
to say that they didn't think much of the town. Nor did they
seem to think much of the girls from the country who stood
around in their colorful dresses and smiled shyly at strangers,
not knowing any better: they were taught to be kind to people,
to smile first, you never knew who it might be. So now Helen
was back in Oriskany, but this time she had come in on a bus

herself. Had ridden alone, all the way from the city of Derby, all alone, and was waiting for her father to pick her up so she could go back to her old life without any more fuss.

It was hot. Flies crawled languidly around; a woman with a small sickly-faced baby had to keep waving them away. The old woman selling tickets looked at Helen as if her eyes were drawn irresistibly that way, as if she knew every nasty rumor and wanted to let Helen know that she knew. Helen's forehead broke out in perspiration and she stood, abruptly, wanting to dislodge that old woman's stare. She went over to the candy machine but did not look at the candy bars; she looked at herself in the mirror. Her own reflection always made her feel better. Whatever went on inside her head—and right now she felt nervous about something—had nothing to do with the way she looked, her smooth gentle skin and the faint freckles on her forehead and nose and the cool, innocent green of her eyes; she was just a girl from the country and anyone in town would know that, even if they didn't know her personally, one of those easy, friendly girls who hummed to themselves and seemed always to be glancing up as if expecting something pleasant, some deliberate surprise. Her light brown hair curled back lazily toward her ears, cut short now because it was the style; in high school she had worn it long. She watched her eyes in the mirror. No alarm there, really. She would be back home in an hour or so. Not her husband's home, of course, but her parents' home. And her face in the mirror was the face she had always seen—twenty-two she was now, and to her that seemed very old, but she looked no different from the way she had looked on her wedding day five years ago.

But it was stupid to try to link together those two Helens, she thought. She went back to the row of seats and sat heavily. If the old woman was still watching, she did not care. A sailor in a soiled white uniform sat nearby, smoking, watching her but not with too much interest; he had other girls to recall. Helen opened her purse and looked inside at nothing and closed it again. The man she had been living with in the city for five months had told her it was stupid—no, he had not used that word; he said something fancy like "immature"—to confuse herself with the child she had been, married woman as she was now, and a mother, an adulterous married woman.... And the word *adulterous* made her lips turn up in a slow bemused smile, the first flash of incredulous pride one might feel when told at last the disease that is going to be fatal. For there were so many diseases and only one way out of the world, only one death and so many ways to get to it. They were like doors, Helen thought dreamily. You walked down a hallway like those in movies, in huge wealthy homes, crystal chandeliers and marble floors and...great sweeping lawns...and doors all along those hallways; if you picked the wrong door you had to go through it. She was dreamy, drowsy. When thought became too much for her—when he had pestered her so much about marrying him, divorcing her husband and marrying him, always him!—she had felt so sleepy she could not listen. If she was not interested in a word her mind wouldn't hear it but made it blurred and strange, like words half heard in dreams or through some thick substance. You didn't have to hear a word if you didn't want to.

So she had telephoned her father the night before and told him the 3:15 bus and now it was 3:30; where was he? Over the telephone he had sounded slow and solemn, it could have been a stranger's voice. Helen had never liked telephones because you could not see smiles or gestures and talking like that made her tired. Listening to her father, she had felt for the first time since she had run away and left them all behind—husband, baby girl, family, in-laws, the minister, the dreary sun-bleached look of the land—that she had perhaps died and only imagined she was running away. Nobody here trusted the city; it was too big. Helen had wanted to go there all her life, not being afraid of anything, and so she had gone, and was coming back; but it was an odd feeling, this dreamy ghostliness, as if she were really dead and coming back in a form that only looked like herself.... She was bored, thinking of this, and crossed her bare legs. The sailor crushed out a cigarette in the dirty tin ashtray and their eyes met. Helen felt a little smile tug at her lips. That was the trouble, she knew men too well. She knew their eyes and their gestures—like the sailor rubbing thoughtfully at his chin now, as if he hadn't shaved well enough but really liked to feel his own skin. She knew them too well and had never figured out why: her sister, four years older, wasn't like that. But to Helen the same man one hundred times or one hundred men, different men, seemed the same. It was wrong, of course, because she had been taught it and believed what she had been taught; but she could not understand the difference. The sailor watched her but she looked away, half closing her eyes. She had no time for him. Her father should be here now, he would be here in a few minutes, so there was no time; she would be home in an hour. When she thought of her father, the ugly bus station with its odor of tobacco and spilled soft drinks seemed to fade away— she remembered his voice the night before, how gentle and soft she had felt listening to that voice, giving in to the protection he represented. She had endured his rough hands, as a child, because she knew they protected her, and all her life they had protected her. There had always been trouble, sometimes the kind you laughed about later and sometimes not; that was one of the reasons she had married John, and before John there had been others—just boys who didn't count, who had no jobs and thought mainly about their cars. Once, when she was fifteen, she had called her father from a roadhouse sixty miles away; she and her best friend Annie had gotten mixed up with some men they had met at a picnic. That had been frightening, Helen thought, but now she could have handled them. She gave everyone too much, that was her trouble. Her father had said that. Even her mother. Lent money to girls at the telephone company where she'd worked; lent her girlfriends clothes; would run outside when some man drove up and blew his horn, not bothering to get out and knock at the door the way he should. She liked to make other people happy, what was wrong with that? Was she too lazy to care? Her head had begun to ache.

Always her thoughts ran one way, fast and innocent, but her body did other things. It got warm, nervous, it could not relax. Was she afraid of what her father's face would tell her? She pushed that idea away, it was nonsense. If she had to think of something, let it be of that muddy spring day when her family had first moved to this part of the country, into an old farmhouse her father had bought at a "bargain." At that time the

road out in front of the house had been no more than a single
dirt lane ... now it was wider, covered with blacktop that smelled
ugly and made your eyes shimmer and water with confusion in
the summer. Yes, that big old house. Nothing about it would
have changed. She did not think of her own house, her husband's
house, because it mixed her up too much right now. Maybe she
would go back and maybe not. She did not think of him—if she
wanted to go back she would, he would take her in. When she
tried to think of what had brought her back, it was never her
husband—so much younger, quicker, happier than the man she
had just left—and not the little girl, either, but something to do
with her family's house and that misty, warm day seventeen
years ago when they had first moved in. So one morning when
that man left for work her thoughts had turned back to home
and she had sat at the breakfast table for an hour or so, not
clearing off the dishes, looking at the coffee left in his cup as if it
were a forlorn reminder of him—a man she was even then
beginning to forget. She knew then that she did not belong there
in the city. It wasn't that she had stopped loving this man—she
never stopped loving anyone who needed her, and he had
needed her more than anyone—it was something else, something she did not understand. Not her husband, not her baby,
not even the look of the river way off down the hill, through the
trees that got so solemn and intricate with their bare branches in
winter. Those things she loved, she hadn't stopped loving them
because she had had to love this new man more ... but something else made her get up and run into the next room and look
through the bureau drawers and the closet, as if looking for
something. That evening, when he returned, she explained to
him that she was going back. He was over forty, she wasn't sure
how much, and it had always been his hesitant, apologetic
manner that made her love him, the odor of failure about him
that mixed with the odor of the drinking he could not stop, even
though he had "cut down" now with her help. Why were so
many men afraid, why did they think so much? He did something that had to do with keeping books, was that nervous
work? He was an attractive man but that wasn't what Helen
had seen in him. It was his staring at her when they had first

met, and the way he had run his hand through his thinning hair, telling her in that gesture that he wanted her and wanted to be young enough to tell her so. That had been five months ago. The months all rushed to Helen's mind in the memory she had of his keen intelligent baffled eyes, and the tears she had had to see in them when she went out to call her father. . . .

Now, back in Oriskany, she would think of him no more.

A few minutes later her father came. Was that really him? she thought. Her heart beat furiously. If blood drained out of her face she would look mottled and sick, as if she had a rash . . . how she hated that! Though he had seen her at once, though the bus station was nearly empty, her father hesitated until she stood and ran to him. "Pa," she said, "I'm so glad to see you." It might have been years ago and he was just going to drive back home now, finished with his business in town, and Helen fourteen or fifteen, waiting to go back with him.

"I'll get your suitcase," he said. The sailor was reading a magazine, no longer interested. Helen watched her father nervously. What was wrong? He stooped, taking hold of the suitcase handle, but he did not straighten fast enough. Just a heartbeat too slow. Why was that? Helen took a tissue already stained with lipstick and dabbed it on her forehead.

On the way home he drove oddly, as if the steering wheel, heated by the sun, were too painful for him to hold. "No more trouble with the car, huh?" Helen said.

"It's all right," he said. They were nearly out of town already. Helen saw few people she knew. "Why are you looking around?" her father said. His voice was pleasant and his eyes fastened seriously upon the road, as if he did not dare look elsewhere.

"Oh, just looking," Helen said. "How is Davey?"

Waiting for her father to answer—he always took his time— Helen arranged her skirt nervously beneath her. Davey was her sister's baby, could he be sick? She had forgotten to ask about him the night before. "Nothing's wrong with Davey, is there, Pa?" she said.

"No, nothing."

"I thought Ma might come, maybe," Helen said.

"No."

"Didn't she want to? Mad at me, huh?"

In the past her mother's dissatisfaction with her had always ranged Helen and her father together; Helen could tell by a glance of her father's when this was so. But he did not look away from the road. They were passing the new high school, the consolidated high school Helen had attended for a year. No one had known what "consolidated" meant or was interested in knowing. Helen frowned at the dark brick and there came to her mind, out of nowhere, the word *adulterous,* for it too had been a word she had not understood for years. A word out of the Bible. It was like a mosquito bothering her at night, or a stain on her dress—the kind she would have to hide without seeming to, letting her hand fall over it accidentally. For some reason the peculiar smell of the old car, the rattling sunshades above the windshield, the same old khaki blanket they used for a seat cover did not comfort her and let her mind get drowsy, to push that word away.

She was not sleepy, but she said she was.

"Yes, honey. Why don't you lay back and try to sleep, then," her father said.

He glanced toward her. She felt relieved at once, made simple and safe. She slid over and leaned her head against her father's shoulder. "Bus ride was long, I hate bus rides," she said. "I used to like them."

"You can sleep till we get home."

"Is Ma mad?"

"No."

His shoulder wasn't as comfortable as it should have been. But she closed her eyes, trying to force sleep. She remembered that April day they had come here—their moving to the house that was new to them, a house of their own they would have to share with no one else, but a house it turned out that had things wrong with it, secret things, that had made Helen's father furious. She could not remember the city and the house they had lived in there, but she had been old enough to sense the simplicity of the country and the eagerness of her parents, and then the angry perplexity that had followed. The family was big—six children then, before Arthur died at ten—and half an hour after they had moved in, the house was crowded and shabby. And she remembered being frightened at something and her father picking her up right in the middle of moving, and not asking her why she cried—her mother had always asked her that, as if there were a reason—but rocking her and comforting her with his rough hands. And she could remember how the house had looked so well: the ballooning curtains in the windows, the first things her mother had put up. The gusty spring air, already too warm, smelling of good earth and the Eden River not too far behind them, and leaves, sunlight, wind; and the sagging porch piled with cartons and bundles and pieces of furniture from the old house. The grandparents—her mother's parents—had died in that old dark house in the city, and Helen did not remember them at all except as her father summoned them back, recalling with hatred his wife's father—some little confused argument they had had years ago that he should have won. That old man had died and the house had gone to the bank, somewhere mysterious, and her father had brought them all out here to the country. A new world, a new life. A farm. And four boys to help, and the promise of such good soil. . . .

Her father turned the wheel sharply. "Rabbit run acrost," he said. He had this strange air of apology for whatever he did, even if it was something gentle; he hated to kill animals, even weasels and hawks. Helen wanted to cover his right hand with hers, that thickened, dirt-creased hand that could never be made clean. But she said, stirring a little as if he had awakened her, "Then why didn't Ma want to come?"

They were taking a long, slow curve. Helen knew without looking up which curve this was, between two wheat fields that belonged to one of the old, old families, those prosperous men who drove broken-down pickup trucks and dressed no better than their own hired hands, but who had money, much money, not just in one bank but in many. "Yes, they're money people," Helen remembered her father saying, years ago, passing someone's pasture. Those ugly red cows meant nothing to Helen, but they meant something to her father. And so after her father had said that—they had been out for a drive after church—her mother got sharp and impatient and the ride was

ruined. That was years ago. Helen's father had been a young
man then, with a raw, waiting, untested look, with muscular
arms and shoulders that needed only to be directed to their
work. "They're money people," he had said, and that had
ruined the ride, as if by magic. It had been as if the air itself had
changed, the direction of the wind changing and easing to them
from the river that was often stagnant in August and September, and not from the green land. With an effort Helen remembered that she had been thinking about her mother. Why did her
mind push her into the past so often these days?—she only
twenty-two (that was not old, not really) and going to begin a
new life. Once she got home and took a bath and washed out the
things in the suitcase, and got some rest, and took a walk down
by the river as she had as a child, skipping stones across it, and
sat around the round kitchen table with the old oilcloth cover to
listen to their advice ("You got to grow up, now. You ain't
fifteen anymore"—that had been her mother, last time), then she
would decide what to do. Make her decision about her husband
and the baby and there would be nothing left to think about.

"Why didn't Ma come?"

"I didn't want her to," he said.

Helen swallowed, without meaning to. His shoulder was thin
and hard against the side of her face. Were those same muscles
still there, or had they become worn away like the soil that was
sucked down into the river every year, stolen from them, so that
the farm Helen's father had bought turned out to be a kind of
joke on him? Or were they a different kind of muscle, hard and
compressed like steel, drawn into themselves from years of
resisting violence?

"How come?" Helen said.

He did not answer. She shut her eyes tight and distracting,
eerie images came to her, stars exploding and shadowy figures
like those in movies—she had gone to the movies all the time in
the city, often taking in the first show at eleven in the morning,
not because she was lonely or had nothing to do but because she
liked movies. Five-twenty and he would come up the stairs,
grimacing a little with the strange inexplicable pain in his chest:

and there Helen would be, back from downtown, dressed up and her hair shining and her face ripe and fresh as a child's, not because she was proud of the look in his eyes but because she knew she could make that pain of his abate for a while. And so why had she left him, when he had needed her more than anyone? "Pa, is something wrong?" she said, as if the recollection of that other man's invisible pain were in some way connected with her father.

He reached down vaguely and touched her hand. She was surprised at this. The movie images vanished—those beautiful people she had wanted to believe in, as she had wanted to believe in God and the saints in their movie-world heaven—and she opened her eyes. The sun was bright. It had been too bright all summer. Helen's mind felt sharp and nervous, as if pricked by tiny needles, but when she tried to think of what they could be no explanation came to her. She would be home soon, she would be able to rest. Tomorrow she could get in touch with John. Things could begin where they had left off—John had always loved her so much, and he had always understood her, had known what she was like. "Ma isn't sick, is she?" Helen said suddenly. "No," said her father. He released her fingers to take hold of the steering wheel again. Another curve. Off to the side, if she bothered to look, the river had swung toward them—low at this time of year, covered in places with a fine brown-green layer of scum. She did not bother to look.

"We moved out here seventeen years ago," her father said. He cleared his throat; the gesture of a man unaccustomed to speech. "You don't remember that."

"Yes, I do," Helen said. "I remember that."

"You don't, you were just a baby."

"Pa, I remember it. I remember you carrying the big rug into the house, you and Eddie. And I started to cry and you picked me up. I was such a big baby, always crying.... And Ma came out and chased me inside so I wouldn't bother you."

"You don't remember that," her father said. He was driving jerkily, pressing down on the gas pedal and then letting it up, as if new thoughts continually struck him. What was wrong with him? Helen had an idea she didn't like: he was older now, he was going to become an old man.

If she had been afraid of the dark, upstairs in that big old farmhouse in the room she shared with her sister, all she had had to do was to think of him. He had a way of sitting at the supper table that was so still, so silent, you knew nothing could budge him. Nothing could frighten him. So, as a child, and even now that she was grown up, it helped her to think of her father's face—those pale surprised green eyes that could be simple or cunning, depending upon the light, and the lines working themselves in deeper every year around his mouth, and the hard angle of his jaw going back to the ear, burned by the sun and then tanned by it, turned into leather, then going pale again in the winter. The sun could not burn its color deep enough into that skin that was almost as fair as Helen's. At Sunday school she and the other children had been told to think of Christ when they were afraid, but the Christ she saw on the little Bible bookmark cards and calendars was no one to protect you. That was a man who would be your cousin, maybe, some cousin you liked but saw rarely, but He looked so given over to thinking and trusting that He could not be of much help; not like her father. When he and the boys came in from the fields with the sweat drenching their clothes and their faces looking as if they were dissolving with heat, you could still see the solid flesh beneath, the skeleton that hung onto its muscles and would never get old, never die. The boys—her brothers, all older—had liked her well enough, Helen being the baby, and her sister had watched her most of the time, and her mother had liked her too—or did her mother like anyone, having been brought up by German-speaking parents who had had no time to teach her love? But it had always been her father she had run to. She had started knowing men by knowing him. She could read things in his face that taught her about the faces of other men, the slowness or quickness of their thoughts, if they were beginning to be impatient, or were pleased and didn't want to show it yet. Was it for this she had come home? —And the thought surprised her so that she sat up, because she did not understand. Was it for this she had come home? "Pa," she said, "like I told you on the telephone, I don't know why I did it. I don't know why I went. That's all right, isn't it? I mean, I'm sorry for it, isn't that enough? Did you talk to John?"

"John? Why John?"

"What?"

"You haven't asked about him until now, so why now?"

"What do you mean? He's my husband, isn't he? Did you talk to him?"

"He came over to the house almost every night for two weeks. Three weeks," he said. Helen could not understand the queer chatty tone of his voice. "Then off and on, all the time. No, I didn't tell him you were coming."

"But why not?" Helen laughed nervously. "Don't you like him?"

"You know I like him. You know that. But if I told him he'd of gone down to get you, not me."

"Not if I said it was you I wanted...."

"I didn't want him to know. Your mother doesn't know either."

"What? You mean you didn't tell her?" Helen looked at the side of his face. It was rigid and bloodless behind the tan, as if something inside were shrinking away and leaving just his voice. "You mean you didn't even tell Ma? She doesn't know I'm coming?"

"No."

The nervous prickling in her brain returned suddenly. Helen rubbed her forehead. "Pa," she said gently, "why didn't you tell anybody? You're ashamed of me, huh?"

He drove on slowly. They were following the bends of the river, that wide shallow meandering river the boys said wasn't worth fishing in any longer. One of its tributaries branched out suddenly—Mud Creek, it was called, all mud and bullfrogs and dragonflies and weeds—and they drove over it on a rickety wooden bridge that thumped beneath them. "Pa," Helen said carefully, "you said you weren't mad, on the phone. And I wrote you that letter explaining. I wanted to write some more, but you know...I don't write much, never even wrote to Annie when she moved away. I never forgot about you or anything, or

Ma.... I thought about the baby, too, and John, but John could always take care of himself. He's smart. He really is. I was in the store with him one time and he was arguing with some salesmen and got the best of them; he never learned all that from his father. The whole family is smart, though, aren't they?"

"The Hendrikses? Sure. You don't get money without brains."

"Yes, and they got money too, John never had to worry. In a house like his parents' house nothing gets lost or broken. You know? It isn't like it was at ours, when we were all kids. That's part of it—when John's father built us our house I was real pleased and real happy, but then something of them came in with it too. Everything is s'post to be clean and put in its place, and after you have a baby you get so tired.... But his mother was always real nice to me. I don't complain about them. I like them all real well."

"Money people always act nice," her father said. "Why shouldn't they?"

"Oh, Pa!" Helen said, tapping at his arm. "What do you mean by that? You always been nicer than anybody I know, that's the truth. Real nice. A lot of them with those big farms, like John's father, and that tractor store they got—they complain a lot. They do. You just don't hear about it. And when that baby got polio, over in the Rapids—that real big farm, you know what I mean?—the McGuires. How do you think they felt? They got troubles just like everybody else."

Then her father did a strange thing: here they were, seven or eight miles from home, no house near, and he stopped the car. "Want to rest for a minute," he said. Yet he kept staring out the windshield as if he were still driving.

"What's wrong?"

"Sun on the hood of the car...."

Helen tugged at the collar of her dress, pulling it away from her damp neck. When had the heat ever bothered her father before? She remembered going out to the farthest field with water for him, before he had given up that part of the farm. And he would take the jug from her and lift it to his lips and it would seem to Helen, the sweet child Helen standing in the dusty corn, that the water flowed into her magnificent father and enlivened him as if it were secret blood of her own she had given him. And his chest would swell, his reddened arms eager with muscle emerging out from his rolled-up sleeves, and his eyes now wiped of sweat and exhaustion.... The vision pleased and confused her, for what had it to do with the man now beside her? She stared at him and saw that his nose was queerly white and that there were many tiny red veins about it, hardly more than pen lines; and his hair was thinning and jagged, growing back stiffly from his forehead as if he had brushed it back impatiently with his hand once too often. When Eddie, the oldest boy, moved away now and lost to them, had pushed their father hard in the chest and knocked him back against the supper table, that same amazed white look had come to his face, starting at his nose.

"I was thinking if, if we got home now, I could help Ma with supper," Helen said. She touched her father's arm as if to wake him. "It's real hot, she'd like some help."

"She doesn't know you're coming."

"But I...I could help anyway." She tried to smile, watching his face for a hint of something: many times in the past he had looked stern but could be made to break into a smile, finally, if she teased him long enough. "But didn't Ma hear you talk on the phone? Wasn't she there?"

"She was there."

"Well, but then..."

"I told her you just talked. Never said nothing about coming home."

The heat had begun to make Helen dizzy. Her father opened the door on his side. "Let's get out for a minute, go down by the river," he said. Helen slid across and got out. The ground felt uncertain beneath her feet. Her father was walking and saying something and she had to run to catch up with him. He said: "We moved out here seventeen years ago. There were six of you then, but you don't remember. Then the boy died. And you don't remember your mother's parents and their house, that goddamn stinking house, and how I did all the work for him in his store. You remember the store down front? The dirty sawdust floor and the old women coming in for sausage, enough to make you want to puke, and pigs' feet and brains out of cows or guts or what the hell they were that people ate in that neighborhood. I could puke for all my life and not get clean of it. You just got born then. And we were dirt to your mother's people, just dirt. I was dirt. And when they died somebody else got the house, it was all owned by somebody else, and so we said how it was for the best and we'd come out here and start all over. You don't remember it or know nothing about us."

"What's wrong, Pa?" Helen said. She took his arm as they descended the weedy bank. "You talk so funny, did you get something to drink before you came to the bus station? You never said these things before. I thought it wasn't just meat, but a grocery store, like the one in..."

"And we came out here," he said loudly, interrupting her, and bought that son of a bitch of a house with the roof half rotted through and the well all shot to hell...and those bastards never looked at us, never believed we were real people. The Hendrikses too. They were like all of them. They looked through me in town, do you know that? Like you look through a window. They didn't see me. It was because hillbilly families were in that house, came and went, pulled out in the middle of the night owing everybody money; they all thought we were like that. I said, we were poor but we weren't hillbillies. I said, do I talk like a hillbilly? We come from the city. But nobody gave a damn. You could go up to them and shout in their faces and they wouldn't hear you, not even when they started losing money themselves. I prayed to God during them bad times that they'd all lose what they had, every bastard one of them, that Swede with the fancy cattle most of all! I prayed to God to bring them down to me so they could see me, my children as good as theirs, and me a harder worker than any of them—if you work till you feel like dying you done the best you can do, whatever money you get. I'd of told them that. I wanted to come into their world even if I had to be on the bottom of it, just so long as they gave me a name...."

"Pa, you been drinking," Helen said softly.

"I had it all fixed, what I'd tell them," he said. They were down by the riverbank now. Fishermen had cleared a little area and stuck Y-shaped branches into the dried mud, to rest their poles on. Helen's father prodded one of the little sticks with his foot and then did something Helen had never seen anyone do in her life, not even boys—he brought his foot down on it and smashed it.

"You oughtn't of done that," Helen said. "Why'd you do that?"

"And I kept on and on; it was seventeen years. I never talked about it to anyone. Your mother and me never had much to say, you know that. She was like her father. You remember that first day? It was spring, nice and warm, and the wind came along when we were moving the stuff in and was so different from that smell in the city—my God! It was a whole new world here."

"I remember it," Helen said. She was staring out at the shallow muddy river. Across the way birds were sunning themselves stupidly on flat, white rocks covered with dried moss like veils.

"You don't remember nothing!" her father said angrily. "Nothing! You were the only one of them I loved, because you didn't remember. It was all for you. First I did it for me, myself, to show that bastard father of hers that was dead—then those other bastards, those big farms around us—but then for you, for you. You were the baby. I said to God that when you grew up it'd be you in one of them big houses with everything fixed and painted all the time, and new machinery, and driving around in a nice car, not this thing we got. I said I would do that for you or die."

"That's real nice, Pa," Helen said nervously, "but I never . . . I never knew nothing about it, or . . . I was happy enough any way I was. I liked it at home, I got along with Ma better than anybody did. And I liked John too, I didn't marry him just because you told me to. I mean, you never pushed me around. I wanted to marry him all by myself, because he loved me. I was always happy, Pa. If John didn't have the store coming to him, and that land and all, I'd have married him anyway— You oughtn't to have worked all that hard for me."

In spite of the heat she felt suddenly chilled. On either side of them tall grass shrank back from the cleared, patted area, stiff and dried with August heat. These weeds gathered upon them-selves in a brittle tumult back where the vines and foliage of trees began, the weeds dead and whitened and the vines a glossy, rich green, as if sucking life out of the water into which they drooped. All along the riverbank trees and bushes leaned out and showed a yard or two of dead, whitish brown where the water line had once been. This river bent so often you could never see far along it. Only a mile or so. Then foliage began, confused and unmoving. What were they doing here, she and her father? A thought came to Helen and frightened her—she was not used to thinking—that they ought not to be here, that this was some other kind of slow, patient world where time didn't care at all for her or her girl's face or her generosity of love, but would push right past her and go on to touch the faces of other people.

"Pa, let's go home. Let's go home," she said.

Her father bent and put his hands into the river. He brought them dripping to his face. "That's dirty there, Pa," she said. A mad dry buzzing started up somewhere—hornets or wasps. Helen looked around but saw nothing.

"God listened and didn't say yes or no," her father said. He was squatting at the river and now looked back at her, his chin creasing. The back of his shirt was wet. "If I could read Him right it was something like this—that I was caught in myself and them money people caught in themselves and God Himself caught in what He was and so couldn't be anything else. Then I never thought about God again."

"I think about God," Helen said. "I do. People should think about God, then they wouldn't have wars and things...."

"No, I never bothered about God again," he said slowly. "If He was up there or not it never had nothing to do with me. A hailstorm that knocked down the wheat, or a drought—what the hell? Whose fault? It wasn't God's no more than mine so I let Him out of it. I knew I was in it all on my own. Then after a while it got better, year by year. We paid off the farm and the new machines. You were in school then, in town. And when we went into the church they said hello to us sometimes, because we outlasted them hillbillies by ten years. And now Mike ain't doing bad on his own place, got a nice car, and me and Bill get enough out of the farm so it ain't too bad, I mean it ain't too bad. But it wasn't money I wanted!"

He was staring at her. She saw something in his face that mixed with the buzzing of the hornets and fascinated her so that she could not move, could not even try to tease him into smiling too. "It wasn't never money I wanted," he said.

"Pa, why don't we go home?"

"I don't know what it was, exactly," he said, still squatting. His hands touched the ground idly. "I tried to think of it, last night when you called and all night long and driving in to town today. I tried to think of it."

"I guess I'm awful tired from that bus. I ... I don't feel good," Helen said.

"Why did you leave with that man?"

"What? Oh," she said, touching the tip of one of the weeds, "I met him at John's cousin's place, where they got that real nice tavern and a dance hall...."

"Why did you run away with him?"

"I don't know, I told you in the letter. I wrote it to you, Pa. He acted so nice and liked me so, he still does, he loves me so much.... And he was always so sad and tired, he made me think of ... you, Pa ... but not really, because he's not strong like you and couldn't ever do work like you. And if he loved me that much I had to go with him."

"Then why did you come back?"

"Come back?" Helen tried to smile out across the water. Sluggish, ugly water, this river that disappointed everyone, so familiar to her that she could not really get used to a house without a river or a creek somewhere behind it, flowing along night and day: perhaps that was what she had missed in the city?

"I came back because ... because ... "

And she shredded the weed in her cold fingers, but no words came to her. She watched the weed-fragments fall. No words came to her, her mind had turned hollow and cold, she had come too far down to this riverbank but it was not a mistake any more than the way the river kept moving was a mistake; it just happened.

Her father got slowly to his feet and she saw in his hand a knife she had been seeing all her life. Her eyes seized upon it and her mind tried to remember: where had she seen it last, whose was it, her father's or her brother's? He came to her and touched her shoulder as if waking her, and they looked at each other, Helen so terrified by now that she was no longer afraid but only curious with the mute marblelike curiosity of a child, and her father stern and silent until a rush of hatred transformed his face into a mass of wrinkles, the skin mottled red and white. He did not raise the knife but slammed it into her chest, up to the hilt, so that his whitened fist struck her body and her blood exploded out upon it.

Afterward, he washed the knife in the dirty water and put it away. He squatted and looked out over the river, then his thighs began to ache and he sat on the ground, a few feet from her body. He sat there for hours as if waiting for some idea to come to him. Then the water began to darken, very slowly, and the sky darkened a little while later—as if belonging to another, separate time—and he tried to turn his mind with an effort to the next thing he must do.

Did You Ever Slip on Red Blood?

D ID YOU? she asked him repeatedly, angrily. *Did you ever? I
mean did you ever slip on red blood yourself, do you know what
it's like?*

She wept and brushed her hair back from her face, her eyes
shut so that he could stare at her, starkly, closely, so that she hid
nothing from him. Her nudeness made her radiant in the dim,
coarse light of a winter afternoon. He felt how her nudeness was
in her face, behind her eyes, in the pressure of her angry eyelids
against her eyes. Everything about her was hard, smooth, stark,
without deception.

"Nobody knows what we know," he said.

She said nothing. Her eyes were still closed.

The sheet had fallen away from her and she was shadowy in
the dim light of this room he had rented for them. It did not look
out onto the sky but across a terrible precipice to another
building. The blinds were always closed; there was nothing to
see. Here he had to see her with his hands, groping anxiously at
her body with his hands. He could not believe in her except
when they were together like this. She slipped from his mind,
slipped out of focus. When they were together in this room she

was brought up close to him, as if centered in the telescopic sight of a rifle.

They met like this for the first time in December. That was six weeks after the day they first had seen each other, at La Guardia Airport, and about nine months after the trial had ended out in Milwaukee—a trial Marian knew little about, involving four young men in their twenties indicted for conspiracy to advocate resistance to induction into the United States Army. Of the four young men only one was well known: the folk singer Jacob Appleman, who was sentenced to three years in jail. Two others were given similar sentences. The youngest of the defendants, Robert Severin, who was twenty-three at the time of the trial and also at the time of his death, had been acquitted. No one knew why.

Why was Severin acquitted? people asked. *Why Severin and no one else?*

Quick, weasellike, nervous, with something melancholic in his expression and in the thin mustache he had refused to shave off for the trial; with a habit of raising his hand to his mouth when he spoke, as if he distrusted his own words or was ashamed of them. "I'm not going to shave it off. I'm not going to misrepresent myself. I don't lie," he told his lawyer. He wouldn't remove the mustache and he wouldn't dress properly and he wouldn't meet anyone's eye, a lifelong habit of his, not even the eyes of his codefendants or of his lawyer, whom his father had retained for him. Severin was short, slender, dark, with a boyish frame and a shallow chest. As he sat, he twisted his body in small, uncoordinated movements, without seeming to know what he was doing. During the trial he had squirmed in his seat, his heart accelerating at strange times—especially during long dull periods in which nothing seemed to be happening. Severin feared that something was really happening at these times, but that no one knew. No one could guess. His heart had gradually increased its beat until it was pounding like mad during one forty-five-minute period when an FBI agent, a stranger, talked about the size and colors and the texture of the paper and the type of print involved in a pamphlet written by the defendants and passed out to several thousand young men in Milwaukee at an antiwar meeting. Minutes and minutes passed as words were pronounced carefully by that man, that stranger, a courteous and handsome American in his thirties who spoke without any hatred or emphasis.... Listening to these simple, incredible words, Severin was afraid he would begin to scream.

But he never screamed so that anyone could hear.

The trial ended on the morning of March 6, after the jury returned its verdict. Severin walked out. He did not say good-by to his lawyer, or to his parents, who had spent the four weeks of the trial at a hotel in Milwaukee, or to the other defendants. He disappeared. He willed himself into disappearing. In his head for many days there had been a vision of himself disappearing, a fading image on a screen, a slow fade-out at the conclusion of a movie.

His mind flashed its thoughts like pictures on a screen, and one of the thoughts was Robert Severin. Always alone. Walking somewhere quickly, alone. Since his boyhood he had imagined himself as a character in a film, a figure pacing across a screen, blown up, enlarged, exaggerated. He could be gigantic sometimes. He knew this even if other people did not. At the age of fifteen he had reached his full growth: five feet seven inches. As if to show that he did not mind being this short, he often stood with his weight balanced on one leg, the other leg bent indifferently. He did not walk with his shoulders back, he did not "observe" good posture. This was one of the things that annoyed his lawyer. "It might be better not to slouch in court," his lawyer said gently. His name was Morton Fisher and he was from New York, not Wisconsin, like the other attorneys; but still Severin did not trust him. He was a lawyer Severin's father had insisted upon. At first Severin had been eager to talk to Fisher, to explain his life, but it turned out that Fisher was not really interested in his life. "We have to concentrate on what is relevant to your case," Fisher kept saying. Finally Severin understood, with a shock, that this man did not like him. He was hurt. And then he was bewildered, for why shouldn't this man like him? Why shouldn't everyone like him? He wanted only to do good and to help others to do good. In the end, Severin hardly spoke to Fisher. He sat with his shoulders slumped, in a green-gray tweed suit with a vest, which he had bought especially for this trial. It was much too large for him, ill-cut, a parody of a suit. He had told the salesman in the discount department store that he wanted a baggy, old man's suit, "a joke of a suit," a proper outfit in which he might be tried by his government, which was displeased with him.

"Do you think that's funny, that suit?" his father asked him.

"Everything is funny," Severin said.

"Is that what you believe?"

"No. I believe that nothing is funny," Severin said in the same tone. "But we have to make certain pretenses."

Why was Severin acquitted and no one else? He could hear everyone ask this question. Making his way up the aisle of the courtroom, out where people stood around in the corridor, ducking when someone seemed to be swinging at him—it turned out to be a student waving a placard—his face darkening, heating; yet he had never screamed. Not out loud. He was free, freed. Time to disappear. *Robert Severin disappearing into the sky.*

When he shut his eyes he could see quite precisely a dark shape drawing into itself, withering, retreating into something that glowed fiercely, like the sun. Then it disappeared. That was peace, that disappearing, that nullity. He wouldn't even have to argue or explain himself. He would have no need for words.

It wasn't until several weeks later that the three others received their sentences; Severin read about it in a newspaper. By then he was in Montreal, where he knew no one. He stared at the photograph of Appleman—Appleman with his bushy hair and glum, sardonic expression and his career "just beginning to catch on," as people said—and Severin heard the voice in his head cry, *I don't know why Severin was acquitted, I don't know why Severin was acquitted, I don't know.* With these words he might have wanted to dissociate himself from Severin.

An incantation: *I don't know why.*

A litany: *I don't know why.*

And he did not know why. He did not understand. His brain replayed for him those hours of the trial, the testimony of FBI agents and the testimony of witnesses and the level, reasoned arguing of the defense lawyers, all of whom had the dark-rimmed, glowing eyes of men drowning for a good cause, and the occasional snorts and interruptions of the judge, whose terrible eyes Severin had never quite seen. He knew that he was guilty, yet he had been found not guilty. He was as guilty as the others; they were as innocent as he. Yet it had not turned out that way.

He had tried to explain some of this to Marian Vernon, who had seemed to understand. "There was no difference between any of us," he told her. His voice had rattled, accelerating. He had not talked for many weeks and now he could not stop. She had nodded, yes, yes, she understood or seemed to understand, staring in prim panic into his face, their faces level, like brother and sister. "That was how I figured out they had me marked for something special," he told her angrily. "That's why I have to get out of the country. I don't have much time left. I'm going to explode if I don't get out." *Yes, yes* she had said dumbly, but she had not really understood. Weeks and months after his death she went around saying she didn't understand, she didn't understand what he had wanted, why he had done it, why, why had it happened? "Jesus, if I could relive that hour," she said. She and Oberon talked about it all the time, talking about "it" as they embraced, closing their eyes upon a fast shocked image of Robert Severin's face. He was a stranger and yet they were close to him, intimate, knowing. He was always with them. His enlarged faced followed them everywhere and excited them almost beyond endurance.

Sometimes she hated Oberon; her love shriveled into something bitter and white-hot and she hated him, she snapped at him, *You don't know what it's like to remember such a thing—did you ever slip on red blood yourself? You don't know what I know!*

And he would take her in his arms to quiet her.

Marian never had time for newspapers, never watched television, picked up important news and catastrophes from other people. Of course she had known nothing about the Milwaukee trial; the name Jacob Appleman was familiar to her, but she had never heard any of his records. She was a young woman of twenty-two, a stewardess with Pan American Airways. She had graduated with a Bachelor of Arts degree from the University of Oklahoma, which qualified her for teaching in the elementary schools of that state, but she had never really planned on teaching. The company of children, other teachers, the confinement of a room and a single building—these things frightened her. She wanted to live.

Her hair was a dark, wavy red, worn to her shoulders. Her face was lightly freckled, very healthy; her posture reflected health and enthusiasm; she had always been a happy child, a happy girl, arguing philosophically to herself that life was a wonderful adventure and that it should be faced with a constant smile. To a magazine reporter who had interviewed her in November she had confided, "That was how I got through that hour without cracking. I told myself that life is a wonderful adventure. I told myself that there is always a good, unexpected side to things, another arrangement we don't know about immediately."

"And did that turn out to be true?" the reporter asked.

She paused. She lowered her eyes, thinking of Oberon. She said finally, "I can't tell you about that."

Oberon had known about the trial, which was always referred to as the "Appleman Case," though three other men had been indicted. Oberon, who was interested in folk music, had followed Appleman's career since his first record, in 1965, and he had been very disappointed at Appleman's political activities—the organization of a series of antiwar demonstrations in Chicago and Milwaukee. In his imagination he had even written Jacob Appleman a letter of warning. "My name is David Oberon and I am a stranger to you, yet believe me when I say that I wish you well. Why are you trying to destroy yourself? Why are you trying to corrupt hundreds of young Americans? Our country is engaged in a certain action in Southeast Asia and it is everyone's duty to support his country...." But he did not dare type the letter. This was in the fall of 1969; Appleman had not been arrested yet, but Oberon knew the government was preparing a case against him. His letter might be confiscated. Even if he sent it anonymously, it might be confiscated and traced back to him.

Oberon had followed the case through the newspapers. He knew the names and a little of the facts concerning the other defendants, so the name Robert Severin was immediately familiar to him. Severin had been the only person acquitted and people had wondered about that. Oberon himself had not wondered, believing the jury had wanted to free someone, just to declare to the FBI and the Department of Justice that they could free a defendant who had probably been guilty of committing a crime against the United States government. It was a harmless act. He had heard, anyway, that Severin, the youngest of the four, had been indicted so that he could be acquitted—the government had had no interest in him, really.

He explained this to Marian, who was rosy, sunny, cheerful by nature, a young American woman with a personality simple as slides shown on a screen, one after another, and yet whose nature changed even as Oberon spoke to her, as if he were teasing her with his words about Severin, his superior knowledge of Severin, drawing her out of herself in a maddening way. "I don't know what you're doing to me," she laughed. "You're making me drunk. I feel drunk. Don't stop talking."

"What else do you want to know?" he asked her.

She hesitated. "What it was like."

"What it was like...?"

"You know. What it felt like. To you. When it happened."

He had fallen helplessly in love with her.

He was fourteen years older than Marian Vernon, a tall, well-built man with brown hair, an amiable anonymous face, with something courteous and predictable in his smile. He was much taller than Robert Severin. If he had had the occasion to stand beside him, he would have towered over him—poor Severin, with his girlish weasellike body, his narrow shoulders! If he had had the occasion to fight with him, he could have picked him up and thrown him down, knocking him senseless. Very deftly and courteously he could have pinned Severin's shoulders to the ground, holding him there safely until he could be arrested.

Oberon sometimes thought of that. He thought, while he lay

with Marian, of holding Severin's squirming body down against the pavement. Once he told her about it. "Like this, and like this...like this...I would have held him down...." he whispered. They had lain together face to face, solemn, grieving, and then one of them had begun to laugh. Another time he hadn't told her what he was thinking of, but he sensed that she too was thinking of Severin, always of Severin. "I love you, I love *you*," she had sobbed, as if arguing.

Seen up close like this, Marian was a stark, beautiful woman. Drained of superficial energy, the friendly charity of her kind of woman, which Oberon had always detested, she was hollow, hungry, almost unmanageable. Her love for him obviously frightened her. It was so violent, so intense, he almost sympathized with her dread of it. *What must a woman feel, to be convulsed like that, to suffer like that,* he thought. No one knew Marian Vernon except him. When she appeared in that Pan American Airways uniform—when she smiled her mechanical little smile—it was a joke, a horror! Only Oberon knew her.

She brushed her hair back from her damp face, impatiently. A strand of her hair stung his eye. He tried to listen to what she was saying: something about his wife. "What does she know? I saw her that evening. Her. She doesn't know. What do ordinary people know?"

"She can sense something...."

"No. She can't. She would have to have been there, where I was. In my place. And she wasn't there, no one else was there except me.... You don't love her. Why do you stay with her?"

They stared at each other. He was perspiring, agitated, always he must stare at her in order to locate himself—his love for this woman, whom he hardly knew, whom he did not really like. There was something coarse about her boldness with him, her near-hysteria. She was younger than his wife, more beautiful than his wife, and he was sick with love for her and yet he did not want to think about divorce, remarriage, the routine intensity of married life.

"Do you love her?" Marian asked.

"No. It's another emotion."

"Another emotion, yes. It's ordinary. I don't want to hear

about it. Ordinary people, ordinary ugly people...I don't want to hear about them.

As soon as he left her she began to slip out of focus. She began to fade back into that neat smiling little stewardess with the uniform, the short skirt, and tight-fitting, buttoned little jacket, with the hat perched cockily on her head. It frightened him, that he might lose her. That he might forget her. And yet he could not locate in his memory of her the passion he always felt in her presence. A kind of energy dominated them, gave them life; it did not belong to either of them.

Sometimes he went to stare at himself in a mirror, at home or anywhere, in a public rest room, but he saw only his public, unpersonal face, which was like a uniform. It was like Marian's uniform. That face took him anywhere, flown in by helicopter to the airport, with his .308 Norma Magnum rifle. *What did it feel like?* Marian asked him, the first night they were together. *Did it have a kick? I felt the kick myself. I felt it. I felt you.* There was something anonymous and symmetrical about Oberon's face. As a younger man he had been annoyed when people were always coming up to him and calling him by the names of strangers—now it no longer bothered him. He could have grown a mustache, like Severin. But he never did. He thought of himself as belonging to a crowd, a crowd of American men as they might be imagined, or collected for a special photograph: not a real crowd of unruly and ugly people, but an ideal crowd of "average" American men, fairly good-looking, of a certain height, in good health. Therefore he was six feet two inches tall, with short, wavy brown hair, a face that was almost handsome, with a strong clean nose and chin. His brown eyes looked ordinary and unalarming, but they were, in fact, extraordinary. His vision was perfect. He had always been proud of his eyesight. Eyes like muscles, tensing, erect, precise, fixing themselves on that stranger's face, adjusting themselves to the face, getting to know it closely, intimately.... The face had been framed by jumbled, spiky hair; it had been partly hidden by sunglasses; its skin was an eerie olive, pale and waxen and yet greasy, sagging with fatigue. The mustache had aged it.

* * *

Severin had bought the sunglasses in a drugstore north of Portland, Maine. It had rained all day and yet the sky glowed; it reminded him of the sky in Milwaukee, that soulless glowering that had pressed upon him for so many months. Swollen gray sky and lake, remote, bulbous, inescapable.... He wanted to break through to a place where the sun shone. He bought the sunglasses for $1.98 and they looked like aviators' glasses, with large lenses and wire frames. They were made of some synthetic material, not glass, a kind of plastic that did not break easily or even crack; they were thrown a dozen yards from his body, and yet they did not break.

Now for the approach: how to approach New York? He had family there, parents. He feared his father and his father's face. It wasn't enough, loving them and then not loving them; somehow they were mixed up with his childhood and the nation itself. Awake, unable to sleep, he began having little split-second dreams out on the highway—going crazy, eh, Severin?—and one of his visions was his father stretched out flat, the face stretched out like a big welcome mat, the bumpy hilly terrain of the United States, all someone's face. That could be. Wasn't there a movie about someone crawling across the faces at Mt. Rushmore? Or had Severin imagined that movie? Or was he an insect himself, crawling across the face of his father, not able to put the various parts of the face together into a whole?

His night dreams did not work. Did not function properly. That was because he couldn't sleep anymore at night—why bother getting a motel room if he couldn't use the bed?—but even when he had been sleeping normally his dreams had not worked. How do dreams *work?* What is there *function?* "My dreams all dissolve and disappear," he told his lawyer, Mr. Fisher. He had no one else to talk to; by then he had quarreled with Appleman and the others, and their attorneys had quarreled with one another; it was no good. The government had already won. A story in *Look* magazine implied that Appleman was a saint, but Severin knew better than that, everyone knew better than that, it was just journalistic crap and yet you couldn't make your way through it: what would turn out to be true, what would turn out to be lies? "Jesus, I can't get myself straight; when I try to think about something it all dissolves. Even my dreams.... My dreams just disappear," he tried to explain to Fisher, who had pretended to be interested. "I don't dream like other people, only pieces of dreams like jigsaw puzzles...."

After the verdict, Severin had walked away without saying good-by.

Not just his dreams but his bowels didn't work. Panic. Pain. Pain like fire. Sitting anxiously in the courtroom, fidgeting in his seat, he heard little of the testimony and fixed his gaze upon sterile, empty space, trying not to show the pain he felt. Small rocks seemed to be passing through his intestines. Yet he had never screamed out loud.... *And now Severin will eradicate himself,* he thought as he walked out of the courtroom and out of the courthouse. *Severin walking fast, a comic figure. Almost running.* During those four winter weeks his weight had dropped from 145 to 128. His skin had grown so sensitive that he could not bear to be touched, and he could feel people breathing on him, he could feel the subtle but very abrasive touch of breath, air, against his skin. Appleman had a habit of gripping his arm, his elbow, as if to make sure Severin wouldn't get away. He hated Appleman's closeness, hated the feel of his breath. If he could get a table between them, good. He couldn't make sense of Appleman's nervous strategies, and after a while he stopped listening.

Anyway, they were all guilty. That was one thing they had agreed upon.

So he sat through the weeks of the trial, sensing how words flowed about him, submerging him, threatening to suffocate him, and yet never quite touching him. How they talked, these adults ... always talking, talking.... His lawyer wouldn't let him testify. None of the defendants was going to testify. All right, then, time would pass and nothing would matter, it was really completed; they were guilty and their punishment was beginning now, right now. That was why his bowels were turning to gas, poisonous rotting gas. That was why he couldn't sleep. In court, already a prisoner at the front of the courtroom, he stared at a certain space in the room, not a person or an object but a space, an invisible point in the air, and tried to hypnotize himself into calmness, silence, into nothing. Otherwise he might explode.

Grappling with the stewardess, the redhead, he had felt the danger of his body colliding with hers: a danger for her, not for himself.

"Don't make me kill you," he begged her.

She was his height, as full in the body as he, her face bleached out beneath her make-up.

As soon as the plane left the runway he stood, stood out in the aisle, and took the rolled-up towel out of his coat. She came toward him, a woman perfectly balanced as in a dream, while around her faces turned and chins creased and outside the windows the jumbled landscape of small houses fell backward and down, in silence. "Don't make me explode us all," he begged.

He had found the flare on a highway outside Montreal; he had laughed to see it so innocently left behind—it looked like a stick of dynamite! Walking in the perpetual drizzle, he had picked it up and hidden it in his jacket; you never knew when you might need dynamite, also you never knew when you might need a knife. He had bought a knife in a sporting goods store in a small town somewhere. He couldn't remember where, but probably someone had been watching him and knew. In grade school and high school he had never played with knives— you didn't "play with" knives in his family—but other boys had had knives and Severin had envied them. Now he had his own knife. And a flare that looked like dynamite. Maybe it *was* dynamite. It had a fuse that could be lit. The fuse was damp, but perhaps it could still be lit.

Outside Boston he took a motel room for a night, but he couldn't sleep. A waste of six dollars. He found a newspaper and looked up the weather report: always raining. From Montreal down to New York: rain. He couldn't remember where he was exactly, but it was always raining, a cold steady drizzle, and yet the sky was light. The weather seemed to him very important. He had stopped thinking about everything in his past, and now he thought about the weather instead. There was a weather map of the United States and also a very helpful list of temperatures in cities around the world. He looked through the list several times and discovered that Algiers was missing. Why was it missing? The FBI had reasons for everything.

In Montreal he had been spie' ⌐n; he knew the feeling and didn't question it. But he had not cared. He walked in the street, up and down the hilly streets, openly. It was a foreign country— Canada—and he was free here. In fact, he was free anywhere. Even in Milwaukee. He sent himself back to Milwaukee, that raw, freezing, ugly city, to the courtroom, to see if Robert Severin was still sitting there; yes, there he was, the size of a boy, pretending to listen while words flooded his head. Yes, he was guilty. Didn't he love his parents? Did he want to destroy his mother? Oh yes. No. Did he want to destroy himself? The first step was dropping out of law school—his father had pointed that out to him. The first step toward self-destruction. And this Appleman, who was Appleman? "Who is this Appleman, that you should follow him blindly?" his father demanded. The irony was that Appleman envied Severin and the others because they had gone to college while he, Appleman, so wealthy and so nervous, had barely managed to graduate from high school; but Severin didn't bother to tell his father that. Was he guilty of certain lies? Of avoiding certain statements? Guilty of a small unmanly body? The young man he had shared an apartment with near Columbia, a twenty-eight-year-old vet- eran of the Vietnam war and, like Severin, a law student, had flown out to Milwaukee to testify for him. *Very serious, very moral . . . a completely moral person. . . . We had little in common and we weren't friends, no, but I admired Bob for his honesty. . . .* Yet, when the courteous businesslike prosecutor had cross-examined him, he had faltered and said, *Yes, Bob is absolutely honest and he would never commit any crime, I mean any dishonest crime. . . .* Any dishonest crime! Severin himself had to laugh; by then he'd sat through one hundred hours of this crap and he knew what was what. Any dishonest crime! *It's a strange distinction for a young man entering the law,* the prosecutor had said gently, with a smile, as if a little embarrassed for the witness, *the division of crimes into honest and dishonest crimes. . . .*

Severin had stopped listening.

The jury spent ten hours discussir ₀ the case, and when they came back Severin stood for them, in honor of them, "at atten- tion," in a parody of a young man in a green-gray tweed suit standing at attention in a courtroom, his face composed for a

smirk and his bowels churning with flame and lava. Bastards!
Bland faces and frank honest souls!

*Mr. Foreman, how say you? Is Jacob Appleman, the defendant at
the bar, guilty or not guilty?*

Guilty.

Is John Harvey, the defendant at the bar, guilty or not guilty?

Guilty.

Is Russell Kurzon, the defendant at the bar, guilty or not guilty?

Guilty.

Is Robert Severin, the defendant at the bar, guilty or not guilty?

Not guilty.

Not guilty.

So he sent himself out of there, on a Greyhound bus up to
Montreal. He was free. He had money. His father was always
giving him money, for good nourishing food and for good hotel
rooms. He tried to sleep on the bus but his skull seemed too
large for his brain. His brain slipped wetly around inside the
bone case, an unpleasant sensation. Were his thoughts dissolving, turning to poisonous intestinal vapors? They kept slipping,
slithering, out of his grasp. He had to rely upon flashes of
dreams in the daylight; that was where he got his best hunches.
He telephoned home just once, collect, from a telephone booth
that looked over and up to McGill University, buildings and
grounds and university students so normal and handsome that
he wanted to cry: his nose ran with envy and he could barely
pay attention to his conversation with his father.... "Bob? Bob?
Is that you, Bob? Are you all right, Bob?" his father had shouted
across the distance. It was terrible to hear his voice. Severin
changed his mind, he didn't want a father again, why hadn't he
remembered what it was like? He hung up.

Anyway, the telephone was probably wiretapped.

"It is not necessary for the accused to have done anything,"
someone was explaining to the jury. It was the judge himself. He
was the most adult of all the adults. "In a case like this, the
prosecution has only to prove that they *agreed* to do something.
The case rests entirely on intent and you must find the defendants guilty or not guilty according to their intent...."

He intended now to blow up the country. He intended to fly

up into the sun, to clean himself in the sun, to escape the rain of
the East Coast. Why did it rain so often? And on clear days his
head ached; he muttered in disgust, *Severin, you're going crazy.*
Why else walk around with a fake stick of dynamite in your
pocket, a kid's jackknife with three blades in your pocket? Oh it
was a joke, like the green suit. People took him too seriously.
Adults took him too seriously. Out in Milwaukee—maybe in the
whole Midwest or the whole country—people thought the White
House might be blown up just because Severin or someone with
a mustache like his did not throw his shoulders back and blew
his nose at the wrong time into a soiled Kleenex. The sunglasses
helped his burning eyes but really they were part of the joke.
You couldn't disguise yourself, of course. The FBI had cameras
that x-rayed you antiseptically as you walked in the street. You
couldn't hide from them; therefore, you joked with them in a
mild and cavalier way.

"You don't joke with these people," Fisher had told him
angrily, as if speaking to a child. "What do you think this is? A
game?"

It turned out that all the defendants, when served with their
indictments, had tried to joke nervously with the men who
brought them. Tried to establish a quick jocular rapport with the
low-level FBI men who questioned them, as if that would help.
Wouldn't it help? A quick jocular alliance against the hierarchy,
the Rulers. Wouldn't it help?

"No, you don't talk. You don't cooperate. You don't try to
win their good favor. They are out to get you whether you can
believe it or not. The government is out to get you.... Do you
think that's a joke?"

It was so hard to believe, so hard to believe, that anyone
wanted to hurt them, even the government that had dared to
arrest them. The government turned out to be men who looked
like Severin's father and his lawyer: that is, good citizens, well
dressed and polite. Of course, they hated the government and
had accused the government of being fascistic, in their speeches,
even in their televised speeches, but somehow it was hard to
believe that these men, the FBI agents and their attorneys and
the prosecutor, really wanted to hurt them.... Like most Ameri-

cans, Severin believed he could make anyone like him if he tried. He had never been popular, in high school or college, but he had always cherished the belief that he could be popular if he worked at it.

The stewardess had smiled at him, her lipsticked lips baring her teeth in a slow numbed grimace, the two of them staring at each other levelly, the same height. He had felt like a brother to her. She was one of those pretty, sisterly girls so popular in high school, grinning hello to everyone in the halls, absolutely confident and shadowless. "I don't want to kill you," he had whispered. "Take me up front. Let me explain myself to the pilot. Let me explain and you can see how clear everything will be."

"Yes, I'll take you. Don't be upset," she said.

"I'm not upset. I'm not going to hurt you, or anyone, unless I have to. I'm very calm," Severin said.

Severin gripped her close. The pilot had a title: Captain. He was a man who resembled one of the other defense lawyers. Severin saw at once that this man was intelligent and would play no tricks on him: were the lives of fifty passengers worth any risk? No. It was logical. You read about it in the newspapers all the time. Yet something in the back of Severin's head told him, *What a joke this is, now, what a laugh! Are you really on this plane? Or still back in Montreal, dreaming a daylight dream?* "My destination is Algeria," Severin stated. "I am defecting. I am demanding diplomatic immunity."

But on the turnpike leaving Boston, he had walked slowly along for several hours before someone stopped. It was an FBI agent in an ordinary car. He joked with the man knowingly, delicately. That was the charm of it: you walked a kind of fence with them, teasing them. This man claimed to be a publisher's representative. Severin laughed and said, "Which publishers? Name one."

The man did give a familiar name. "I'm in the college department. Textbooks. Are you a college student?"

"Ha ha," Severin said. "Are you offering me a scholarship if I turn over all the evidence? I wouldn't mind going back to law school."

"I don't understand," the man said slowly.

"No, never mind. It's just a joke. I'm on my way out of the country, I'm just going to say good-by to my family."

"Where does your family live?"

Severin glanced at the man, sizing him up. A big man, like all of them. If it came to a fight, he'd have to use his elbows and feet to paralyze the bastard. He wouldn't want to use the knife; then it would be murder. Still, it would probably not come to a fight. They rarely touched you. Why should they?

"New York," Severin said. He felt helpless, telling the truth like this; but when they already knew the truth you had no choice but to say it.

He put on his sunglasses carefully, hooking them behind his ears. The earpieces were made of wire and quite pliable. When Marian Vernon looked into his face for the first time—welcoming him frankly on board the plane—she did not see him. She did not remember seeing him. But after the takeoff, when he stumbled to his feet and opened his oversized coat, she looked at him again and this time she saw him.

Out of his baggy green suit coat he drew a white towel, rolled up, and he unrolled it to show her a stick of dynamite. Mutely he raised it to her, his eyebrows arching. They walked together to the front of the plane. She felt his breath on the back of her neck, so close.

"I don't like violence. I don't like blood. I don't like knives and this is the first knife I ever bought," he told her earnestly. She glanced back to see that he had a knife in his hand. She went cold. *I went cold. The dynamite I couldn't believe in, it was so ... so extreme.... But the knife was just the right size.... But he was very polite, very nice to me.... No. I wasn't afraid. I went cold, I was numb and like a robot, but I wasn't afraid. I would have been afraid to do what Mr. Oberon did ... that really took courage....*

"You don't resent the FBI risking your life, then?" they asked her.

"Oh, no. No. I don't consider it that, that they risked my life. I mean, it was their job. It was Mr. Oberon's job. He was given orders. It was all done very carefully. I had faith in them. I prayed and I had faith in them. I wasn't afraid."

"How close did he stay to you?"

"Oh, very close. He held me from behind, my arm. His fingers were very tight around my arm, my upper arm, and he kept asking me if he was hurting me; he was very polite and didn't talk loud, he was sort of short, no taller than I was, and all along I could feel the knife in my back, like a fingernail, a man's fingernail.... He wanted to go to Algeria, he said. Something about the sun. He was tired of rain. The Captain told him, of course, this plane was headed for Cleveland and it wasn't a transatlantic plane and if he wanted that he would have to wait...."

"And did he believe that?"

"Oh, yes, he believed that at once. He was very polite and apologetic about hurting me."

Why are you working with planes? Severin asked her. *This is no job for a woman. Planes explode in the sky all the time, disintegrate in the sky....* She seemed to be listening to him intently. She nodded. He could see a droplet of perspiration on her forehead. She was a pretty young woman, like a sister, so pretty, so eager to please him, docile and not argumentative, as he had feared she might be.... *The sky is for men, it's dangerous. After this you should stay on the ground. Are you listening?*

Oh yes I'm listening, yes I'm listening....

The other passengers had filed out. Severin stood with her just inside the door, at the top of the ramp, squinting out into the drizzle. Someone was speaking to him through a loudspeaker. But the loudspeaker did not work very well. "Where is that plane? That big plane? I'm waiting for it," he yelled out into the rain. He held the stewardess back against him, an embrace and yet not an embrace; it was an impersonal embrace. Minutes passed. He had the idea that an hour had passed and could not be retrieved. He saw a large jetliner being moved toward him, far away in the rain, and then he wondered if he had seen correctly. Would they give him a pilot and a crew? All that expense, just for him?

"You might like Algeria yourself," he told the girl. "There, you could stay on the ground and forget about all this crap, this fooling around. You could stay there with me."

"You won't hurt me?"

"I don't want to hurt you."

"When will you let me go?"

"In Algeria."

They were calling to him: the plane is ready, the crew is ready. He saw the plane but it was some distance away. "Closer, bring it closer! Don't you hear me?" he yelled.

The little knife, with one blade stuck out, pressed against the girl's back. Against the uniform. His face was hot from being so close to her hair. He breathed in and out, against the back of her neck. Her ear. He said, "I don't want to hurt you or kill you, I'm not in favor of violence or blood.... Tell them to bring that plane closer."

She cupped her hands to her mouth and tried to call to them, but she could not speak. He heard a sob from her. *I thought I would break down then, and that he would kill me, just slide the knife in me because he was disgusted....* She sobbed, her shoulders shook; he relented and said, "All right, forget it, let's go. Let's go."

Stiffly he walked her down the ramp. She nearly slipped and he held her steady, his fingers tightening around her arm. She cried out with the surprise of it, the pain. He knew that people were watching him, from inside the hangars and from behind the steel fences; perhaps a camera crew was filming this. He imagined himself on film, on a television screen. An image of Robert Severin walking across a screen jerkily, streaks of rain on the camera lens. It would be so realistic. He could see his own figure, holding the stewardess tight against the front of him, walking her down the ramp carefully, stiffly, Robert Severin in his dirty, baggy suit wearing his aviator's sunglasses as if he were prepared for the sun of Algeria, his hair bunched and spiky from not having been washed for a month. *Robert Severin centered on a screen. Robert Severin centered in a telescopic sight.*

At the bottom of the ramp the girl slipped and stumbled two steps down, to the pavement. She turned as if to apologize to him and at that moment there was a shot. Severin jerked backward against the steps, away from her. Then another shot. His face exploded: she was looking up into his face when it exploded. It was as if something had been thrown against his face, an object stuffed with blood, and now the blood had burst out and was pouring from him. Did she hear him scream? Any sound at all? She caught the fullness of his weight as he fell, his body gone heavy, the blood gushing from him and onto her. She fell, she tried to get to her feet, screaming, but she slipped in his blood, she slipped to her knees and then pushed herself up, frantic to get away, to get away....

I thought I was shot myself. I thought we were both shot.
Does this alter your plans?—your plans for a career?
Oh no. No.
You'll have something to tell your grandchildren, won't you?
Oh yes.
What do you think of the FBI man who did the shooting?

She studied the photographs in that evening's newspaper: a picture of herself, two microphones extended toward her, her face looking good enough, even her hair good enough; and a picture of the man at the steel wall, aiming his rifle. She stared. He had such dark hair, he held the gun so firmly, so certainly.... Other men stood below him, watching. They seemed such ordinary men. They watched him and he leaned over the wall, his back to them, aiming the rifle and peering through the scope, staring at her and Severin through the scope.... And yet neither she nor Severin had known about the rifle! She marveled at this, tracing with her forefinger her own face and then the outline of the FBI man's body and the rifle, aimed out of the picture, at that face of hers. Past her face. Over her shoulder and into Severin's face.

It was so confusing, so hard to think about....

Powerfully, she felt the blow again: Severin slammed back from her, against the steps of the ramp. She had slipped on the wet steps. And then the shot, then the second shot. How she loved him! "Tell me what you felt," she said.

"I had the idea that the two of you could see me. Right back through the scope," he said.

"Did you? Did it seem as though I was watching you? What did I look like?"

"Very beautiful," he said.

"Was I beautiful? Was I? Even in the rain, even after that hour with him? Was I beautiful to you?"

"Yes, you were beautiful. . . . For fifteen minutes I was watching you, you and him. You. I had never seen a face like yours. . . ."

"Were you afraid?"

"No. I took my time. I knew how it would turn out. I had only to wait for the right moment in order to make it turn out that way. As soon as they flew me in, as soon as I got propped up on that wall, he was a dead man. But it took a while to kill him."

"Did you ever kill anyone before?"

"Never an American."

With his deer rifle he had shot the young man with the sunglasses, the first shot catching him squarely in the chest, the second shot squarely in the face. Excellent shots. For ten, fifteen minutes he had watched through the sight, hardly breathing, waiting patiently. He had been given his orders. Ah, that girl! That white, gasping face of hers!

The boy had bounced back. Blood had sprung out of his face like an exclamation.

One day Oberon sought her out, rang the doorbell to her apartment. He introduced himself. He heard her breathing inside the door, a few inches away. Silence. "You know who I am," he said. He was very excited; there was even an odor about him of intense excitement. The girl stood inside her door, which was latched with a safety lock, a chain, and he brought his smiling face to the crack in the door so that he could look at her. She was staring up at him.

"You know why I'm here," he said.

The Lady with the Pet Dog

S TRANGERS PARTED as if to make way for him.
There he stood. He was there in the aisle, a few yards away,
watching her.

She leaned forward at once in her seat, her hand jerked up to
her face as if to ward off a blow—but then the crowd in the aisle
hid him, he was gone. She pressed both hands against her
cheeks. He was not there, she had imagined him.

"My God," she whispered.

She was alone. Her husband had gone out to the foyer to
make a telephone call; it was intermission at the concert, a
Thursday evening.

Now she saw him again, clearly. He was standing there. He
was staring at her. Her blood rocked in her body, draining out
of her head...she was going to faint.... They stared at each
other. They gave no sign of recognition. Only when he took a
step forward did she shake her head *no—no—keep away*. It was
not possible.

When her husband returned, she was staring at the place in
the aisle where her lover had been standing. Her husband
leaned forward to interrupt that stare.

"What's wrong?" he said. "Are you sick?"

Panic rose in her in long shuddering waves. She tried to get to her feet, panicked at the thought of fainting here, and her husband took hold of her. She stood like an aged woman, clutching the seat before her.

At home he helped her up the stairs and she lay down. Her head was like a large piece of crockery that had to be held still, it was so heavy. She was still panicked. She felt it in the shallows of her face, behind her knees, in the pit of her stomach. It sickened her, it made her think of mucus, of something thick and gray congested inside her, stuck to her, that was herself and yet not herself—a poison.

She lay with her knees drawn up toward her chest, her eyes hotly open, while her husband spoke to her. She imagined that other man saying, *Why did you run away from me?* Her husband was saying other words. She tried to listen to them. He was going to call the doctor, he said, and she tried to sit up. "No, I'm all right now," she said quickly. The panic was like lead inside her, so thickly congested. How slow love was to drain out of her, how fluid and sticky it was inside her head!

Her husband believed her. No doctor. No threat. Grateful, she drew her husband down to her. They embraced, not comfortably. For years now they had not been comfortable together, in their intimacy and at a distance, and now they struggled gently as if the paces of this dance were too rigorous for them. It was something they might have known once, but had now outgrown. The panic in her thickened at this double betrayal: she drew her husband to her, she caressed him wildly, she shut her eyes to think about that other man.

A crowd of men and women parting, unexpectedly, and there he stood—there he stood—she kept seeing him, and yet her vision blotched at the memory. It had been finished between them, six months before, but he had come out here...and she had escaped him, now she was lying in her husband's arms, in his embrace, her face pressed against his. It was a kind of sleep, this love-making. She felt herself falling asleep, her body falling from her. Her eyes shut.

"I love you," her husband said fiercely, angrily.

She shut her eyes and thought of that other man, as if betraying him would give her life a center.

"Did I hurt you? Are you—?" her husband whispered. Always this hot flashing of shame between them, the shame of her husband's near failure, the clumsiness of his love— "You didn't hurt me," she said.

II

They had said good-by six months before. He drove her from Nantucket, where they had met, to Albany, New York, where she visited her sister. The hours of intimacy in the car had sealed something between them, a vow of silence and impersonality: she recalled the movement of the highways, the passing of other cars, the natural rhythms of the day hypnotizing her toward sleep while he drove. She trusted him, she could sleep in his presence. Yet she could not really fall asleep in spite of her exhaustion, and she kept jerking awake, frightened, to discover that nothing had changed—still the stranger who was driving her to Albany, still the highway, the sky, the antiseptic odor of the rented car, the sense of a rhythm behind the rhythm of the air that might unleash itself at any second. Everywhere on this highway, at this moment, there were men and women driving together, bonded together—what did that mean, to be together? What did it mean to enter into a bond with another person?

No, she did not really trust him; she did not really trust men. He would glance at her with his small cautious smile and she felt a declaration of shame between them.

Shame.

In her head she rehearsed conversations. She said bitterly, "You'll be relieved when we get to Albany. Relieved to get rid of me." They had spent so many days talking, confessing too much, driven to a pitch of childish excitement, laughing together on the beach, breaking into that pose of laughter that seems to eradicate the soul, so many days of this that the silence of the trip was like the silence of a hospital—all these surface noises, these rattles and hums, but an interior silence, a befuddlement. She said to him in her imagination, "One of us should die." Then she leaned over to touch him. She caressed the back of his neck. She said, aloud, "Would you like me to drive for a while?"

They stopped at a picnic area where other cars were stopped— couples, families—and walked together, smiling at their good luck. He put his arm around her shoulders and she sensed how they were in a posture together, a man and a woman forming a posture, a figure, that someone might sketch and show to them. She said slowly, "I don't want to go back.... "

Silence. She looked up at him. His face was heavy with her words, as if she had pulled at his skin with her fingers. Children ran nearby and distracted him—yes, he was a father too, his children ran like that, they tugged at his skin with their light, busy fingers.

"Are you so unhappy?" he said.

"I'm not unhappy, back there. I'm nothing. There's nothing to me," she said.

They stared at each other. The sensation between them was intense, exhausting. She thought that this man was her savior, that he had come to her at a time in her life when her life demanded completion, an end, a permanent fixing of all that was troubled and shifting and deadly. And yet it was absurd to think this. No person could save another. So she drew back from him and released him.

A few hours later they stopped at a gas station in a small city. She went to the women's rest room, having to ask the attendant for a key, and when she came back her eye jumped nervously onto the rented car—why? did she think he might have driven off without her?—onto the man, her friend, standing in conversation with the young attendant. Her friend was as old as her husband, over forty, with lanky, sloping shoulders, a full body, his hair thick, a dark, burnished brown, a festive color that made her eye twitch a little—and his hands were always moving, always those rapid conversational circles, going nowhere, gestures that were at once a little aggressive and apologetic.

She put her hand on his arm, a claim. He turned to her and smiled and she felt that she loved him, that everything in her life had forced her to this moment and that she had no choice about it.

They sat in the car for two hours, in Albany, in the parking lot of a Howard Johnson's restaurant, talking, trying to figure out their past. There was no future. They concentrated on the past, the several days behind them, lit up with a hot, dazzling August sun, like explosions that already belonged to other people, to strangers. Her face was faintly reflected in the green-tinted curve of the windshield, but she could not have recognized that face. She began to cry; she told herself: *I am not here, this will pass, this is nothing.* Still, she could not stop crying. The muscles of her face were springy, like a child's, unpredictable muscles. He stroked her arms, her shoulders, trying to comfort her. "This is so hard . . . this is impossible. . . ." he said. She felt panic for the world outside this car, all that was not herself and this man, and at the same time she understood that she was free of him, as people are free of other people, she would leave him soon, safely, and within a few days he would have fallen into the past, the impersonal past. . . .

"I'm so ashamed of myself!" she said finally.

She returned to her husband and saw that another woman, a shadow-woman, had taken her place—noiseless and convincing, like a dancer performing certain difficult steps. Her husband folded her in his arms and talked to her of his own loneliness, his worries about his business, his health, his mother, kept tranquilized and mute in a nursing home, and her spirit detached itself from her and drifted about the rooms of the large house she lived in with her husband, a shadow-woman delicate and imprecise. There was no boundary to her, no edge. Alone, she took hot baths and sat exhausted in the steaming water, wondering at her perpetual exhaustion. All that winter she noticed the limp, languid weight of her arms, her veins bulging slightly with the pressure of her extreme weariness. *This is fate,* she thought, to be here and not there, to be one person and not another, a certain man's wife and not the wife of another man. The long, slow pain of this certainty rose in her, but it never became clear, it was baffling and imprecise. She could not be serious about it; she kept congratulating herself on her own good luck, to have escaped so easily, to have freed herself. So much love had gone into the first several years of her marriage that there wasn't much left, now, for another man.... She was certain of that. But the bath water made her dizzy, all that perpetual heat, and one day in January she drew a razor blade lightly across the inside of her arm, near the elbow, to see what would happen.

Afterward she wrapped a small towel around it, to stop the bleeding. The towel soaked through. She wrapped a bath towel around that and walked through the empty rooms of her home, lightheaded, hardly aware of the stubborn seeping of blood. There was no boundary to her in this house, no precise limit. She could flow out like her own blood and come to no end.

She sat for a while on a blue love seat, her mind empty. Her husband telephoned her when he would be staying late at the plant. He talked to her always about his plans, his problems, his business friends, his future. It was obvious that he had a future. As he spoke she nodded to encourage him, and her heartbeat quickened with the memory of her own, personal shame, the shame of this man's particular, private wife. One evening at dinner he leaned forward and put his head in his arms and fell asleep, like a child. She sat at the table with him for a while, watching him. His hair had gone gray, almost white, at the temples—no one would guess that he was so quick, so careful a man, still fairly young about the eyes. She put her hand on his head, lightly, as if to prove to herself that he was real. He slept, exhausted.

One evening they went to a concert and she looked up to see her lover there, in the crowded aisle, in this city, watching her. He was standing there, with his overcoat on, watching her. She went cold. That morning the telephone had rung while her husband was still home, and she had heard him answer it, heard him hang up—it must have been a wrong number—and when the telephone rang again, at 9:30, she had been afraid to answer it. She had left home to be out of the range of that ringing, but now, in this public place, in this busy auditorium, she found herself staring at that man, unable to make any sign to him, any gesture of recognition....

He would have come to her but she shook her head. *No. Stay away.*

Her husband helped her out of the row of seats, saying, "Excuse us, please. Excuse us," so that strangers got to their feet, quickly, alarmed, to let them pass. Was that woman about to faint? What was wrong?

At home she felt the blood drain slowly back into her head. Her husband embraced her hips, pressing his face against her, in that silence that belonged to the earliest days of their marriage. She thought, *He will drive it out of me.* He made love to her and she was back in the auditorium again, sitting alone, now that the concert was over. The stage was empty; the heavy velvet curtains had not been drawn; the musicians' chairs were empty, everything was silent and expectant; in the aisle her lover stood and smiled at her— Her husband was impatient. He was apart from her, working on her, operating on her; and then, stricken, he whispered, "Did I hurt you?"

The telephone rang the next morning. Dully, sluggishly, she answered it. She recognized his voice at once—that "Anna?" with its lifting of the second syllable, questioning and apologetic and making its claim— "Yes, what do you want?" she said.

"Just to see you. Please—"

"I can't."

"Anna, I'm sorry, I didn't mean to upset you—"

"I can't see you."

"Just for a few minutes—I have to talk to you—"

"But why, why now? Why now?" she said.

She heard her voice rising, but she could not stop it. He began to talk again, drowning her out. She remembered his rapid conversation. She remembered his gestures, the witty energetic circling of his hands.

"Please don't hang up!" he cried.

"I can't—I don't want to go through it again—"

"I'm not going to hurt you. Just tell me how you are."

"Everything is the same."

"Everything is the same with me."

She looked up at the ceiling, shyly. "Your wife? Your children?"

"The same."

"Your son?"

"He's fine—"

"I'm glad to hear that. I—"

"Is it still the same with you, your marriage? Tell me what you feel. What are you thinking?"

"I don't know...."

She remembered his intense, eager words, the movement of his hands, that impatient precise fixing of the air by his hands, the jabbing of his fingers.

"Do you love me?" he said.

She could not answer.

"I'll come over to see you," he said.

"No," she said.

What will come next, what will happen?

Flesh hardening on his body, aging. Shrinking. He will grow old, but not soft like her husband. They are two different types: he is nervous, lean, energetic, wise. She will grow thinner, as the tension radiates out from her backbone, wearing down her flesh. Her collarbones will jut out of her skin. Her husband, caressing her in their bed, will discover that she is another woman—she is not there with him—instead she is rising in an elevator in a downtown hotel, carrying a book as a prop, or walking quickly away from that hotel, her head bent and filled with secrets. Love, what to do with it?... Useless as moths' wings, as moths' fluttering.... She feels the flutterings of silky, crazy wings in her chest.

He flew out to visit her every several weeks, staying at a different hotel each time. He telephoned her, and she drove down to park in an underground garage at the very center of the city.

She lay in his arms while her husband talked to her, miles away, one body fading into another. He will grow old, his body will change, she thought, pressing her cheek against the back of one of these men. If it was her lover, they were in a hotel room: always the propped-up little booklet describing the hotel's many services, with color photographs of its cocktail lounge and dining room and coffee shop. Grow old, leave me, die, go back to your neurotic wife and your sad, ordinary children, she thought, but still her eyes closed gratefully against his skin and she felt how complete their silence was, how they had come to rest in each other.

"Tell me about your life here. The people who love you," he said, as he always did.

One afternoon they lay together for four hours. It was her birthday and she was intoxicated with her good fortune, this prize of the afternoon, this man in her arms! She was a little giddy, she talked too much. She told him about her parents, about her husband.... "They were all people I believed in, but it turned out wrong. Now, I believe in you...." He laughed as if shocked by her words. She did not understand. Then she understood. "But I believe truly in you. I can't think of myself without you," she said.... He spoke of his wife, her ambitions, her intelligence, her use of the children against him, her use of his younger son's blindness, all of his words gentle and hypnotic and convincing in the late afternoon peace of this hotel room ... and she felt the terror of laughter, threatening laughter. Their words, like their bodies, were aging.

She dressed quickly in the bathroom, drawing her long hair up around the back of her head, fixing it as always, anxious that everything be the same. Her face was slightly raw, from his face. The rubbing of his skin. Her eyes were too bright, wearily bright. Her hair was blond but not so blond as it had been that summer in the white Nantucket air.

She ran water and splashed it on her face. She blinked at the water. Blind. Drowning. She thought with satisfaction that soon, soon, he would be back home, in that house on Long Island she had never seen, with that woman she had never seen, sitting on the edge of another bed, putting on his shoes. She wanted nothing except to be free of him. Why not be free? *Oh, she thought suddenly, I will follow you back and kill you. You and her and the little boy. What is there to stop me?*

She left him. Everyone on the street pitied her, that look of absolute zero.

III

A man and a child, approaching her. The sharp acrid smell of fish. The crashing of waves. Anna pretended not to notice the father with his son—there was something strange about them. That frank, silent intimacy, too gentle, the man's bare feet in the water and the boy a few feet away, leaning away from his father. He was about nine years old and still his father held his hand.

A small yipping dog, a golden dog, bounded near them.

Anna turned shyly back to her reading; she did not want to have to speak to these neighbors. She saw the man's shadow falling over her legs, then over the pages of her book, and she had the idea that he wanted to see what she was reading. The dog nuzzled her; the man called him away.

She watched them walk down the beach. She was relieved that the man had not spoken to her.

She saw them in town later that day, the two of them brown-haired and patient, now wearing sandals, walking with that same look of care. The man's white shorts were soiled and a little baggy. His pullover shirt was a faded green. His face was broad, the cheekbones wide, spaced widely apart, the eyes stark in their sockets, as if they fastened onto objects for no reason, ponderous and edgy. The little boy's face was pale and sharp; his lips were perpetually parted.

Anna realized that the child was blind.

The next morning, early, she caught sight of them again. For some reason she went to the back door of her cottage. She faced the sea breeze eagerly. Her heart hammered.... She had been here, in her family's old house, for three days, alone, bitterly satisfied at being alone, and now it was a puzzle to her how her soul strained to fly outward, to meet with another person. She watched the man with his son, his cautious, rather stooped shoulders above the child's small shoulders.

The man was carrying something, it looked like a notebook. He sat on the sand, not far from Anna's spot of the day before, and the dog rushed up to them. The child approached the edge of the ocean, timidly. He moved in short jerky steps, his legs stiff. The dog ran around him. Anna heard the child crying out a word that sounded like "Ty"—it must have been the dog's name—and then the man joined in, his voice heavy and firm.

"Ty—"

Anna tied her hair back with a yellow scarf and went down to the beach.

The man glanced around at her. He smiled. She stared past him at the waves. To talk to him or not to talk—she had the freedom of that choice. For a moment she felt that she had made a mistake, that the child and the dog would not protect her, that behind this man's ordinary, friendly face there was a certain arrogant maleness—then she relented, she smiled shyly.

"A nice house you've got there," the man said.

She nodded her thanks.

The man pushed his sunglasses up on his forehead. Yes, she recognized the eyes of the day before—intelligent and nervous, the sockets pale, untanned.

"Is that your telephone ringing?" he said.

She did not bother to listen. "It's a wrong number," she said.

Her husband calling: she had left home for a few days, to be alone.

But the man, settling himself on the sand, seemed to misinterpret this. He smiled in surprise, one corner of his mouth higher than the other. He said nothing. Anna wondered: *What is he thinking?* The dog was leaping about her, panting against her legs, and she laughed in embarrassment. She bent to pet it, grateful for its busyness. "Don't let him jump up on you," the man said. "He's a nuisance."

The dog was a small golden retriever, a young dog. The blind child, standing now in the water, turned to call the dog to him. His voice was shrill and impatient.

"Our house is the third one down—the white one," the man said.

She turned, startled, "Oh, did you buy it from Dr. Patrick? Did he die?"

"Yes, finally...."

Her eyes wandered nervously over the child and the dog. She felt the nervous beat of her heart out to the very tips of her fingers, the fleshy tips of her fingers: little hearts were there, pulsing. *What is he thinking?* The man had opened his notebook. He had a piece of charcoal and he began to sketch something.

Anna looked down at him. She saw the top of his head, his thick brown hair, the freckles on his shoulders, the quick, deft movement of his hand. Upside down, Anna herself being drawn. She smiled in surprise.

"Let me draw you. Sit down," he said.

She knelt awkwardly a few yards away .1e turned the page of the sketch pad. The dog ran to her and she sat, straightening out her skirt beneath her, flinching from the dog's tongue. "Ty!" cried the child. Anna sat, and slowly the pleasure of the moment began to glow in her; her skin flushed with gratitude.

She sat there for nearly an hour. The man did not talk much. Back and forth the dog bounded, shaking itself. The child came to sit near them, in silence. Anna felt that she was drifting into a kind of trance while the man sketched her, half a dozen rapid sketches, the surface of her face given up to him. "Where are you from?" the man asked.

"Ohio. My husband lives in Ohio."

She wore no wedding band.

"Your wife—" Anna began.

"Yes?"

"Is she here?"

"Not right now."

She was silent, ashamed. She had asked an improper question. But the man did not seem to notice. He continued drawing her, bent over the sketch pad. When Anna said she had to go, he showed her the drawings—one after another of her, Anna, recognizably Anna, a woman in her early thirties, her hair smooth and flat across the top of her head, tied behind by a scarf. "Take the one you like best," he said, and she picked one of her with the dog in her lap, sitting very straight, her brows and eyes clearly defined, her lips girlishly pursed, the dog and her dress suggested by a few quick irregular lines.

"Lady with pet dog," the man said.

She spent the rest of that day reading, nearer her cottage. It was not really a cottage—it was a two-story house, large and ungainly and weathered. It was mixed up in her mind with her family, her own childhood, and she glanced up from her book, perplexed, as if waiting for one of her parents or her sister to come up to her. Then she thought of that man, the man with the blind child, the man with the dog, and she could not concentrate on her reading. Someone—probably her father—had marked a passage that must be important, but she kept reading and rereading it: *We try to discover in things, endeared to us on that account, the spiritual glamour which we ourselves have cast upon them; we are disillusioned, and learn that they are in themselves barren and devoid of the charm that they owed, in our minds, to the association of certain ideas....*

She thought again of the man on the beach. She lay the book aside and thought of him: his eyes, his aloneness, his drawings of her.

They began seeing each other after that. He came to her front door in the evening, without the child; he drove her into town for dinner. She was shy and extremely pleased. The darkness of the expensive restaurant released her; she heard herself chatter; she leaned forward and seemed to be offering her face up to him, listening to him. He talked about his work on a Long Island newspaper and she seemed to be listening to him, as she stared at his face, arranging her own face into the expression she had seen in that charcoal drawing. Did he see her like that, then?— girlish and withdrawn and patrician? She felt the weight of his interest in her, a force that fell upon her like a blow. A repeated blow. Of course he was married, he had children—of course she was married, permanently married. This flight from her husband was not important. She had left him before, to be alone, it was not important. Everything in her was slender and delicate and not important.

They walked for hours after dinner, looking at the other strollers, the weekend visitors, the tourists, the couples like themselves. Surely they were mistaken for a couple, a married couple. *This is the hour in which everything is decided,* Anna thought. They had both had several drinks and they talked a great deal. Anna found herself saying too much, stopping and starting giddily. She put her hand to her forehead, feeling faint.

"It's from the sun—you've had too much sun—" he said.

At the door to her cottage, on the front porch, she heard herself asking him if he would like to come in. She allowed him to lead her inside, to close the door. *This is not important,* she thought clearly, *he doesn't mean it, he doesn't love me, nothing will come of it.* She was frightened, yet it seemed to her necessary to give in; she had to leave Nantucket with that act completed, an act of adultery, an accomplishment she would take back to Ohio and to her marriage.

Later, incredibly, she heard herself asking: "Do you . . . do you love me?"

"You're so beautiful!" he said, amazed.

She felt this beauty, shy and glowing and centered in her eyes. He stared at her. In this large, drafty house, alone together, they were like accomplices, conspirators. She could not think: how old was she? which year was this? They had done something unforgivable together, and the knowledge of it was tugging at their faces. A cloud seemed to pass over her. She felt herself smiling shrilly.

Afterward, a peculiar raspiness, a dryness of breath. He was silent. She felt a strange, idle fear, a sense of the danger outside this room and this old, comfortable bed—a danger that would not recognize her as the lady in that drawing, the lady with the pet dog. There was nothing to say to this man, this stranger. She felt the beauty draining out of her face, her eyes fading.

"I've got to be alone," she told him.

He left, and she understood that she would not see him again. She stood by the window of the room, watching the ocean. A sense of shame overpowered her: it was smeared everywhere on her body, the smell of it, the richness of it. She tried to recall him, and his face was confused in her memory: she would have to shout to him across a jumbled space, she would have to wave her arms wildly. *You love me! You must love me!* But she knew he did not love her, and she did not love him; he was a man who drew everything up into himself, like all men, walking away, free to walk away, free to have his own thoughts, free to envision her body, all the secrets of her body. . . . And she lay down again in the bed, feeling how heavy this body had become, her insides heavy with shame, the very backs of her eyelids coated with shame.

"This is the end of one part of my life," she thought.

But in the morning the telephone rang. She answered it. It was her lover: they talked brightly and happily. She could hear the eagerness in his voice, the love in his voice, that same still, sad amazement—she understood how simple life was, there were no problems.

They spent most of their time on the beach, with the child and the dog. He joked and was serious at the same time. He said, once, "You have defined my soul for me," and she laughed to hide her alarm. In a few days it was time for her to leave. He got a sitter for the boy and took the ferry with her to the mainland, then rented a car to drive her up to Albany. She kept thinking: *Now something will happen. It will come to an end.* But most of the drive was silent and hypnotic. She wanted him to joke with her, to say again that she had defined his soul for him, but he drove fast, he was serious, she distrusted the hawkish look of his profile—she did not know him at all. At a gas station she splashed her face with cold water. Alone in the grubby little rest room, shaky and very much alone. In such places are women totally alone with their bodies. The body grows heavier, more evil, in such silence. . . . On the beach everything had been noisy with sunlight and gulls and waves; here, as if run to earth, everything was cramped and silent and dead.

She went outside, squinting. There he was, talking with the station attendant. She could not think as she returned to him whether she wanted to live or not.

She stayed in Albany for a few days, then flew home to her husband. He met her at the airport, near the luggage counter, where her three pieces of pale-brown luggage were brought to him on a conveyer belt, to be claimed by him. He kissed her on the cheek. They shook hands, a little embarrassed. She had come home again.

"How will I live out the rest of my life?" she wondered.

In January her lover spied on her: she glanced up and saw him, in a public place, in the DeRoy Symphony Hall. She was paralyzed with fear. She nearly fainted. In this faint she felt her husband's body, loving her, working its love upon her, and she shut her eyes harder to keep out the certainty of his love— sometimes he failed at loving her, sometimes he succeeded, it had nothing to do with her or her pity or her ten years of love for him, it had nothing to do with a woman at all. It was a private act accomplished by a man, a husband or a lover, in communion with his own soul, his manhood.

Her husband was forty-two years old now, growing slowly into middle age, getting heavier, softer. Her lover was about the same age, narrower in the shoulders, with a full, solid chest, yet lean, nervous. She thought, in her paralysis, of men and how they love freely and eagerly so long as their bodies are capable of love, love for a woman; and then, as love fades in their bodies, it fades from their souls and they become immune and immortal and ready to die.

Her husband was a little rough with her, as if impatient with himself. "I love you," he said fiercely, angrily. And then, ashamed, he said, "Did I hurt you?..."

"You didn't hurt me," she said.

Her voice was too shrill for their embrace.

While he was in the bathroom she went to her closet and took out that drawing of the summer before. There she was, on the beach at Nantucket, a lady with a pet dog, her eyes large and defined, the dog in her lap hardly more than a few snarls, a few coarse soft lines of charcoal...her dress smeared, her arms oddly limp...her hands not well drawn at all.... She tried to think: did she love the man who had drawn this? did he love her? The fever in her husband's body had touched her and driven her temperature up, and now she stared at the drawing with a kind of lust, fearful of seeing an ugly soul in that woman's face, fearful of seeing the face suddenly through her lover's eyes. She breathed quickly and harshly, staring at the drawing.

And so, the next day, she went to him at his hotel. She wept, pressing against him, demanding of him, "What do you want? Why are you here? Why don't you let me alone?" He told her that he wanted nothing. He expected nothing. He would not cause trouble.

"I want to talk about last August," he said.

"Don't—" she said.

She was hypnotized by his gesturing hands, his nervousness,

his obvious agitation. He kept saying, "I understand. I'm making no claims upon you."

They became lovers again.

He called room service for something to drink and they sat side by side on his bed, looking through a copy of *The New Yorker*, laughing at the cartoons. It was so peaceful in this room, so complete. They were on a holiday. It was a secret holiday. Four-thirty in the afternoon, on a Friday, an ordinary Friday: a secret holiday.

"I won't bother you again," he said.

He flew back to see her again in March, and in late April. He telephoned her from his hotel—a different hotel each time—and she came down to him at once. She rose to him in various elevators, she knocked on the doors of various rooms, she stepped into his embrace, breathless and guilty and already angry with him, pleading with him. One morning in May, when he telephoned, she pressed her forehead against the doorframe and could not speak. He kept saying, "What's wrong? Can't you talk? Aren't you alone?" She felt that she was going insane. Her head would burst. Why, why did he love her, why did he pursue her? Why did he want her to die?

She went to him in the hotel room. A familiar room: had they been here before? "Everything is repeating itself. Everything is stuck," she said. He framed her face in his hands and said that she looked thinner—was she sick?—what was wrong? She shook herself free. He, her lover, looked about the same. There was a small, angry pimple on his neck. He stared at her, eagerly and suspiciously. Did she bring bad news?

"So you love me? You love me?" she asked.

"Why are you so angry?"

"I want to be free of you. The two of us free of each other."

"That isn't true—you don't want that—"

He embraced her. She was wild with that old, familiar passion for him, her body clinging to his, her arms not strong enough to hold him. Ah, what despair!—what bitter hatred she felt!—she needed this man for her salvation, he was all she had to live for, and yet she could not believe in him. He embraced her thighs, her hips, kissing her, pressing his warm face against her, and yet she could not believe in him, not really. She needed him in order to live, but he was not worth her love, he was not worth her dying.... She promised herself this: when she got back home, when she was alone, she would draw the razor more deeply across her arm.

The telephone rang and he answered it: a wrong number.

"Jesus," he said.

They lay together, still. She imagined their posture like this, the two of them one figure, one substance; and outside this room and this bed there was a universe of disjointed, separate things, blank things, that had nothing to do with them. She would not be Anna out there, the lady in the drawing. He would not be her lover.

"I love you so much..." she whispered.

"Please don't cry! We have only a few hours, please...."

It was absurd, their clinging together like this. She saw them as a single figure in a drawing, their arms and legs entwined, their heads pressing mutely together. Helpless substance, so heavy and warm and doomed. It was absurd that any human being should be so important to another human being. She wanted to laugh: a laugh might free them both.

She could not laugh.

Sometime later he said, as if they had been arguing, "Look. It's you. You're the one who doesn't want to get married. You lie to me—"

"Lie to you?"

"You love me but you won't marry me, because you want something left over— Something not finished— All your life you can attribute your misery to me, to our not being married— you are using me—"

"Stop it! You'll make me hate you!" she cried.

"You can say to yourself that you're miserable because of *me*. We will never be married, you will never be happy, neither one of us will ever be happy—"

"I don't want to hear this!" she said.

She pressed her hands flatly against her face.

She went to the bathroom to get dressed. She washed her face and part of her body, quickly. The fever was in her, in the pit of her belly. She would rush home and strike a razor across the inside of her arm and free that pressure, that fever.

The impatient bulging of the veins: an ordeal over.

The demand of the telephone's ringing: that ordeal over.

The nuisance of getting the car and driving home in all that five o'clock traffic: an ordeal too much for a woman.

The movement of this stranger's body in hers: over, finished.

Now, dressed, a little calmer, they held hands and talked. They had to talk swiftly, to get all their news in: he did not trust the people who worked for him, he had faith in no one, his wife had moved to a textbook publishing company and was doing well, she had inherited a Ben Shahn painting from her father and wanted to "touch it up a little"—she was crazy!—his blind son was at another school, doing fairly well, in fact his children were all doing fairly well in spite of the stupid mistake of their parents' marriage—and what about her? what about her life? She told him in a rush the one thing he wanted to hear: that she lived with her husband lovelessly, the two of them polite strangers, sharing a bed, lying side by side in the night in that bed, bodies out of which souls had fled. There was no longer even any shame between them.

"And what about me? Do you feel shame with me still?" he asked.

She did not answer. She moved away from him and prepared to leave.

Then, a minute later, she happened to catch sight of his reflection in the bureau mirror—he was glancing down at himself, checking himself mechanically, impersonally, preparing also to leave. He too would leave this room: he too was headed somewhere else.

She stared at him. It seemed to her that in this instant he was breaking from her, the image of her lover fell free of her, breaking from her . . . and she realized that he existed in a dimension quite apart from her, a mysterious being. And suddenly, joyfully, she felt a miraculous calm. This man was her husband, truly—they were truly married, here in this room—they had been married haphazardly and accidentally for a long time. In another part of the city she had another husband, a "husband," but she had not betrayed that man, not really. This man, whom she loved above any other person in the world, above even her own self-pitying sorrow and her own life, was her truest lover, her destiny. And she did not hate him, she did not hate herself any longer; she did not wish to die; she was flooded with a strange certainty, a sense of gratitude, of pure selfless energy. It was obvious to her that she had, all along, been behaving correctly; out of instinct.

What triumph, to love like this in any room, anywhere, risking even the craziest of accidents!

"Why are you so happy? What's wrong?" he asked, startled. He stared at her. She felt the abrupt concentration in him, the focusing of his vision on her, almost a bitterness in his face, as if he feared her. What, was it beginning all over again? Their love beginning again, in spite of them? "How can you look so happy?" he asked. "We don't have any right to it. Is it because...?"

"Yes," she said.

The Turn of the Screw

*T*UESDAY, JULY 6.

Tuesday, July 6.

A wide stony beach. Pebbles big as hands. Here the sky is bluer than it is at home. Got out of the hotel before anyone could say hello—need to be alone after last night. Uncle and his hacking cough! Stayed up most of the night with him. His coughing is like the noise of the earth, its insides shifting. I imagine the earth splitting to draw the old man down, his body tumbling into the crater, into Hell. . . .

(Curious about Hell: will the flames make much noise?)

Had to read the Bible to him

Alone here, hidden, sick at heart. Away from that horrible numerosity. The oppression of the London sky, terraces bathed in evil light, the tonnage of history, too many horizons brought up short. . . . Chimneys that mock, beckon. Stained and weathered like cheeses. . . .

The stern demanding sea. It, too, mocks. But it does not know me. *Idle now for weeks, for a month and a half.*

Dying by the sea. Wearing the same two or three sets of clothes—no need to change—

while he lay there coughing and spitting. Didn't pay attention to me. Finally he slept—around five. I fell onto my bed fully dressed and slept until seven. Sleep like death. In the morning I got out fast, my head echoing with Uncle's awful noises... so glad to be alone! And then a strange thing happened....

A mile from the hotel. Me walking fast, enjoying the air, the smell of the sea. Great gulping breaths of air. My new boots slick with mud, my eyes fixed on the ground before me... glancing up I saw a girl, hardly more than a child. Twelve, thirteen years old.

Staring at me!

She called out something to me, a stranger. A high wheedling voice. Words I couldn't hear. My senses rushed together, stinging. I was deaf. A pull to my insides. Pain. Ah, that girl!—not pretty but full-faced, full-bodied, her eyes gleaming slits above her coarse pinkened cheeks—eyes gleaming as if there were already a secret between us!

anonymous gentleman dark-ringed about the eyes with failure—afraid of new arrivals at the hotel: but they are all strangers. This morning I nearly collided with the young man I had noticed last night—he and an older man, probably his father, arrived yesterday, the old man apparently quite ill— Saw him walking along the beach, alone. Rather finely dressed and yet with a look—how strange that I should feel so certain of this!—of being doubtful of his clothes, as if they belonged to someone else. A waistcoat of pale satin. Excellent boots. Hatless, dark red hair, very strong features—the eyebrows are especially dark and firm—the eyes downcast as if searching out his fate *there*, on the ground. Something heraldic about him—a figure for art— My senses stung at the sight of him—

Then I saw, standing farther up the bank, near a thicket, that poor little girl who runs loose in the town some-times—"not right in the head"—she was beckoning to the young American. Some shy instinct made me halt,

A dress of some green material, shapeless over her full hips and thighs; her plump little feet in boots, splattered with mud; her cheeks red as if pinched, very excited, strange dark eyes gleaming.... A head of curls—dark blond, depths of blond and shadow, enough to make my body ache. Licking her lips. One foot extended slightly as if in a dance. Cried out to me—a question—her voice tilting upward shrilly— but the noise of the waves drowned her out, my blood drowned her out, pulsing in my ears. Her gleaming eyes. The mist seemed to thicken and cloak us both. My eyes filmed over, filmed over....

Bell-like tone to her voice. I could see now the veins in her throat.

Behind her, half a mile from the beach, a building like a fortress—is it a church? A barn? Stinging film over my eyes...my heart is pounding violently.... Around us on the beach: no one. Empty. Heart pounding, temples pounding, a dense dewlike moisture on every part of my body, cold and slick as fog,

back up—what would happen? I wanted to turn and hurry away. Befuddlement everywhere about us—the crashing of the waves—the young man's agitation— His smart clothes suddenly the clothes of an actor. *I must leave, must leave!*

Flushed face—the girl's frizzy blond hair—my own strange elation— *She is putting her hand out to him, she is calling to him,* but I am too far away to hear.

He will touch her, take hold of her arm. He will approach her and touch her. The three of us stand on the beach in total silence.

Waiting.

It is too late for me to turn and hurry away—my own face flushed and dangerously heated—something churns in my brain and fixes me here to the spot— *His back is to me: what does his face show?* She is staring up into his face—she *sees*—what words are passing between them? What words are spoken at such a time?

He approaches her. His stiff

my insides in pain.... Suddenly I thought of my uncle back in the hotel: *he might be dying.*

A thicket for us. Giant bushes, spongy ground. The pebbles fade. The girl backs away from me. Wide staring smile. Her face protruding, plump. Something about her wet mouth that is fearful... but I cannot stop, it is too late, I cannot stop my hand from reaching out to her.... There! Her arm, her elbow. My fingers close about her elbow. Giggling, backing away... a branch catches in her hair and then snaps away again, snaps straight... my fingers sliding up her arm to the shoulder and she is laughing faintly, breathily, the down on her upper lip is gleaming as if with cunning, she is very young, no more than twelve or thirteen years old... her chest rising and falling... little body stumbling backward, drawing us both backward into the thicket....

She gave a jump. A little scream. Jerked away from me—pointed somewhere behind me—what was it? I couldn't see anything. What?

back. She draws away, teasing. Giant bushes will hide them from me. Panting, dizzy. I will be sick. He has taken hold of her now—yes, he has touched her—the two of them drawing back, back, almost out of my sight—they will hide themselves from me—it is going to happen, it is going to happen—

The girl screamed suddenly. Leaped back.

Must have seen me.

I hurry up the bank, must hide. Must get out of their sight. Heart sickened with fear, panic... I must not stumble....

Reddening terrible face.

The dowdy room I have taken: its small charms and beguilements, etched glass, lace curtains, the dust of sorrow, sorrow, sorrow....

In the mirror my face surprises me. So pale, so frightened! I thought it to be, for one confused moment, the face of that young man

Overcome with panic—*I have
made a terrible mistake. My
uncle has followed me.* The girl
ran away. Behind me on the
beach there was nothing, no
one, I stood there trembling
and staring back up the
beach, no, nothing, no one,
and yet I had the idea that
someone had been standing
there watching us only a few
seconds before....

Not my uncle?...

Slick with sweat. Oh, reeking.
My head is still pounding. If
anyone had seen...if any-
one.... Uncle would abandon
me, like the rest, if he had
seen....

God, help me to get through
each day.

Wednesday, July 7.

Papers still filled with
Victoria's Jubilee. Uncle
Wallace at breakfast, robust
and scornful, an excellent
mood. Eggs, ham, toast,
marmalade, buns. Snatches
up the paper to read me an
item; snorts with disgust.
Breakfast takes an hour and a
half. The dining room has a
high cavernous ceiling:

Wednesday, July 7.

Sleepless. Preoccupied. Idle
now for a month and a half.
My life: turned over and over
as I turn this paperweight in
my hand, something to be
flung down, forgotten.

Breakfast. Careful not to stare
at *him.* Hot, hot tea. There is
a delightful family at a
window table—rather hazy

everything echoes. The room is not much used, the hotel not much used. Everyone looks English except us. Cold mealy independent faces.

A woman in her early fifties at a near table ... dull red-blond hair, brusque mannish gestures ... but her face is attractive as she glances toward me, past her husband. Uncle does not see. Reading the third newspaper, grunting, coughing up something into his napkin.... By the seaside windows an English family with three children— the oldest a girl about ten. A child. Alone at another table is a middle-aged man in a rough tweedy jacket, too big for him, sipping tea. Reading a paper. Very British. Lifting the paper to turn it, he glances toward Uncle and me—our eyes meet—then he looks away. A large rigid face. Eyes piercing.

With Uncle at the seaside. Grunts, clearing his throat vigorously, staring out at the sea. It disappoints him. Spits something up in his handker-chief. *What if he dies?* ... My first trip to Europe; three months of travel ahead; what light—rain today? No matter. I will bicycle out into the isolation.

My heart has been turning inside me, tugging to one side. A leaden sickish tug. I surrender.... He is sitting with the old gentleman, wearing clothes that fit him splendidly. Yet somehow not *his.* I turn my paper very briskly, neatly, to draw his attention.... An instant of our exchanging a glance ... perhaps he recognizes me from yesterday?

His eye wanders away from me.

Close-curling red hair. Handsome, pale, American face. Sits erect at the table like a son. I imagine he is perhaps twenty-five years old, and most dreadfully bored in the company of that old man, somehow thrown in with him for a trip, yet I don't believe that they are father and son....

Absurdly sad: they are leaving the dining room. Yet an elation—the prospect lies ahead of further meetings, if he sickens and dies and leaves me alone? No. Behind him is my father. His brother. Dying also, dying very slowly. Decades of it. In Boston they take decades. *Quarles Ltd., Dry Goods.*

Loosed, what would my body do? ... Run from this wreck of a man. Run. Noble wreck, ruined noble face. Cascades of wrinkled shriveled flesh on his neck! Back in Boston they are frowning sourly over us— two of a kind, two failures. Uncle and nephew. When Uncle Wallace was my age he was already a father.... Then the children died. First the boy, then the girl. Then the wife. Now I am his son, maybe. Two failures.

Uncle in a chair below the hotel. Attendants eager to please. Cool for July, they talk of the chance of clearing by this afternoon, always squinting at the sky and making prophecies. The middle-aged lady greets us doubtfully; yes, it is cool for July, she says. I am bored, bored. In a canvas chair beside Uncle. Staring at the sea. More blue here than back home—choppy distances— I cannot stop think-

accidental meetings. Is there a mysterious and perhaps incomprehensible alliance here?

Subdued. A solitary break- fast. The family has left the dining room now—I hear excited talk of a carriage, an excursion—two girls and a boy, beautiful children. The boy is by far the youngest and walks with a bold stride. To be a father, a father of that particular boy.... What would that mean? How could it be experienced, so deep and terrifying a condition? Beautiful children!

Idle. Yet a small fever begins in me, as if I were about to start work. Idle and nervous. But I see that I am not head- ing for my room, no, I am walking quite reasonably headlong into a kind of hush—postbreakfast solem- nity in this droll old hotel, all a kind of hush, the fixtures overdone and pompous and hushed, a held breath, as in that eerie moment when something gathers or crouches in preparation for an attack. ...

Ah, the beach. Poor helpless

ing of that girl of yesterday, that child on the beach. My body tries to shrivel. I think of my cousin Madeline—that face of hers. Accusing me. *He said things to me! Said things!*

Like a girl of twelve herself. But she was twenty-four.

Next week I will be thirty.

Uncle clearing his throat loudly, spreading a blanket across his knees; more newspapers. Brings the edge of his fingers hard across his mustache. Someone pauses near him. Cane in hand, jaunty for a man his age, his beard trimmed to a spadelike shape. Dark. Neat. He is a gentleman but nervous— wears a polka-dot bow tie and a golfing cap. Heavyset in the thighs and torso.

Uncle Wallace and he are talking— "...north of Boston?..." "...the Clintons, Arnold Clinton, finance ...imports?..." "...crowds in London?...awful!"

My eye is drawn out to the edge of the sea.

Women: the girl of yesterday.

eyes bobbing about—from horizon to shore—there they are, seated. The old man humped and tyrannical. The young man with legs crossed; white trousers, handsome high-button shoes, an air of indolence and impatience. The son of a wealthy father, certainly.

Approaching the old gentleman. His sudden raised face—querulous watery eyes—yet I introduce myself quite easily. Ah, yes, they are Americans; should I seem surprised? From Boston. It turns out that we know someone in common. I chat quite happily, quite easily with the old man. My agitation seems to have subsided. Ignore the young man's stare—it is good to hear my own voice again—too conscious of Self, too haunted, driven by Self, always Self. I must overcome myself.

Patrick Quarles II. His name.

I think of Dickens—for we are near David Copperfield's country—no, I think of Stendhal: a young man lounging idly, restlessly, ambitious and yet not strong

Eyes secretive as slits. Her
foot—the mud—the ankle—
the pale stockings—the calf of
the leg inside the stocking—
the knee—the thigh—

Old men chattering: of
London, of crowds, *this
screaming, clumsy overdoing of
a fine thing,* the man in the
golfing cap says.

Ah, the cords of her little
throat were taut with concentration! Cheap material of the
dress drawn tight across the
small bosom, tight as the
veins of the throat, the tense
arteries of the stomach, the
loins . . . blue-veined thighs,
the shadowy soft insides of
thighs. . . . *London defaced: an
atrocious sight. Miles of un-
sightly scaffolding . . . a sudden,
new vision of our age, an
unwelcome perspective of the
century that lies ahead. . . .
Machinery . . . that infuriates
and deflowers and destroys. . . .*

Walking slowly down the
beach. Why do I want to run,
run away from the chatter of
old men!—a root is alive in
me, stirring in me. Trembling.
Ugh. I am alive and the old
men are dying or are dead, if
I glance over my shoulder at

enough to direct the progress
of the story he is in. Con-
demned almost and never to
be quite *real,* quite sympathetic. *He seems to be listening
as I speak of London. . . .* He is a
man marked for some strange
destiny. For women? Yes, but
more. He does not know
what his fate will be. *Nervous,
I am beginning to be nervous. . . .*

He is like a young animal: no
history.

The old man contains all their
family history. Draws it up
into him. We chatter wonderfully, two Americans, he
seems to be impressed with
my denunciation of the
Jubilee nonsense. Can understand best harsh abrasive
words.

The young man gets to his
feet suddenly, unaccountably,
and strolls away. . . .

The old man is a large
monument; the nephew a
small marker. In a flash I see
their family gravesite. Yes. I,
standing here so helplessly
and timidly, cane tucked
through my arm, smiling and
smiling, a gravestone of too
fragile a substance: the wintry

them I would see only two
aging gentlemen—one in a
canvas chair, bundled up for
a cool July morning, the other
with a cane thrust through his
arm, words that do not
matter, a flow of words that
do not matter the way the
pebbles of this wide wet
beach matter—and behind
them, in America, my own
father stands like a monument, his shadow rooted to
him at his base, unshakable.
Can you shake them? You
walk away from them.

I light a cigar.

Thursday, July 8.

Was informed of a letter for
me—took it from the clerk,
surprised, for who would
write to me?—having left
home as I did—could not
recognize the handwriting—
walked confused out the front
of the hotel, almost slipped
on the steps that were wet
from the morning's rain—
tore open the envelope
nervously—

My Dear Boy,
I am anxious for this letter to do
nothing except soothe you,

gusts from this sea would
destroy me.

Thursday, July 8.

Walking quickly along the
shore. Unable to think. *Must*
think. Not fit for company
now—my face a mask of
grimaces, taunts, smirks,
bewilderments, small pains
and pleasures, featureless as
the sea. Not human now. Not
human. To have dared what I
did!... A sleepless night,
palpitating heart. Absurd
attempts at prayer. Godless
prayer. But something,
something must aid me, must
beguile me out of myself...
out of the memory of what I

encourage you, insist upon the simple joy you have given me by existing so innocently and so nobly as yourself. From my timid post of observation, your future strikes me as rich and enormously open, wide as the ocean—and I beg that you do not destroy it by any impulsive act—for, you see, I was a most reluctant and helpless witness to Tuesday's small episode—or by any systematic and perhaps more wasteful surrender of your youth to another's age. Be free: I rejoice in your very being. But: Caution!

No signature.

I stumbled along the street—cobbled street—row upon row of small blank houses, shops, the tower of the church and its crumbling ivy wall—mind in a whirl—panic—must tear up this letter and get rid of it—

Went into a pub. Seated, my eyesight blotched. Din inside my head. Last night Uncle kept me awake again, reading the Bible to him. Words kept rising in my head: *Why doesn't he die!* My fear of him, my love for him. *Why don't they*

have done ... memories of Father's fits of madness, the Imaginary seizing his throat, the Demon always beside him, squatting, leaping up when he did not, could not, have expected it.... Am I my father's son, after all?

Heroism: acquiescing to that madness.

At the bottom of my soul it squats, like that dwarf of a demon: the fear that I am mad, evil, reckless, sick, corrupting, contaminating, loosed, formless, sucking like the waves here upon the packed sand, desolate, inexhaustible, damned....

Why did I write him that letter?

Yet—the joy of this morning! The utter abandoned joy of the writing, the sealing of the envelope, the very slow, slow, firm addressing of a name that suddenly seems to have been my own invention, to have been known to me all my life: *Patrick Quarles II.*

What is he? A disinherited son—so I have gathered. He

all die, die! I order a small
beer and drink it at once and
in the instant in which I close
my eyes I can see their bodies
bobbing and ebbing in a tide,
the bodies of the old, old men,
tossed up toward an anonymous shore that is neither
American nor English, just a
shore, just bodies of the dead.
*Why don't they die and free us
from them?—free us to life?*

Spent the afternoon. Seagoing
men here—retired men—
noisy in their greetings—
"What ho!" they call out to
each other when they meet—
ther. fall into silence—but the
silence is not awkward.
Women. Moving about. They
glance at me and my heart
feels enormous, suffocating.
One woman stares openly at
me. A broad smile, straggly
hairs on her forehead... skin
not pale like Madeline's but
opaque, blunt... *easing the
stocking from her muscular leg,
heavy flesh, dark hairs growing
out of the flesh*... but I stand
suddenly, hurry away. Must
get back to the hotel before
Uncle is angry.

I tore the letter up into small
pieces and threw it away.

has the look of a London
urchin grown and clothed
splendidly—an actor—a
nervous flitting consciousness
that no clothes can define—*I
will clothe you.*

What will happen when our
eyes meet? That fateful
terrifying instant of our
common *knowledge!* I will bow
to him, I will acknowledge
everything meekly.... Breath
in ragged spurts. Aging. My
best work is behind me. Now,
ahead of me, is work of
another kind.... He is so
young, he is pure instinct.
The old man, the uncle, wants
to suck his energy. Ignorant
old man!

I am mad to have such
thoughts... sharp pain in my
chest as I climb the hotel
steps, which seem suddenly
steep, mountainous.... Is he
here, waiting? The letter in
his hand, waiting?

Friday, July 9.

Excursion by carriage. Out along the country roads in spite of the drizzle. Uncle's sour cough. Forgave me for leaving him yesterday: his heir.

Women. Foul and sluggish in their evil. Mud on my boots, scummy feel of my own skin. My cousin's tears and red-rimmed eyes. The woman in the tavern: the veins of her flesh would have been hidden deep inside that opaque fatty skin.

Afternoon tea: Uncle gorges himself. Buns, jam. Beer. Whiskey. Coffee. Small meat pie. My duty to rise obediently as a son, to seek out more food. Which village are we in? What is its name? The map I studied is marked with names of places I had wanted to explore—Blundeston, Great Yarmouth, Bournemouth itself—but everything passes now before my eyes in a mist, my senses sting, the machinery of my brain races ahead to what, to what?—

Caution, the letter advised.

Friday, July 9.

Sleepless. Feverish and very happy. Three letters composed for him, and I hardly know which to select. All of them?

The chambermaid listens with her good plain worried gaze upon me. I begin explaining carefully, but end by stammering, my eyes filled with moisture—"Mr. Quarles is an extremely sensitive gentleman...and he would be distressed to be told that he walked off with my letters this morning...he quite simply picked them up by accident, when we paused to chat together.... I called after him, of course, but as you may know, he doesn't hear quite so well...and...and I would actually prefer not to bring the matter up to him, and certainly I would prefer never to see the poor letters again if it were a question of...a question of insulting him, however indirectly...." Nods in sympathy with me. Grimly. Out of her mild gaze I think I see something growing—sharp and deadly and cunning—but no, I must be imagining it. Imagining it.

What does that mean?—why caution?—Am I about to do something I must be urged against? *Uncle's piggish grunts. The Royal Park Hotel. Will I outlive him?* Sat in the pub with him, a lonely pub. Thought of hell. Spirits brushing against us in daylight, the damned. What could they tell us about hell if they could speak?

Dutiful nephew to a sick man.

Nothing more.

She replies that it is out of her control. Only the manager, perhaps.... Very hard for her to know what to do.... But no, no, I say at once, the manager must absolutely not be bothered; I will surrender the letters—gaily I tell her this, ready to back away— She frowns, blinks slowly and stupidly at me— Suddenly she consents.

Ah, she consents! And within five minutes we are *there*, in that room! The Quarleses have taken a rather grand suite of rooms. A sitting room of really lavish proportions— excellent furniture—a carpet in much finer condition than the one in my sad little room—a balcony that stares out wonderfully at the sea and sky. There is a little old antique of a writing desk that I approach, under the chambermaid's watchful eye, for my letters would be here if Mr. Quarles had really walked off with them—and humbly, timidly I bend over the desk, in that good lady's sight, and do not touch anything on it. Only yesterday's *Times*. A letter tucked into its envelope, postmarked Boston. I shake

my head—nothing here—and
with a slight questioning rise
of my eyebrows, indicate that
I will take just one step inside
this bedroom—

Staring at me impassively.
What is she thinking? Can she
guess? The forbidden rises to
one's face in the presence of
such women, they positively
draw guilt out, expose
everything— But though I am
nervous, extremely nervous, I
smile rather bravely back at
her—how she stands watch-
ing me!— And so I open the
door to one of the bedrooms
and simply lean inside—my
heart is pounding— It is *his*
room.

Scent of pomade. Tobacco.

For a long icy moment I stand
there—my body rigid with
the necessity of showing
nothing, absolutely nothing,
as if the hunters and their
dogs will be upon me if I
flinch— I feel his strange
heedless presence everywhere
about me, rushing upon me.
So much closer and dearer
than he might ever be in his
own person—

"No luck, sir?" the chambermaid calls out.

Saturday, July 10.

Three letters.

That dark demanding hand—
not a lady's hand—it is
someone like myself, shouting
at me—trying to make me
hear—

A young woman and her
mother brush past me with a
scent of something harsh and
flowery about them—my
nerves are jumping—people
are beginning to notice me.
An elderly man is staring
quite openly at me—did he
write these letters?

I walk out quickly. Must be
alone.

My Dear Boy,
Understand only that I wish you
well—only well!—and that I
should not communicate so
strangely and so secretively if
other means were open to me....

The last sentence is crossed
out, I can't make out anything. No signature.

My Dear Boy,
You are generous to allow me to
write, knowing that it is the
only manner in which I may

Saturday, July 10.

Another sleepless, aching
night. The chambermaid's
face hovering in my private
darkness—witness of my
folly!—this morning I will
press upon her a small sum,
hopefully not a bribe—or
have I come to that? A gift, a
sign of my gratitude for her
kindness, her—

No breakfast this morning.
My stomach is so weak, I am
so preoccupied...I am
terrified.... Must imagine
him. Him. I stand on the
balcony and think of him,
envision him, only him. The
sea is choppy and leaden
today. Everything disappoints
us that is not human.

Few people strolling out.
Ladies with their long
dresses, so drastically protected. Gentlemen. Hats,
gloves, pipes. *Must imagine*
him. No freedom. Fallen upon
evil days, sick days—signs of
vastation all around me,
inside me—

Ah, he is there!

Wooden steps. The board-
walk. Ah, he is reading...he

hold you close, lay upon you—
oh, so soothingly!—the most
respectful of hands— I see in
your face a terrible need. I fear
for you. Will you stand on the
shore and accept these frail
words of mine, will you accept
the only gift I dare give you—
words, prophecies—

For a long moment I cannot
think. What is happening? It
is as if a secret Self—my own
Self—were writing to me like
this, hinting at a terrible
knowledge—*prophecies:* what
does that mean?— Are there
spirits, ghosts? Is there a
future Self—a future Patrick
Quarles—gazing back upon
me, seeing me, from the
future—the 1900's, when we
may all be free!—and reaching back to bless me—

And so I stand on the shore,
yes. I accept. In this dour
chilling breeze I am very
happy, and I turn slowly to
look back at the hotel—that
monster of a hotel!

Who is watching me?

He must be gazing at me
from one of the windows. But
I dare not wave. What does
he think? Is he there? Is there

is reading my letters.... He is
reading what I have written
to him, in such anguish!

Disgust? Shame? Or can he
sense the human wish behind
it, the wish to speak kindly to
another soul, a solitary
soul?...

Feverish. The wind inside my
head, not cooling it. Wind.
Fever. My head is swimming.
He is standing there with his
back to me—his figure blurs
and swims in my vision— I
want to cry out to him, "Must
I grow old? Must I die? If you
walk away from me I will
die—"

No—he is turning—

His figure against the somber
water. Unimagined—such
splendor! He is looking
toward me but I draw back at
once, into the shadow of the
room—my eyes brimming—

Across that space he seems to
bless me. I must put my
hands out against the French
doors, I must steady myself
or I will fling myself forward,
outward, to my death—

Yes, he looks at me. It has

really anyone there? I stare into space, smiling.

Across the distance something passes into me, like a breath.

Lighting a cigar, I stroll down the beach and open the third letter. A letter from a friend, one who wishes me well and knows me, knows me.

My Dear Boy,
You are without history and so
you must free yourself from it.
But caution. Am I speaking
madness? Am I offending you?
Or can you understand how I
should, if I dared, quite openly
invite you to lean upon me as a
kindly father? . . . The sense that
I cannot speak to you, cannot
reveal myself to you—this
torments me, makes me ache at
the bitterness of things. I reach
out toward you—I let go—I
abandon you—

More words crossed out.

Something tries to come through those X-ed out words. A command. Angry urgent words. *Utter caution.* A voice has spoken. I know there are ghosts. I understand them. I feel them in this

happened. The distance between us is holy. A hush. . . . He is my living Self: I see that now. Living as I have never lived. He is magnificent. I am alive in him and dead, dead in myself, but alive in him, only in him—

In a lifetime there are few moments of such bliss.

Trembling, hiding, in the shadows of my room . . . safe. Saved. My heart lunges backward into safety. Must hide. Must remain hidden. I am growing old, yes, soon I will be as old and as ugly as his uncle—yes, and it is right, we must be pushed aside, we must die—must acquiesce to darkness— Our heirs demand the future. They demand that history be turned over to them.

In this moment of joy I am transformed.

He, he is myself: walking away! Free to walk away! I must strain to see him, his handsome figure about to fade into the low heathery bareness of the country, that shy purple and gold that runs nearly to the edge of the sea. . . .

medieval town, on all sides of me, harsh and innocent with their cold piercing eyes and their victories—their terrible victories—

I will kill him.

No. The words are not mine. I will never lay hands upon him. The mark of my hands would show upon him, it would scream out that I was his murderer— *I will suffocate him, I have been given permission to suffocate him, to destroy him*— I will not come near him, no. No. I will sit quietly at his bedside as he strangles in his own phlegm—the poison that bubbles up out of his ugly soul—

Will I sit at his bedside? Will I watch him die? Will I dare to do what those letters instruct? Will I outlive him? Will I outlive all these old men?

A moment too deep for any utterance.

It takes me an hour to dress. I am still shaky. A little feverish. Soon I will be working again—I will work through *him*. He will possess me. I am ready to work, ready even to return to the coal-gray skies of London, that sky that encloses and entraps the mind—

He has understood my message. My love. I will live through him and he through me: born again in my writing, in something I will, must write, something I will begin soon in honor of his youth and the perfect power of his face. . . .

I hurry downstairs. I must feed the birds in the garden— I have forgotten them for days— The garden is deserted, hushed. Everyone is elsewhere. Only *he* is with me, his presence close to me, our minds beating with the beauty of this somber garden and its wide gravel paths and its pinched roses and weathered walls—

In a lifetime there are few moments of such bliss.

The Dead

*U*SEFUL IN ACUTE AND CHRONIC DEPRESSION, *where accompanied by anxiety, insomnia, agitation; psychoneurotic states manifested by tension, apprehension, fatigue....* They were small yellow capsules, very expensive. She took them along with other capsules, green-and-aqua, that did not cost quite so much but were weaker. *Caution against hazardous occupations requiring complete mental alertness.* What did that mean, "complete mental alertness?" Since the decline of her marriage, a few years ago, Ilena thought it wisest to avoid complete mental alertness. That was an overrated American virtue.

For the relief of anxiety and the relief of the apprehension of anxiety: small pink pills. *Advise against ingestion of alcohol.* But she was in the habit of drinking anyway, always before meeting strangers and often before meeting friends, sometimes on perfectly ordinary, lonely days when she expected to meet no one at all. She was fascinated by the possibility that some of these drugs could cause paradoxical reactions—fatigue and intense rage, increase and decrease in libido. She liked paradox. She wondered how the paradoxical reactions could take place in the same body, at the same time. Or did they alternate days? *For the relief of chronic insomnia:* small harmless white barbiturates. In the morning, hurrying out somewhere, she took a handful of mood-elevating pills, swallowed with some hot water right from the faucet, or coffee, to bring about a curious hollow-headed sensation, exactly as if her head were a kind of drum. Elevation! She felt the very air breathed into her lungs suffused with a peculiar dazzling joy, worth every risk.

Adverse reactions were possible: *confusion, ataxia, skin eruptions, edema, nausea, constipation, blood dyscrasias, jaundice, hepatic dysfunction, hallucinations, tremor, slurred speech, hyperexcitement....* But anything was possible, after all!

A young internist said to her, "These tests show that you are normal," and her heart had fallen, her stomach had sunk, her very intestines yearned downward, stricken with gravity. Normal? Could that be? She had stared at him, unbelieving. "The symptoms you mention—the insomnia, for instance—have no organic basis that we can determine," he said.

Then why the trembling hands, why the glitter to the eyes, why, why the static in the head? She felt that she had been cheated. This was not worth sixty dollars, news like this. As soon as she left the doctor's office she went to a water fountain in the corridor and took a few capsules of whatever was in her coat pocket, loose in the pocket along with tiny pieces of lint and something that looked like the flaky skins of peanuts, though she did not remember having put peanuts in any of her pockets. She swallowed one, two, three green-and-aqua tranquilizers, and a fairly large white pill that she didn't recognize, found in the bottom of her purse with a few stray hairs and paper clips. This helped a little. "So I'm normal!" she said.

She had been living at that time in Buffalo, New York, teaching part-time at the university. Buffalo was a compromise between going to California, as her ex-husband begged, and going to New York, where she was probably headed. Her brain burned dryly, urging her both westward and eastward, so she spent a year in this dismal Midwestern city in upstate New York, all blighted elms and dingy skies and angry politicians. The city was in a turmoil of excitement; daily and nightly the city police prowled the university campus in search of trouble-some students, and the troublesome students hid in the bushes alongside buildings, eager to plant their homemade time bombs and run; so the campus was not safe for ordinary students or ordinary people at all. Even the "normal," like Ilena, long wearied of political activism, were in danger.

She taught twice a week and the rest of the time avoided the university. She drove a 1965 Mercedes an uncle had willed her, an uncle rakish and remote and selfish, like Ilena herself, who had taken a kind of proud pity on her because of her failed marriage and her guilty listlessness about family ties. The uncle, a judge, had died in St. Louis; she had had to fly there to get the car. The trip back had taken her nearly a week, she had felt so unaccountably lazy and sullen. But, once back in Buffalo, driving her stodgy silver car, its conservative shape protecting her heavily, she felt safe from the noxious street fumes and the darting, excitable eyes of the police and the local Buffalo taxpayers—in spite of her own untidy hair and clothes.

The mood-elevating pills elevated her several feet off the ground and made her stammer rapidly into the near, dim faces of her students, speaking faster and faster in the hope that the class period would end sooner. But the tranquilizers dragged her down, massaged her girlish heart to a dreamy condition, fingered the nerve ends lovingly, soothingly, wanted only to assure her that all was well. In her inherited car she alternately drove too fast, made nervous by the speedier pills, or too slowly, causing warlike sounds from the rear, the honking of other drivers in American cars.

In the last two years Ilena had been moving around constantly: packing up the same clothes and items and unpacking them again, always eager, ready to be surprised, flying from one coast to the other to speak at universities or organizations interested in "literature," hopeful and adventurous as she was met at various windy airports by strangers. Newly divorced, she had felt virginal again, years younger, truly childlike and American. Beginning again. Always beginning. She had written two quiet novels, each politely received and selling under one thousand copies, and then she had written a novel based on an anecdote overheard by her at the University of Michigan, in a girls' rest room in the library, about a suicide club and the "systematic deaths of our most valuable natural resource, our children"—as one national reviewer of the novel said gravely. It was her weakest novel, but it was widely acclaimed and landed her on the cover of a famous magazine, since her *Death Dance* had also coincided with a sudden public interest in the achievement of women in "male-dominated fields." Six magazines came out with cover stories on the women's liberation movement inside a three-month period; Ilena's photograph had been exceptionally good. She found herself famous, and fame made her mouth ironic and dry with a sleeplessness that was worse than ever, in spite of her being "normal."

The pills came and went in cycles—the yellow capsules favored for a while, then dropped for the small pink pills, tranquilizers big enough to nearly knock her out taken with some gin and bitter lemon, late at night. These concoctions were sacred to her, always kept secret. Her eyes grew large with the prospect of all those "adverse reactions" that were threatened but somehow never arrived. She was lucky, she thought. Maybe nothing adverse would ever happen to her. She had been twenty-six years old at the start of the breakup of her marriage; it was then that most of the pills began, though she had always had a problem with insomnia. The only time she had truly passed out, her brain gone absolutely black, was the winter day—very late in the afternoon—when she had been in her office at a university in Detroit, with a man whom she had loved at that time, and a key had been thrust in the lock and the door opened—Ilena had screamed, "No! Go away!" It had been only a cleaning lady, frightened off without seeing anything, or so the man had assured Ilena. But she had fainted. Her skin had gone wet and cold; it had taken the terrified man half an hour to bring her back to normal again. "Ilena, I love you, don't die," he had begged. Finally she was calm enough to return to her own home, an apartment she shared with her husband in the northwestern corner of the city; she went home, fixed herself some gin and bitter lemon, and stood in the kitchen drinking it while her husband yelled questions at her. "Where were you? Why were you gone so long?" She had not answered him. The drink was mixed up in her memory with the intense relief of having escaped some humiliating danger, and the intense terror of the new, immediate danger of her husband's rage. Why was this man yelling at her? Whom had she married, that he could yell at her so viciously? The drinking of that gin was a celebration of her evil.

That was back in 1967; their marriage had ended with the school year; her husband spent three weeks in a hospital half a block from his mother's house in Oswego, New York, and Ilena had not gone to see him, not once, being hard of heart, like stone, and terrified of seeing him again. She feared his mother, too. The marriage had been dwindling all during the Detroit years—1965–1967—and they both left the city shortly before the riot, which seemed to Ilena, in her usual poetic, hyperbolic, pill-sweetened state, a cataclysmic flowering of their own hatred. She had thought herself good enough at hating, but her husband was much better. "Die. Why don't you die. *Die,*" he had whispered hypnotically to her once, as she lay in bed weeping very early one morning, before dawn, too weary to continue their battle. Off and on she had spoken sentimentally about having children, but Bryan was wise enough to dismiss that scornfully—"You don't bring children into the world to fix up a rotten marriage," he said. She had not known it was rotten, exactly. She knew that he was jealous of her. A mutual friend, a psychiatrist, had told her gently that her having published two novels—unknown as they were, and financial failures—was "unmanning" to Bryan, who wanted to write but couldn't. Was that her fault? What could she do? "You could fail at something yourself," she was advised.

In the end she had fallen in love with another man. She had set out to love someone in order to punish her husband, to revenge herself upon him; but the revenge was forgotten, she had really fallen in love in spite of all her troubles . . . in love with a man who turned out to be a disappointment himself, but another kind of disappointment.

Adverse reactions: *confusion, ataxia, skin eruptions, edema, nausea, constipation, blood dyscrasias, jaundice, hepatic dysfunction, hallucinations. . . .* Her eyes filmed over with brief ghostly uninspired hallucinations now and then, but she believed this had nothing to do with the barbiturates she took to sleep, or the amphetamines she took to speed herself up. It was love that wore her out. Love, and the air of Detroit, the gently wafting smoke from the manly smokestacks of factories. Love and smoke. The precise agitation of love in her body, what her lover and her husband did to her body; and the imprecise haze of the air, of her vision, filmed-over and hypnotized. She recalled having loved her husband very much at one time. Before their marriage in 1964. His name was Bryan Donohue, and as his wife she had been *Ilena Donohue*, legally; but a kind of maiden cunning had told her to publish her novels as *Ilena Williams*, chaste Ilena, the name musical with *l*'s. Her books were by that Ilena, while her nights of sleeplessness beside a sleeping, twitching, perspiring man were spent by the other Ilena. At that time she was not famous yet and not quite so nervous. A little insomnia, that wasn't so bad. Many people had insomnia. She feared sleep because she often dreamed of the assassination of Kennedy, which was run and rerun in her brain like old newsreels. Years after that November day she was still fresh with sorrow for him, scornful of her own sentimentality but unable to control it. How she had wept! Maybe she had been in love with Kennedy, a little.... So, sleeping brought him back to her not as a man: as a corpse. Therefore she feared sleep. She could lie awake beside a breathing, troubled corpse of her own, her partner in this puzzling marriage, and she rehearsed her final speech to him so many times that it became jaded and corny to her, out of date as a monologue in an Ibsen play.

"There is another man, of course," he had said flatly.

"No. No one."

"Yes, another man."

"No."

"Another man, I know, but I'm not interested. Don't tell me his name."

"There is no other man."

"Obviously there is. Probably a professor at that third-rate school of yours."

"No."

Of course, when she was in the company of the *other man*, it was Bryan who became "the other" to him and Ilena—remote and masculine and dangerous, powerful as a nightmare figure, with every right to embrace Ilena in the domestic quiet of their apartment. He had every right to make love to her, and Gordon did not. They were adulterers, Ilena and Gordon. They lost weight with their guilt, which was finely wrought in them as music, precious and subtle and prized, talked over endlessly. Ilena could see Gordon's love for her in his face. She loved that face, she loved to stroke it, stare at it, trying to imagine it as the face of a man married to another woman.... He was not so handsome as her own husband, perhaps. She didn't know. She only knew, bewildered and stunned, that his face was the center of the universe for her, and she could no more talk herself out of this whimsy than she could talk herself out of her sorrow for Kennedy.

Her husband, Bryan Donohue: tall, abrupt, self-centered, amusing, an instructor in radiology at Wayne Medical School, with an interest in jazz and a desire to write articles on science, science and sociology, jazz, jazz and sociology, anything. He was very verbal and he talked excellently, expertly. Ilena had always been proud of him in the presence of other people. He had a sharp, dissatisfied face, with very dark eyes. He dressed well and criticized Ilena when she let herself go, too rushed to bother with her appearance. In those days, disappointed by the low salary and the bad schedule she received as an instructor at a small university in Detroit, Ilena had arrived for early classes— she was given eight-o'clock classes every semester—with her hair barely combed, loose down to her shoulders, snarled and bestial from a night of insomnia, her stockings marred with snags or long disfiguring runs, her face glossy with the dry-mouthed euphoria of tranquilizers, so that, pious and sour, she led her classes in the prescribed ritual prayer—this was a Catholic university, and Ilena had been brought up as a Catholic—and felt freed, once the prayer was finished, of all restraint.

Bad as the eight-o'clock classes were, the late-afternoon classes (4:30–6:00) were worse: the ashes of the day, tired undergraduates who needed this course to fill out their schedules, high-school teachers—mainly nuns and "brothers"—who needed a few more credits for their Master's degrees, students who worked, tired unexplained strangers with rings around their eyes of fatigue and boredom and the degradation of many semesters as "special students." When she was fortunate enough to have one or two good students in these classes, Ilena charged around in excitement, wound up by the pills taken at noon with black coffee, eager to draw them out into a dialogue with her. They talked back and forth. They argued. The other students sat docile and perplexed, waiting for the class to end, glancing from Ilena to one of her articulate boys, back to Ilena again, taking notes only when Ilena seemed to be saying something important. What was so exciting about Conrad's *Heart of Darkness*, they wondered, that Mrs. Donohue could get this worked up?

Her copper-colored hair fell in a jumble about her face, and her skin sometimes took a radiant coppery beauty from the late afternoon sun as it sheared mistily through the campus trees, or from the excitement of a rare, good class, or from the thought of her love for Gordon, who would be waiting to see her after class. One of the boys in this late-afternoon class—Emmett Norlan—already wore his hair frizzy and long, though this was 1966 and a few years ahead of the style, and he himself was only a sophomore, a small precocious irritable argumentative boy with glasses. He was always charging up to Ilena after class, demanding that she explain herself—"You use words like 'emotions,' you bully us with your *emotions!*" he cried. "When I ask you a question in class, you distort it! You try to make everyone laugh at me! It's a womanly trick, a *female* trick, not worthy of you!" Emmett took everything seriously, as seriously as Ilena; he was always hanging around her office, in the doorway, refusing to come in and sit down because he was "in a hurry" and yet reluctant to go away, and Ilena could sense by a certain sullen alteration of his jaw that her lover was coming down the hall to her office. . . .

"See you," Emmett would say sourly, backing away.

Gordon was a professor in sociology, a decade or more older than Ilena, gentle and paternal; no match for her cunning. After a particularly ugly quarrel with her husband, one fall day, Ilena had looked upon this man and decided that he must become her lover. At the time she had not even known his name. *A lover. She would have a lover.* He was as tall as her own husband, with a married, uncomfortable look about his mouth—tense apologetic smiles, creases at the corners of his lips, bluish-purple veins on his forehead. A handsome man, but somehow a little gray. His complexion was both boyish and gray. He did not dress with the self-conscious care of her husband Bryan; his clothes were tweedy, not very new or very clean, baggy at the knees, smelling of tobacco and unaired closets. Ilena, determined to fall in love with him, had walked by his home near the university—an ordinary brick two-story house with white shutters. Her heart pounded with jealousy. She imagined his domestic life: a wife, four children, a Ford with a dented rear fender, a lawn that was balding, a street that was going bad—one handsome old Tudor home had already been converted into apartments for students, the sign of inevitable disaster. Meeting him, talking shyly with him, loving him at her finger tips was to be one of the gravest events in her life, for pill-sweetened as she was, she had not seriously believed he might return her interest. He was Catholic. He was supposed to be happily married.

When it was over between them and she was teaching, for two quick, furtive semesters at the University of Buffalo, where most classes were canceled because of rioting and police harassment, Ilena thought back to her Detroit days and wondered how she had survived, even with the help of drugs and gin: the central nervous system could not take such abuse, not for long. She had written a novel out of her misery, her excitement, her guilt, typing ten or fifteen pages an evening until her head throbbed with pain that not even pills could ease. At times, lost in the story she was creating, she had felt an eerie longing to remain there permanently, to simply give up and go mad. *Adverse reactions: confusion, hallucinations, hyperexcitement....* But she had not gone mad. She had kept on typing, working, and when she was finished it was possible to pick up, in her fingers, the essence of that shattering year: one slim book.

Death Dance. *The story of America's alienated youth ... shocking revelations ... suicide ... drugs ... waste ... horror ...* $5.98.

It had been at the top of the *New York Times* best-seller list for fifteen weeks.

Gordon had said to her, often, "I don't want to hurt you, Ilena. I'm afraid of ruining your life." She had assured him that her life was not that delicate. "I could go away if Bryan found out, alone. I could live alone," she had said lightly, airily, knowing by his grimness that he would not let her—surely he would not let her go? Gordon thought more about her husband than Ilena did, the "husband" he had met only once, at a large university reception, but with whom he now shared a woman. Two men, strangers, shared her body. Ilena wandered in a perpetual sodden daze, thinking of the . . . the madness of loving two men . . . the freakishness of it, which she could never really comprehend, could not assess, because everything in her recoiled from it: this could not be happening to her. Yet the fact of it was in her body, carried about in her body. She could not isolate it, could not comprehend it. Gazing at the girl students, at the nuns, she found herself thinking enviously that their lives were unsoiled and honest and open to any possibility, while hers had become fouled, complicated, criminal, snagged, somehow completed without her assent. She felt that she was going crazy.

Her teaching was either sluggish and uninspired, or hysterical. She was always wound up and ready to let go with a small speech on any subject—Vietnam, the oppression of blacks, religious hypocrisy, the censorship haggling over the student newspaper, any subject minor or massive—and while her few aggressive students appreciated this, the rest of her students were baffled and unenlightened. She sat in her darkened office, late in the afternoon, whispering to Gordon about her classes: "They aren't going well. I'm afraid. I'm not any good as a teacher. My hands shake when I come into the classroom. . . . The sophomores are forced to take this course and they hate me, I know they hate me. . . ." Gordon stroked her hands, kissed her face, her uplifted face, and told her that he heard nothing but good reports about her teaching. He himself was a comfortable, moderately popular professor; he had been teaching for fifteen years. "You have some very enthusiastic students," he said. "Don't doubt yourself, Ilena, please; if you hear negative things it might be from other teachers who are jealous. . . ." Ilena pressed herself gratefully into this good man's embrace, hearing the echo of her mother's words of years ago, when Ilena would come home hurt from school for some minor girlish reason: "Don't mind them, they're just *jealous.*"

A world of jealous people, like her husband: therefore hateful, therefore dangerous. Out to destroy her. Therefore the pills, tiny round pills and large button-sized pills, and the multicolored capsules.

There were few places she and Gordon could meet. Sometimes they walked around the campus, sometimes they met for lunch downtown, but most of the time they simply sat in her office and talked. She told him everything about her life, reviewing all the snarls and joys she had reviewed, years before, with Bryan, noticing that she emphasized the same events and even used the same words to describe them. She told him everything, but she never mentioned the drugs. He would disapprove. Maybe he would be disgusted. Like many Catholic men of his social class, and of his generation, he would be frightened by weakness in women, though by his own admission he drank too much. If he commented on her dazed appearance, if he worried over her fatigue—"Does your husband do this to you? Put you in this state?"—she pretended not to understand. "What, do I look so awful? So ugly?" she would tease. That way she diverted his concern, she bullied him into loving her, because he was a man to whom female beauty was important—his own wife had been a beauty queen many years ago, at a teachers' college in Ohio. "No, you're beautiful. You're beautiful," he would whisper.

They teased each other to a state of anguish on those dark winter afternoons, never really safe in Ilena's office—she shared the office with a nun, who had an early teaching schedule but who might conceivably turn up at any time, and there was always the possibility of the cleaning lady or the janitor unlocking the door with a master key—nightmarish possibility! Gordon kissed her face, her body, she clasped her hands around him and gave herself up to him musically, dreamily, like a rose of rot with only a short while left to bloom, carrying the rot neatly hidden, deeply hidden. She loved him so that her mind went blank even of the euphoria of drugs or the stimulation of a good, exciting day of teaching; she felt herself falling back into a blankness like a white flawless wall, pure material, pure essence, a mysterious essence that was fleshly and spiritual at once. Over and over they declared their love for each other, they promised it, vowed it, repeated it in each other's grave accents, echoing and unconsciously imitating each other, Ilena carrying home to her apartment her lover's gentleness, his paternal listening manner. Maybe Bryan sensed Gordon's presence, his influence on her, long before the breakup. Maybe he could discern, with his scientist's keen heatless eye, the shadow of another personality, powerful and beloved, on the other side of his wife's consciousness.

Ilena vowed to Gordon, "I love you, only you," and she made him believe that she and Bryan no longer slept in the same bed. This was not true: she was so fearful of Bryan, of his guessing her secret, that she imitated with her husband the affection she gave to Gordon, in that way giving herself to two men, uniting them in her body. *Two men. Uniting them in her body.* Her body could not take all this. Her body threatened to break down. She hid from Bryan, spending an hour or more in the bathtub, gazing down through her lashes at her bluish, bruised body, wondering how long this phase of her life could last—the taunting of her sanity, the use of her rather delicate body by two normal men. *This is how a woman becomes prehistoric,* she thought. *Prehistoric. Before all personalized, civilized history. Men make love to her and she is reduced to protoplasm.*

She recalled her girlhood and her fear of men, her fear of someday having to marry—for all her female relatives urged marriage, marriage!—and now it seemed to her puzzling that the physical side of her life should be so trivial. It was not important, finally. She could have taken on any number of lovers, it was like shaking hands at a party, moving idly and absent-mindedly from one man to another; nothing serious about it at all. Why had she feared it so? And that was why the landscape of Detroit took on to her such neutral bleakness, its sidewalks and store windows and streets and trees, its spotted skies, its old people, its children—all unformed, unpersonalized, unhistoric. Everyone is protoplasm, she thought, easing together and easing apart. Some touch and remain stuck together; others touch and part.... But, though she told herself this, she sometimes felt her head weighed down with a terrible depression and she knew she would have to die, would have to kill her consciousness. She could not live with two men.

She could not live with one man.

Heated, hysterical, she allowed Gordon to make love to her in that office. The two of them lay exhausted and stunned on the cold floor—unbelieving lovers. Had this really happened? She felt the back of her mind dissolve. Now she was committed to him, she had been degraded, if anyone still believed in degradation; now something would happen, something must happen. She would divorce Bryan; he would divorce his wife. They must leave Detroit. They must marry. They must change their lives.

Nothing happened.

She sprang back to her feet, assisted by this man who seemed to love her so helplessly, her face framed by his large hands, her hair smoothed, corrected by his hands. She felt only a terrible chilly happiness, an elation that made no sense. And so she would put on her coat and run across the snowy, windswept campus to teach a class in freshman composition, her skin rosy, radiant, her body soiled and reeking beneath her clothes, everything secret and very lovely. Delirious and articulate, she lived out the winter. She thought, eying her students: *If they only knew....* It was all very high, very nervous and close to hysteria; Gordon loved her, undressed her and dressed her, retreated to his home where he undressed and bathed his smallest children, and she carried his human heat with her everywhere on the coldest days, edgy from the pills of that noon and slightly hung over from the barbiturates of the night before, feeling that she was living her female life close to the limits, at the most extreme boundaries of health and reason. Her love for him burned inward, secretly, and she was dismayed to see how very soiled her clothes were, sometimes as if mocking her. Was this love, was it a stain like any other? But her love for him burned outward, making her more confident of herself, so that she did not hesitate to argue with her colleagues. She took part in a feeble anti-Vietnam demonstration on campus, which was jeered at by most of the students who bothered to watch, and which seemed to embarrass Gordon, who was not "political." She did not hesitate to argue with hard-to-manage students during class, sensing herself unladylike and impudent and reckless in their middle-class Catholic eyes, a *woman* who dared to say such things!—"I believe in birth control, obviously, and in death control. Suicide must be recognized as a natural human right." This, at a Catholic school; she had thought herself daring in those days.

Emmett Norlan and his friends, scrawny, intense kids who were probably taking drugs themselves, at least smoking marijuana, clustered around Ilena and tried to draw her into their circle. They complained that they could not talk to the other professors. They complained about the "religious chauvinism" of the university, though Ilena asked them what they expected— it was a Catholic school, wasn't it? "Most professors here are just closed circuits, they don't create anything, they don't communicate anything," Emmett declared contemptuously. He was no taller than Ilena herself, and she was a petite woman. He wore sloppy, soiled clothes, and even on freezing days he tried to go without a heavy coat; his perpetual grimy fatigue jacket became so familiar to Ilena that she was to think of him, sharply and nostalgically, whenever she saw such a jacket in the years to come. The boy's face was surprisingly handsome, in spite of all the frizzy hair and beard and the constant squinting and grimacing; but it was small and boyish. He had to fight that boyishness by being tough. His glasses were heavy, black-rimmed, and made marks on either side of his nose—he often snatched them off and rubbed the bridge of his nose, squinting nearsightedly at Ilena, never faltering in his argument. Finally Ilena would say, "Emmett, I have to go home. Can't we talk about this some other time?"—wondering anxiously if Gordon had already left school. She was always backing away from even the students she liked, always edging away from her fellow teachers; she was always in a hurry, literally running from her office to a classroom or to the library, her head ducked against the wind and her eyes narrowed so that she need not see the faces of anyone she knew. In that university she was friendly with only a few people, among them the head of her department, a middle-aged priest with a degree from Harvard. He was neat, graying, gentlemanly, but a little corrupt in his academic standards: the Harvard years had been eclipsed long ago by the stern daily realities of Detroit.

The end for Ilena at this school came suddenly, in Father Hoffman's office.

Flushed with excitement, having spent an hour with Gordon in which they embraced and exchanged confidences—about his wife's sourness, her husband's iciness—Ilena had rushed to a committee that was to examine a Master's degree candidate in English. She had never sat on one of these committees before. The candidate was a monk, Brother Ronald, a pale, rather obese, pleasant man in his thirties. His lips were more womanish than Ilena's. The examination began with a question by a professor named O'Brien: "Please give us a brief outline of English literature." Brother Ronald began slowly, speaking in a gentle, faltering voice—this question was always asked by this particular professor, so the candidate had memorized an answer, perfectly—and O'Brien worked at lighting his pipe, nodding vaguely from time to time. Brother Ronald came to a kind of conclusion some fifteen minutes later, with the "twentieth century," mentioning the names of Joyce, Lawrence, and T. S. Eliot. "Very good," said O'Brien. The second examiner, Mr. Honig, asked nervously: "Will you describe tragedy and give us an example, please?" Brother Ronald frowned. After a moment he said, "There is *Hamlet*...and *Macbeth*...." He seemed to panic then. He could think of nothing more to say. Honig, himself an obese good-natured little man of about fifty, with a Master's degree from a local university and no publications, smiled encouragingly at Brother Ronald; but Brother Ronald could only stammer, "Tragedy has a plot...a climax and a conclusion.... It has a moment of revelation...and comic relief...." After several minutes of painful silence, during which the only sounds were of O'Brien's sucking at his pipe, Brother Ronald smiled shakily and said that he did not know any more about tragedy.

Now it was Ilena's turn. She was astonished. She kept glancing at O'Brien and Honig, trying to catch their eyes, but they did not appear to notice. Was it possible that this candidate was considered good enough for an advanced degree, was it possible that anyone would allow him to teach English anywhere? She could not believe it. She said, sitting up very straight, "Brother Ronald, please define the term 'Gothicism' for us." Silence. Brother Ronald stared at his hands. He tried to smile. "Then could you define the term 'heroic couplet' for us," Ilena said. Her heart pounded combatively. The monk gazed at her, sorrowful and soft, his eyes watery; he shook his head *no*, he didn't know. "Have you read any of Shakespeare's sonnets?" Ilena asked. Brother Ronald nodded gravely, *yes*. "Could you discuss one of them?" Ilena asked. Again, silence. Brother Ronald appeared to be thinking. Finally he said, "I guess I don't remember any of them...." "Could you tell us what a sonnet is, then?" Ilena asked. "A short poem," said Brother Ronald uncertainly. "Could you give us an example of any sonnet?" said Ilena. He stared at his hands, which were now clasped together. They were pudgy and very clean. After a while Ilena saw that he could not think of a sonnet, so she said sharply, having become quite nervous herself, "Could you talk to us about any poem at all? One of your favorite poems?" He sat in silence for several seconds. Finally Ilena said, "Could you give us the *title* of a poem?"

A miserable half minute. But the examination was nearly over: Ilena saw the monk glance at his wristwatch.

"I've been teaching math at St. Rose's for the last five years...." Brother Ronald said softly. "It wasn't really my idea to get a Master's degree in English...my order sent me out...."

"Don't you know any poems at all? Not even any titles?" Ilena asked.

"Of course he does. We studied Browning last year, didn't we, Brother Ronald?" O'Brien said. "You remember. You received a B in the course. I was quite satisfied with your work. Couldn't you tell us the title of a work of Browning's?"

Brother Ronald stared at his hands and smiled nervously.

"*That's my last duchess up there on the wall....*" O'Brien said coaxingly.

Brother Ronald was breathing deeply. After a few seconds he said, in a voice so soft they could almost not hear it, *"My last duchess? ..."*

"Yes, that is a poem," Ilena said.

"Now it's my turn to ask another question," O'Brien said briskly. He asked the monk a very long, conversational question about the place of literature in education—did it have a place? How would he teach a class of high-school sophomores a Shakespearean play, for instance?

The examination ended before Brother Ronald was able to answer.

They dismissed him. O'Brien, who was the chairman of the examining committee, said without glancing at Ilena, "We will give him a B."

"Yes, a B seems about right," the other professor said quickly.

Ilena, whose head was ringing with outrage and shame, put her hand down flat on the table. "No," she said.

"What do you mean, no?"

"I won't pass him."

They stared at her. O'Brien said irritably, "Then I'll give him an A, to balance out your C."

"But I'm not giving him a C. I'm not giving him anything. How can he receive any other grade than F? I won't sign that paper. I can't sign it," Ilena said.

"I'll give him an A also," the other professor said doubtfully. "Then ... then maybe he could still pass ... if we averaged it out...."

"But I won't sign the paper at all," Ilena said.

"You have to sign it."

"I won't sign it."

"It is one of your duties as a member of this examining board to give a grade and to sign your name."

"I won't sign it," Ilena said. She got shakily to her feet and walked out. In the corridor, ghostly and terrified, Brother Ronald hovered. Ilena passed by him in silence.

But the next morning she was summoned to Father Hoffman's office.

The story got out that she had been fired, but really she had

had enough sense to resign—to write a quick resignation note on Father Hoffman's memo pad. They did not part friends. The following year, when her best-selling novel was published, Father Hoffman sent her a letter of congratulation on university stationery, charmingly worded: "I wish only the very best for you. We were wrong to lose you. Pity us." By then she had moved out of Detroit, her husband was in San Diego, she was living in a flat in Buffalo, near Delaware Avenue, afraid of being recognized when she went out to the drugstore or the supermarket. *Death Dance* had become a selection of the Book of the Month Club; it had been sold for $150,000 to a movie producer famous for his plodding, "socially significant" films, and for the first time in her life Ilena was sleepless because of money—rabid jangling thoughts about money. She was ashamed of having done so well financially. She was terrified of her ability to survive all this noise, this publicity, this national good fortune. For, truly, *Death Dance* was not her best novel: a hectic narrative about college students and their preoccupation with sex and drugs and death, in a prose she had tried to make "poetic." Her more abrasive colleagues at the University of Buffalo cautioned her against believing the praise that was being heaped upon her, that she would destroy her small but unique talent if she took all this seriously, etc. Even her new lover, a critic, separated from his wife and several children, a fifty-year-old ex-child prodigy, warned her against success: "They want to make you believe you're a genius, so they can draw back and laugh at you. First they hypnotize you, then they destroy you. Believe nothing."

The flow of barbiturates and amphetamines gave her eyes a certain wild sheen, her copper hair a frantic wasteful curl, made her voice go shrill at the many Buffalo parties. She wondered if she did not have the talent, after all, for being a spectacle. Someone to stare at. The magazine cover had flattered her wonderfully: taken by a Greenwich Village photographer as dreamily hung over as Ilena herself, the two of them moving about in slow motion in his studio, adjusting her hair, her lips, her eyelashes, the tip of her chin, adjusting the light, altering the light, bringing out a fantastic ethereal glow in her eyes and cheeks and forehead that Ilena had never seen in herself. The cover had been in full color and Ilena had looked really beautiful, a Pre-Raphaelite virgin. Below her photograph was a caption in high alarmed black letters: ARE AMERICAN WOMEN AVENGING CENTURIES OF OPPRESSION?

Revenge!

Death Dance was nominated for a National Book Award, but lost out to a long, tedious, naturalistic novel; someone at Buffalo who knew the judges told Ilena that this was just because the female member of the committee had been jealous of her. Ilena, whose head seemed to be swimming all the time now, and who did not dare to drive around in her Mercedes for fear of having an accident, accepted all opinions, listened desperately to everyone, pressed herself against her lover, and wept at the thought of her disintegrating brain.

This lover wanted to marry her, as soon as his divorce was final; his name was Lyle Myer. He was the author of twelve books of criticism and a columnist for a weekly left-wing magazine; a New Yorker, he had never lived outside New York until coming to Buffalo, which terrified him. He was afraid of being beaten up by militant students on campus, and he was afraid of being beaten up by the police. Hesitant, sweet, and as easily moved to sentimental tears as Ilena herself, he was always telephoning her or dropping in at her flat. Because he was, or had been, an alcoholic, Ilena felt it was safe to tell him about the pills she took. He seemed pleased by this confidence, this admission of her weakness, as if it bound her more hopelessly to him—just as his teen-aged daughter, whose snapshot Ilena had seen, was bound to be a perpetual daughter to him because of her acne and rounded shoulders, unable to escape his love. "Drugs are suicidal, yes, but if they forestall the actual act of suicide they are obviously beneficial," he told her.

With him, she felt nothing except a clumsy domestic affection: no physical love at all.

She was so tired most of the time that she did not even pretend to feel anything. With Gordon, in those hurried steep moments back in Detroit, the two of them always fearful of being discovered, her body had been keyed up to hysteria and love had made her delirious; with Bryan, near the end of their marriage, she had sometimes felt a tinge of love, a nagging doubtful rush that she often let fade away again, but with Lyle her body was dead, worn out, it could not respond to his most tender caresses. She felt how intellectualized she had become, her entire body passive and observant and cynical.

"Oh, I have to get my head straight. I have to get my head straight," Ilena wept.

Lyle undressed her gently, lovingly. She felt panic, seeing in his eyes that compassionate look that had meant Gordon was thinking of his children: how she had flinched from that look!

The end had come with Gordon just as abruptly as it had come with Father Hoffman, and only a week later. They had met by accident out on the street one day, Gordon with his wife and the two smallest children, Ilena in a trench coat, bareheaded, a leather purse with a frayed strap slung over her shoulder. "Hello, Ilena," Gordon said guiltily. He was really frightened. His wife, still a handsome woman, though looking older than her thirty-seven years, smiled stiffly at Ilena and let her gaze travel down to Ilena's watermarked boots. "How are you, Ilena?" Gordon said. His eyes grabbed at her, blue and intimidated. His wife, tugging at one of the little boys, turned a sour, ironic smile upon Ilena and said, "Are you one of my husband's students?" Ilena guessed that this was meant to insult Gordon, to make him feel old. But she explained politely that she was an instructor in the English Department, "but I'm leaving after this semester," and she noticed covertly that Gordon was not insulted, not irritated by his wife's nastiness, but only watchful, cautious, his smile strained with the fear that Ilena would give him away.

"In fact, I'm leaving in a few weeks," Ilena said.

His wife nodded stiffly, not bothering to show much regret. Gordon smiled nervously, apologetically. With relief, Ilena thought. He was smiling with relief because now he would be rid of her.

And so that had ended.

They met several times after this, but Ilena was now in a constant state of excitement or drowsiness; she was working out the beginning chapters of *Death Dance*—now living alone in the apartment, since her husband had moved out to a hotel. Her life was a confusion of days and nights, sleepless nights, headachy days, classes she taught in a dream and classes she failed to meet; she spent long periods in the bathtub while the hot water turned tepid and finally cold, her mind racing. She thought of her marriage and its failure. Marriage was the deepest, most mysterious, most profound exploration open to man: she had always believed that, and she believed it now. Because she had failed did not change that belief. This plunging into another's soul, this pressure of bodies together, so brutally intimate, was the closest one could come to a sacred adventure; she still believed that. But she had failed. So she forced herself to think of her work. She thought of the novel she was writing—about a "suicide club" that had apparently existed in Ann Arbor, Michigan—projecting her confusion and her misery into the heads of those late-adolescent girls, trying not to think of her own personal misery, the way love had soured in her life. Her husband. Gordon. Well, yes, men failed at being men; but maybe she had failed at being a woman. She had been unfaithful to two men at the same time. She deserved whatever she got.

Still, she found it difficult to resist swallowing a handful of sleeping pills.... Why not? Why not empty the whole container? There were moments when she looked at herself in the bathroom mirror and raised one eyebrow flirtatiously. *How about it?... Why not die?...* Only the empty apartment awaited her.

But she kept living because the novel obsessed her. She had to write it. She had to solve its problems, had to finish it, send it away from her completed. And, anyway, if she took sleeping pills and did not wake up, Gordon or Bryan would probably discover her before she had time to die. They often telephoned, and would have been alarmed if she hadn't answered. Gordon called her every evening, usually from a drugstore, always guiltily, so that she began to take pity on his cowardice. Did he fear her committing suicide and leaving a note that would drag him in? Or did he really love her?... Ilena kept assuring him that she was all right, that she would be packing soon, yes, yes, she would always remember him with affection; no, she would probably not write to him, it would be better not to write. They talked quickly, sadly. Already the frantic hours of love-making in that office had become history, outlandish and improbable. Sometimes Ilena thought, *My God, I really love this man*, but her voice kept on with the usual conversation—what she had done that day, what he had done, what the state of her relationship with Bryan was, what his children were doing, the plans his wife had for that summer.

So it had ended, feebly; she had not even seen him the last week she was in Detroit.

Bryan called her too, impulsively. Sometimes to argue, sometimes to check plans, dates. He knew about the pills she took, though not about their quantity, and if she failed to answer the telephone for long he would have come over at once. Ilena would have been revived, wakened by a stomach pump, an ultimate masculine attack upon her body, sucking out her insides in great gasping shuddering gulps. . . . So she took only a double dose of sleeping pills before bed, along with the gin, and most of the time she slept soundly enough, without dreams. The wonderful thing about pills was that dreams were not possible. No dreams. The death of dreams. What could be more lovely than a dreamless sleep? . . .

In late April, Bryan had a collapse of some kind and was admitted to a local clinic; then he flew to his mother's, in Oswego. Ilena learned from a mutual friend at Wayne Medical School that Gordon had had a general nervous collapse, aggravated by a sudden malfunctioning of the liver brought on by malnutrition—he had been starving himself, evidently, to punish Ilena. But she worked on her novel, incorporating this latest catastrophe into the plot; she finished it in January of 1968, in Buffalo, where she was teaching a writing seminar; it was published in early 1969, and changed her life.

Lyle Myer pretended jealousy of her—all this acclaim, all this fuss! He insisted that she agree to marry him. He never mentioned, seemed deliberately to overlook, the embarrassing fact that she could love him only tepidly, that her mind was always elsewhere in their dry, fateful struggles, strung out with drugs or the memory of some other man, someone she half remembered, or the letters she had to answer from her agent and a dozen other people, so many people inviting her to give talks, to accept awards, to teach at their universities, to be interviewed by them, begging and demanding her time, her intense interest, like a hundred lovers tugging and pulling at her body, engaging it in a kind of love-making to which she could make only the feeblest of responses, her face locked now in a perpetual feminine smile.... With so much publicity and money, she felt an obligation to be feminine and gracious to everyone; when she was interviewed she spoke enthusiastically of the place of art in life, the place of beauty in this modern technological culture— she seemed to stress, on one national late-night television show, the tragedy of small trees stripped bare by vandals in city parks as much as the tragedy of the country's current foreign policy in Vietnam. At least it turned out that way. It was no wonder people could not take her seriously: one of the other writers at Buffalo, himself famous though more avant-garde than Ilena, shrugged her off as that girl who was always "licking her lips to make them glisten."

She did not sign on for another year at Buffalo, partly because of the political strife there and partly because she was restless, agitated, ready to move on. She sold the Mercedes and gave to the Salvation Army the furniture and other possessions Bryan had so cavalierly—indifferently—given her, and took an apartment in New York. She began writing stories that were to appear in fashion magazines, Ilena's slick, graceful prose an easy complement to the dreamlike faces and bodies of models whose photographs appeared in those same magazines, everything muted and slightly distorted as if by a drunken lens, the "very poetry of hallucination"—as one reviewer had said of *Death Dance*. Lyle flew down to see her nearly every weekend; on other weekends he was with his "separated" family. She loved him, yes, and she agreed to marry him, though she felt no hurry—in fact, she felt no real interest in men at all, her body shrinking when it was touched even accidentally, not out of fear but out of a kind of chaste boredom. So much, she had had so much of men, so much loving, so much mauling, so much passion....

What, she was only twenty-nine years old?

She noted, with a small pang of vanity, how surprised audiences were when she rose to speak. *Ilena Williams looks so young!* They could not see the fine vibrations of her knees and hands, already viciously toned down by Librium. They could not see the colorless glop she vomited up in motel bathrooms, or in rest rooms down the hall from the auditorium in which she was speaking—she was always "speaking," invited out all over the country for fees ranging from $500 to a colossal $2000, speaking on "current trends in literature" or "current mores in America" or answering questions about her "writing habits" or reading sections from her latest work, a series of short stories in honor of certain dead writers with whom she felt a kinship. "I don't exist as an individual but only as a completion of a tradition, the end of something, not the best part of it but only the end," she explained, wondering if she was telling the truth or if this was all nonsense, "and I want to honor the dead by reimagining their works, by reimagining their obsessions...in a way marrying them, joining them as a woman joins a man...spiritually and erotically...." She spoke so softly, so hesitantly, that audiences often could not hear her. Whereupon an energetic young man sitting in the first row, or onstage with her, would spring to his feet and adjust the microphone. "Is that better? Can you all hear now?" he would ask. Ilena saw the faces in the audience waver and blur and fade away, sheer protoplasm, and panic began in her stomach—what if she should vomit right in front of everyone? on this tidy little lectern propped up on dictionaries for her benefit? But she kept on talking. Sometimes she talked about the future of the short story, sometimes about the future of civilization—she heard the familiar, dead, deadened word *Vietnam* uttered often in her own voice, a word that had once meant something; she heard her voice echoing from the farthest corners of the auditorium as if from the corners of all those heads, her own head hollow as a drum, occasionally seeing herself at a distance—a woman with long but rather listless copper-red hair, thin cheeks, eyes that looked unnaturally enlarged. *Adverse reactions: confusion, edema, nausea, constipation, jaundice, hallucinations....* Did that qualify as a legitimate hallucination, seeing herself from a distance, hearing herself from a distance? Did that qualify as a sign of madness?

During the fall and winter of 1969 and the spring of 1970 she traveled everywhere, giving talks, being met at airports by interested strangers, driven to neat disinfected motel rooms. She had time to write only a few stories, which had to be edited with care before they could be published. Her blood pounded barbarously, while her voice went on and on in that gentle precise way, her body withdrawing from any man's touch, demure with a dread that could not show through her clothes. She had been losing weight gradually for three years, and now she had the angular, light-boned, but very intense look of a precocious child. People wanted to protect her. Women mothered her, men were always taking her arm, helping her through doorways; the editor of a famous men's magazine took her to lunch and warned her of Lyle Myer's habit of marrying young, artistic women and then ruining them—after all, he had been married three times already, and the pattern was established. Wasn't it? When people were most gentle with her, Ilena thought of the tough days when she'd run across that wind-tortured campus in Detroit, her coat flapping about her, her body still dazzled by Gordon's love, damp and sweaty from him, and she had dared run into the classroom, five minutes late, had dared take off her coat and begin the lesson.... The radiators in that old building had knocked as if they might explode; like colossal arteries, like her thudding arteries, overwhelmed with life.

In the fall of 1970 she was invited back to Detroit to give a talk before the local Phi Beta Kappa chapter; she accepted, and a few days later she received a letter from the new dean of the School of Arts—new since she had left—of her old university, inviting her to a reception in her honor, as their "most esteemed ex-staff member." It was all very diplomatic, very charming. She had escaped them, they had gotten rid of her, and now they could all meet together for a few hours.... Father Hoffman sent a note to her also, underscoring the dean's invitation, hoping that she was well and as attractive as ever. So she accepted.

Father Hoffman and another priest came to pick her up at the Sheraton Cadillac Hotel; she was startled to see that Father Hoffman had let his hair grow a little long, that he had noble, graying sideburns, and that the young priest with him was even shaggier. After the first awkward seconds—Father Hoffman forgot and called her "Mrs. Donohue"—they got along very well. Ilena was optimistic about the evening; her stomach seemed settled. As soon as they arrived at the dean's home she saw that Gordon was not there; she felt immensely relieved, though she had known he would not come, would not want to see her again . . . she felt immensely relieved and accepted a drink at once from Father Hoffman, who was behaving in an exceptionally gallant manner. "Ilena is looking better than ever," he said as people crowded around her, some of them with copies of her novel to sign, "better even than all her photographs. . . . But we don't want to tire her out, you know. We don't want to exhaust her." He kept refreshing her drink, like a lover or a husband. In the old days everyone at this place had ignored Ilena's novels, even the fact of her being a "writer," but now they were all smiles and congratulations—even the wives of her ex-colleagues, sturdy, dowdy women who had never seemed to like her. Ilena was too shaky to make any sarcastic observations about this to Father Hoffman, who might have appreciated them. He did say, "Times have changed, eh, Ilena?" and winked at her roguishly. "For one thing, you're not quite as excitable as you used to be. You were a very *young* woman around here." She could sense, beneath his gallantry, a barely disguised contempt for her—for all women—and this knowledge made her go cold. She mumbled something about fighting off the flu. Time to take a "cold tablet." She fished in her purse and came out with a large yellow capsule, a tranquilizer, and swallowed it down with a mouthful of Scotch.

Father Hoffman and Dr. O'Brien and a new, young assistant professor—a poet whose first book would be published next spring—talked to Ilena in a kind of chorus, telling her about all the changes in the university. It was much more "community-oriented" now. Its buildings—its "physical plant"—were to be open to the neighborhood on certain evenings and on Saturdays. The young poet, whose blond hair was very long and who wore a suede outfit and a black silk turtleneck shirt, kept interrupting the older men with brief explosions of mirth. "Christ, all this is a decade out of date—integration and all that crap— the NAACP and good old Martin Luther King and all that crap—

the blacks don't want it and I agree with them one hundred percent! King is dead and so is Civil Rights—just another white middle-class week-night activity the blacks saw through long ago! I agree with them one hundred percent!" He seemed to be trying to make an impression on Ilena, not quite looking at her, but leaning toward her with his knees slightly bent, as if to exaggerate his youth. Ilena sipped at her drink, trying to hide the panic that was beginning. Yes, the NAACP was dead, all that was dead, but she didn't want to think about it—after all, it had been at a civil-rights rally that she and Bryan had met, years ago in Madison, Wisconsin.... "I haven't gotten around to reading your novel yet," the poet said, bringing his gaze sideways to Ilena.

Ilena excused herself and searched for a bathroom.

The dean's wife took her upstairs, kindly. Left alone, she waited to be sick, then lost interest in being sick; she had only to get through a few more hours of this and she would be safe. And Gordon wasn't there. She looked at herself in the mirror and should have been pleased to see that she looked so pretty— not beautiful tonight but pretty, delicate—she had worked hard enough at it, spending an hour in the hotel bathroom steaming her face and patting astringent on it, hoping for the best. She dreaded the cracks in her brain somehow working their way out to her skin. What then, what then? . . . But beauty did no good for anyone; it conferred no blessing upon the beautiful woman. Nervously, Ilena opened the medicine cabinet and peered at the array of things inside. She was interested mainly in prescription containers. Here were some small green pills prescribed for the dean's wife, for "tension." Tension, good! She took two of the pills. On another shelf there were some yellow capsules, per- haps the same as her own, though slightly smaller; she checked, yes, hers were 5 mg. and these were only 2. So she didn't bother with them. But she did discover an interesting white pill for "muscular tension," Dean Spriggs's prescription; she took one of these.

She descended the stairs, her hand firm on the bannister.

Before she could return safely to Father Hoffman, she was waylaid by someone's wife—the apple-cheeked Mrs. Honig, a very short woman with white hair who looked older than her husband, who looked, in fact, like Mrs. Santa Claus, motherly and dwarfed; Mrs. Honig asked her to sign a copy of *Death Dance*. "We all think it's so wonderful, just so wonderful for you," she said. Another woman joined them. Ilena had met her once, years before, but she could not remember her name. Mr. Honig hurried over. The conversation seemed to be about the tragedy of America—"All these young people dying in a senseless war," Mrs. Honig said, shaking her white hair; Mr. Honig agreed mournfully. "Vietnam is a shameful tragedy," he said. The dean's wife came by with a tray of cheese and crackers; everyone took something, even Ilena, though she doubted her ability to eat. She doubted everything. It seemed to her that Mrs. Honig and these other people were talking about Vietnam, and about drugs and death—could this be true?—or was it another hallucination? "Why, you know, a young man was killed here last spring, he took part in a demonstration against the Cambodian business," Mrs. Honig said vaguely; "they say a policeman clubbed him to death...." "No, Ida, he had a concussion and died afterward," Mr. Honig said. He wiped his mouth of cracker crumbs and stared sadly at Ilena. "I think you knew him ... Emmett Norlan?"

Emmett Norlan?

"You mean—Emmett is dead? He died? He died?" Ilena asked shrilly.

The blond poet came over to join their group. He had known Emmett, yes, a brilliant young man, a martyr to the Cause—yes, yes—he knew everything. While Ilena stared into space he told them all about Emmett. He had been an intimate friend of Emmett's.

Ilena happened to be staring toward the front of the hall, and she saw Gordon enter. The dean's wife was showing him in. Flakes of snow had settled upon the shoulders of his gray coat. Ilena started, seeing him so suddenly. She had forgotten all about him. She stared across the room in dismay, wondering at his appearance—he wore his hair longer, his sideburns were long and a little curly, he even had a small wiry brown beard— But he did not look youthful, he looked weary and drawn.

Now began half an hour of Ilena's awareness of him and his awareness of her. They had lived through events like this in the past, at other parties, meeting in other groups at the university; a dangerous, nervous sensation about their playing this game, not wanting to rush together. Ilena accepted a drink from a forty-year-old who looked zestful and adolescent, a priest who did not wear his Roman collar but, instead, a black nylon sweater and a medallion on a leather strap; Ilena's brain whirled at such surprises. What had happened? In the past there had been three categories: men, women, and priests. She had known how to conduct herself discreetly around these priests, who were masculine but undangerous; now she wasn't so sure. She kept thinking of Emmett dead. Had Emmett really been killed by the police? Little Emmett? She kept thinking of Gordon, aware of him circling her at a distance of some yards. She kept thinking of these people talking so casually of Vietnam, of drugs, of the death of little Emmett Norlan—these people—the very words they used turning flat and banal and safe in their mouths. "The waste of youth in this country is a tragedy," the priest with the sweater and the medallion said, shaking his head sadly.

Ilena eased away from them to stare at a Chagall lithograph, "Summer Night." Two lovers embraced, in repose; yet a nightmarish dream blossomed out of their heads, an intricate maze of dark depthless foliage, a lighted window, faces ghastly-white and perhaps a little grotesque.... Staring at these lovers, she sensed Gordon approaching her. She turned to him, wanting to be casual. But she was shaking. Gordon stared at her and she saw that old helplessness in his eyes—what, did he still love her? Wasn't she free of him yet? She began talking swiftly, nervously. "Tell me about Emmett. Tell me what happened." Gordon, who seemed heavier than she recalled, whose tired face disappointed her sharply, spoke as always in his gentle, rather paternal voice; she tried to listen. She tried to listen but she kept recalling that office, the two of them lying on the floor together, helpless in an embrace, so hasty, so reckless, grinding their bodies together in anguish.... They had been so close, so intimate, that their blood had flowed freely in each other's veins; on the coldest days they had gone about blood-warmed, love-warmed. Tears filled Ilena's eyes. Gordon was saying, "The story was that he died of a concussion, but actually he died of liver failure. Once he got in the hospital he just disintegrated . . . he had hepatitis . . . he'd been taking heroin. . . . It was a hell of a thing, Ilena. . . . "

She pressed her fingers hard against her eyes.

"Don't cry, please," Gordon said, stricken.

A pause of several seconds: the two of them in a kind of equilibrium, two lovers.

"Would you like me to drive you back to your hotel?" Gordon said.

She went at once to get her coat. Backing away, always backing away . . . she stammered a few words to Father Hoffman, to the dean and his wife, words of gratitude, confusion. Goodby to Detroit! *Good-by, good-by.* She shook hands. She finished her drink. Gordon helped her on with her coat—a stylish black coat with a black mink collar, nothing like the clothes she had worn in the old days. Out on the walk, in the soft falling snow, Gordon said nervously: "I know you're going to be married. Lyle Myer. I know all about it. I'm very happy. I'm happy for you. You're looking very well."

Ilena closed her eyes, waiting for her mind to straighten itself out. Yes, she was normal; she had gone to an internist in Buffalo and had been declared normal. *You are too young to be experiencing menopause,* the doctor had said thoughtfully; *the cessation of menstrual periods must be related to the Pill or to an emotional condition.* She thought it better not to tell Gordon all that. "Thank you," she said simply.

"I'm sorry they told you about Emmett," Gordon said. "There was no reason to tell you. He liked you so much, Ilena; he hung around my office after you left and all but confessed he was in love with you . . . he kept asking if you wrote to me and I said no, but he didn't believe me . . . he was always asking about you. . . . "

"When did he die?"

"Last spring. His liver gave out. Evidently it was just shot. Someone said his skin was bright yellow."

"He was taking heroin? . . . "

"God, yes. He was a wreck. The poor kid just disintegrated, it was a hell of a shame...."

He drove her back downtown. They were suddenly very comfortable together, sadly comfortable. Ilena had been in this car only two or three times in the past. "Where is your wife?" she asked shyly. She watched him as he answered—his wife was visiting her mother in Ohio, she'd taken the children—no, things were no better between them—always the same, always the same— Ilena thought in dismay that he was trivialized by these words: men were trivialized by love and by their need for women.

"I've missed you so much... " Gordon said suddenly.

They walked through the tufts of falling snow, to the hotel. A gigantic hotel, all lights and people. Ilena felt brazen and anonymous here. Gordon kept glancing at her, as if unable to believe in her. He was nervous, eager, a little drunk; an uncertain adolescent smile hovered about his face. "I love you, I still love you," he whispered. In the elevator he embraced her. Ilena did not resist. She felt her body warming to him as toward an old friend, a brother. She did love him. Tears of love stung her eyes. If only she could get her head straight, if only she could think of what she was supposed to think of... someone she was supposed to remember.... In the overheated room they embraced gently. Gently. Ilena did not want to start this love again, it was a mistake, but she caught sight of Gordon's stricken face and could not resist. She began to cry. Gordon clutched her around the hips, kneeling before her. He pressed his hot face against her.

"Ilena, I'm so sorry... " he said.

She thought of planets: sun-warmed planets revolving around a molten star. Revolving around a glob of light. And the planets rotated on their own private axes. But now the planets were accelerating, they wobbled on their axes and the strain of their movement threatened to tear them apart. She began to sob. Ugly, gasping, painful sobs.... "Don't cry, please, I'm so sorry," Gordon said. They lay down together. The room was hot, too hot. They had not bothered to put on a light. Only the light from the window, a dull glazed wintry light; Ilena allowed him to kiss her, to undress her, to move his hands wildly about her body as she wept. What should she be thinking of? Whom should she remember? When she was with Lyle she thought back to Gordon...now, with Gordon, she thought back to someone else, someone else, half-remembered, indistinct, perhaps dead.... He began to make love to her. He was eager, breathing as sharply and as painfully as Ilena herself. She clasped her arms around him. That firm hard back she remembered. Or did she remember?... Her mind wandered and she thought suddenly of Bryan, her husband. He was her ex-husband now. She thought of their meeting at that civil-rights rally, introduced by mutual friends, she thought of the little tavern they had gone to, on State Street in Madison, she thought of the first meal she'd made for Bryan and that other couple...proud of herself as a cook, baking them an Italian dish with shrimp and crabmeat and mushrooms...yes, she had been proud of her cooking, she had loved to cook for years. For years. She had loved Bryan. But suddenly she was not thinking of him; her mind gave way to a sharper thought and she saw Emmett's face: his scorn, his disapproval.

She stifled a scream.

Gordon slid from her, frightened. "Did I hurt you? Ilena?"

She began to weep uncontrollably. Their bodies, so warm, now shivered and seemed to sting each other. Their hairs seemed to catch at each other painfully.

"Did I hurt you?..." he whispered.

She remembered the afternoon she had fainted. Passed out cold. And then she had come to her senses and she had cried, like this, hiding her face from her lover because crying made it ugly, so swollen.... Gordon tried to comfort her. But the bed was crowded with people. A din of people. A mob. Lovers were kissing her on every inch of her body and trying to suck up her tepid blood, prodding, poking, inspecting her like that doctor in Buffalo—up on the table, naked beneath an oversized white robe, her feet in the stirrups, being examined with a cold sharp metal device and then with the doctor's fingers in his slick rubber gloves—checking her ovaries, so casually— *You are too young for menopause,* he had said. Was it the pills, then? The birth-control pills? *This kind of sterility is not necessarily unrelated to the Pill,* the doctor had conceded, and his subtlety of language had enchanted Ilena....

"Don't cry," Gordon begged.

She had frightened him off and he would not make love to her. He only clutched at her, embraced her. She felt that he was heavier, yes, than she remembered. Heavier. Older. But she could not concentrate on him: she kept seeing Emmett's face. His frizzy hair, his big glasses, his continual whine. Far inside her, too deep for any man to reach and stir into sensation, a dull, dim lust began for Emmett, hardly more than a faint throbbing. Emmett, who was dead. She wanted to hold him, now, instead of this man—Emmett in her arms, his irritation calmed, his glasses off and set on the night table beside the bed, everything silent, silent. Gordon was whispering to her. *Love. Love.* She did not remember that short scratchy beard. But she was lying in bed with an anxious, perspiring, bearded man, evidently someone she knew. They were so close that their blood might flow easily back and forth between their bodies, sluggish and warm and loving.

She recalled her husband's face: a look of surprise, shock. She had betrayed him. His face blended with the face of her student, who was dead, and Gordon's face, pressed so close to her in the dark that she could not see it. The bed was crammed with people. Their identities flowed sluggishly, haltingly, from vein to vein. One by one they were all becoming each other. Becoming protoplasm. They were protoplasm that had the sticky pale formlessness of semen. They were all turning into each other, into protoplasm.... Ilena was conscious of something fading in her, in the pit of her belly. Fading. Dying. *The central sexual organ is the brain,* she had read, and now her brain was drawing away, fading, dissolving.

"Do you want me to leave?" Gordon asked.

She did not answer. Against the hotel window: soft, shapeless clumps of snow. She must remember something, she must remember someone...there was an important truth she must understand.... But she could not get it into focus. Her brain seemed to swoon backward in an elation of fatigue, and she heard beyond this man's hoarse, strained breathing the gentle breathing of the snow, falling shapelessly upon them all.

"Do you want me to leave?" Gordon asked.

She could not speak.

Concerning the Case
of Bobby T.

*J*UNE *28, 1952*

Bobby T. struggled with Frances Berardi and yanked her to
the side, as if trying to knock her over. But she twisted her small
body to keep from falling. She was screaming. They were near
the boarded-up cabin in Reardon Park—a refreshment stand
not open this summer, though painted a tart black-green that
still smelled fresh—and three friends of Frances, girls her own
age, were on the wide dirt path nearby, watching, and other
people in the park turned to watch, hearing the noise. Bobby T.
noticed nothing. He shook Frances so her head swung forward
and back and her long black hair flicked into his face, stinging
his eyes.

This seemed to drive him into a frenzy, her hair stinging his
eyes. She fell to her knees. Bobby T. was gripping her by the
upper arm, and he yanked her back up onto her feet again and
gave her a final shove, back at her friends. She collided with one
of the girls. The girls were so surprised by all this that they
hadn't had time to cry for help until it was all over and Bobby T.
was running. By then people were coming—a man who had

been sitting on a blanket nearby, with his wife and baby and a portable radio, and some Negro men who were fishing at the river, and some boys on bicycles, attracted by all the yelling. But by then Bobby T. had run crashing through the bushes and was gone.

That was around seven-thirty on a very hot evening in Seneca, New York.

August 9, 1971

Frances Berardi, thirty-one years old, separated now for nearly two months from her husband, stood behind the counter in her father's music store and thought about Bobby T. Cheatum.

In spite of the airless heat of the store, she was shivering. She stared, fascinated and contemptuous, at the prickly flesh on her bare arms.

She was helping out at Berardi's Music Store, in its "new location"—since 1969—on Drummond Avenue. Her father was giving an organ lesson to a widow named Florence Daley, in the soundproof room at the rear of the store. Twelve free lessons came with each purchase of an organ; Mrs. Daley's son and his wife had bought her an organ for her birthday. From time to time Frances could hear the muffled breathless shrieks of the organ, though maybe she was imagining it. The room was supposed to be soundproof. She inclined her head, listening. Yes, she did hear the shrieks. She heard something.

If Bobby T. walked through the door she would say to him, *I'm not Frances Berardi any longer. I'm Frances Laseck.*

Her father's store was small, only half the size of the shoe store on one side of it and perhaps one-third the size of the drugstore at the corner. He had crowded it with merchandise— pianos and organs lining the walls and out in the middle of the floor. It was hard to walk around in here. There were several counters of smaller musical instruments—accordions and guitars and drums—and racks of sheet music and records, though Frances's father made no effort to compete with the discount department stores that sold popular records so cheaply. He wouldn't compete with them, he said angrily; there, records were stocked "by the foot" according to what sold fast, and nobody cared what kind of music was being sold. He didn't want to compete on that level, he said. But Berardi's Music Store kept going, year after year. Frances liked helping her father because the store was so familiar, so contained, like a box seen from the inside. There were no surprises here. She loved the smell of the clean polished wood, the pianos and organs that looked so perfect, handsome and mute and oiled, with their white and black keys.

If she had to wait for Bobby T., she was safer here than at home.

Her eyes felt bright and glittery, her neck strangely long and thin. She had not slept well for several nights. She knew that her collar bones showed in this dress, and that she looked wispy and shrill in it, like a bird, but she had worn it anyway. If Bobby T. did come to look her up, after so many years, he might take pity on her when he saw how thin she was. After the baby she had never gained weight. After the trouble with her husband she had never gained weight.

Frances checked her watch: four-thirty. A very long, hot, quiet afternoon. She looked at the clock on the wall behind her: four-thirty. Outside, people strolled by on the sidewalk and did not come in, sometimes didn't even glance into the window. Now someone was slowing down, lingering—a middle-aged woman in a housedress, who stared at the small $898 organ for sale there, and at the music books displayed on a velvet cloth, *Gershwin's Finest Hours, Two on the Aisle, Songs from South Pacific.* The woman's name was Mrs. Fuhr; Frances knew her daughter Maude from high school. She hoped that Mrs. Fuhr wouldn't come in the store.

Only an hour and a half, Frances thought. Then they could close the store.

July 2, 1952

Again and again they asked Frances what had happened. Her face was hot and stiff from crying. If she cried hard enough they might let her alone. Why wouldn't they let her alone? Her mother sat broad and creaking in a cane-backed chair, ashamed, silent. Her father was unable to stay in one place, kept jumping up from his seat and pacing around, making everyone nervous. "Just tell them, Frannie. Tell them again. Speak up nice and tell them, please," he said.

They were in the downtown police station, in one of the back rooms. The police station! Frances knew that Bobby T. was locked up somewhere nearby.

"Repeat, please, what you told us. Then what? Then, after he knocked you down, then what?" a man was asking her.

Frances went through it all again.

Her upper arm was bruised, ugly orange and yellow and purple bruises—look at that, her father said, turning Frances's arm for the man to see. Yes, he saw it. Her knees were scratched bad. The policeman tried not to look at Frances's knees. Anyway the scratches were covered with bandages and adhesive tape her mother changed several times a day.

"She could get infection—bad infection—" her father muttered.

"Yes," said the policeman. He was a sizable man with a gleaming bald head, her father's age. He did not wear a uniform like the other policemen who were listening. As he talked, Frances stared at the grim creases around his mouth. From time to time he rubbed a handkerchief into these sweaty creases because it was so hot, even with the fan going. It had been hot now, up in the nineties, for over a week. Everyone in Seneca was sick of the weather.

"Bobby T. Cheatum was always a wise guy, smart-assing around," the policeman said, "but I never thought he'd go crazy like this."

"You just keep him locked up," Frances's father said loudly. "If he breaks out—"

"He isn't going to break out."

"No? Who says so, a jail like this? I know this town. I know how my kids and my neighbors' kids get chased around—boys or girls, it don't matter— Look, you see this goes to a trial—in a courtroom, with a judge and all that," he stammered, "because there are some things this town should learn—"

"Yes, Mr. Berardi, that's right. I happen to agree with you," the policeman said, wiping his face.

Frances had no more tears left. She wondered if they had

come to the end of the questioning. For four days now she had been kept in the house, her father had closed up the store and stayed home, sometimes weeping angrily in the bedroom, sometimes storming out of the house, bypassing Frances, not even looking at her. As if he hated her. Frances had cried until she was worn out. She thought in a flash of anger that Bobby T. was a stupid goddam nigger, though he thought he was smarter than the other niggers, and the next time she saw him she would tell him so.

November 19, 1956

"My name is Herbert Ryder from Legal Aid. I came out here the other time with your sister Bonnie. Do you remember me, Bobby?"

Bobby T. Cheatum sat with his arms listless on his big knees, knees parted and tilting to either side of his body. His face was oily with a peculiar sweatless perspiration, especially the wings of his broad nose. His eyes were yellowed. Sometimes his lips were pursed, sometimes slack. He did not glance at Herbert Ryder.

"Bobby, I want to ask you a few questions. Are you listening, Bobby?"

They were in a visitors' room, an alcove off the veranda used for arts and crafts instructions on certain days of the week. This was a Wednesday evening, the only time Ryder could come to the hospital. The alcove was quite cold. There was no one around except a nurse at the reception desk in the foyer; she was typing in brief, hacking spasms, and listening to music on a small transistor radio.

"As soon as you can be examined again and released from here we'll get you on the court docket. I'm confident the charges will be dismissed. Bobby, are you listening?"

Bobby did not reply.

"Why aren't you listening? Don't you trust me? Your sister Bonnie came to me for help—don't you remember, she introduced me to you? You know who I am. You want to get out of here, don't you?"

Bobby shrugged his shoulders. "Hell," he mumbled.
"What?"
"Hell with it," he said hoarsely.
"What do you mean? Don't you want to get out of here?"
Bobby stared at the floor. His hair was oily and very woolly.
The tight, tiny curls gave his face a look of tension that was
misleading. Really he was very relaxed, slack, almost unconscious. He sat sunk into himself, his beefy bare arms heavy on
his thighs, his big hands loose on his knees. Though it was
drafty in the alcove he appeared warm; the large pores of his
nose glowed.
"Everything will be cleared up...I'm confident the charges
will be dismissed. But you have to get well. I mean you have to
be declared well. If you would only make an effort...."
Suddenly Bobby appeared to be listening.
"When you're scheduled to be examined, if you would only
try to be...try to... If you would only make an effort to act
normal...."
The nurse in the foyer began typing again, interrupting the
music. Bobby T. flinched: it had been the music he was listening
to, not Ryder.
"Do you want to rot in here?" Ryder asked impatiently.
Bobby T. did not bother to reply.

July 6, 1952

Bounding on and off the prison cot at the downtown Seneca
jail, shouting. On and off the bars, throwing himself against the
bars, which he couldn't believe in. They had dragged him here
and locked him in! Bobby T. Cheatum himself!
When he got out—
He mashed his sweating face against the iron bars. His
eyeballs itched with the heat and this way he could scratch
them. Roll them hard against the bars, then harder, and then he
knocked his forehead against them—it maddened him to think
of how he was locked up while everyone else was loose.
Probably laughing at him. Shaking their heads over him. His
mother had predicted all this, with her used-up sour laugh.
Bobby T., your troubles and mine are set to begin soon, with that lip of

yours. She wouldn't come visit him. But she sent him a message through his sister: *I give you my undivided love and attention. God bless you always.*

He kept hearing Frances Berardi's scream. Why had that little bitch made so much noise? And when he looked around, sure enough Roosevelt had run, and the girls started to scream for help— Where had those girls come from, anyway? Dawdling on the path, holding back and then walking forward, fast, right up out of the awful waves of heat, heat like air easing out of an oven, and no place to hide from it. He had worked all day at Allied Storage, loading and unloading vans, and what he looked forward to was the evening—strolling down to Reardon Park to see who was around.

He could shut his eyes and see everyone there, hanging around the concrete abutment, telling jokes about how Bobby T. had gotten dragged off to jail.

He banged his head against the bars to see what would happen. Suddenly he liked the hard-soft feel of the iron, its cool flatness, the way it pushed back at his hot face. There was something to respect in those bars.

...He remembered the little brash-faced Italian girls from when he'd been in school, how they joked with him and didn't even mind sitting next to him on the Uptown bus. He had gotten along with all of them. Everyone liked him. The kids from Lowertown all stuck together, riding the bus three or four miles up to Lawrence Belknap School. Frances Berardi hadn't been on that bus—she was younger than Bobby T. and his friends—he wasn't sure what age she was, but she was young. The little white bitch, with that yell of hers....

His mouth had been cut on the inside and he'd spat out blood, but no doctor would come to see him.

He pressed his face, his cheek, his jaw against the bars. An idea came to him slowly. He could see it, beginning as a pinprick in his head, then swelling. He watched it swell until it was too large to stay inside his head.

"You let me out!" he yelled.

The noise of his voice astonished him. It was the noise he'd heard in the fight with Frances—not really his own voice, but

another, that pushed its way out of him. Now that it was free it
yelled again: "You're listenin'! You guys're listenin'! You let me
out—you—"

He paused, panting. His heart was pounding now as if it had
gotten away from him, jubilant and wild. *Yes, yes, Bobby T.,* he
thought to himself, a thought that was like a shout, and something seemed to burst in his head. He picked the mattress off his
cot and, grunting, threw it against the wall. Then he wheeled
around and saw the frame and seized it—it wasn't heavy, it was
disappointing, but anyway it was something to grab, a real
opponent. Not like little Frances Berardi who turned out to
weigh almost nothing, for all her smart-aleck taunts—he could
have snapped her neck in a second—

That face of hers froze in his head. He remembered the
sudden springing madness he'd felt, Frances's face, how she'd
turned against him and slapped him, right for everybody to
see— He began slamming the cot against the wall. Again. And
again. Beating the cot against the wall and the bars and yelling
for them to let him out, until he couldn't stop, didn't want to
stop—

"Let me out 'n' I'll kill you—the goddam bunch of you—"

July 9, 1952

Nine-thirty in the morning. He knew that from seeing a clock.
All night long Bobby T.'s eyes were rolling like crazy in his
head, wanting to get loose. Leather belts kept him in bed. To
spite the nurse he wet the bed on purpose—let her clean it up.
Sponge it up. She was a claw-handed white bitch, afraid of him,
wouldn't come near him if she could help it. He tried to throw
up on her but it caught somewhere inside him—wouldn't come
up. So he had to taste it, seeping back down his throat. That
drove him wild.

A shot in the left buttock and then he was up and into
somebody's clothes, not clothes he recognized. Now his head
was very heavy, though he knew it was only nine-thirty in the
morning and he had a long day ahead. They walked him out to
an ambulance and helped him up and closed the door on him,
with more leather straps to keep his arms against his sides and

an attendant sitting by the door to guard him. A white punk of maybe twenty, staring at Bobby T. as if he expected Bobby T. to leap at him.

So they really thought he was crazy!

He had to laugh, that was such a joke. The white boy by the back door, sitting on a little stool, stared at him and said nothing.

So he was mentally unfit to stand trial—so they said—so he had fooled them, all of them—

Mentally unfit to stand trial! He was fooling them all.

June 28, 1952

Frances Berardi and some friends of hers, girls her own age, were cutting through Reardon Park, it was after supper and everyone was out. They talked for a while with some boys they knew, and Frances took a few puffs of a cigarette from one of them—a small, dark, ferret-faced boy named Joe Palisano. She smoked with a squinting, adult detachment, as if assessing the taste of the smoke carefully and finding it not bad. She and Joe were not older than the others but they acted older; but then he started to tease her about certain things, about something that had been written about her on a viaduct nearby, and she told him to go to hell.

She led her friends away, walking stiffly and angrily. "I don't like guys who talk dirty," she said. "I don't have to put up with that crap from anybody's mouth."

She spoke with a tart philosophical air. She and her friends wandered down to the river, where people were fishing—most of them Negroes, boys and older men, even a few heavy black women, sitting on upended boxes and sighing with the heat. There was no one here that Frances was interested in. She and her friends walked along the abutment, kicking Mallow Cup wrappers and popsicle wrappers into the water. It was a very hot, airless evening.

Frances was wearing jeans cut off high on her thighs and a jersey blouse that pulled tight over her head, pink and white stripes and a white stretch collar; she had bought it just the Saturday before, at an Uptown store. She knew she looked good in it. She was twelve years old but mature for her age, her black hair glossy and loose, her bangs falling thick over her forehead so that they brushed the tops of her thick eyebrows. She was short, trim, athletic, with quick eyes and a brief upper lip, a little loud in her laughter and joking. You could always hear Frannie from a distance, one of her sisters complained—at school or hanging around the grocery store or here in the park, always Frannie Berardi with her big mouth, fooling around. Her friends stood around her, envious and uneasy.

There was nothing to do by the river so they headed back up toward Market Street. Joe Palisano and his friends were gone. Frances regretted walking away like that, but she had thought maybe he would follow her. Right now she might be riding on the crossbar of his bicycle, hot-faced and excited.... "The hell with him," she muttered. She and her friends walked slowly, scuffing their feet. They all wore moccasins made of imitation leather, a bright tan, and decorated with small colored beads, bought at the same store Uptown. It was a thing they did, scuff their feet, especially when they walked on the pavement. They scuffed their feet now in the dirt. They all had the same dark-bright faces, dark eyes moving restlessly. Their minds were tipped in one direction by someone honking a horn up ahead—but it was nobody they knew—and then another way by a blast of music from someone's radio—but it was just a married couple with their baby, lying on a blanket nearby, a cousin of Frances's and her husband—and then in another direction by two Negro boys up ahead. Frances knew one of them, Bobby T., a big boy wearing jeans and a buckled belt and a white T-shirt tucked into the jeans.

"Look who's hanging around," Frances called out to him in a drawl.

He turned to her with a surprised grin. "I see a cute little fox," he said, raising his hand to sight her through his fingers, a circle made by his thumb and forefinger.

Frances laughed. "That's all you got to do, huh, hang around here? I thought you had a car. How come you're hanging around here?"

"Taking in the sights," Bobby T. said.

Frances looked Bobby T. straight in the eye. He was nineteen and had been in the same class with her brother Salvatore. But he acted younger and was always lots of fun. He was a good-looking black boy.

"Out for any special sight?" Frances said. She was hot-faced and bold. Her friends giggled at the way Frances walked right up to him with her hands on her hips, like someone in a movie.

"Could be we might take a drive Uptown. Want to come along?" Bobby T. said.

"Not tonight." Frances saw that he was barefoot and that his feet were powdery with the dust. She giggled at the size of his feet. "Anyway, I heard your car broke down. That's what I heard."

"How come not tonight? You got some special business?"

Frances shrugged her shoulders. She was very excited, almost giddy. It was as if someone were pushing her from behind, pushing her toward Bobby T. *Come on, don't be afraid! Stand right up to him!*

"Hell, my father would kill me," Frances said.

"Who's gonna tell him?"

"I heard your car broke down and anyway I got better things to do."

"Your father ain't gonna know about it—he never knew about it the other time, did he?"

Frances hoped her friends hadn't heard that. A kind of flame passed over her face and she poked Bobby T. with her forefinger, right in the center of his chest.

"Somebody's got a big mouth," she drawled.

Bobby T. just grinned.

That made Frances mad. Something was beating furiously in her. She had to stand back on her heels, with her head tilted, in order to look up straight into Bobby T.'s face. She wasn't going to back down from him.

"I got better things to do than ram around with you," she said.

"How come you so fussy? That's never what I heard about Frannie Berardi."

She almost laughed. Then, lit by a sudden giddy excitement,

a daring she had rehearsed in her imagination many times—
slapping Joe Palisano's face in front of everyone—Frances reared
back and struck Bobby T. on the side of the face, with the flat of
her hand, slapping her palm hard against his cheek—

April 23, 1960

"So I slapped his face. I was just kidding around. And he
grabbed my wrist and started shaking me . . . and I tried to kick
him . . . and . . . "
    Frances hesitated, staring at Father Luciano as if she expected
him to nod, to remember. But he couldn't remember. He couldn't
see that summer evening, the park and the wide dirt path and
the boarded-up refreshment stand and Bobby T. and her. . . .
    "Didn't this all happen a long time ago, Frances? Years ago?"
he asked.
    "Yes, before we all moved Uptown, a whole lot of us moved,"
Frances said slowly. "It was like the kids themselves decided to
move—you know—kids who were friends with one another—
now it's mostly all Negro down there. By the river. Eddie drives
me by there sometimes and I look at our old house and it's all
colored, a big family. . . . Lowertown used to be all Italian and
colored, now it's just colored. . . . It's funny how that changed."
    Father Luciano smiled a pursed little smile. His expression
looked out of focus, not quite right. Wasn't he listening? Frances
sat forward. She had to make him understand. There was
something urgent she had to explain, she must ask his forgiveness and his absolution, she must confess it and get it all
straightened out so that she could forget about it and get
married and pass beyond that part of her life.
    "It was a long time ago, yes," she stammered, "and I was
such a brat, it makes me sick to remember myself! I was such a
show-off. . . . We'd go roller-skating on Saturdays, and kid around
with the Uptown boys, and ride our bicycles all over. . . . It
makes me so ashamed to remember myself," she said. She took
a tissue out of her purse and wiped her forehead. "And Bobby
T.—Bobby T. Cheatum—he was a neighborhood kid a little
older than we were. He went to school with my brother but

dropped out. Everybody played together, you know, white and colored, in the park and at school and all over, and Bobby T. was always a nice kid—kind of daring, the way he would climb across the railroad bridge when a train might come at any time, and you know how that thing wobbles—"

Why was she saying all this? Father Luciano didn't know what she was talking about. Probably he had never even driven down to Lowertown. He was new to the city of Seneca itself and his parish was nowhere near the hill. He was from Buffalo, forty miles away. Frances was confused. She wanted to make him understand, she wanted to make him remember—those years in the cinder playgrounds, in the park, at Lawrence Belknap school, she wanted to make him remember again the kids in the neighborhood, who were all grown up now, a lot of them married, some still in the Navy or the Army, a few of them gone on to college, or disappeared, two of them killed in car accidents, and a few of them with crazy bad luck—like Bobby T., locked up in the state hospital all these years.

"Would you like to begin your confession now?" Father Luciano asked.

"No, not yet, no, wait.... I want to explain something...." she said slowly, confused. Out in the anteroom Eddie was waiting and she could imagine him smoking a cigarette, frowning. This was taking too long. She knew what was coming: a little lecture on birth control, the paper she would have to sign swearing that she would not use any artificial methods of birth control and that her children would be brought up Catholic. Yes. She was ready for that. But first she had to explain something about those years of her childhood, her young girlhood, when she was twelve years old and had bought that pink and white blouse she liked so much, when she had walked up to Bobby T. Cheatum that night in the park....

"You said that the boy is in the hospital," Father Luciano said, when Frances did not speak for a while. "Don't you think he's in good hands there? He's out of danger and he can't cause danger to others.... I'm sure they have an excellent staff there to help him. If he were out on his own he'd just be a threat to himself and to others."

"But I was such a brat, I was always shooting my mouth off...."

"And the court showed the proper wisdom, I believe. I'm sure of it. Does anyone else ever talk about this incident, Frances? Does anyone else even remember except you?"

"Oh, no. No," Frances said at once. "Not in my family. We stopped talking about it right away. And Eddie used to live outside Seneca, he's from the country where his parents have a farm.... The kids are all sort of scattered now, except for some girls I see around, you know, shopping. We all moved Uptown. And Bobby T.'s people, well, I didn't know them.... His father died a few years ago, I heard...but probably people don't remember...."

Father Luciano shifted his weight in his chair. Over his shoulder Frances could see the lawn out front and the grilled iron gates decorated with golden crosses, cross after cross stretching along the sidewalk. She looked down at her hands, at the frayed damp tissue. She couldn't remember having taken it out of her purse.

"If he were out on his own," Father Luciano said gently, "he'd just be a threat to himself and to others. Isn't that so?"

"I thought if I could visit him...maybe I could explain it to him.... But that would drive my father wild, I couldn't even bring it up. Once some lawyer came to see me, he was from Legal Aid. I think that's what it was called. He was trying to get Bobby T. set for a trial or something. He asked me questions but my father was right there with me, so I had to keep saying the old answers.... And... Oh, I don't know. That was a long time ago too, three or four years ago. I suppose people don't remember now."

"I'm sure they don't," Father Luciano said.

August 9, 1971

Frances answered the phone on the first ring.

"Frannie? How is it there?"

"What do you mean, how is it?" she said irritably. "The four o'clock lesson came and went—the lady with the organ lessons—and it's dead as hell in here, and hot. Why he wants to stay open till six is beyond me."

"You sure nobody came in?"

"If you mean Bobby T., he's nowhere in sight and what's more no Negro is in sight or has even looked in the window all day. So. How's everything at home?"

"Frannie, I just happened to mention that this colored boy was being released today, you know, I just happened to mention it to Edith Columbo, and she said maybe we better notify the police. I don't mean to be asking for trouble, Frannie—but just to be sensible—to give warning—"

"No."

"You should let Eddie know, anyway. He would want to know. He would be worrying about you right now."

Frances made a despairing droll face that her mother should be so stupid! That her mother should think Eddie gave a damn about her!

"How's Sue Ann?" Frances asked flatly.

"Outside playing with the kid next door.... You sure nobody's hanging around there? Out on the sidewalk?"

Frances's father came out of the back room, looking at her. She mouthed the word "Mama" to him and he nodded, his face closing up. He walked to the front of the store and gazed out at the street. Traffic passed slowly. After a few minutes Frances said, "Mama, I got to hang up, a customer is coming in—"

She stared at her father's back, his damp white shirt, and wondered what he was thinking. Not of Bobby T. No. He wouldn't spend five minutes in all these years thinking of him: that black bastard, that maniac, beating his daughter up the way he did, and then running so wild it took three policemen to drag him away.... Frances took out her compact and checked her face. It was always a surprise, that she should look so cute. *Cute.* That's all you could say for her face but it was enough—with her short upper lip and her long thin nose and her dark, darting eyes, and the way her hair didn't turn kinky even in this hot weather. Yes, she was cute. Short and cute. What had someone said to her once?—Bobby T. himself?—*The best things come in small packages.*

Once she had been under the awning at the Rexall Drugs on Main Street, waiting for rain to stop, and cruising along the curb in his rattletrap jalopy was Bobby T. and that friend of his with the funny name—she couldn't remember it now—and Bobby asked her how'd she like a ride home? Because they lived near each other. Frances hesitated only a second, then said Okay. Great. And she had jumped in the back seat. She had always had a lot of nerve. They drove right down the big hill to Lowertown, Bobby T. showing off a little bit, thumping on the steering wheel as if it were a drum, but putting himself out to be nice to her. Yet he let you know, that Bobby T., that he was always thinking around the edges of what he shouldn't be thinking. That was the day he had said, teasing her, *the best things come in small packages.*

Bobby T.'s friend—his name was Roosevelt—couldn't keep up with her and Bobby T., the way they kidded each other. What a nerve she had! She knew her father would kill her if he saw her in a car with any boys, let alone colored boys. But she had jumped in the car anyway.

Then, as they approached her own neighborhood, she began to wonder if this had been a good idea. Someone on the street might see her and tell her father. So she poked Bobby T. on the shoulder and said, "Hey, maybe you better let me out here."

"In the rain, honey? You'll spoil that high-class outfit of yours!"

She snorted at this—she was wearing shorts and a soiled blouse.

But Bobby T. let her out anyway, near a grocery store so that she could wait for the rain to stop. Nobody had seen her, evidently. Nobody told her father. And yet now, today, so many years later, she wanted to tell her father about that ride. How they had all giggled together....

"I've been thinking about Bobby T. all day...." she said softly.

Her father stood with his back to her, blunt and perspiring. He had grown heavy and bald: once a good-looking man, even when his hair had thinned unevenly, now he sagged with worry and irritability. Frances was a little afraid of him. She feared his peevish scowl, that scowl that had been directed at her over the years—because she was no good at the piano, because her marriage had been bad from the start, most of all because she had a pert, impatient, unserious scowl herself.

"What did you say?" her father said, turning suddenly.

His face warned her: *Better shut up, Fran. Shut your cute little mouth.*

"Nothing," she said.

"It better be nothing," her father said.

August 9, 1971

They had located Bobby T.'s older sister, Bonnie, who was married and living now in Buffalo. At first she had said no, no, she couldn't take him in, she was afraid of him, and her husband was in and out of trouble himself.... What would Bobby T. do around the house? Wouldn't he be dangerous?

A woman social worker told her: "Bobby has ten years' experience working in the hospital laundry. He'll be able to get a good job in a laundry. He only needs to adjust himself to society again. He needs a friendly home for a while, to get him started again."

"How long's that gonna take, to get him started again?" Bonnie asked suspiciously.

She was a grave-faced, thick woman in her mid-forties, with a habit of shaking her head negatively as she thought, as if nothing seemed right to her. But in the end she agreed to take Bobby T. in.

So they brought Bobby T. to her one Monday afternoon. He turned out to be a tall, thin black man with a slight stoop, shy and apologetic. He was carrying a small suitcase. He had five dollars release money.

"Well, Bobby T.," she said awkwardly. "Such a long time...."

They shook hands like people in a movie. Bonnie didn't know what to do: she remembered her brother as taller and heavier, and maybe this man was someone else.

"Hello," he said.

A voice like a whisper, so hoarse! She didn't recognize that either.

She cleared off a place for him to sit on the sofa and he set the suitcase primly at his feet. So this was her crazy put-away brother Bobby Templar, the one nobody in the family liked to talk about.... He had a curious way of ducking his head. He would not meet her gaze, not directly. A tall thin scrawny bird, birdlike in his nervousness, with a glaze to his dark skin that was like permanent sweat, and a smell in his clothes of panic. Bonnie stared at him, her heart sinking. This was a mistake and she couldn't get out of it.

"Been a lot of time since we seen each other," she said slowly. "They treated you okay there, huh?"

"Yes," Bobby said.

"The big trouble—you know—the courtroom and all—I mean the trial—that got all cleared up, huh?"

"The charges were dismissed," Bobby T. said softly.

"Charges were dismissed, oh yes," his sister said seriously, nodding. That was an important fact. That was good news.

She couldn't think what to do—start supper with him sitting here?—so after a while she suggested that they go down to the corner to get some things she needed. "Just a five-minute walk," she said.

Bobby got to his feet self-consciously and followed her out of the building—she had an apartment on the first floor, a good location—and she noticed out of the corner of her eye that he walked in a kind of crouch, leading with his forehead. He didn't look crazy, not the way some people on the street looked, but he didn't look quite right either, with that stiff walk of his, like an old man's walk and not a man of—what was he now?—thirty-eight? He kept staring out at the street, at the buses and trucks.

At the intersection he froze and didn't seem able to move. "It's just across the street, that's the grocery right over there," Bonnie said, panicked herself. *Oh Jesus,* she thought, *they brought him to me still crazy and they drove away again!* "Look, Bobby T., it ain't nothing to get across this street—nobody's going to hurt you—"

What was wrong with him? He stood on the curb, sweating, and wouldn't step off onto the street. He was staring ahead, his eyes wide. He stood in that crouched-over, crazy way, his shoulders hunched as if for battle. Bonnie broke out into a sweat, standing beside him. She didn't know if she should touch his arm, or what. He looked paralyzed. And all around them people were passing, some of them staring at him—didn't he have any shame, to act like this on the street?

"Bobby T., there just *ain't* no trouble getting over there...."

He didn't look at her but he seemed to be listening. After a long wait he took one step forward, off the curb and into the gutter. Bonnie drew in her breath slowly, cautiously.

"See, how there ain't any trouble? It's real easy," she said.

He took another step, slow as hell; at this rate it would take them an hour to cross the street, but anyway it was a start.

She took hold of his arm and led him. "Okay, Bobby T., you see how easy it is, huh...? See how easy...?" He was slow as hell and she was burning hot with the shame of it, but he was her brother, after all. Her baby brother. Anyway, today was a start.

In the Warehouse

"WHY DOES YOUR MOTHER DO THAT TO HER HAIR? Does she think it looks nice or something?"

"Do what to her hair?"

"Frizz it up or whatever that is—she's such an ugly old bag! If I looked like that I'd stick my head in the oven!"

The two girls are standing out on the sidewalk before a house, at twilight. The taller one makes vast good-humored gestures in the air as she talks, and the other stands silently, her lips pursed. She has a small, dark, patient face; her brown hair falls in thick puffy bangs across her forehead. The taller girl has hair that is in no style at all—just messy, not very clean, pulled back from her big face, and fixed with black bobby pins, which are the wrong color for her dark blond hair. She has a lot to talk about. She is talking now about Nancy, who lives a few houses away. Nancy is eighteen and works uptown in a store; she thinks she's too good for everyone—"I could show her a thing or two, just give me a match and let me at that dyed hair of hers"—and her mother is grumpy and ugly, like everyone's mother, "just an old bitch that might as well be dead."

It is autumn. Down the street kids are playing after supper, running along between houses or all the way down to the open area that is blocked off because of an expressway nearby. "You don't want to go in already, do you?" the taller girl whines. "Why d'ya always want to go in, you think your house is so hot? Your goddam mother is so hot? We could walk down by the warehouse, see if anybody's around. Just for something to do."

"I better go in."

"Your mother isn't calling you, is she? What's so hot about going in that dump of a house?"

I am the short, dark girl, and my friend Ronnie is laughing into my face as she always does. Ronnie lives two houses away. Her mother has five children and no husband—he died or ran away—and Ronnie is the middle child, thirteen years old. She is big for her age. I am twelve, skinny and meek and incredulous as she jumps to another subject: how Nancy's boyfriend slapped her around and burned her with his cigar just the other night. "Don't you believe me? You think I'm lying?" she challenges me.

"I never heard about that."

"So what? Nobody'd tell you anything. You'd tell the cops or something."

"No I wouldn't."

"Some cop comes to see your father, don't he?"

"He's just somebody—some old friend. I don't know who he is," I tell her, but it's too late. My whining voice gives Ronnie what she needs. It's like an opening for a wedge or the toe of her worn-out old "Indian" moccasins. She pinches my arm and I say feebly, "Don't. That hurts."

"Oh, does it hurt?"

She pinches me again.

"I said don't—"

She laughs and forgets about it. She's a big strong girl. Her legs are thick. Her face is round and her teeth are a little crooked, so that she looks as if she is always smiling. In school she sits at the back and makes trouble, hiding her yellowish teeth behind her hand when she laughs. One day she said to our teacher—our teacher is Mrs. Gunderson—"There was a man out by the front door who did something bad. He opened up his pants and everything." Mrs. Gunderson was always nervous. She told Ronnie to come out into the hall with her, and everyone tried to listen, and in a minute she called me out too. Ronnie said to me, "Wasn't that Mr. Whalen out by the front door? Wasn't it, Sarah?" "When?" I said. "You know when, you were right there," Ronnie said. She was very excited and her face had a pleasant, high color. "You know what he did." "I didn't see anything," I said. Mrs. Gunderson wore ugly black shoes and her stockings were so thick you couldn't see her skin through them. Ronnie wore her moccasin loafers and no socks and her legs were pale and lumpy, covered with fine blond hairs. "Mr. Whalen stood *right out there* and Sarah saw him but she's too afraid to say. She's just a damn dirty coward," Ronnie said. Mr. Whalen was the fifth-grade teacher. Nobody liked him, but I had to say, "There wasn't any man out there." So Mrs. Gunderson let us go. Ronnie whispered, "You dirty goddam teacher's pet!"

That day at noon hour she rubbed my face in the dirt by the swings, and when I began crying she let me up. "Oh, don't cry, you big baby," she said. She rubbed my head playfully. She always did this to her little brother, her favorite brother. "I didn't mean to hurt you, but you had it coming. Right? You got to do what I say. If we're friends you got to obey me, don't you?"

"Yes."

Now she talks faster and faster. I know her mother isn't home and that's why she doesn't want to go in yet—her mother is always out somewhere. No one dares to ask Ronnie about her mother. In our house my mother is waiting somewhere, or maybe not waiting at all but upstairs doing something, listening to the radio. The supper dishes are put away. My father is working the night shift. When he comes home he will sleep downstairs on the sofa and when I come down for school in the morning there he'll be, stretched out and snoring. When my father and mother are together there are two currents of air, like invisible clouds, that move with them and will not overlap. These clouds keep them separate even when they are together; they seem to be calling across a deep ditch.

"Okay, let's walk down by the warehouse."

"Why do you want to go down there?"

"Just for the hell of it."

"I got a lot of homework to do—"

"Are you trying to make me mad?"

The first day I met Ronnie was the first day they had moved into their house, about two months ago. Ronnie strolled up and down the street, looking around, and she saw me right away sitting up on our veranda, reading. She was wearing soiled white shorts that came down to her knees and a baggy pullover shirt that was her brother's. Her hands were shoved in her pockets as she walked. She said to me on that first day: "Hey, what are you doing? Are you busy or can I come up?"

Now she is my best friend and I do everything she says, almost everything. She keeps talking. She likes to touch people when she talks, tap them on the arm or nudge them. "Come on. You don't have nothing to do inside," she says, whining, wheedling, and I give in. We stroll down the block. Nobody sits outside anymore at night, because it is too cold now. I am wearing a jacket and blue jeans, and Ronnie is wearing the same coat she wears to school: it used to be her mother's coat. It is made of shiny material, with black and fluorescent green splotches and tiny white umbrellas because it is a raincoat. As we walk down the street she points out houses we pass, telling me who the people are. "In there lives a fat old bastard, he goes to the bathroom in the sink," she says, her voice loud and helpful like a teacher's voice. "His name is Chanock or Chanick or some crappy name like that."

"How do you know about him?"

"I know lots of things, stupid. You think I'm lying?"

"No."

We walk on idly. We cross the street over toward Don's Drugstore. A few boys are standing around outside, leaning on their bicycles. When they see us coming they say, "Here comes that fat old cow Lay-zer," and they all laugh. Ronnie sticks out her tongue and says what she always says: a short loud nasty word that makes them laugh louder. When she does this I feel like laughing or running away, I feel as if something had opened in the ground before me—a great gaping crack in the sidewalk. The boys don't bother with me but keep on teasing Ronnie until we're past.

This street is darker. The houses are older, set back from the sidewalk with little plots of grass that are like mounds of graves in front of them. There are "boarders" in these houses. "Dirty old perverts," Ronnie calls them if we ever see them. One of the houses is vacant and kids come from all over to break windows and fool around, even though the police have chased them away. "In this next house is a man who does nasty things with a dog. I saw him out in the alley once," Ronnie says, snickering.

I have to take big steps to keep up with her. We're headed out toward the warehouse, which is boarded up, but everyone goes in there to play. I am afraid of the warehouse at night, because bums sometimes sleep there, but if I tell Ronnie, she'll snort with laughter and pinch me. Walking along fast, she says, "I sure don't want to miss that show on Saturday. You and me can go early," and then, whistling through her teeth, "One of these days that big dumpy warehouse is going to burn down. Wait and see."

Ronnie once lit a little fire in someone's garage, but it must have gone out because nothing happened. She wanted to get back at the people because she didn't like the girl who lived there, a girl ahead of us in school. At noon hour Ronnie and I sat alone to eat our lunches. If she was angry about something she could stare me down with her cold blue eyes that were like plastic caps; but other times she has to wipe at her eyes, saying, "This bastard who came home with her last night, he— He—" Or she talks bitterly of the other girls and how they all hate her because they're afraid of her. She has dirty hair, a dirty neck, and her dresses are just...just old baggy things passed down from someone else. At noon she often whispers to me about kids in the cafeteria, naming them one by one, telling me what she'll do to them when she gets around to it: certain acts with shears, razors, ice picks, butcher knives, acts described so vividly and with such passion that I feel sick.

Even when I'm not with Ronnie I feel a little sick, but not just in my stomach. It's all through my body. Ma always says, "Why do you run out when that big cow calls you? What do you see in her?" and I answer miserably, frightened, "I like her all right." But I have never thought about liking Ronnie. I have no choice.

She has never given me the privilege of liking or disliking her, and if she knew I was thinking such a thought she would yank my hair out of my head.

Light from the street lamp falls onto the front and part of the side of the old warehouse. There is a basement entrance I am afraid of because of spiders and rats. Junk is stored in the warehouse, things we don't recognize and never bother to wonder about, parts from machines, rails, strange wheels that are solid metal and must weigh hundreds of pounds. "Let's climb in the window," I say to Ronnie. "The cellar way's faster," she says. "Please, let's go in the window," I beg. I have begun to tremble and don't know why. It seems to me that something terrible is waiting inside the warehouse.

Ronnie looks at me contemptuously. She is grave and large in the moonlight, her mother's shiny coat wrinkled tight across her broad shoulders. The way her eyes are in shadow makes me think suddenly of a person falling backwards, falling down—onto something hard and sharp. That could happen. Inside the warehouse there are all kinds of strange, sharp things half hidden in the junk, rusty edges and broken glass from the windows that have been smashed. "Please, Ron, let's climb in the window," I beg.

She laughs and we go around to the window. There is an important board pulled out that makes a place for your foot. Then you jump up and put one knee on the window ledge, then you slide inside. The boards crisscrossing the window have been torn down a long time ago. Ronnie goes first and then helps me up. She says, "What if I let you go right now? You'd fall down and split your dumb head open!"

But she helps me crawl inside. Why do we like the warehouse so much? During the day I like to explore in it; we never get tired of all the junk and the places to hide and the view from the upstairs windows. Machines—nails and nuts and bolts underfoot—big crates torn apart and left behind, with mysterious black markings on their sides. The moonlight is strong enough for us to see things dimly. I am nervous, even though I know where everything is. I know this place. In my bed at night I can climb up into the warehouse and envision everything, remem-

ber it clearly, every part of it—it is our secret place, no grownups
come here—I can remember the big sliver of glass that is like a
quarter moon, a beautiful shape, lying at the foot of the steps,
and the thing we call the "tractor," and a great long dusty
machine that is beside the stairs. When you touch it you feel first
dust, then oil; beneath the dust there is a coating of oil. Three
prongs rise out of one end like dull knives.

Ronnie bumps into something and says, "Oh Christ!" She is
always bumping into things. One time when she hurt herself—
fooling around with some bricks—she got angry at me for no
reason and slapped me. She was always poking or pinching or
slapping.... It occurs to me that I should kill her. She is like a
big hulking dead body tied to me, the mouth fixed up for a grin
and always ready to laugh, and we are sinking together into the
water, and I will have to slash out at her to get free—I want to
get free. So I say, beginning to shiver, "Should we go upstairs?"

"What's upstairs but pigeon crap?"

"We can look out the window."

"You and your goddam windows—"

She laughs because I like to look out of the windows; she likes
to grub around instead in corners, prying things loose, looking
under things for "treasure." She told me once that she'd found a
silver dollar in the warehouse. But now I go ahead of her to the
stairs, a strange keen sensation in my bowels, and she grumbles
but comes along behind me. These old steps are filthy with dust
and some of the boards sag. I know exactly where to step.
Behind me, Ronnie is like a horse. The stairs are shaking. I wait
for her at the top and in that second I can see out a window and
over to the street light—but past that nothing, there is nothing to
see at night! The street light has a cloudy halo about it, something that isn't real but seems real to my eye. Ronnie bounds up
the stairs and I wait for her, sick with being so afraid, my heart
pounding in a jerky, bouncy way as if it wanted to burst—but
suddenly my heart is like another person inside me, nudging me
and saying, "Do it! Do it!" When Ronnie is about two steps from
the top I reach down and push her.

She falls at once. She falls over the side, her voice a screech
that is yanked out into the air above her, and then her body hits

the edge of that machine hard. She is screaming. I stand at the top, listening to her. Everything is dry and clear and pounding. She falls again, from the edge of the machine onto the floor, and now her scream is muffled as if someone had put his hand over her mouth.

I come down the stairs slowly. The air is hard and dry, like acid that burns my mouth, and I can't look anywhere except at Ronnie's twisting body. I wait for it to stop twisting. What if she doesn't die? At the base of the stairs I make a wide circle around her, brushing up against something and getting grease on my jeans.

There is this big girl half in the moonlight from the shattered window and half in the dark. Dust rolls in startled balls about her, aroused by her moans. She is bleeding. A dark stain explodes out from her and pushes the dust along before it, everything speeded up by her violent squirming, and I feel as if I must walk on tiptoe to keep from being seen by her.... Blood, all that blood!—it is like an animal crawling out from under her, like the shadows we drag around with us, broken loose now and given its own life, twisting out from under her and grabbing her, big as she is. She cries out, "Sarah! Ma!" but I don't hear her. I am at the window already. "Ma!" she says. "Ma!" It does not seem that I am moving or hearing anything, but still my feet take me to the window and those words come to me from a distance, "Ma, help me!" and I think to myself that I will have to get to where those words won't reach.

At home our house is warm and my head aches because I am sleepy. I fall asleep on my bed without undressing, and the next day we all hear about Ronnie. "Fooling around in that old dump, I knew it was going to happen to somebody," my mother says grimly. "You stay the hell out of that place from now on. You hear?"

I tell her yes, yes. I will never go there again.

There is a great shadowy space about me, filled with waiting: waiting to cry, to feel sorry. I myself am waiting, my body is waiting the way it waited that night at the top of the steps. But nothing happens. Do you know that twenty years have gone by? I am still dark but not so skinny, I have grown into a body that is approved of by people who glance at me in the street, I have grown out of the skinny little body that knocked that clumsy body down—and I have never felt sorry. Never felt any guilt. I live in what is called a "colonial" house, on a lane of colonial houses called Meadowbrook Lane. Ours is the sixth house on the right. Our mailboxes are down at the intersection with a larger road.... I am married and have children and I am still waiting to feel guilty, to feel some of Ronnie's pain, to feel the shock of that impact again as I felt it when she struck the prongs of the machine—but nothing happens. In my quiet, pleasant life, when my two boys are at school, I write stories I hope may be put on television someday—why not, why couldn't that miracle happen?

My stories are more real than my childhood; my childhood is just another story, but one written by someone else.

Small Avalanches

I KEPT BOTHERING MY MOTHER FOR A DIME, so she gave me a dime, and I went down our lane and took the shortcut to the highway, and down to the gas station. My uncle Winfield ran the gas station. There were two machines in the garage and I had to decide between them: the pop machine and the candy bar machine. No, there were three machines, but the other one sold cigarettes and I didn't care about that.

It took me a few minutes to make up my mind, then I bought a bottle of Pepsi-Cola.

Sometimes a man came to unlock the machines and take out the coins, and if I happened to be there it was interesting—the way the machines could be changed so fast if you just had the right key to open them. This man drove up in a white truck with a license plate from Kansas, a different color from our license plates, and he unlocked the machines and took out the money and loaded the machines back up again. When we were younger we liked to hang around and watch. There was something strange about it, how the look of the machines could be changed so fast, the fronts swinging open, the insides showing, just because a man with the right keys drove up.

I went out front where my uncle was working on a car. He was under the car, lying on a thing made out of wood that had rollers on it so that he could roll himself under the car; I could just see his feet. He had on big heavy shoes that were all greasy. I asked him if my cousin Georgia was home—they lived about two miles away and I could walk—and he said no, she was babysitting in Stratton for three days. I already knew this but I hoped the people might have changed their minds.

"Is that man coming today to take out the money?"

My uncle didn't here me. I was sucking at the Pepsi-Cola and running my tongue around the rim of the bottle. I always loved the taste of pop, the first two or three swallows. Then I would feel a little filled up and would have to drink it slowly. Sometimes I even poured the last of it out, but not so that anyone saw me.

"That man who takes care of the machines, is he coming today?"

"Who? No. Sometime next week."

My uncle pushed himself out from under the car. He was my mother's brother, a few years older than my mother. He had bushy brown hair and his face was dirty. "Did you call Georgia last night?"

"No. Ma wouldn't let me."

"Well, somebody was on the line because Betty wanted to check on her and the goddam line was busy all night. So Betty wanted to drive in, all the way to Stratton, drive six miles when probably nothing's wrong. You didn't call her, huh?"

"No."

"This morning Betty called her and gave her hell and she tried to say she hadn't been talking all night, that the telephone lines must have gotten mixed up. Georgia is a goddam little liar and if I catch her fooling around..."

He was walking away, into the garage. In the back pocket of his overalls was a dirty rag, stuffed there. He always yanked it out and wiped his face with it, not looking at it, even if it was dirty. I watched to see if he would do this and he did.

I almost laughed at this, and at how Georgia got away with murder. I had a good idea who was talking to her on the telephone.

The pop made my tongue tingle, a strong acid-sweet taste

that almost hurt. I sat down and looked out at the road. This
was in the middle of Colorado, on the road that goes through,
east and west. It was a hot day. I drank one, two, three, four
small swallows of pop. I pressed the bottle against my knees
because I was hot. I tried to balance the bottle on one knee and it
fell right over; I watched the pop trickle out onto the concrete.
I was too lazy to move my feet, so my bare toes got wet.

Somebody came along the road in a pickup truck, Mr. Watkins,
and he tapped on the horn to say hello to me and my uncle. He
was on his way to Stratton. I thought, *Damn it, I could have
hitched a ride with him.* I don't know why I bothered to think this
because I had to get home pretty soon, anyway, my mother
would kill me if I went to town without telling her. Georgia and
I did that once, back just after school let out in June, we went
down the road a ways and hitched a ride with some guy in a
beat-up car we thought looked familiar, but when he stopped to
let us in we didn't know him and it was too late. But nothing
happened, he was all right. We walked all the way back home
again because we were scared to hitch another ride. My parents
didn't find out, or Georgia's, but we didn't try it again.

I followed my uncle into the gas station. The building was
made of ordinary wood, painted white a few years ago but
starting to peel. It was just one room. The floor was concrete, all
stained with grease and cracked. I knew the whole place by
heart: the ceiling planks, the black rubber things hanging on the
wall, looped over big rusty spikes, the Cat's Paw ad that I liked,
and the other ads for beer and cigarettes on shiny pieces of
cardboard that stood up. To see those things you wouldn't
guess how they came flat, and you could unfold them and fix
them yourself, like fancy things for under the Christmas tree.
Inside the candy machine, behind the little windows, the candy
bars stood up on display: *Milky Way, O Henry, Junior Mints,
Mallow Cup, Three Musketeers, Hershey.* I liked them all. Sometimes *Milky Way* was my favorite, other times I only bought
Mallow Cup for weeks in a row, trying to get enough of the
cardboard letters to spell out *Mallow Cup.* One letter came with
each candy bar, and if you spelled out the whole name you
could send away for a prize. But the letter "w" was hard to find.

There were lots of "1's," it was rotten luck to open the wrapper up and see another "1" when you already had ten of them.

"Could I borrow a nickel?" I asked my uncle.

"I don't have any change."

Like hell, I thought. My uncle was always stingy.

I pressed the "return coin" knob but nothing came out. I pulled the knob out under *Mallow Cup* but nothing came out.

"Nancy, don't fool around with that thing, okay?"

"I don't have anything to do."

"Yeah, well, your mother can find something for you to do."

"She can do it herself."

"You want me to tell her that?"

"Go right ahead."

"Hey, did your father find out any more about the guy in Polo?"

"What guy?"

"Oh, I don't know, some guy who got into a fight and was arrested—he was in the Navy with your father, I don't remember his name."

"I don't know."

My uncle yawned. I followed him back outside and he stretched his arms and yawned. It was very hot. You could see the fake water puddles on the highway that were so mysterious and always moved back when you approached them. They could hypnotize you. Across from the garage was the mailbox on a post and then just scrub land, nothing to look at, pasture land and big rocky hills.

I thought about going to check to see if my uncle had any mail, but I knew there wouldn't be anything inside. We only got a booklet in the mail that morning, some information about how to make money selling jewelry door-to-door that I had written away for, but now I didn't care about. "Georgia has all the luck," I said. "I could use a few dollars myself."

"Yeah," my uncle said. He wasn't listening.

I looked at myself in the outside mirror of the car he was fixing. I don't know what kind of car it was, I never memorized the makes like the boys did. It was a dark maroon color with big heavy fenders and a bumper that had little bits of rust in it, like sparks. The running board had old, dried mud packed down inside its ruts. It was covered with black rubber, a mat. My hair was blown-looking. It was a big heavy mane of hair the color everybody called dishwater blond. My baby pictures showed that it used to be light blond.

"I wish I could get a job like Georgia," I said.

"Georgia's a year older than you."

"Oh hell...."

I was thirteen but I was Georgia's size, all over, and I was smarter. We looked alike. We both had long bushy flyaway hair that frizzed up when the air was wet, but kept curls in very well when we set it, like for church. I forgot about my hair and leaned closer to the mirror to look at my face. I made my lips shape a little circle, noticing how wrinkled they got. They could wrinkle up into a small space. I poked the tip of my tongue out.

There was the noise of something on gravel, and I looked around to see a man driving in. Out by the highway my uncle just had gravel, then around the gas pumps he had concrete. This man's car was white, a color you don't see much, and his license plate was from Kansas.

He told my uncle to fill up the gas tank and he got out of the car, stretching his arms.

He looked at me and smiled. "Hi," he said.

"Hi."

He said something to my uncle about how hot it was, and my uncle said it wasn't too bad. Because that's the way he is— always contradicting you. My mother hates him for this. But then he said, "You read about the dry spell coming up?—right into September?" My uncle meant the ranch bureau thing but the man didn't know what he was talking about. He meant the *Bureau News & Forecast.* This made me mad, that my uncle was so stupid, thinking that a man from out of state and probably from a city would know about that, or give a damn. It made me mad. I saw my pop bottle where it fell and I decided to go home, not to bother putting it in the case where you were supposed to.

I walked along on the edge of the road, on the pavement, because there were stones and prickles and weeds with bugs in them off the side that I didn't like to walk in barefoot. I felt hot and mad about something. A yawn started in me, and I felt it coming up like a little bubble of gas from the pop. There was my cousin Georgia in town, and all she had to do was watch a little girl who wore thick glasses and was sort of strange, but very nice and quiet and no trouble, and she'd get two dollars. I thought angrily that if anybody came along I'd put out my thumb and hitch a ride to Stratton, and the hell with my mother.

Then I did hear a car coming but I just got over to the side and waited for him to pass. I felt stubborn and wouldn't look around to see who it was, but then the car didn't pass and I looked over my shoulder—it was the man in the white car, who had stopped for gas. He was driving very slow. I got farther off the road and waited for him to pass. But he leaned over to this side and said out the open window, "You want a ride home? Get in."

"No, that's okay," I said.

"Come on, I'll drive you home. No trouble."

"No, it's okay. I'm almost home," I said.

I was embarrassed and didn't want to look at him. People didn't do this, a grown-up man in a car wouldn't bother to do this. Either you hitched for a ride or you didn't, and if you didn't, people would never slow down to ask you. This guy is crazy, I thought. I felt very strange. I tried to look over into the field but there wasn't anything to look at, not even any cattle, just land and scrubby trees and a barbed-wire fence half falling down.

"Your feet will get all sore, walking like that," the man said.

"I'm okay."

"Hey, watch out for the snake!"

There wasn't any snake and I made a noise like a laugh to show that I knew it was a joke but didn't think it was very funny.

"Aren't there rattlesnakes around here? Rattlers?"

"Oh I don't know," I said.

He was still driving right alongside me, very slow. You are not used to seeing a car slowed down like that, it seems very strange. I tried not to look at the man. But there was nothing else to look at, just the country and the road and the mountains in the distance and some clouds.

"That man at the gas station was mad, he picked up the bottle you left."

I tried to keep my lips pursed shut, but they were dry and came open again. I wondered if my teeth were too big in front.

"How come you walked away so fast? That wasn't friendly," the man said. "You forgot your pop bottle and the man back there said somebody could drive over it and get a flat tire, he was a little mad."

"He's my uncle," I said.

"What?"

He couldn't hear or was pretending he couldn't hear, so I had to turn toward him. He was all-right-looking, he was smiling. "He's my uncle," I said.

"Oh, is he? You don't look anything like *him*. Is your home nearby?"

"Up ahead." I was embarrassed and started to laugh, I don't know why.

"I don't see any house there."

"You can't see it from here," I said, laughing.

"What's so funny? My face? You know, when you smile you're a very pretty girl. You should smile all the time.... " He was paying so much attention to me it made me laugh. "Yes, that's a fact. Why are you blushing?"

I blushed fast, like my mother; we both hated to blush and hated people to tease us. But I couldn't get mad.

"I'm worried about your feet and the rattlers around here. Aren't there rattlers around here?"

"Oh I don't know."

"Where I come from there are streets and sidewalks and no snakes, of course, but it isn't interesting. It isn't dangerous. I think I'd like to live here, even with the snakes—this is very beautiful, hard country, isn't it? Do you like the mountains way over there? Or don't you notice them?"

I didn't pay any attention to where he was pointing, I looked at him and saw that he was smiling. He was my father's age but he wasn't stern like my father, who had a line between his eyebrows like a knife-cut, from frowning. This man was wearing a shirt, a regular white shirt, out in the country. His hair was dampened and combed back from his forehead; it was damp right now, as if he had just combed it.

"Yes, I'd like to take a walk out out here and get some exercise," he said. His voice sounded very cheerful. "Snakes or no snakes! You turned me down for a free ride so maybe I'll join you in a walk."

That really made me laugh: *join you in a walk.*

"Hey, what's so funny?" he said, laughing himself.

People didn't talk like that, but I didn't say anything. He parked the car on the shoulder of the road and got out and I heard him drop the car keys in his pocket. He was scratching at his jaw. "Well, excellent! This is excellent, healthy, divine country air! Do you like living out here?"

I shook my head, no.

"You wouldn't want to give all this up for a city, would you?"

"Sure. Any day."

I was walking fast to keep ahead of him, I couldn't help but giggle, I was so embarrassed—this man in a white shirt was really walking out on the highway, he was really going to leave his car parked like that! You never saw a car parked on the road around here, unless it was by the creek, fishermen's cars, or unless it was a wreck. All this made my face get hotter.

He walked fast to catch up with me. I could hear coins and things jingling in his pockets.

"You never told me your name," he said. "That isn't friendly."

"It's Nancy."

"Nancy what?"

"Oh I don't know," I laughed.

"Nancy I-Don't-Know?" he said.

I didn't get this. He was smiling hard. He was shorter than my father and now that he was out in the bright sun I could see he was older. His face wasn't tanned, and his mouth kept going into a soft smile. Men like my father and my uncles and other men never bothered to smile like that at me, they never bothered to look at me at all. Some men did, once in a while, in

Stratton, strangers waiting for Greyhound buses to Denver or Kansas City, but they weren't friendly like this, they didn't keep on smiling for so long.

When I came to the path I said, "Well, good-by, I'm going to cut over this way. This is a shortcut."

"A shortcut where?"

"Oh I don't know," I said, embarrassed.

"To your house, Nancy?"

"Yeah. No, it's to our lane, our lane is half a mile long."

"Is it? That's very long. . . ."

He came closer. "Well, good-by," I said.

"That's a long lane, isn't it?—it must get blocked up with snow in the winter, doesn't it? You people get a lot of snow out here—"

"Yeah."

"So your house must be way back there . . . ?" he said, pointing. He was smiling. When he stood straight like this, looking over my head, he was more like the other men. But then he looked down at me and smiled again, so friendly. I waved good-by and jumped over the ditch and climbed the fence, clumsy as hell just when somebody was watching me, wouldn't you know it. Some barbed wire caught at my shorts and the man said, "Let me get that loose—" but I jerked away and jumped down again. I waved good-by again and started up the path. But the man said something and when I looked back he was climbing over the fence himself. I was so surprised that I just stood there.

"I like shortcuts and secret paths," he said. "I'll walk a little way with you."

"What do you—" I started to say. I stopped smiling because something was wrong. I looked around and there was just the path behind me that the kids always took, and some boulders and old dried-up manure from cattle, and some scrubby bushes. At the top of the hill was the big tree that had been struck by lightning so many times. I was looking at all this and couldn't figure out why I was looking at it.

"You're a brave little girl to go around barefoot," the man said, right next to me. "Or are your feet tough on the bottom?"

I didn't know what he was talking about because I was worried; then I heard his question and said vaguely, "I'm all right," and started to walk faster. I felt a tingling all through me like the tingling from the Pepsi-Cola in my mouth.

"Do you always walk so fast?" the man laughed.

"Oh I don't know."

"Is that all you can say? Nancy I-Don't-Know! That's a funny name—is it foreign?"

This made me start to laugh again. I was walking fast, then I began to run a few steps. Right away I was out of breath. That was strange—I was out of breath right away.

"Hey, Nancy, where are you going?" the man cried.

But I kept running, not fast. I ran a few steps and looked back and there he was, smiling and panting, and I happened to see his foot come down on a loose rock. I knew what would happen—the rock rolled off sideways and he almost fell, and I laughed. He glanced up at me with a surprised grin. "This path is a booby trap, huh? Nancy has all sorts of little traps and tricks for me, huh?"

I didn't know what he was talking about. I ran up the side of the hill, careful not to step on the manure or anything sharp, and I was still out of breath but my legs felt good. They felt as if they wanted to run a long distance. "You're going off the path," he said, pretending to be mad. "Hey. That's against the rules. Is that another trick?"

I giggled but couldn't think of any answer.

"Did you make this path up by yourself?" the man asked. But he was breathing hard from the hill. He stared at me, climbing up, with his hands pushing on his knees as if to help him climb. "Little Nancy, you're like a wild colt or a deer, you're so graceful—is this your own private secret path? Or do other people use it?"

"Oh, my brother and some other kids, when they're around," I said vaguely. I was walking backward up the hill now, so that I could look down at him. The top of his hair was thin, you could see the scalp. The very top of his forehead seemed to have two bumps, not big ones, but as if the bone went out a little, and this part was a bright pink, sunburned, but the rest of his face and his scalp were white.

He stepped on another loose rock, and the rock and some stones and mud came loose. He fell hard onto his knee. "Jesus!" he said. The way he stayed down like that looked funny. I had to press my hand over my mouth. When he looked up at me his smile was different. He got up, pushing himself up with his hands, grunting, and then he wiped his hands on his trousers. The dust showed on them. He looked funny.

"Is my face amusing? Is it a good joke?"

I didn't mean to laugh, but now I couldn't stop. I pressed my hand over my mouth hard.

He stared at me. "What do you see in my face, Nancy? What do you see—anything? Do you see my soul, do you see *me*, is that what you're laughing at?" He took a fast step toward me, but I jumped back. It was like a game. "Come on, Nancy, slow down, just slow down," he said. "Come on, Nancy...."

I didn't know what he was talking about, I just had to laugh at his face. It was so tense and strange; it was so *important*.

I noticed a big rock higher up, and I went around behind it and pushed it loose—it rolled right down toward him and he had to scramble to get out of the way. "Hey! Jesus!" he yelled. The rock came loose with some other things and a mud chunk got him in the leg.

I laughed so hard my stomach started to ache.

He laughed too, but a little different from before.

"This is a little trial for me, isn't it?" he said. "A little preliminary contest. Is that how the game goes? Is that your game, Nancy?"

I ran higher up the hill, off to the side where it was steeper. Little rocks and things came loose and rolled back down. My breath was coming so fast it made me wonder if something was wrong. Down behind me the man was following, stooped over, looking at me, and his hand was pressed against the front of his shirt. I could see his hand moving up and down because he was breathing so hard. I could even see his tongue moving around the edge of his dried-out lips.... I started to get afraid, and then the tingling came back into me, beginning in my tongue and going out through my whole body, and I couldn't help giggling.

He said something that sounded like "—won't be laughing—" but I couldn't hear the rest of it. My hair was all wet in back where it would be a job for me to unsnarl it with the hairbrush. The man came closer, stumbling, and just for a joke I kicked out at him, to scare him—and he jerked backward and tried to grab onto a branch of a bush, but it slipped through his fingers and he lost his balance and fell. He grunted. He fell so hard that he just lay there for a minute. I wanted to say I was sorry, or ask him if he was all right, but I just stood there grinning.

He got up again; the fleshy part of his hand was bleeding. But he didn't seem to notice it and I turned and ran up the rest of the hill, going almost straight up the last part, my legs were so strong and felt so good. Right at the top I paused, just balanced there, and a gust of wind would have pushed me over—but I was all right. I laughed aloud, my legs felt so springy and strong.

I looked down over the side where he was crawling, down on his hands and knees again. "You better go back to Kansas! Back home to Kansas!" I laughed. He stared up at me and I waited for him to smile again but he didn't. His face was very pale. He was staring at me but he seemed to be seeing something else, his eyes were very serious and strange. I could see his belt creasing his stomach, the bulge of his white shirt. He pressed his hand against his chest again. "Better go home, go home, get in your damn old car and go home," I sang, making a song of it. He looked so serious, staring up at me. I pretended to kick at him again and he flinched, his eyes going small.

"Don't leave me—" he whimpered.

"Oh go on," I said.

"Don't leave—I'm sick—I think I—"

His face seemed to shrivel. He was drawing in his breath very slowly, carefully, as if checking to see how much it hurt, and I waited for this to turn into another joke. Then I got tired of waiting and just rested back on my heels. My smile got smaller and smaller, like his.

"Good-by, I'm going," I said, waving. I turned and he said something—it was like a cry—but I didn't want to bother going back. The tingling in me was almost noisy.

I walked over to the other side, and slid back down to the path and went along the path to our lane. I was very hot. I knew my face was flushed and red. "Damn old nut," I said. But I had to laugh at the way he had looked, the way he kept scrambling up the hill and was just crouched there at the end, on his hands and knees. He looked so funny, bent over and clutching at his chest, pretending to have a heart attack or maybe having one, a little one, for all I knew. This will teach you a lesson, I thought.

By the time I got home my face had dried off a little, but my hair was like a haystack. I stopped by the old car parked in the lane, just a junker on blocks, and looked in the outside rearview mirror—the mirror was all twisted around because people looked in it all the time. I tried to fix my hair by rubbing my hands down hard against it, but no luck. "Oh damn," I said aloud, and went up the steps to the back, and remembered not to let the screen door slam so my mother wouldn't holler at me.

She was in the kitchen ironing, just sprinkling some clothes on the ironing board. She used a pop bottle painted blue and fitted out with a sprinkler top made of rubber, that I fixed for her at grade school a long time ago for a Christmas present; she shook the bottle over the clothes and stared at me. "Where have you been? I told you to come right back."

"I did come right back."

"You're all dirty, you look like hell. What happened to you?"

"Oh I don't know," I said. "Nothing."

She threw something at me—it was my brother's shirt—and I caught it and pressed it against my hot face.

"You get busy and finish these," my mother said. "It must be ninety-five in here and I'm fed up. And you do a good job, I'm really fed up. Are you listening, Nancy? Where the hell is your mind?"

I liked the way the damp shirt felt on my face. "Oh I don't know," I said.

The Widows

WHY WAS SHE DRAWN TO THE TELEPHONE?—it was not ringing. She found herself walking out of her way, through the narrow hall, where the telephone was kept on a small pedestal table beneath the stairs. Even during the day it was dark in this part of the house; there were not many windows and she didn't want to waste money on electricity. She knew the passageway so well that she moved through it with the stiff, alert confidence of the blind. Why bother with a telephone? She meant to have it disconnected.

Sometimes it did ring. And she listened to it, bitterly. She might be in the kitchen, at the table: a small cleared-off space at one corner of the table, *her* space. She ate there, absentmindedly, quickly, while she read. If the telephone rang, she listened to it with a kind of respectful distaste: a call could be only a disappointment or an insult. Or a wrong number. It was strange, it might even have been exhilarating—she would have to think about the possibilities—the fact that no one in the world, no one at all, could have anything valuable to tell her.

Yet she found herself wandering along the passageway, distracted and vaguely expectant. As if she were about to receive an important call. When the telephone call had come from the hospital, some months before, of course she had not expected it—she might have been expecting a call from someone else, in fact, a house painter with his estimate of what it would cost them to have this shabby little house repainted—so she had answered it easily enough, neither eager nor terrified. Now she drifted near the phone and stood there, in the dark. If it rang, she had the option of answering or not answering: that was freedom. Her mother, her in-laws, anyone who cared to communicate with her could write to her—if they liked—if they imagined that anything they might say would mean much to her. She might even reply eventually.

One evening in late August she went to the telephone, and as she approached it, it began to ring. She smiled. She smiled knowingly. For a few moments she resisted; then she picked up the receiver. She said nothing. She hoped it might be a wrong number so that she could replace the receiver gently, in the middle of a stranger's query. But it was someone who called her by name, a woman, a woman people had wanted her to meet— another young widow—and before Beatrice could cut her off, the woman was suggesting that they meet for lunch sometime. Was she free? Would she be interested?

"Why are you telephoning me?" Beatrice stammered. "Why— What is it— Why are you harassing me?"

The woman paused. Then she began again, in a rather warm, aggressive voice, apologizing for bothering Beatrice—explaining that friends of friends had suggested she call—Manitock was such a small city, as Beatrice knew, of course people talked about one another constantly. And they were saying that Beatrice was not looking well; that she had resigned her teaching job; someone had even said she was—

Beatrice interrupted. She said calmly: "Who are these people? I don't know these people. I don't know you. You're a stranger— why are you telephoning me? Haven't you anyone else to telephone tonight? There's no connection between us. This is insulting. It's degrading. If people worry about me, it isn't me they are worrying about—is it?—I'm onto their games! If they want to worry about me, let them discover what it is in themselves they are afraid of. Where is the fear? It isn't in me; it's in all of you. The thought of death isn't in me, it's never in me; it's in the rest of you. If—please don't interrupt, Mrs. Greaney—if you have nothing else to do but gossip about me and clack your teeth about me, if Manitock is really so impoverished, that's unfortunate, but it's hardly my fault, is it? Good night."

She dropped the receiver into place. She began to sob, pounding at her thighs and belly with her fists, not knowing what she did. The sobs were dry, hoarse; like laughter. She took the receiver off the hook so that the woman could not call her back. She whispered: *Let me alone! Let him die! ... Let me die!*

A few days later someone approached her, someone's wife, evidently a woman Beatrice had known in her former life—she had been *Mrs. Kern* in that life—and began reproving her, gently scolding her, for what she had said to Moira Greaney. The woman was middle-aged, maternal. Perhaps she had a right to speak to Beatrice and even to suggest that a misdeed, a crime of some kind, had been committed. "Why, what did I say?" Beatrice asked. "Did I say something? What did I say? I don't remember. Were you listening in on an extension?—are you someone I'm supposed to know?"

It was the drug that asked these questions, the aftermath of a drug—barbiturates, because of her insomnia—and not Beatrice herself. Beatrice was angry. The drug altered her voice, made it sound confused and innocent. She might have been lost in a foreign city instead of standing helpless in the Village Pharmacy, staring at a woman whose name she could not recall. Fortunately, the woman did not touch her. That might have meant she was really Beatrice's mother, a few pounds heavier, disguised crudely as a blond. Beatrice herself was angry, outraged, but the sounds she made were really quite childlike. So many short, abrupt, baffled questions—surely she was innocent of any crime, and must be forgiven.

Innocent. Always so innocent. She no longer knew whether her extraordinary innocence was genuine, as much a part of her as her small, frail body, or whether it was a form of savage irony. Had she been less intelligent, her open-eyed bewilderment, her ceaseless questioning, might have been genuine. But she was too intelligent. Some part of her had developed too shrewdly, like a head that has grown out of the drowsy earth and can now gaze down upon it—a head on a long stalk—an eerie drunken-swaying stalk of a neck! But Wallace had not judged her so harshly. He had forbidden her to judge herself in those censorious terms. Now he was dead; now the dates of his death and of his funeral were retreating, day by day, pages back on the calendar, so she had the freedom to say whatever she liked about herself. Other people talked about her, other people stated their opinions. Whispering. Worrying. Gleefully "worrying." She had the freedom to judge herself however she liked, as cruelly as she wished; she wanted no pity, not even from herself. But she could not quite imagine herself. *Beatrice Kern.* Before her marriage she had been *Beatrice Egleston,* but she was finished with that. That was done.... She could not analyze herself thoroughly enough, could not be certain that she understood the nature of the being she evidently inhabited. A face, a body. Yes. Fine. As usual. If the insides are secrets no one especially cares to know, the outside can at least be contemplated: that was the basis of life. But—what are the visions a mirror offers? The mirror is too friendly, demoniacally friendly, always distorting reality in order to give us back our own expectations. Always lying, always slanting, muffling....

So Beatrice did not know if she was that young woman whom everyone pitied, and who seemed pitiful indeed. A young wife who had lost her husband. *Lost her husband.* Other people lost gloves, books, tickets; or they lost at a game of cards. But Beatrice had lost her husband, which was tragic or freakish, depending. Across town was the *other widow,* who had also "lost" her husband, months before Wallace's death. A coincidence, in such a small town...among so small a circle of acquaintances. Two young widows, in their late twenties. Inevitable, hideous, that they should rush together, should embrace each other, should weep together while the rest of the community watched with solemn approval....

Beatrice wandered around the house, a rented single-bedroom frame house not far from the University, murmuring to herself—not arguing, not angry—only befuddled. Sometimes she wept. Sometimes no tears came, only that dry wracking sob, a kind of chuckle. She taunted herself with the thought that perhaps she was weeping, mourning, because of the role she had to play—people were spying on her, demanding tears. She was a widow, childless. She was deathly, like all widows; she must acknowledge it.

She wondered when it would be concluded—when her husband would really die.

"Do you ever imagine—he might by trying to contact you?"

"No."

"Do you ever—do you— Would you want it, would you want him to communicate with you, if it were possible?"

"You're insane."

"*But would you want it?*"

"Want what? What are you saying?"

"—want *it*—"

"What is *it*? What kind of a joke is this? You're teasing me, you're trying to drive me crazy—you're crazy yourself and want me to become like you—"

"No. You can't become like me. You have to be yourself—you can only become yourself."

She was frightened of the other widow. Though she went out rarely—no more than three or four times in an entire week—she seemed to meet Moira Greaney all the time. But they were not friends, not even acquaintances. They knew each other only by sight. Manitock was not really so small, but it seemed small: once a mill town, a factory town built upon the banks of a river in upstate New Hampshire, now a university town in which everyone connected with the University knew everyone else. And most of them lived in town, in the radius of a few miles, because the mountains were so steep, the foothills so unfriendly, the only houses or farms available outside Manitock were very poor. Some were hardly more than shanties. The University itself was losing money. Beatrice had resigned her part-time position, teaching art history in night school, and no one had tried to argue her into keeping it. Possibly she would have been dismissed anyway—except for the embarrassing fact that she was the wife of a man who had died suddenly, in an automobile accident. The other widow was not so poor as Beatrice ... not even childless, exactly, because her husband had a son somewhere, from his first marriage. *Do you wish you had had a baby? No. Yes. Were you waiting . . . ? Yes, we were waiting. Do you regret it now? . . .* She regretted nothing. She had very few emotions, no more than two or three. They narrowed, they expanded. They narrowed again. She took a book out of the town library, an income-tax guide, and saw that Moira Greaney had taken it out before her—the name printed in small block letters, in green ink.

She hiked out to the cemetery, north of town. It had an older section, for the natives; the newer section looked cheap, with tombstones and markers of polished stone, slick and neat. The old gravestones were battered, gray, some of the very old ones even encrusted with bird droppings—entirely natural, proper. What could be said about the newer graves, the newer deaths?— the younger people? A shame they died, that was about all. Beatrice considered the marker on her husband's grave adequate. It was adequate. She had already forgotten its price—it had been the least expensive of those markers currently available—and she could never remember what it was made of, perhaps granite. . . . The Greaney grave was nearby, slightly uphill from the Kern grave. Better drainage. A better location. The stone was fairly large, must have been costly, but its front was black-gleaming and highly polished—so that it looked too prosperous for this place. It looked hearty, smug. There were potted geraniums around it and Beatrice detested geraniums and she taunted herself with the possibility of kicking them over . . . and hearing a cry . . . turning to see Mrs. Greaney running at her, running up the incline to her. *Why, you're a murderer!—only pretending to be in mourning!*

More sanely, she considered the ugly possibility of meeting the woman out here, in the cemetery. There was only one entrance, one way out. It could happen. . . . Once, on a Sunday, she lingered in the vicinity of her husband's and Mr. Greaney's graves, as if waiting. But no one came along.

That was in September. By November, she had given in.

* * *

"I am the catastrophe, the ugly disaster," Beatrice laughed. "My husband died in an accident. An eighteen-year-old boy ran into him broadside, he hit the driver's side of our car—going over seventy miles an hour, they said—running a four-way stop. The boy died and so did my husband. Instantly, they said. How did they know? With what authority do people say such things?... *Instantly. So he didn't suffer. It isn't much of a consolation, Mrs. Kern, but*... When people see me now, they think of disaster. The impact of one car on another, seventy miles an hour, the noise, the smashed metal, the way bodies must be ruined, so strangely, being only flesh.... They dread seeing me because what happened to my husband could happen to them, and it's an insult. They can't control it... it's a betrayal of their civilized lives... of sanity itself. My face reminds them of the closed casket. Their imaginations run wild, they're sickened, excited, they rush forward to pity me, but they wish I had died in the accident along with him. This place is too small to absorb me.... I remind them of something demonic, that goes against their God. Because they do have versions of God, their own kind of God, having to do with their brains, their reason. Their careers. All that is godly to them, because they have to worship something and so they worship themselves. But it can be changed in a few seconds. I don't blame them for hating me."

"They don't hate you. They're just a little frightened of you," Moira said. She was two years older than Beatrice, twenty–nine, but she looked younger—that wide, frank, freckled face, those blue eyes that protruded slightly, charmingly, as if everything fascinated her. She stared. She stared at Beatrice. Her stare came first, then her slow, friendly smile. Was she pleased? Always. Curious? Always. "Nobody hates you, Beatrice," she said "...It's what I represent they really fear. It isn't so bad now, because he's been dead quite a while, but while he was dying, the last six weeks especially, I walked around like a criminal, I pitied people who happened to see me, because they were genuinely frightened of me.... That long, slow, protracted death... eighteen months of it... he wasn't as young as your husband, but he was too young to die, only forty-four, and whenever anyone saw me I knew he wanted to duck away, to hide. And the strained, absurd conversations!—their eyes grabbing at me, hoping I wouldn't say anything obscene. They dreaded the very word *cancer.* They dreaded me.... But now that he's dead, people can see I'm still alive. I'm not a leper, I'm not contaminated with his disease. After all, death isn't contagious."

"Isn't it?" Beatrice said.

She was getting drunk. Her voice was wild, unpredictable.... She had noticed a mirror in the foyer, by a coat rack; she went to observe herself in this new role. But what was there to say?— whether "Beatrice" was an attractive woman or whether she was obscene, ugly, contaminated by death, she could not judge. Her skin was pale. But it was always pale, especially when she was tired. Her hair was dark, almost black. She had not bothered to remove the several silvery hairs she had discovered one morning, but no one noticed anyway. A delicate woman, hardly more than a girl. Her eyes were slanted or gave the appearance of being so, especially when she was intense or suspicious. Very dark eyes. But their expression was usually dreamy, inward, contemplative, as if she were engrossed with images inside her head.

Moira's face hovered near hers in the mirror. But Moira was careful to stand some distance from Beatrice, not touching her. She was a tall woman—at least five feet nine—with broad shoulders, a wide, clear forehead, and ash-blond hair that stuck out around her head in clumps of curls. Sometimes her hair was frizzy, messy. At other times it was striking; Beatrice had seen her on the street occasionally, and had noticed how other people glanced at her, especially men. Her manner was brisk, hearty, almost oppressively healthy. "Nobody hates us, Beatrice. You shouldn't allow yourself to think that," she said. There was a subtle edge to her voice, as if the two of them had been quarreling off and on all their lives.

Beatrice had telephoned the Greaney woman one night in November.

Unable to sleep, she had wandered downstairs, barefoot, thinking that she would sit in the kitchen for the rest of the night. She would be quite safe there. Walls painted a very light yellow, a refrigerator that hummed and rattled, linoleum tile of orange and brown. Warm colors. At her usual place, her feet primly up on the chair, arms around her knees. Like a child. She could sit there until dawn. It was well known that consciousness alters with daylight. She had faith in that.... From a distance she heard the dry, heaving sobs. She heard her own voice, lifting in a question. *But when will it not be mad, so that I can return to it?* She closed her eyes. Listened. It was her own voice, cheerful and witty. Evidently time had passed. There was some confusion. When the sleeping pill did not work, confusion followed: like a storm at every window, while you are trying heroically to close one window. Resist? Give in?... She heard her own voice and the voices of others. She realized they were at a party. Of course. One of the many parties she had attended. She and her husband had had many friends, especially when they were in graduate school in Boston. Sitting in one another's apartments, late into the night. Talking. Arguing. Rarely getting drunk, because the value of their being together lay in their conversations.

Some of them, men and women both, had been daring, iconoclastic. Some had taken other roles: Beatrice herself had always sounded fairly conservative. All this was conversation. Personalities expressed in talk, in words. There was a kind of psychological chastity to it, harmless. Of course none of them had known this at the time. How energetically they had discussed all things, even the topics that dismayed their parents— even the forbidden things, the taboos. Sexual behavior. Sexual promiscuity. Deviance. The possibility of divorce. Of death. Of madness. Of suicide. Quite calmly, fearlessly, they had assumed the world was mad anyway. What did it matter?—governments, social programs, philosophical principles. They knew everything. They knew everything in essence, if not in detail. And they were totally unmoved, undismayed, as if anything that might be expressed in words was already rendered quaint, its power to wound thwarted. It was even the fashion, for a while, not to know very much, to avoid reading newspapers. A young man, a close friend of Wallace's, had encouraged Beatrice to do graduate work involving a Maine artist of the nineteenth century and to turn her back on the "madness" of the contemporary world. Beatrice had replied wittily that the world has always been mad: one crisis after another, wars and the preludes to war, treaties, peace pacts, agreements, and then war again. How could he expect her, or anyone, to hide until the world returned to normal? It would never return to what he considered normal. In fact it was normal at the present time; it was always normal. And when would it not be mad, so that she could safely return to it?

Anyway, she had said, she had no interest in dead men.

She remembered this conversation. Horrible, that she should both recall it from the outside, as if she had been a third person observing the scene, and animate it, give life to her own words. She was not ashamed of herself, she was terrified. There was nothing for her to claim; nowhere to retreat to. She realized that she might possibly not survive. She had no interest in the dead and yet she had nothing else, no one else, except a dead man whose features were already unclear, his voice dubious and vague, his love for her in all probability based upon a misunderstanding of her nature, which she had deliberately cultivated.

"I want...I don't want...I...I'm not going to... "

It was very late, nearly three o'clock in the morning, when she telephoned Moira Greaney.

Moira's husband had disappeared long before his death. Whoever remained had put up a struggle of some kind, assisted by the hospital staff, and he was now buried in the Manitock cemetery; she should sell the house on Fort Street, people advised, and return to her own life. But he was buried nearby. How could she leave? She had been very happy with him and was very happy now. No, she would not betray him. She paused before the windows of the local tourist agencies, staring at brightly colored advertisements for travel. *Fly Away to India. Africa the Golden Continent.* No, she would not betray him, not again.

"Really. *Really.* Is that true."

"Is that *really true.*"

She stared at people, absorbed their remarks, marveling with a vague note of protest at the most ordinary of disclosures. She could not help herself. An intensity of interest in other people, an exaggerated respect for whatever they said or did, had characterized her almost since childhood. Because she was big-boned, her shoulders quite wide for a woman, people expected her to be ungainly, but in fact she was graceful; she had the effortless grace of the natural athlete. Her feet were rather large. Her hands were large also, but she filed her nails carefully and even polished them, and wore a number of rings that she changed from day to day, except for her wedding ring. *How pretty Moira is!* people sometimes said, as if surprised. Seeing her at close range, they were often surprised. *How pretty your wife is!* people had told her husband, meaning to flatter him.

He liked her with her hair tied up behind. Or in blouses with frilly, fussy collars and cuffs. Or in those outfits she had pieced together, years before, from secondhand shops: crushed-velvet skirts, furred vests, shoes with odd heels and straps, felt hats shaped like buckets or shovels. She was taller than her husband, a golden-glowing girl with a daughterly manner, both robust and shy. It had been years since she had played on girls' hockey and basketball teams, yet her husband often alluded to her skill at sports; he complimented her, embarrassed her, as if to explain to her—however obliquely—why she was not maternal and should not take that risk. She told Beatrice about the humiliating visits of the son, her husband's boy, up from New York City for weekends; she had told no one else, had never dared complain, because of course people would have told Edgar. Everyone in Manitock was his friend. Everyone was loyal to him. He was respected, admired, possibly because he looked so much older than he was—in his early forties he had lost most of his hair except for a few blond-white strands that floated about his head like a halo or an aura, and his face was furrowed, the indentations around his mouth both severe and kindly. He looked like a man who has suffered. He looked like a man who fully expects to suffer. His son was totally unlike him, but he seemed to love the boy very much, whenever he remembered him. So Moira had tried to love the boy too.

"I even practiced basketball shots with him," Moira told

Beatrice. Her tone was lightly sardonic. "There was a playground a few blocks away with a basketball hoop, so we trudged over there and practiced shots while my husband worked.... We didn't talk at all. He had nothing to say to me. He wasn't friendly to anyone; he wasn't even boyish. I couldn't remember him now if I met him on the street. He wouldn't know me; he rarely looked at me." The wife, the other Mrs. Greaney, had fattened the boy up, so that at the age of eleven he was thirty pounds overweight, a sullen child who admired athletes and hunters. He had no interest in his father's work—never looked through the encyclopedias and world books and almanacs his father owned. He confided in Moira only once, begging her to talk his father into buying him an air rifle. He wanted to hunt in the field behind his father's house, a hilly area that was partly wooded, where starlings and grackles and cardinals and blue jays and occasionally even pheasants might be found. He carried around with him, folded many times, full-color advertisements from *Boy's Life* that he showed Moira, displays of handsome air rifles. He could not have a gun in the city, could not hunt or kill in the city. His eyes glistened, with pain or desire, as he spoke to Moira. She had told him it was hopeless. If she even brought up the subject to his father, which she would not, his father would be angry with them both; it was hopeless. So he had turned away from her and had not seemed to like her much after that.

"I didn't hate him," Moira said. "I have never hated anyone.... I felt him hating me, but I didn't hate him. Instead I forgot him. After the funeral, I forgot him. I'm forgetting everything. Sometimes I think...I halfway think that my husband didn't have any children, that the child he had was *me*. I was his child. I wasn't his daughter, necessarily, but his child. He was twelve years older than I was; he ended his marriage for me, in order to marry me, because I loved him so much. He loved me too. But he realized how much I loved him, how I needed him; so he ended his marriage with that other woman. He..."

"He loved you very much," Beatrice interrupted. "Obviously

he loved you very much. My husband would never have married me, he would never even have noticed me, if he had already been married...."

"No, he did it out of kindness, out of charity," Moira said. "I loved him so much it made him feel guilty. I was only twenty-two.... He gave up living in the city, all his friends there and his position at the University, to move up here to Manitock, where everyone admired him but didn't know him...and he was contemptuous of nearly everyone here, because of course he couldn't talk to them. But he never accused me, he never blamed me. He was a wonderful man."

Beatrice tried to remember Edgar Greaney: she could recall only one rather large gathering, Greaney in a wing chair by a fireplace, surrounded by younger men, and the wife, Moira, sitting with other wives, a woman with ash-blond hair who might have been pretty, even beautiful, had she not smiled so persistently. Greaney was a small man with a dapper, brusque manner; his skin was pitted, perhaps from acne or smallpox, but this did not detract from his good looks. In a way he was ugly, in another way quite charming. Beatrice had disliked him at once—she noted how everyone stood at attention around him, stiff and silent, respectful, while he explained something, speaking in a logical, precise way, developing a statement to its inevitable conclusion. Not only would no one dare interrupt, but the possibility of an interruption was grotesque. Edgar Greaney was the author of a number of books, both introductory and advanced, on the subject of logical positivism...he had been brought to Manitock as chairman of the philosophy department. Beatrice had liked the man's certainty, she had liked his slightly British accent, believing him to be a European who had spent some time in England and was now trying, with some success, to speak American English. She had even admired, in a way, his method of bringing an evidently abstract argument to a powerful, emotional conclusion that surprised his listeners, but she had no interest in meeting him; his crossed leg, his twitching foot, the explosive laughter he seemed to force in others, had annoyed her. *I can see the thoughts rising in your mind,* he had said to someone playfully. A joke, yet a serious joke.

"I loved him so much," Moira said. "I don't want to forget him."

Beatrice confessed to Moira. She confessed her jealousy, her envy. For months she had seen Moira at a distance, had dreaded her, had been bitterly envious of her. But why? Because Moira had been a widow five months before Beatrice and had always been so healthy, so intelligent about her fate. No one pitied her. No one worried about her. "There was an outfit you wore last summer, yellow trousers and a striped pullover shirt, like a sailor's shirt, that made me think... Forgive me," Beatrice said, "but it made me think that you couldn't possibly be a widow. Not like me."

"People wanted us to meet, did you know that?" Moira said. "I drove by your house a few times, though it was out of my way, thinking that if you were out in the yard ... I must say that everything you wore, even the expression on your face, did seem to indicate you were a widow. Or an older woman. Like some of the mill-workers' wives or mothers, those older Italian women who like to dress in black. I envied you, that you could disguise yourself like that. Sometimes you seemed almost dowdy, almost ugly, did you know that? You looked so pale, almost greenish-white. You looked sick. But you did it deliberately. That was courageous, really; you went down into the grave with him. I was afraid to do that. I thought I might not return again."

Beatrice was offended. *Went down into the grave with him.* What was the woman talking about, was she crazy?... But Beatrice pretended not to mind, she even laughed. They were having coffee together at Beatrice's one afternoon, and her hand shook so that coffee spilled into her saucer, but she did not mind.

"Cancer of the throat," Moira said without hesitation. "Didn't you know?"

"I didn't know, not specifically...."

"Yes, it was strange how at first everyone seemed to know," Moira said in her amused, sardonic voice, though her expression showed that she blamed no one, "at least all our friends knew. All his friends. He went to Boston for treatments, he came back, and for a while the news seemed to be optimistic; or he lied a little. People were anxious about him. They cornered me, telephoned me when he was at school, wanted to know how he was. But as time passed they no longer asked. There's a moment at the very start of a conversation when the person you've just met asks how you are, how things are with you, and this moment was almost intolerable—I could see the question in the person's mind, I could see it there almost before he could—"

"How strange," Beatrice said.

"—and I could also see the instant in which the person realized he must not ask that question. So—there was nothing to be asked, no question, except a clumsy substitute. But I pretended to notice nothing, I filled in the gaps in conversations; after all, I was an independent, healthy person, not at all sick; I didn't even get a bad cold last spring when everyone was sick with the flu, do you remember? —Yes, it was cancer of the throat. The preliminary months were the worst in a way, since there was some hope. Afterward, when there was no hope ... "

She began to cry. She cried openly, almost irritably, like a child.

" ... people came to visit him in the hospital, but I could tell they dreaded the visits. They were terrified and bored at the same time. Because he wouldn't talk. He didn't even seem to be listening. If I was there I had to talk in his place ... I felt as if my soul were being drained out of me in all those spurts of conversation, trying to make other people feel halfway at ease. There was one awful visit when an associate of his ... when ... the man had come alone, without his wife, and he was so miserable, so naively miserable, he believed he had to stay until visiting hours were over at seven, so he was there an hour and a half ... ashen-faced. ... He kept staring at me, directing questions to me, and I kept replying and asking him questions, an hour and a half of it, and so pointless. ... "

Beatrice was moved by the woman's tears. And the sound of her voice, which was no longer well-modulated, but had the unashamed, undignified whine, the ugly unmusical noise, of angry grief. Beatrice was panicked that she might begin to cry as

well. And they would be united involuntarily by their tears—
like young girls, like children, like sisters. She stared at Moira,
whose face was contracted almost like an infant's, and was
upset that Moira should allow herself to appear so ugly.
"Don't do that! —Your face, you'll ruin your face!" Beatrice
cried.

By January, the two of them were so obviously friends, so
often seen together in Manitock, that when people invited either
of them to parties and dinners, they always added, as if inciden-
tally, that the other was also being invited. But Beatrice always
declined. She was gracious, but she declined. She wanted no
part of social life; for years she had hated it without ever
comprehending the depth of her hatred, always imagining it
was a particular evening, a particular set of people, that had
disappointed her. But no: it was the commotion and strain of
social life itself. Especially, she had come to dislike the ritual
remarks women made to one another, even in the presence of
men—always complimenting one another on their clothes, their
hair, their physical appearance. They did not know how insulting such remarks were to her, as if she were to be continually
assessed from the outside, as an aesthetic phenomenon; they did
not sense how, unconsciously, they were setting one another up
for the routine, perfunctory admiration of men, which was
always slightly contemptuous. And of course she was frightened of their pity. When someone said that it was good she had
a teaching job—teaching was so absorbing, wasn't it—she had
replied angrily that she no longer had the job. She had quit. And
why was it "good," why might anyone imagine it was "good"
for her to have something to absorb her?
    That time, Moira had interrupted, had gracefully intervened.
Like an older sister. She had turned the conversation onto
something else, while Beatrice stood, smarting, angry and remorseful at the same time, knowing herself a stranger to all
these people.... Like an older, wiser, more worldly sister, Moira
seemed to precede her; she might have made the social events
tolerable, but Beatrice thought it better to withdraw. She knew
that people were not to blame, that they meant only well; she
knew it was selfish of her to dislike them. So she declined

invitations. But when the telephone rang, she was no longer worried—most of the time it was Moira.

"People ask about you," Moira reported. "Men ask about you."

Beatrice laughed. "You're lying."

"I'm not lying; I never lie."

"They ask about you, not me. They crowd around you, not me.... I have no interest in men."

"Still, they ask about you."

"I don't want to hear it," Beatrice said.

"I've had to decline invitations from certain people," Moira said slowly, "...men I knew in the past...I mean, men I was very friendly with.... Before Edgar's death, I mean."

Beatrice wondered what she meant. But she did not ask: the subject of men sickened her. She was still a young woman, only a few months from her twenty-eighth birthday, but she felt aged, soured by too much experience. She and Wallace had been married only five years. But it seemed much longer—more than half her lifetime. He had drawn her spirit out of her and into him, partly, and then he had been killed, one ordinary afternoon. It was as if her right arm had been yanked off. And now she walked around, her arm gone at the socket, bloodless, a scar healing over it, and people asked her cheerfully about how things were going, wasn't it good to be teaching, shouldn't she get out more, shouldn't she have more interests? Even Moira hinted that she should go out. The two of them could go out together, Moira laughed, so men could approach them both, openly....

"And then what?" Beatrice asked.

"Then we could explain how we don't need them," Moira said.

"It was worse for you, the fact that he died so slowly," Beatrice said.

"...no, I think it was worse for you. You weren't prepared for it. You had the worst shock."

"But you had to endure him changing. His personality must have changed."

"Yes, it changed. He changed. The man who died wasn't the same man I knew," Moira said. "So in fact it was easier for me.... I mean, people seem to die a while before their actual deaths, their physical deaths. It was the same way with my father. They seem to leave themselves. Do you know what I mean? I don't know if I believe in a soul, a soul detachable from the body, but the personality seems to leave...or disappear...and someone else is there, left behind. It's very strange. About the third week before he actually died, my husband seemed to leave. He even said good-by to me.... I mean, in a way, in a way I can't explain.... You don't understand! I can see that you don't understand and I'm frightening you. I meant only to tell you that I think you had the worst of it, a sudden death. You're very brave. "

Beatrice remembered the night she had gone mad. She thought of it that way, as madness. Hearing the voice of a former self, hearing her party voice, her social self, going on and on and on so happily and witlessly about the tragic madness of the world, which could not, of course, have any effect upon an intelligent person.... And then the terror, the utter, blank, deathly terror. She had experienced a sensation that was indescribable. There were no words for it, nothing. Yet, stammering her anguish over the phone to Moira, to a stranger whom she believed she disliked, she managed to say it was like the empty silence after the *click* of an automatic phonograph, when the last record has been played and the machine neatly shuts itself off.

"You haven't gone mad," Moira said gently. "You didn't go mad. It's just the shock of it, of his death. It was so much worse for you because he died instantly."

Beatrice pressed her fingertips against her eyes. No, she could not allow her friend to be so generous. No. They argued late into the night, in voices that grew strident at times; at other times, quite tender. "No, I think it must have been more torturous for you, because he died so slowly.... "

Beatrice would never forget how Moira had come to her house. Three in the morning, awakened by the telephone, able to recognize Beatrice's voice in spite of the hysteria...without

hesitating she had put on ski pants and a sweater, slid her bare
feet into boots, snatched a parka from wherever she had tossed
it the day before...trudged through the brittle snow to her
car...driven all the way across town on the desolate, icy streets,
to Beatrice. She had even known where Beatrice lived.

Beatrice wept that anyone should be so generous. She knew
she herself was not that generous. Something had been left out
of her soul, perhaps. Again and again she thanked Moira. And
she could not resist saying: "Would I have done that much for
you? Or for anyone?... Of course not."

"Certainly you would," Moira said warmly.

"Then you don't know me," Beatrice said.

"I know you very well!" Moira laughed. "I know you in a
way you don't know yourself.... Yes, it's possible," she said
seriously, "in fact, my husband always claimed to know me in a
way I didn't know myself. Because he could sense what I was as
a possibility, while I only knew myself from the inside, in terms
of what I was."

"Your husband was a genius," Beatrice said. "I always admired him...."

"Yes, everyone admired him," Moira said. "...Did you like
his voice, his accent?"

"Was he European?"

"Born in Columbus, Ohio," Moira laughed. "His parents
were from Warsaw; they were Jews, they escaped just before the
war. They lived in New York for a while; evidently they were
very poor; then somehow ended up in Columbus—I don't know
the details because Edgar didn't tell me. Of course his name was
another name. It wasn't Edgar Greaney. He changed it when he
went to England, he was a Rhodes scholar at Oxford...so in a
way, yes, you could say he was European," Moira said thoughtfully. "Yes. But obliquely. He was always around the corner
from where anyone stood...and if you turned the corner, he'd
duck around another corner."

Beatrice looked away. She hoped that Moira would say
nothing further.

"...toward the end he even spoke in Yiddish," Moira said. "I
didn't know what on earth he was saying. I didn't know it was

a language—any language—I didn't know the sounds of it. Somehow it came back to him, words and phrases. Names. Prayers. I can't be certain, but I think they were prayers, mixed in with other words. English, Polish, Yiddish, German, even French...I sat there by his bedside and experienced these sounds, these various struggling sounds, and I came to know what language adds up to. Then, at the very end, he couldn't speak at all. I think he was at peace then; he'd managed to say what he wanted to say, so he was at peace.... He was a genius, yes," Moira said dreamily, "but that had nothing to do with his death."

"I don't think we should talk about these things," Beatrice said.

"No," said Moira. "But we will."

They fell into each other's lives as if, all along, they had known about each other. Parallel lives, parallel habits. Both woke early, around dawn, and could not get back to sleep. In the kitchen at seven, making coffee, Beatrice felt no dismay when the telephone rang. If it did not ring by seven-thirty, she went to call Moira.

They shopped together. They had lunch at one of the three or four good restaurants in town—were seen together as late as two-thirty in the afternoon in the dining room of the Ethan Allen Inn, discussing something that must have been of vital importance to each. Moira with her ash-blond hair, her turtleneck sweaters, her tweed skirts and leather boots...Beatrice small, dark, so unaware of her surroundings that she sometimes raised her voice in an incredulous whine, like a child. They evidently argued a great deal. Then Moira would laugh, husky-voiced, totally at ease.... In the ski shop adjacent to Manitock's only department store, a man who had known Wallace Kern fairly well tried to have a conversation with them, but it seemed to him that Beatrice was not even listening and that the Greaney woman, whom he did not know, was simply waiting for him to go away, aggressively gracious, nodding before he even finished what he had to say. Moira evidently was going skiing; she was trying to talk Beatrice into going along, up into Canada, into the Laurentians. But Beatrice was silent, even a little sullen.

"It would be good for her, wouldn't it," Moira said to the man, "to get away from Manitock for a few days...? And nothing could happen. She wouldn't have to ski, not even the beginners' slopes, if she didn't want to."

The man agreed. He said clumsily that it would be good for Beatrice.

"Why should I want what's good for me?" Beatrice asked him, smiling. "Is that what you want for yourself—only what's good for you?"

Yet when Moira had a dinner party in the big, Victorian-Gothic house on Fort Street—built by one of the mill owners at the turn of the century—Beatrice was not there. Someone asked about her and Moira explained gravely that Mrs. Kern wasn't well, that she regretted very much having to miss the party—since she liked the other guests—she enjoyed small parties and serious, intelligent conversations. But she wasn't well.

Moira telephoned her from her bedroom upstairs while the party was still going on; she told Beatrice that everyone missed her and was asking about her and, yes, she had to admit that Beatrice was right: these people were too busy, too distracting, they talked loudly and tried to joke, even about matters that were not funny—like the University's financial problems— Beatrice had made the correct decision to stay away. Even though it was almost rude of her.

"Rude? Why is it rude?" Beatrice cried. "...Did I hear you right? *Rude?*"

"Isn't it? Deliberately rude?"

They argued for several minutes. Moira was whispering angrily. She wanted to know what Beatrice was doing—was she in bed? No? Then she wasn't ill; it had been a lie. But Beatrice protested, saying she had never claimed to be ill. What was going on? Ill? When? She had simply refused to come to the party because other people made her nervous, even people she liked; she could not endure their forced cheerfulness. Moira paused, then said that Beatrice's husband had been a very extroverted person, hadn't he—he had enjoyed parties? Beatrice did not reply; she might have been trying to remember. "I can see him in my mind's eye," Moira said. "He had brown curly hair...he was tall...he laughed a great deal, didn't he?...he liked to drink, didn't he? And...and... And his eyes were heavy-lidded, he was handsome, his mouth was...he was... You're at home tonight thinking about him, aren't you? Aren't you?"

"He didn't like to drink," Beatrice said. "No more than anyone else. He—"

"He might have been let go at the University, did you know that?" Moira said. "There were rumors. Of course it wouldn't have had to do with his professional competence—but the budget is being cut back— Did you know that? Did he tell you?"

"He told me everything," Beatrice said.

"Did he tell you that?"

"He kept nothing from me!" Beatrice said.

She hung up.

When Moira telephoned her back, she let the phone ring.

"How many weeks has it been?" Moira asked.

"Weeks? I think in terms of months," Beatrice said, ashamed.

"I think you loved him more than I loved my husband. I get that impression."

"No. No, really. I loved my husband very much, but...but I don't think I'm as mature a person as you; I don't think I'm capable of love in the way you are."

They sat together in the dining room of Moira's house; Beatrice had come over for dinner at six and it was now eight-thirty. They were finishing a bottle of wine.

"I envy you," Beatrice said, "because he was so much older than you. He taught you so much. He even taught you how to die.... Wally was too young, he left me too young. He was just a boy. It was said about him...this is a secret, Moira, I know you won't tell anyone...it was said about him that he was immature, in spite of being so intelligent. Yes, I actually saw it, the word *immature*. The chairman of his department called me in one day, meaning to be kind, and was very sweet to me...praised Wallace...told me how the entire department was grief-stricken, and many students...because he was very popular with students, especially underclassmen. And the chairman actually showed me the files he and the Dean kept on Wallace, meaning only to be kind...a very sweet, nervous man...and though most of the comments on the forms were very good, excellent, I happened to notice that word *immature* down in the left-hand corner of the page." She began to laugh. "He may have tried to cover it with his thumb, I don't know, but in any case I saw it.... Isn't that funny?"

Moira seized her wrist to make her stop. She never allowed Beatrice to laugh in that dry, self-mocking way; she found it intolerable. "But you never betrayed your husband. Did you? You were never unfaithful to him, were you? So you did love him more than I loved my husband, regardless of whether some ignorant sons of bitches labeled him *immature*.... You were faithful; you were never unfaithful. You're better than I am."

"I don't want to hear about it," Beatrice said.

"I don't want to talk about it. I won't talk about it," Moira said.

One day in February the telephone rang very early, a few minutes after six in the morning. Moira wanted to know if Beatrice had had disturbing dreams. Beatrice had confided in her, as she had never confided in anyone else, that she some-times suffered from extraordinarily ugly dreams. "What were they? What did you dream? Maybe you should tell me," Moira said.

"They're degrading. I can't talk about them."

Moira said nothing for several seconds. Then, hurt, she mumbled something about the fact that she slept without dreams: blunt and big and healthy as a horse, she was. A clumsy, ugly creature.

"That's ridiculous," Beatrice said sleepily. "You're not ugly. You're not clumsy."

"Sometimes Edgar said I was clumsy. And my mind...my imagination...he said it was crude. That's why I don't dream. I would welcome even nightmares, I'd be happy to share your nightmares. That would be better than nothing."

"When were you unfaithful to your husband?" Beatrice asked.

"When he was dying."

"Did you tell him?"

"Tell him! No, of course not.... And you were never unfaithful to Wallace?"

"Never."

"And now...?"

"What do you mean, *and now?*"

"Are you still faithful to him?"

"...last night I dreamed that someone was trying to get into bed with me, he'd climbed through the window.... I was paralyzed with fear, I was sick with fear, I tried to scream because I knew I was sleeping and I had to wake up, I had to escape...."

"Yes?" Moira said sharply. "Why are you telling me this? Was the man your husband, is that it?"

"I think—I think— Yes, I think it was my husband."

For a moment Moira was silent. Then she said sullenly, "I thought that might be happening. With you. I don't dream, myself, but I sense dreams elsewhere...I sense *your* dreams.... And so, Beatrice, did you allow him in your bed?"

Beatrice murmured something unintelligible. She was very embarrassed.

"I want to know," Moira said. "Did you allow him in? Did he actually—?"

"I woke up terrified," Beatrice said. "I told you: I was sick with fear."

"All right, Beatrice," Moira said slowly. "But would you have allowed him in your bed if you'd known who he was? I mean to say—did you know, at the time, that the man was your husband?—or did you think it was a stranger, an intruder?"

"It happened too quickly," Beatrice said. "I had no time to think. All I knew was that someone had crawled through the open window and was trying to get into bed with me, moaning, making a hideous moaning noise, as if he were pleading with me, trying to pronounce my name—and I was terrified, I began to scream in my sleep, and somehow—somehow I managed to wake up. And I was grateful to know that I'd been sleeping. And that I was alone."

Moira was silent for a long, strained moment. Then she said simply, strangely, "Yes."

THE MANITOCK MILL
Manitock, New Hampshire

This 3-story gristmill was built by Dawson Cody and Robertson Wesley Turner and began operation in 1854. Restored in 1956, the mill is open to the public. One set of original millstones still exists and the six turbines are still in operation.

The inauguration of the mill in 1854 was marred by a tragic accident. The bride of the co-owner, R. W. Turner, was accidentally killed in the machinery.

Beatrice read the plaque and immediately turned away. She did not approve of the prose style. She was alone, out for a long walk, the mill was not open this late in the afternoon, she had no interest in seeing it or in anything else. Moira was not with her. But she was talking to Moira, under her breath, muttering. "Loathsome. Disgusting.... No one of them will ever...not with me, not again. Never. No man.... No one."

"...he did something terrible once. Terrible. You won't tell anyone?... We had seen his son off at the airport, and on the way back, at the entrance to the expressway...well, there was a girl in a Volkswagen just ahead of him, going rather slowly, because there was so much traffic out on the expressway. And...and evidently he was angry about something or just impatient, because he honked his horn a number of times, furiously, and forced the girl out onto the expressway. Because she was just a girl, a frightened girl, and not certain about driving. And a truck rammed her from behind, and...and he didn't stop but just pulled out around the wreck and sped home...he forbade me ever to speak of it. He was upset, yes, and guilty and remorseful, and sick about what he had done...but he forbade me ever to speak of it."

* * *

" ...but you loved him, of course?"

"Didn't you? ...love *your* husband?"

Beatrice felt illness coming gradually upon her, as if from a distance: the way light sometimes moved across the late-winter hills, patches of inexplicable sunlight that appeared ... and disappeared ... and appeared again while she held her breath. The exact route this sunshine would take could not be predicted, but it moved with a strange blithe certainty, as if it had happened innumerable times in the past. She could feel the sickness in her throat and in her bowels. And in her head: a quick darting piercing pain. She lay in bed, propped up with pillows. Was she, now, going to die? Was this the beginning of death? How little it seemed to matter ...! She read books of a kind one reads in bed, mildly sick. Too weakened to be alarmed. She read poetry for hours and could not always judge—were such lines exquisitely beautiful, or were they terrifying?

> *Such consciousness seemed but accidents,*
> *Relapses from the one interior life*
> *In which all beings live with god, themselves*
> *Are god, existing in the mighty whole*
> *As indistinguishable as the cloudless east*
> *Is from the cloudless west, when all*
> *The hemisphere is one cerulean blue.*

She wanted to read these lines aloud to another person. To Moira. Her voice would shake, her absurd terror would be exposed, yet she wanted to match her emotions with another person's—for how could she know, being so sick now, so weak, what was terror and what was awe? What was beauty?

In the end she did not read the lines to Moira. She closed the book, put it aside. It was beautiful, yes, but inhuman. Earlier in her life, when she had known so little, she might have rejoiced in the poet's massive vision, assuming—smugly, and wrongly— that it was a vision one might easily appropriate. And perhaps later in her life, near its completion, she might approach such a vision without any fear at all. But now: no. It wasn't possible. Not now, not yet.

Instead she craved an art that defined limits, a human, humble, sane art, unashamed of turning away from the void, unashamed of celebrating what was human and therefore scaled down; an art of what was possible, what must be embraced.

"As you probably know, I nursed my husband for months. I was his nurse. He didn't want anyone else and I didn't want anyone else around him. It wasn't easy, in fact I dreaded it at first...I dreaded not only him but myself in that role, I was afraid something irrevocable might happen to me. After a while, though, I came to almost like it, to feel fulfilled by nursing him. I'm ashamed of that now. I can hardly believe it. Then, near the end, when he was very sick, I dreaded it again and resented it, I think, and I was very, very unhappy. I was ashamed of that too.... But what do these emotions matter? We do what we must do. He died. Whether I was ashamed or not, happy or unhappy, the poor man died.... But *you're* not going to."

"Of course I'm not," Beatrice said softly. "You've been so generous, Moira, coming over here so often, fixing meals for me.... I'm not really sick. Not really. You must be neglecting your own life, aren't you?"

Moira gazed down at herself contemplatively. She took in the length of her body: that day she was wearing a cable-stitched ski sweater and faded blue jeans. So tall, so confident!—Beatrice had always admired women like Moira. Moira said strangely, "How can I be neglecting my own life? This *is* my life here. We inhabit our own lives constantly."

" ... he did like parties, yes, and he liked to drink. He couldn't seem to control it. The color of his skin actually changed, it got pink, rosy, flushed...and he would start to laugh over nothing...he liked to be happy, he liked to laugh. It was a mistake for him to come here, to this place; it wasn't right for him.... The accident wasn't his fault, but I was told he had been drinking; he had a bottle in the glove compartment and it flew out and was smashed and the smell of it was everywhere...so I believed, I tried to believe, that it was just that, the smell of liquor, they were going by. I've never told anyone.... He was hardly more than a boy, really. He wasn't an adult. You would have liked him so much, he could make anyone laugh once he got going. He could even make me laugh.... But most of the time I don't see anything amusing in the world."

"There isn't anything amusing in the world. It's in your head."

"...I mean the world in itself," Beatrice said uncertainly.

"...in your head. The world is. The world," Moira said, as if imitating someone else, "...is in your head. The world is your idea."

"But I can't alter it."

"Why not?"

"Don't frighten me," Beatrice said. "It must be the pills, but I can't seem to understand you."

"We understand everything," Moira said. She had brought Beatrice some soup and tea on a tray; she squatted at the bedside. Her hair had been brushed carelessly and sprang out in all directions. "We know and foresee and remember simultaneously."

Beatrice shuddered.

"The past is gone, but the future is gone too—it's inaccessible. It's completed and inaccessible. Today is February twenty-seventh; we can talk about the past and the future today; we can talk about our dead husbands or we could talk about ourselves; we could make plans for leaving this part of the world together...or even singly...escaping together or singly. But it doesn't matter because everything has already happened. That's why you feel like a corpse: in a sense you're already dead."

"I don't feel dead," Beatrice said.

"Nobody ever does," Moira laughed.

"I don't know what you mean," Beatrice said.

"Would you get married again?"

"And have him die again?"

"But they have to die! It's what must happen."

"It won't happen again," Beatrice whispered.

Moira's eyes were blue, that cerulean blue. She told Beatrice it did not matter in the slightest, she would not hold it against

Beatrice that Edgar had not seemed attractive to her. "He was a bastard. He would have hurt you," Moira said.

"I did admire him...."

"He hadn't time for women, really. I don't know why he fell in love with me. It would have upset me terribly if that man had taken advantage of you.... No, he wasn't right for you. He may have appeared to be a genius, but...he wasn't quite human; he'd forget about his own son for weeks at a time. Yes, you were right to avoid him."

"...I was afraid of him," Beatrice said.

"Yes, and you should have been. He would have hurt you. You're not as tough as I am.... I am tough, I'm strong. Don't underestimate me. He always underestimated me because he didn't know how to value women.... You were afraid of him, then? But you admired him?"

"Yes. Yes."

"But nothing came of it."

"Nothing came of it...."

"You didn't ever see him in private?"

"No."

"So nothing came of it.... And now he's dead. I should sell the house; it's my property. This house is rented, isn't it? We could move back to Boston. We could move all the way out to San Francisco. Would you like that? When you're well again?"

"I'm not sick," Beatrice said. "It's just a cold."

"People think you're ill; they say the most absurd things about you," Moira said. "They do nothing but gossip. We have to leave, don't we? Either together or each of us singly.... I'll have to leave him there, in the cemetery. I'll have to leave everyone and so will you.... No, you're not sick; you look a little pale and you've lost weight, but there's nothing wrong with you."

"I'm afraid to leave," Beatrice said.

"Do you still dream about him?"

"Yes. No. I dream about many things."

"What did you dream last night?"

Beatrice shook her head, as if not wanting to remember.

"Was he trying to get back to you, trying to...?"

"No," Beatrice said. "It was someone else. I think it was you...but then it was a stranger...it was you, Moira, but also someone else, a stranger. You were pushing me out somewhere, out onto a highway. It was so noisy, the traffic and horns and people screaming and...and I was terrified...."

Moira seized her wrist and shook it. "What do you mean?"

"...I don't mean anything," Beatrice said. "The dream doesn't mean anything.... But it was so vivid."

"It was only a dream, it doesn't mean anything," Moira laughed. "In fact, I forbid it to mean anything."

"I don't want to go to Boston," Beatrice said. "Or San Francisco either. I'm afraid...."

"I can forbid that too," Moira said.

"Who was your lover, here in Manitock?"

"It isn't important. It doesn't matter. I never see him."

"Who was he?"

It was late March now: they had hiked out to the cemetery. The earth was moist, the wind chilly and fragrant; miles away, in the mountains, sunlight and shadow moved restlessly together, apart, together. Beatrice was frightened of the cemetery, but she had come out anyway. She dreaded the little marker— *Kern*—and there was something about the *Greaney* stone, that highly polished black rock, that made her uneasy. Yet she had walked the two miles just the same. And now she felt invigorated.

"...people came to visit him at the hospital..." Moira was saying slowly. "...especially on Sundays...and...and it was such a horror for them, and so boring, that... Well, a friend of Edgar's came one day without his wife, and I felt so sorry for him because he was miserable.... In the elevator going down, I started to cry and he... So it happened. But it isn't important."

"And he what?"

"He comforted me. I comforted him too, in a way, because he was frightened of what was happening to my husband, and...and so it happened. But it isn't important. It has no meaning."

"You saw the man again, though?"

"A few times."

Beatrice looked at Moira wonderingly.

"I didn't know what I was doing exactly," Moira said. "I was very upset and so was he and... But it's over now. I never see him now."

"He was married, your lover? Who was he?"

"It isn't important.

"Was he...my husband?" Beatrice asked.

Her eyes filled suddenly with tears. She had been angry all along, without knowing it; and now her body pulsed with excitement. Moira stared at her, utterly amazed. There were faint lines on her forehead, her skin looked bleached out, the ash-blond hair was coarse as a horse's mane...yet she was an attractive woman, certainly; Wallace would have been drawn to her. Beatrice tried to smile.

"*Your husband?*" Moira whispered.

"Was it? You can tell me. You can admit it."

"Beatrice, are you joking?"

"Was it—?"

"Of course not."

"But why do you look so guilty?"

" ...I didn't even know your husband, Beatrice. Edgar didn't know him. The four of us weren't friends, were we, we didn't know one another, did we...? It was someone else, someone you don't know. It doesn't matter."

Beatrice was trembling. "But I can see the two of you to-gether, you and my husband. I can see you. Yes, it's like something I've already dreamed, something that has already happened.... Were you happy with your lover while your husband was dying?"

Moira turned away.

"Weren't you happy, at least occasionally?"

"No."

"Moira—"

"Frankly, no!"

"Why don't you say *yes?*" Beatrice said.

Moira looked at her, frowning. Then she laughed. "All right. *Yes.*"

"So you were happy betraying your husband?"

"If you insist."

"And it was my husband ...?"

"Beatrice, please. You're frightening me. You look so strange ... you're not going to be sick again, are you? Of course it wasn't—"

"He was going to die anyway in a few months. But he didn't know it. Why shouldn't he have loved you? Why shouldn't the two of you have been happy?.... He liked life, he liked laughter, I wasn't right for him. Obviously he fell in love with you and I don't blame him."

She was shouting. Moira backed away.

"I don't blame him! I don't blame either of you!"

"Beatrice, please," Moira said. "The man was someone you don't even know—you and Wallace didn't know him—and it didn't matter, we never loved each other—"

"I don't believe that," Beatrice said.

"We never—"

"No. I know Wallace too well. I know *you*." She pressed her hands against her face. The wind must have drawn tears out of her; her cheeks were wet. "Don't you deny it, Moira ... don't you deny him ... he was going to die anyway and why shouldn't he have been happy ... why would it have mattered? ... I don't mind. I don't mind."

"Beatrice, it wasn't your—"

"I don't mind!"

She turned away. *Don't you deny it ... don't you resist....*

Moira said nothing; she simply stood there. Then she said softly, "I knew you would understand, Beatrice, all along. It was your husband, yes."

Beatrice saw that her friend's expression had changed; the tension was gone, the guilt gone.

They walked back to town in silence. It was a wild, windy day.

Eventually, both women left Manitock. Beatrice got a job in the public school system in Albany, New York, teaching part-time in junior high, and enrolled in a graduate program in art history at the State University there. Moira, after selling her house, moved to San Francisco where she bought into a small bookstore. On an impulse Beatrice sent her a note one day: *Thank you, Moira.* Months passed. When she received a reply on a stiff oatmeal-colored piece of paper, she had nearly forgotten about the note she had sent. *You're welcome, Beatrice,* Moira had said. And that was all.

The Translation

WHAT WERE THE WORDS for *woman, man, love, freedom, fate?*—
in this strange land where the architecture and the countryside and the sea with its dark choppy waters and the very air
itself seemed to Oliver totally foreign, unearthly? He must have
fallen in love with the woman at once, after fifteen minutes'
conversation. Such perversity was unlike him. He had loved a
woman twenty years before; had perhaps loved two or even
three women in his lifetime; but had never fallen in love, had
never been *in love;* such melodramatic passion was not his style.
He had only spoken with her for fifteen minutes at the most,
and not directly: through the translator assigned to him. He did
not know her at all. Yet, that night, he dreamed of rescuing her.

"I am struck and impressed," he said politely, addressing the
young woman introduced to him as a music teacher at the high
school and a musician—a violist—herself, "with the marvelous
old buildings here . . . the church that is on the same street as my
hotel . . . yes? . . . you know it? . . . and with the beauty of the parks,
the trees and flowers, everything so well-tended, and the manner of the people I have encountered . . . they are friendly but not
effusive; they appear so very . . . so very healthy," he said, hearing his voice falter, realizing that he was being condescending;

as if it surprised him, the fact that people in this legendary, long-suffering nation were not very different from people anywhere. But his translator translated the speech and the young woman appeared to agree, nodding, smiling as if to encourage him. Thank God, he had not offended her. "I am very grateful to have been allowed a visa," he said. "I have never visited a country that has struck me in such a way ... an immediate sense of, of ... how shall I put it ... of something like nostalgia ... do you know the expression, the meaning? ... nostalgia ... emotion for something once possessed but now lost, perhaps not now even accessible through memory...."

If he was making a fool of himself with this speech, and by so urgently staring at the woman, Alisa, the others did not appear to notice; they listened intently, even greedily, as Oliver's young translator repeated his words, hardly pausing for breath. He was a remarkable young man, probably in his early twenties, and Oliver had the idea that the translator's presence and evident good will toward him were freeing his tongue, giving him a measure of happiness for the first time since he had left the United States. For the first time, really, in many years. It was marvelous, magical, to utter his thoughts aloud and to hear, then, their instantaneous translation into a foreign language—to sit with his translator at his left hand, watching the effect of his words upon his listeners' faces as they were translated. An eerie, uncanny experience ... unsettling and yet exciting in a way Oliver could not have explained. He had not liked the idea of relying upon a translator; one of his failings, one of the disappointments of his life, had always been a certain shyness or coolness in his character, which it was evidently his fate not to alter, and he had supposed that travel into a country as foreign as this one, and as formally antagonistic to the United States, would be especially difficult since he knew nothing of the language. But in fact the translator was like a younger brother to him, like a son. There was an intimacy between them and a pleasurable freedom, even an unembarrassed lyricism in Oliver's remarks that he could not possibly have anticipated.

Of course his mood was partly attributable to the cognac and to the close, crowded, overheated room in which the reception was being held and to his immediate attraction for the dusky-haired, solemn young woman with the name he could not pronounce—*Alisa* was as close as he could come to it; he would have to ask the translator to write it out for him when they returned to the hotel. It would not last, his mood of gaiety. But for the present moment he was very happy, merely to hear these people speak their language, a melodic play of explosive consonants and throaty vowels; it hardly mattered that his translator could manage to translate only a fraction of what was being said. Oliver was happy, almost euphoric. He was intoxicated. He had to restrain himself from taking one of Alisa's delicate hands in his own and squeezing it, to show how taken he was by her. *I know you are suffering in this prison-state of yours,* he wanted to whisper to her, *and I want, I want to do something for you ... want to rescue you, save you, change your life. ...*

The Director of the Lexicographic Institute was asking him a courteous, convoluted question about the current state of culture in his own nation, and everyone listened, frowning as if with anxiety, while, with one part of his mind, Oliver made several statements. His translator took them up at once, transformed them into those eerie, exquisite sounds; the Director nodded gravely, emphatically; the others nodded; it seemed to be about what they had anticipated. One of the men, white-haired, diminutive, asked something in a quavering voice, and Oliver's translator hesitated before repeating it. "Dr. Crlejevec is curious to know—is it true that your visual artists have become artists merely of the void—that is, of death—they are exclusively morbid, they have turned their backs on life?" The translator blushed, not quite meeting Oliver's gaze, as if he were embarrassed by the question. But the question did not annoy Oliver. Not in the least. He disliked much of contemporary art anyway and welcomed the opportunity to express his feelings warmly, knowing what he said would endear him to these people. It pleased him most of all that Alisa listened so closely. Her long, nervous fingers toyed with a cameo broach she wore at her throat; her gray eyes were fixed upon his face. "Art moves in a certain tendril-like manner ... in many directions, though at a single point in history one direction is usually stressed and acclaimed... like the evolutionary gropings of nature, to my way of thinking. Do you see? The contemporary pathway is but a tendril, a feeler, an experimental gesture... because it is obsessed with death and the void and the annihilation of self it will necessarily die... it pronounces its own death sentence."

The words were translated; the effect was instantaneous; Oliver's pronouncement seemed to meet with approval. The Director, however, posed another question. He was a huge man in his fifties, with a ruddy, beefy face and rather coarse features, though his voice seemed to Oliver quite cultured. "...But in the meantime, does it not do damage?... to the unformed, that is, to the young, the susceptible... does it not do irreparable damage, such deathly art?"

Oliver's high spirits could not be diminished. He only pretended to be thinking seriously before he answered, "Not at all! In my part of the world, 'serious' art is ignored by the masses; the unformed, the young, the susceptible are hardly aware of its existence!"

He had expected his listeners to laugh. But they did not laugh. The young woman murmured something, shaking her head. Oliver's translator said to him, "She says she is shocked... unless, of course, you are joking."

The conversation shifted. Oliver was taken to other groups of people, was introduced by his translator, was made to feel important, honored. From time to time he glanced back at the young woman—when he saw her preparing to leave, he was stricken; he wanted to tell his translator to stop her, but of course that would have been indecorous. *I want to do something for you. Anything. I want*... But it would have been indecorous.

"She is a fine person, very hard-working, very trustworthy," Liebert was saying slowly. "Not my friend or even acquaintance, but my sister's... my older sister, who was her classmate. She is a very accomplished violist, participated in a festival last spring in Moscow, but also a very fine teacher here, very hardworking, very serious."

"Is she married?" Oliver asked.

They were being driven in a shiny black taxicab along an avenue of trees in blossom—acacia, lime—past buildings of all sizes, some very old, some disconcertingly new, of glass and poured concrete and steel, and from time to time the buildings fell back and a monument appeared, sudden, grandiose, rather pompous—not very old either, Oliver noted. Postwar.

"There is some difficulty, yes," the translator said, "with the husband... and with the father as well. But I do not know, really. I am not an acquaintance of hers, as I said. She lives her life, I live mine. We meet a few times a year, at gatherings like the one last night... she too does translations, though not into English. Into German exclusively."

"Then she is married? You mentioned a husband...?"

Liebert looked out the window, as if embarrassed by Oliver's interest. He was not unwilling to talk about the young woman, but not willing either. For the first time in their three days' acquaintance, Oliver felt the young man's stubborn nature. "They have not been together in one place for many years, as I understand it," he said. "The husband, not an acquaintance of my own, is some years older than she... a doctor, I believe... a research specialist in an area I know nothing of. He is in another city. He has been in another city, and Alisa in this city, for many years."

"I'm sorry to hear that," Oliver said sincerely. "She struck me as sweet, vulnerable... possibly a little lonely? I don't like to think that she may be unhappy."

Liebert shrugged his shoulders.

"Unhappy, so?" he murmured.

They drove through a square and Oliver's attention was drawn to an immense portrait of a man's face: a poster three stories high.

"Amazing!" he said without irony.

"It is not amazing, it is ordinary life," Liebert said. "We live here."

"...She isn't unhappy then? No more than most?"

"There is not the—what is the word?—the compulsion to analyze such things, such states of mind," Liebert said with a vague air of reproach. "It is enough to complete the day—

working hard, carrying out one's obligations. You understand? Leisure would only result in morbid self-scrutiny and the void, the infatuation with the void, which is your fate."

"My fate?" Oliver said. "Not mine. Don't confuse me with anyone else."

Liebert mumbled an apology.

They drove on in silence for a few minutes. They were approaching a hilly area north of the city; in the near distance were mountains of a peculiar magenta color, partly obscured by mist. Oliver still felt that uncharacteristic euphoria, as if he were in a dream, a kind of paradise, and on all sides miracles ringed him in. He had not been prepared for the physical beauty of this place, or for the liveliness of its people. And his translator, Liebert, was quite a surprise. He spoke English with very little accent, clear-voiced, boyish, attentive to Oliver's every hesitation or expression of curiosity, exactly as if he could read Oliver's thoughts. He evidently took it as his solemn duty to make Oliver comfortable in every way. His manner was both shy and composed, childlike and remarkably mature. He had a sweet, melancholy, shadowed face with a thick head of dark curly hair and a widow's peak above a narrow forehead; his cheekbones were Slavic; his complexion was pale but with a faint rosy cast to it, as if the blood hummed warmly close beneath the skin. Large brown eyes, a long nose, ears too large for his slender face...something about him put Oliver in mind of a nocturnal animal, quick, furtive, naturally given to silence. In general he had an ascetic appearance. No doubt he was very poor, in his ill-fitting tweed suit and scuffed brown shoes, his hair crudely cut, so short that it emphasized the thinness of his neck and the prominence of his Adam's apple. Not handsome, perhaps, but attractive in his own way. Oliver liked him very much.

"If you would like, perhaps another meeting could be arranged," he said softly. "That is, it would not be impossible."

"Another meeting? With her?"

"If you would like," Liebert said.

Love: loss of equilibrium. Imbalance. Something fundamental to one's being, an almost physical certainty of self, is violated.

Oliver had loved women in the past and he had felt, even, this distressing physical urgency, this anxiety, before; but it had never blossomed so quickly, based on so little evidence. The night of the reception at the Institute he had slept poorly, rehearsing in his sleep certain phrases he would say to Alisa, pleading with her, begging her. For what? And why? She was a striking woman, perhaps not beautiful; it was natural that he might be attracted to her, though his experiences with women in recent years had been disappointing. But the intensity of his feeling worried him. It was exactly as if something foreign to his nature had infiltrated his system, had found him vulnerable, had shot his temperature up by several degrees. And he rejoiced in it, despite his worry and an obscure sense of shame. He really rejoiced in it. He woke, poured himself some of the sweet-tasting brandy he had left on his night table, lay back upon the goose-feather pillows, and thought of her. Was it possible he could see her again? Under what pretext? He was leaving in four days. Possibly he could extend his visit. Possibly not.

He recalled her bony, broad cheekbones, the severity of her gaze, her rather startled smile. A stranger. One of many strangers. In this phase of his life, Oliver thought, he met only strangers; he had no wish to see people he knew.

I love you. I want . . . what do I want? . . . I want to know more about you.

A mistake, but he could not resist pouring more brandy into the glass. It tasted like sweet, heavy syrup at first and then, after a few seconds, like pure alcohol, blistering, acidic. One wished to obliterate the strong taste with the sweet—the impulse was to sip a little more.

According to his clock in its small leather traveling case it was three-fifteen.

I want . . . what do I want? he murmured aloud.

Liebert translated for Oliver: "She says that the 'extravagance' you speak of in Androv's chronicles . . . and in our literature generally . . . is understood here as exaggeration . . . metaphors? . . . metaphors, yes, for interior states. But we ourselves, we are not extravagant in our living."

"Of course I only know Androv's work in translation," Oliver

said quickly. "It reads awkwardly, rather like Dreiser?... do you
know the name, the novelist?... one of our distinguished American novelists, no longer so popular as he once was.... I was
enormously impressed with the stubbornness, the resiliency, the
audacity of Androv's characters, and despite his technique of
exaggeration they seemed to me very lifelike." He paused, in
order to give Liebert the opportunity to translate. He was
breathing quickly, watching Alisa's face. They were having a
drink in the hotel lounge, a dim, quiet place where morose
potted plants of a type Oliver did not recognize grew more than
six feet high, drooping over the half dozen marble tables. Oliver
was able to see his own reflection in a mirror across the room;
the mirror looked smoky, webbed as if with a spider's web; his
own face hovered there indistinct and pale. His constant, rather
nervous smile was not visible.

In the subdued light of the hotel lounge Alisa seemed to him
more beautiful than before. Her dark hair was drawn back and
fastened in an attractive French twist; it was not done carelessly
into a bun or a knot, the way many local women wore their hair;
it shone with good health. She wore a white blouse and, again,
the old-fashioned cameo broach, and a hip-length sweater of
some coarse dark wool, and a nondescript skirt that fell well
below her knees. Her eyes were slightly slanted, almond-shaped,
dark, glistening; her cheekbones, like Liebert's, were prominent.
Oliver guessed her to be about thirty-five, a little older than he
had thought. But striking—very striking. Every movement of
hers charmed him. Her mixture of shyness and composure, her
quick contralto voice, her habit of glancing from Oliver to
Liebert to Oliver again, almost flirtatiously—he knew he was
staring rudely at her, but he could not look away.

"She says—Of course we have a reputation for audacity; how
else could we have survived? The blend of humor and mor-
bidity... the bizarre tall tales... 'deaths and weddings,' if you
are familiar with the allusion?... no?... she is referring to the
third volume of *The Peasants*," Liebert murmured. Oliver nodded as if he were following all this. In fact he had lost track of
the conversation; the woman fascinated him; he was vexed with
the thought that he had seen her somewhere before, had in some

way known her before.... And he had read only the first two volumes of Androv's massive work. "From the early fifteenth century, as you know, most of the country has been under foreign dominion...the most harsh, the Turks...centuries of oppression...between 1941 and 1945 alone there were two million of us murdered.... Without the 'extravagance' and even the mania of high spirits, how could we have survived?"

"I know, I understand, I am deeply sympathetic," Oliver said at once.

He could not relax, though he had had two drinks that afternoon. Something was urgent, crucial—he must not fail—but he could not quite comprehend what he must do. An American traveler, not really a tourist, prominent enough in his own country to merit the designation of "cultural emissary"—the State Department's term, not his own—he heard his own accent and his own predictable words with a kind of revulsion, as if, here, in this strange, charming country, the personality he had created for himself over a forty-three-year period were simply inadequate: shallow, superficial, hypocritical. He had not suffered. He could pretend knowledge and sympathy, but of course he was an impostor; he had not suffered except in the most ordinary of ways—an early, failed marriage; a satisfactory but not very exciting profession; the stray, undefined disappointments of early middle age. He listened to the woman's low, beautifully modulated voice, and to his translator's voice; he observed their perfect manners, their rather shabby clothing, and judged himself inferior. He hoped they would not notice. Liebert, who had spent so many patient hours with him, must sense by now his own natural superiority; must have some awareness of the irony of their relative positions. Oliver hoped the young man would not resent him, would not turn bitterly against him before the visit came to a conclusion. It seemed to him an ugly fact of life: that he, Oliver, had money, had a certain measure of prestige, however lightly he valued it, and had, most of all, complete freedom to travel anywhere he wished. The vast earth was his—as much of it as he cared to explore. Other cultures, other ways of life were open to his investigation. Even the past was his, for he could visit places of antiquity, could assemble countless books and valuable objects, could pursue any interest of his to its culmination. As the editor and publisher of a distinguished magazine, which featured essays on international culture, with as little emphasis as possible upon politics, Oliver was welcome nearly anywhere; he knew several languages—French, Italian, Spanish—and if he did not know a country's language a skillful interpreter was assigned to him and there was rarely any difficulty. Though he was accustomed to think of himself as colorless, as a failure—as a young man he had wanted to be a poet and a playwright—it was nevertheless true that he was a public success, and that he had a certain amount of power. Alisa and Liebert, however, were powerless; in a sense they were prisoners.

Of course they proclaimed their great satisfaction with post-war events. The Nazis had been driven back, another world power had come to their aid, the government under which they now lived was as close to perfection as one might wish. Compared to their tumultuous, miserable past, how sunny their present seemed!—of course they were happy. But they were prisoners just the same. They could not leave their country. It might even be the case that they could not leave this particular city without good cause. Oliver happened to know that nearly one-third of the population was involved, on one level or another, in espionage—neighbors reporting on neighbors, relatives on relatives, students on teachers, teachers on supervisors, friends on friends. It was a way of life. As Liebert had said the other day, it was nothing other than ordinary life for them.

Oliver knew. He knew. The two of them were fortunate just to have jobs that weren't manual; they were fortunate to be as free as they were, talking with an American. He believed he could gauge their fate in the abstract, in the collective, no matter that the two were really strangers to him. He knew and he did sympathize and, in spite of his better judgment, he wished he could help them.

At dusk they walked three abreast along the sparsely lit boulevard, the main street of the city; Oliver was to be taken to a workingman's café; he was tired of the hotel food, the expensive dinners. They spoke now of the new buildings that were

being erected, south of the city, along the sea cliff; they told
Oliver that he must take time to visit one of the excavations
farther to the south—he would see Roman ornaments, coins,
grave toys, statuary. "Alisa says—the evidence of other centuries and other civilizations is so close to us," Liebert murmured,
"we are unable to place too much emphasis upon the individual,
the ephemeral. Do you see? I have often thought along those
lines myself."

"Yes, I suppose so—I suppose that's right," Oliver said
slowly.

Alisa said something to him, looking up at him. Liebert, on
his right side, translated at once: "Future generations are as
certain as the past—there is a continuity—there is a progress, an
evolution. It is clear, it is scientifically demonstrable."

"Is it?" Oliver said, for a moment wondering if it might be so.
"Yes—that's possible—I'm sure that's possible."

Liebert translated his words and Alisa laughed.

"Why is she laughing? What did you say?" Oliver asked,
smiling.

"I said—only what you said. I translated your words faithfully," Liebert said rather primly.

"She has such a ready, sweet laugh," Oliver said. "She's so
charming, so unconscious of herself.... Ask her, Liebert, where
she's from ... where she went to school ... where she lives ... what
her life is like."

"All that?" Liebert asked. "So much!"

"But we have all evening, don't we?" Oliver said plaintively.
"... All night?"

That day he had been a guest at the District Commissioner's
home, for a two-hour luncheon. He had been driven to the
village where the poet Hisjak had been born. Along with another guest of honor, an Italian novelist, he had been shown
precious documents—the totally illegible manuscripts of an
unknown writer, unknown at least to Oliver—kept in a safe in a
museum. The first two evenings of his visit had been spent at
endless dinners. He had witnessed a troupe of youthful dancers
in rehearsal; he had admired the many statues of heroes placed

about the city; he had marveled over the Byzantine domes, the towers and vaulting roofs and fountains. But his hours with Alisa and Liebert were by far the most enjoyable; he knew he would never forget them.

They ate a thick, greasy stew of coarse beef and vegetables, and many slices of whole-grain bread and butter, and drank two bottles of wine, of a dry, tart nature, quite unfamiliar to Oliver. The three of them sat at a corner table in an utterly unimpressive restaurant; it was crude and brightly lit and noisy as an American diner. At first the other patrons took notice of them, but as time passed and the restaurant grew noisier they were able to speak without being overheard. Oliver was very happy. He felt strangely free, like a child. The food was delicious; he kept complimenting them, and asking Liebert to tell the waitress, and even to tell the cook; the bread, especially, seemed extraordinary—he insisted that he had never tasted bread so good. "How can I leave? Where can I go from here?" he said jokingly. They were served small, flaky tarts for dessert, and Oliver ate his in two or three bites, though he was no longer hungry and the oversweet taste, apricots and brandy and raw dark sugar, was not really to his liking.

"You are all so wonderful... " he said.

Alisa sat across from him, Liebert sat to his left. The table was too small for their many dishes and glasses and silverware. They laughed together like old friends, easily, intimately. Alisa showed her gums as she laughed—no self-consciousness about her—utterly natural, direct. Her eyes narrowed to slits and opened wide again sparkling. The wine had brought a flush to her cheeks. Liebert too was expansive, robust. He no longer played the role of the impoverished, obsequious student. Sometimes he spoke to Oliver without feeling the necessity to translate his English for Alisa; sometimes he and Alisa exchanged remarks, and though Oliver did not know what they were saying, or why they laughed so merrily, he joined them in their laughter. Most of the time, however, Liebert translated back and forth from Oliver to Alisa, from Alisa to Oliver, rapidly, easily, always with genuine interest. Oliver liked the rhythm that was established: like a game, like a piece of music, like the bantering of love. Oliver's words in English translated into Alisa's language, Alisa's words translated into Oliver's language, magically. Surely it was magic. Oliver asked Alisa about her background, about the village she had grown up in; he asked her about her parents, about her work. It turned out that her father had been a teacher also, a music teacher at one of the colleges—"very distinguished and well loved"—but he had become ill, there was no treatment available, he had wanted to return to his home district to die. Oliver listened sympathetically. There was more to it, he supposed, there was something further about it...but he could not inquire. And what about the husband? But he could not inquire; he did not dare.

"You are all so remarkably free of bitterness," he said.

Liebert translated. Alisa replied. Liebert hesitated before saying: "Why should we be bitter? We live with complexity. You wish simplicity in your life...good divided sharply from evil, love divided from hate...beauty from ugliness. We have always been different. We live with complexity; we would not recognize the world otherwise."

Oliver was staring at Alisa. "Did you really say that?" he asked.

"Of course she said that. Those words exactly," Liebert murmured.

"She's so...she's so very... I find her so very charming," Oliver said weakly. "Please don't translate! Please. Do you see? It's just that I find her so... I admire her without reservation," he said, squeezing Liebert's arm. "I find it difficult to reply to her. Central Europe is baffling to me; I expected to be meeting quite different kinds of people; your closed border, your wartime consciousness that seems never to lift, your reputation for...for certain inexplicable..." Both Liebert and Alisa were watching him, expressionless. He fell silent. Absurdly, he had been about to speak of the innumerable arrests and imprisonments, even of the tortures reported in the West, but it seemed to him now that perhaps these reports were lies. He did not know what to believe.

"Freedom and constraint cannot be sharply divided, the one from the other," Liebert said coldly. "Freedom is a relative

thing. It is relative to the context, to the humanity it serves
...shelters. For instance, your great American cities, they are so
famed, they are 'free'; you would boast citizens can come and
go as they wish...each in his automobile—isn't that so? But, in
fact, we know that your people are terrified of being hurt by one
another. They are terrified of being killed by their fellow citizens. In this way," Liebert said, smiling, "in this way it must be
judged that the nature of freedom is not so simple. But it is
always political."

"There's a difference between self-imposed restrictions and
...and the restrictions of a state like yours," Oliver said, obscurely hurt, blinking. He had no interest in defending his
nation. He did not care about it at all, not at the moment. "But
perhaps you are correct, the issue is always political, even when
it is baffling and obscure.... In America we have too much
freedom and the individual is free to hurt others, this is an
excess of...am I speaking too quickly?...this is an excess rather
than... But I don't wish to talk of such things," he said softly.
"Not tonight. It is more important, our being together. Do you
agree? Yes? Ask Alisa—does she agree?"

They agreed. They laughed together like old friends.

"Alisa says—We must live our lives in the interstices of the
political state," Liebert said slyly, "like sparrows who make
their nests on window ledges or street lamps. They are happy
there until the happiness stops. We are happy, until it stops. But
perhaps it will not stop for many years—who can predict?
Political oppression is no more a disaster than an accident on
the highway or a fatal disease or being born crippled—"

"Disaster is disaster," Oliver said thickly. "What do we care?
There isn't time. I must leave in a few days.... I admire you
both so very, very much. You're noble, you're brave, you're
attractive...she is beautiful, isn't she?...beautiful! I've never
met anyone so intelligent and beautiful at the same time, so
vivacious, good-natured.... Will you tell her that? Please?"

Liebert turned to her and spoke. She lowered her head,
fussed with her hair, reddened slightly, frowned. A long moment passed. She glanced shyly at Oliver. Seeing the desperation in his eyes, she managed to smile.

"Thank you," Oliver whispered. "Thank you both so very much."

Something was stinging him.

Bedbugs?

His arms were curiously leaden; he could not move; he could not rake his nails against his sides, his abdomen, his buttocks, his back. He groaned but did not wake. The stinging became a single sweeping flame that covered his body, burned fiercely. "Alisa?" he said. "Are you here? Are you hiding?"

He was in the Old City, the City of Stone. Much of it had been leveled during the war, but there were ancient buildings—fortresses, inns, cathedrals. The weight of time. The weight of the spirit. On all sides voices were chattering in that exquisite, teasing language he could not decipher. They were mocking him, jeering at him. They knew him very well. He was to be led to their shrine, where a miracle would be performed. The holy saint of Toskinjevec, patron saint of lepers, epileptics, the crippled and the insane and the fanatic.... He was being hurried along the cobblestone streets. There were heavy oak doors with iron hinges; there were rusted latches and locks; walls slime-green with mold, beginning to crumble. Footsteps rang and echoed. Liebert held his hand, murmured words of comfort, stroked his head. He wanted only to obey. "Where is she? Is she already there?" he whispered. Liebert told him to be still—he must not speak! Someone was following them. Someone wished to hurt them. Oliver saw, in a panic, the greenish-copper steeple of an old church; he could take refuge in its ruins; no one would find them there. The main part of the building had been reduced to rubble. A wall remained and on this wall were posters of the great President—charmingly candid shots that showed the man with one of his children, and in a peasant's costume, and with a rifle raised to his shoulder, one eye squinted shut, and on the ledge above a waterfall, his arm raised in a salute to the crowd gathered below. Oliver hurried. Someone would stand guard for them—one of the men he had seen in the restaurant, had seen without really considering; a young black-haired man who had been playing chess with a friend, and who had not glanced up a single time at Oliver and his friends. But now he would stand guard. Now he was to be trusted.

They descended into a cellar. Everywhere there were slabs of stone, broken plasterboard, broken glass. Weeds grew abundantly in the cracks. "Hurry," Liebert urged, dragging him forward. Then Oliver was with her, clutching at her. By a miracle they were together. He kissed her desperately, recklessly. She pretended to resist. "No, there isn't time, there isn't enough time," he begged, "no, don't stop me...." She went limp; she put her arms around his neck; they struggled together, panting, while the young translator urged them on, anxious, a little annoyed. Oliver's entire body stung. Waves of heat swept over him and broke into tiny bits so that he groaned aloud. He wanted her so violently, he was so hungry for her, for her or for something.... "How can I bring you with me?" he said. "I love you, I won't surrender you." She spoke in short melodic phrases. He could not understand. Now she too was anxious, clutching at him, pressing herself against him. Oliver could not bear it. He was going mad. Then, out of the corner of his eye, he happened to see someone watching them. The police!... But no, it was a poorly dressed old man, a cripple, peering at them from behind a broken wall. He was deformed: his legs were mere stumps. Oliver stared, in a panic. He could not believe what he saw. Behind the old man were two or three others, half crawling, pushing themselves along through the debris by the exertions of their arms, their legs cut off at the thigh. They were bearded, wide-eyed, gaping, moronic. He understood that they were moronic. Oliver tried to lead Alisa away, but she resisted. Evidently the men were from a nearby hospital and were harmless. They had been arrested in an abortive uprising of some sort, years before, and punished in ways fitting their audacity; but now they were harmless, harmless....

His sexual desire died at once. The dream died at once.

He could not sleep. The dream had left him terrified and nauseous.

During the past few years life had thinned out for Oliver. It had become insubstantial, unreal, too spontaneous to have much value. Mere details, pieces, ugly tiny bits. Nothing was connected and nothing made sense. Was this "life"?—an idle pointless flow? He had watched it, knowing that one must be attentive, one must be responsible. But he had not really believed in it. There was no internal necessity, no order, only that jarring spontaneity, a world of slivers and teasing fragments. Ugly and illusory.

Here, however, things seemed different. He could breathe here. There were travelers who could not accept the reality of the countries they visited, and who yearned, homesick, for their own country, for their own language; but Oliver was not one of them. He would not have cared—not for a moment!—if the past were eradicated, his home country destroyed and erased from history.

He poured brandy into a glass, his fingers steady.

"Would I mourn...? Never."

The dream had frightened him, but it was fading now. It was not important. He had had too much to eat, too much to drink. His emotional state was unnatural. Love was an imbalance: he was temporarily out of control. But he would be all right. He had faith in himself.

The woman lived in a one-room apartment, Liebert had informed him. She shared it with another teacher at the high school, a woman. Should Oliver wish to visit her there—how could it be arranged? She could not come to the hotel. That was out of the question. Liebert had muttered something about the possibility of the other woman going to visit her family...though this would involve some expenses...she would need money. It would be awkward, but it could be arranged. If so, then Alisa would be alone and Oliver would be welcome to visit her. There might be danger, still. Or was there no danger? Oliver really did not know.

"And what of her husband?" Oliver had asked hesitantly.

"Ah—there is no risk. The man is in a hospital at Kanleža, in the mountains...he is receiving treatment for emotional maladjustment...a very sad case. Very sad. It is tragic, but he is no risk; do not worry about him," Liebert said softly.

They looked at each other for a moment. Oliver warmed,

reddened. He did not know if he was terribly ashamed or simply excited.

"I love her," he whispered. "I can't help it."

Liebert might not have heard, he had spoken so softly. But he did not ask Oliver to repeat his words.

"How much money would the woman need?" Oliver asked helplessly.

They had been here, in this room. The money had changed hands and Liebert had gone and Oliver had undressed at once, exhausted from the evening, from all the eating and drinking and talking. He had wanted only to sleep. His fate was decided, he would meet Alisa the following day, he would extend his visit for another week perhaps, in order to see her every day; but now he must sleep, he was sick with exhaustion. And so he had slept. But dreams disturbed him: in them he was trying to speak, trying to make himself understood, while strangers mocked and jeered. The last dream, of Alisa and the deformed old men, was the most violent of all, a nightmare of the sort he had not had for years. When he woke, he felt debased, poisoned. It was as if a poison of some sort had spread throughout his body.

He sat up, leafing through a guidebook in English, until dawn.

"But I don't understand. Where is Mr. Liebert?"

His new translator was a stout, perspiring man in his fifties, no more than five feet four inches tall. He wore a shiny black suit with a vest and oversized buttons, of black plastic. Baldness had enlarged his round face. His eyebrows were snarled and craggy, his lips pale, rubbery. With a shrug of his shoulders he dismissed Liebert. "Who knows? There was important business. Back home, called away. Not your concern."

He smiled. Oliver stared, thinking: He's a nightmare. He's from a nightmare. But the man was real, the bright chilly morning was real, Oliver's dismay and alarm were real. He tried to protest, saying that he had liked Liebert very much, the two of them had understood each other very well; but the new translator merely smiled stupidly, as before. "I am your escort now and your translator," he repeated.

Oliver made several telephone calls, but there was nothing to be done.

"I do not have the acquaintance of Mr. Liebert," the new translator said as they walked out together. One eyelid descended in a wink. "But there is no lack of sympathy. It is all the same. —A nice day, isn't it? That is acacia tree in blossom; is lovely, eh? Every spring."

The man's accent was guttural. Oliver could not believe his bad luck. He walked in a trance, thinking of Alisa, of Liebert—Liebert, who had been so charming, so quick. It did not seem possible that this had happened.

That day he saw the posters of his dream. He saw a tarnished coppery-green steeple rising above a ruined church. He saw, in the distance, long, low, curiously narrow strips of cloud or mist rising from the sea, reaching into the lower part of the city. Beside him, the squat, perspiring man chattered in babyish English, translated signs and menus, kept asking Oliver in his mechanical chirping voice, "It is nice, eh? Spring day. Good luck." From time to time he winked at Oliver as if there were a joke between them.

Oliver shuddered.

The city looked different. There was too much traffic—buses, motorbikes, vans of one kind or another—and from the newer section of the city, where a number of one-story factories had been built, there came invisible clouds of poison. The sky was mottled; though it was May fifteenth, it was really quite cold.

"Where is Liebert?" Oliver asked, more than once. "He and I were friends... we understood each other...."

They went to a folk museum where they joined another small group. Oliver tried to concentrate. He smiled, he was courteous as always, he made every effort to be civil. But the banalities!—the idiotic lies! His translator repeated what was said in a thick, dull voice, passing no judgment—as Liebert would have done, slyly—and Oliver was forced to reply, to say something. He stammered, he heard his voice proclaiming the most asinine things—bald, blunt compliments, flattery. Seven or eight men in a group for an endless luncheon, exchanging banalities, hypocritical praise, chatter about the weather and the blossoming trees and the National Ballet. The food was too rich, and when

Oliver's came to him it was already lukewarm. The butter was unsalted and tasteless. One of the men, a fat, pompous official, exactly like an official in a political cartoon, smoked a cigar and the smoke drifted into Oliver's face. He tried to bring up the subject of his first translator but was met with uncomprehending stares.

Afterward he was taken, for some reason, to the offices of the Ministry of Agriculture; he was introduced to the editor of a series of agricultural pamphlets; it was difficult for him to make sense of what was being said. Some of these people spoke English as well as his translator, and he had the idea that others merely pretended not to know English. There was a great deal of chatter. He thought of Alisa and felt suddenly exhausted. He would never get to her now—it was impossible. Beside him the fat sweating man kept close watch. What was being said?— words. He leaned against a gritty windowsill, staring absently out at the innumerable rooftops, the ugly chimneys and water tanks, the banal towers. He remembered the poison of his dream and could taste it in the air now; the air of this city was remarkably polluted.

"You are tired now? Too much visit? You rest, eh?"

"Yes."

"You leave soon, it was said? Day after tomorrow?"

"Yes. I think so."

There were streetcars and factory whistles. Automobile horns. In the street someone stared rudely at him. Oliver wondered what these people saw—a tall, sandy-haired man in his early forties, distracted, haggard, rather vain in his expensive clothes? They looked at his clothes, not at him. At his shoes. They did not see him at all; they had no use for him.

"You are maybe sick...?"

"A little. I think. Yes."

"Ah!" he said, in a parody of sympathy. "You go to room, rest. Afterward perk up. Afterward there is plan for evening— yes? All set?"

"Evening? I thought this evening was free—"

The man winked. "She is friend—old friend. Sympathizes you."

"I don't understand," Oliver stammered.

"All understand. All sympathize one another," the man said cheerfully.

"Is wealthy? Own several automobiles? What about house—houses? Parents are living? How many brothers and sisters? Is married, has children? How many? Names?"

The three of them sat together, not in Alisa's room but in another café. Oliver was paying for their drinks. He was paying for everything. The woman's curt, rude questions were being put to him in clusters and he managed to answer, as succinctly as possible, trying not to show his despair. When his translator repeated Oliver's answers, Alisa nodded emphatically, always the same way, her eyes bright, deliberately widened. Wisps of hair had come loose about her forehead; it annoyed Oliver that she did not brush them away. She was a little drunk, her laughter was jarring, she showed her gums when she laughed—he could hardly bear to watch her.

"Say like our country very much? Good. New place going up—there is new company, Volkswagen—many new jobs. When you come back, another year, lots new things. You are friendly, always welcome. Very nice. Good to know...."

The conversation seemed to rattle on without Oliver's intervention. He heard his voice, heard certain simple-minded replies. Alisa and the fat man laughed merrily. They were having a fine time. Oliver drank because he had nothing else to do; whenever he glanced at his watch, the others looked at it also, with childish, open avarice. Time did not pass. He dreaded any mention of the room, of the alleged roommate who had left town, but he had the idea that if he refused to mention it, the others would not mention it either. They were having too good a time drinking. They murmured to each other in their own language and broke into peals of laughter, and other patrons, taking notice, grinned as if sharing their good spirits.

"Is nice place? All along here, this street. Yes? Close to hotel. All close. She says—Is wife of yours pretty? Young? Is not jealous, you on long trip, take airplane? Any picture of wife? Babies?"

"No wife," Oliver said wearily. "No babies."

"No—? Is not married."

"Is not," Oliver said.

"Not *love?* Not once?"

"Not," he said.

The two of them exchanged incredulous looks. Then they laughed again and Oliver sat, silent, while their laughter washed about him.

Being driven to the airport he saw, on the street, a dark-haired cyclist pedaling energetically—a young long-nosed handsome boy in a pullover sweater—Liebert—his heart sang: *Liebert.* But of course it was not Liebert. It was a stranger, a boy of about seventeen, no one Oliver knew. Then, again, at the airport he saw him. Again it was Liebert. A mechanic in coveralls, glimpsed in a doorway, solemn, dark-eyed, with a pronounced widow's peak and prominent cheekbones: Liebert. He wanted to push his way through the crowd to him. To his translator. He wanted to touch him again, wanted to squeeze his hands, his arm. But of course the young man was a stranger—his gaze was dull, his mouth slack. Oliver stared at him just the same. His plane was loading; it was time for him to leave, yet he stood there, paralyzed.

"What will I do for the rest of my life...?" he called to the boy.

Bloodstains

H E SAT. He turned to see that he was sharing the bench with
a young mother who did not glance around at him. The
park they were in was a small noisy island around which traffic
moved in a continual stream. Aged, listless men sat on other
benches—a few women shoppers, pausing to rest, their eyes
eagle-bright and their gloved fingers tugging at the straps of
shoes or at hemlines—a few children, urchins from the tenement
homes a few blocks off this wide main street. Great untidy
flocks of pigeons rose and settled again and rose, startled,
scattering. Lawrence Pryor looked at everything keenly. He
knew he was out of place here; he had come down from his
office because his eleven o'clock appointment had canceled out;
he was free for half an hour. The only place to sit had been
beside this pretty young mother, who held her baby up to her
face and who took no interest at all in the pigeons or the
chattering children or Lawrence himself. He was sitting in a
patch of sunlight that fell upon him through the narrow channel
between two tall buildings, as if singling him out for a blessing.

All these women shoppers! He watched them cross quickly to
the island, and quickly over to the other curb, for they rarely
had the time to sit and rest. They were in a hurry. Because of
them, hurrying across the street, traffic was backed up waiting

to make right-hand turns. Out of the crowd of shoppers he saw a blond woman appear, walking briskly and confidently. She hurried against a red light, and a horn sounded. How American she was, how well-dressed and sure of herself! Lawrence found himself staring at her, imagining the face that might reveal itself to him if he were to approach her—startled and elegant and composed, seeing by his face that he was no danger to her, no danger.

She did not cross the little park but took the sidewalk that led around it. Avoiding the bench-sitters and the pigeons. Lawrence was disappointed. And then, watching her, he saw that the woman was familiar—her brisk, impatient walk, her trim blue coat—and, indeed, he knew her well; the woman was his own wife! He tapped his jaw with the tips of his fingers in a gesture of amused surprise. Of course! Beverly! As if acting out embarrassment for an audience, he smiled up toward the sky...and when he looked back, his wife was already hurrying across the street, moving bravely against the light while buses and taxicabs pressed forward.

He got to his feet to follow her. But an extraordinarily tall man got in front of him, walking quickly, and then a small crowd of women shoppers, everyone hurrying now that the light had turned green. Something held Lawrence back. The tall man was hurrying as if to catch up with Beverly. He was strangely tall, freakishly tall, with silver-gray hair that was bunched around his head in tight little curls, like grapes. He wore a dark coat and, on the back of his neck, there was a vivid red birthmark, a stain in the shape of a finger. The shoppers moved forward, in front of Lawrence, and the tall man and Lawrence's wife moved into the distance. All this motion made Lawrence feel slightly dizzy.

The legend about him was his fanaticism about work: Beverly complained of this, she worried about it, she was proud of it. He was a doctor and his patients were sacred to him. And so he had better not run after his wife, because she would be alarmed to see him out on the street at this time of day and because it might be ten or fifteen minutes before he could get away again. She might want him to have lunch with her. She might want him to go into stores with her. Better to stay behind, to stay hidden. So he watched her disappear—his wife hurrying into the midst of the city—and he sat down again, feeling oddly pleased and excited. He felt as if something secret had been revealed to him.

Beside him the young woman was leaning her face to her child, whispering. She had a pale, angular face, illuminated by love, or by the child's reflecting face, or by the narrow patch of sunlight that was moving slowly from Lawrence and onto her. Women, seen like this, were gifts to men.

He considered smiling at her. But no, that might be a mistake—this was not a city in which people smiled freely at one another.

Herb Altman came into the office, striding forward with his head slightly lowered. Bald, but only forty-five. He had a portly, arrogant body and his clothes were always jaunty—today he wore a bright yellow necktie that jumped in Lawrence's vision.

Shaking hands.

"How are you?"

"Not well. I can't sleep. I never sleep, you know that," Altman said.

He sat and began to talk. His voice was urgent and demanding. As he spoke he shook his head so that his cheeks shivered. Altman's wife, Connie, was a friend of Lawrence's wife. It seemed to Lawrence that the women in their circle were all close friends; in a way they blended into one another. The husbands too seemed to blend into one another. Many of them had several lives, but the lives were somehow shared. They lived in one dimension but turned up in other dimensions—downtown late in the afternoon or in downriver suburbs. Their expensive homes and automobiles and boats could not quite contain them. Too much energy. Urgent, clicking, demanding words. While Altman talked angrily about his insomnia and switched onto the complaints of his wife and then onto the complaints of his girl, Lawrence again saw his wife in the distance of his imagination, a dream he had dreamed while awake, moving freely and happily along the sidewalk of this massive city.

What mystery was in her, this woman he had lived with for

so long? They had one child, a daughter. They had known each other for two decades. And yet, seeing her like that, Lawrence had been struck by the mystery of her separateness, her being. . . .

Altman said in a furious whisper, "I'm going to have her followed!"

"Your wife?"

"Evie. *Evelyn*. Twenty-five years old, a baby, and she tells me the plans she dreams up! She wants me to marry her next year!"

The numerals of Lawrence's watch were greenish-white, glowing up out of a dark face. They were supposed to glow in the dark, but they glowed in the light as well.

"All right," Altman said, seeing Lawrence look at his watch, "so I'm wasting your time. So. Check my heart, my blackened lungs, tap me on the back to see if I have echoes inside, to see what's hollowed out—I'm a sick man, we both know that. Here I am."

In the end Lawrence did as he always did: refilling Altman's prescription for barbiturates. It was for six refills and Altman would be back again in a few weeks.

At the door Altman paused dramatically. His white shirtfront bulged. "Why do they keep after me?" he said. "Larry, what is it? Why are they always after me? I can't sleep at night. I'm planning a trip in my mind, but when I get up I can't remember it—I don't sleep but I don't remember what I think about— Why are they always after me, those women? What are they doing to me?"

Lawrence and his wife and daughter lived a few blocks from the lake in a brick home that had been painted white. The house glowed in the air of twilight. It had the ghostly weightless look of something at the bottom of a lake, made perfect. It was a place in which Lawrence might sleep soundly, as he had never slept in his parents' oversized, combative home in Philadelphia. No more of that life! He had blocked out even the memory of that life.

Behind him in the city were his patients and the unhappy memories of his patients. Ten, sometimes twelve hours of ailments—the shame of being sick, of being weak, of uttering words better left unsaid. Office hours were worse than hospital hours. During the day Lawrence's hand turned shaky and reluctant, writing out so many prescriptions, smiling with his prescribed smile, a forty-year-old face that was in danger of wearing out. His patients had too many faces. They were blotched or sullen or impatient or, like Altman's, familiar but eerily distant, demanding something Lawrence could not give and could not understand.

Many of the ailments were imaginary. They existed, yes, but they were imaginary; how to cure them?

The telephone was ringing as he entered his home. He had the idea that it had been ringing for some time. When he went to answer it, in the kitchen, it stopped ringing and he stood with his hand out, a few inches above the receiver, listening to the silence of the house.

His mother is coming to visit, due the next morning on the nine-thirty flight from Philadelphia.

Beverly and Edie are going out again; they get in each other's way by the closet. Edie, fourteen years old and taller than her mother, sticks her arms angrily into her coat. The coat is khaki-colored and lined with fake wool, years old; Edie will not give it up in spite of her mother's pleas. Lawrence stands with the evening newspaper, watching them. It is six-thirty. "Do you have to go out now?" he says.

"I forgot to get new towels. I wanted to get new towels for your mother, I can't let her use those old ones," Beverly says.

"New towels? You're going out now for new towels?"

"Everything is old. It isn't *good enough for her.*"

Beverly's jaws are hardening. Her eyes are bright, alert, restless. Edie is shiny-faced and almost pretty, but always in a hurry, always bumping into things. It is obvious to Lawrence that his wife and daughter have been arguing about something. Edie knocks against a chair in the foyer and screws up her face. "God!" she winces.

"Did you go shopping downtown today?" Lawrence asks his wife.

She is frowning into her purse, looking for something. "No."

"I thought I saw you."

"Saw me? When?"

"A little before noon."

She stares at him, closing her purse. There is a cold, bright look around her eyes, a look Lawrence cannot understand. Then she smiles. "Oh yes, I was downtown...I just drove down and back, looking for some things I couldn't get out here.... I've been running around all day. I had to pick Edie up at school and take her to the dentist and now...now I have to go out again."

"You're making too much out of it. My mother doesn't expect you to fuss over her."

She shakes her head and avoids his eye. He thinks of the tall, silver-haired man with the birthmark, hurrying along after her as if to catch up with her.

His mother. The airport. They have met his mother like this many times and each time they say the same things; it seems that the same crowds are at the airport. His mother begins at once to tell him about the news at home and she will continue to tell him of funerals and weddings, births, illnesses, surgery, unpleasant surprises, all the way home, though she has written him about these things in her weekly letters.

"Oh, look at this!" she says in disgust.

She holds up her hands for them to see her white gloves, which are soiled and even stained with something that looks like rust or blood, a very faint red-brown color.

"I'll wash them out for you, Mother," Beverly says at once.

"Traveling is so dirty. Filthy," Lawrence's mother says.

He recalls her having said that before.

While his mother and his wife talk, Lawrence drives in silence. He is happy that his mother is visiting them. She comes often, several times a year. Lawrence has the idea that she blames him for having left Philadelphia and come to this city of strangers where he has no relatives. The letters they write to each other do not seem to express them. Beneath his neat, typed lines, and beneath her slanted lines in their lavender ink, there seems to be another dimension, a submerged feeling or memory, that the two of them can only hint at but cannot express.

They are approaching Lawrence's home. "I like that house,"

his mother says flatly, as she always does. This seems to settle something. Lawrence and Beverly both feel relieved.

The old family home had been white also. Now Lawrence's mother lives in an apartment favored by other widows, but for decades of her life she lived in a house the size of a municipal building. In his dreams Lawrence sometimes climbs the stairway to the third floor, which had been closed off, to look through the stacks of his father's old medical journals, as he did when he was a child. There were bundles of journals. Small towers. He had spent many hours looking through them, fascinated.

His mother's presence in his house, his own house, makes Lawrence feel a little displaced. It seems to him that time is confused. His own age is uncertain. But he is a good host to his mother; he makes an effort to be gallant. After dinner that night they look through snapshots—another ritual. The snapshots are passed around. Then, leaning toward him, in a sudden stiff motion that makes him realize how his mother is corseted—his wife, also, her body slim and deft but smoothly hard to the touch—she hands him a photograph that had been taken years ago. That photograph again! It is Lawrence, Larry Jr., sitting on a spotted pony at some forgotten fair, a rented pony, Lawrence's dark hair combed down onto his forehead in a way that makes him look like a moron, his stare startled and vacuous, his mouth too timid to smile. Lawrence stares at the photograph. Why does his mother treasure it so much? Why does she always bring it along with the more recent snapshots, as if she doesn't remember she has shown it to him on her last visit?

"Look at that, isn't that darling? A darling boy?" she says stubbornly.

Lawrence stares down at his own face, which is blank and stark in the photograph. It was a face that might have become anything. Any personality might have inhabited it. It was so blank, that face—anything could inhabit it.

He stands suddenly. His mother and his wife stare at him in alarm.

"Larry? What's wrong?" Beverly says.

He passes his hand over his eyes. He sits down again.

"Nothing."

"Did you hear something—?"

"No. Nothing."

Two evenings later he is driving home when a car veers out around him, passing him with its horn blaring. The car is filled with kids—boys and girls—and he thinks he sees Edie in with them. His heart jumps. But he cannot be sure.

When he gets home, it is nearly dark. His mother kisses him on the side of the face. She is powdery and yet hard, a precise, stubborn little woman. What do they talk about all day, women? His mother and his wife? They are telling him now about what they have done today. Their chatter is like music, rising in snatches about them, airy and incomplete. It never quite completes itself; it has to continue.

"Is Edie home yet?" he says.

"No, not yet," says Beverly.

"Where is she?"

"She had something after school—choir practice—"

"All this time?"

"No, not all this time. She's probably at someone's house. She'll be home in a few minutes."

"But you don't know where she is?"

"Not exactly. What's wrong? Why are you so angry?"

"I'm not angry."

When she comes in he will find out nothing from her. Nothing. She will move her body jerkily through the kitchen and to the front closet, she will take off her coat, she will sit slouching at dinner and stare down into her plate, or stare dutifully up at him, and he will find out nothing about her, nothing. His heart pounds angrily. Once Beverly had said of Edie, "She has all that stuff on her face, but you should see her neck—she never washes. Oh, she's hopeless—what can I do?"

What can they do?

His mother asks him about his day. Did he work hard? Is he tired?

He answers her vaguely, listening for Edie to come in. But

when she does come in, he will find out nothing from her. His mother switches to another topic—complaints about one of his aunts—and he can't follow her. He is thinking of Edie, then he is thinking of his wife. Then he finds himself thinking of one of his patients, Connie Altman. She had wept in his office that morning. "I need something to help me sleep at night. I lie awake thinking. Then in the morning I can't remember what I was thinking about. I'm so nervous, my heart pounds, can you give me something stronger to help me sleep? Everything is running out...."

This had puzzled him. "What do you mean, everything is running out?"

"There isn't any point. I don't see it. We are all running out, people our age, things are running out of us ... draining out of us.... I will have to live out my life in this body...."

She was a woman of beauty, very small, with childish wrists and ankles. But her face had begun to harden in the last few years.

"I need something to help me sleep. Please. I know that in the other room *he* is awake, he can't sleep either, it drives me crazy! I prefer the nights he stays out. At least he isn't in the house, lying awake like me, I don't care who he's with.... I need something to help me sleep, please. I can't stand my thoughts all night long."

His daughter's room. Saturday afternoon. The house is empty for a few hours and he may walk through it, anywhere, because it is his house and all the rooms are his, his property.

Edie's room is piled with clothes, schoolbooks, shoes, junk. Two of the three dresser drawers are pulled out. The top of the dresser is cluttered. Lawrence's reflection moves into the mirror and he looks at himself in surprise—is that really him, Dr. Pryor? He is disappointed. He is even rather alarmed. The man reflected there in the smudged mirror bears little resemblance to the image of himself he carries with him in his imagination; it does not even resemble the man of recent snapshots. He stares, frankly bewildered. Why does his shirt appear to be rumpled when he put it on fresh only that morning—why is his face sallow, lined, why do his hands appear to be strangely empty, loose at his sides? For a moment he doubts that the man in the mirror is really Dr. Pryor. He doubts the necessity of his continuing to exist in that body, waking each morning to that particular face and body, out of all the multitudes of human beings. Is existence itself an illusion? he thinks. He smiles. In the mirror the sallow-skinned man smiles with him as if mocking him. No: perhaps he is sympathetic, perhaps he is in agreement. Is existence an illusion? A commonplace illusion?

He wakes from his trance and goes quickly to his daughter's dresser. Must not hesitate. Must move swiftly, confidently. He tugs at the first drawer: a jumble of stockings, black tights, bright red tights, knee-length woollen socks of various colors and designs; filmy, gauzy things tangled together; some stiffly new as if just taken from packages, some rather soiled, thrown into the drawer in a heap. A spool of black thread rolls noisily about. Lawrence is about to close the drawer when he remembers that it wasn't closed, it was open a few inches. Good. Good he remembered. He pulls out the second drawer, which sticks; he tugs at it and it nearly falls out; he exclaims in vexation. Here there are underclothes of various colors that release an air of freshness—clean from the laundry; but they too are rudely jumbled together.

Lawrence has never come into his daughter's room alone. Never. He would not violate her privacy; he would not dare anger her. But being here this afternoon, so close to her, so strangely intimate with her, he feels oddly pleased. She is very real to him at this moment. She might be standing close behind him, about to break into one of her breathless greetings—"Hi, Friend!" has been a maddeningly frequent greeting of hers this past month; perhaps it is in common usage among children her age—she might be about to hum into his ear one of her slangy, banal, mysterious little tunes.

He finds himself looking through the silky underclothes. Things stick together; there is the crackle of static electricity. He holds up a half-slip of mint green with tiny white bows on it. Pretty. It is very pretty. Probably a birthday or Christmas gift from her mother, probably not something she would have

bought for herself. He wants to rub it against his face. Very
carefully he folds it and puts it back, and discovers a book
hidden against the side of the drawer—a journal, a diary—is it a
diary?—but he's disappointed to see that it isn't a diary: instead
it is a small hardcover book, *Edgar Cayce and the Miracle of
Reincarnation*.

He does no more than leaf through the book, irritated. What
trash. How dare such books be published and sold. One sentence especially angers him: *Modern medical science has lagged
shamefully behind.* . . . He snaps the book shut and eases it back
into its hiding place. And now a kind of despair weakens him,
he doesn't know quite why. He touches the green slip again,
and a very silky—satiny?—pair of panties, pale blue with an
elastic band. He tries to see his daughter's face but she eludes
him. Oh Father, she might say, drawling, oh Daddy. For God's
sake! This afternoon she is at the shopping mall with her girl
friends. What do you do there all day? he asks, and she shrugs
her shoulders and says, Go through the stores and buy a few
things and sit around, and meet people, you know; have a few
Cokes; sit around and meet people and have a good time. Is
there anything wrong with that?

It is a mystery, his having a daughter. He cannot quite
comprehend it. He looks through the drawer farther, this sense
of despair rising strongly in him. . . . Rolled up in a ball, stuck
back in a corner of the drawer, is a pair of white underpants. He
picks them up. They have several bloodstains on them, thick
and stiff, almost caked. He stares. Why bloodstains? Why here?
For a moment he feels nothing, he thinks nothing. He is not even
surprised. Then it occurs to him that his daughter was ashamed
to put these soiled underpants in the wash, that she had meant
to wash them herself but had forgotten, and weeks, maybe
months have gone by . . . the blood grown old and hard, the
stains impossible to get out . . . she has forgotten about
them . . . balled up, rolled up and stuck in the corner of the
drawer, forgotten. . . .

His mother is talking with some friends of theirs who have
dropped in. An ordinary Sunday afternoon. Beverly is handing

drinks around. In the mirror above the fireplace his mother's bluish-white hair bobs weightlessly. On the mantel, long white candles in holders of silver, the wicks perfectly white, never burnt. What are they talking about so earnestly? Lawrence tries to listen. Beverly is chiding him gently for working so hard—it is a familiar pattern, almost a tune, the words of his mother to his father years ago—and he nods, smiles, he is Dr. Pryor, who works hard. The fact is that he has done nothing all day except sit in his study, at his desk, leafing through medical journals. He has not been able to concentrate on anything.

Ted Albrecht, a friend of many years, is talking in his usual fanciful manner. He is a stockbroker but thinks of himself as a social critic. A short man, with glasses and lively eyebrows, he is considered a friend of Lawrence's, and his wife is a friend of Beverly's. They have known each other for some time, which is why they are friends. They always meet at parties, in someone's living room, with groups of other people close about them.

Ted says, "I guarantee you, disaster is on its way for this nation!"

Lawrence has not been able to concentrate on the conversation. He thinks that he may not be able to endure this minute, this very minute.

Voices ring around him. It is a ring of concentric rings, a ring of voices and breaths and bright glances, circling him. Like music, the voices do not come to rest. They pause shrilly; they pause in expectation. Lawrence accepts a drink from his wife, a woman whose face looks oddly brittle. The ice cubes in his glass make him think of the Arctic—pure crystal, pure colorless ice and air, where no germs survive. It is impossible, this minute. Impossible. Impossible to stand with these people. He does not know what is wrong and yet he understands that it has become impossible, that his body is being pushed to the breaking point, that to contain himself—his physicalness, his being—would take the strength of a wrestler, a man not himself.

The minute expands slowly. Nothing happens.

Again, the airport. The reversal of the meeting last Monday: now she is going home. The airliner will draw up into it a certain number of people, Lawrence's mother among them, and then it will be gone. Now there is a rush of words. Things to be said. His mother complains bitterly of one of his aunts—he nods in agreement, embarrassed that she should say these things in front of Beverly—he nods yes, yes, he will agree to anything. "What could she know? She was never married!" Lawrence's mother says, twisting her mouth. Of Lawrence's father, who died in a boating accident when Lawrence was eighteen, she does not ever speak, exactly; she speaks of other misfortunes and disasters, glibly, routinely, with petulant jerks of her stiff little body. Lawrence's father died on the lake, alone. He drowned, alone. The boat must have capsized and he had drowned, alone, with no one to witness the death or to explain it.

Lawrence's mother begins to cry. She will back off from them, crying, and then at a certain point she will stop crying, collecting herself, and she will promise to telephone them as soon as she lands in Philadelphia. The visit is concluded.

Though it was a weekday evening, they went to Dorothy Clair's art gallery, where a young sculptor was having an opening. Dorothy Clair was a widow some years older than the Pryors, a wealthy woman on the periphery of their social group. It was a champagne opening. Lawrence and his wife were separated, drawn into different groups; Lawrence was not really taking part in the conversation, but he appeared enthusiastic. The champagne went to his head. His mother had stayed with them for seven days, seven nights; the visit had gone well, everything was over. Good. It was a weekday evening, but they had gone out as if to reward themselves.

Next to Lawrence there was a piece of sculpture—a single column of metal, with sharp edges. It looked dangerous. A woman seemed about to back into it and Lawrence wondered if he should warn her. He could see his own reflection in its surface, blotchy and comic. All the pieces of sculpture were metallic. Some hung from the ceiling, heavily; others hung from the walls. Great massive hulks—not defined enough to be shapes—squatted on the floor. People drifted around the sculpture, sometimes bumping into pieces. A woman stooped to disentangle her skirt from some wire, a thick ball of wire that had been sprayed with white paint.

What were these strange forms? They were oppressive to Lawrence. But no one else seemed to be uneasy. He went to examine the wire—it looked like chicken wire—and he could make no sense of it. Elsewhere in the crowded room there were balls of metal that were distorted, like planets wrenched out of shape. Their shiny surfaces reflected a galaxy of human faces, but the faces were not really human. They were cheerful and blatant and flat, as if there were no private depths to them.... How they were all chattering away, those faces! No privacy at all, nothing but the facial mask of flesh; no private depths of anguish or darkness or sweetness, nothing. The faces are all talking earnestly to one another.

Lawrence looked for his wife. He saw her across the room, talking to a tall man with silvery hair. It was the man he had seen downtown! Astonished, Lawrence could not move. He stood with his drink in his hand, as metallic and fixed as the pieces of sculpture. These columns punctuated the gallery, each reaching to the ceiling, with flat, shiny surfaces and edges that appeared razor-sharp. They made him think suddenly of the furniture in his parents' house that he had stood up on end as a child—allowed by his mother to play with the furniture of certain rooms, upending tables and chairs so that he could crawl under them and pretend they were small houses, huts. He had crouched under them, peering out past the legs of tables and chairs. Sometimes his mother had given him a blanket to drape over the piece of furniture.

The man with the silver hair turned and Lawrence saw that it was not the stranger from downtown after all—it was someone he'd known for years. Yet he felt no relief. He was still paralyzed. Beverly, not seeing him, was looking around cautiously, nervously. The man was about to drift into another conversation and leave her. He had a big, heavy, handsome head, his silver-gray hair curly and bunched, his face florid and generous and a little too aggressive—too sure of itself. Lawrence felt a sudden dislike for him. And yet he was grateful that he had not become that man—grateful that, in the moment of paralysis and panic, his soul had not flown out of him and into that man, into that other body.

He went out. He walked quickly out of his building and into the midday crowd, in a hurry, and once on the sidewalk he stayed near the curb so that he could walk fast. The day was cold and overcast. He walked several blocks to the end of the street and across the street to the riverfront. There were few people down here, only the most hardy of tourists. No shoppers bothered to come this far. There were no stores here, only concrete and walls and a ferry landing and the water, the grim cold water. He leaned over a railing. He stared down at the lapping water. It was not very clean; there were long streaks of foam in it, as long as six or eight feet, bobbing and curling and twisting like snakes.

The discontent of the past two weeks rose in his mind. What was wrong? What had happened? It had begun on that sunlit day when he'd seen his wife from a distance. His wife. His mother arrived the following morning; they picked her up at the airport as always. And his daughter—there had been something about his daughter as well—but he could not remember. In the dirty, bouncy water he saw Edie's face, grinning up at him. But she did not really see him. There was nothing there. He was alone.

He thought in a panic of himself and the river: the fact of being alone like this, with the river a few yards beneath him.

There was a sensation of deadness around his eyes. His eyes had become hardened, crusted over; like crusts of blood; the wounds where eyes had once been. And now they might fall off...? Another face was pushing its way through. He must scratch at the scabs of his eyes and scratch them off, to make way for the new face, digging the crusts of blood away with his nails. He must tear at himself. He must do it now, this minute... for at this minute his body could no longer contain itself; it was like a wrestler with superbly developed muscles bursting through his clothing, tearing his clothing with anger and impatience and joy—

He saw, suddenly, that the river beneath him was a river of souls: the souls of all the children he had been meant to father, flowing out of him and helplessly, ferociously downstream. He stared at the water. All of these his children! Sons and daughters of his body! He had been meant to father these thousands, these thousands of millions of souls, and yet he was on the concrete walk, leaning against the guard rail, and the children of his body were flowing by him, lapping noisily against the abutment, becoming lost.

For some time he stood in silence. His eyes ached. He tried to think of what he must do—had he planned something? Why had he come down here? If he were to drown, perhaps scenes of his past life would flash to him. He would see the upended furniture again—the clumsy gold-covered chair with its curved legs and its gauzy bottom, the springs visible through the dark gauze—he would crawl between the legs again, drawing his knees up to his chest, hiding there, sly and safe. He would see the big house, he would see the piles of magazines and he would smell the acrid, lovely odor of loneliness on the third floor of that house; he would pass into that room and live out his life there chastely and silently.

But perhaps he would fall into the water screaming. He would thresh his arms and legs—he would sink at once, screaming—and no one could save him. People might come to gawk, but they could not save him. And perhaps he would see nothing at all, no vision, no memories; perhaps it was only a lie about a drowning man living his life again and he would see nothing, nothing; he would drown in agony and be washed downstream, lost.

He glanced at his watch. After one.

He hurried back to his office. The receptionist, a pretty black woman, chided him for walking in the rain. She took his trench coat from him, shook it, hung it up. In the waiting room—he could see through two partly opened doors—a few people were sitting and had been sitting for a while. He went into his private office. In a few minutes his nurse showed in his first patient of the afternoon: Herb Altman.

"I'm back a little faster this time, but everything is the usual.

Diagnosis the usual," Altman said flatly. He wore a stylish, wide green tie, mint green. There were tiny white streaks in it that bothered Lawrence's vision.

Shaking of hands.

"Maybe somebody should just shoot me. I should croak, eh?" Altman laughed. "Anyway, I still can't sleep, Larry. The same damn thing. Give me something strong to help me sleep, eh? And did you hear about that bastard, that investigator I got to follow Evie? He was a friend of hers! It turned out he was a friend of hers! He told her everything, he tipped her off. I fired him and I'm dumping her, believe you me, I think even she and my wife are comparing notes on me and laughing and it's no goddam wonder I can't sleep. Maybe I should just drop over, eh? Make things easier for everybody? What is your opinion?"

"Let me do just a routine examination," Lawrence said carefully. "You do look a little agitated."

Daisy

D<small>AISY,</small>
Daisy,
Give us your answer, sweet!
We're half-crazy
Wondering what you'll eat....

Purse-lipped, she would not speak to the young waiter but pointed at the items on the menu, one two three. And to drink? Tea, coffee—? No. Nothing. Milk? No. Nothing.

"The June bugs have arrived, not quite on schedule," he announced. "It's July. Shall we send them back, Daisy?"

She laughed. She snickered.

"Those bugs aren't going to listen to *you*," she said.

Defiant. But shivering. She was frightened of certain insects and so it was best to speak openly of them, to jest, to ridicule. Where laughter prevailed, he thought, there shall terror quaver and die.

"Ah but maybe they will," he said lightly. "I know their secret name—*Phyllophaga. Phylloflyofleeophagohgaga!* —An ancient curse."

She laughed in delight. She was his girl, his sweetheart, his pet, his nuisance, his little one, his angel, his wanton, his scrabble-dabble, his kitten, his flibbertigibbet of old. And a genius. No small part of the riddle that she was a genius.

When they walked out along the sprinkled gravel path, between the banks of flowers, it was noted by all how attentive he was to her, how courtly; and wouldn't she try your patience, that one? When they walked above the sea cliff, fast-paced, never minding the strident northeast wind, it was noted how frequently he glanced at her in amazement, as if she uttered remarkable things and then turned defiantly and mischievously away. Her dark eyes gleamed. Glowed. Glittered. She was a hobgoblin, a fairy. At the age of four she had been the loveliest of the fairies in a production of *Midsummer Night's Dream*, staged by friends of her father's in Majorca, summer friends, a summer fantasy, the raising of funds for a cause now forgotten. She walked with her weight thrust forward, on the balls of her feet, as if ready to run or even to fly—to spring in the air. Once out of sight of the hotel, she often ran. And circled back to him. And ran ahead again, teasing for him to join her. "Old scarecrow! Old bag of bones! You're just pretending you can't run because you're *lazy*."

"I own that I am lazy, bone-aching lazy," he sighed.

Often he fumbled in his pocket for the small black notebook he carried everywhere. And paused to record, in his tiny near-microscopic hand, certain treasures that skittered into his mind. It might be a word of Daisy's or a phrase evoked by her or a sudden explosive memory that came from nowhere, though probably he could trace it—as he often did when he was in that mood—back to Daisy. He wrote in abbreviations, almost in code. Perhaps he did write in code. He was fairly certain that no one could break that code, for it changed from day to day and sometimes even from hour to hour. Music, it was, the act of memory and of recording memory a kind of music, enigmatic and fluid.

"Father, what did I say?" Daisy sometimes asked. She would peer at him with her head held back, eyes half closed, so that she could look at him across her cheekbones. She was haughty. But a little anxious. Lovely girl with dark, dark eyes and windblown dark hair, a thick brush of hair she feared the spiders might someday seize for a home if she wasn't vigilant. "What did I say? It was something that surprised you, wasn't it, something you will put in a poem, wasn't it, something you'll boast about when people come to visit you, wasn't it? And you'll tell them about me, won't you?"

It made him uncomfortable when anyone watched him write. Even she. He would close the little notebook and slip it back in his pocket as negligently as if it were a crumpled handkerchief.

"I always tell them about you," he said.

He carried an umbrella. Never bothered to open it—had it ever been unsnapped? Used it as a cane sometimes. The steep path, the wind, the frequent euphoria of these walks, and the nearly as frequent jumps of his heart when he sensed danger: exhausting. But a cane would have embarrassed them both.

His little girl did not mind if they were caught in the rain. She would sometimes raise her arms, sometimes hold her face up and her tongue far out, to receive the raindrops. Like a communicant, he realized. And his eyes misted over with love.

"I always tell them about you," he murmured.

Tall and scarecrow-thin, he was; but did not mind. Did not pay much attention to his appearance. Which was ironic, people had noted, since he paid such scrupulous attention to the appearance of others and of things...to a universe of detail, beautiful clamorous inexhaustible detail. He was in love with surfaces, he claimed. Meaning by surfaces everything there was: layer upon layer upon layer. But his own physical existence did not interest him. It was a means, a medium. A vehicle. At times a burden: because he could not trust it. Suddenly tired, so bone-weary he believed himself on the brink of utter extinction, he would laugh nervously and berate himself for being lazy or "out of condition." No, the physical being was untrustworthy, an inferior Siamese twin stuck to the soul, a clownish Doppelgänger one could not—unfortunately—do without. He clothed this creature in mismatching trousers and vests and coats, he shod its bunion-prone feet in custom-made shoes that soon became muddy and scuffed, he jammed a shapeless hat upon its head, and sometimes added fey decorative touches: an ascot tie of flamboyant purple, a marigold in his buttonhole, one or two or even three of his famous big rings. For the past several years he had worn a copper bracelet to ward off the evil spirits that bring rheumatism, and it gave to his bony wrist a certain dash he rather liked.

Daisy dressed carefully. Not quite with style but with care, elaborate care. It had begun as a game between them, years ago, that she would have to ask her father permission for various things, and have to stand inspection by him before going out; gradually it had become a ritual and though Bonham did not care what the girl wore, so long as it was decent and appropriate to the season, he was unable to extricate himself from the ritual without upsetting her. He had tried, he had tried. God knows. *He* knew. But once imprinted in Daisy's imagination, the clothing-inspection ritual, like a number of other rituals, had become a permanent feature of their life together.

"Do I look all right, Father?" she would ask anxiously. "Are the colors right? They aren't too daring, are they? You won't be ashamed of me, will you? Is the blouse too big? Are the trousers baggy? Will people laugh? Will *you* laugh?"

"If you don't laugh at me, I vow not to laugh at you," he said gravely.

And they smiled happily at each other, in perfect understanding.

For their hikes out along the sea cliff Daisy wore sports clothes, attractive outfits that were nevertheless sturdy, so that she would not be hurt by briars or thorns, or if she happened to fall on the path. Bonham liked her dusky-rose slacks, though they were rather loose on her, and the caftanlike beige top she usually wore with them; he did not at all like a certain pair of trousers that were black and shiny with age and comically baggy, which Daisy would have worn most of the time if he hadn't expressed disapproval. On her feet were tennis shoes, once white but now dark with age. They were the most practical shoes for these walks because, from time to time, Daisy felt the compulsion to scramble down the bank to the water and wade out in it. Like Bonham she wore a hat, but her hat, unlike his, was wide-brimmed and tied beneath the chin, a pretty maidenish sun hat to protect her delicate complexion: she had two, one of a gauzelike white with a bright yellow ribbon band, and the other of new, greenish straw with a white band. When she ran, the hat would slip off and bounce behind her head, secured by the tie around her neck. One morning Bonham, watching her, had the involuntary and really quite silly vision of a girl running with part of her head fallen back. He had not liked the idea but, dutifully, religiously, had noted it in his little book. It had eventually found its way into one of his poems.

Father and daughter both favored rings. All her rings were gifts from him, and she wore them in rotation, except for the antique ring on her left hand that had belonged to his mother. It was not so precious as it looked—in fact, Bonham had pawned it in one of the squalid epochs of his earlier life, quite astonished at how little money he had been able to get for it—but it was very beautiful. Small diamonds arranged around an oval amethyst, in a setting of gold. It was her special ring, her sacred ring. It could never, never be taken off. Not even to be cleaned. Not even for a moment! No! If he had commanded her to take it off, he supposed she would have done so, but he could not bear to use his power so arbitrarily and so cruelly; and the gesture would have been futile anyway.

"What if a thief comes into my room and takes the ring while I'm asleep?" Daisy asked. "What if he slips it off my finger?"

"That won't happen, dear. You know it won't happen."

"But what if it *does*? There was a burglary in town the other day, I read about it, I read about it in the newspaper. Thieves like hotels. Don't they? You know they do!"

Bonham whistled and shrugged his shoulders languidly.

"That time in Istanbul thieves got into Uncle Eli's room, didn't they? They took something of his, didn't they? So they could get into our ugly old hotel—they could get in anywhere— *and take whatever they want.*"

"Sweet my girl," Bonham said, showing not a quiver of the surprise he felt that Daisy should remember an event that had happened so long ago, and which was nearly forgotten by everyone concerned, "it just isn't going to happen. I have spoken. *Voilà.*"

"Do you *know* it isn't going to happen?"

It was a serious question. She squinted at him, her expression childlike with interest.

"Do I *know*...? Well, dear, am I omnipotent? Am I God? Am I the author of creation? Not quite. Not *quite*. You'll grant me a little marginal humanity, a little leeway to err now and then? Daisy, please! Don't look so anxious. You know very well no one can get into your room once you've locked it from inside."

"People do, though," she said.

"But they're dreams."

She shrugged her shoulders in imitation of him.

"They're only dreams," he said, still smiling.

But the anxiety in her eyes was fading, as if she had simply forgotten it. That often happened when he distracted her or when he spoke in his light, bantering, rather musical voice, and reached out to tap her beneath the chin.

She whirled and ran, and the straw hat was blown from her head and fluttered at the nape of her neck. Wind! Sunshine! The wild gray Atlantic! Rocks thistles clouds gulls waist-high weeds with tiny blue flowers and behind her Father musing, staring, brooding. Poor Father! She knew his fear. She knew his dread. That she might fall and hurt herself or suddenly feel the need to wade in the surf, and what if the bank was too steep for her to clamber down? Daisy might be hurt—might be very, very badly hurt.

One terrible night he had wept, had wept. Had wiped at his nose with his fingers. Francis Bonham! Bonham himself! He who quivered at bad manners, who could not bear Daisy to sniffle in his earshot—he had wiped at his nose with his fingers. Daisy had seen and had wanted to giggle. So funny! Shivering fearful broken whiskey-smelling Father, wordless for once as he wept, not even noticing—he with his keen cruel eye—the uniformed people exchanging glances. Ah hah, they were thinking, *Ah hah.* He crouched above her and wept that she was his life, his soul, his dear one, his most precious girl, his only baby, and she must never never do this again—never—*never*—otherwise he would be destroyed and they would take her away and she would be theirs.

She did not giggle. There was nothing funny. She saw the others approaching. She saw her father's blue eyes washed pale with tears. What had happened? Did she remember? No. Yes.

There was a movie and people had been screaming. Ugly, ugly. Someone caught in quicksand. Sucked down. Screaming. In the movie there was screaming and in the theater there was screaming and Daisy had tried to get away but was fixed to her seat. So there was nothing to do but scream and scream and scream.

But maybe she had mixed that with something else. Or maybe she had dreamed it. Or painted it. Or one of those nasty children had told her about it, to confuse her. Only her father knew what was real and what was error.

"You won't ever do this again, Daisy? Won't ever run away again?"

She shook her head, mute. Why did he ask her when he already knew? He knew what she would do, and what would be done to her, so why did he pretend not to know—why did he pretend to be so frightened?

"We'd love to see you, of course," he said, "but at the moment we're still not quite settled into a routine. The trouble in March, you know.... No, no, she's nearly recovered now. She's made quite a comeback. Back to her drawing again, even a few paintings, though nothing too ambitious. Has to guard against excitement.... Yes, like her father; yes. That's right. I've always said that, since the start, haven't I?—she's no different from me. Our temperaments are identical. If anything, Daisy is more sensitive, possibly more original.... Yes, we'd love to see you, but maybe Christmas would be the best time. Christmas. That isn't too distant, really. You see, for one thing, I've had some difficulty getting back to work. I *work*, yes, I labor away, my usual eight hours, but I'm not at all satisfied with the results. Another problem is your girls. Daisy loves them, of course, she feels very close to her cousins, but at the same time she's a little... she's a little uneasy in their presence, I think; a little jealous. It's quite natural. Her life has been so eccentric and theirs have been so beautifully, formidably *normal;* and too much conversation, too much stimulation, you know how it excites her and she's back on the pill routine again, which is repulsive to me.... Yes, we're fine, really. Our move to this hotel was a good idea, in spite of the cost.... The strangest thing, today on our walk Daisy began speaking of you, of that theft in your hotel room in Istanbul, so many years ago—isn't that odd?—it must have been in connection with your call tonight . . . she must have sensed you were going to call. Really. Really! It's more than just a coincidence, obviously. With Daisy these odd little things happen constantly. We make light of them, she and I, it's best to skim the surface of such things, otherwise one grows frightened. . . . For instance, she has an astonishing memory. It seems to be growing sharper. The other evening at dinner we could hear a string quartet in another part of the hotel, where there was a wedding party, and Daisy suddenly began telling me how vividly she could remember the little pieces I had played on the violin for her, when she was in her crib . . . only an infant, think of it! . . . in her crib. So long ago. I used to entertain her and her mother, just nonsense tunes, nursery tunes . . . and now, three decades later, my daughter claims she can remember. . . . And there have been even more remarkable things, Eli, almost unbelievable things. . . ." But he was speaking rapidly. Too rapidly. He stood in his shabby dressing gown by a mirror, turned away from his reflection so that he need not look at himself. At the same time, he was conscious of himself twinned in the mirror, the telephone receiver clutched tightly in his left hand. He forced himself to speak in a more normal voice. "Of course I'll make all the arrangements, Eli, and you and Florence and the girls will be my guests for Christmas. . . . No, please. Don't argue. Please. I'm not that seriously in debt, don't believe the rumors, and in any case I'm your elder brother and your host and I insist, I *insist*. We'll have a fine Christmas. By then Daisy should be settled down and I should, I fully expect, have my interminable poem finished and ready for publication. Yes. . . . Yes. Of course I'm telling the truth: Daisy and I are both in excellent health."

"Did you dream, Daisy?"
"Did I dream? He wants to know did I dream. . . . Yes, I did but I won't tell you," she says smugly.
Arm in arm along the corridor. Soft muffling rugs. Hands that emerge from the pale wallpaper, lace at cuffs, holding aloft

torches that are really electric lights with small salmon-colored shades. So silly. Silly. The elevator is too dangerous so they take the stairs. Seven flights. Daisy's dark bright-gleaming bush of hair has been tied back from her face with a velvet ribbon. She is pretty. Her complexion is almost clear again. She is sprightly. Sly. She is the Day's Eye. The Night's Eye as well. She sleeps, but her eyes are open all night, stony and merciless. The night air burns her eyes. The ceiling is crowded with lights. People appear—sometimes her mother appears—and instruct her; hour after hour she stares at them, unable to look away. They show her what to draw. They take her hand and guide it through the secret patterns so that, in the morning, she can repeat these patterns. Father never appears: that is because he controls everything. He is the author. He controls the night and he controls the day. Only lesser beings appear at his bidding.

"The telephone rang last night in your study," Daisy says. "Was it Uncle Eli?"

"No. Not at all," Bonham says. "It was no one important."

"It wasn't Uncle Eli?" she asks, squinting at him.

"A young man who had gotten my number from an editor, an arrogant little soul, wanting to come up here for an interview— no one important, as I said. No, it wasn't your uncle."

Daisy smiles. Daisy is relieved. Daisy thinks it didn't happen that time.

At the age of three Daisy Bonham had drawn a remarkably detailed picture of hundreds of butterflies. Her first poem accompanied it, as a caption: *The Butterflies lick Butter from the Buttercups.* The words were childlike, but the drawing had not seemed childlike. The butterflies were not laboriously drawn, as a child might draw them, but were mere sketches, thin and insubstantial, as if in motion; they were a cloud narrow at one end and swollen at the other, and there had been something disturbing about them. When she was finished with the drawing, Daisy had no interest in it, not even any pride; she told her mother it was Daddy's—it belonged to him.

She recited his poetry. She made up little melodies and accompanied herself on the piano, singing his words. Friends and visitors were amazed, charmed. They were eager to praise her. They noted how Francis Bonham stared at her, his expression rapt, his customary restlessness gone. He loved her, did he?—loved her. Doted on her. An artist-friend painted their portrait together. A fellow poet, once close to Bonham and then banished, inexplicably, sought to regain Bonham's favor by writing a dense little lyric about the two of them. Bonham's wife retained her position in his household for years simply because she was the mother of his daughter and he was absurdly and sentimentally grateful; had she not chosen to leave, he would never have expelled her—it would have been impossible. Even after their quarrels. Even after their celebrated fights.

But that lovely little girl! How was it possible, Bonham asked everyone, that *he* had fathered so exquisite a child?

She had a private tutor. He refused to send her to school, even to a private school. What did it matter, the expense? The debts? People came along and helped him out, people were always appearing to help him out, magically, as if by an act of his will. He might be destitute—the three of them literally hungry—but someone came along, or a grant or an award came through, and all was well. Money spent on Daisy did not really count to Bonham, just as money spent on drinking or restaurants or houseguests or books did not really count; he never considered himself extravagant and was always rather hurt when people criticized him for certain expenses. Daisy loved costumes, loved to put on little shows, dancing and singing and acting in dramas she had written; her mother took her to theatrical supply shops and old clothes shops in New York, to outfit her, and sometimes Bonham himself accompanied them. What did the expense matter? It did not matter at all.

At the age of six Daisy put on a puppet show for the children of Bonham's friends and for children in the apartment building they were living in, having made the puppets herself, and the puppets' costumes, and the small portable stage. She did the voices beautifully, with an almost eerie, adult precision. Afterward one of Bonham's friends told him that his daughter was the most precocious, gifted child he had ever encountered—and that she would go beyond Bonham himself. He had been de-lighted. He had been wonderfully moved. It annoyed him that the other children could not appreciate her and that she hadn't any friends her own age—but that was to be expected, after all. Other children were so clearly her inferiors. Bonham, as a boy, had been very much alone, usually in frail health, and he had had few friends. It was the burden of a certain sort of genius, the genius that develops early, flooding the child personality with another, more complex, less easily accommodated personality. But where Bonham had been lonely, his daughter did not seem to be lonely at all. Throughout her childhood she expressed quite emphatically her preference for the company of adults rather than children; she mocked other children, imitated their voices and behavior and silly little repetitive routines. She provoked quarrels, even provoked fights. And she never cried, not even if her hair was pulled or her face slapped. She glared at her small enemies, flushed and victorious. "I despise you," she sometimes shouted. If their parents were friends of the Bonhams, it was necessary for them to apologize, explaining always that Daisy was high-strung and sensitive; if the children were insig-nificant, or the children of people Bonham disliked, he often winked at Daisy and gave her the old Roman sign of approval.

Ah, the secrets between them! The pantomimes, the parodies, the burlesques of fools they knew; the ingenious mimicry of affectations, mannerisms, voices, patterns of speech. Years later, when the first of Daisy's troubles began, a psychiatrist sug-gested that he had spent too much time with her. But that struck Bonham as preposterous. The children of many of his friends and acquaintances had been miserable because their fathers had neglected them, or had moved out of their households alto-gether; he, Bonham, had made every effort to be an attentive, loving father. He had been enchanted by her drawings and paintings more than by anything else, for it seemed to him that in these she was not merely talented, but genuinely gifted; hadn't it been wise of him, as her father, to recognize her genius and to encourage it? His wife had been enthusiastic as well, but her praise had often seemed forced and unconvincing, and as her drinking increased, the quarrels between mother and daughter increased, and Daisy was all the more dependent upon her father. And he had not really spent that much time with her, not in actual hours. Most of his life was his poetry. He worked alone, in absolute sacred solitude, and no one—not even Daisy—ever dared to disturb him.

"She's like me. She has a temper," he said.

After her mother's death Daisy's tantrums became more protracted, and more physical. She smashed things. She tore at one of her most beautiful paintings—an intricately detailed forest of leaves and animals' eyes and feathers and what might have been human organs—with a scissors in one hand and a kitchen knife in the other. She could no longer work with clay—the feel of the clay seemed to enrage her. Bonham had taken his wife's death hard, though they had been separated for years. He had had a kind of breakdown, in spite of his resolution to remain completely calm, and it was thought that his mourning for his wife infuriated Daisy. "*Him?* That idiot?" she would say over the telephone if someone called to ask after her father. "*He's* playing games."

In her fourteenth year she often refused to eat, to bathe, to undress for bed, to leave the house even on special outings Bonham arranged for her to theaters and museums. It was clear to him that she wasn't sick but merely stubborn. "I won't. I won't," she said, her voice inflectionless. Even when she refused to speak and lay there unmoving in her rumpled, dirty bed, arms and legs rigid, eyes stony-cold, it seemed to Bonham that her soul cried out *I won't.*

Stubborn, she was. And capricious. And sly. Pretending to be in a heavy, unstirring sleep, she would nevertheless be aware of his every movement, and if he left the apartment—if he met friends at a tavern nearby, or simply went out for a night walk—she was waiting for him when he returned, angry and babbling. At such times she often destroyed work of her own or ripped her clothing. Her senses were so keen, she could even hear him dial the telephone in his study, though she was rooms away. She accused him of meeting with her mother, of making plans to go away and leave her. She accused him of listening to her thoughts. She accused him of not loving her.

Bonham drank, forgot to eat, couldn't afford a housekeeper, so the apartment grew shabby and filthy. He quarreled with his family, who offered unwanted advice. He emptied a glass of wine into his brother's face and ordered him out—out of the apartment and out of his life. His friends knew enough to stay away. He had no friends. They were all opportunists, all out to betray him. They were delighted that he was finished as a poet: he could imagine their jubilant conversations about him. The sons of bitches! But he knew they were right, he knew he was finished. For nearly two years he didn't write a single good line.

Instead, his energies went into coaxing Daisy out of bed, or encouraging her to eat, or to take a bath. He composed rollicking little songs and limericks in her honor, some of which remained in his repertoire permanently, sung to Daisy at appropriate times. She wasn't ill, only stubborn. And hot-tempered. If he could make her laugh, she usually gave in, seemed to melt, suddenly tractable and sweet as a little girl.

The psychiatrists and psychotherapists enraged him with their jargon, their fixed imaginations, their relatively unexceptional minds. It astounded him to realize that these people were—quite ordinary. Some of them were personally charming and could no doubt help troubled people simply by seeming to know what they were doing, but Daisy was too sharp for them; afterward she mimicked them savagely. And there were the magical therapies, seized hopefully and then rejected, one by one: bioenergetics, the Alexander technique, music therapy, light-and-color therapy, eurythmy, massage, desensitization, hypnosis, a high-protein diet, a low-protein diet, a vegetarian diet, a diet of fruits and grain, a diet that required the drinking of ten glasses of water daily. Exercises. Regulated breathing. A form of meditation taught by a disciple of Krishnamurti.

"She isn't ill," Bonham said sullenly. "No more than I am ill. No more than any exceptional human being is ill."

She was the only person he trusted. He spoke to her of the books he wanted to write—read aloud to her from journals and notebooks, or from old crumbling books he delighted in, for their sheer irrelevance to his own life. His first book of poems had celebrated the austere madness of Cotton Mather; it had contained an ingenious five-hundred-line journey to Hades, praised by some critics as one of the most remarkable things ever written by an American. His second book had been a free improvisation on the theme of *succubi*, with a long, gorgeous, highly allusive passage about Saint Anthony in the desert. His third book would not write itself—would not emerge. One evening, reading animatedly to Daisy from an old, eccentric book on Egyptian mythology by Sir Gaston Camille Charles Maspero, he had happened to glance up—saw a curious half-smile on his daughter's face, and a glassy, utterly entranced look to her eyes—and it struck him, with the ease of a knife-blade slipping into his heart, that his subject was there: was Daisy herself.

Many years later she fixes the napkin about her left hand, as if it were a skirt, and walks two fingers comically across the table toward him.

"Silly," he murmurs.

"How small it's all! How cruel, you fool! How silly, you dilly!"

"Daisy, hush."

"*You* hush. You're the one."

Sunday brunch. Leisurely lazy luxurious Sunday. The terrace a little crowded but pleasant, sunny, warm. Daisy's eyes sparkle. Daisy's tempo is faster than his. He hopes she won't suggest a walk along the sea cliff until he feels better. Slight indigestion— mild hangover—a headache concentrated in the area above his left eye. He never tells her when he's unwell because it alarms and excites her to a peculiar scoffing amusement. "Hugger-mugger!" she will say, shaking her forefinger, as if he were a naughty deceiving child.

Day's Eye, his Daisy. His girl. His princess. His Eye of Night as well.

"Mother was bothering me last night," she says suddenly.

"Oh? Yes?"

His interest is so quick and unguarded that she naturally

turns aside, smiling smugly. He knows better—should have replied in a light bantering tone if he really wanted to explore the subject—but she caught him napping.

"You don't want to walk, do you?" she says flatly, accusingly. "You just want to sit here."

"It's lovely here, isn't it? You said you liked it out on the terrace. Why don't you sketch something, Daisy? Sit in the sun and relax.... Daisy? Why are you frowning? That's better. That's a good sweetling. *For looks kill love and love by looks reviveth.*"

She is wearing his mother's dainty ring on her left hand and a large, ungainly "good luck" ring of inexpensive garnet on her right hand. He sees it is too large for her finger—she has put a turn or two of adhesive tape through it. Because it is Sunday he is wearing the ring of hammered gold that is his own good-luck charm—for certain occasions at least—which he bought one day many years ago in another seaside town. That day there had come to him, almost perfectly arranged, line after line of one of his poems; the one about Hermes, Mercurius, he of the prankish double nature. One of his forms is a lion and, by chance, Bonham happened upon a ring with a lion's head on it, rather nicely done. He bought it without hesitation, though he had only enough money in his pockets for a down payment and had to borrow the rest.

"What did your mother have to say?" he asks lightly.

But she snubs him. She is sketching in the sketchbook, frowning, completely absorbed. A droplet of saliva in the corner of her mouth. She is his girl, his baby, and so it sometimes startles him to see that she is no longer young—no longer girlish. A woman of thirty-six. Slight coarsening of her features, around the mouth especially. But charming. Charming. Thank God the skin eruptions are nearly gone. He wishes she would not frown so, as if she were in agony, but he knows better than to scold.

Sometimes she draws her dream-visions and they are elaborate, knotty things, curlicues like thought itself, hopelessly snarled. Sometimes she draws faces, strangers' faces. Sometimes she draws stark, mysterious designs. Bonham feels he can almost interpret them. But in the end he cannot—he merely stares at them, feeling the prick of excitement, of wonder. He knows he is in the presence of something remarkable, but he does not know what it is. Must be careful. Very careful. As if in a god's presence, must give no sign of being moved by an emotion.

It occasionally happens that Daisy cannot get the drawing right. This morning she is having trouble. Again and again she draws a small, fairly simple design, stares at it, then crosses it out violently or turns the page of the sketchbook. She is becoming overheated. He wishes she would sketch their surroundings—the clouds, which she does so beautifully, or the other diners, whom she can render in realistic or in parodistic tones. Sometimes the two of them play a game. Bonham, who can draw with a fine amateur flair, will begin a caricature, and Daisy will finish it, laughing excitedly. Over the years they have drawn wicked caricatures of everyone they know and of many strangers who happen to be in the vicinity. The other day, at this very table, they immortalized the pathetic obese woman with the Southern accent, who often sits as long as they do at breakfast, sipping coffee thick with sugar; they have immortalized most of the waiters, the hotel manager, the black wide-hipped woman who cleans their suite; a few of the more obnoxious children staying at the hotel; Bonham's editor and long-suffering champion, named Stanton, a man with a horse's face and morose droopy eyes; and Bonham's brother Eli and his smiley gat-toothed wife Florence—Eli as a befuddled pelican, his wife as a pig with plump cheeks and lots of lipstick. Gay as children they have done hundreds of these drawings and saved each one. It chills Bonham, however, to see how quickly—almost instantaneously—Daisy guesses whom he is caricaturing. Sometimes he draws no more than one or two lines before she snatches the sketchbook away. And she is never wrong: never.

"Don't push yourself, Daisy," he says uneasily. So far as he can see, she is drawing utterly simple designs, hardly more than lines and circles. Yet none is quite right. She crosses it out and begins again, her lips pressed tight together. At the next table a woman is eying her, a bitch with a crusty made-up face, and Bonham begins to tremble with irritation. "We could go for a walk now if you'd rather...."

As she draws she mutters half-audibly. Then purses her lips shut. Then mutters again, as if the words come unbidden from her, without her consent. "Always. Allggoes. Butterfly. But/Or Fly. Draggingfly. Firefly. Jewelfly. Diamond Eye. Day's Eye. Ose Eoseye. Eee eee eee. Earth's Eee. June bug. June flood. June mud. Bud. Bed. Slug. Sweet."

Bonham's head trembles on his thin stalk of a neck. He remembers—remembers— Suddenly he remembers— Himself a young man, joyous with love, teasing his bride on a sunny lost morning because she slept late and he had been up for hours, prowling about some long-forgotten street, impatient for her, teasing her with these lines of Herrick's, which he knew by heart:

> *Get up, get up for shame! The blooming morn*
> *Upon her wings presents the god unshorn.*
> *See how Aurora throws her fair,*
> *Fresh-quilted flowers through the air.*
> *Get up, sweet slug-a-bed, and see*
> *The dew bespangling herb and tree!*

But of course, Bonham thinks carefully, the memory is only an accident. It has nothing to do with Daisy or with her frantic drawings.

Something terrible had happened once. And he was to blame.

Without telling Daisy he had slipped from the apartment—they had lived in New York at the time—and gone to a ceremonial dinner in his honor. Bonham scorned such awards, and certainly scorned the people who presumed to hand them out to their betters; but this particular award carried with it an extraordinary prize—fifteen thousand dollars. He had not wanted to take Daisy with him. So he had gone, had told her he would be in his study all evening, and since his study was the one room she never entered, out of a superstitious awe he had done his best to evoke, he had presumed he would be safe. But of course she sensed his absence, sensed fraud.

She ran out into the winter street. Coatless, with thin bedroom slippers on her feet, unwashed hair wild about her face. Ran on the icy pavement. Darted through traffic. Eluded people who tried to stop her. Babbling, weeping angrily. His daughter! His dear one! She had run and run like a maddened animal and a patrolman chased her and another joined him and people on the sidewalk stared and smirked and giggled and she tried to hide in an alley, a filthy alley, whimpering, crouched behind garbage cans, hugging herself and rocking from side to side. It took both policemen and another man to subdue her. "I'm going to punish you!" she screamed. "I'm going to slay you all! You'll see! Give me one hundred years! I'll slay you—I can't be stopped—I am the greatest genius of the century—"

Bonham was forced to commit her to a hospital. They had not allowed him to take her back home.

"She isn't crazy," he protested. Nevertheless they forced him to commit her. In his weakened state he signed a certain paper. And, in the hospital, where he could not watch over her, they did terrible things.

Pills and injections. Electro-convulsive treatment. Solitary confinement. Torture. By the time of Bonham's first visit the powerful drugs had dulled her eyes, thickened her speech, caused her delicate skin to break out in ugly boil-like eruptions. Of course he had not known at once what was wrong. Gradually she grew worse: double vision, constant headaches, nausea. When she reported her symptoms, the staff retaliated by subjecting her to a series of brutal tests, including a spinal tap which was evidently poorly administered by a young resident. For several days she was partly paralyzed. He was going to sue them, was in the process of suing them, the bastards, the crude ignorant sadistic incompetent bastards! He would avenge himself and his daughter, he would punish them if it took every penny of his and all his energy. How she had suffered, and for what crime? Seeing her, he had burst into tears and demanded that she be released into his custody at once. No more of this!— no more. "From this day forward," he had shouted at them, "let everyone be free of pain! Let there be no more agony inflicted on human beings by human beings—do you hear? Do you hear? I'll make you hear!"

* * *

So he had taken her from the hospital in New York City to a small rented frame house in Springfield, Massachusetts, aspiring to an absolute anonymity, an obliteration of *Bonham* in any public sense; from there they had moved to the enormous estate of an acquaintance, who provided them with a handsome guest cottage and fine, private meals, near Lake Placid, New York; and from there to Cambridge, Massachusetts, to an apartment sublet by an old friend. Under threat of imprisonment and torture Daisy maintained a remarkably alert and responsible sanity, edged with cynicism, and Bonham believed she had never been more lucid in her life—capable of lengthy, sustained conversations, devoted to his work and to her "play," as she called her art, and rarely compulsive or manic. He took her to the seashore. He took her to a small resort town in northern Massachusetts, a once-fashionable watering place, and there they rented by the month a suite with a balcony in an old, attractive hotel with Gothic pretensions. There they were happy. Are happy. "The sea," Bonham says, "is a place for the birth of visions. Thus Venus rises from the sea: the Eternal Feminine rising in a man's carnal mind. Thus the eagle in *Esdras* rises from the sea, and the vision of Man himself comes up 'from the midst of the sea.' And so we are here, at the edge of the great American continent, looking out."

Daisy has failed to reproduce the design. She lays down her pencil carefully on the table; she does not throw it down. She allows her father to take the sketchbook from her. In the old days she would have ripped its pages but now she surrenders it sullenly.

As he examines the torturous, inconclusive, and seemingly inconsequential marks on the paper, his girl mutters, "Nought.

Rien. Zed. Zed. Zed." She begins to mimic his voice, fluttering all ten fingers in what must be a parody of his paternal concern. *"She isn't ill but in the process of discovering the fount of creativity! She isn't sick, she's a genius! The world isn't yet ready for her! Not crazy, our Daisy! Not—"*

"Hush," Bonham says. "People are listening. You and I are not public entertainers."

"Passencore," says Daisy. "...My life, Mother says, was invisible. That's why she clutches at me in the night. She. She wants to be born again, she says. This time she would escape you, she says, she would live and live and live and live."

Bonham forces himself to continue examining the little drawings. He does not dare show his daughter the sick apprehension he feels, nor does he dare ask her what she means. Her mother? In the night? The dead come back to suck at the vitality of the living? Wishing to be born again? But of course it is nonsense: an ugly dream merely. Very ugly. In life he had easily won the struggle between himself and his wife for the rare Daisy, he had scarcely thought of it as a struggle, his opponent was so readily flummoxed and dismissed.

Daisy is singing under her breath in a gross guttural mockery of Bonham: *"Not crazy our Daisy, not ill our Jill, not dross our ghost, not Daisy our lazy.... Gentlemen I forbid you to touch her! Nay, not a hair on her head! Nay, not even a tick on her scalp! She isn't ill, gentlemen, no more than I am ill....* Oh, I hate her! I hate her. She crawls under the covers with me and whispers in my ear. Wants to turn me against you. Tear up his little notebook, she says. Snatch his glasses from his face and break them in two. Run out into the street at noon and tell everyone what he has done. I hate her, I don't want her back, I don't know what to do, I said I would show you what she wanted," Daisy says, striking the sketchbook, "and maybe she would let me alone...but I failed. I don't know how to draw it. What she wants. I tried but I failed," she says, rolling her eyes comically. "Bad Daisy! Hazy Daisy! Big fat lazy! She said for me to ask you, she said, give me your big big hand for my tiny one, Daddy, don't shut the door against me, don't leave me ever again. She wants to be born— she held me in both arms last night—strapped me in so that I couldn't move. Crossed my arms in front of me and held them tight. She is strong now, very strong. Stronger than before. Oh very strong! But you are stronger. You are always stronger. Will you kill her again...?"

"Hush, Daisy, for God's sake," Bonham mutters.

"We are not public entertainers. But are you? Are you?"

"Leave the table. I forbid you to speak to me in this fashion."

She throws her napkin down with a snort of angry triumph and rises from her chair, unsprung, all arms and legs, spidery, energized and frantic and gleeful. Boldly she strides across the terrace, blind, glowing, her countenance so terrible that the staring multitudes are forced to look aside. Bonham sits frozen, his ringed hand to his face, watching to see which direction his daughter will take:

LEFT to the hotel and the cloistered safety of the room
RIGHT to the path high above the tumultuous sea

Left. Right. Left? To the path, to the sea, to death? *Daisy,* he commands, his eyes shut tightly and every atom of his spirit reaching out to her, *Daisy, I order you to turn left, I order you to turn left, go up to your room and go to bed and sleep and no more of this no more of this no more of this ever.*

He opens his eyes to see his gangling galloping daughter turn abruptly to the left, nearly colliding with one of the waiters.

She will be safe. Is safe.

She will sleep, and forget. And awake. And all will be as it was.

Bonham gives the impression of relaxing. He is being watched, he is acutely conscious of being watched, and so he turns the pages of the sketchbook slowly and languidly. He will not satisfy the gawking fools of the world by showing the distress he feels, or by wetting a napkin and pressing it against his forehead to ease the alarming pain. Not at all. Not he. He finishes his coffee without hurrying, he signs the check with his usual gay flourish, rises from the table with an ironic little smile. "What do you know of *us*?" he seems to say. "You know nothing. 'Like as thou canst neither seek out nor know the things that are in the deep of the sea, even so can no man on earth see my daughter....'"

Later that afternoon they are strolling along the sea cliff and Bonham scribbles in his tiny notebook, held up close to his eyes, and Daisy pauses to gather buttercups in great clumsy charming bunches and all is well is well.

The Molesters

I AM SIX YEARS OLD. There, at the end of the porch, is the old lilac tree. Everything is blurred with misty light, because there was a fog the night before and it is lifting slowly. I am sitting on the porch step playing with something—a doll. It has no clothes and is scuffed. It is neither a boy nor a girl; its hair was pulled off; its body is smooth and its eyes staring as if they saw something that frightened them. In the lilac tree some blackbirds are arguing. Not too far away is the cherry orchard; the birds fly over from the cherry trees and in a minute will fly back again. My father has put tinfoil up in the trees to scare the birds away, but it doesn't work. If I lean forward I can see the brilliant tinfoil gleaming high up in the trees—it moves with the rocking of the limbs, in the wind. My father has gone to work and does not come home until supper. The odor of supper and the harsh sound of my father's car turning into the cinder drive go together; everything goes together.

I climb up into the lilac tree. The first branch is hard to hold. The birds fly away. The doll is back there, by the steps. My grandmother gave me that doll, and the funny thing about it is this: I never remember it or think about it until I see it lying somewhere, then I pick it up and hug it. There is a little chair in the lilac tree made by three branches that come together. I like to sit here and hide. Once I fell down and cried and Mommy ran out onto the porch, but that was a long time ago when I was little. I am much bigger now. My legs dangle beneath me, scuffed like the doll's skin. My knees are marred with old scratches that are about to flake off and one milky white scar that will never go away.

My mother comes outside. The chickens run toward her even though they know it isn't time to be fed; they come anyway. My mother puts something up on the clothesline. The clothesline is always up, running from tree to tree.

"What are you doing?" Mommy says. I thought she couldn't see me but she can.

"Can I go down to the crick?" I ask her.

There, in the grass, her feet are almost hidden. The grass is jagged and seems like waves of water. "Tommy isn't home," she says, without looking around. She finishes hanging the towels up—she has clothespins in her pocket and they make her stomach look funny. "Why do you always want to play there?" she says. "Can't you play up here?"

"Tommy can go down anytime—"

"Tommy's bigger, Tommy doesn't fall down." She looks past me. There is something soft about her face—nothing bad stays in it. When I was little I kept going back into the kitchen to make sure she was there and she was always there. The big kids teased me and said she was gone, but she was always there. She would pick me up with a laugh.

I take the path through the field to the creek. There is more than one path: a path from our house and the Sullivans' house, and a path for fishermen who come from the road. Our path runs along flat but curves around, and there are prickly bushes that scratch you. By the creek the path dips downhill and goes to the bank. The fishermen's path comes down from the road, alongside the bridge. Fishermen leave their cars up on the road and come down the path, slipping and sliding because it is so steep. When fishermen come we have to leave. Mommy says we have to leave. One of the big boys threw stones in the creek once, to scare the fish away, and the fisherman ran up to the Sullivans' house and was mad. He was from the city.

The creek has a smell I like. I always forget it until I come back to it; there it is. There are big flat white rocks by the shore, covered with dried-up moss that is green in the water but white outside. This is what smells. It smells dry and strange; there is something dead about it. There are dead things by the creek. Little fish and yellow birds and toads; once a garter snake. The fishermen throw little fish down on the stones and let them rot. When the fishermen are from around here we can stay and watch—they're like my father, they talk like him. When they're from the city they talk different.

Everybody has their rocks. Tommy's rock is the biggest one and nobody can sit on it but him. I have a rock too. I sit on it and my feet get in the water by mistake. That's bad. My mother will holler. I try not to let them slip in but my rock is too little, I can't sit on it right. I let my feet go back in the water. I like the way the water feels.

I have a dam made out of stones, between two rocks. When I look around I see the fisherman behind me.

He has a strange dark face; I saw someone like him in a movie once. He has a fishing pole and a paper bag and some things in his pockets. His hat looks dusty. "Do you live up there?" he says. He has a nice voice.

That makes me think of my mother. I don't know how to talk to grownups. They talk too loud to you, and something is always wrong. I don't say anything to him. There are two crabs behind the dam, little ones. Their bodies are soft to touch but they'd bite you if they could; their pincers are too little. Tommy and the boys use them for fishing, instead of worms.

"Do you live close by here?"

The fisherman is squatting on the bank now. His hat is off and next to him. He has dark hair. I tell him yes. My face is prickly, because of him looking at it. There is something funny about him.

"How old are you?" he says.

They always ask that. I don't answer but let a stone fall in the water to show I'm not afraid of him.

"Are you fishing?"

"No."

"What are you doing?"

He is squatting on the bank and calling over to me. A grown-up would just walk out and see what I had, or he would walk away; he wouldn't care. This man is squatting and watching me. The bank is bare from people always standing on it. We play here all the time. When I was little I could look down from higher up and see the boys down here, playing. Mommy wouldn't let me come down then. Now I can come down by myself, alone. I am getting big. The bank tilts down toward the creek, and there are a whole lot of stones and rocks where the creek is dried up, then the water begins but is shallow, like where I am, but then farther out it is deep and only the big rocks stick up. The boys can wade out there but not me. There are holes somewhere too; it is dangerous to walk out there. Then, across the creek, is a big tangle of bushes and trees. Somebody owns that land. On this side nobody owns it, but that side has a fence. Farther down where the bushes are gone, cows come down to the creek sometimes. The boys throw stones at them. When I throw a stone it goes up in the air and comes down right away.

"What have you got there?"

"A dam."

He smiles and puts his hand to his ear. "A what?"

I don't answer him, but pretend to be fixing something.

"Can I come look?" he says.

I tell him yes. Up there, nobody cares about what I do, except if I break or spill something; then they holler. This man is different. He is like my father but not like him because he talks to me. My father says things to me but doesn't talk to me, he doesn't look at me for long because there are too many other things going on. He is always driving back and forth in the car. This man looks right at me. His eyes are dark, like Daddy's. He left his hat back on the bank. His hair is funny. He must have been out in the sun because his skin is dark. He is darker than Tommy with his suntan.

"A little dam," he says. "Well, that's real nice."

The crabs are inside yet. He doesn't see them.

"I got two crabs," I say.

The man bends down right away to look. I can smell something by him, something sweet. It makes me think of the store down the road. "Hey, look at that—I see them crabs. They'd like to bite a nice little girl like you."

I pick up one of the crabs to show him I'm not afraid. I am never afraid of crabs but only of fish that they catch and tear off the hook and let lie around to die. They flop around on the grass, bleeding, and their eyes look right at you. I'm afraid of them but not of crabs.

"Hey, don't let him bite you!" The man laughs.

"He can't bite."

The crab gets away and falls back into the water. It swims backward in quick little jerks and gets under a rock. It is the rock the man has his foot on. He has big black shoes like my father's, but caked with mud and cracked. He stands with one foot on a rock and the other in a little bit of water. He can do that if he wants to, nobody can holler at him.

"Do you like to play down here?"

"Yes."

"Do you go to school?"

"I'm going next year."

The sun comes out and is bright. When I look up at him my eyes have to squint. He is bending over me. "I went to school too," he says. He smiles at me. "Hey, you got yourself dirty," he says.

I look down and there is mud on me, on my knees and legs and arms. It makes me giggle.

"Will your mommy be mad?" he says. Now, slowly, he squats down. He is leaning over me the way some of them in town do, my mother's people. You can smell smoke or something in their breaths and it isn't nice, it makes me not like them. This man smells of something like candy.

"Little girls shouldn't get dirty," he says. "Don't you want to be nice and clean and pretty?"

I splash in the water again because I know it's all right. He won't holler.

"Little boys like to be dirty but little girls like to be clean," he says. He talks slow, like he was doing something dangerous— walking from rock to rock, or trying to keep his balance on a fence.

"You've got some stuff in your hair," he says. He touches my hair. I stop what I'm doing and am quiet, like when Mommy takes burrs out. He rubs the top of my head and my neck. "Your hair is real nice," he says.

"It's got snarls underneath. She has to cut them out."

"It's real pretty hair," he says. "Hey, you know in the city little girls have two daddies. One goes to work and the other stays home to play. Do you know that?"

Something makes me giggle. His hand is on my shoulder. He has dark, staring eyes with tight lines around them. He looks like he is staring into a lamp.

"Would you like another daddy?" he says.

"I got a daddy."

He touches my arm. He looks at me as if he was really seeing me. He is not thinking about anybody else; in a minute he won't stand up and yell out to somebody else, like my mother does. He is really with me. He puts his finger to his mouth to get it wet and then he rubs at the dirt on my arm. "I wouldn't never spank no little girl of mine either," he says. He shifts forward. His legs must ache, bent so tight like that. "You think they'd spank you at home for being dirty?"

"I can wash it off." I put my arm in the water. When you knock over a stone in the water a little puff of mud comes and hides the crabs that jump out—that saves them. When you can see again they're all hid.

"Maybe you better get washed up down here. I sure wouldn't want you to get spanked again," the man says. His voice is soft, like music. His hands are warm and heavy but I don't mind them. He is holding my arm; with his thumb he is rubbing it. I look but can't see any dirt where he is rubbing it.

"Hey, don't touch your hair. You'll get mud in it," he says. He pulls my hand away. "You can wash right here in the crick. They won't never know you were dirty then. Okay? We can keep it a secret."

"Tommy has some secrets."

"It can be a secret, and we'll be friends. Okay? Don't you tell anybody about it."

"Okay."

"I'll get you all nice and clean and then we'll be friends. And you won't tell them about it. I can come back here to visit sometimes." He looks back at the bank for something. "I got some real nice licorice in there. You like that, huh?"

I tell him yes.

"When you get cleaned up you can have some then. I bet you like it."

He smiles when I say yes. Now I know what the smell is about him—licorice. It reminds me of the store down the road where the licorice sticks are standing up in a plastic thing and when you touch them they're soft. They stick to your teeth.

"Little girls don't know how to wash themselves," he says. He pats water on my arm and washes it. I sit there and don't move. There is nothing that hurts, like there is sometimes with a washcloth and hot water. He washes me slow and careful. His face is serious; he isn't in a hurry. He looks like somebody that is listening to the radio but you can't hear what he hears.

He washes my legs. "You're a real pretty little girl," he says. "They shouldn't spank you. Shouldn't nobody spank you. I'd kill them if I saw it." He looks like he might cry. Something draws his face all in, and his eyes seem to be going in, looking somewhere inside him.

"But I'll get you clean, nice and clean," he says. "Then you can have some licorice."

"Is it from the store?"

He moves his hand on my back, slow, like you pet a cat. The cat makes his back go stiff and I do the same thing. I understand what it is like to be a cat.

"Do you want to walk in the water a little?"

"I can't do that."

"Just here. By these rocks."

"They don't let me do it."

I look at him, waiting for permission. My shoes are already soaked. But if I play out in the sun afterward then they will get dry.

"Sure. They ain't nowhere around here. *I* say you can do it," he whispers. He leans back and watches me. Because he is so close I am safe and it's all right to wade in the water. Nobody else ever sat and watched me so close. Nobody else ever wanted me to walk in the water and would sit there to catch me if I tripped.

"Is it nice? Does the water feel nice?"

The water comes up to my knees in the deepest place. I can't go out any farther than this. I was swimming somewhere, but not here; we go to a lake. There they have sand and people lying on blankets, but here there isn't anything except stones. The stones are sharp sometimes.

After a while the man stands up. His face is squinting in the sun. He walks alongside me, watching me; his feet will get wet. Something makes me yawn. I feel tired. I look down and see that I am making clouds of mud underwater.

"You better come out now," he says.

When I step out on the stones my shoes make a squishy noise. It makes me laugh to see the water running out. Inside my shoes my toes are cold.

He takes my hand and walks with me back to the bank. His hand is very warm. "You had a real nice time out there, didn't you?" he says. "Little girls like to play in the water and get clean."

He wets his finger and rubs something on my face. I close my eyes until it's clean.

The licorice stick isn't as good as the ones at the store. I want to take it back home but the man says no, I have to eat it down here. I keep yawning and want to go to bed. When I play in the water I get tired, the sun makes my eyes tired.

The man washes my hands with creek water, his own hands wet and rubbing with mine like he was washing his own.

"This is our own secret and don't never tell anybody," he says.

He wipes our hands on his shirt. He is squatting down all the time to be just as tall as I am. He has a black comb he combs my hair with, but there are snarls underneath and he has to stop. He pulls the hairs out of the comb.

"Now you have another daddy, and don't never tell them," he says.

When I turn around to look at him from higher up on the path, he is bending to get his fishing pole. I forgot about looking at the pole and want to run back to see it, if it's a glass pole like some of them, but now he looks like somebody I don't know. With his back to me he is like some fisherman from the city that I don't know and am afraid of.

II

I am six years old. At this time we are still living in the country; in a few years we will move to the city, in with my grandmother. But now my father is still well enough to work. My brother and his friends have gone on a bike trip. They have mustard sandwiches wrapped in wax paper and emptied pop bottles with water in them. I went out to the road and watched them ride away. Nobody cared about me; the boys call me baby if they are nice and push me away and tease me if they're bad. I hate my brother because he pushes me with his hand, like people do in the movies when they want to knock somebody out of the way. "Move it, kid," he says and pushes me. If I run to Mommy it won't do any good. He is four years older than me and so I can never catch up to him.

The day is hot. It's August, in the morning. The high grass in the orchard is dried up; the birds are always fighting in the trees; the leaves churn to show their sleek black wings. Tommy has a BB gun and shoots the birds sometimes, but when they hear the noise they fly away; birds are smart. The cat ate one of the dead birds and then threw up the feathers and stuff, right on the kitchen floor.

I am playing with my doll. Inside, Mommy is still canning cherries. On Sundays Daddy sits out front under the tree and tries to sell baskets of cherries to people that drive by. You can't go out by him and talk because he is always mad. The kitchen is ugly and hot. There are steamed jars everywhere, and bowls of cherries. Once I liked cherries, but the last time they made me sick. I saw a little worm in a cherry, by the pit. Twenty-five years from now I will drive by cherry orchards and the nausea will rise up in me; a tiny white worm. My mind will always be pushed back to this farm, and there is nothing I can do about it. I will never be able to get away.

Today is a weekday. Later on I will learn the number of it, from hearing so much about it. But now I know nothing except there are two or three days until Sunday, when Daddy stays home and sits out in front and waits for cars to stop.

My mother comes outside to see where I am. She wears an old dress with cherry stains on it. The stains make me look at them, they remind me of something. Of blood. She has her hair pushed back. Her hair is streaked up in front, by the sun, but brown everywhere else. There is a picture of her when she had long hair; she isn't my mother but somebody else. Around the house she is barefoot. Her legs look strong; she could probably run fast if she wanted to but she never wants to. Everything is slow around her. The chickens are nervous, picking in the dirt and watching her for food. They jerk their heads from side to side. If she raises her hand they will flutter their wings, waiting to be fed.

My mother comes over to me where I am sitting on the branches. She brushes my hair out of my eyes. "Can't you wait for Tommy to come back, to go down there?" she says.

"I want to play with my dam," I tell her. I lean back so she can't touch my hair. When she works in the kitchen her pale hands are stained from cherries. I don't like them to touch me then. When she gives me my bath they're like that too. I don't always like her. I can like her if I want to, but I don't have to. I like Daddy better, on purpose, even though Mommy is nicer to me. She never knows what I am thinking.

"I can take you down in a while, myself," she says. "Okay?"

I stare down at nothing. My face gets hard.

"What the hell is so good about playing in that dirty water?" she says.

This makes my heart beat hard, with hating her.

Her eyebrows are thin and always look surprised. I see her pluck at them sometimes. That must hurt. She stands with her hands thrust in her pockets, and her shoulders slump. I always know before she does what she is going to say.

"All right, then, go on down. But don't get wet."

I run around back of our orchard and through the next-door neighbor's field. Nothing is planted there. Then a path begins that goes down the big hill to the creek. In August the creek is shallow and there is filth in little patches in it, from sewers up-creek. Fishermen fish anywhere along the creek, but there are some spots they like more than others. We always play by the rocks. There are also pieces of iron lying around, from when the new bridge was built. I can't remember any other bridge, but there was one.

I have my own little rock, that Tommy lets me have. It is shaped like a funny loaf of bread and has little dents in it. It looks like birds chipped at it, but they couldn't do that. When I come down and run through the bushes, some yellow birds fly up in surprise. Then everything is quiet. I walk in the water right away, to get my shoes wet. I hate my mother. Yesterday she was sitting on Daddy's lap; she was barefoot and her feet were dirty. They told me to come by them but I wouldn't. I ran outside by myself. Down at the creek I am happier by myself, but something makes me shiver. It is too quiet. If I was to fall in the water and drown nobody would know about it or care.

A man drowned in this creek, a few miles away. It was out back of a tavern. I heard my father talk about it.

When I look around there is a man standing on the bank. His car is parked up on the road but I didn't see it before. The man waves at me and grins. I can see his teeth way out here.

"Real nice day to play in the water," he says.

I narrow my eyes and watch him. Something touches the back of my neck, trying to tell me something. I start to shiver but stop. He reminds me of the man that drowned. Maybe his body wasn't taken out of the creek but lost. This man is too tall. His arms hang down. He has a fishing pole in one hand that is long and gawky like he is. There is something about the way he is standing—with his legs apart, as if he thought somebody might run and knock him down—that makes my eyes get narrow.

"You live around here?" he says.

He takes off his hat and tosses it down as if he was tired of it. Now I know what he is: a colored man. I know what a colored man is like. But this one isn't black like the one my grandmother pointed out when we were driving. This one has a light brown skin. When Tommy gets real brown he's almost that dark.

"How old are you?" he says.

I should run past him and up the hill and go home. I know this. Mommy told me so. But something makes me stay where I am. To make Mommy sorry, I will stay here, right where I am. I think of her watching me, standing up on top of the hill and watching and feeling sorry for me.

"I'm six," I tell the man. With my head lowered I can still see him through my lashes. My eyes are half closed.

Everything is prickly and strange. Like when you are going to be sick but don't know it yet and are just waiting for something to happen. Something is going to happen. Or like when there is a spider on the ceiling, in just the second before you turn your head to see it. You know it's there but don't know why. There is something between us like a wet soft cobweb that keeps us watching each other, the colored man and me. I can tell he is afraid too.

"What are you doing?" he says. He squats down on the bank. He puts the fishing pole and the bag behind him. He looks like a dog waiting for his dish; he knows he can't come until it's ready. I could throw a stone at him, and he could reach out and catch it with a laugh.

"Can I come look?" he says.

He gets up slowly. His legs are long and he walks like he isn't used to walking. He comes right out to where I am and looks at what I have: a little dam made with stones between my rock and another rock. The water is running slowly through it. Nothing can stop that water. There is scum on it, greasy spots, and I touch them with my finger even though I hate them.

"I got two crabs in here," I tell the man.

I can hear him breathing when he bends down to look. A smell of licorice by him—and this makes me know I should run away. Men smell like smoke or something. They smell like beer, or the outside, or sweat. He is different from them.

"A crab would like to bite a nice little girl like you," he says. Right in the middle of talking he makes a swallowing sound. I keep playing in the water just like I was alone. I seem to see my mother coming out on the porch, frowning and making that sharp line like a cut between her eyebrows. She looks down and sees my doll on the steps, by itself. If she would come down to get me I would be all right. But she won't. She will just go back in the house and forget about me.

Now the colored man squats beside me. He is still taller than I am. I am sitting with my feet in the water, and it makes me think of how the water might stop me, pulling at my feet, if I wanted to run. The water is quiet. If an airplane would fly past we could look up at it, but nothing happens. After a while the man starts to talk to me.

He says I have mud on me. Yes, this is right. It is like in a dream; maybe he put the mud on me somehow when I wasn't watching. I'm afraid to look at him, but his voice is soft and nice. He talks about little boys and little girls. I know he is not a daddy from the way he talks.

"Your hair is real nice," he says.

As soon as he touches me I am not afraid. He takes something out of my hair and shows me—a dried-up leaf. We both laugh.

He is bending toward me. His eyes are funny. The eyelid is sleepy and would push down to close the eyes, except the eyeball bulges too much. It can't see enough. We are so close together that I can see tiny little threads of blood in his eyes. He smells nice. Dark skin like that is funny to me, I never saw it so close. I would like to touch it but I don't dare. The man's mouth keeps moving. Sometimes it is a smile, then it gets bigger, then it changes back to nothing. It is as if he doesn't know what it's doing. His teeth are yellowish. The top ones are big, and when he smiles I can see his gums—a bright pink color, like a dog's. When he breathes his nostrils get small and then larger. I can almost see the warm air coming out of him, mixed with the smell of licorice and the dark smell of his skin.

He touches my shoulders and arms. He is saying something. He talks about my father and says he knows him, and he would like to be my father too. But he is not like any of the fathers because he talks in a whisper and nobody does that. He would not hit me or get mad. His eyelids come down over his big eyes and he must see me like you see something in a fog. His neck has a cord in it or something that moves; my grandmother has that too. It is the only ugly thing about him.

Now he is washing me. His breath is fast and warm against my skin. "They'll spank you if you're not clean. You got to be clean. All clean," he says. When he pulls my shirt off over my head the collar gets stuck by my nose and hurts me, but I know it is too late to run away. The water keeps coming and making a noise. "Now this. Hold on here," he says, with his voice muffled as if it was pushed in a pillow, and he pulls my shorts down and takes them off.

I can't stop shivering now. He stares at me. His hand is big and dark by my arm. I say I want to go home, and my voice is a surprise, because it is ready to cry. "Now you just be nice," he says. He moves his hand on my back so that I am pressed up by him. I wait for something to hurt me but nothing hurts me. He would never hurt me like they would. His breath is fast and he could be drowning, and then he pushes me back a little. "Why don't you walk in the water a little?"

His forehead is wrinkled, and in the wrinkles there are drops of sweat that won't run down. I wouldn't want to touch his hair. He stares at me while I wade in the water. Everywhere he touched me I feel strange, and where he looks at me I feel strange. I know how he is watching. I can feel how he likes me. He would never hurt me. Something that makes me want to laugh comes up into my throat and almost scares me.

The sun is hot and makes me tired.

He takes my clothes and dresses me on the bank. He is very quiet. He drops my shirt and picks it up again, right away. Then with his long forefinger he rubs my arm down to the wrist, as if he doesn't understand what it is. His hands are real funny inside—a pink color, not like the rest of him. His fingernails are light too but ridged with dirt.

"Don't leave yet," he says. "Please. Sit and eat this with me."

When we eat the licorice he seems to forget about it, even when it's in his mouth. He forgets to chew it. I can see something coming into his eyes that makes him forget about me; he is listening to something.

We have a secret together that I won't ever tell.

When I come home Mommy is still in the kitchen. But everything looks different. It is the same but different. The air is wet. The way Mommy looks at me when I come in is different. She is smoking a cigarette.

"For Christ's sake, look at your shoes!"

She might be going to hit me, and I jerk back. But she just bends down and starts to unlace my shoe. "Just lucky for you these are the old ones," she says. The top of her head is damp. I can see her white scalp in places right through her hair. "Come on, put your foot up," she says, tugging at my shoe.

When the shoes are off she straightens up, and her face shows that she feels something hurt her.

"What the hell is that?" she says.

My heart starts to pound. "What?"

"On your teeth."

She stares at me. I can see the little lines on her face that will get to be like Grandma's.

"I said what is that? What have you been eating?"

I try to pull away from her. "Nothing."

"What have you been eating? Licorice? Who gave it to you?"

Her face gets hard. She leans down to me and sniffs, like a cat. I think of how I hate her because she can know every secret.

"Who gave it to you?"

"Nobody."

"I said who gave it to you!"

She slaps me. Her hand moves so fast both of us are afraid of it. She makes me cry.

"Who gave it to you? Who was it? Was it somebody down at the creek?"

"A man . . . a man had it—"

"What man?"

"A man down there."

"A fisherman?"

"Yes."

Her head is moving a little, rocking back and forth as if her heart began to pound too hard. "Why did he give it to you? Were you alone?"

"He liked me."

"Why did he give it to you?"

Her eyes are like the cat's eyes. They are too big for her face. What I see in them is terrible.

"Did he ... did he do anything to you?" she says. Her voice is getting higher. "What did he do? What did he do?"

"Nothing."

She pulls me in from the door, like she doesn't know what she is doing. "God," she says. She doesn't know I can hear it. "My God. My God."

I try to push against her legs. I would like to run back out the door and away from her and back down to the creek.

"What did he do?" she says.

I am crying now. "Nothing. I like him. I like him better than you!"

She pulls me to the kitchen chair and knocks me against it, as if she was trying to make me sit on it but forgot how. The chair hurts my back. "Tell me what he did!" she screams.

She knocks me against the chair again. She is trying to hurt me, to kill me. Her face is terrible. It is somebody else's. She is like somebody from the city come to get me. It seems to me that the colored man is hiding behind me, afraid of her eyes and her screaming, that awful voice I never heard before. She is trying to get both of us.

"What did he do? Oh, my God, my God!" Her words all run together. She is touching me everywhere, my arms, my legs. Her fingers want to pinch me but she won't let them. "He took your clothes off, didn't he?" she says. "He took them off. He took them off—this is on backwards, this is ..."

She begins to scream. Her arms swing around and one of the jars is knocked off the table and breaks on the floor. I try to get away from her. I kick her leg. She is going to kill me, her face is red and everything is different, her voice is going higher and higher and nothing can stop it. I know from the way her eyes stare at me that something terrible happened and that everything is changed.

III

I am six years old. Down at the creek, I am trying to sit on a rock but my feet keep sliding off. Am I too big for the rock now? How big am I? Am I six years old or some other age? My toes curl inside my shoes but I can't take hold of the rock.

The colored man leans toward me and touches my hair. "I'm going to be your new daddy," he says.

The colored man leans toward me and touches my shoulders. His hand is warm and heavy.

The colored man leans toward me and puts his big hand around the back of my neck. He touches me with his mouth, and then I can feel his teeth and his tongue all soft and wet on my shoulder. "I love you," he says. The words come back inside my head over and over, so that I am saying that to him: "I love you."

Then I am in the water and it touches me everywhere. I start to scream. My mouth tries to make noises but I can't hear them until somebody saves me.

"Honey, wake up. Wake up!"

My mother is by the bed. She pulls me awake.

"What's wrong, honey?" she says. "What did you dream about?"

In the light from the lamp her face is lined and not pretty.

I can hear myself crying. My throat is sore. When I see her face it makes me cry harder. What if they all come in behind her, all those people again, to look at me? The doctor had something cold that touched me. I hated them all. I wanted them to die.

But only my father comes in. He stumbles against the bureau. "Another one of them dreams, huh?" he says in a voice like the doctor's. He is walking fast but then he slows down. The first night he was in here before my mother, to help me.

My mother presses me against her. Her hands rub my back and remind me of something...the creek again, and the dead dry smell and the rush of terror like ice that came up in me, from way down in my stomach. Now it comes again and I can't stop crying.

"Hey, little girl, come on now," my father says. He bends over me with his two hands on his thighs, frowning. He stares at me and then at my mother. He is wondering who we are.

"We better drive her back to the doctor tomorrow," he says.

"Leave her alone, she's all right," my mother says.

"What the hell do you know about it?"

"She wasn't hurt, it's all in her head. It's in her head," my mother says sharply. She leans back and looks at me as if she is trying to look inside my head. "I can take care of her."

"Look, I can't take this much longer. It's been a year now—"

"It has not been a year!" my mother says.

My crying runs down. It always stops. Then they go out and I hear them walk into the kitchen. Alone in bed, I lie with my legs stiff and my arms stiff; something bad will happen if I move. I have to stay just the way I am when they snap off my light, or something will happen to me. I have to stay like this until morning.

They are out in the kitchen. At first they talk too low for me to hear, then louder. If they argue it will get louder. One night they talked about the nigger and I could hear them. Tommy could hear them too; I know he was awake. The nigger was caught and a state trooper that Daddy knows real well kicked him in the face—he was kicked in the face. I can't remember that face now. Yes, I can remember it. I can remember some face. He did something terrible, and what was terrible came onto me, like black tar you can't wash off, and they are sitting out there talking about it. They are trying to remember what that nigger did to me. They weren't there and so they can't remember it. They will sit there until morning and then I will smell coffee. They are talking about what to do, what to do with me, and they keep trying to remember what that nigger did to me.

My mother's voice lifts sleepily. "Oh, you bastard!" she says. Something made of glass touches something else of glass.

The rooster out back has been crowing for hours.

"Look," says my father, and then his voice drops and I can't hear it. I lie still with my legs and arms stiff like they were made of ice or stone, trying to hear him. I can never hear him.

"... time is it?" says my mother.

The room is starting to get light and so I know everything is safe again.

Silkie

WELL, HERE WE ARE standing side by side on the bridge, and who's going to speak first? Getting here was one thing; it's easy to stay quiet when you're walking and pretending you have somewhere to go. But when you get there the clumsiness sets in.

It is late summer. Evening. If there were something to say about the river—the "river"—down below I'd say it, or Nathan would say it. But it just moves on beneath us the way it has for years and years, nothing new, the same old river we've been seeing since we played in this park as kids or took the long way home from school to get horse chestnuts from the front yards of the Park Drive houses. Those were houses we never even thought of as houses people might live in, people like us—big brick houses with doors painted a bright happy yellow and windows framed with that yellow, and old big colonials with shutters painted dark blue or dark green, and lawns that rose up from the street so that you couldn't see in the front windows if you tried.

Maybe Nathan is thinking about this, or maybe he is thinking about my trouble. I am conscious of everything about him. For a few years his family rented on our street, a little soiled-white frame house like Mama's, and we played in the same gang; then his father ran off and what was left of the family moved to the outskirts of town to live with his mother's sister. But our town has just one high school, of course—that big old brick monstrosity across from the building that has both the police station and the library in it—so Nathan and I stayed friends all along. He always "liked" me, even when he was a kid and could be teased about it. He was always waiting for me to get tired of the boy I was going with so I could go out with him a few times, then he'd be waiting again while I got tired of the next one or he got tired of me. Some of them were nowhere near as nice-looking as Nathan, either. He is nice-looking, yes. If you look at him the right way, without him knowing, there is something about his dark hair and the serious straightness of his eyebrows that catches at your heart.

"What's the matter?" he says, seeing me watching him.

I raise my shoulders to indicate I don't know, and try to laugh. My laughter is a little thin but Nathan smiles to make it easier for me.

"You're silly," he says.

This is how he shows affection. In school I was one of the flighty, silly girls, just the way Bernice Chamberlain and Alice Dwyer were hardworking, serious girls. You got in one of those categories in ninth grade and never got out, even if you wanted to. Being one of the "silly" girls was nice; it meant I could go out all the time and make dates with two boys for the same time and pretend to be sorry, and everyone thought it was cute. All my girlfriends were the same way and we spent afternoons after school being driven up and down the highway by boys lucky enough to have cars, or by men young enough to take us out and not get into trouble for it, or we wandered through the five-and-ten looking at things and winding up by the magazine rack where we could read through *True Romance* and *True Confessions*. The sales girls were our older sisters or cousins and never hollered at us.

"I was just thinking that you didn't used to look so handsome," I say to him. "You used to be skinny. Your skin wasn't nice."

Nathan laughs. Because I am taking this particular line—

imitating myself—it is easier for him. He takes out a pack of cigarettes and selects one. The guys in our town always took
smoking seriously. It was the one serious thing they did, along
with drinking and joining the navy.

"Well, you look the same. Better," he says.

He lights the cigarette with his Ronson lighter, his Christmas
present to himself a few years back. He was always proud of
that lighter. When the cigarette is lit he lets his eyes move onto
mine, shyly, and I can see that he means what he says—he is in
love with me, what can he do?

"Yeah, well, I could do something with my hair. I could cut
it."

This is just talk but he says, "Don't you ever cut it, Silkie," as
serious as if we'd come out tonight just to discuss my hair.
"Don't you cut it, never. I'll get mad."

Because he speaks like that of the future, slipping it in, we
both have to look away. There is nothing to stare at but the river
and we lean against the railing together. In late August the river
is down, of course, and the banks are strewn with napkins and
beer cans and other junk. It surprises me, all this mess. When we
were little kids the river was always exciting and we didn't
compare it to a real river—the Shedd River, for instance, about
ten miles away. It was our own river and that was that. But now
Nathan and I are stranded here, grown up, like two people
drawn down to the shore to get some mysterious gift from the
sea, but it just turns out to be a dried-up creek in a park that is
running down. And some of the big old places on Park Drive
need paint and one of them is even boarded up. There are some
things that catch at my mind and want to make me think about
them, like cockleburs you can't shake off, but I can never get
those things into focus. I can never understand all there is.

"Give me a cigarette too," I say to Nathan. He takes out the
pack at once even though he hates to see me smoke. He was
always a polite boy, even years ago, and where it comes from
nobody could say—his brothers are all pretty wild and his
mother drinks and of course his father ran off and left them. But
here's Nathan, a surprise. A gift. "Thank you, honey," I say. He
smiles at this, fast to hide his surprise; that word pleases him.

He lights the cigarette for me and it takes a few seconds, giving us time to think about what to say next. What is safe? But how can we stay safe and still get said what is unsaid between us?

I rest my hand on top of his, like a woman in a movie, framed by sweet overdone colors and backed with music coming out of the air itself. It does not mean anything. But Nathan's gaze drops and he purses his lips the way he does when he is not quite ready to acknowledge something. He works in a gas station all day long and from two to eight on Sundays, so he has to have two parts to himself—the one that takes everything in clearly and the one that stays drawn back and hidden, not open to receive the loud hellos and how-are-yous people are so free with when they drive in. It's his face that makes people friendly and open. There are some boys' faces that look as if they'd been shaped by razors, all sharp lines and sharp, icy eyes. Not Nathan. Mama always liked him, the best of all the boys who came around to the house. She'd say, "Why don't Nathan come around anymore?" and I'd have to make up some excuse. "He's a real nice boy. He never kept you out too late," she would say. Poor Mama—cleaning the house up and down, washing the walls, scrubbing the floors and stairs, out on the front porch in cold weather and leaning around to wash the windows no matter if she risked her neck—all because of my crabby old grandmother. Poor Mama is sitting at home right now watching television and trying to make herself see the figures on the screen and not other people—for instance me—and trying to remember where she went wrong. Where did she make her mistake with me? Why did it happen? I love Mama because she didn't scream at me the way other mothers would, and then what could you do? Nothing else but run away from home. But Mama did not get angry. If she'd gotten angry I could have talked back, but she was just sorry, just sad as if it was her the same as me, and I wasn't alone in it. That was the second biggest shock of my life: finding out how much Mama loved me, after all.

"Well, how's old Marsh?" Nathan says. Mr. Marsh owns the drugstore I work in. "Still kicking around?"

"Still kicking."

"He must be eighty-five, or something."

"I guess so."

"How's your job going?"

I shrug my shoulders again in a way I must have picked up from someone. It isn't a habit I like. So to make it softer I brush my hair back from my face and let it fall down behind my shoulders. It's long, long hair, not as blond as I'd like it, but enough to make men stare around even if they're driving by fast. I was going to get it cut the last three summers but each time Mama got the newspapers down on the kitchen floor and got ready I changed my mind; I felt like crying. Old as I am I'm still silly. I could lie on my bed and cry for hours, even before I had something to cry about. Now that I do have something worthwhile to cry over I find there's no point in it—better to sit dry-eyed and do a little thinking. Last night after I talked on the phone to Nathan I couldn't sleep for all the thinking I did, which was probably more thinking than I ever did before in my life. And, like Mama said, making a hard-mouthed little joke, if I had done some thinking a few weeks back I wouldn't need to be wearing myself out with it now.

"Oh, Mama!" I said, and in spite of everything I laughed. There are times when a laugh forces its way out of you no matter what the situation. When Pa died it was all so strange, the house was upset and Mama's sisters were running in and out, my Aunt Bea looked so foolish with her reddened eyes and frizzy hair that I almost—almost—laughed. But lucky for me I didn't because it would be one more thing I'd never hear the end of.

Right now I'm afraid I might laugh too, because I am so silly. Silly or exhausted—or beaten down—or terrified. I don't know which. If only I could go back to the way I was a few years ago, before I quit school, and we'd all drive out to the Moonlight Rotunda on Saturday nights where they'd serve the boys and let us dance, then I'd be safe. I did so much laughing then, so much giggling. I had a pretty laugh. The boys would make jokes and we'd sit giggling helplessly, our long hair falling into our faces, our eyes shut tight and our heads tilted back a little so that the pink light from the neon tubing came to us blurred and mixed up with the music from the jukebox and the smell of our own perfume. It seems to me that the hundreds of times I did things like that were just one single time, locked safe somewhere with me, still that age and safe from growing up, and I could maybe get back to it if I knew how. Like an old photograph, maybe, everyone in it locked together in one instant and kept young and safe. But here I am standing with Nathan and we aren't even touching, as if we were already married and had been married for ages....

"Well," Nathan says slowly. He is awkward and shy, beginning. If we could spend this time the way we spent so many hours, in each other's arms, he would forget his shyness like all boys. And if I could get that close to him so that I could almost forget who he was, the way I did with all of them except Johnny, everything would flatten out and there would be no clumsy talk to get through. There would be no need to talk. Johnny had never talked much and that was one of the ways he kept himself from me, no matter how many times we were together. He never gave himself to me by saying the words Nathan is getting ready to say. "Well, what do you want to do? It's up to you," he says.

I let the cigarette fall down into the water, to let him know that I am not afraid. "You said to me, if I wanted to see you or anything, if I needed help—you would always be there." Saying this is awful; I can't look at him. But I force myself to look around, a gentle sideways glance that fastens itself right on his eyes.

"Well, yes, ma'am," Nathan says, trying to smile. He has dark, dark eyes and a patient face, and how I want to hurt him! How I want to punish him for not being the right person! But he knows nothing of this. "Say, Silkie," he says, off on another subject, "you remember when Davey died? You remember that?"

He slides his arm around my shoulders. "Of course I remember."

"And all the kids went to the funeral and I kept watching you.... You had a white hat on. You had white gloves."

"Oh, Nathan—"

"I don't know why I thought of it. It's funny, Davey seemed so old but now we're older than he was. He never got this old."

We are silent for a while. Finally I say, "You have to get up at six tomorrow?"

"Yeah."

"My job, God...Mr. Marsh is getting real bad. He says everything three times and gets mad over nothing."

"He hadn't better get mad at you."

This is all so nervous, so brittle. His arm around my shoulders isn't just anyone's arm but is so much Nathan's that I want to push him away. I want to escape. But I say, slowly, "I guess I need you, after all. You can figure out what I mean."

"I already know that," he says. He sounds slow, tired, as if he had planned all these words and practiced them too much. Or maybe he is noticing how warm and desperate I am and is thinking, "This is Silkie! *This* is Silkie—" for the first time in his life. Not just an idea of a girl or someone waving at him from a car going past, and not just a face that was lucky enough to be born pretty, but the real person standing here in black flat shoes worn over at the heel and a skirt that already feels too tight even if it is my imagination, both of us maybe thinking ahead to the same thing: a room in somebody else's house, Nathan up at six to drive out to the gas station, me left alone with straightening up and maybe sick because of the baby or, later on, feeding the baby and changing it and fixing myself up nice enough to take a walk downtown or out to see Toni or Laney or even Mama. I can even see the General Electric clock on the wall that somebody is sure to give us, a nice bright red like a sun gone screaming crazy, nailed up on the wall over the kitchen table, and I can see the rumpled bed and the dishes in the sink from the night before, and that's that. I know that I will die in that room, that I will live out my life and die there or in a room just like it somewhere else or in a rented house with three or four rooms like it, and we'll go to the show when it changes and out drinking with our friends, who'll be getting married too, and we'll have more kids, and he'll spend his life showing how he loves them all the same, the first one just as much as the ones that are really his.

"Well, he didn't want to stay around here," I tell Nathan. He is touching my hair and pretending a need to smooth it down. "He said he'd go crazy in this dump, but he never said anything about taking me along and I didn't bother telling him there was any special reason for him to do it. I didn't know him that well."

"Okay."

"He's got all kinds of ideas about traveling around. And him going on thirty, and already one wife behind him—he said she was a nice little girl but didn't go on to say what he found wrong with her. How do you like that?" And I make myself laugh to show how ugly it is. "So I thought what the hell, let him go. There's nothing going to keep him in one place anyway."

"Yes," Nathan says.

"You want me to tell you about it, don't you?"

"I don't know."

"But if you're—if we—"

"You don't need to make it hard for me," he says. I can hear him swallow, as if he's afraid. Why is he so shy, why is he so weak? Does love make people like that? Because he never loved me Johnny was strong and it was his strength I had to love, I couldn't help it, even the way he left and never even bothered to lie about writing to me....

"Don't you want to know what happened?" I ask him.

We look at each other. It is getting dark. He is a year older than I am and we have known each other all our lives, but the way we stand not touching, with our faces tightened and pale, you'd think we were two strangers who happened to meet on this bridge for the first time in our lives.

His face tells me No, but he says, "All right."

"I don't want no secrets between us. Mama said I had no need to tell but I'm not Mama, I'm myself."

"Yes."

"I made some mistakes," I tell him. My heart is pounding so hard I am afraid he will hear it and pity me. "I got hurt pretty bad for them, and I wouldn't do all of it again. I—"

"Why don't you forget it?" Nathan says.

"But later on you would think about him and get mad at me—"

"I won't get mad at you, Silkie."

"You don't know. Look at your father."

"Oh, the hell with him."

"Some men are like that."

"So what?"

A few kids are coming by on bicycles. I don't want to look at them so I lean on the railing. There is no reflection down below, just dark. The kids yell at each other and their bikes thump up on the wood floor of the bridge and then they're gone.

"Well, I was with Riley Summers when I met him. You know Riley, he's Baxter's cousin? We were at this place in Hampton that's by a lake, and you can dance out by the lake. It was real nice. I had on my pink dress. Toni and her boyfriend were with us, then when Johnny came we went off by ourselves, we shook Riley—he's a real nice guy but—Johnny was there alone and came right over to me, we danced a few times and decided to leave for somewhere else. I never did that before with a guy, like that."

"Okay. I know it."

"I couldn't do anything about it," I tell him. I would like to scream this at him to make him understand, but he can't understand because he can't know what that night was like or what Johnny was like. "I didn't want to go but I did anyway and—and Riley was mad like you heard—and I couldn't ever stop it, all the different times I was with him. He was—"

"For Christ's sake!" Nathan says.

"But don't you want to know? Are you afraid?" My voice is higher than I would like it to be but I can't control it. It keeps getting thin and shrill as if it wants to fly at Nathan and punish him for something that isn't his fault and he couldn't ever help. "Don't you want to know?"

He is staring at me in a way I have never seen before.

"You're a coward, you don't want to hear about him!" I scream into his face. "You're afraid of him! You don't want it hard for you, coming in where another man was, you want to pretty it up and forget about it—you don't want to think how I was with him all those different times. He took me all the way to the beach once—he was—"

"What the hell do you want from me?" Nathan shouts.

"I want—I want—I don't know what I want—" I turn away from him, crying now, and the ugly little park and the first row of houses just beyond it are all broken up in the dusk, smeared and ruined. I feel as if I could snatch up Nathan and me and squeeze us into a tiny ball, crumple us up and throw us away and not ever give a damn.

Nathan turns me around. I can see his hand moving fast and then my head jerks back. Where his hand struck my face is burning. Nathan stares down at me and I have to see so much in his eyes, in his face, that is sick with watching and listening to me all these years. Maybe he's going to spit in my face or hit it again, I've never seen him like this, or maybe he's going to strangle me and push me over the railing—

"Are you coming with me or not?" he says angrily.

He doesn't mean just back to my house. We both know what he means. He starts off the bridge and I watch him go and think, all wild inside where the slap is just getting to me, that I could let him walk away and go home by himself and then what would happen? What would happen to me? But when he hears me coming he waits for me to catch up. He doesn't look around at me; his shoulders are a little slumped.

When I finally get home it's late and there's one light on in the parlor, waiting for me. But Mama wakes up and calls out from the back bedroom, "Joan? Joan?"

"Yes, Mama, it's me."

I snap off the light on the table as if I'd like to snap off her voice forever, and that name "Joan" along with it. The fringe from the stupid old lampshade tickles my hand.

"Is it—is it all settled?" she says.

"Yes."

"Is it? Is it all settled?" I can almost hear her breathing, waiting for me to answer. "I prayed to God that—"

"It's all settled, Mama," I say, to cut her short. "We don't need to worry anymore, either one of us." I stand there with my eyes shut tight even though it's dark and hope to God I won't hear the springs in her bed, meaning she's on her way out here and to me.

AFTERWORD

What does it mean to "love" an art or a craft, like writing? And to "love" the primary materials (people, landscapes, events) that the effort of writing evokes? Is this a "love" that can be measured ethically?—in any way practicably? How strange to claim that the artist's love for his or her work is so passionately bound up with the artist's life in its deepest, most mysterious sense that this "love" *is* the life; and the means by which the artist expresses his or her gratitude to the world for having been born into it.

My lifelong love of writing is underlaid by a great love of reading, itself rooted in childhood. So to me any act of the imagination, no matter how coolly calibrated or layered in that uniquely adult vision we call irony, is first of all an act of childlike adventure and wonder.

Over a period of three decades I seem to have published somewhere beyond four hundred short stories—a number as daunting, or more daunting, to me, as to any other. The motives have nearly always to do with memorializing people, or a landscape, or an event, or a profound and riddlesome experience that can only be contemplated in the solitude of art. There is the hope too of "bearing witness" for those who can't speak for themselves; the hope of recording mysteries whose very contours I can scarcely define, except through transforming them into structures that lay claim to some sort of communal permanence. For what links us are elemental experiences— emotions—forces—that have no intrinsic language and must be imagined as art if they are to be contemplated at all.

It's instructive for me, in assembling these early stories, to see how, from the first, such motives underlay my fiction. My earliest publications, "In the Old World" (not included here:

written when I was nineteen, and collected in *By The North Gate*)
and "The Fine White Mist of Winter" (the oldest story in this
volume, originally published in 1962) dramatize white-black (or,
in the idiom of those days, white-"Negro" relations); my current
novel-in-progress, *Corky's Price*, begun in June 1992, also drama-
tizes, in very different form, such relations. And what I perceive
to be the subterranean philosophical query of much, perhaps all,
of my writing, is there from the first, leaping to my eye at a
casual rereading as if no time at all had passed between 1962
and 1993—

> Murray stared out at the great banks of white, toppled
> and slanted in the dark. Beyond his surface paralysis,
> he felt something else, something peculiar—a sense,
> maybe, of the familiarity of the landscape. He had
> watched such scenes as this almost every night in the
> winters of his childhood farther north, when he used
> to crouch at his bedroom window in the dark and
> peer out at the night, at the snow falling or the fine
> whirling mist, which held no strangeness, he felt,
> except what people thought strange in it—the chaos
> of something not yet formed.... The earth seemed to
> roll out of sight, like something too gigantic to con-
> ceive of.
> —"The Fine White Mist of Winter"

This is autobiography in the guise of fiction, for the protagonist
is not only my young, yearning, questing self (who so often
crouched at the single window of my bedroom at home in
Millersport, New York, peering out into the night at the "chaos
of something not yet formed") but my self of this very day, this
hour. The harsher tonalities of such stories as "At the Seminary"
(a pre-feminist work, indeed!), "Unmailed, Unwritten Letters,"
and "How I Contemplated the World from the Detroit House of
Correction and Began My Life Over Again," as well as the
sexual tensions of other stories, are also qualities of my present
work, though subjects, landscapes, types of characters, and
modes of telling have changed.

Like tributaries flowing into a single river, and that river into the ocean, a writer's individual works come to seem, from the impersonal perspective of time, a single effort; as the individual personality, undergoing its inevitable modulations through time, is first and last unique.

My earliest collections of short stories, *By the North Gate* (1963) and *Upon the Sweeping Flood* (1966), contained all, or nearly all, the stories I had written and published up to that time. With *The Wheel of Love* (1970), having more short stories in reserve, and being in a position to shape my collections more deliberately, I included only stories that were thematically related. From that point onward, my books of stories were not assemblages of disparate material but wholes, with unifying strategies of organization; so I was forced to omit more and more stories I might otherwise have wished to preserve.

And now, this further "selection" of the "selected"—yet another opportunity for abridgment, an opportunity and a challenge. The frequently anthologized ("Where Are You Going, Where Have You Been?" is by far the title of mine most reprinted in anthologies) have been included with a story virtually no one could know, "Silkie," which never found its way into any hardcover collection of mine; experimental fictions like "The Turn of the Screw" (imagined as a further turn of the screw beyond Henry James's—the secret inspiration for the great Gothic novella itself) and "Daisy" (a rhapsody, playing with the ecstatic loss of control that is madness, involving the tragic relationship between James Joyce and his schizophrenic daughter Lucia) included with the seemingly straightforward and naturalistic "Small Avalanches" (a story of which I remain peculiarly fond, perhaps for its unimpeded forward motion— so different from the prose of my current work). "The Molesters," never reprinted in any story collection, is a part of my novel of 1968, *Expensive People,* where it was presented as the work of a fictional alter ego, a doomed woman writer; yet I may as well acknowledge it as my own, especially since its setting, its "Eden County"/western New York landscape, is so clearly my own.

The historian of the short story will perceive that the majority of these stories belong to a contemporary mode that might be designated as the "literary-oral." Such stories are literary-minded, in some cases quite elaborately *written;* at the same time, they share characteristics in common with the storyteller's story, which is *told.* The "telling" is generally through a protagonist with whom the reader is asked to identify, and in most cases the identification is a reasonable one. (Though in such stories as "How I Contemplated...," "Daisy," "The Turn of the Screw," and others, the role of the narrator in itself should be assessed.) A number of these stories were constructed to move toward, and to illuminate, what I've called "moments of grace"—dramatic turns of action, as at the end of "Where Are You Going..." when the presumably doomed Connie makes a decision to accept her fate with dignity, and to spare her family's involvement in this fate. And there are more commonplace moments of grace, as, for example, at the conclusion of "The Lady with the Pet Dog," when the lovers realize that, since nothing has been decided, and everything will remain the same, they *are* happy: these are the terms of their love.

All writers are time travelers to whom no time is merely "present" or "past," for memory is a transcendental function. These stories of the 1960's and 1970's remain so close to my heart as to constitute not just a part of my career as a writer but much of my private identity as a person. I think of them as, somehow, concentric; unfolding in time, thus seemingly linear and chronological, yet, in their essence, forming rings upon one another, rings that emerge out of rings, with *By The North Gate,* my first book, at the core.

—JOYCE CAROL OATES
January 1993